THE YEAR OF THE

HYDRA

A NOVEL BY

WILLIAM BROUGHTON BURT

grey gecko press

Published by Grey Gecko Press, Katy, Texas.

www.greygeckopress.com

Printed in the United States of America

Design by Grey Gecko Press

Library of Congress Cataloging-in-Publication Data
Burt, William Broughton
The year of the hydra / William Broughton Burt
Library of Congress Control Number: 2014951636
ISBN 978-1-9388211-0-3
10 9 8 7 6 5 4 3 2 1
First Edition

*A deep bow of thanks
to the beneficent people of
Zhonghua, the Middle Kingdom.*

*And apologies all around
for our runaway narrator,
whom I tried and failed to tether.*

—the author

Part One
The Year of the Horse

1

"So?" says the beautiful woman with the steam iron. "What's it going to be?"

"I'm formulating a reply," I say, stalling.

"Formulate faster."

Her red-nailed thumb changes the setting from cotton to silk.

The money was attractive at the time. Researchers are always casting about for identical twins, say nothing of mixed-sex polar-body twins such as Lillian and myself, *la crème de la crème* of gender factor elimination and control group fulcruming and just general number cookery.

So of course Lillian and I accepted the occasional dollar or two as research subjects during our lean college years, and when Hydrangea Laboratories stepped forward with an offer of nine dollars an hour *each* to do stupid telepath tricks, we bit hard. At the time, nine dollars purchased three monaural record albums of your choice. With her first check, Lillian purchased the complete works of both Liberace and Andy Williams, in stereo.

I bought drugs.

"Spit it out," says my twin sister. "I always know when you're hiding something from me."

"You're steaming your bangs, dear."

Lillian lowers the steam iron. "Don't tell me Hydrangea Labs called. They did, didn't they? Why would those awful people call us completely out of the blue?"

"They faxed," I correct her. "And the sky above Beijing hasn't been blue since the Ming dynasty. Good job, otherwise."

"What did they say?"

"To call Chicago."

Frowning, Lillian flips the blue silk dress she's ironing. A Chinese bed makes for a very fine ironing board. An ironing board, conversely, is far too soft for a Chinese bed. And you can unstop an obdurate squat toilet with a small Chinese child. Not everyone knows that.

"Are you going to call them?" asks Lillian.

"Of course not."

"Good."

This hotel room is nearly identical to mine, down to the pink, peach, and gold color scheme, except for the roach electrocution device plugged in near the floor lamp. My room doesn't have a roach electrocution device, thank God. I'd have tried making coffee on it by now. I smuggled a half-pound of multi-grind into this country, but there's nothing here to brew it in. Tomorrow I'll be dipping it like snuff.

Beijing Telecommunications of Postal Sanitarium. That's the name of my hotel. I think this place, mid-campus of Peking University where Lillian rooms with Tree Carter, is called Splendid Auspicious of Tubercular Travelodge.

"How did Hydrangea find out where we are?" asks Lillian.

I don't roll my eyes. It requires an effort. "Our passports were just swiped at four airports in three countries, dear. There really are very few secrets in the world."

Especially with my sister around. I note with satisfaction that the inquisitive one has required an entire day to pick my brain about the fax from Hydrangea. Maybe putting garlic in my socks is actually working. And thus far she seems to have gleaned nothing at all of that nasty business with the singing condom machine earlier today.

Best not think about that right now.

The Year of the Horse is supposed to be about charging ahead with great and purposeful spirit. Deep into August, however, our 2002 seems to be *veering.*

"Why didn't you tell me?" asks Lillian coolly.

"You asked me to handle the research people," I reply with equal aplomb. "So I'm handling the research people."

And absolutely nothing happened today directly or indirectly involving a condom-vending machine, singing or non-singing.

I watch Lillian drape her blue dress over a hanger. She packed business this trip, meaning grey, blue, and white, the only colors my sister imagines she doesn't look astonishing in. She's wrong about the blue. Lillian still has the radiant thing going, the platinum mane and milk skin. We're both more or less the same creature, one that doesn't seem to be ageing in any particular hurry. Lil's arms and neck are still long and slender, and when the sun catches the emerald in her eyes—no wonder the Chinese are driving their cars into lampposts.

Slight touch of narcissism. My twin sister and I each stand one point nine three meters in height, which works out to six feet and four inches. When we decide to really light it up, say on Oscars night, she and I dress as one, down to our matching black-out shades and expressionless stares. The Mancer twins. Lillian and Julian. Identical in every way but sexual category. Very rare. Very sought after. Look for us between Madonna and Marilyn Manson in *Who's Who*. I'm the one on the left.

"Doo, would you be a doll and get us some take-out?" says Lil, spreading a white blouse across the bed. *Doo* is baby talk for Julian. Depending on the baby, I suppose.

I tell her it's out of the question.

"Please please please?" she begs.

I ignore her.

Hydrangea Labs got their money's worth. We were telling them what they'd had for breakfast. I sent and Lil received. She turned out to be especially clever at identifying postage stamps of the world. There was one streak where we were hitting very close to twelve hundred percent above random. After that, no more postage stamps of the world. Suddenly Lillian was being asked to describe the contents of filing cabinets and prison cells and missile facilities and leopard-skin panties and God only knows what.

I was shunted off meanwhile to crude medical experiments I'd rather not recall in any detail. We were told it was all "hypothetical," whatever that was supposed to mean. Then Bob's Appliance Repair and Lawn Mower Emporium discovered a hypothetical listening device in Lillian's toaster oven. We resigned at Hydrangea the following day, never to hear from them again until twenty-seven hours ago, going on twenty-seven point three three three.

With a loud electronic click, the door opens and Tree Carter enters, wheezing heavily.

"What did the doctor say?" asks Lil.

"To stay close to the toilet," pants Tree, dropping her purse onto a nightstand. In a single rolling motion, Tree casts her considerable mass onto the nearer twin bed. It doesn't even flinch. You could play pocket billiards on a Chinese bed. And with a small Chinese child . . .

"That's all he said?" asks Lil. "Stay close to the toilet?"

"That's all he said. I told him I already had that part figured out. When do I get better? He said *mmm very difficult know this.*"

Tree does a not-bad Chinese man for a three-hundred-seven-pound African American woman with a case of the canters. I found her weight online. Tree's famous. Not in *Who's Who* but famous.

"I guess that's why he's a hotel doctor," says Lil.

Still panting, Tree shakes her head of close-cropped curls, and her ear hoops dance. "This mess is diabolical with a capital di-. A capital *di-.*"

Tree is short for Shatrina. Shatrina is short for New Age radio diva gone totally mad on organic lettuce wraps and pickled pigs' feet and books channeled from the left bank of the

Milky Way. Her weekly talk show, *Shatrina*, is aired in over three hundred American cities and five foreign countries, counting the free state of Texas. Tree's popularity is due less to the predictable line of New Age pap, I'd say, than to the woman's voice which at most moments is an emphatic purr, sweet yet gritty like the honey at the mouth of the jar.

"Qing's revenge," I say.

Both women look at me.

"Jia Qing was the emperor forced to sign the Unequal Treaties with the West," I say. "In China, travelers' diarrhea would be Qing's revenge."

"We're so fortunate to know that," says Lil.

"Wasn't my doing," says Tree.

All of this is Tree Carter's doing. It was she who told my sister that their soul destinies awaited them in China, so of course they rush to sign one-year contracts to teach Conversational English to the young and post-commie at a Shenzhen public high school. "It's about the kids, the Indigos," Tree is fond of trilling. "China has gone totally Indigo, and those kids need our guidance now if they're to guide us later."

If the authorities don't seize Tree's mini satellite uplink, she will feed her weekly radio show from Shenzhen. She got the uplink past customs by saying it was a personal medical device. If my sister could get her hands on it for one night, it would be.

Tree says the soul destinies of all three of us await in China, mine included, not that I'd be caught dead or maimed anywhere near my soul destiny. I'm just here for the jet lag. And of course to watch over the girls as they settle in for their year of teaching abroad. It's the least I can do.

I shoot my sister a suspicious stare. I'm almost certain I smell cigarette smoke in this room.

Actually I'm in Beijing because Miriam, my editor at *Magazine Mariposa*, wants something Chinese-y for September and I supposedly work for her glossy tax write-off of a *haut prótention* magazine. Miriam is dangling airfare if I produce two thousand words of Chinese-y before the September deadline which, factoring in the international date line, the eleven-hour time differential and the stray wormhole, I think was two and a half days ago. Too bad. I was just about to work up something on China's singing condom machines. Melodies not maladies, something along that line.

Okay, the real reason I'm in Beijing is I owe money to some people in Memphis, which is a long and tortured story but suffice it to say I could use a little financial aid just now, and only Tree Carter is in a position to provide it, which matter I hope to broach with her as quickly as I can wrest Her Tree-ness away from my sister for a moment's time.

"Lots of water," I tell Tree.

Without opening her eyes, she holds up her liter of Binihana purified water.

"Good girl."

"Doo's going for take-out," says Lil, seating herself at an impossibly small desk, towering stork-like above her notes on survival Mandarin. "Please please please? Tree and I have a huge test tomorrow and you can see she's in no condition to go anywhere."

"And I," I reply, "am in no condition to order food in this country. I can't even whistle in Mandarin."

"Buffet place," says Tree, eyes still closed. "Outside the West Gate."

"Yeah," says Lil, turning to bat her eyes at me. "The buffet place. Easy-schmeasy."

I mull this over. In Beijing, easy-schmeasy may require an hour and a half of perplexing, draining, and sweat-dripping toil, and finally outright begging—half the struggle is fighting your way forward through the mob. There are no lines here, no taking of numbers, no politeness at all among strangers. But the acrobats are outstanding.

"Please please *please*?" says Lil.

I mull a little more, asking myself which is likely to be worse, humiliating myself in yet another Beijing restaurant or remaining here while my sister goes through my head like it's her sock drawer. Lillian was once quite free with remote viewing my journal before I got my hands on two leaves of a NASA-grade titanium alloy as light as aluminum and impervious as adamantium. This stuff is resistant to penetration of almost any imaginable kind, so I had a jeweler fashion the two leaves into a binder for my journal.

Girl can't get in.

I turn to gaze at my stork of a sister at her little desk. Lil so resembles our mother that I sometimes catch myself staring, not that Mom and I were ever particularly close. The senility helps. Now that she has no idea who I am, she seems to like me a good deal more.

Lil and I do seem to be ageing reasonably well, I reflect. Not a grey hair on either platinum head, nor a cavity in either chilly smile. Neither my sister nor I have ever so much as sneezed, when I stop to think about it, nor have we ever reacted in any way to the brute incursions of the sun. But who is without his or her little peculiarity? I once knew a woman with a dread of seeing her own feet. She was nearing thirty years of age and had yet to encounter them visually. I married that woman for some reason.

Suddenly Lil draws herself taller. "Why am I suddenly thinking about vending machines?"

I stand a bit too abruptly and lose my balance. I have to grab the floor lamp, which nearly goes down with me. Both Lil and Tree stare.

"Anybody feel like Chinese?"

Peking University is better by night, but outside Provo, Utah, what place isn't? I feel practically at home within these seething shadows where lovers stroll and cicadas trill and utopian dreams molder beneath pressure of familial duty and sweet-and-sour exam scores. Curious how a windless summer night can transform a world-renowned university into a string of scruffy villages, randomly and dimly lit, un-weed-eaten, human infested, a slowly composting oasis of warm-beer–softened reflection within the glaring, blaring urban desert called Beijing. Unfortunately these collegiate meanderings have thus far produced no description of a gate nor even a real good screen door, East West North South Garden nor Pearly, let alone one with a buffet place.

"Just get us something—anything," was Lil's injunction.

"It better be good," she added.

"It better be dead," said Tree.

"It'll be dead," I assured them both, "if I have to kill it myself."

As I turn back toward the lotus pond, a cool breeze stirs the dank summer scents and I think *Canadian air mass moving in* before I remember where I am. The breeze against my cheek would be a postcard from Siberia, and I'd do well to read it. To winter in Beijing, I'm given to understand, one wears all one's clothes and several members of one's family, not that I intend to hang around long enough to find out. Once Lillian and Tree have concluded their two-week intensive in survival Mandarin, off they go to teaching posts in Shenzhen—and I return to my small nest in Memphis with a new ending for *The End of Day*, which I must now wheedle out of Tree Carter.

That's the title of my newest novel. *The End of Day*. I came up with it myself. The rest of the novel was channeled by Tree from the disincarnate soul of a late Pulitzer laureate with a lot of time on his hands and no way to order a martini. Like every other writer worth mentioning, the poor man was claimed by a wastrel's death before he could deliver his best work, so would I please please please give it to the world beneath my own name, as my style of Southern Noir and his are all but indistinguishable—said he. A sly accusation, I believe.

The thing is, this guy doesn't even exist outside Tree's general hoodoo-ness, and I have gambling debts in Memphis where aggravated assault is considered a form of aerobic exercise.

Besides, this material isn't half bad. In fact, it's pretty good.

Once more at the lotus pond, I study the approach of a sleeveless and bespectacled young man bearing a basketball beneath one arm. "Excuse me," I say to him. "Could you possibly direct me to the West Gate?"

The student, tall and broad-shouldered, points out an arched footbridge partially shrouded in willows. "West Gate closs the blidge. You see?"

"The blidge?"

He nods pensively. "Closs and just go some more. You see later."

"See later the glate? Closs first the blidge?"

"Yes," says the young man, nodding earnestly.

"Who's your favorite basketball player named Billy? Never mind. I have to go now. Best of luck with your studies."

"Thank you very much," says the young man.

"No, thank you."

"You're welcome."

"It's *you* who are welcome, my friend."

I head toward the arched footbridge. Students. More worthless with each generation.

I'll be completely candid about those twelve chapters channeled by Tree Carter. I could no more produce prose of that quality than poo brown-and-serve rolls. So why *not* be a good sport and present Truman's best work to the world beneath my own name, thereby reaping the critical and monetary rewards that life has thus far so miserably denied? But I will not accept his title. I have my artistic limits.

Dipping Between the Dip Slopes. That's Truman's title.

Beyond all that and central to the current dilemma, said material stopped coming after Chapter Twelve of what is clearly a thirteen chapter book. Just. Stopped. "Finish it yourself," said Tree.

True, I have three novels out there, the most recent of them named Best Southern Novel of 1999 by the Greater Birmingham, Alabama, Regional Library. "Focus inward on the native magic of your unique artistic voice," said Tree.

"Get off your ass and write," said Lillian. So I got off my ass and focused on my native whatever it was and handed the result to my agent, Bernie, who *instantly* lined up a prime New York publisher who was not totally wild about the ending, beginning more or less with the first letter of the first word of Chapter Thirteen. All of which coincides very awkwardly with a personal cash-flow issue that we needn't go into now but I, like, really need for Tree Carter to rediscover whatever snarly queer little splinter-personality it was that produced Chapters One through Twelve and pronto.

The night before I left Memphis, I discovered a cricket's head in my bed. Could have been a coincidence, but how do you know?

Atop the arched footbridge, I pause to enjoy a moonlit vista of floating lotus pods in lurid, faintly pink bloom. Steadying myself against the wooden railing, I gaze straight up at the usual Beijing sheetrock and think *completion*. I've known all along that China is about completion. I boarded the plane in Memphis with a very clear sense that the various strands of my dishevelment were soon to meet in some kind of nonstandard knot, hopefully sans the sort of pointless and painful catharsis I do my best to experience only when sleeping.

That same unbidden thought, completion, returned yesterday at a street market where I stood waiting to purchase four brown-dappled bananas. All at once the fruit merchant experienced a whole-body spasm that could have been Drunken Fruit Merchant Kung Fu before raising something to my face. It was a squealing rat impaled on an ice pick. I'm afraid I didn't show the proper appreciation. Everyone else within earshot chuckled happily as the rat did the *eeek*-ing upside-down death dance.

China's the endgame. I'm pretty clear on that. I'm just not sure what game it is we're into here.

Go toward the light. Moth-like I allow myself to be drawn toward a luminescence beyond the trees, one more felt than seen.

Daddy was an anonymous sperm donor. Which I'm quite sure is the first line of at least one country song. It was Father dearest who provided the *identicon* and myself with our slightly different spins, our delightful little quirks, our semi-imprisonable offenses against norms and memes and baas. As how could those qualities have possibly flowed from dread, cold, and unimaginative Mother? Cue the cellos.

I start across a broad, empty plaza, all the while picturing Lillian hunched over her survival Mandarin notebook in the Roach Electrocution Suite, a burning cigarette in each hand and another in the ashtray. I went through hell to get that woman off cigarettes. Absolute. Hell.

On balance, I suppose I owe Lillian a lot. When we were scarcely more than babes, my sister came to the place where I was—just out there somewhere—and brought me in for a landing in consensus reality, or I'd probably be in *What's What* rather than *Who's Who*. My twin sister imagines that she still caretakes me, and I humor her. "Have you taken your meds, dear?" she asks offhand. Yes, dear. Thanks for caring, dear. See you in the glow, dear.

Beyond this dark plaza is a shadowy grove of trees pierced by a faintly glowing walkway. Entering, I shudder for no particular reason. As though one needs a particular reason in this twenty-five-dynasty-old city. That includes the commic one that's going end-of-life as we speak. Which is to say, there are considerably more dead people in this town than living ones.

As a child in Memphis, a place most rich in unnatural death, I had my occasional little problem with bumps in the night before learning that I could exit the glow anytime I wished. Then at age twelve I discovered the liquor cabinet above the fridge and learned to exit a lot more than that.

Nothing much goes bump in the night anymore. Except for the occasional doorframe. Thanks for asking.

While we're passing along deep soul secrets, there's a small gambling addiction I'd like to own here. Though I'm not the least attracted to sports betting, nor the standard fifty-two-card deck, let alone anything directly or indirectly involving a revolving wheel, there is one particular amusement that does address me in a siren's wail in one or another of my weaker moments. The result is the occasional financial quandary such as the current one—*easily* resolved once I obtain that final chapter.

I enter a tunnel of trees that becomes a tangle of handlebars. Parked jammed and stacked all around me, some of them two and three high, are more bicycles than could possibly exist. I've stumbled upon the world's bicycle graveyard. Either that or I'm drawing closer to one of this campus's four flood-lit gates.

A noble number, in its way, Four. Stodgy. Pointy-headed. An excellent basis for tables and chairs. I stopped at four marriages because of the importance of stability in an often unsteady world. Not to mention the many problems awaiting at Five and Six. I should explain that there was no television in our home during the tender interval between Lillian's bringing me *in* and my acquisition of the liquor cabinet. My chief means of engagement during those years was to disappear into math. I was pretty good at it.

We arrive at the West Gate and we are impressed. Each of Peking U's grandiose and lavishly turned-out portals is manned twenty-four-seven by uniformed guards, their primary duty being to intimidate bicyclists into dismounting as they *closs* the threshold where a young Mao Zedong once strode, *Das Kapital* beneath his arm. Mao worked at the campus library, there to discover the diverse worlds of ideas obtainable from books he would later find occasion to burn, actually padlocking the four gates of this university that now honor the memory of his footsteps.

My belly tightens as I scuttle past the guards. Why does Beijing need so many gates and guards? A casual stroll anywhere in this town requires passing through all kinds of portals of permission. I suppose it goes back to the days when Beijing was composed of *hutongs* or professional neighborhoods. You had one called Woodcutter, another called Wash Clothes or Wet Nurse or Make Soup, which may explain all these walls and gates. Or maybe the government just likes the idea of being able to lock Beijing down anytime they feel like it.

Nah.

Just beyond the spotlights of the gate, I'm swallowed by the swirling chaos of the street, the beeping and *br-rr-ringing* menagerie of bicycles and motorbikes and flat-bed trikes and all their weird hybrid children. And always the teeming footsore hordes, the dull faces and sightless eyes, the over-brimming kiosks and pee-smelling paving stones of a thoroughfare as broad as a city zoo and pointless as a chicken yard—all of it lit by the ugly brown-out haze of what the Chinese call public lighting. Beijing isn't much brighter by day. On cloudless days you still can't find the sun. You can scarcely see buildings two blocks away.

This town likes to go for forbidding Albert Speer-like scale, but you never quite leave the funky ferment of the stained little alleyways where shirtless old men sleep upright in wooden chairs and summer-sweet scents of simmering noodles and open sewers cavort with those of old fruit stalls and one-legged beggars and half-rotted mops. Everywhere you've got the violent collision of a millennia of failed ideas in urban planning and three millennia of no planning at all.

But what's this? Across the broad boulevard are the paired lions and bobbing red lanterns of what seems to be the buffet place. Encouraged, I head for the double doors. They are flanked on either side by four red-uniformed women. Again I feel my belly tighten. Why does Beijing need so many doors and red-uniformed women? I brace myself and at half a furlong all eight girls explode with greetings, throwing open the double doors and inundating me with forward-leaning giggles that practically become kisses.

Cringing, I enter a crowded restaurant practically as rich in noise as in cigarette smoke. Clawing my way through those and the syrupy aromas of courses five through nine, I ascertain that our buffet place is in fact a *lunch* buffet place, and here it is nearly eleven p.m. Back out I scuttle, shrinking back from the red-clad octa-girlie gauntlet just outside the doors.

Skulking south along whatever *lu* this is, I begin scouting for a picture menu taped to a window. Failing a buffet place, the next best option is a picture-menu place. Otherwise you're reduced to pointing toward someone's plate and saying *that*.

Beijing passes before me like a cough-syrup dream.

Just one more deep soul secret and I'll be finished owning for the night. Sometimes Tree's cheek-kisses come a little close to the corner of my mouth and I find myself transported to a climax beech forest on the second day of spring. I'll be the first to admit I don't have Dr. Shatrina Carter figured out even on the most basic of levels, but listen to me. Whatever's brewing within the hormonal soup kitchen of that Hummer body of hers I'd like to have in smokable form. Radio listeners the world over are in love with Tree Carter on the basis of *purr* alone, and many of those careless enough to take a hit of her pheromones are discovered three months later unshaven and bad-smelling wandering Highway 277 outside Wichita Falls.

Two men dodder arm-in-arm along the sidewalk, their newly lit cigarettes glowing brightly. One of them is singing "Yesterday Once More" at the top of his one good lung, cigarette bobbing in time.

Ehhh-veee sha-ra-ra-raaaaaaaah . . .

This afternoon along this same stretch of sidewalk, I encountered five women beneath five black parasols, spaced as regularly as Magritte's derbied Englishmen. For one or two eerie moments, they walked in perfect sync and I knew I'd just wandered into some other room. Sure enough, not three minutes later I encountered the singing condom machine. Five women. Five parasols. Beware.

Then, I haven't taken my meds today.

It's all rooms, you know. One moment you're in this one. Next you're in that one. Before me now, for example, sprawls a vast intersection where several hundred Chinese surge at eight curbs, daring the multi-lane traffic to show the least sign of hesitation. Do I even want to cross here, I ask myself forlornly, peering in one direction and the other. No matter. Soon the traffic lights will change and so will everything else. There's little to be done about it.

The lights do change and I allow myself to be swept along by a human tsunami that engulfs a wooden cart and the hunched man laboring behind it. Next category, one hundred points. Things your sister has whined you into going out for. Two hundred points. Dishes you cannot place anywhere on the USDA food pyramid. Five hundred points. Chinese words that mean something / anything as long as it's dead. Suddenly appear the headlights of left-turning taxis, their horns blaring. Pedestrians scatter in every direction, but I continue my arrogant saunter.

Take me.

The traffic lights glow a unanimous green now and little commuter cars begin honking at my ankles like so many enraged geese. To hell with them. I'm walking here.

There are nearly four million cars in Beijing and not a single old beater among them, for the simple reason that there were no passenger cars at all in this country until very recently. Boxy trucks, yes, and medieval buses and comical donkey-ish agricultural vehicles, all of which are still available for view.

Chinese eighteen-wheelers have fourteen wheels. We'll let that serve as your introduction to Chinese logic.

I make it to the other curb. Nobody ever takes me when I say take me.

But we find ourselves in another room. Suddenly everyone is wearing polyester pajamas. Little kids are pedaling plastic trikes and women are ballroom dancing to boom-boxes and old men are hocking and spitting at one another's feet. Somehow I have entered a residential area. No bobbing red lanterns. No basic food groups.

But wait. My eyes catch sight of a string of weather-skewed lanterns sagging in a nearby alley. We seem to have discovered a second- or third-tier restaurant of some stripe. We begin walking purposefully toward imagined scents of shark's fin and cow's spleen and piggie index finger. I don't care if this place offers up leg of librarian, I'm going in there and coming out with little white boxes.

Inside our eatery are dismal smells of overheated peanut oil and under-cleaned ashtrays. The waitress gives me a gape as she scurries to deliver longnecks to a table of rowdies. We may actually be talking tier number four here. I scan the tables for something / anything dead but discover only beer bottles and smoldering butts.

Suddenly a voice in my right ear. "Excuse me. May I be of assistance?"

Though the accent is West End, London, I turn to encounter the smile of a Chinese man in his forties.

"The score of the Braves game?" I say. "Games, actually. It's a twi-night doubleheader. Or maybe you could help me order a little take-out?"

The stranger laughs apologetically. "This is only a neighborhood restaurant. Not very good I'm afraid. I just come here for the soup. Very good for the health. Please allow me to show you a more splendid place."

Herding me back onto the street, the stranger says, "There is a restaurant close by that's very famous for Peking Duck. Do you like Peking Duck?"

I lie. What else can you do when the man's national dish eats like a Rockport soaked in bacon drippings? So far, my favorite Chinese dish would be Egg Foo Kellogg's Corn Flakes.

The stranger leads me across the same street I just floated my very life to cross. He hands me a business card. "My name is Chen. If you ever need anything, anything at all, call me. I will be happy to help. Please, where are you from?"

Ah. The first of the three splendid questions. Next comes: how long have you been in China, followed closely by: what do you think of China. I provide the usual antiseptic answers and Chen celebrates the fact that I arrived here on an auspicious day. "This is very lucky for you. That day is Cowherd and Weaving Maiden Festival. You have heard of this?"

I haven't heard of this.

"There is a legend about this day," says Chen brightly. "Very long ago, a lonely girl just worked at her weaving all the time. The heavenly father took pity on her and sent her across the stars to marry a cowherd boy. They were very happy together but unfortunately the girl neglected her weaving, so the heavenly father sent her back home, saying you can visit your husband on the seventh day of the seventh month. Ever since, on that night many birds fly together and make a bridge so the weaving maiden can walk across the sky to visit her husband."

Chen turns to beam at me. "Now Chinese women celebrate this night by climbing a hill to offer flowers to the sky."

I stare at him. I'm still waiting for the lucky part. I'm also beginning to suspect this man of taking me back to the house of eight hi-theres. Eight is not my favorite integer.

"Personally," I tell Chen, "I would call this a rather unhappy story."

He laughs. "I think also. This is why only women go to the top of the hill. The men think this is not such a good deal."

Chen knits his brow and sucks his teeth. Among the Chinese this means I-am-now-thinking-very-deeply. A Chinese may also place one hand near his mouth and say, "Nigga, nigga, nigga," which means there's a word on the tip of his or her tongue. Don't try this in Memphis.

"But maybe every romantic story is also very sad," says Chen, "like the play by William Shakespeare."

"*Romeo and Juliet*?"

He nods eagerly. "I think everyone enjoys this play so much because of the suffering. It is the same in life. The love is only as great as the suffering, like in the story of the weaving maiden. For three hundred sixty-four days, nothing but suffering. Then one night of love and—" He beams again. "All was worth it!"

"That goes a long way toward explaining Chinese novels," I tell Chen, gazing dejectedly ahead. He *is* taking me back to the house of eight hi-theres.

As though sensing my urge to bolt, Chen seizes my arm. "This restaurant I think will be more to your enjoying."

Again at half a furlong the double doors fly open and eight identical women explode into scarlet delight. When I open my eyes once more, we are inside the restaurant. The noise and smoke are even denser than before. Now ten minutes of intense negotiations—this is ordering in China—and Chen asks if I'd like to take a seat.

"I'd like to take a beer," I reply, a bit dazed.

We claim the only available table, still covered in mountains of dinner detritus, the wooden chairs still warm. Chen orders two bottles of Hsingtao. "How long will you be in China?" he asks politely. That would be splendid question number four, unless it comes after how do you like Chinese food.

"I don't know," I reply. "I may decide to travel a little."

"Oh! You must see Xi'an and Yunnan."

I've no interest at all in Xi'an and its one thousand terracotta whatevers, but for some reason my ears prick up at the other mention. "Yunnan?"

Chen gestures toward the far end of the restaurant. "Yunnan Province. Southwest. Very far from Beijing. Yunnan is— what is the word? I think *frontier*."

"China has a frontier?"

Chen watches me jot a note in my titanium-plated journal and says, "May I ask what you do, Mr. Mancer?"

"I write."

His posture straightens. "Ah. You are here to write about China's economic growth."

"I'm not that kind of writer."

Chen thinks for a moment. "Then you are here to write about preparations for the 2008 Olympic Games."

I shake my head.

"I think you are being very modest," says Chen with a smile. "Probably you write some very famous books in the USA."

I picture my three very famous novels in discount bins, their upper right-hand corners missing. Shaking my head, I close my journal but don't yet put it away.

"Please," says Chen, "what are you writing about now?"

"Actually I'm here to visit my sister."

After what seems a cool silence, Chen offers his pack of Panda cigarettes and I shake my head. Unhurriedly he lights up then smiles. "I think my countrymen will find your journal very interesting."

"Oh?" I say.

"We Chinese are very affected by the written word. To study the old books is considered the greatest thing a man can do."

Three uniformed Chinese did, in fact, take a very keen interest in my journal just this morning. I don't think it was because they were very affected by the written word.

"In America," I say, "a book is just an opinion. That makes an old book somebody's outdated idea. You know something else? It's a little smoky in here. My nose hairs are beginning to smolder."

"Why don't we wait outside?"

"Why *don't* we wait outside?"

Chen and I push through the doors, and all eight uniformed girls gush a cathartic farewell. It's all I can do to keep from cold-cocking the nearest of them.

Chen and I cast about for an appealing place to drain our beers. Finding none, we turn to face each other.

"May I ask what you do, Mr. Chen?"

With a slight bow, he says, "I teach International Politics at Peking University."

"As soon as you understand America's foreign policy," I say, "I hope you'll explain it to me."

Chen laughs politely. "Fortunately American foreign policy is very easy to understand. Have you read *Rebuilding America's Defenses: Strategies, Forces and Resources for a New Century?*"

I look away. "Missed that one."

"Every American should read this," says Chen. "It describes your country's global policy very clearly."

"So," I say, "what is my country's global policy?"

Chen composes himself before continuing. "According to this document, published in September of 2000, America will dominate the world by attacking every country strong enough to become a potential threat."

"Attacking?" I say.

"Yes, with subversion and if necessary with the military."

I look at him. "You say 'every country.' What about our allies?"

Chen shakes his head. "America will have no more allies. Your leaders believe that you are strong enough to no longer need them."

"Perhaps I should read this book," I say without conviction.

"It is not a book but a position paper written by some conservatives of your country. Several of those men are now in your White House. One is your secretary of state. Another is your vice-president."

We exchange an uncertain gaze and I say, "This seems to concern you, Mr. Chen."

He smiles softly. "China is a very powerful country. This can only mean that the United States will attack us very soon. We can only ask ourselves how it will come."

A shout from the restaurant door.

"Your food is ready," says Chen.

We duck once more beneath the eight cooing young women, their enthusiasm finally beginning to wane. Inside, Chen loads me down with plastic bags containing white boxes of something/anything, and I follow him back out through the doors *and* a final crimson chorus of farewells.

"In China," says Chen, shaking my hand in the brown-out gloom, "we have a saying. 'A wise rabbit has three openings to its den.' May you always be this wise rabbit."

I study the broad, impenetrable grin for a moment before muttering my thanks and turning toward the West Gate. I am hurried along by mingled scents of rice and veggies, shrimp and chicken, pork and bean sprouts. All that's missing are fortune cookies, which the Chinese have never heard of. Just as well, I think. One more Chinese proverb would be exactly two too many.

2

If I admitted it, our mother wasn't too bad with numbers. During her peak years anyway. She lectured at Memphis State Teachers' College and did everyone's taxes in April. Her colleagues probably saw her as somewhat heroic. Unwed mother for science or something of the kind. It was she who introduced me to Zeno's Motion Paradox—out of malice, I believe, as I was a hideously overgrown and under-cooked eleven-year-old in need of some means of believing in himself.

By the time I solved Zeno, I was a hollow-eyed twelve point five, but solve it I did. When I handed the solution to my mother, she gave it a disinterested glance and announced that the problem had been solved quite satisfactorily a century earlier. I began wetting the bed shortly thereafter. But only on nights that were primes.

Just so you'll know, Zeno's Motion Paradox has been around for over two thousand years, and my solution, conceived when I was twelve point five years old, is among the most elegant ever proposed. I didn't say that. A reviewer said that of the article my mother wrote presenting my solution under her name. I've never been troubled by the Oedipus complex. What I have is the Menendez Brothers complex.

I am standing on a street corner awaiting Ralpho, a fellow I met late last night in an Irish pub on Third Ring Road. Why we chose this corner to reconvene eludes me, as its one claim to charm seems to be the smelly one-legged and one-armed burn victim who lies twitching and contorting across the sidewalk so that passersby have to step over or around him.

His begging bowl is as filthy as his clothes, not that *Mongo* is paying much mind to either just now, as he seems to be in some kind of open-mouthed drug-induced stupor. Which in general terms I greatly admire in a man. Still, I'm keeping one eye on this fellow, as I imagine he could really cover some ground should he take a mind to, differently abled though he is.

Ralpho and I didn't set this up very precisely. I don't know whether he's to appear in a taxi or on foot, or even whether I'm awaiting him on the proper street corner, Ralpho not having said anything at all about Mongo, and I'd certainly have. I'm pretty sure we established four-thirty as the meeting time, and here it is nearly five and I'm beginning to worry.

When I met Ralpho last night, he was half-eating half-wearing a plate of wet ribs, for which he admits a keen fondness. Thus Ralpho's belly precedes him by about a minute and a half. He has a habit of chewing his reddish-orange beard—conveniently the same color as barbeque sauce—when excited, which appears to be frequently. You can see where he's bitten parts of it off.

Ralpho speaks with the restrained swagger of an East Texan who is confident that he knows considerably more than you but sees no reason to rub it in. On balance, he smells a good deal better than Mongo and has offered to introduce me to a Triad-operated steam-bath brothel that offers happy hour from five to six.

It's two minutes till five.

The lips of a donkey, the Chinese are fond of pointing out, do not fit on the mouth of a horse. Based on that same general logic, I began this day by stuffing my long, lustrous mane into a stocking cap to minimize the visual impact of appearing in public with both my sister, ponytailed and wearing grey sweats, and Tree, in sunglasses. We exited the girls' hotel at separate moments to meet at a nearby corner where their fellow teacher, Arnie, was quite punctually waiting. The idea was to spend a morning viewing the sights of Beijing as inconspicuously as could be arranged.

Arnie flagged two taxis for us but before we could arrange ourselves in either, a crowd had formed and photos were being snapped. Tree, being Tree, became ebullient and gave the masses a few bars of "I Loves You, Porgy" to delighted cheers. Meanwhile I spotted a video surveillance camera above our heads—they're everywhere in this town—and deduced that the edge-recognition software had most likely kicked in and the black panel trucks were headed our way. I back-loaded Tree, still singing, into the rear of one of the taxis, and we booked out of there.

We saw Wax Mao in his Mao-soleum. You couldn't really tell much. They don't let you poke him or sniff him or anything. At least Tree Carter didn't break out into "Oh Danny Boy." Our next stop was the overcrowded and heat-oppressed Temple of Heaven Park, which I found interesting in a highly statistical kind of way. The Circular Mound Altar in particular turns out to be some kind of algorithm cut from white marble, every tiny detail elaborated in multiples of nine, Nine being symbolic among the Chinese of completion and heaven, not to mention the soup course.

The airless heat finally got to Tree, who is at all moments dehydrated, if she admitted it. She refuses to take on water outside the hotel, due I'm quite sure to squat-toilet issues. I was afraid the others of us were going to have to bear her to a taxi. Back at the hotel, she insisted she'd been overcome by the energy of that place, which bore unusual and spiteful signatures. "One more minute," Tree told us, "and I would've passed dead out." And we would've been faced with discovering the Mandarin word for U-Haul.

I now have independent confirmation of the singing condom machine. I thought you'd want to know. I even have a translation of the jingle. "Always remember because it's your duty and keeps your wife and parents smiling. Also smells good."

And pleases Wax Mao.

I check my watch again. It's five-oh-four. Fifty-six minutes of happy remaining. This sidewalk is so hot meanwhile, a wind is rising off it. I've been warned that summer in Beijing can be hallucinatory. Its vast stretches of concrete absorb more solar radiation than the dense atmosphere can begin to disperse. You can use Beijing air as a building material. You want to gnaw on the number-two German-made pencil in your shirt pocket just for the oxygen content.

Finally deciding that I can't remain here a moment longer, I turn and begin planning my negotiation around a whimpering Mongo when a very small taxi screeches to a stop, in the passenger seat, his belly crowding the dashboard, Ralpho. His nose is pressed against the side window. His lips seem to be saying, "Get in."

I do my level best, crawling headfirst into the rear and pulling the door closed with one of my feet. "Is this a means of transport," I ask, "or of preserving foodstuffs?" At least it's air-conditioned.

"We're headed for Nanshan District," says Ralpho, trying to turn in the seat. "You wanna help me out with the cab fare? Shouldn't be more than a hundred yuan altogether. We're paying extra for air."

Ralpho is short for Ralph O'Malley, ex-military. Army *and* Navy. Evidently the Air Force wouldn't have him. Ralpho now teaches English wherever he can score a contract, this year Taipei, next year Singapore. His main reason for being in Beijing just now, he has confided, has less to do with gainful employment than with hard research for his blog on China's secret moon bases.

"Yeah, sure I know about the bases," he told me last night, his pale blue eyes reaching for casual understatement. "In the military they're a known fact to everyone above pay grade three, and I was way above that." Ralpho's tongue was beginning to toy with his beard. Before the evening was over, I'd learned of an extraterrestrial plot to annex the world by covertly funding anti-gun legislation and vegetarianism. "When we no longer have guns," said Ralpho, cold-eyed, "or eat meat, what's the difference between us and a cow?"

The spots?

The mini-taxi stops on a quiet side street, and I labor to open the rear door with my foot. Ralpho, meanwhile, initiates an argument with the driver in hopelessly bad Mandarin— even I can tell—before reporting, "We're gonna have to over-pay this asshole. It's less hassle than calling the transit cops. He says it's a hundred eighty. Can you do the hundred? I can do the eighty."

Now on the superheated sidewalk, Ralpho pushes open an unmarked steel door and we scale two narrow flights of concrete steps, at the top of which is another unmarked steel door. Leaning on the buzzer, Ralpho tells me over his shoulder, "I'll take care of everything. They know me here."

The door pops opens and we encounter a burly green-eyed Chinese man in a gold silk suit. Another argument. It seems that, yes they know Ralpho here, but they don't partic-ularly like him. After ten minutes of hand-waving and finger-pointing and a two-hundred-yuan payoff from my pocket, we get past the portal guardian.

"Fucking jerk," mutters Ralpho, now leading me along another corridor. "Said I owe a tab. Usual Chinese bullshit. Fucking highway robbery every step of the way. You see those green contacts, man? You fucking *see* that?"

Once, in Queens, New York, I heard a man generate the following sentence: Fuck that fucking fuck up the fucking fuckhole. Interestingly the man was not at all upset at the time but actually appeared to be in good spirits.

The corridor takes us back down to street level and around a corner before ascending once more to a second-floor landing where a well-dressed woman smiles behind a large teak desk that displays nothing but her own folded hands. After a brief discussion, Ralpho and I place six hundred yuan at the center of the desk. The two hands sweep the bills away in favor of a pair of keys, two white bath towels, matching white terry robes and four hopelessly small blue plastic sandals.

I follow Ralpho into a dressing room where a sound system oozes Montivani. Several men are toweling off and donning street clothes. All of them are Chinese and all have pubic hair. One question answered. I scan their expressions for evidence of happy but find only inscrutable.

Following Ralpho's lead, I use my key to open an empty locker and place my clothes and shoes inside. My terry robe turns out to approximate the size of a handkerchief. I manage to get my shoulders inside and tie it around my sternum. Ralpho frowns at me through his glasses and tries to pull the robe down a little. "Perfect," he says. "You just need a little sun."

We pass through a swinging wooden door into what appears to be the golden age of Pompeii. I pause for a moment, letting my eyes adjust to the dim light. Half concealed by a drifting, herb-scented veil of vapor are various pools of emerald water. Vague human forms seem to cavort there, doing things I can't quite make out but would really like to.

"Come on," calls Ralpho, walking ahead. "I'll show you around."

Toes squenched up in my blue sandals, I follow Ralpho past a long line of wooden doors. "Saunas," he informs me. "The ones on the right are, like, Japanese only. Same with the herbal baths. Stay to the left."

Ralpho opens an anonymous door and I recoil from a blast of hot, dry air. "Sauna *with* company," says Ralpho. As the door auto-closes, I catch sight of two dripping young women tucked into a corner, wrapped in red towels.

Pressing on, Ralpho says, "Don't get carried away. Everything here goes on a tab and nothing's cheap."

"But it's Happy Hour, right?"

Shrugging, Ralpho pushes through a massive swinging door. We enter a large humidity-controlled room filled with billiards and ping-pong tables. Along one wall, several white-robed men smoke cigarettes and study a row of computer monitors. Everything is spotless.

"It's early," says Ralpho. "Nobody's here yet. C'mon, I'll show you the library."

I glance at my watch. Thirty-seven minutes of happy remaining, and Ralpho wants to show me the library. I follow him through a massive Mandarin, Japanese, Korean, and English library and three adjoining television rooms. There's also a tea room with its own bamboo garden, plus various massage rooms, reflexology tables, and other spaces I don't fully comprehend. Some of the male clients, I notice, are accompanied by demure young women in robes of flaming red.

Asian women wear red *so* well.

Now we're touring a fern bar heavy with oak. At one side, a carpeted staircase leads to rooms that Ralpho assures me we cannot afford.

"Didn't you tell me Happy Hour is from—"

Before I can finish, Ralpho gives me a two-handed shove and I stumble through a massive wooden door.

I find myself enclosed by a wall of vapor so shockingly hot that I'm momentarily blinded. Before I find my bearings, I feel several small hands pulling at my robe. As my eyes clear, I find that I'm one of several naked humans in a Fellini-esque landscape of coy giggles, towering statuary and slowly swirling steam. The first thing I make out with any certainty is the sight of two slender women wrapped around a man, one of them sucking intently on his face, the other similarly employed somewhat farther south.

Watching with interest are two silver-haired men seated on contoured wooden benches, their yellow shoulders kneaded by a pair of full-lipped young women who now offer me a single stare. Looming eerily above the scene is an enormous golden Buddha perhaps two stories tall, his pudgy features set in a deliberate Elvis-like sneer. On either side of the statue, massive Roman columns seem to rise forever amid upward-spiraling clouds of pure devilment.

I turn to look for Ralpho. Instead I discover three wispy Asian women who approach tentatively as though never having seen a body at once so large and so white. Apparently they're getting used to it. Opening my arms, I allow all three to press their superheated bodies against mine.

Ah. Happy.

Bending to sniff the wet hair of each golden child, I find their skin generously oiled, allowing my hands to glide along each warm curve as on a raceway. I bend a little farther to investigate the subtle differences in the muscle tone of each little bum—when a gruff voice calls, *"Bie!"*

Instantly the three girls grab red towels and exit through the swinging wooden door, followed by all the others, lastly the two silver-haired men, their escorts helping them into white robes as they jog past.

Considerably less happy now, I turn and peer into the steam, wondering whose voice I'd heard and why it couldn't have waited a bit longer. As I watch, an unclothed, short, and pudgy Chinese man emerges from between the golden legs of the Buddha, a damp unlit cigarette hanging from his lips. Stopping directly before me, feet widely set, he gazes up at my face then unhurriedly down to my toes and back again.

"Big," he says at last and chuckles.

I watch the man remove the unlit cigarette from his lips as though to dust an ash. "You like steam?" he asks roughly.

I've no idea how to reply.

After a moment, the naked man nods and returns the cigarette to his mouth. "Don't like to talk? Good. Don't need to talk. Don't need to talk nobody. You okay? Talk nobody? You understand?"

The man gazes at me for a long moment before stepping aside and pointing to the steam-swirling gap between the Buddha's legs. I walk mechanically in that direction, glancing up to note the *very* enlightened hard-on lifting the awakened one's tunic. Ducking beneath the prodigious set of golden balls, I enter a shadowed space of redwood benches where, by slow degrees, I make out the form of a seated Westerner wearing the tormented expression of a newly condemned man and a hopelessly wet British-cut three-piece suit. In the man's lap is an overstuffed briefcase, its papers wilting.

"Mr. Mancer? Are you Julian Mancer?" the man says eagerly. "Mr. Mancer, forgive me for not getting up but I fear that I have lost the strength of my limbs. Please be assured that this meeting place is not, I repeat, *not* of my choosing. In point of fact, I had to practically fight to retain my clothes, which I am sorry to see you were unable to do. Won't you please have a seat?"

Too bewildered to respond, I watch the stranger, sweat dripping from his nose, fumble in the soggy briefcase. For a moment I fully expect him to propose the merits of a variable universal life insurance policy with critical illness.

"I am fully aware," says the man, still fumbling, "that the *gentlemen* here are mocking me, but as I told them repeatedly and tell you now, I am a devoted lifetime Latter Day Saint—most people say Mormon because of *The Book of Mormon*—and would no sooner take off my clothes among these—well—"

"Who *are* you?" I ask.

He sits taller. "My name is Jerry Scribner. I represent various international companies in East Asia, among them Hydrangea Laboratories of Chicago, Illinois. It would appear they are very interested in contacting you, as they have overnighted me here to deliver this message, which I cannot do quickly enough if you would—"

"You're from Savannah," I interrupt.

Scribner nods appreciatively. "Very, very good. I am from Charlestown, fifty miles from Savannah."

"Why would Hydrangea Labs want to talk to me?" I ask, sweat stinging both my eyes. "More to the point, why would I want to talk to them?"

"Mr. Mancer, if you would just *sit* for a moment—" Scribner says irritably, trying to avoid the sight of a certain parsnip.

Reluctantly I take a seat beside Jerry Scribner. The last time a man with a briefcase invited me to sit, I came away with the blue copy and the pink copy and he with three-quarters of my portfolio—something to do with my then-wife and the narrowest possible interpretation of our wedding vows.

"Thank you," says Scribner, extracting a cell phone from his briefcase and pressing a button. He holds the phone out to me.

I hear one ring, then: "Hello? Mr. Mancer? Are you on the line?"

Sighing, I accept the phone. "This is Julian Mancer."

"Thank God," says a reedy voice. "Mr. Mancer, we have turned over heaven and hell to find you. I do hope you're well this eve—uh, morning."

"It's late afternoon. May I ask who I'm speaking to?"

"I am Edgar Spears, a research fellow at the University of Chicago. We haven't met but I do look forward to meeting you at the earliest possible moment. Would you like me to come directly to the point?"

"I would appreciate that."

"Mr. Mancer, we are at a very crucial crossroads in a research project of some importance, and it would be incredibly, incredibly helpful if you and your sister, Lillian—"

"Dr. Spears," I cut in, "surely you know where my sister and I are, geographically?"

"I do."

"And that we have moved on to other things professionally?"

"Yes, yes," says the voice on the phone. "We are very sensitive to that, I assure you."

Wiping my eyes, I ask, "What happened to the Sullivan twins? Isn't Hydrangea working with Edna and Elsa Sullivan?"

"Not for some time," comes the answer. "But even if that were the case—"

"What about Nelga and Helga Olszewski? Have you called them?"

"I'm sorry. We have no interest at all in the Olszewskis."

"Kyung-Ho and Gung-Ho Seok?"

"No, no."

"Flossie and Freddie Bobbsey?"

"Mr. Mancer. There is no one except yourself and your sister, no one whatsoever, who can take us where we must now go."

I close my eyes. I want to be angry with this man but I can't quite find it. Finally I say, "You came to the point for me, Doctor. I'll do the same for you. My sister and I do not want to work for Hydrangea, nor Gardenia, nor Creeping Myrtle, nor any other zone-nine ornamental. In fact, we're very busy people these days, so—"

"You still manage to find Dr. Fenwick's lab from time to time," says Spears. "I should congratulate you. The Mancer twins are putting parapsychology on the map just as you once did for polar-body genetics."

"Lillian and I have *retired*," I say carefully. "Our work with Beth Fenwick is highly sporadic, completely voluntary and absolutely tax-deductible, so—"

The voice on the phone changes. "Mr. Mancer, the gentleman who gave you the phone has an envelope. Ask him for it."

"An envelope? For me? How thoughtful."

On cue, the South Carolina lawyer produces a damp letter-sized envelope.

Spears almost whispers, "I think you will find this project extremely well-funded. We are prepared to fly you and Lillian, first class, all expenses—"

"Have you heard of Mancer's law?" I ask, ignoring the envelope.

"Uh, no, I don't think so."

"The higher the funding, the lower the ethics. Those are Lillian's words, but I like to say them. And I really should be going now. Only thirteen minutes of happy left."

Spears says, "Mr. Mancer, I understand you're experiencing some personal financial issues. Why not let us help you with that?"

"Look, you people totally blew it with my sister, okay? When it comes to listening devices in the toaster oven, Lillian's limit is one. By the way, what happened to me on the street yesterday?"

"Happened to you?" says Spears.

"It's your duty? Keeps the wife and parents smiling? Pleases Wax Mao?"

"Julian. Listen to me. Come home. Complete your work. There's only so much I can tell you on the phone."

"Well, I'm not coming to Chicago to hear it," I say. "And if you even *think* about contacting my sister, you are going to meet our attorney, and he does get naked. Good morning—uh, night. Uh, bye."

I punch End Call and offer the phone to the unsmiling attorney.

"Sorry about that last part," I say.

3

Reading alone in the tea room is Ralph O'Malley. On the table before him is half a Heineken and an untouched pack of Kools. At my approach, he breaks into a boyish grin.

"So how was it?" he asks, turning his paperback novel face-down. It's *The Loins of a Princess* by Lowell P. Nightsong.

I stop to give him a stare. "How was what? I had less than two minutes of happy. Who told you to bring me here?"

The grin disappears, and Ralpho looks away. "It's your first time. Place grows on you."

I take a seat across from him. "Ralpho, who told you to bring me here?"

Pushing his glasses higher on his nose, Ralpho says, "Look, I'm sorry if it didn't work out. It's got nothing to do with me, okay? Let me buy you a good German beer."

"Ralpho, who told—"

"I don't know and I don't care," he fires back. "This is a big town, okay? I don't know what happened in there, and I don't want to know. Come on, forget about it."

"What exactly happened to me on the street yesterday?"

"I got no fucking idea what you're talking about," says Ralpho.

"On the street," I say slowly, my voice rising. "Yesterday. Something happened. What was it?"

Ralpho takes an unhurried inhalation and lets it out. "Know what I just did? I counted to ten. Know why? You're shouting at me. When people shout at me, my blood pressure goes up and I make bad decisions." He picks up his paperback novel. "I don't even know who the fuck you are."

I sit back in my chair and try to arrange my robe so that it covers a third of me. It's a scary thought, but Ralph O'Malley could be the closest thing to a reliable source of information I currently have.

"I'll take the beer," I say.

Three and a half Heinekens later, Ralpho knows all about the singing condom machine, or what little I know to tell. Here I am walking along the street when I hear this god-awful screeching that roughly approximates the human voice. I turn to discover a condom-vending machine attached to a masonry wall, just crooning its little hiney off. Since I'm putting something together for October, I quite naturally stop to jot a note in my journal. Suddenly this very pale Westerner in a red Ohio State tee is grabbing me around the shoulders and saying, "Hey, guy, let's go have a beer!" Now he's *hauling* me along the sidewalk and whispering, "Keep walking. Don't turn around. You're about to be arrested."

Naturally I did turn around, and walking straight toward me were three well-starched military uniforms. Mr. Buckeye stepped in front of a cab and we dove inside. "You picked a bad place to jot notes," I was told as the cab sped away. "You were standing in front of a military installation. Something important must be going down there. Those guys were definitely going to grab you." All the while, the stranger was throwing blue-eyed glances through the rear window of the cab. Adrenaline-charged. Completely calm. Neck like a sycamore. Not exactly my picture of a Fulbright scholar, which was the story he gave me. Oh, and his name. His name was *John.*

John, the Fulbright scholar.

The taxi dropped me at Tiananmen Square and disappeared. I haven't seen Mr. Buckeye since. End of story, or so I hope.

Ralpho frowns. "So, what are you saying? You think this guy's a spook?"

"I don't know. What do you know about spooks?"

He shrugs. "Probably is a spook. Beijing's full of them. But that doesn't explain why he'd want to grab you off the sidewalk like that."

"His adrenaline fix of the day?" I say. "Maybe he just goes around doing good deeds. Maybe he's Agent Double-O Nice."

"Maybe he was following you," says Ralpho. "You know any reason why someone would be following you?"

"I could come up with a number of reasons, none of them particularly rational."

"Then he probably wasn't. Maybe he was on his way to lunch. Spooks eat lunch. He saw the bad guys coming and decided to save your ass. I would've done the same thing."

I try to picture Ralph O'Malley saving someone's ass.

"Or," he continues, "he might have been surveilling the army base and you just happened along. Either way, it's not about you."

"Why," I ask, "would you surveil something in Beijing in a red Ohio State tee and skin the approximate color of copy paper?"

Ralpho adjusts his glasses. "I didn't say he was smart."

"And why would he blow his cover like that, assuming the poor man had any to begin with?"

"I used to drink beer with a couple of spooks when I was in the service," Ralpho says with a touch of swagger. "They're just guys. They can screw up."

"This guy didn't impress me as a screw-up."

Ralpho shifts in his chair. "Okay, let's look at it from another perspective. You're a writer. Maybe you're looking into something the US government's a little nervous about."

"I'm not that kind of writer."

"Nobody has a file on you? Think about it. Have you ever picketed? Signed a petition? It's not that hard to get on a list."

"In that case," I argue, "the list would be too long to mean anything. Your grandmother would be on it."

My sister's on it, if anyone is. Lillian has herself arrested at various political protests as frequently as her schedule permits. The Memphis police love hauling her in. They call her Long Tall.

Lil also has a sizable *pro bono* law practice related to a personal mission to assist immigrant Honduran women with multiple personality disorder.

"Maybe they're worried you'll be approached by one of the dissident groups here," suggests Ralpho, lighting a fresh cigarette. He's starting to enjoy this.

I grimace. "I'm probably not on the short list of many dissident groups."

"Could you have some kind of information? Is there anything we wouldn't want the Chinese to get their hands on?"

"No," I answer quickly, but my blood chills a half degree.

"You sure?" asks Ralpho.

"Why do you ask me if I'm sure?"

"I don't know," he replies. "You just looked like you weren't sure."

"You want another one of those high-class beers?" I ask.

"I can drink another one."

As I look around for the waiter, I ask myself what just happened. It was almost too subtle to notice, yet somewhere inside me a circuit closed, a single piece of information flowed, and my response was fear.

Lillian and I go out of our way to not think about it. Who wants to imagine that your names are tucked into file folders in gun-metal–grey cabinets in every capital of the world. Ralpho's right about one thing. It's not that hard to get your name on a list. What's hard is getting it off again.

The beers arrive. After the waiter goes, I clear my throat. "Uh, there may be one other possibility. It's probably nothing. In fact, I'm sure it's nothing."

Ralpho waits.

"From time to time, my sister and I work as research subjects. We have a reputation of sorts."

"Are you identical twins?" asks Ralpho.

I look at him disappointedly. "Identicals are same-sex. Lillian and I are polar-body twins. Identical genetic material from the mother, different from the father."

"Is that pretty rare?" asks Ralpho.

I nod. The odds against having twins of any description are thirty-three to one. Against having identicals, it's two hundred eighty-five to one. The odds against polar-body twins, say nothing of a mixed pair—well, let me put it this way. Lillian and I have met all the other such pairs known to exist. Both of them.

"What kind of research do you do?" asks Ralpho.

"Remote viewing, remote influencing, that sort of thing."

Ralpho's head jerks up. "Are you talking about psychic research? Jesus, are you serious?"

"It's not that big a deal."

"Don't you read?" he asks. "Don't you know how big the CIA is into all that shit? No wonder they're crawling all over you."

Ralpho looks over both his shoulders. "Listen, the Russians have been into psychic research forever, and we're busting our ass to catch up with them. I'll bet the CIA funded every dime of those research projects."

I stare at my German beer. More likely NSA than CIA, if that makes a difference.

For a moment I consider asking Ralpho what he knows about a certain pharmaceutical consortium beginning with H and ending with –ydrangea. My mouth can't quite form the words.

"We're retired," I tell Ralpho. "When Lil and I work now, it's for a little university lab about three blocks from my apartment. They have no money at all. They can't buy paper clips."

"That's even worse," says Ralpho. Raking book, cigarettes, and ashtray to one side, he leans toward me. "Listen, Mancer, if the Russians are doing it and we're doing it, you can bet your ass the Chinese are doing it. So here's the question. How do we know you aren't here to fucking defect?"

I think for a moment. "Americans can defect?"

"You just told me you aren't making any money," says Ralpho. "So maybe you and your sister are shopping yourselves around. Think about it."

I close my eyes wearily. "Look, maybe I gave you the wrong idea. We aren't *that* well known."

"It doesn't even matter how good you are," says Ralpho. "All that matters is the perception. If the Americans have the perception that the Chinese have the perception—"

Two white-robed men walk very near our table, and Ralpho stops himself. I take a tiny sip of beer. There's a knot in my stomach the size of a fist. Lil and I put all that Hydrangea crap behind us for a very good reason. It was creeping us out.

"If there's even the perception," continues Ralpho, "that the Chinese might be interested, agents are going to be climbing hand-over-hand up your ass, okay? Look what happened yesterday. It looked like the Chinese were going to grab you, so we grabbed you."

"Stop," I tell him.

"And you know the Russians are watching," he goes on. "And the Brits. And the fucking North Koreans."

"Ralpho, stop."

"It becomes a circus, I'm telling you."

"How do you know all this?"

Ralpho's face slams shut. "I can't tell you."

"That's probably best," I say weakly.

He leans a little closer. "Look, why didn't you just read that guy's mind? That John guy? I mean, you could read it right now, couldn't you?"

"Actually, no."

"All I can tell you is," says Ralpho, stubbing out his cigarette, "it's going to be weird the whole time you're over here. If I were you, I'd take care of business and get the hell out of China."

"And one more thing," he adds, his pale blue eyes sharpening. "That Arnie guy you were hanging with this morning? I don't think I'd tell him what you just told me."

"Arnie? Arnie's just a teacher in Lil's group."

I watch Ralpho munch a bit of moustache. I should never have brought this up. Sighing, I rise from the table.

"Gimme a call sometime," says Ralpho. "We'll talk some more."

"I don't do phones."

"Buy yourself a phone," he says flatly. "Keep it with you. Weird shit happens in this country."

I turn away. Once all the squirrels are dead, the Chinese are fond of saying, the dogs that tracked them will be cooked. I'm not sure why that comes to me just now. They also say it's bad luck to walk beneath a pair of trousers, but I think that depends on who's wearing them.

Outside, evening has become night. The prevailing aroma seems to be one part honeysuckle, two parts bus exhaust, and three parts inscrutable Chinese sewage. Overhead is the searing roar of jet engines, but when I look up I see only the usual Beijing sheetrock. I've been in this town for four days and I've yet to see either the sun or a bird.

Take care of business, said Ralpho, and get out of China. I ask myself just how much credence to give a man who blogs about moon bases. I'd love to hear his theories on Bat Boy. And how exactly did Ralpho know I spent the morning with Arnie? I don't remember saying a word.

Frowning, I pass a row of bicycle shops, their greasy overflow of tools and spare parts half-covering the sidewalk. In each shop is a little shelf with a Taoist altar with blinking red lights. One features a rearing horse cut from paper. The Year of the Horse. Shocking new developments. Rapid advancement. Unexplained cravings for oats.

Hitchcock said there has to be a MacGuffin. It doesn't matter what the MacGuffin is, as long as everyone wants it.

Or maybe, it occurs, nobody wants it but only imagines that everyone else does.

Nearby, an old man pauses to hock up a lung, repeating his extended shhhhree-*eee*-aughk until everyone in East Rutherford knows all about it. Beyond him, an eight-stories-tall Yao Ming enjoys a Pepsi. I find myself once more searching the sky. I never knew that I liked the sight and sound of birds. When the Chinese go to the park, they bring their own, hanging their cages in the trees. I suppose it reminds them a little of the world.

I cast about for a taxi, and of course there is none. Stuffing my hands into my pockets, I encounter something and pull out the fax from Hydrangea Laboratories. Exactly four words: Please call Chicago immediately. Listed are four phone numbers. I especially like the *please*.

The Hydra, you may recall, was a nine-headed monster that could neither be killed nor induced to vote split-ticket. Even Hercules was reduced to trapping the revolting thing under a rock. My hands begin to crumple the fax but instead return it to my pocket. I've a feeling this particular nine-headed monster isn't going back under its rock quite yet.

4

I discovered dominos at the tender age of two. There was a boxed set on a lower shelf in our mother's living room. I'll never forget the first time I dumped them onto the thirsty pine floor and heard that arresting *clatter*, that precise brilliance, each note exactly the same. The tiles themselves looked quite identical, each an elegant response to a single perfectly articulated idea.

At last, I thought. Civilization.

I seated myself and carefully lifted one of the glossy, impossibly smooth tiles and gazed into the eyes of a sinister reptile with oversized claws. It stood out, black on black, in relief. On the other side were white dots in two groupings, each dot identically recessed. I used the tip of a forefinger to explore one dot, feeling every detail of its contour.

Surveying the other upturned tiles, I discovered that each tile was divided into two segments of equal measure, and the concepts *half* and *double* appeared in my mind. The tiles, I quickly gathered, varied one from another only in terms of the dots. The concept *quantity* appeared in my mind. In that singular moment, holding that first tile in my fingers, I knew I'd encountered the most perfect thing in existence. Platonic. Cold. Alien. Like myself.

And it was clean. Very clean.

It wasn't long before Mother appeared in the living room and re-boxed the dominos—they fit the box *exactly*—and placed them on a higher shelf. But as small children go I was reasonably resourceful and soon was rising from my bed while the house slept to, with the aid of a broom and a bathmat, reacquire the dominos and continue my work in theoretical math. I learned to arrange the tiles in ascending and descending order, and to form number loops that fed one into the other, gradually evolving a personal understanding of mathematics that would result in failing marks in arithmetic in grades one through four. Fifth grade is when you realize that either you dumb it down really fast or you'll never kiss a girl.

By that time, I had acquired four boxes of dominos of my own and was combining them into arrays that required the entire floor of my bedroom. Unfortunately, there was no lock on my door and our mother was fond of trumping up reasons to impound my dominos while I was away at school.

Still, I discovered that I could lie on my back on the pine floorboards and gaze upward to visualize the tiles floating upon the air, first along two-dimensional planes and then three. Just once, at age thirteen, shortly after my discovery of coffee, I successfully incorporated a fourth dimension. It was around that time that I encountered double dominos and, well, I didn't kiss a girl until I was twenty. She was unconscious at the time.

All of this eventually went into two papers, or all except that last bit, entitled *The Nature of Integer as Revealed by Dominos*, which was published but not widely appreciated, and *Double Dominos as a Self-Enfolding Revelation of Implicit Order*, which was neither appreciated nor published. All of which is a way of saying-without-saying there is a mental illness to which the genius is more susceptible than the fool. A wealth of them, actually, and I am prey to most—but to none quite so much as *one*.

The vague smear of the moon makes an appearance low in the east, and a waiter materializes from the gloom to give my table a swipe. I request a glass of red in honor of the ghost of Li Bai (rhymes with *be high*). If anyone haunts the moonlit nights of Cathay, it's the Bacchus-laureate of the

High Tang dynasty who, it's said, drowned one night trying to embrace the reflection of the moon on the water.

Gotta know how to die.

Personally, I'm feeling better all the time. My few days of sweats and tremors have passed, along with the whole jet lag thing. I think it was for the most part a case of too much railroad gin back in Memphis, which served as a port of refuge over the past eight or nine months of my life. Not Memphis. Railroad gin. Now it's warm Chinese beer and metallic Aussie wine, and not in the trendiest of nightspots.

This outdoor bar, roughly mid-campus of Peking University, is comprised of three unsteady tables, a few weather-ravaged wooden chairs, a refrigerator, and a dirty candle that sputters heroically as I ask myself what is keeping Her Treeness. It wasn't easy scheduling this tête-à-tête without tête number three horning in. Lillian and Tree met at a prayer vigil on the original Harmonic Convergence, thereafter to harmonically converge at the hip. You get one, you get the other. I did manage to catch Tree alone this afternoon just long enough to cajole her into a little bonding time beneath the splendid sheetrock sky.

The Cabernet arrives, and I hoist it to the indistinct moon, recalling Li Bai's immortal words:

> Amidst these flowers, a jug of wine.
> I pour myself the cup of aloneness.
> Raising it high, I invite the bright moon
> Then turn to my shadow, which—

"Hello, how *ahhh* you?"

A polite distance from my table stands a smiling young couple, prodigious stacks of books beneath their scrawny arms. Chinese scholars, I've learned, take every opportunity to converse with Westerners, which is very flattering until they bring up Hemingway and Joyce and Keats and Elliot and

Melville. These kids have not only read all the books you fully intended to, but quote from them and would like to compare their impressions with, mmm, yours.

"Fine," I tell them, "and you?"

The young man replies, "Fine and you?" before catching himself. They both fan the air and laugh.

I invite the couple to sit but they refuse, actually backing up a step. Both man and woman wear glasses, *de rigueur* for Chinese scholars, the most respected of whom have totally wrecked their eyes by fifth grade.

We don't use the word *scholar* in the States, and I suppose we shouldn't. We have *students*, guys and gals in baseball caps who attend most of their classes, read half their texts and, as seniors, if faced with locating the university library, inquire at the student help desk. At Peking U, you can hardly walk for people studying. They're on benches, bridges, boulders, every horizontal surface, slumped over their books or pacing feverishly, reading aloud to themselves.

The closest American parallel would be a really serious gym, wordless people sweating at this or that machine, each alone in his pool of suffering. It's scholarship as athleticism. Go into one of the buildings at Peking U and you'll find a yellow butt in every chair, a jar of tea on every desk, and such rip-throat intensity you're convinced that finals must be going on. Finals aren't going on. Classes aren't going on. This is summer holiday. You're looking at Chinese scholars on vacation.

From the smiling young couple, I learn that fall semester begins in two weeks. "We go home to visit only the short time," the man tells me, "then go here again very quick." Now he laughs apologetically. "My English is only reading. Very sorry."

"The economy is very . . . is very . . . ," begins his companion, but she stalls out and laughs to cover her embarrassment. "I think the jobs in China is very few, and so many students."

"*So* many students," echoes the young man, sucking his teeth.

I nod amenably, as though I can fathom what it's like to grow up in a place where even the arts are reduced to numbers and rankings. In China everything finally goes back to *the* number: one point three billion. You've got a quarter of the world's population here trying to make a living boiling bird's nest soup for one another.

I'm handed two business cards. All Chinese students carry them, networking having been basically invented by this culture. The Mandarin word is *guanxi*, and success without it is wholly unimaginable. The young man, I learn, is an investment broker to-be. The young woman is studying law, specializing in women's issues. I'm as unprepared for the one as for the other. Who's going to drive the tractor, I want to ask.

"My father," she tells me, "is very important in the Party. I can use my, mmmm, my in-fru-nace?"

"Influence?" I say.

"My in-fru-ance, I think, can help someone. Chinese women is *so* hard to have the life. I visit a women's shelter in Cambridge, Massachusetts. Now I open here in Beijing."

"First shelter woman child in all China," the young man says proudly. "Four beds."

I nod approvingly. Nine hundred million Chinese women and children and four beds. I hope they're willing to share.

Meanwhile, our budding social reformer pays for her meals by washing dishes at the university dining hall—a punishment from her father, who wanted her in business law.

The smiling young couple inquires of my plans. I tell them I'm going to Yunnan. They seem as surprised as I to hear it.

"Yunnan?" asks he. "Yunnan Province?"

"You are going to Yunnan?" asks she. "That is my home province!"

Apparently this is quite the coincidence, as they're practically dancing around in circles. Before it's over, I have three names and phone numbers of English speakers I'm to ring as soon as I arrive in the capital city of Kunming. Not quite satisfied with this, the young woman writes a formal note of introduction and signs it with a flourish.

"This say, 'Please help this person every courtesy,'" she smiles, presenting the note with a bow.

Off go the two young scholars, waving emphatically. I give the note of introduction a dull glance before tucking it into my wallet. Who knows when a little *guanxi* might come in *handxi*? I toss down the last drop of my wine and glance left and right, hoping to catch sight of an approaching Shatrina Carter, who, I remind myself, was born three weeks late only to fall ever farther behind. Once she does arrive, I resolve quite firmly, either *Madame* turns out to be in the mood for a nice little séance or it's going to get ugly out on the veranda.

The indistinct, bitten moon has all but cleared the treetops. Again I lift my glass.

> . . . I pour myself the cup of aloneness.
> Raising it high, I invite the bright moon
> Then turn to my shadow, which makes of us three.
> Because the moon does not know how to drink wine,
> She has given me this shadow for company . . .

Li Bai was a lonely man, a banished government official, and a drunkard. His good moments were private ones, small affairs with scraps of paper, graceless dances with luminescent bodies, failed encounters with reflections of reflections of light. I'm afraid I understand him too well. I wave for another red.

Bernie says all my problems are the fault of acrid Mother, which is fine by me. Bernie, I should point out, is both my literary agent and my psychiatrist, which is a primary conflict of interest if ever there was one. I write best when least focused in consensus reality. It's a situation. But Bernie doesn't make me talk to chairs as though someone were sitting there, and I don't report him to the Board of Mental Health Professionals for introducing me to Peruvian marching powder.

The second Cabernet appears, and I glance about once more for Tree Carter before tipping the glass. Last night we tried out her mini uplink. Fired up like a champ. Tree's shooting for live-feeding her first program three evenings from now. Not quite sure what the focus will be. I think she came here fully expecting to find Indigo children locked inside little cages like rhesus monkeys. She still harbors a fantasy of finding herself dining in the same restaurant as Bi Yu Nu, the shadowy New Age sci-fi king said to be sulking somewhere in Beijing.

I tried reading one of Bi's (rhymes with *knees*) stories. It was about a guy whose consciousness was stolen one morning by the air vent above the kitchen stove. He was frying two eggs, over easy, when he turned the vent fan on. Unexpectedly, it yanked his consciousness from his body and pulled it hurtling through the complex of ducts behind the walls of his seventy-three-story apartment building. The guy's consciousness wound up lodged in a dirty air filter, one of those buck-fifty replaceable filters that had been ignored by the maintenance crew forever and a day. The last thing we see is a spider whose web is at the edge of the filter methodically mincing its way over.

Tree did a whole month of radio shows on that story. A month.

Incoming English. I look up to see Tree Carter fretting her way toward my table, my sister *quite* close at her side.

"We were just kurbitzed," says Lillian, her face flushed.

"Lord God Almighty," pants Tree, picking up one of the spindly wooden chairs and giving it a suspicious shake.

"So sorry to hear it," I say, waving for the waiter.

I've learned it's best to indulge the girls when they've been *kurbitzed*, a term coined by themselves to refer to engagements with non-friendlies of the other-than-physical variety. Lil and Tree once swore they'd been importuned for two and a half hours by tourists from a low-rent alternative reality with a fetish for human pancreatic function. I told them I was sorry to hear it.

"Tree was walking me to the hotel," says Lil, settling warily into one of the chairs, "and we decided to cut through the bamboo grove. Big mistake. There was something waiting in there."

"Will this thing hold me?" asks Tree, setting the chair down. It leans to the left like Michel Pablo.

"Absolutely," I say, still looking about for the waiter.

"It was getting dark," continues Lil, "and we feel this *really* creepy energy. We got out of there fast, man. Tree says we have to Center, Seal, and Clear."

I give Tree a scowl. I *hate* Center, Seal, and Clear.

Borrowing a chair from the other table, Tree lowers herself onto both chairs at once. "This was no ordinary kurbitz," she tells me. "Listen, we're close. We're *close* close. They're getting scared."

"Is it the Three-three-three?" asks Lil, voice hushed. "Is that what's got them spooked?"

"The Three-three-three's six months away, baby," says Tree, mopping her brow with a hand towel from her purse. "Okay, here we go. Center, Seal, and Clear."

"Is this absolutely—" I begin.

"Julian," says Lil.

"Yes, darling. Of course, darling. Baa-aaa, darling."

As one, we check the time on our wristwatches and remove them. Lil places all three at the far edge of a nearby table, hopefully out of range. We've cooked several perfectly good digital watches over the years, plus a couple of laptops and one digital pedometer—mine. Now we reach beneath our shirt collars and extract matching pendants of translucent green moldavite, and Tree takes them into her palm. The three jagged gemstones interlock perfectly, forming a single, almost egg-shaped stone, actually a shard of an enormous meteorite that struck Eastern Europe fifteen million years ago, give or take a three-day weekend. It took my sister six months of nagging to get one of those pendants around my neck. Now I can't take it off without feeling a discomfiting drift into the *reds*.

Now resting against our chair backs, Tree, Lil, and I exhale as one, close our eyes, and focus on the image of a sphere of green-tinged amber light that gradually grows in size till it encloses us.

Her voice rich and rhetorical, Tree says, "We send a voice to the *highest* of our highest selves, and to those who work with us and through us on behalf of the brightest of the light and the lightest of the bright, and say *be* here with us now and help us in this which we do, Lord God Almighty Jesus."

Lil and I repeat, "Lord God Almighty Jesus."

"We go to the centermost of our centermost hearts," continues Tree, voice rising, "to that place where we are the strongest and the purest, and call *unto* ourselves every soul part that has separated and wandered, diverged and divested, turned out and turned away, that we may be gathered and strong, all praise Aphrodite Aditi."

"All praise Aphrodite Aditi," Lil and I say together.

"Here and now we *seal* this space," says Tree, "in all its dimensions and divestitures, its ways and means, its varieties and vagaries, its every turning and *re*-turning, that none may come unto us except he and she who bear the light, to enter into and *unto* its glorious and glendiferous work, Immortal Soul of Emanuel Jeremiah Jerusalem."

"Immortal Soul of Emanuel Jeremiah Jerusalem."

I open my eyes to peek at Tree, her forehead glistening with sweat. A deep line forms between her eyebrows as she continues, "We now clear from our midst and our doing, *clear* from our comings and our goings, any and all who would by intention thought deed or deception, hinder harm or delay us in that great work which we embrace and which embraces us, Holy Lord God Nimbutsu Nimbutsu."

"Holy Lord God Nimbutsu Nimbutsu."

"Thanks be unto all who shine," says Tree, "and all who shine and *all* who shine. Be it hereby and forevermore so."

"Be it hereby and forevermore so."

Jesus Jerusalem Jehosephat.

"Give me my watch," I say irritably, stuffing the moldavite pendant back into my shirt. My head hurts beginning somewhere around the nipples.

All three wristwatches indicate that forty-nine minutes have elapsed. Time really flies when you're casting out debils.

I look at Tree. "I have a question. If this little ceremony works so well, why do we have to keep doing it? Especially as it takes actual time off our lives? Shouldn't we be the most centered of all God's children by now? And I've never replaced that digital pedometer."

Lil gives me a look.

"Not that I really used it that much," I add.

Tree wraps me in her warmest smile. "We have to center and clear, again and yet again, because everything changes, Julian, including change itself. Sine waves within sine waves, nested one within another *ad infinitum infinitum*, each a footnote to evolution, revolution, devolution, and change."

I gaze for a moment at this wanked-out hoodoo of a second-day-of-spring woman with a voice like the right hand of God Almighty and an anterior like most people's posterior. "That's your answer?" I say. "Sine waves within sine waves? Wasn't that the same thing you said when I asked who the bad guys are?"

"Could you possibly chill?" suggests Lil.

"They are the Opponent," says Tree, still smiling. "That's all. They shape-shift. They adapt like a virus. All I can tell you for certain is, the closer we get to what we came here to do, the nearer at hand they will be."

That's another thing I've never quite gotten. What we came here to do. I let it pass. Tree's starting to sound like her radio show, Lillian's sending me her little *looks*, and my head feels like it just spent forty-nine minutes fisting Aileen Carol Wuornos. And I think we may have dematerialized our waiter.

"I know you don't get it," Tree tells me. "I don't either, baby, not on the intellectual level. But I know what's true, and so do you. Our bones know."

I avoid Tree's eyes. I think my bones and hers may have attended different meetings. Tree once announced quite importantly that she was the Chohan of the Sixth Ray and went into quite some detail about why she'd taken physical form at this time. It was the usual laundry list. Saving the world, eliminating corporations and diagonally-striped ties, establishing an International Day of the Worm. The usual. She said nothing at all about channeling final chapters of really promising novels, but she was in trance at the time. Afterward, Tree denied having said anything at all.

"My blood sugar's hitting bottom," says Lil. "Does this place have a kitchen?"

"This place has a refrigerator," I tell her. "It may be full of lemon ice-box pie. Why don't you ask?"

"I don't know the word for lemon ice-box pie," she says.

"That was a joke, Lillian."

"I *know* it was a joke, asshole. I was just saying I don't know the word."

I look at my sister. "You think there's *one* Chinese word for lemon ice-box pie?"

"Kids . . . ," says Tree.

Lil's voice rises. "Like you know jack *shit* about lexical syntax in Mandarin."

"This meeting was not intended to be a general assembly," I say through my teeth. "I invited Tree for a drink. Tree. For a drink."

"Like I'm supposed to control being kurbitzed, you totally self-absorbed—"

"Kids . . . ?"

I turn to Tree. "Shatrina. Dr. Carter. Her Hoodoo-ness. I need a new ending for that book."

"Ain't none of me," says Tree, turning away.

"Well, it ain't none of me *neither*," I say irritably, "which I believe to be the salient point. I tried writing that final chapter. I couldn't do it. It's going to have to come from the same place as the previous twelve."

"Jules," says Tree, "Truman never intended to write that whole book for you, and you know it. He gave you an idea and that's all, baby. An *idea*. But you kept asking him for more and more till finally he quit."

"She's right," says Lil. "You totally blew it with Truman, man."

I close my eyes and try to count to ten. I make it to two.

"You're both right, of course," I say, my voice perfectly controlled. "But, as our little friend Truman may not actually *exist* outside of Tree's lovely head, so far as can be objectively determined, and as I have bills that are quantifiable, I'd kind of like to give it another go."

Tree says, "Truman comes when he comes, and he gives what he gives. If I were you, Jules, I'd concentrate less on that book and more on getting my situation together, if you know what I'm talking about."

I don't reply. What's to say, finally, about my situation.

"Look, kids," says Tree, "why don't we just put ourselves to bed? Tomorrow's a brand new day."

"With sine waves within sine waves," I mutter, searching again for the dematerialized waiter.

"Why don't you, like, go *write* something?" says my sister. "Isn't that what writers, like, do?"

"As a matter of fact," I say importantly, "I'm on assignment. I leave tomorrow for Yunnan Province, and I'm not sure when I'll return."

I throw down the last of the red, and the two women stare.

Beijing just doesn't seem the place for me right now. It's beginning to wear that a city of this size doesn't have a Chinatown.

5

On the occasion of my third birthday, I received notification from our mother that being two was no longer a possibility. I took it badly, Two having been my identity for as long as I could recall. All I'd had to do was pronounce its name to be heartily congratulated by whomever was present. I was no taller than a footstool, and I had the world dicked. All you had to do was say *two*. Then one day all of that is gone and there's nothing to be done about it.

Three, I found, had an entirely different sound, energy, and color. Two had been a solid, grounded navy blue. Three I found to be a floaty canary yellow. Three was expansive and ephemeral and just generally unacceptable as a representation of myself. And the audience response was nothing like before. Actually I remained a secret Two for quite some time. I did eventually discover the important information hub that Three constitutes, but by then I was thirty-three years old.

Point three three three.

There's no escaping Kenny J's dimly expectant saxophone anywhere on this southbound train, but tree mammals were never intended to possess sound-amplifying devices, say nothing of saxophones. This particular track I'd describe as a slightly perplexed line of self-aggrandizing male emotio-logic extended to the high B breaking point that *sutures* the bridge to the remaining six or seven grumpy minutes of failed rationalization—as you finish the oversweet Chinese ice-cream cone you wish you'd never begun. Which is to say, I got out of Beijing just in time. I was starting to have acid spit.

You never know what's going to stir your dusts. It can be as simple as a corner turned or a tunnel of trees taken by moonlight, or a train ticket purchased because someone spoke the word *Yunnan* and it lodged inside you.

A bit stupidly, I watch as the window of this first-class cabin frames a brilliant cloudless sunset, then a sunrise followed by another sunset and sunrise, as the steel tracks undulate, rising and falling to hug this mute mountainside, that delicate dale. "The curved line belongs to God," said Gaudi but it was borrowed freely by the French who laid these rails a century ago, keeping to the mountainsides, high above the fields and their muds and floods as did the Taoists with their immortality highways, always a tasteful distance from the torpid valleys where the misery of history wends and no one's the wiser.

My non-English speaking cabin-mate wakes himself by snoring and responds by sitting upright, yawning loudly, belching a couple of times, and lighting a cigarette, as, along the narrow corridor, a blue-uniformed woman pushes an overloaded fruit cart. I decide to dart in front of her before the cart blocks the forward corridor. A sorely needed visit to the loo—I shudder at the thought—then I'll return to the cabin to wash my hands the requisite three times, dry them on a shirt from my bag, and settle into the dining car for an early dinner and the day's final view to the east.

Past the advancing fruit cart and around a sheet-metal corner are three other people awaiting the same mournful toilet, a same-sex squatter with a metal floor floating in pee. No toilet paper. No soap. No running water. No towel. "No Occupying While Stabling." That's what the sign above the door says, meaning when the train stops, so do you. There's no holding tank.

Earlier today, I found myself corridor-waiting behind another Westerner, a most fetching one who smelled deliciously of bed. She seemed to have just awakened, the whole tousled tresses thing, *lots* of brunette hair, her body radiating heat, her breath not yet entirely regular, and I asked myself what conversation one makes while awaiting the same toilet on a southbound Chinese train. "Do you think you'll be long?" Or maybe, "Ever occupied while stabling?" Quite certainly, "May God be with you."

Now, after taking my turn then purging my hands to the elbows, I seat myself at the only available table in the crowded dining car, which is oak-handsome with little white curtains and white tablecloths. I order a bottle of Zinfandel with tonight's seafood one-course, and why not? There's a subtly reassuring back-and-forth sway to the dining car, my number-two German-made pencil is deliciously sharp, and the background music is a cheerful trombone deformation of "Auld Lang Syne," perfect for a mid-August evening. If this were prime Hitchcock, Eva Marie Saint would walk into the dining car exactly now, a pensive expression on her face, and I'd have a perfect line on the tip of my tongue.

No sooner does the thought occur than the door opens, and in walks our lady of the tousled tresses, the fetching Westerner I'd encountered this morning in the corridor. Even more amazing, the only available chair is at my table, making it all too easy for me to rise and say, "Would you like to join me? I've ordered a bottle of wine, and I'd hate to drink it alone."

Damn, that was a good line.

"A glass of wine would be perfect," replies tousled lady, extending her hand. "I'm Ana Manguella."

She uses the Spanish soft-a pronunciation of her first name. The surname comes out *mahn-gay-yuh*, also quite Spanish, though the accent is crisply British.

Ana Manguella takes a seat, and I find myself gazing into eyes of astonishing blue-green. When I open my mouth to speak, nothing comes out because, my God, this woman's eyes are not blue-green. One is blue. One is green. In their setting of bone-white skin, the eyes blaze like two cold jewels.

"I'm sorry," I say. "I'm sure you hear compliments about your eyes all the time. They are very beautiful. I'm Julian Mancer."

"So nice to meet you, Julian."

Ana is in her thirties, I'd say, and unmarried if rings still mean anything. The treasonable brunette hair is now gathered into a rough ponytail. At her throat is a silk scarf, azure in color, which brings forward the left eye. She's wearing at least one tinted contact, I decide.

"Please help me place the accent," I say. "I want to say Edinburgh, but I'm wrong a lot."

"Glastonbury," says Ana. "And you would be an American? From the South?"

"Yes and yes. What do you think of our background music?"

Ana cants her head to listen, and I notice her small porcelain hands. Yet the fingertips are blunt and strong. Close-cropped nails. I can easily see Ana Manguella pulling a pack of Gauloises from her bag.

"Oh, Robert Burns," she says. "Don't often get to hear that one in summer, do we?"

I say, "The Chinese love Burns. Any man who can father seven sons and drink himself to death before turning forty clearly has something going for him."

"Really? Seven sons?"

"And three daughters," I add, hoping I'm somewhere near right.

The Zinfandel arrives, and I request a second glass before asking Ana's destination.

"Hong Kong," she replies. "And you?"

"I fly from Hong Kong to Kunming in the morning."

Ana tells me she's taken a post with a Hong Kong consulting firm. "Boring stuff," she says.

"Then what do you find interesting?"

After an appraising glance, she answers, "Actually I enjoy the study of mythology very much. And you?"

"Some say that myth is the most direct way to describe reality," I reply, playing my most promising card. "Or, conversely, that reality is a clumsy way of describing myth. Either way, we do enjoy telling ourselves stories, don't we?"

"Indeed we do. And what do you do, Julian?"

"Write them. Stories, that is. I also play pointless math games. Do you wear a tinted contact?"

Ana blinks before replying, "What kind of pointless math games?"

"Very pointless ones. Actually, math may be the purest form of myth, and vice versa—once the cultural coloration is stripped away. It all reduces to a handful of corroborating equations, doesn't it? Sorry about that last question, by the way, but the next will likely be far worse. I've no manners at all. "

Our waiter appears with a second wine glass and deftly fills it.

"So, you're a philosopher then?" asks Ana.

"I hope not. Philosophers are still working on the same four or five questions that came to mind two thousand years ago. I'd rather devote myself to something with a bit more promise, such as rehabilitating career criminals. Meanwhile, let's hope we can endure this Zinfandel. The Chinese are very able counterfeiters, but a good dinner wine is something they're still working on."

We each sip the Zinfandel. The taste changes after a moment, only to change once more. Not for the better, I'd say.

"What do you think?" I ask.

"I've had worse in Spain. You?"

"Woody," I say, squinting, "with just a touch of pomegranate and all-weather motor oil. Do you know the median lifetime for members of the animal kingdom?"

"Am I supposed to?"

"It's not very long," I say. "Fifteen point two days. Some insects cycle in a single day, as you probably know."

"And you bring this up because—?"

"Exactly. Because. But enough about me. Why the interest in myth, Ana Manguella?"

"Passion," she replies. "Unpredictability. There's no telling what the gods will do on a given day, but it's certain to be interesting."

"And naughty," I add.

"Oh, of course naughty. Why be a god if you're just going to behave?"

I let Ana Manguella's question glisten for a moment, as do each of her eyes. The yellowing light is hitting the green one just right to reveal that it harbors no contact lens, tinted or otherwise. I really do have no manners. I once asked a woman on a plane whether her hinder parts included a tattoo of a gull in flight. A simple enough question, I'd thought, and it might have been, had the answer been no.

The seafood one-course arrives. Ana is as hungry as I, and we willingly drop the conversation until the table has been cleared. Night seems to have fallen. Pushing away from the table, I say, "So, you're leaving Glastonbury in your dust? Why?"

Sitting back, Ana says, "I hated going, but Hong Kong is such a rare opportunity. Have you been?"

"Is there a pack of Gauloises in your bag?" I ask.

Ana stares at me. "Would you like one?"

"Just wondering. I visited Hong Kong some years ago when it was still a proper British colony. I understand you can still get your hands on a blood pudding. What was with Hermaphroditus, by the way, since we're discussing myth?"

Ana's shoulders sag a little. "Julian, why don't we just go for normal train conversation? It's better for the digestion. You can tell me what you found enjoyable about Beijing, and I can tell you which tourist attractions to avoid in Glastonbury. And Hermaphroditus was every aspect of herself. Himself if you prefer."

"Itself," I suggest. "Beijing was horrid. I did find the Diligent Administration Hall somewhat appealing, though Mao's three GE refrigerators are no longer on display. Did you visit the Temple of Heaven?"

She shakes her tresses.

"Pure numerology," I say. "Nines, all of it."

"Didn't the emperor pray there once a year?" asks Ana. "To ensure good crops and the like?"

"Three times a year, after a night of fasting and praying in the Hall of Abstinence. Next morning he took a stroll to the Circular Mound Altar where bits of human sacrifice simmered in the—"

"Human sacrifice? Really?"

"No one you or I know personally. Actually I doubt whether the emperor himself knew what that temple complex was designed to accomplish. Not that I do, mind you, but I did come away with the impression that I'd encountered an engine of some kind, one powered by a very intentional mathematics. Math is all well and good, if you're asking me, so long as it remains theoretical. More wine?"

"Half, please."

"There's an example for you—half. Hugely theoretical. According to this notion, no matter what you have, it can continue to be divided into identical halves forever. Poppycock. Still, a harmless enough notion in itself—until someone decided to halve an atom. Applied mathematics. Not recommended. Here's your half-glass of wine just the same."

"Thanks."

"Take this Temple of Heaven," I continue. "All those dovetailed nines in one place. To me, that has to constitute some kind of probability antenna, some means of separating out a specific outcome, though who's to say what."

"Could I ask you something personal?" asks Ana.

"Would you?"

"What exactly is your interest in flowers?"

I gaze into the flawless white face. "I've an interest in flowers?"

"Or they in you," says Ana. "You're practically wrapped head-to-toe in a floral display of some kind. I read auras. Hope you don't mind."

My eyes tip down to her blouse for an instant. "I'm more of a fauna man, actually. But lately I have developed a mild curiosity concerning hydrangeas."

Ana blinks, consulting her memory. "Sun. Lots of moisture. Sandy soil. You're not to over-prune them."

"Really? Surprising. You could hack at the Hydra all day and never get its attention."

"The Hydra?" says Ana. "I'd never thought to connect the hydrangea to the Hydra. I should have. The Twelve Labors of Heracles is one of my favorite stories."

"Do you mean Hercules?"

"Oh, the Romans gave him that name," says Ana. "To the Greeks, he'd been Heracles for quite some time. Before that, he was Osiris. He has also been known as Horus and Krishna and Jesus. Amazing, really, how many civilizations have been shaped by this single story of a man who couldn't handle his own power. A man with a god for a father and a mortal for a mother."

"Dangerous mix."

"Evidently," says Ana. "Heracles awoke from a stupor one morning to find that he'd murdered his whole family. His only chance for redemption was to accomplish a number of tasks, as you know, the last of which was subduing the Hydra."

"And the Hydra would represent . . . ?"

"Symbolically? Well, with all the new heads sprouting and so forth, I'd have to say the Hydra represents endless and pointless propagation. Horror, really. Look at modern corporations, which cannot die because they do not live, yet they're everywhere, propagating endlessly, consuming everything in sight. A bit like cancer, really. Or a virus. You know, a virus is not a living thing in the classical sense, but more like a self-replicating code. But I'd rather hear what you think."

"All things being equal," I say, lifting the nearly empty bottle, "I prefer not to. A little more all-weather motor oil?"

Ana's eyes hold mine for a moment. "You seem to have a bit of Heracles going yourself, Julian, if you don't mind my saying so. That is, you possess a great deal of power, but you're not quite present with it. There's a curious disconnect. Actually I'm not sure what to make of it."

"It's called apathy," I tell her. "Very unpopular those days, apathy, but if humans had any less of it we'd have annihilated each other twelve times over by now. It may still be our last best hope. I'm ordering a second Zinfandel."

"Oh, no. I'm perfectly fine."

Waving for the waiter, I say, "Don't worry. I'm entirely capable of drinking it myself."

"If you're going to get drunk," says Ana, "I'm going to smoke. Do you mind? You Americans *are* funny."

"Yes we are, and yes you may."

With a wooden match, Ana lights an oblong Gaulois and pulls on it with relish. After the second draw, she smiles and says, "So, why are you really in China, Julian?"

I gaze at the woman across the table, enjoying the way she holds the cigarette between the bases of two fingers like a man, letting the ash grow.

"Isn't that something we discover later?" I say. "Why we really did this thing or that one?"

"You're hedging," says Ana.

"I'm a master hedger. It comes with being my sister's brother. There's no other way to have a moment's privacy. To answer your question, I've no idea why I'm really in China, any more than I knew why I was really in Memphis. The more serious questions I leave to Tree. I carry the suitcases."

"Tree?"

"Short for Shatrina. She says the three of us have been together hundreds of lifetimes, mostly in the galaxy Cetus, which geographically I think is somewhere near Orion's left clavicle."

The waiter brings the second bottle and begins to open it.

"So," says Ana, freshly interested, "a three-soul group. And what exactly is a pod from Cetus doing on Earth just now?"

I pause to absorb the fresh turn in the conversation. It's not unusual to find myself in a dialogue I'd no intention of entering, often concerning beliefs to which I don't subscribe yet which have a way of appearing in the mails nonetheless. There's something about this woman. that tells me I'm already in the trap, and I've yet to so much as sniff the cheese. What *am* I doing on Earth now?

I give Ana Manguella a cool smile. "Saving it, I believe."

"All of it?"

I nod agreeably. "And why are you really in China, Ana?"

"To meet you," she says without missing a beat. Ana exhales a shaft of white smoke, gives her thick ponytail a toss and returns my gaze.

I ponder her words for a full minute. I'd like to believe that this woman is coming on to me.

"Might I ask," says Ana, "what you and your friends are saving Earth from? Or is that a deep Cetian secret?"

"Voice mail. Saxophone music. The whole tight-underwear military-industrial sort of thing. Which is to say, Tree doesn't exactly know yet. Things are supposed to become clearer on the Three-three-three."

Ana gives me a blank look.

"March third, 2003," I say. "All threes. New Age Groundhog Day or something of the kind."

"A ceremony then? The three of you will perform a ceremony on the Three-three-three? Very thoughtful of you, actually, but would you mind telling me how—no, never mind. You're just going to toy with me, and I'll be bothered."

I lean closer. "Promise that you'll be bothered."

"Julian, I wish you'd take our conversation more seriously or else say nothing at all. You toss these conflicting little *snippets* about and it's all so clever, but you're committed to none of it, which I find entirely offensive. If you must know, it doesn't become you at all."

"Are we having a quarrel?" I ask. "I'd say things are moving right along, wouldn't you?"

"I think I'd like my check."

Setting down my empty glass, I give it a half turn and say, "Every argument makes an equal amount of sense within the context of its devices, wouldn't you say?"

"Julian . . ."

"No, this is just getting good. It all cancels out in the end, don't you see? Are we biochemical accidents in a blind and random universe? Obviously. Is there some kind of grand evolutionary scheme afoot in which we're all invited to play a role? Obviously." I shrug. "It's just rooms. Alternative realities, faux-realities. People talk about what's true and what isn't, what's crucial and what's not, and there's none of that. Situations arise and you choose a place to stand. There's nothing more. Myself, I choose to stand where it's most comfortable, thank you, preferably in the shade with a drink in my hand."

Ana takes a last weary pull on the Gaulois and puts it out. "So nice to hear it. Would you please ask for my check?"

I exhale resignedly. "Okay, you've teased it out of me. I am the narrator."

Ana doesn't respond.

"Are you surprised?" I ask.

"It depends on what you mean."

"I convey the experience stream. I see to it that all this will be remembered."

"But everyone witnesses reality, Julian," says Ana.

"Do they? Can you absolutely ensure that, were I not here to describe the dinner we have just enjoyed, it would be available for others to know?"

"Thanks so much," says Ana, lifting her purse, "for all that you do. Now—"

"One more question. When I asked why you'd come to China, you said, 'To meet you.' What did you mean by that?"

Ana very nearly blushes. "It seemed true enough when I said it. Sometimes I open my mouth and out it comes. Really, Julian, I'm quite tired. Would you ask—"

"I've got it."

"No. Please don't."

"It's the custom," I tell her. "You're in China now. Best get used to it. When will I see you again, my dear? In the morning, perhaps, in front of the loo?"

Ana rises and I with her. "We were put together once," she says. "It can happen again."

"But just to be on the safe side, I'd like an e-address."

Her voice softens. "Julian, there's no such thing as a safe side. You're on Earth now. Best get used to it."

6

The first thing is, I purchased a copy of Mao's little red book yesterday from the guy now dozing just outside my window at Dali Guesthouse Number Four. I'd seen the stack of rain-stained Condensed Maos from this lumpy bed whose window opens to the upper reaches of Foreigner Street where hemp halter blouses swing in a wind straight off Zhonghe Peak and a half-dozen trinket merchants nod off at most hours of the day.

Second, there's a badly broken bone in my right hand, and I've no idea why. From time to time, I gaze longingly at my backpack on the dresser, a full water bottle visible in one pocket. I've ached for a drink for hours, but my legs haven't quite arrived yet. I don't know where my wallet is, or my passport.

I'd never gotten around to reading Mao, which felt increasingly wrong, as here I was writing articles on modern China—or fully intending to. I'm not that kind of writer. So I fed fifteen yuan through the steel bars of this window and received in return my own English pocket edition of *Quotations*, whose frontispiece contains thirty-one pix of Glorious Chairman in wool hat, Glorious Chairman in bathrobe, Glorious Chairman in gray wool suit, on and on, the same face-splitting smile on every page.

Someone's knocking. At the room next door, I believe.

I then passed another four yuan through the bars in exchange for a butane lighter that caught both the sun and my eye. The lighter bore the image of a slender, swaying woman, her colors iridescent in the bright midday. It was Quan Yin,

Goddess of Mercy and Inflammable Petroleum Byproducts and spiritual matriarch to this atheistic patriarchy.

The knocking continues. Finally the guy next door answers hoarsely. He and his companion have overslept, having spent the night alternately arguing, watching TV at maximum volume, and slamming their bed against our common wall.

My eyes go to a scrap of cardboard in the wastebasket, and I ask myself once more whether I might fashion a splint from the cardboard and a few turns of dental floss—but how to tie the knot? It's challenge enough just stringing subject and predicate together in my armored journal while awaiting the return of my legs, if indeed they come back this time. I keep thinking I'll just this moment emerge from the gray-purples and shit-browns of this decidedly non-lucid dream and—

And what?

I often lucid dream, if you must know. I generally find it agreeable despite the sorting out process that accompanies re-entry. It may require a half-hour of tormented puzzlement to finally determine whether I'm in a room or a *room*. It's nearly always one or the other.

This particular habitation I call the Marigold Suite because of the yellow-gold flowering plant erupting from a crack in the concrete just outside the door, beyond which a row of porcelain sinks and dim, flaking mirrors summon humorless men and women by dawn to comb and shave beneath a vanished sky.

The Marigold Suite has a water boiler that doesn't work and a reading light with no switch, though you can turn off the latter by yanking the in-series extension cords stretched knee-high all the way across the room—which I found strangely satisfying, as I do reading the hand-lettered sign on my bathroom door ("Keep the ground towel in order be careful for slippery floor otherwise accept the result"). Then there are the blue batik bedspreads tacked over the crumbling bedroom walls and the two used condoms stuck as though glued to the lower shelf of the nightstand. It all comes together in a statement of some kind.

I was resting here yesterday, browsing my newly purchased *Quotations* and its thirty-one pictures of Cherubic Chairman, when I came upon two black-and-whites of a lean young Zedong, unsmiling, brooding, as though behind the broad, clear eyes, the inner landscape were already rent like the severely parted hair. Turning the pages, I watched the two hairlines recede ever farther.

When I was a child, I couldn't get past the 'do and the mole. Now I couldn't get past the 'do and the mole and the smug self-delight, the pudgy, seemingly rouged relief-map of monstrous conceit that somehow passed for a human face. I saw all the Caesars in that face, I saw Deputy Sheriff Cecil Ray Price, I saw the perfected Las Vegas Elvis of the final Babylon.

I see that the trinket merchant has snored himself awake. As I watch, he takes a sip from his jar of tea, re-secures the lid, and rolls up a shirtsleeve, exposing a long line of junkie welts. He ties off with a woven belt and disinterestedly gives himself an injection. Within a minute, he's nodding again.

What really dotted the *i* for me about the Marigold Suite was the moment I opened my nightstand drawer to browse the tourist information, and *there* between the brochure offering tour packages up the Cangshan Mountains and the menu of the nearby treehouse café was a Polaroid taken in this room of a young Bai woman wearing pink bikini panties and a Mona Lisa smile. She'd been photographed lying on this bed. *So* much better than discovering the Gideon Bible, I noted, closing the drawer.

I wish I'd left it at that.

Now through the wall comes the day's first argument from the couple next door. Mostly it's the guy who argues. The woman just bleats every now and then. Now the TV comes on. It can only be a matter of time before the bed starts up. At one moment last night, they had it revving so hard that *my* bed was in motion, the in-series extension cords bobbing like a rope bridge.

Neither of them uttered a sound.

I lift my trembling right hand and take a good look at it. Could take Best Overall at the Iowa Rutabaga Show. What the hell is happening to me. I close my eyes and sigh. My legs will come back as they always do, and so will the memory of last night, at this point a badly haunted landscape of glimpsed grotesques. A woman pacing with an antenna-ed telephone. A recurring beeping sound. But the dots don't connect.

Head in his lap, the trinket merchant is in danger of tipping over. This corner of China, often called the Burma Triangle, was deeply invested in drug trafficking before Jessie James robbed his first train. It remains a clearinghouse for most of the world's opium, flowing to processing centers in Hong Kong then shipping points in northern China—none of which I have mentioned to Miriam, telling her only that Yunnan Province is a treasury of one-third of China's ethnic minorities and half of its remaining plant and animal species. Though the Han race accounts for ninety percent of China's population, fifty-eight tribal peoples—conquered peoples, actually—still cling to their old ways along the indifferent borders. It's a China I'd never thought to inquire about.

From the first moment, the pristine peaks and pines of Yunnan Province have been a surprise, as have the hewn-stone villages and rippling rivers, the mingled Brazilian smells of horse shit and strong coffee in the alpine air, and the disparate strands of Tibetan, Burmese, Vietnamese, and Han traditions that weave a coat of many curiosities. Stepping off the train in yesterday's dawn just outside Dali, I sensed all of that swirling in the chill mist and felt, too, the vague apprehension that I was drawing very close to something.

That's the third thing. I'm getting close to something. Or maybe I encountered it somehow last night. Maybe that was the problem.

Next door, the bed is beginning to rev once more. Outside my window, the s-shaped fellow mimics Beijing politics by leaning ever farther to the right without quite falling over. I wonder if he has tied himself upright somehow. His tribe, the copper-skinned Bai, have hung tough in these mountains for millennia, even whipping the ass of Beijing's imperial army seventeen centuries ago.

The Bai still speak their Sino-Tibetan language, bear their woven baskets on their backs, and practice a casserole religion that simmers native polytheism, Buddhism and Roman Catholicism with a little yam and wild onion. Hopefully all this will come together in a magazine article of some stripe, as Miriam still dangles airfare by the finest of threads.

I gaze achingly at the water bottle across the room. Everything sparkled with such *promise* yesterday when I tucked the book of quotations into my daypack and mounted a shaggy pony en route to Zhonghe Peak, two Bai guides leading the way on foot. It was to be a working day, one of clear-headed research beneath a cobalt sky, accumulating field notes with tidy vertical margins and clear pronoun reference. I would be proud of myself.

As my pony traced the raw edges of Dali, the two men hollered helloes to distant farmers hoeing fields of corn, squash, and cabbage, my pony reaching for the occasional mouthful of a star-shaped leaf I was certain I'd seen before. True enough, *cannabis sativa* lined every stray ditch bank, providing new teeth for the old saw, "The sky was high and the emperor was far away."

At midmorning, the trail turned sharply upward into mature stands of short-leaf pine where muddy switchbacks led into a rude cemetery, slowly toppling east-facing vaults mutely awaiting the next sunrise. At the summit, a paint-flaking Buddhist temple offered a tilted, dizzying view of Dali.

The temple I found to be entirely innocent of structural agendas, a definite comfort after Beijing and its many examples of intentional architecture. Lil, Tree, and I had toured one centuries-old Buddhist complex widely known for its thousand carved human figures, each expressing a different shade of emotion. I found that less intriguing than the string of adjoining structures that led quite purposefully, I thought, to a hill's summit.

That series of structures connected the collection of carved figures to a ponderous hilltop tower that jutted skyward, topped by odd protruding masonry orbs that suggested clumsy antennas. It's probably just me. In fact, I'm sure it's me, but that place certainly looked the part of a brick-and-mortar broadcast station designed to depict and disseminate highly detailed information about the vagaries of human feeling.

The earthling channel.

Before heading back down the mountain yesterday, I joined my guides for a simple lunch of rice and veggies in the shade of a red masonry wall. Afterward, I had the guides arrange an interview with the head monk, a smiling old man with a silver crewcut. I dutifully jotted down his nonsense, the elder guide serving as interpreter. At one point, the guide registered surprise before telling me, "You come here receive the teaching. Quan Yin give this teaching to you." At that, all three men gave me a significant gawk. Whatever. In truth, I was distracted by the memory of a certain star-shaped leaf. Clearly, additional field research would be in order once I touched back down on Foreigner Street.

In this country, one joint equals a pistol bullet above the left ear, after which you are gutted like a pig, every transplantable organ is harvested for resale, and a letter is composed on a manual typewriter dunning your family for the cost of the bullet. Which is to say, pot-smoking isn't particularly widespread.

Personally, back in Memphis, I usually keep a small pinch on hand. I find it to be a great comfort during serious life crises such as waking up each morning. And later on, when the arc of the day has flattened out a little, say around two or three p.m., a puff or two oftentimes helps one regain the necessary traction. And then there's the weary eventide and the often lonely bedtime experience, not to mention those nasty moments when one awakes in the horse latitudes of night. In general, I'd have to say that marijuana handsomely finishes the business that alcohol begins. Or is it the other way around?

Anyway, no sooner was I down from Zhonghe Peak and freshly showered than a gaggle of Bai women was trotting beside me along Foreigner Street flashing laminated pix of saddled horses and penile temples and glass-bottomed boats, and finally someone uttered my favorite Sanskrit word.

"Ganja?"

Minutes later, that woman and I stood before a wooden door whose knob rattled as it turned. A dark eye appeared in the crack. Words were whispered, and the door closed once more. My accomplice, a hefty Bai woman in blue homesewns, said, "Wait," and wait we did. Finally the door opened wide and we entered an airless space incongruously brimming with shelves of brightly painted native handicrafts. A slender woman in a towering headdress triple-bolted the door behind us and dragged two wooden stools to a spot between twin beds. I watched her take a seat on one stool and gesture toward the other.

As quickly as I seated myself, a cardboard box appeared from beneath the bed. "Ganja," said the woman, untying a black garbage bag. "Very good." Placing a sprig of marijuana between her palms, she rubbed her hands together vigorously and thrust the crushed leaves beneath my nose. I sniffed and shrugged. Crap weed. Seeds galore. But there is a thing called supply and demand, and in the end the lady in the headdress had some twenty bucks of my money and I had a quarter ounce of crap marijuana plus a rough biscuit of hashish that looked like it had come off the underside of a lawnmower. There was also a dark sticky nugget of opium that looked somewhat promising.

Field research.

At that point, the woman in the headdress leaned closer and said, "Peeee-nis. You want?"

"*Peeeee*-nis," cooed the other woman, handing me a length of bamboo covered with Kama Sutra engravings. Her long fingernail indicated a man and woman copulating with disinterested expressions.

"Okay?" asked headdress woman. "You want?"

I glanced from pair of eyes to pair of eyes, wondering exactly what I was being offered by whom.

"You are an *utter* addict," my sister enjoys telling me from time to time. "Alcohol, gambling, sex, hard drugs, soft drugs—is there anything you aren't hooked on?"

Phonics.

Again, knocking. No answer comes from the couple in the next room. Apparently they're dozing.

Actually, I occasionally have my moments, such as yesterday when I pulled the brim of my cap a little tighter and told the two Bai women, "No, thank you," and rose to leave.

I should have left it at that.

I remember returning to the Marigold Suite as dark clouds abruptly gathered. I remember barely making it back before the sky broke open in a fragrant thundershower. Beyond that, I can't say. If I could get to that water bottle, my mind might clear. I just recall seeing, through the barred window, tourists giddily running toward shelter and vendors hurrying to unfold patched canvas tarps. After that, I think I must have poured myself a maotai and cleared the wooden table. There was a quarter ounce of grass to clean. Then there was the question of rolling papers. You can't find them in this country. And then—

And then I remembered Mao's little red book.

Examining *Quotations* with new eyes, I noted that its pages were admirably thin. I chose the page that read "Workers of the World Unite!" in revolutionary red, carefully worked it free of the binding, and creased it along the center. Then I applied a generous amount of freshly cleaned buds, sprinkling in a few crumbs of lawnmower gleanings for good measure. Before sealing my work, I decided a pinch or two of opium probably wouldn't hurt anything. I remember the dull taste of the paper as I licked and sealed a joint shaped more or less like Chairman After Banquet. The revolutionary slogan was displayed in bright red along the side. Pleased with myself, I placed the joint in my mouth and patted myself down in search of a lighter bearing the image of Quan Yin, Goddess of Mercy and Inflammable Petroleum Byproducts.

The knock comes again, and I lift my head to see the silhouettes of four feet beneath the door of the Marigold Suite. Two people. Double the reason to pretend I'm not here. Which arguably I'm not, though I do seem to be leaving a recognizable number-two graphite trail along the pages of my journal. I fear that trail may be leading me ever closer to a recollection I'd prefer not to have. I'm likely better off with random shards and stray shrapnel bursts.

Again I look up from my bed. The silhouettes have vanished from beneath the door. Good.

I'm sure I promptly smoked *Unite!*. Then it doubtless seemed a good idea to burn *the World*. At that point, I probably celebrated with another maotai and attempted to produce a couple more joints. Problem was, there was only a single decent page remaining. Minutes later, I was admiring a slightly bent doobie that read, "Our Glorious Chairman Mao Zedong" along one side. But now what? I certainly wasn't smoking Chairman in Bathrobe. I seem to remember rummaging through the nightstand drawer, looking for any description of blank paper, when—what should fall into my hands but the Mona Lisa smile?

It's all coming back to me now.

Again the knocking, this time more insistent. The four silhouettes re-materialize beneath my door. Now comes a man's voice, chillingly authoritative as he mispronounces both my name and the word "police."

Shit.

Setting the journal aside, I place one bare foot then the other on the cold plank floor. Rising unsteadily, I tilt my weight forward and shuffle past the backpack and its full water bottle, limping a bit from an unexpected aching in my ass. I open the deadbolt with my good left hand and peer into the sober gazes of two police officers. Some part of me recognizes the face on the left and a bolt of fear crashes through me. I have to struggle to not pee myself. The other officer taps his wristwatch and says, "Bus."

7

A few crumpled bills secure me a seat on the next minibus to Lijiang, three hours and a gutful of dust away along a lane-and-a-half road. Surrendering myself to a wooden bench to wait in partial shade, I clamp the water bottle between my knees and try pitifully to unscrew the cap. On my third try, the cap finally submits with a dry crack and I drain the warm contents, losing more than a little down my chin. Now, panting, I look up to discover the same two policemen staring at me through the windshield of their patrol car. I must have made quite the impression last night.

Closing my eyes, I consider the probability of Lijiang's having both a competent Western-trained doctor and an X-ray machine that doesn't also make noodles. At the thought, a bright visual image of an X-ray machine appears in my mind and shimmers there for a few seconds, the little steel rivets along its edges standing out in perfect relief. We seem to be packing some serious alkaloids.

If I *just* hadn't opened that nightstand drawer. A little hot apple pie and ice cream at the tree-house café, a little Aussie wine to wash it down, and a pleasant leaden sleep. I'd have awakened to a chill mountain morning bearing in its hands every bright possibility for clear-headed research beneath a cobalt sky. But no. My fingers lifted the Polaroid, and my eyes collected all they could of the warm Venusian swell beneath the scrap of pink polyester.

I studied the perilous fall between the two golden legs, and I was undone, stuffing things into pockets, pulling shoes onto the wrong foot, every cell, each sentient circuit aswim with detailed schematics of *pelvic morfi, obturator inter-nus, iliac crest.* I was hurrying through the tilted gate of Dali Guesthouse Number Four to stumble along unlit cobble-stones, past weathered woodwork and tousled roof shingles, beneath moon-scatting clouds and unwavering stars, few people out, it being Hungry Ghost Month when the door to the other world is slightly ajar. I was drawing closer to some-thing. So close that I was practically on its farther side.

I'm seeing it all now, in no particular order. The haggard face of another Bai woman. An damp unlit alley. A flight of cold steel stairs. A sorrow of stale cigarette smoke. Red velvet chairs with cigarette burns. Nearby, two dapper men smoke cigarettes, their thin legs crossed. They're studying me. A woman in her thirties paces with an antenna-ed telephone at her ear. Somewhere, a smoke detector beeps.

"Three girls. You pick."

A door opens. I'm gazing at a nondescript Han woman with chopped hair and a light blue dress. Her spike heels are loud on the wooden floor. Her eyes are turned away. As she stands there, the door opens again and a second woman ap-pears, this one in black. Otherwise she is indistinguishable from the first. I feel nothing. The two stand there unsmiling, looking at no one. The smoke detector beeps again. I struggle to summon that moment of exquisitely focused sexual greed that had fetched me to such an awful place. I can't find it.

In China, age of consent is fourteen, prostitution laws are unenforced, condoms are eschewed, and life expectancy for sex workers is rather less than that of a Shi Tzu. Did I think about that? I doubt it.

Suddenly the pacing woman puts away her phone and stalks into the adjacent room. Shouting. The two dapper men and I exchange a look. A moment later the woman re-emerges, holding the door open. And—

Striding barefoot into the room, her long raven hair sail-ing behind her, is a *wisp* of a young girl in Bai homesewns and a broad embarrassed smile. I watch her choose a spot between the two Han women but farther back, evidently hoping not to be noticed.

She is noticed.

My eyes lick every inch of the svelte teenager whose fine-textured skin is of a single chestnut tone. Her long hair is clean and carefully parted. Her features are fine and precise. Gone is every troubling thought.

Here. Is the flower of Dali.

I approach the barefoot girl, who steps back, eyes darting. The two Han women stalk away, throwing poisonous glares at homesewn girl, slamming the door behind them. Someone yanks a stack of bills from my palm. I am alone with the wisp of a chestnut girl who turns now and motions for me to follow.

Spellbound, I trail the whisperings of bare footfalls along a dim corridor of creaking boards, past endless identical doorways, each opening upon a raw single-bunk room beneath an uncovered red bulb. The chestnut girl's steps are irregular and playful. At one point, she even turns to share a conspiratorial grin, as though an old friend's daughter were taking me to the kitchen for lemonade. Finally she stops and points into a room indistinguishable from the others. Bunk. Nightstand. Red bulb. I step inside.

"What's your name?"

No reply. Her long, dark hair hanging forward, home-sewn girl is pouring tea into two cellophane cups. No steam. I watch her feel the side of the teapot then open the lid to peer inside.

"Name?" I ask. "*Mingza?*"

She looks up.

I point to her. "*Mingza?*"

"Wa," she answers quietly.

I watch Wa set down the teapot, return the cold tea to it and squat to look beneath the nightstand. Hooking her hair behind her ears, she opens a jar of petroleum jelly, finding it almost empty. In a flash, she has taken jar and teapot and vanished. I hear her bare feet running along the dark hallway.

Somewhat pensively, I take a seat on the edge of the bed, remove my watch cap and set it beside me. Now I take off my shoes and place my socks inside them. I pull off my sweater and shirt, fold them neatly and set them beside the cap. The smoke detector beeps, nearer this time.

So. Here it is.

The minibus has arrived. I'm one of four people handing tickets to the driver and crawling over baggage piled hip-deep in the aisle. Struggling to protect my swollen hand, I tumble into a seat on the shady side of the bus and, panting with exhaustion, wedge out a small space in the aisle for my knees. Minibus now in motion, I turn to see the patrol car pull out to escort us to the city limit.

I *have* made quite the impression.

Across the aisle from me, two Mao-capped old men stare at my face in unguarded fascination, as behind them a teenage boy munches sunflower seeds from a brown paper bag, his right hand delivering each with the regularity of a piston, mouth jettisoning each empty hull onto the floor just as the new one arrives.

I fall back against the vinyl seat as Zhonghe Peak, rough-swirled with rain-bearing clouds, tumbles in through the open windows. Sparkling mountain air rushes into my nostrils as the bus driver finds another gear. Along each side of the highway twelve-inch stands of rice nod their graceful farewells. The patrol car slows and turns around.

I've escaped.

Panting with relief, I sag in my seat and close my eyes. Again, the tiny ocher room. The stale air. I watch a barefoot Wa bound in through the open doorway, a careless smile on her face. In her hands are an unopened jar of petroleum jelly and a steaming teapot.

As though I've never seen it done before, I watch her pour tea into two cellophane cups, the vapor framing her profile in wavering red. I can't take my eyes off her. Who could? Wa is what every woman longs to be. Young, elegant, gathered. Animated by a country sweetness that lifts even this vile dungeon. Lifts even my own poisoned marrow. No longer pensive, I am possessed. I want the trailing raven hair. I want the tiny waist. The pert bottom. I want to feel all of her warmth against my skin. What that might cost and who must pay—matters not at all.

Suddenly rising full height, Wa gives me an uneasy glance, slings the door closed behind her and throws her hair behind her shoulders. She draws a deep breath and I see the small breasts rise and fall beneath the homesewns. With a brusque gesture, Wa orders me to lie down. Quickly she undresses me and rolls my clothes into a bundle that she places beneath my head.

Now she steps back from the bed and her facial features seem to disappear. In one motion, she lifts the tunic over her head. Even in the dim ocher light, I see the deep lines of Wa's collarbones. I see the twin swells of her ribcage, the vanishing v of her waist. Now the bra is gone. Two small, dark nipples appear and then are gone. Wa has wrapped herself in her own embrace. I hear what sounds like a shudder. She is cold.

The wisp of a chestnut girl dives into my arms, warming me as she finds warmth. Suddenly I am holding my daughter. I am comforting a stranger. I am enclosing my lover. I am accepting acceptance. I am doing all, and none, of these things. It's a moment that belongs nowhere yet creates a place for itself. Part of me notices a commotion in the hallway, but now Wa is moving her small hips against mine, describing ever larger circles. Hungrily, my hands search for the tie at her waist.

There is a story about a woman named Wa and a very bad historical moment when the sky was in need of repair and no one quite knew what to do about it. The story is called "Wa Mends the Sky" because it was this woman Wa who solved the problem by making a fire, melting together stones of five different colors, and using the iridescent magma to fill all the gaps. It worked beautifully, Wa's solution, and everyone said very nice things about her.

My hands find the tie.

The historical Wa, we're told, travels these days on a thunder chariot drawn by a double-winged dragon and two hornless dragons. With auspicious objects in her hands, she sails among golden clouds with a white dragon leading the way and a flying snake following behind. Which is definitely the way to go if you can't get a cabin next to the dining car.

Loosening the cotton ribbon of Wa's homesewn pants, I slide my long cold hands inside. I feel her muscles tighten. I'm definitely drawing closer to something. Burying my nose in the nape of Wa's neck, I find her skin to smell faintly of almonds. My hands want to reach a little farther beneath the homesewn pants, and I begin to lift one shoulder. Instantly Wa throws her weight against the shoulder as would a wrestler, pinning me.

She now spreads her legs to hold my hips in place, and my fingers take full advantage, describing the warm divide of her bottom. Again, noises in the hallway, but Wa's hips are describing circles once more. The chestnut girl is ever warmer the farther my fingertips stretch. I sense that I'm drawing *very* close to something now, close enough to feel the vague beginnings of a glow in my thighs when—

When I realize I'm being watched.

My eyes open upon a most unexpected sight. A ghostly and fiery-eyed Shatrina Carter is hovering like a flaming zeppelin at the ceiling of the room. Her mouth opens, and I hear Truman whisper, "This is mahhhch bigger than you and me, Julian. It's about the *chuuul*-run."

With each word, the glowing coals of Tree's eyes glow brighter. "It's about the destiny of the wooooild."

"Uh, could we talk about this later?" I murmur.

Wa's hips cease to circle.

"You get your chap-tuh," whispers Truman. "In return, the *wooooild* gets your help."

Wa lifts her head. Maybe she, too, hears noises in the hall.

"Fine," I tell Tree's hovering image. "I like the world. I like it a lot. But just now—"

"Beware the *sheen*," says Truman, Tree's fiery eyes beginning to fade, "of the blue and the *greeeen.*"

As the image of Tree Carter fades overhead, the door crashes open and into the room spill several people, some of them wearing uniforms. Two shrieking women point at Wa, who scrambles off the bed into a corner. They are the two Han sex workers I'd just spurned. One of the uniformed men lurches to the corner where Wa cowers and seizes her by the hair. I watch him drag her from the room. Another policeman points to the roll of clothes beneath my head. The smoke detector beeps.

The two Han women disappear. I put my pants on backwards and the uniformed men laugh. Outside are two patrol cars. As I lower myself into one, the other drives away, its red light strobing. I wonder if Wa is inside.

At the police station, I am shut inside a white room empty but for two chairs and a small desk. Glass-encased on one wall is the blood-red flag of the People's Republic of China. The walls have recently been painted. There is no air in the room. I'm horribly thirsty. My hands keep feeling for my wallet and journal, both of them gone.

Later, perhaps hours later, a grey-haired man with Han features enters the room, his uniform immaculate. In his hand is a large ziplock bag. I watch the man, obviously an officer, take a seat behind the small desk, unzip the bag and remove from it a thin white object. He shows it to me. Along one side are the words "Our Glorious Chairman Mao Zedong."

I swallow hard.

After staring at me for a moment, the man sets down the joint and produces, sequentially, a roach bearing the words "Workers of . . ," a quarter-ounce bag of crap marijuana, an irregular cake of hashish, a small grey nugget of opium, and a torn, defiled book of the maxims of Mao Zedong. The bag also contains some crumpled photos of Mao lifted from a trash can.

Another long gaze.

Unhurriedly the grey-haired man returns each object to the bag, zips it closed, and places it on the desk between us.

"Mr. Mancer," says a mild voice, its accent both British and Chinese, "do you know how old that girl is?"

A bit hoarsely, I reply, "No."

"Thirteen," he says, his gaze fixed on me.

My throat tries to swallow again. It lacks the spit.

The officer says, "You seem to be having a good time in Dali. Would you say that's so?"

He waits. I don't know how to answer.

"No?" he asks evenly. "Is there something additional we can do to make your stay more enjoyable?"

"Uh, if I may," I manage, "I'm a writer for an American magazine. If you'll just call Miriam Goldfarb at—"

"Oh? You're a writer?" he interrupts. "What is your assignment here in Dali?"

"Actually, I'm researching China's ethnic minorities."

He stares, unblinking.

"I know that sounds a little funny," I say.

After a moment, the officer replies, "No, that's not funny. I'll tell you what's funny. That thirteen-year-old girl has been charged with prostitution. She'll remain here until she reaches fourteen years of age. Then she will begin a prison sentence of ten years. In a Chinese prison, Mr. Mancer, life expectancy is a little more than eight."

I avoid his gaze.

Abruptly the officer sits back. The chair squeaks. "I am married to a Bai woman. They were once a very strong people, the Bai. So were the Naxi, and the Dai, and the Mosou and the other peoples in these mountains. They received everything they needed from the lakes and the forests. Then outsiders came with their tourist money. Their drug money. Their sex money. Now these same people are criminals and drug addicts. Their children have HIV. That girl you were with tonight? I know her family. Her father has a drug habit. He sold his daughter to that—"

"That place," he says almost too softly to hear.

The grey-haired man picks up the ziplock bag, gazes at it, then sets it down again. "There's no need to call your magazine. Someone has already spoken to me concerning your . . . situation."

I look at him blankly.

"In any event, my government doesn't approve of placing Americans in jail for anything short of axe murder." He looks up at me. "Do you plan to murder anyone with an axe, Mr. Mancer?"

He awaits an answer.

My "no" is almost inaudible.

The officer gazes at me, nodding slowly for what seems a full minute. Finally he rises and leaves the room. The ziplock bag is still on the table. I can't bring myself to look at it. A few minutes later, two bronze-skinned policemen enter and lock the door behind them. They aren't smiling.

Except for the little red book and its endearing photos, everything in the ziplock bag is forced up my ass. The next thing I remember is the long, bitter struggle to awake. Slowly, by awful degrees, I realize that I am sprawled on the bed of the Marigold Suite, my right arm twisted beneath me. It is hours before I understand anything. I understand now. I understand now.

The young man across the aisle has finished with the sunflower seeds. He wads the brown paper bag and tosses it out my window, missing my nose by an inch. The two Mao-capped men are leaning against each other, asleep. I no longer feel that I'm drawing closer to anything.

My hand is throbbing viciously. I grope for the tin of aspirin that may be in my left pants pocket. It isn't there. Adjusting my posture, I try digging in the right pocket with my left hand. It's impossible. Exhausted, I give up.

If only I could stop thinking about her. Could stop catching the scent of her or imagining that I do. Soon I'll put some distance between myself and this degradation. I'll cease to know quite so clearly that I have failed even my lowest instincts and, without some stranger's intercession, would be utterly and finally undone. It's a situation.

I'll arrive in another town. I'll locate my meds. I'll find my equilibrium. I'll shower all this off me. I'll walk into a Western medical clinic smelling of honest wood alcohol and have this throbbing horror of a right hand properly X-rayed and set. I'll produce field notes with tidy vertical margins and clear pronoun reference. I'll vanish without a trace into Julian Mancer.

Refocusing on the tin of aspirin, I decide to search my backpack. Sighing, I snake my good left hand into the nearest pocket of the backpack. The hand closes around an unfamiliar shape, and I pull out a butane lighter imprinted with the image of Quan Yin, Goddess of Mercy and Inflammable Petroleum Byproducts. "You come here receive the teaching," I was told in a paint-flaking temple. "Quan Yin give this teaching to you."

I stare dully at the lighter.

It begins to rain. The passengers scramble to throw the bus windows up. They're laughing, giddy from the negative ions and the sudden burst of activity. The bus reaches the end of the fertile valley and hurls itself up the side of a mountain. The pavement changes from blacktop to a noisy pebbled concrete. Through my window, I look down on a churning mist denser with each switchback. We are leaving the place where we have been. Maybe that's the same as going somewhere.

8

It's not as though Joseph Campbell wasn't alert to the situation. Though a lesser one than you might have guessed from the boring pants and wheezy voice that something short of *fraichement coupe* was going on here, but believe as you must. We are each free to choose our own décor, our most representative room in which to die our death, and die it we do. Just don't undershoot the landing strip. The hissing serpents and run-afoul seraphim of deepest night retreat not before our misunderstanding, friend. All is other than. All is deeply rooted in a foreign soil.

Which is to say, I still don't know where my meds are. I'm increasingly loathe to look for them, actually, as my fingers have tired of the same stuttering zippers, the same dutiful snaps, only to discover once more the forlorn and ill-loved items encountered before. *Syzygy.* That's what the zippers say to me of late. I don't know what it means.

Dawn is Lijiang. That much seems clear enough. The first rays over Eastern Mountain hit this tangle of stone and weathered pine planking at just the right angle to deepen every shadow and roughen every texture, adding a cast of pink to the chiseled stone and dabbed plaster of an ethnic village in many ways unchanged for eight centuries.

Just this instant, the sun is high enough to roll the morning chill into little whorls of warmth, inducing mini-slumbers as I curl around my cup of yak-butter tea at this rooftop café of no name. I'm awaiting my guide and interpreter, Zhu (pronounced *Jew*), a tall, somber widower who late yesterday promised me a competent doctor for my right hand. "Is best doctor Lijiang," said Zhu. "We go very early. Dr. Wang always so busy."

British travel writer Bruce Chatwin once stopped in Lijiang to see a doctor. Suffering from appendicitis, Chatwin was given poisonous mushroom spores to inhale. The appendix got better. The rest of him died. It's probably a good thing I'm not that kind of writer.

Trotting to my table, my young waitress poses a question in Mandarin with great formality. I nod agreeably, and off she goes. I wonder what I have just agreed to. Hopefully nothing to do with mushrooms.

The café of no name is, in fact, no café at all but the rooftop of the Yu family's ancestral home overlooking Lijiang's dense quilt of grey-tiled roofs. As the Yus' gate opens upon the most frequented foot route to a park of eight-hundred-year-old cedars, it was a simple enough matter to place a hand-lettered sign at the gate offering tea and pastries.

Now when a stranger wanders into their courtyard, as have I, Grandmother Yu looks up from her gardening, takes note of you, and shouts to the granddaughter who comes running, tying on an apron and pointing to the narrow staircase. But not before you have glimpsed a centuries-old rhythm of living and read the silent messages of worn stone and unplaned pine, the clutter of often-used things, the three bird-cages of tiny flutterings, the slowly turning wheel of morning chores, the self-renewing drama of *anthropos muddle-os,* the hero's journey sans hero.

I take a look at my swollen right hand and ponder the likelihood of our Dr. Wang's having an X-ray machine. As likely, he's just received word of the thermometer.

At least my thinking has cleared a bit this morning, or so I self-congratulate as I lift the broad-handled ceramic cup and note its gloss finish. Granddaughter Yu brings me a croissant hard enough to produce a *thunk* as it hits the plate, over her shoulder the eighteen-thousand-foot preponderance called Jade Dragon Snow Mountain. Such a charming name for a volcano whose next stirring will cheerfully cook everyone here alive. You feel the threat with your eyes closed.

My good left hand trembles a bit as it lifts the ceramic cup.

Syzygy is a dangerous word. All those consonants and not a single standard American vowel. *Thunk* I find much easier to be around.

This particular tea—of Tibetan origin, as are most things Naxi—contains egg, ground sesame seeds and walnuts, and milk of yak. My hand trembles again as I set down the cup, and I wonder how long before the analgesic properties of certain recent excesses wear off entirely and what exactly happens to me then. Reasonable question, as I see it, but before I can conjure a suitable answer, a navy baseball cap pulses up the narrow stairs, followed by an unsmiling face behind thick glasses. This would be guide and interpreter Zhu.

Reaching my table, Zhu says, "Hello. Please we go now." He declines to sit, preferring to wait dolefully at the head of the stairs as Granddaughter Yu runs to fetch my change.

My legs are a bit wobbly as I rise to follow my guide into the street. Right away I'm panting two and three strides behind Zhu as we press through the charcoal smells of morning. I fight the urge to look over my shoulder. Just because someone in red socks is following you doesn't mean you have to turn and look at him.

Yesterday I was certain I'd spotted Ana Manguella in a street market. A blanket-wrapped woman, her face turned away, was buying fruit, and from the thick ponytail and my own fusty mind, she was exactly Ana until she wheeled, revealing a face something like a knee. We were put together once, a crisp voice once told me. It can happen again. And Mao's missing testicle may materialize in my left shirt pocket.

Zhu and I skirt around a pile of lime that has caught fire at center. Unhurriedly three construction workers carry buckets of water from the river. As each bucket is dumped onto the pile, a burst of steam erupts, hissing and popping violently.

Just to be sure, I check my left shirt pocket. No testicle.

Zhu leads me across an arched bridge of cut stone. To know Lijiang, Zhu has told me, kneeling at yesterday's dusk to touch a paving stone, one must know Five Flower Stone. Centuries ago Naxi stonemasons used the pebble-studded rose granite to lift their village from the mud, stone-channeling the Jade River into canals that reached every home, installing waterwheels and self-brimming public wells, laying streets and bridges smooth enough for wheeled carts, even creating a system of locks that make it possible still to flood and scrub down entire sections of Lijiang. All of this was constructed without mortar, resulting in a city all but earthquake-proof, scarcely noticing a seven point two a few years back.

At just past seven, Dr. Wang is in. I pay the receptionist the two point nine yuan required for an office visit—less than twenty-five cents. Following Zhu into a large frumpy office, I discover an old man behind a cluttered desk beneath two vast unscreened windows open to the busy sidewalk, the passersby practically close enough to donate blood. Behind the desk, Dr. Wang is preoccupied with opening a fresh pack of Hong Ta cigarettes.

I study the smooth-skinned face beneath the blue Mao cap. Wild salt-and-pepper eyebrows flare two and three inches from his brow, the scattered chin whiskers every bit as seditious. You can't look at Dr. Wang and not think *wizened*. As though hearing the thought, he glances up and points to a chair. Unhurriedly the doctor lights a cigarette, sits back, and gives me a calm, appraising look.

Zhu seats himself at my left and says in a hushed voice, "You can ask Dr. Wang something. I tell you the meaning."

"I have a broken hand," I say irritably.

The doctor says something.

"Dr. Wang ask," Zhu translates, "what is happen to your hand?"

I turn to look at Zhu. "I broke it. I have a broken hand."

Zhu translates timidly, taking forever. I survey the office, hoping to discover something recognizably medical. Aside from the stethoscope around the doctor's neck, this place could be a really bad church rummage sale. On one table is a fishbowl filled with dried insects. Next to it is an unstrung tennis racket.

"Would you please ask the doctor if he knows how to set a bone," I interrupt Zhu. "Has he ever done it before?"

Zhu is speechless for a moment. Finally he says, "Yes, Dr. Wang is know."

The doctor guffaws and blows Hong Ta smoke toward the ceiling.

Patience gone, I place my right elbow on the cluttered desk, hold up my rutabaga of a right hand for Dr. Yang to see, and rotate it slowly for full effect. Even the people on the street are getting this.

"Please tell Dr. Wang," I say carefully, "that I broke my smallest finger, and possibly one or more bones of the palm, *two* nights ago and therefore must have the bones set immediately or they will heal improperly. Can you translate that?"

Zhu sets his feet carefully on the floor and begins in earnest. I fall back in my chair, my beleaguered heart hammering, meanwhile pretending not to notice the two adolescent girls seated half-inside the windows, listening. A very thin man stands near them, studying me. I can't see whether he's wearing red socks.

As Zhu rattles on, Dr. Wang sets down his Hong Ta, takes a sip from the spout of a brass teapot, and hurries around the desk to grab my left wrist. Immediately, a frown. He's checking the three pulses. Ah. So much better than an X-ray.

Dr. Wang sticks out his tongue. I return the favor and he examines my tongue with an expression of distaste. Now he's dabbing at my chest with his stethoscope.

Zhu asks, "Do you have the high, uh, high . . ."

"Blood pressure?" I say. "No, but I can feel it coming on."

Dr. Wang goes back to my pulses, still scowling.

"Dr. Wang say your heart is like a very young man."

"Clean living," I reply.

Now the doctor's fingertips are probing beneath my ribs. I feel that he's half-inside my body cavity.

"He say something is make the liver tired," reports Zhu. "Also say something is on your head."

"I'm sorry?"

"On your . . . thinking," says Zhu.

"On my mind?"

"Yes. Something on your mind."

"There's always something on my mind," I inform him.

When Wang hears the translation, he stops examining me. Speaking to Zhu in a near-falsetto, he returns to his chair.

"Dr. Wang say," Zhu translates, "this is why your body have the problem. Stop the problem in the mind, is fix the problem in the body."

I look from face to face. "I have a problem with the body because I fell off the damn bed."

Zhu stares at me for what seems a full minute before breaking into peals of laughter. His laugh is eerily like that of Desi Arnaz.

Wang leans across the desk, eager for the translation. When he finally gets it, he begins slapping the desk, his wheezy laugh almost inaudible. On cue, the girls in the windows practically fall into the office laughing. Now they're telling a couple of other people. A crowd is forming.

I look down at my throbbing hand. I'd have been better off wrapping the goddamn thing in frozen fish.

Finally, Dr. Wang says something to Zhu, who's wiping his tears on a rag from his pocket. Zhu blows his nose twice before continuing. "Doctor say, if no problem is in the mind, why you do this to yourself?"

I look across the desk. Wang, no longer laughing, stares awaiting my answer.

I sigh. It's a long story, okay? Forcing a smile, I say, "Well, it's done now, isn't it? Why don't we just concentrate on fixing it?"

After the translation, Wang answers listlessly, lighting a second Hong Ta from the first.

Zhu says, "Doctor say, no fix your hand today. Give you some kind of tea, some kind of leaf make your hand go small. Bone is stay very soft."

I give Wang a glance. I feel mushroom therapy coming.

Now the doctor speaks at length, shrugging his shoulders with every other sentence, pausing once or twice to sip tea from the spout of his dirty teapot. The half-dozen people at the windows are leaning in, holding their collective breath. It must be quite a speech.

Finally Zhu turns to me. "Dr. Wang say fix the problem too quick like put bone together wrong. Is need keep soft. Is need—" Zhu pauses to search his mind for appropriate words. "Is need fix the *mind* or next time break the neck of your head."

I'm still forcing a smile. "But it isn't *easy* to fix the mind."

As this is translated, the doctor's face seems to expand in surprise. Now he chortles merrily. The people in the windows think it's pretty funny, too.

Zhu translates, "Many things not so easy. You want the advice, Dr. Wang tell you something very true answer."

I close my eyes for a moment and try to focus. Forget the people in the windows. Forget the swollen hand. Forget everything except what these two men are struggling to offer me. When I open my eyes, I find them moist. "Please tell the doctor that I am a very sad man. So sad that I've no idea how I remain alive."

I can't believe that I'm saying this. I check short-term memory to be sure. I'm saying it all right.

"Something is . . . turned wrong," I tell the two men. "I can't feel anything. I drink. I snort. I smoke. I—"

"You *what*?" asks Zhu.

I enunciate the words carefully. "Snort. Smoke. Ganja. Shit. Spliff."

"You mean," he asks in amazement, "some kind of drugs?"

"Some kind of drugs."

Zhu's voice is a little different as he translates. Dr. Wang's face is impassive. Finally the doctor replies. Lots of words, lots of shrugs, lots of puffs on Hong Ta. The people in the windows are losing interest.

"Dr. Wang is say," Zhu tells me, "need to regulate the mind. Once mind is regulate . . ."

Zhu drones on. I look at the doctor, who is still giving me this endlessly patient expression, yet I feel that he has yet to see me at all. I know perfectly well what's going on here. Of the three people in this room, not counting those half-inside the windows, two are healthy, centered, well-balanced humans who inhabit their lives with simple, direct grace.

Are you doing it wrong? Well then, begin doing it right. What could be simpler? And what could be more impossible for these two men to understand than human being number three, the one somehow removed from his offices, somehow outside looking in, gesturing to those inside and warm, saying how do I get in there? And they, in their innocence, their maddening ingenuousness, can only reply: why you're just *in* here.

The street is quiet as Zhu and I step out into the harsh sunlight. There's no one in red socks. Zhu is darkly silent during the long walk to my hotel. At the construction site, the lime is no longer burning. Workers are mixing it with water and sand, re-laying Five Flower Stone over new sewer line. Walking ahead of us are two women with ponytails. Neither is Ana Manguella.

I think there was once a time when things mattered. A boyish interval, an awkward interlude, less than a summer, more than a pity. I can almost remember the taste of it but could no more call it back than serve it on a wedge of rye, that too-simple and overly angular abstraction, *virtue*, which my sister clings to as to a porcelain doll while denying the smallest portion to me. Nor am I entirely certain that I would call it back if I could, just to see it perish once more beneath the bone-splintering press of the world's baseline indifference.

And my own. At times I feel its weight like a cement truck, the antipathy of this doomed race of smelly flesh-ripping monkeys whose deepest devotion is to the sniffing of paint cans. "I find that entirely offensive," said Ana Manguella. "If you must know, it doesn't become you at all." Nor does the color orange. When she bid me farewell at the Guangzhou train station, the Englishwoman offered up a piece of advice, and my stomach drew in protectively.

"If you really want to contribute something here, you simply must find a way to ground yourself. You could begin by taking off that moldavite. It's from outer space, you know. I can't imagine how you intend to accomplish anything at all here, Julian, when you've yet to acknowledge that you've arrived."

For a moment, the two cool eyes held me almost tenderly and I wondered how this woman could have known about the moldavite pendant hidden beneath my shirt. I felt a sudden urge to tear it off my neck and hand it to her, to wrap it in the cool porcelain fingers just to discover what moment it might bring to her face. I think I would've had she not so quickly turned away.

I've no idea what I think anymore. I've yet to completely claw my way out of the stupendous stupor of two nights ago, let alone the teeming *hideom* of my days and nights since boarding a plane in Memphis with a quarter-formed apprehension and a half-pound of multi-grind. Here I am panting at ten thousand feet, my shattered right hand pulsing with each step, while the other clutches a bundle of pungent herbs wrapped in a Beijing Daily from eleven months ago.

"I know sometimes is very hard," Zhu's hoarse whisper says to me now as he walks dolefully at my side. His eyes don't rise to meet mine. "Sometimes I too feel this way. Don't have the wife. Don't have the job. Daughter go away. I start get old. Think about this only make me feel sad, so just get up, put on the shoes, go walk somewhere."

Zhu turns to peer at me, his eyes enormous in the thick lenses. "Julian, please don't take the drugs. Just go out some-place. Go walk, talk to somebody have the trouble more than you. You feel better like me."

My eyes hold the melancholy face for a moment, unex-pectedly touched by the concern of this gaunt man I'll never see again. If only his kindness didn't make me feel that much worse. Zhu and I continue up the hill, each of us gazing thoughtfully at Five Flower Stone as though at any moment one of us will say something encompassing. It doesn't come.

9

This is the day it hits me square in the big American nose. I can feel it coming. I'm leaning into it, a lifetime's experience having established just how long one can paddle blithely up de' Nile before the crocodile surfaces beneath the boat. Whether that will turn out to have much or little to do with recent errors in judgment, as opposed to those of yore, probably matters not at all. It is, at least, a comfort to know that all I have to do is paddle a wee bit farther before the answers come quite obligingly to *me*.

This is situational depression, I tell myself, abetted by the laconic three-day rain that has re-enlivened old Kunming scents and left my very soul to question what is sweat and what precipitation, what ambient hydrogen sulfate and what just the Kunming *film*.

As the drizzle seems to have abated for the moment, I pause at a street corner to wrestle my double-jointed umbrella closed. Not easily done with one hand. As I struggle pitifully, a gap-toothed man in a Chicago Bulls cap studies my face from about nine inches away, as rapt and unselfconscious as if watching two dogs screw in the park. Now another man joins him, leaning forward seemingly to count my nose hairs. Now the two men turn to discuss.

Kunming, one more horridly huge and hugely horrid Han city, is the capital of Yunnan Province and home to two million people innocent of additional options. It is home, as well, to a functioning X-ray machine. Thus, finally, three-plus days after one very nasty fall from grace, my right hand is now embraced by a white plaster cast as clean as the dreams of an unfevered child. No one has signed it. I feel so unpopular.

Simple clean break, I was told, and thanks to Dr. Yang's poultice, completely unknitted.

As I cannot possibly close this umbrella and the gap-toothed fellow and his friend are too deep in conversation to assist, I give up and cross the intersection against the light, hopeful that my steps will bear me in the general direction of *edible*. The charcoal grill at the overcrowded and under-cleaned Kunming train station didn't particularly beckon. Just beside the counter was a pile of garbage as high as a horse's back.

All around lay damp, miserable Chinese elbow-to-elbow on blankets and newspapers like war dead, most of them awaiting the same squalid train, a hard sleeper to Guangzhou outbound in two and a half hours. Until then, I get to skulk along these pitted and rain-fouled streets, clinging to my double-jointed umbrella and muttering Bro' Foucault beneath my breath while scouting for a semi-hygienic restaurant or a particularly nasty massage parlor, whichever comes first. Not that I haven't learned my lesson.

Then, it may have been a situational lesson.

It hurts, by the way. The hand beneath the handsome white cast. More so all the time, as my beleaguered liver seems finally to have cleared all traces of pain-dulling substances—which begs the question, why do I still awake each morning with no clue as to where I am, not even the continent whereupon I *dip* among these inimitable dip slopes. On this particular morning it was at least five minutes before I constructed a line of logic and ten before I was willing to buy in. Just because something runs in a straight line doesn't make it true, no more than being unable to locate my meds for three consecutive days means they are lost.

I wish I had a little more of that sticky black opium.

A hard sleeper, I have learned, is a cramped bunkhouse on steel wheels. There are no assigned bunks, thus "boarding" is far too kind a word for what happens when the train hisses to a near-halt. Hopefully I'll wind up with a lower berth with no all-night card games left or right— the players sit on your bed—and no additional war wounds. From Guangzhou I'll take a first-class train to Shenzhen where Lillian and Tree now await placement for their concurrent one-year sentences in separate but equal high schools. There I shall inquire of the higher angels of Tree's nature as to when and where I'm to receive that passel of pages that our little strumpet Truman seems now to be dangling, and for which I've evidently bartered my immortal soul.

Personally I don't care whether I'm to comfort the world's *chuul*-ren or deliver them on a skewer. That New York publisher is practically panting for the final chapter of *The End of Day* and I'm at pains to come up with a fresh excuse for not delivering it. Meanwhile I'd do well to place another parcel of Chinese-y with Miriam and quickly, before she disremembers my airfare.

Magazine Mariposa is a tax shelter for an arms manufacturer. Grenade launchers. I haven't mentioned this to Lillian, nor should you. It's a situation. Life's full of them.

And I should petition Bernie for another little bottle of syzygy. I mean another little bottle of meds. Bernie writes me the good pills, and I get him into the B parties in New York. Actually they're the C parties, but Bernie doesn't know that. Not that I'm particularly *disturbed* just this moment. Situationally depressed is all. One point nine, maybe one nine five, is all. The coping mechanisms kick in at two.

This particular dreary stretch of Kunming seems long on butchers and sheet-metal shops and short on sanitary eating establishments, say nothing of particularly nasty massage parlors. I'd settle just now for a clean one. Chinese men are fond of paying young women to stroll up and down the backs of their legs—which explains the plumbing above Chinese massage tables, I'm happy to have learned.

The masseuse clings to the pipes while making Wan Fan Shan squeal like a widdle pig. Afterward comes an hour of the most exquisite pressure-point torture followed by the kind of

spirited steaming-towel rub-down that Chairman Mao pre-
ferred to bathing the last two decades of his life. Which is
exactly the kind of vector Bro' Foucault warned us about, not
that we were listening.

We should have been.

Whether we hang our hat on circumstance or our balls
out on chance, there's still this seething background *murmur*
that one can but notice between his/her little wheezes, his/*her*
lame saxophone rationalizations while struggling one-handed
with a two-handed umbrella. Or whilst going through the
pockets of one's backpack the thirty-third time, unsure whether, when last we triple-checked for the meds, they were *there*,
clearly there, but we somehow failed to recognize them.

I just spent an hour in a soggy internet café where I
checked my various email accounts, alternative realities, faux
realities, and all such like. They were all fine. Lillian notified
me that Shenzhen has palm trees. A former associate reminded me that I owe him money. There was an email from Ralpho
that provided a link to his article on "the real truth about glo-
bel [*sic*] warming." Catastrophic climate change, says Ralpho,
turns out to have less to do with petro emissions than biological ones.

Human flatulence, we're gradually learning, contains an
organic compound that combines with elements of the upper
atmosphere in a way that traps radiant heat like a black Lin-
coln Town Car. This information is being suppressed, says
Ralpho, as there seems no real alternative to a massive die-
off. So while the privileged few will hunker in their bunkers,
the rest of us will be left to fart ourselves into oblivion.

Happily, Ralpho's article proposes a kinder solution, namely the establishment of two days per week—Tuesdays and
Thursdays are suggested—when we all hold it. If everyone
were to participate, emissions could be reduced by nearly
thirty percent, which is not an insignificant amount. Re-
fraining from the consumption of beans on those same days
might go farther still, suggests Ralpho. Personally I think he

was absent from school the day they taught Newton's Fourth Law concerning the conservation of gaseous matter. Anyway, I've always held it on Tuesdays and Thursdays. It's my contribution.

Good thing I was unable to close my umbrella. The low clouds are once more beginning to *ooze*, to the chagrin of my bladder which is nearing the point of no return. China has no public restrooms—none at all—thus, the defining sensation of being in this country is an unending sorrowful cramp in the midsection, and as I have left the train station a dozen blocks behind, it seems time to embrace an eatery.

I pause amid the puddles to look both ways, and I briefly consider the three phone numbers moldering in my wallet. Please help this colorless foreign devil every courtesy. Too bad I don't do telephones. Neither did e. e. cummings, as you may know. His feeling, and I understand utterly, was that if someone really wanted to speak to him, he had a front door with a serviceable bell. Still I can't quite bring myself to throw those numbers away, nor the tattered note of introduction stuck fast to them. Tree would accuse me of harboring an intuition, but it's likely more a case of undifferentiated fear. I'm less and less interested in separating these things out.

Her Tree-ness is excited, said Lillian's email, as the movie version of Bi (rhymes with *pee*) Yu Nu's latest book debuts tonight in Beijing amid rumors that the author himself may appear, ending three decades of speculation as to his identity. As tickets are impossible to come by, Tree plans to be part of the mob in front of the theater. *A Room of Eyes*. That's the title of both the book and the movie. I once visited a room constructed entirely of antonyms. Eyes, no. But there seems to be a room for pretty much everything.

I pause in front of a small diner. It's gloomy, fly-swirling, and oppressively wet, which probably makes it the finest restaurant in all of Kunming. Stepping inside, I find myself hydroplaning on deposits of cooking oil from the Xin dynasty. I steady myself on a table and its plastic cover, precipitating a *sssschlllp* sound when I peel my hand off. Taking a seat, I discover that the menu is just as sticky. I order a beer and a number-one, whatever that is, and mime to the waitress that I'd very much like to wash my hands.

Follow me, she signals.

I follow, grease-skating, through a tiny door and its frayed curtain into a wretched hole of a kitchen. Amid piles of unwashed pots and pans is a metal sink beneath a dirty rubber hose. The startled expression of the cook informs me that I'm the first patron to ever ask to wash his hands. My present needs call for an actual restroom, however, so I grudgingly produce the requisite word, the only Mandarin one I know.

Follow me.

Tree blames it all on little René Descartes. From the red tides of Tobago to the blue moons of Kentucky, from our tiny beads of sweat as we strain against the multiplication tables in fourth grade, to smart bombs that aren't quite smart enough to not go off—it all goes onto little René's account. The conquest of the world, he was told in a dream, was to be accomplished through number. Not integer, mind you. It was an angel who hot-whispered these flawed words, fluttering down to the edge of town to pop the clutch and send the world fishtailing into Act Three of either farce or tragedy, you choose. As though there remains much of a choice, dear ones.

Neither x axis, nor y, let alone that zany z, proffers a place to lay weary head on cold night, you may have noticed—and where exactly do we *go* with these issues, having saved neither the original packaging nor the sales slip. But never mind. The waitress is leading me slip-sliding back through the diner and out once more to the sidewalk from whence I came. Giggling in the rain, she points across the street, forefinger indicating an entire hectare of jumbled doors and signs, not one of which even suggests a restroom, and I use my best Charlie Chaplin to complain about this. She just keeps giggling and pointing.

Disgusted, I muck my way back inside to fetch my backpack and double-jointed umbrella, waitress all the while shouting insults at what appears to be a teenage boy asleep beneath a table. He emerges stupidly to fuss with his hair, which had evidently been a spiked Mohawk at some earlier moment of the day, now resembling nothing so much as a sun-dried dead animal. The waitress, still yammering, shoves the boy toward me and a moment later I'm following him across the street.

The rain comes down heavier. Torpid teen tosses his head, and the spikes send off shimmering arcs of droplets, thin rivulets meanwhile running down narrow neck to disappear beneath black vinyl to seek the earth's center along the path of least developmental disability. He's wearing forty zippers at the least. In front of each ear meanwhile hangs a thin lock of hair in hopeful suggestion of sideburns.

Despite the downpour, he is stubbornly unhurried, sauntering, hands in pockets, and why hasten through a world wherein one moment you're snoring beneath a table and the next leading a monochrome giant through the stinking rain, no difference between the texture of the day and that of your undies. Which I think speaks to the growing tendency among retirement-age banking executives to sniff their secretaries' office chairs just after they've left in a good mood, for lunch.

Marvel not that Bro' Foucault says unto you: the world we view is nothing like the one we inhabit but only its shadow, a timid footnote to discourses among gods far too fair to imagine, nor do they imagine us save when in sudden and dire need of a little pussy *wussy*. All of reality, its flotsam and jetsam, its unsigned scorecards and unfinished masters theses, *all* of this improbable hurdy-gurdy oompah occurs not at center stage at all, nor even off-off Broadway but in some fly-swirling diner in a neighborhood where the taxis don't slow down. Which perhaps puts it a little negatively. But I'm pushing a one point nine. Maybe one nine five.

Obediently following zipper-boy into soggy alleyway, I'm careful to hold the double-jointed umbrella directly above the new plaster cast. Otherwise, I take it, we have so much oatmeal without any real description of a spoon. Abruptly the boy stops among chicken droppings and dog spare parts at the foot of an improbably massive staircase of rusted steel, at its top a moldering wooden third-floor balcony. He points toward the balcony, which features an anonymous door at either end.

I mime the question, "Up then left, or up then right?"

The teenager nods soberly and continues to jab his fore-finger toward the balcony.

Again, more emphatically: up then *left*? Or up then *right*?

The boy continues pointing upward, and even shoves me a little closer to the staircase as though I don't quite see it yet.

With exquisite annoyance, I start up the metal stairs. Be-fore reaching the top, I glance over my shoulder. Zippered teen is slouching away in the rain, having accomplished his worthy deed of the day. For a long moment, I stand panting just below the top of the stairs, looking out across the jumbled tiled rooftops of *phantasmagorium eyesorium* and suddenly it's one of those unexpected crystalline travel moments. An-noyance gone, I discover myself panting above a sodden alley in Kunming, China, bladder cramping, raindrops tapping out an umbrella melody.

For a moment everything is transfigured.

Before leaving Lijiang, I convinced a reluctant Zhu to take me to the ruins of a Buddhist monastery on Paintbrush Moun-tain. "Is just some pile of stones," said he. I told Zhu I was very fond of piles of stones. In truth I was tiring of the streets of Lijiang and its throngs of red-stockinged men with a hard-on for my best-kept secrets. Zhu and I endured a succession of mini-buses then a half-hour uphill hike through pine forest to . . . a pile of stones. I'm not sure what I'd expected. Wenfeng Monastery looked less like a historical site than a very recent demolition.

"What happened here?" I asked.

"Is Red Guard destroy it," said Zhu.

"Ah. El Cultural Revolution."

It wasn't really a revolution, as you probably know, but a government-sanctioned lynch mob loosed against anyone/everyone whose thoughts were trending the wrong way. During the Cultural Revolution, a joke uttered over beers decades earlier could get you a life sentence. Having a brother-in-law who'd told such a joke could get you a public flogging. And if your next-door neighbor had laughed at the joke, you *and* he were forced to do the side-straddle hop.

"Red Guard is destroy many, many place. I know this," said Zhu. The eyes behind the thick lenses searched my face. "When I am a young man, I am Red Guard."

I turned to peer at my guide and interpreter. You don't hear this admission every day.

"I am nineteen years old," continued Zhu, "and I think Mao is some kind of god. Everybody is believe this. All of the school is closed, so nothing to do. Mao is tell all the young men go do something. You can have this nice uniform. Everybody says just go burn some bad books, so I do this. I take the uniform. After we burn the books, now somebody is say go to some temple. We go there, burn the temple. Now somebody say this man is say something bad. Everybody go to this man's house. Is very wrong but you cannot stop it. You say something, tomorrow they come drag your mother and father on the ground."

And force drugs up their cracks, or I miss my guess.

With a sigh, I step from the wet staircase onto the wooden balcony and approach the door at right, my bladder so swollen that my teeth hurt. Turning the knob, I peer inside at a gray-haired woman silently leading some thirty others in Taiji. I close the door at right.

The door at left is swollen from the rain. It drags as I push it. I peer down a dark hallway. The air inside seems oddly empty, no sounds at all nor any hint of the sharp odor that customarily announces a Chinese toilet. The building seems to be abandoned. Stepping inside, I find that the corridor extends in both directions. At one end is a large room suggestive of pointless meetings, at the other a row of doors, one of them partly open. I take a few steps and look inside the half-open door, discovering a janitor's closet that features a low concrete basin designed to accommodate a mop.

Actually this may be the finest public restroom in all of Kunming, I reason, approaching the mop basin and opening my fly. I wait for my cramping abdomen to unknot itself, gazing meanwhile at a three-pronged electrical outlet above the basin. Last night's inelegant departure from the village of Baisha comes to mind.

It wasn't entirely my fault.

Many Chinese hotels provide voltage adaptors, some of them—including the one in last night's wayside inn—bearing inscrutable switches. I must have bumped it. Minor smoke damage was all, but management suggested that I continue my science experiments a little farther down the road.

My first Chinese fire drill. What you'd expect, for the most part. Lots of discussion.

Closing my fly, I reach for the faucet handle to rinse the mop basin and perhaps wash a little Kunming off my hands—and the handle breaks off in my hand. I stare at it for a moment then try to put it back on, and of course it doesn't go back on. As I puzzle over this, a most unwelcome sound comes to my attention, that of a rain-swollen wooden door scraping against a floor, followed by two weighty footsteps.

Faucet handle still in hand, I listen for what seems a long time, hoping to hear additional footsteps fade to some distant part of the building, but there is no sound at all. Gradually it registers that the person standing motionless in the entry is listening as well. Listening for me.

I watched a television program in my room last night. Before the fire drill. I think it was a beauty contest. There must have been a hundred colorless Chinese women with long straight hair, all wearing the same white two-piece bathing suit. Each contestant walked to the front, bumped left then right, spun on the right heel, and walked away. It was the Miss

Identical Pageant. Miss Instant Replay. Miss White Is Not My Color. Three-digit numbers had been pinned to the left hip of each contestant so they could tell themselves apart. Just look down at your number, honey.

I don't know who won the contest. There was a commercial break, after which a panel discussion appeared, government officials with reassuring smiles giving long, unhurried speeches that cascaded like mountain streams and fried lie detectors on the far side of Neptune. Maybe they were discussing how impossible it was to tell those women apart. That was when I first smelled the smoke.

The heavy footsteps continue. Fortunately they lead in the opposite direction, toward the meeting room. There they abruptly stop. Call me psychic, but I've no doubt that those two feet will quite soon turn in this direction. There's only a moment to act. Instead I luxuriate in the sudden silence, finding it more content-laden than I might have reasonably expected. I feel qualitatively different. I try to name the difference but discover that I can't recall how things were before.

Bad, most likely.

A floorboard creaks and then another. At this, three realizations appear in my mind in no particular order. One is, I'm holding a faucet handle in my left hand. Two, I may have tucked my meds into my heavy wool socks, which I've had no occasion to wear of late. The third thing that occurs to me is that people in Westerns get out of situations very like this one by throwing an object, a rock or a stick, whatever comes to hand, thus creating a diversion that bad guys find irresistible, sometimes turning and firing two or three bullets in the wrong direction entirely.

I toss the faucet handle through the open door.

I once saw an actual crocodile surface no farther away than the end of this paragraph. Miriam had evidently decided that the most economical way to get rid of me was to assign an article on any endangered species capable of unhinging its jaw. I was dispatched to East Africa with a pad and pencil and a camera lacking a functional zoom. Unfortunately for both Miriam and the crocodile, I was neither paddling nor swimming at the time but on the deck of a forty-three-foot Bayliner, where I was receiving the attentions of a young woman very nearly capable of unhinging hers. All at once, the yellow eyes of the croc were clearly in view. I tilted my head to one side and said, quite sagely I thought at the time, "I wish I had a little more of that sticky black opium."

I watch the faucet handle crash against the side of the door frame, bounce a few times, and roll to a stop exactly at my feet.

Could I do that again? I want to ask, but that would give away my location.

As expected, the footsteps resume, aggressively loud now and growing ever more so. I decide that the best idea is to panic and dash wild-eyed into the hallway where—

I collide head-on with Julian Mancer. Our bulbous noses meet at dead-center of the hallway, and we each emit a surprised *oomph*. Panicked, I try to step around Julian Mancer, but the same idea occurs to him and we meet face-on once more. It's the Keystone Doos. Finally, my mirror image turns away and flees toward the center of the abandoned building. I make for the fire escape, taking the rusting steps two at a time. Aiming myself in the direction of the diner, I make haste to put a little distance between myselves.

I never knew how silly I look in epaulets.

10

My first encounter with music must surely have occurred very early on, monaural strains drifting into crib from kitchen radio, or however it was. I do recall one timeless moment—I was sitting on a chill black-and-white tiled floor—when I became aware of an active organizing principle materializing around my tenderest of regions and imploring them to surrender all notion of order and consequence unto an entirely novel scheme.

The experience was too altogether abstract to do anything with except register a category of hoodoo later to be labeled *music*, or what I then supposed music to be. It was in point of fact *recorded* music, the experiential difference being roughly the same as that between eating a cheeseburger and eating a photo of a cheeseburger.

I wish I were eating a photo of the number-one. As far as I can tell, it's an omelet with a side of boiled dumplings. The brown bottle of beer that came with it was warm, but it was beer. So was the second one. The third one seemed to be kind of like beer, too. Numbers four through seven haven't specifically registered, but my hands don't feel quite so dirty now and I no longer feel bad about ignoring the phone numbers in my wallet.

I think I'm adjusting rather well to what just happened in that abandoned building, whatever it was and whomever it happened to. You hear the occasional metaphorical reference to unexpected encounters with one's evil twin, or dark side, shadow-self, whatever. I liked it better when it was a metaphor. This wasn't even a real good simile. That was a *person* in there. I felt his nose against mine. I smelled his Altoid. Whoever it was, if not for the grey eyes, he would have been a better me than me. What remains unclear is whether I have just met my evil twin or he has just met his.

I'm going to check my wool socks for those meds.

There are stories about twins separated at birth and placed with families on opposite coasts, only to meet head-on as adults in circumstances as unlikely as today's or quite nearly, thereafter to learn they'd both married a woman named Agnes with Rett syndrome. Still in all, having viewed Lillian's and my birth records on more than one occasion, I think we can be relatively certain that our mother did not drop more than two offspring on the occasion of Lil's and my birth. Which leaves us where?

And then there's the matter of the envelope.

When I returned to this sticky table, awaiting me was an uncapped bottle of warm beer, a saucer of limp noodle crisps, a plastic jigger of soy sauce with enough MSG and corn sweetener to disable a nuclear submarine, and a sealed letter-sized envelope of exceptional quality with my name laser-printed across the front in twelve-point Courier New. I haven't opened it. I'm waiting for the right moment.

Zippered teenager is sleeping again, his upper body sprawled across a table. There's something stuck in his hair. It looks like a price sticker. At another table, an old man buries his face in a bowl of noodles. He's making more or less the same sounds as a Bangkok airport hooker with Rett syndrome.

Chairman Mao once tried waiting for the right moment but found it entirely onerous. So many gratifications so near to hand, and here he'd survived the Long March for what, a grey wool suit? So, as his right hand stirred the egg-flower soup, the left one unbuttoned his fly and the misshapen map-of-China face twisted into something like an appeasing grin as the three young women across the table tittered uncertainly, still believing they were the Chairman's ballroom dance partners for the evening—but where were the musicians? And why did the Chairman *smile* so as he lowered the warm soup bowl to his lap? And what did come first, anyway, the flower or the egg?

But easy answers are for easy minds. This shadow was given *me* for company, not some other wastrel, and it is I who must sing that the moon may reel.

> . . . Because the moon does not know how to drink wine,
> She has given me this shadow for company.
> So let our mirth keep pace with the spring!
> I sing and the moon begins to reel,
> I dance and the shadow lurches grotesquely . . .

I lift the envelope, and the world tilts a little to the right. Too thin to contain ready cash, I decide, which doesn't preclude the possibility of a nice cashier's check. Not that I'm ready to assume at this tender point that the current envelope connects in any way to that proffered in a Beijing steam brothel, but for a moment I let myself wonder just how well-financed this hypothetical research project might be, and whether the ethical pain associated with accepting money for something I've no intention of actually doing might not be easier to bear than that of swindling good prose from a dead queer, or at least giving it a really nice try before both knees are shattered with a corked Louisville Slugger in the warehouse district along Old Summer Ave.

Good question, however lengthy, but one better suited to a mind that does not slip like a loose bicycle chain. I expect any moment to awaken from all this in a lumpy bed beside a barred window, trinket merchant nodding just beyond, no paired silhouettes of shoed feet at door, no horrors to recall nor fail to recall, no alternative *selves* to go bump in the broad and scent-enlivened afternoon, no Bro' Fou' theorems to boldly cast forth then methodically reel back in, nothing at all to hold on Tuesdays and Thursdays, nor any room of eyes to shed self-witnessed tears in statuary silence in that great getting-up morning fare-thee-well oh fare-thee-well.

Lillian says Tree just broadcast her first radio show from Shenzhen. Shatrina informed a spellbound world that China is, as expected, the place where it all be going down, whatever *it* turns out to be. She said a lot of former Atlanteans are milling about here, hoping to avert the same kind of disaster as before. "Uh, Atlantis didn't exist," I told Tree not so long ago. "It's been proven by plate tectonics."

"Everything existed," replied Lillian, to whom I wasn't speaking. "That's been proven, too."

"You're always talking about rooms, Jules," concurred Tree. "There's one for everything, right?"

I told her I wasn't sure about an Atlantis room, besides which wouldn't you, like, need a lot of extra towels?

"Pi," I say to the waitress (rhymes with Bi) and she dashes to the kitchen for another brown bottle of warm beer while I return my attention to the disturbingly perfect envelope on the plastic table cover. Most likely there's nothing inside but two plane tickets to Chicago and a gift certificate to Luby's. To hell with these people and their shoddy recruitment techniques. Next time I squat a Chinese toilet, I'm quite sure that Jerry Scribner's head will emerge from my ass to inform me that it was not *he* who chose this meeting place but if I would just excrete his briefcase, I might find that it contains a most interesting proposal.

The last really interesting proposal I received came late yesterday as I bade farewell to Zhu just outside the Lijiang train station. He was still in his little pout and so avoided eye contact until the very moment of goodbye when, as he tucked my money into his wallet, he extracted a small card and handed it to me.

"I carry this always to wait for some time I need it. I think you need it more."

I gazed at a purple and gold image of Guan Yin, Goddess of Mercy and Inflammable et cetera. She stood on a luminous cloud, the ribbons in her hair flowing in a breeze that I could not detect. On the reverse side of the card were three long strings of Chinese characters in the usual dull red. The card was stiff, as though a metal core lay beneath the high-gloss paper, which was worn around the edges as though it had ridden in Zhu's wallet for some time. For a moment, I was thrown back upon the careworn deck of cards with which my one grandmother had often amused herself at a folding table as I hovered out-of-body nearby, pondering Fermat's Last Theorem and my own dread mortality.

Zhu frowned at the card I cradled in my hand. "Is for make the miracle. Just put on your hand and ask the miracle something. My daughter give it on the Spring Festival some time. Every day I think don't need the miracle today, maybe need it more tomorrow, so just go take the walk, do something feel better."

Zhu's eyes met mine timidly. "You remember me same time you use the miracle, maybe make two miracle." He shrugged. "Or maybe just don't do nothing."

Returning his wallet to his pocket, Zhu pointed his baseball cap into the late afternoon sun and vanished in the glare.

I think I over-tipped him. It's so hard to know.

Again I stare at the white envelope and wonder whether this might be the right moment. I hesitate, knowing all too well the consequences of drawing when holding might better serve. What nourishes one instant may very well kill you the next, which Fermat never understood and I learned only at great cost, humbled, hounded, and harried practically to the point of tears and *only* because of a boyish love for numbers and one or two bad spots of luck and having fallen in with the wrong crowd.

Rich people who gamble.

It was very nearly miraculous that I had gained access to that particular society of degenerates at all, but I tumbled

through the sash of an improbable window of circumstance—
a rich person who gambles having just passed out on his sofa,
his last coherent words: *you go*. I thought he was proposing
a discussion on the relative merits of inexpensive East European automobiles, but as the man fell to snoring I caught the
glint of something metallic in his right hand.

Curious, I extracted a handsome gold-inlayed invitation.
The man's name—I can't recall it now—was engraved into the
card, along with an address in Memphis's most exclusive
neighborhood. Okay, Memphis's *only* exclusive neighborhood.
There was also the current day's date and the time 11 p.m. I
looked at my watch. It was twenty till eleven. At that precise
moment, a sharp knock came at the door where I discovered a
formally-dressed limo driver. He glanced at the card in my
hand and said, "Are you ready, sir?"

I said yes.

Always say yes.

Lillian knows nothing of this particular matter, despite
her charming approach to wondering what I'm thinking, which
is to suck it out of my brain with a Dyson DC07 vacuum. Co-
semi-existent is the word her shrink prefers to codependent in
our case, and he's one of the few who's gotten it right. Imagine
being tethered for life to someone no more free than yourself
to be the sum of her constituent parts. You're walking around
in each other's genomes. You're entangled kite strings on a
March afternoon. You're the funhouse mirrors minus all the
fun. You're the whipping boy and the whipping post, oh *such* a
fine story for olives and toast.

It's the right moment.

I slam down my longneck on the plastic table cover, and
the waitress's head swivels. At the same instant, the old man
looks up from his noodles, and Fermat attempts to turn over
in his grave but lacks the requisite smooth muscle mass. Only
zippered teenager doesn't stir. I lift the envelope and give the
expensive paper stock an appreciative sniff. Mitsumata, I decide, though the weight is a bit more Schurman. I may yet

discover that I am lucid-napping in my garage apartment in Memphis, nothing at all in my hand but my favorite constituent part. But it seems so real.

We all live within the flickering shadows of Plato's cave, or at least time-share with the Wilsons, wondering whether we out-picture the picture or the picture out-pictures us, as though it matters one way or the other at the end of the billing cycle. All is tethered. All is other than. Something somewhere rears its head, or nine of them, and not one of us is free to not taste its sour breath in our mouths. Screw Fermat. He invented something that fits absolutely nowhere, whereas—and here is the juicy nougat center or so it seems after those warm brown bottles of *pi*—I fit everywhere.

Especially naked.

One yank on the silk pull-thread, and the envelope parts effortlessly, revealing a single tri-folded page. No check. No tickets. No gift certificate to Luby's. Just a single folded sheet of paper which I pop open. One sentence in twelve-point Courier New:

"China is no longer safe for you and your sister."

I wave for my check. It's pointless, I know, to consider such matters within the context of a moment no more finely textured than this—the word *brackwurst* suggests itself—but at this juncture, one hypothesis seems difficult to dismiss. China may no longer be safe for myself and my sister.

11

Don't give the Chinese money. They'll build something hideous. It's like giving money to Elvis, only worse because you can ignore a pink sofa. Try ignoring a pink sixty-three-story building. With fins. You look up and say to yourself *man* anything with that much chrome should come with AM radio. But there are dozens of structures in this brave new city that if erected in the States would result in angry citizens' committees.

But what can you expect from the people who invented Stir Fried Pork with Egg and Black Fungus? Welcome to Shenzhen, pronounced roughly *sun zun*, the city hailed by the Limey Guidebook as "a soulless assemblage of obscene architecture and Chinese camp." But every country should have an Orlando.

I'm journaling on a plastic park bench in Dongmen Shopping District, which is best described as six hundred acres of convoluted shopping malls and department hives that offer up all the expensive crap that modern man can't possibly live without, from ugly German stereos to TVs too large to deliver without a crane.

Twenty-three years ago, there was nothing here but a sleepy fishing village and an uncanny silence. This whole fuchsia and chrome skyscraper-ripped conglomeration of greed portals—China's first Special Economic Zone—popped up like a bad mushroom in 1980 and shows no signs of relenting. Yesterday I stopped at a random street corner and looked up, wondering how many under-construction high-rises I could count from that spot.

Twenty-two.

This plastic bench is imprinting my ass with longitudinal bars, making me feel uncomfortably like Old Glory, but it's not yet time to meet Arnie for a late breakfast at the restaurant of our too-expensive hotel. I shift my position diagonally on the plastic bench and go for something more along the lines of the Union Jack.

It burns when I pee. I thought you'd want to know. The meds were indeed inside my wool socks. Thought I'd pass that nugget along, as well. The cast comes off my right hand in three weeks. Thanks for asking.

At nine in the morning, Dongmen Shopping District looks like Coney Island in February, so boarded up and grease-mucked you'd swear it would take a league of men in white spacesuits to re-open it. But an hour from now, yawning nine-teen-year-old women with orange hair will throw open garage doors and drag loudspeakers outside, and food vendors will begin whacking chicken, beef, and pork, and the smells of overheated woks will begin to compete with the seasoned yowl of the sidewalk.

By nightfall, Dongmen will be a tornadic frenzy of buying and selling, over-amped music blaring from every other store-front, women with megaphones hyperventilating beside bins heaped like Iowa haystacks with rayon fashion knock-offs from Hong Kong, and throngs of shoppers, mostly girls in threes and fours, will choke every avenue of escape. Or so it may feel if you are fresh from a village whose entire nightlife centered around one thirty-watt bulb in a grocery store half the size of your too-expensive hotel room.

I think I know why it burns when I pee.

There are probably eleven million people in this town, though officially it's a third that number. So splendiferous are the get-rich tales erupting from this semi-tropical jewel of a city that the government has surrounded Shenzhen with a very substantial electrified fence, a modern-day Great Wall against China's restless hordes of toothless ex-farmers. In the coming decade more humans will be drifting into Chinese cities with a bedroll and a sack of turnips than live in most countries of the world, and all I can say is, the Party had better come up with a war to send all these Wangs and Fangs to, or somebody's looking at one ugly electric bill.

Unable to tolerate this plastic bench a moment longer, I rise and it kisses me goodbye. I wobble past the hocking and farting old men of morning, carefully dodging the yellow-brown gobs that, on high acid days, are capable of dissolving closed-cell polyurethane on contact. I check in all directions for signs of red-stockinged men, evil twins in epaulets, Mormons with satchels, and all such. None of the above, but the day is young. I turn toward my too-expensive hotel and breakfast with Arnie.

Understand, the Chinese don't spit for effect alone. Regular vehement hocking is considered crucial to one's internal wellbeing. And it really builds the abs. Most health-conscious Chinese begin each day by stepping out into the syrupy air of morning to dredge up as much sedimentation as their tragic lungs can afford and directing it downward, preferably at some living thing, be it a rhododendron or the neighbor's three-year-old.

Say what you will, Shenzhen has actual birds. Living ones. And cartoonish palm trees. And a sky. It also has the same red taxis as in Beijing—I was hoping for something in a powder blue. Shenzhen features the same basic odor package as Beijing, I find, minus the ageing. The latter has had thousands of years for that distinctive *munge* to cross-reference and micro-acclimatize and just generally become disgusting.

Shenzhen just needs a little time.

After the late breakfast with Arnie, the plan is to take a city bus to Lil's apartment, on-campus at her school, and help her hang the living room curtains. My sister says the other tenants—most of the thousand-plus employees of the school live on campus—amuse themselves by pressing their noses against her living room window, cupping their hands for a better view.

"See," I told her. "They love you already."

"Then why are they laughing?" asked Lil.

"They're a happy people."

True, actually, despite every reason to the contrary. Even the overburdened, under-sighted, and massively guilt-tripped schoolchildren of this country, their spindly legs bearing forty-pound book-bags hither and yon, seem to be perfectly well-adjusted. We are *Chinese*, seems to be the basic reasoning, so what could be so bad? I could provide a short list but why spoil a perfectly good mass delusion?

I definitely know why it burns when I pee. It's the *how* I haven't figured out. She never had her pants off, for the love of Mike. We seem to be looking at a case of immaculate contagion here. That's unless those two nice policemen were kind enough to night-deposit something I've yet to recall, there to silently accumulate interest.

Nah.

After I help Lillian with the curtains, Tree will arrive for a highly anticipated and well-overdue séance. "I can't promise," she has said, "to produce Truman, or Schuman, or anybody else. Spirit is what it is, and it gives what it gives."

It's the *new* material, the shall-we-say bordello papers, that have reacquired the good doctor's interest. Save the world, beware chartreuse and purple, hang garlic and dried mice around your neck—Tree eats that stuff up. My own interest lies more along the lines of fresh pages of high-quality prose, and I don't intend to leave my sister's apartment without them, whatever I have to night-deposit or where.

I round a corner and my too-titanium hotel swings into view. The prospect of a late breakfast with Arnie doesn't particularly beckon. This chrome-sunglassed veteran of unnecessary wars and I have yet to discover anything in common beyond country of origin, number of toes, and acquaintance-ship with Lillian—for whom I suspect this man of certain *stirrings*. At the thought, I shudder so hard that I almost lose a contact. Anyway Arnie invited me, which assumedly means he's paying.

A valet opens the too-grandiose door, and I enter a hotel lobby brimming with the usual white faces. Lil and Tree have already moved to their appointed schools, but most of the other fifty-odd American teachers still giddily await placement. This many Americans in a single spot constitutes a micro-culture, a floating suburb of Cincy complete with sporty shades, khaki shorts with too many pockets, and far too many sentences ending "sucks."

You also hear a lot of "sucks ass" from the young American women but only those who smoke cigarettes, which is a correspondence some psycho-linguist should definitely burrow into. Most of these teachers aren't actually teachers but college kids with a healthy sense of the absurd. There's also the middle-aged contingent consisting of Tree, Lil, Arnie, and one brassy, whiskey-voiced woman—I believe she's from Sphincter, Ohio—who last night decided to take on the whole hotel staff because one of her placemats was missing.

She'd bought a matching set of four in Dongmen Shopping District, and by God one of them was gone. If she'd screamed at those people another eleven seconds, I'd have emerged from my room with a throat lozenge and a Chinese dime and said, "Here, go buy seven more just like it." But I'm always thinking of ways to be helpful.

I walk past the hotel business center where a gaggle of Americans waits to use one of the three computers. Unable to sleep last night on my too-billiard-table bed, I downed the two complementary beers in the mini-fridge and took the elevator down to the business center to see if the net was up. It was, more or less. Table Tennis Weekly was available in nine languages. There wasn't a whole lot else. In China, every international news site is blocked roughly one day in ten.

The only news you can reliably get is government-penned and thus peppered with happy lies that absolutely everyone

oooo through. The Chinese know about government censor-
ship and find it more or less agreeable. You develop a sense
of things after a while. If the article says thirty-seven people
died in the mine explosion, you pretty much know that the
number was around a hundred. When you read that tens of
thousands of rural health clinics are initiating vigorous education campaigns concerning STDs—I read such a story in
yesterday's English edition of the Beijing Daily complete
with photos of triumphantly beaming doctors and nurses—
you pretty much know that Chinese dicks are rotting off by
the boatload and no one has a clue what to do about it. I don't
know why that image comes to mind just now.

Anyway, after perusing Table Tennis Weekly in the morning's wee hours, I checked my three email accounts and discovered fresh mailings from Miriam, each with the same basic
thrust. *Magazine Mariposa* requires another article on Chinese ink painting, and fast—not that I wrote the first one. I
lifted most of it from a museum brochure. I'm that kind of
writer. And yes, Miriam, there's more where that came from.

There was also an email from Jeremy, a drinking companion back in Memphis who wants to know where I've vanished to. I owe Jeremy a bit of money, but he knows I'm good
for it. Besides which, who ever had his nose slit open by someone named Jeremy?

That particular financial setback, if you must know, came
on the heels of a truly ugly one that occurred in a poorly decorated and altogether humorless game room in Tunica, Mississippi, and certainly *they* have noticed that my front porch is
accumulating newspapers. And then there's the really painful
part. Just as I was about to pay off Jeremy and the game room,
I was nailed for forty-nine large ones. Forty-nine thousand
dollars in a single night, and this wasn't to a drinking buddy or
a poorly decorated game room but some pitted-faced guy from
Kansas City named Louie.

I kid you not. His name was Louie. Somebody named
Louie will take your whole nose home as a trophy. He'll give it

to his dog for a chew toy. And that's just a Louie from Gainesville. This came to pass during the aforementioned night of the gilded invitation and the limo driver and the improbable window of circumstance. I may or may not have mentioned the glass-topped table in the rear of the limo and the small lacquered box filled with—I think it was Twenty Mule Team Borax.

By the time I arrived at the party, I was beyond intimidation by Jehovah *or* his big brother, tossing the gilded invitation to the three gym rats guarding the grand entry, sweeping a goblet of wine off a silver tray beneath the Chloe Sabine iron candelabra, and striding through the over-tanned crowd in search of the gaming table that I could smell as clearly as though it were stapled to my philthrum.

Unfortunately, I found it.

Now I'm thinking maybe I should look into a loan consolidation. They can take a little out of my check each month. Miriam actually does cut me a monthly check, though why anyone would put me on straight salary is beyond both B.F. Skinner's comprehension and my own. I haven't made a deadline since James Taylor had a hairline, and I find myself increasingly drawn to the repugnant theory that Miriam must have some kind of thing for me.

Before returning to my too-firm bed in this morning's weensy hours, I took a moment to net-search everyone's favorite cuddly, the Hydra, which besides the whole nine-heads thing also turns out to have a bit of a breath problem. One whiff of the Hydra's breath and you run with the dogs of Hades. All told, not the kind of enemy you'd choose even if you're Hercules, not that I'm *concerned* about Hydrangea Laboratories.

All we have here is a normal everyday profit-making enterprise with a black-box government contract or twelve, and if the Mancer twins provide somewhat cleaner data than the Sullivans or the Spullivans or the Stooligans, of course they're going to apply a teensy bit of pressure till it becomes massively clear to them and anyone idly watching that the Mancers are not going to do the locomotion. Which, happily, is the case.

No sooner do I push through the doors of the too-expensive restaurant than I'm hit in the face by a sour blast from Kenny J's saxophone. I'm momentarily blinded. All I can see is the fleeting image of the ooze dribbling from a brass spit-valve.

"So," announces Arnie's voice, "what does Lillian think of her apartment?"

"It's air-conditioned," I reply, eyes slowly adjusting. Finally I make out Arnie, his usual mirrored aviator shades in place. The booth where he sits almost has room for one of my knees.

"Want a menu?" asks Arnie.

"Coffee," I say, struggling to seat myself.

"You're joking, right?"

"I just like saying it," I tell him. "Order me a pot of tea at least as black as yours, though that may require steeping a pair of army boots for a fortnight. So, tell me. How are you exactly?"

"What's a fortnight?" asks Arnie.

"In Britain, two weeks. Everywhere else, fourteen days. You aren't actually considering it, are you?"

"Considering what?"

"Soaking the boots."

Arnie stares at me for a moment then turns away.

This is starting out well. Maybe I should tell him straight-away where my sister has moles and skin tags. Then again, that may intensify his *stirrings*. Another shudder goes through me. That's two shudders inside twenty minutes. I haven't come this close to an aerobic workout since being thrown off the high-school basketball team—something to do with shaving points in return for old copies of *Tease* magazine.

The teapot arrives, and I request a few additional teabags. You don't usually get bags in this country, let alone a pot, but rather a chaos of tea leaves floating at the top of a half-molten cellophane cup. Once the tea cools, you take tiny sips and spit the leaves across the room like everyone else.

"When does the cast come off?" asks Arnie.

"Three weeks. And yes, it itches, but that's what chopsticks are for."

Arnie points his aviator shades at me. "I met my headmaster yesterday. Total military freak. Reads the Tom Clancys in English as soon as they come out. When he found out I was a pilot, right away he's all over my ass about the P-3 deal."

I give Arnie a blank look.

"The P-3 deal," he says. "The spy plane the Chinese captured. Happened a couple of years ago."

"Sorry to hear about it."

"They tried to force down one of our recon planes," he says. "Assholes sideswiped it. Their plane crashed. Ours managed to land at a Chinese airfield. It was a huge mess."

"And this guy was razzing you about it?"

Arnie shrugs. "So we have spy planes. Everybody has spy planes. What pisses you off is when somebody like China or North Korea scrambles jets to force you down. They've been doing that since the fifties. They put one plane under your wing and another behind you, missiles locked on. When you hear that *whoop whoop whoop* in your headphones?" says Arnie. "I'll tell you something. Recon suddenly means reconsider."

I comment that the dirty commie reds probably want to reverse-engineer our technology, and Arnie laughs. "The Chinese have military technology we can only dream about. They caught Russia in a weak moment and bought a shitload of their SU-30s. Best fighter plane in the world. And they're about to launch an Aegis destroyer. You see that in the papers?"

I shake my head.

"*And* a manned spacecraft," says Arnie. "Pure military mission, no matter what they call it."

And you wondered what they were going to do with the thirteen million we gave them for Yao Ming.

"Napoleon was right when he called China a sleeping giant," Arnie tells me. "He said, 'Let her sleep, for when she wakes she will shake the world.' Bitch is awake, man."

"I didn't know Napoleon spoke English."

Arnie gives me a look. "It's a translation."

More teabags arrive on a saucer lined with tangerine sections. Eyeing one of the latter with something approximating hunger, I extract a set of wooden chopsticks from my pants pocket. The slippery plastic ones provided by restaurants are useless. At about the same time comes a sound not unlike the mating cry of an all-in-one copy machine. Arnie pulls out a cell phone. "Quick Comebacks," he barks into the phone. He listens for several seconds then says, "Yeah, well, you and Elmer Fudd seem to have more in common than your neck size." A moment later, he says, "Unh," and hangs up.

Turning to me again, Arnie says, "I guess you know that we're going to war with Iraq. American boots in Baghdad by the end of the year. Write it down."

"And our excuse will be . . . ?"

"Chemical weapons, probably. Of course, it has nothing to do with that. The plan was in place five years ago. Clinton wouldn't sign off, or we'd be in Iraq right now." Arnie levels his twin mirrors. "If we controlled Baghdad and Tehran, the world would instantly be a better place."

"World peace through American strength?" I say. I know the catch-phrases.

"Here's the question," says Arnie, rolling his shoulders. "With no Soviet Union anymore, what's our place in the world? Do we sit on the sideline, or do we see to it there are no more Soviet Unions?"

"Which we would accomplish how, exactly?"

"It wouldn't be easy. Easy means staying home and minding our own business. Easy means keeping our allies happy and placating our enemies. Problem is, that policy has already resulted in two world wars that we didn't start but had to finish."

I set down my personal wooden chopsticks. "Let me get this straight. What made the Soviets so bad was that they invaded and occupied other countries and installed puppet governments. So what we're going to do to prevent that from ever happening again is to invade and occupy other countries and install puppet governments."

"That kind of distorts it, actually," says Arnie. "Obviously there's a fine line, but somebody's got to walk it. Who's it going to be? Do we leave it to the Saddam Husseins? History says—"

Again Arnie lifts his trumpeting phone. "Quick Comebacks," he barks. A few seconds later, he says, "Forgive me, but your actions speak so loudly that I can't quite hear your words." After muttering, "Unh," he hangs up.

"Good line," I say.

"Thanks," says Arnie, suppressing a smile.

"You make money like this? Supplying people with comebacks?"

Arnie nods. "You know how it is. You can never think of what to say till an hour or two later. My service cuts lag time to less than a minute. Where were we?"

"We were walking a fine line," I say. "You know, my fifth-grade teacher said there's one thing that makes us different from the bad guys. They believe the end justifies the means. We don't."

The mirrored shades lock onto my face. "I don't want to argue with your fifth-grade teacher, Julian, but I'll say this. Actually I'll ask this. If you can prevent the next world war and you don't, how do you live with yourself?"

I have my methods.

Arnie and I decide on the breakfast buffet, which is mostly unrecognizable pastries and even less recognizable fruit. There's also a congealed pile of scrambled eggs, a haystack of boiled greens, and something more or less resembling hashbrowns.

No grits.

Arnie and I dine in relative silence, thank God. I think I just quoted my fifth-grade teacher. Actually my fifth-grade teacher was pretty hot. Mrs. Culpepper. She had two tight sweaters, the lilac one and the pink one.

Ah, the pink one.

Ignoring Chinese etiquette, Arnie and I split the tab. I yank a few colorful currency notes from my wallet. The blues, I've noted, have a picture of two women with scarves tied over their heads. The orange ones feature a lone crane standing in a bamboo grove. I think that means a blue is worth two oranges.

"Give me another blue," says Arnie, making a small pile of bills at the center of the table. As always, we leave no tip. In China, your waitress will chase you down the street to return any and all gratuities. The first time that happened, I thought I'd been nailed for stealing the little packets of soy sauce. In my hotel room, I add them to hot water and pretend I'm drinking coffee.

As Arnie and I part in the hotel lobby, he suggests we do the clubs sometime. "I've found a cool Triad club in the Shikou District," he says. "They love Americans. They take you straight to the back room."

Where I assume everyone's learning macramé.

Arnie asks for my cell number. I tell him I don't do telephones.

"Why not?"

"I don't like them."

"Name three things that you do like," says Arnie.

I stare at him.

Arnie places a cigarette in his mouth. "What can I say, Julian? You've got a bit of a negative attitude. I'd get that phone if I were you. I don't know if you've noticed, but you're not in Memphis anymore."

"In one week," I tell him, "I will be."

I've been saying that for three weeks. I'm going to keep saying it. Sooner or later, it'll be true.

12

Following my sister's instructions, I exit Bus 101 at the edge of vast and charmless Lichee Park with its ranked, filed, and popsicle-identical lichee trees. To my surprise, there's also a huge expanse of actual lawn grass, upon which wander various disoriented locals. Along the broad sidewalk, meanwhile, a row of downcast men slump cross-legged behind hand-lettered cardboard signs that go into great detail about, it would appear, some very sad stories. Passersby idly browse the signs, smoking, hocking, farting, all the usual.

It's interesting actually. Here you're talking to a Chinese gentleman over dinner about, say, the recent death of your mother—wishful thinking there—when Hong Dong Wong looses a multisyllabic jet of colonic gases requiring six or seven seconds of your rapt attention. At which point Hong breaks into a bright smile and says *excuse me!* and just like that, everything is fine. *Excuse me!* erases the entire event.

So you go on to describe your tearful tribute at Ma's memorial service, during which entire interval Hong is straining visibly, ripping the air four, five, six additional times *while* chewing his food with his mouth open and emitting little involuntary urps. Not to worry though. Again Hong utters the magic words and everything is once more perfectly fine. It's wonderful. If you say *excuse me!* afterward, you can cornhole Granddad at the dinner table over Hay Wrapped Fragrant Ribs.

Before I've covered much of Lichee Park, a freakish wind rises up and the sky darkens. September is typhoon season along the South China coast. Nothing severe enough to require mass evacuation, thanks be unto God, as how exactly does one evacuate fifty million people who don't know how to form a line?

And no, I'm not anti-Chinese. I'm anti-human.

Present company excepted.

Just past Lichee Park, I have been alerted, awaits the grandly arched gate of Shenzhen High School of Electronic Excellence upon whose campus my sister will both live and toil over the course of the next ten months. Tree has been placed at Primary School Focus Youth Shenzhen, a half-hour bus ride across town. Tree, too, will abide on-campus and from there covertly satellite-feed New Age gabble to a meaning-starved world. I'll meanwhile spend the next several months being wined and *lined* by the plethora of Hollywood studios soon to be jockeying for film rights to *The End of Day*. I may do the screenplay myself. I haven't decided.

Sci-fi author Bi Yu Nu, by the way, didn't show up for the debut of *A Room of Eyes*. Tree says he lives anonymously in Beijing and writes under a pen name. Only his secretive London publisher knows how to contact him. Doubtless, Bi fears arrest. His stories are considered counter-revolutionary even today. The government permitted only two screenings of *Eyes*, one in Beijing and one in Shanghai, which of course only added to the general frenzy. Tree wasn't able to get within a block of the theater. I intend to remember every bit of this when it's time for advance publicity for *The End of Day*. Widespread disapproval has always been golden, but actual governmental sanctions? How do you put a price on that?

Bi's next project is rumored to delve into what *really* happened in Atlantis, which island continent, if you believe what you hear, sank to the bottom of the sea some twelve thousand years ago due to poorly thought-out applications of technology and the unavailability of annotated Bibles. I think Bi's title will be *A Room of Floating Atlanteans*.

Now entering the cartoonish forest of identical lichees, I ask myself what manner of room I seem to be meandering into now. The gust of wind and its accompanying cloud have vanished as quickly as they appeared. I give a glance in each direction but discover nothing overt, no synchro-stepping women beneath identical umbrellas, yet I do feel somewhat odd. Tree likes to say I'm the most second-sighted of the three of us, were I to actually see everything that I see but then I'd find it quite difficult to not know everything that I know, and as I know something that I don't yet agree to see, I'm left to drink a lot. Says she. Lillian, it now comes to mind, has promised me a glass of decent English gin before this evening's séance.

I've no idea what Tree is talking about. Alcohol is an attribute of the blood, right along with platelets and colorful corpuscles. If it makes the liver work a little, well, what is a liver for? I find that alcohol supplies a willing predicate for whatever the subject, and it's *just* such a grammatical sabbatical that each day requires at a certain point, sometimes early, sometimes late. Say what you will, alcohol frees the spirit to soar like an eagle among the chair legs and dust bunnies, revealing human dignity to be more or less the rag that it is. Is alcohol a crutch? I just wish it were a better one. I am a man moving through life on two shattered knees.

Pay no attention, by the way, to anything I may have let slip about unexpected limousine rides to exclusive neighborhoods, there to fail dramatically at stupid math games. When under duress, I am apt to lie and quite badly, even to myself. I'm at least as likely to have lost that money down a pant leg. Make no mistake. If I had, in fact, stolen into the midst of a secret society of lewdly moneyed gamblers, there'd have been no one in that room who could have topped me. I'm not joking when I say that. I *should* be joking when I say that.

Tree says all my problems go back to primordial misbehaviors in a distant galaxy where even now my face is displayed in post offices from asteroid belt to icy outer-orbit satellite. Could be true, for all I know. But as no extradition agreements currently exist between those jurisdictions and these, I find the discussion both moot and bothersome. I'm more interested in focusing on primordial misbehaviors of the here and now.

Through the thinning lichee forest before me comes the hum, then the roar, of high-speed multi-lane traffic. I find myself standing before a twelve-lane. On the other side is the arched gate of what appears to be an institution of mid- to lower-learning. That huddle of tall grimy buildings would be Shenzhen High School of Electronic Excellence. About three blocks from where I stand is a concrete pedestrian overpass, but that's quite a stroll from here.

I give another long look to the sizzling traffic, composed mostly of boxy Chinese-made trucks en route to Hong Kong. Gazing at the school on the opposite side with something that almost approximates longing, I ask myself what's happening to me. I'm still registering an odd feeling. It's almost as though I've seen this charmless and butt-ugly place somewhere before. Only not before. After. Maybe after I kill myself trying to cross this twelve-lane. Ah, the traffic seems to have thinned just this moment. As running seems an absurd idea, I decide to saunter.

Take me.

As usual, nobody takes me. But by the time I've sauntered all twelve lanes, I know something about Chinese air horns and four-character Mandarin salutes. Ears ringing slightly, I arrive at the gate of Lil's school and tiptoe past a uniformed guard asleep in a wooden chair. Beyond the guardhouse, I aim myself at a tenement building described by Lil as "five stories of bathroom tile in powder blue and pink. You like actually can't miss it." No, but I'd like a second try.

I pass an empty school cafeteria, its rows of wooden chairs bottoms-up on long tables, the scent of chlorine wafting through the open windows. Last night Lil and Tree took me to a formal banquet. I had to borrow a tie from Arnie. But nine free courses are nine free courses. The wait staff was really on top of levels, making it impossible for anyone to know how much they were drinking, and along about course number seven things began to get really unsightly. I found myself talking spiritedly to both the nineteen-year-old Lutheran at my left and the elderly non-English-speaking gentleman across the table.

I think the Lutheran and I were discussing Affine Geometry, or I was anyway. All I remember clearly was his way of smiling generously until I spoke, at which point the smile faded as though someone had drawn off a pint of his blood. He began every declarative sentence with *actually* and ended each interrogative with *or*. Nice Lutheran. The elderly non-English-speaker and I were discussing armpit sex. Or I was.

Lil and Tree were seated all the way across the dining hall, but I could hear them more clearly than my own thoughts. Lil and Tree do not attend a party. They are the party. By the final course, every man in the room was huddled around their table toasting The Splendid Large American Bosom of Woman and Humour.

During the rounds of drunken toasts that capped the evening, I was handed a business card by a man with a hooked nose and tiny black-rimmed spectacles. He called himself Bellamy. Bellamy's publishing company could use a proofreader for its latest English text, he informed me in very decent English, the clear implication being that unless I turn out to be wholly illiterate I can have as much work as I want, off-site, and get paid in fat pink hundred-yuan notes.

I told Bellamy I'd call Monday. Between now and then, I need to learn how to make a phone call. It seems to require expertise in the use of scratch n' sniff phone cards. I also need to get into a cheaper hotel. After paying four dollars a night in Yunnan Province, I can't quite see a hundred and four. Besides, they steal your placemats. And don't restock the mini-fridge with complimentary beer.

Arriving at the stairs of Lil's pink-and-powder-blue tenement building, I pause to gather my strength. Lil has warned that visitors often become confused because the stairs meet the building midway between floors, so how exactly do you count them? I want fourth floor, room three. How complicated can it be?

Instantly I'm puffing. I really have to cut back on the r-and-r.

There's one really scary half-memory from last night's banquet. I'm standing close enough to the brassy whiskey-voiced woman to measure her goiter. She's advocating yanking the arms and legs off Saddam Hussein with four Abram M1-A2 tanks because we didn't get around to doing it in the last war. This is before we confiscate his placemats of mass destruction, or maybe it was the other way around. I think I advocated more armpit sex. It probably wasn't much of a conversation.

Finally, panting furiously, I knock at a metal door marked with a Roman 3. Nearby along the clothesline-strewn balcony, two small children stare at me. I stare back, and they vanish into a curtained doorway.

The door pops opens and I'm surprised at the sight of a graying Chinese woman in powder-blue cat's-eye glasses. After a moment, she points to the ceiling and says, "You go up. Okay?"

"Oh, sorry," I say, backing away. I've met the illustrious Madam Wu who, Lil has told me, occupies the room directly below hers and so gets to meet everyone in search of the American Teacher's Apartment.

More climbing. More puffing. More knocking.

"You're here!" Lil says brightly. Her air conditioning hits me like a Midwest snowstorm. "Did you see all the commotion on the street?" asks my sister, securing the steel door with her hip.

"Commotion?"

"They must have finally taken him away," says Lil. "A man was knifed right in front of the school. Isn't that nice?"

I tell her I'm sorry to hear it.

"You almost couldn't walk for the crowd," says Lil. "Murder must be, like, really big news here. Isn't it a misdemeanor now in Memphis? So, what can I get you to drink? I have everything."

"You promised me a nice English gin," I remind her, "and I'm here to collect it."

"Sour? Light on the sugar?"

I nod. "I just met your Madam Wu."

Lil titters. "'You go up, okay?' Isn't she precious?"

My sister begins making noises in the kitchen. I claim one of two uncomfortable chairs at the settee by the window. No roach electrocution device.

I finally made good on my smuggled half-pound of multigrind, if you care to know. It occurred to me that one might simply use the hot water from the boiler/purifier—there's one in every hotel room in this country—and strain the grounds through a paper towel. This is after you take the plastic bag from the waste basket, tear a hole in one corner, place the paper towel inside the bag and place the grounds in the paper towel. Next you hold the plastic bag above a bowl and, chanting, "Cof-FEE, cof-FEE, cof-FEE," pour and watch with increasing anticipation as a liquid more or less the color of a reggae artist forms in the bottom of the bowl. Then you throw the liquid away and eat the paper towel.

Lillian's new curtains lie spread across the double bed. Yellow flowers on an emerald field. I guess there was nothing in pink.

"Did you say something about coffee, dear?" calls Lil from the kitchen.

"No, I didn't. I want a gin sour, light on the sugar."

Through the front window, I see much of the campus, such as it is. Shenzhen High School of Electronic Excellence is composed of two five-story classroom buildings, an eleven-story office building, two concrete dormitories, and a regulation soccer field ringed by an asphalt track. Directly below the balcony are two tennis courts in a soft green. The office building owes to the fact that the school is fully endowed by China's government-owned telephone company. The students here, mouth-breathers all we're assured, will be fed into low-paying jobs at Wa Bell. Like all the other apartments on this campus, Lil's is composed of a modest studio, a postage-stamp kitchen, and an abbreviated john. But there's air-conditioning and an actual Western toilet—which the Chinese prefer, by the way, when and wherever they're able to get their little bee-hinds onto one.

My sister returns with my drink and a green tea for herself.

"I can't believe," she says, squeezing into the other settee chair, "that classes start in two days and my boss doesn't even know what classes I'm teaching, let alone when or where. I'll find out when I walk in Monday morning. And I don't get my own classroom. And I teach in a five-story walk-up with no heating or cooling. And the power has gone out in this apartment twice today. And anyway it's the new moon, and you know how I always get."

"I know."

"And Tree says Mercury's in retrograde, which just . . ."

I stop listening to my sister. Who over-sugared my drink. I'm anticipating Tree's arrival and the subsequent appearance of everyone's favorite world savior and lover of small children and randy lapdogs—whom Tree has not actually promised, but at least she's willing to sit down and let her eyes roll back.

I can feel the weight of those new pages in my hands.

". . . And I was promised I wouldn't have to keep rolls or give grades, so now it turns out I get to do *both*, plus I have fifty kids per class, which if I teach fifteen classes is how many grades?"

"Seven hundred fifty," I tell her.

If this gin is English, I'm Lithuanian.

"Seven hundred *fifty*," says Lil. "And they all look alike, which I hate to say, but everybody wears the same uniform and has exactly . . ."

Again, I tune out my sister while maintaining eye contact, having learned years ago that Lillian equates being looked at with receiving attention. Frankly, I enjoy the sense of control, those nice secret serotonin *puffs* that come from successfully misleading my nemesis just a tiddly-tad. And honestly there are worse things than listening to my sister's voice without following the strained lines of Lillian-logic. It's a case of a seasoned musical instrument in the hands of a child. When my sister is really wound up, which is usually, her words tumble over one another in a mad unself-conscious dash, little gasps between. Pure proximal differentiation. I haven't gasped since fifth grade. See earlier reference to lilac and pink sweaters.

Proximal differentiation, for the uninitiated, means that twins who grow up together polarize. One becomes the talker, the other the recluse. One becomes the achiever, the other the neuroser. Good twin, bad twin, basically. I'm holding up my end of the bargain.

"...Anyway, it's a good thing I'm not freaking out," says Lil, falling silent.

I reach for a reassuring tone. "It's just the Chinese way of doing things, dear. You'll get used to it."

Lil looks unreassured.

Our Dr. Carter is facing the stray challenge, as well, I'm told. Tree has a PhD in Ed Psych, a string of publications, and a strong classroom background, so the headmaster of Primary School Focus Youth Shenzhen takes one look at her and assigns her to an office. Clearly here is a woman way too scary-looking to put in front of small children.

"Look at Tree," I tell Lil. "They don't want her anywhere near the kids, and is she freaking out? No. She's just going to charm them all into submission."

"If anybody can," says Lil drearily, "she will."

"And so will you."

True, actually. My sister's a charmer. More proximal differentiation.

Two neighbors' faces appear in the window, hands cupped, mouths sagging open. After a glance at them, Lil says glumly,

"Didn't we read that the Temple of Heaven is the navel of the world?"

"The Heaven's Heart Stone inside the temple, specifically," I say, waving to the people outside. They wave back.

"Shenzhen is a thousand miles south of there. What body part do you suppose that would be?"

I take it for a rhetorical question.

Hanging the curtains turns out to be easy enough. First you drink the gin sour, then you complain of your aching broken hand. Then it's a simple matter of watching your sister thread the new curtains onto the old rod. Outside meanwhile is an increasingly unruly mob of neighbors who cheer happily as Lil closes the curtains. At the same moment, the power goes off. Suddenly we hear the traffic on the nearby thoroughfare.

"Three times," says Lil.

I picture three blackened farmers smoking atop Shenzhen's electric fence.

Seconds later, the power returns. Again the roar of the air-conditioner consumes everything. I ask Lil for another sour, lighter on the sugar this time, and follow her to the kitchen. It's too small for both of us, so I lean against the doorway to ask, "So, who was the dead guy?"

"Dead guy?" says Lil, slicing a lemon. "Oh, the dead guy. Nobody seems to know. All I can tell you is he wore red socks."

There's a knock at the door.

"Must be Tree," says Lil, dropping the knife and hurrying past my stunned expression.

Dr. Shatrina Carter sweeps into the American Teacher's Apartment. "Air conditioning! *Ahhhhhgh*! I've died and gone to heaven! And here's my Julian!"

"No hugs," I say.

She hugs me anyway, practically lifting me off my feet. While Lil shows Tree the apartment, I fill my glass with straight gin—Filipino, it turns out—while asking myself why anyone would want to find himself freshly murdered in broad daylight in front of the building where my sister has just opened her suitcases, say nothing of political affiliation, insurance plan, or stocking preference. Say what you will. Even in the basic Crayola box of twelve, red constitutes a mere eight percent probability, which begs the question: do rival groups now *vie* for the viewing grounds surrounding the lives of my sister and myself, and what exactly might that mean in terms of normalcy, privacy, and daily pursuit of dalliance?

A question for another time. A séance seems to be forming in the front room.

"You want to extinguish that drink, Doo?" says Lil. "Tree wants to get started."

I down the gin and go into my bag for two freshly sharpened German number-two pencils and an official Gregg ministeno notebook in institutional green. I'm not half bad at shorthand. A hundred eighty words per minute, depending on the minute. A hundred ninety when tipsy.

Tree wrinkles her nose. "I still smell alcohol in here."

"I'll light some incense," says Lil.

"Incense contains saltpeter," I inform her, "besides which, if the idea is to attract Truman, shouldn't we be dousing ourselves with martinis?"

As Lady Shatrina arranges herself cross-legged on the center of the double bed, Lil and I pull up settee chairs at either side. In my lap are the two number-twos and the ministeno, open to a fresh page. Across the top, in near-perfect Gregg's shorthand, I write, "Chapter Thirteen" and stare fixedly at Tree. Lil asks for my moldavite. I hand it to her. She places mine and hers in Tree's palm where the third pendant awaits. Deftly, Tree arranges them into one roundish stone.

"Listen, Jules," says Tree, closing her eyes, "I have no idea what this session is going to be about. I'm just willing. You say something new came in when you were out in the countryside. What involves you, involves all three of us, okay? I hope you're beginning to understand that. You are in this country for a reason, Jules, just the same as your sister and myself."

Tree's eyes slide open, and I realize that she's been staring at me through the lids. "You *decided* to come here. Now you're here, and it's time you started to be here."

I turn away from Tree's gaze. When I glance at her again, the brown eyes are once more closed.

"We send a voice to the highest of our highest-most selves," begins Tree, the mahogany voice deepening as it rises in volume, "and to all those who work on behalf of the brightest of the light and the lightest of the bright, and say *be* here now and help us in this which we do, Lord God Heavenly Jesus Uma Sofia."

"Lord God Heavenly Jesus Uma Sophia," drone Lil and I.

"Here and now, we seal this space in all its dimensions and times, ways, varieties and vacuities, expanses expressions *and* dominions," say Tree, voice dropping still farther till it's etching the floor tiles, "that no one shall come unto us now except that lamb of the immortal blessed dawn known to us as Truman—be he now present and accounted for, Holy Lord God Immortal Soul of Abraham Wagga Wagga."

Lil and I look at each other. "Holy Lord God mmmm . . . Wagga Wagga."

"Be it hereby and forevermore so," says Tree.

"Be it hereby and forevermore so."

Pulling myself a bit taller in my chair, I watch as Tree sinks into her signature trance by slow and, it would appear, tender degrees, dropping her head farther and farther till it hangs on the bone and her breathing becomes ragged.

It shouldn't be long now.

I remember one stretch when Tree brought in a series of deceased professional wrestlers who'd entered the next world with serious maladaptations to soul-evolvement in the absence of leotards. Attachment, the Buddhists call it. The whole thing was touching, actually. I'll never forget the moment when Minter the Tormenter first admitted he'd been dragged along the tunnel of light kicking and begging for his Capezios. Not that I've ever believed that Tree is actually bringing in spirits of the dead. But there was and *is* no better entertainment value in west Tennessee, outside the summer tent-revival circuit, than Tree's channeling sessions, drinkable English gin or no.

Suddenly Tree rears her head. A frown-line forms between her eyebrows, and she opens her mouth to speak.

"Gweeeeetings," caws Truman's voice.

Oddly, Tree's mouth did not move. Truman's thin nasal voice seemed to have leached from some other place entirely. Tree opens her eyes in confusion, and we stare at one another.

"It's twuuuue," says Truman. "I have chosen another medium this time."

Tree and I turn in the direction of Lillian, whose eyes are closed and lips moist and parted. "I come through Lady Lillian for a weeeeason," says my sister's mouth. "Your *doubts*, Julian. Your doubts are holding everything back. All that must end here and now. Are you listening?"

"Write," says Tree, jostling me.

I begin to transcribe.

"I'm just some fwaaaagment of Tree's personality? Is that what you believe, Julian? And all those wonderful chapters. Do you think those could have come from just anywhere? You still believe that you're in China for your petty personal weeeasons, but the time for doubting is over. The battle is joined. Your wake-up calls will no longer be gentle ones."

"Awesome," I say. "Now, about *The End of Day*? I think we were just beginning Chapter Thirteen."

"I gave you the title of the novella."

"*Dipping Between the Dip Slopes* is a title?"

"It's allegorical," says Truman.

"Allegorical is a nice word for that title," I reply. "It happens that I've found a publisher very happy with *The End of Day*. Now if we can just—"

"You'll get your final chapter, Julian. But first you must *pwoove* your intentions."

"My what?"

"You will be tested, Julian. Be weady."

"Wait. How about proving your intentions?" I say. "Give me a page. A compound sentence. A gerund."

"Be weady, Julian. And remember. Beware the sheeeeen of the blue and the greeeeen."

With a gasp, Lillian opens her eyes and says, "But Arnie, I hardly know you."

Tree puts her hand on Lil's shoulder. "Baby, you just *channeled*. You were beautiful."

"I can't believe it," I say, slamming down my number-two pencil. At the same moment, the overhead lights blink and go out. The air-conditioner dies. Four times.

"We need you," says Tree, looking straight at me.

In the semi-darkness, Tree Carter leans forward to gaze into my eyes. Her voice is soft. "Julian. We can't do this without you, okay? I wish to God we could, baby, but we just can't. No one can say what you'll choose when the moment comes, not even yourself. But the moment's coming, and you'll have to live with your choice for a long, long time. Like you've had to do since the last time you chose."

My belly tightens. I don't know what Tree is talking about. And I do.

Lillian gives her head a shake. "Why do I have this sudden urge to visit death row?"

"Just be ready," Tree says to me with a smile. "That's all, baby. Just get yourself ready, okay?"

Who is this woman kidding? I was born weady.

PART TWO
THE YEAR OF THE RAM

13

Lillian just called to say she's ringing in the New Year by admitting our mother to Baptist Memorial Hospital of Memphis—or is that ringing out the old? Anyway it's just Chinese New Year, not the real one. We're now entering 2003, the Year of the Ram. Fortuitous perhaps for the Dodge Truck Division. The rest of us will have to wait and see.

"There's no other way I can leave Memphis," said Lil's voice on her bunny phone. My sister's bedroom telephone is pink and shaped like a young rabbit. You speak into its little rabbit ear. "Golden Acres isn't set up for really sick people, and Mom's really sick, okay? She's literally green."

Vital signs are stable, said my sister, but our mother's weight is dropping like a semi-precious stone, and she has no aura at all. It's a good thing Lil went. I'm sure I wouldn't have known what to do. Some withered someone is curled on a bed. And she's *green*. So I'm holding down the American Teacher's Apartment, where Lil's plants need watering and her pirated DVDs need watching, especially the three dirty ones. I have the whole dorm to myself actually. Because of Spring Festival—a colloquialism for Chinese New Year—Shenzhen High School of Electronic Excellence is shut down like Enron. Everyone is out visiting relatives. Chinese ones, most probably.

"You know," I told my sister, "it's possible that Mom's just checking out."

"Yes, that's possible," replied Lil, "but since she can't tell us that, we have to assume that she wants to live—and that's *just* the kind of statement I'd expect from you. Throw her off a bridge and save the money."

"Did I say anything about a bridge?"

"I wish you'd settle your Mom issues before she—"

"What? I can't hear you for the fireworks."

"I *said*, you'd better settle your Mom issues before she crosses over. You'll be sorry if you don't."

"Write down her meds," I said. "I'll go online and see what does what. It's always the meds."

"How are yours holding out?"

"Fine," I lied. "And you can stop reading me."

Lil let a moment pass before saying, "Who'd want to read you? Anyway you've been blocking me since forever. You have your own personal Great Wall now. I hope you're happy."

"I'm always happy," I said. "I'm a happy guy. So, you plan on making your flight this time?"

"Can't. I'll have to fly out Saturday."

Lillian's trip to Memphis was supposed to be four days, including eleven-hour time differential, date change, New Year, wormhole, whatever. It's now seven days and counting. Not that I really care. My sister's apartment beats the altogether out of mine. I have a key to a one-room cold-water flat with a view of the hiney of a dumpster. Really. There's a rusty crack near the bottom of the dumpster where brown ooze drips out.

Hiney.

The flat belongs to my employer, the snappily-named Shenzhen Textbook Publishing Company, from whom Bellamy swears I'll get a paycheck any day now. He's been saying that for over a month. I'm starting to make excuses for not returning his discs.

I bet he has copies.

Credit where it's due, Bellamy scored me some antibiotics or I'd be peeing from my navel by now. He also turned me onto ma huang, which I find *really* hits the mark when you don't skimp on the dose. Weight loss has nothing to do with it. Ma huang is about diamond-studding the moment.

"Somebody came here looking for you," Lil told me on the phone. "He said something about you owing some money."

"Who was he?"

"How many people do you owe money to? I told him to never come to my house again. I think he was from one of the casinos."

"Small misunderstanding. Forget about it."

"You seem to have a lot of small misunderstandings," said Lil. "Are you watering my plants?"

"Every day," I lied.

I told my sister about the large animal droppings in the American Teacher's Kitchen. I could hear her shudder.

"Take care of it, please, please, please?" said Lil. "You know I can't deal with mice."

I told her we aren't looking at a mouse. "From the scat, I'd place it somewhere between a mature wolverine and a very young yeti."

"Kill it," said Lillian, who was once arrested protesting animal testing in the manufacture of baby wipes.

"Consider it dead," I told her. "I got a New Years present from that girl you tutor."

"Which one?"

"Pie face. When she smiles, her eyes disappear."

"Oh, Nancy Drew. What did she give you?"

"Some kind of bell-pepper plant. I put it in the kitchen window."

"It's about the New Year," explained Lil. "In Guangdong Province it's customary to buy a plant that symbolizes the kind of year you want to have."

"I think I'm leaning toward a bell-shaped year," I replied. Actually that particular plant, said Nancy Drew, represents the *woid*. I think she meant the world.

"Gotta go," said Lil.

"Already? You haven't said a word about world peace. Or asked about Arnie."

"Arnie's an asshole," said Lil, "and there *is* no world peace. Our secretary of state is at the United Nations right now giving a slide show on Iraqi weapon plants. The war's a fucking done deal. The White House is just greasing everybody for it."

Which is only considerate, if you're asking me. Lil told me that anti-war demonstrations are going on everywhere in the *woid*. "I'm helping with the one at Overton Park this weekend, which is why I gotta go. Love you, love you. Kiss, kiss."

So began the day. And the year, though not the real one.

I'm now engaged in coaxing breakfast out of Lillian's postage-stamp kitchen, which consists of a water boiler, a rice cooker, and a combination refrigerator/clothes-washer. I've learned that I can dump some oatmeal into the rice cooker—Lil discovered actual oatmeal at the nearby supermarket, which looks like an eight-story '58 Studebaker running a little hot. Anyway, what I do is put the oatmeal into the rice cooker along with water and a dash of salt, then break a couple of eggs on top and forget about the whole thing for a while. When I think to go back and check, *voila*, an Iraqi chemical-weapons war chest.

Tonight I accumulate field notes. At nine o'clock this evening, I will put a sweater under my jacket and take to the streets with a hundred fifty thousand euphoric Chinese, which is sure to either illuminate or eliminate me. I'm definitely ready for one or the other. I never dreamed I'd be in this wacked-out country for six months, nor did I pack for same, and frankly it's beginning to wear on me. But returning moneyless to Memphis doesn't seem like much of an option.

That *hypothetical* publishing deal with the gaudy up-front money seems now to be finally and permanently dead. I did make one more lame-ass attempt at finishing *The End of Day* myself, but it dipped rather badly among the various dip slopes, and the publisher-to-be informed Bernie that they were moving on to other projects, and all I can say is, I wish that ill-humored casino would do the same. And that former drinking buddy of mine is *still* sending me emails with subject lines like WHERE R U???

Say nothing of that Louie guy from Kansas City with the nose collection. That I haven't heard from him at all strikes me as slightly ominous. I don't know why some people can't just make a fresh start. And I don't know what came of all that *China is no longer safe for you and your pet hamster* business. No follow-through at all in this country. I've seen more commitment among hedgehogs.

The oatmeal's beginning to boil. I unplug the rice cooker and take a look inside. I've seen a lot worse. I break Lil's last two eggs over the top, yellows running generously and egg-shell bits mixed in, all the usual, and close the lid.

Arnie keeps inviting me to a brothel he's discovered in Shikou (rhymes with *jerko*). It has a bowling theme. Pin-girls in black lingerie help you in and out of your green-and-tan bowling shoes. But that kind of evening requires actual money, and I'm waiting for this hook-nosed Bellamy guy to come up with what's now nearly a thousand bucks. He tap-dances all over the office every time I bring it up. He's got the top hat, the cane. This guy and Shirley Temple would make a really mean pair. Meanwhile I'm rationing my meds. I catch myself slipping little double entendres into the new textbook. Marvelous veiled sexual references and political commentaries that I'm sure no one will ever pick up on. But I'm fine. Really.

Tomorrow I get to eat my fill at a wedding in the Chinese countryside, courtesy of a golden lovely whom I recently came upon, though not literally, at an English salon. Read: cheesy night school with door prizes where a down-and-out American can pick up the occasional half-pocketful of yuan, if not the stray wedding invitation. The golden lovely calls herself Phoebe. No Chinese can resist an English name. Did you know that during the last decade of his life, Dung Xiaoping went by Chester?

Of course, Phoebe is married to some guy with more money than Slim Whitman, but you expect that with a woman like

Phoebe who could be the most beautiful Chinese woman I've ever seen, beginning with the Manchurian cheekbones and ending more or less everywhere else. A little pallid for my blood—which constitutes the Asian definition of beauty, as you may know. Half the ads on TV are for skin-whitening creams. Phoebe wants me to experience a traditional Chinese wedding in the countryside. I think you know what I want to experience.

First I have to survive tonight's mass celebration, whose purpose I fail to understand on even the most basic level. Why, for example, is the new year so widely assumed to be an improvement over the old one? Given that the world has been around for roughly thirteen billion years, if each in turn were even marginally superior to the former—wouldn't this be, like, a really fun place by now?

Look at last year. If I remember right it was the Year of the Moose. The high point of the Year of the Moose I don't expressly recall, but the low point was definitely the bust of my sister's apartment for marijuana that nobody ever found. Yes. The police. Raided. This apartment. There was a loud knock at Lil's door, and when she opened it there must have been twenty men on the balcony waving papers and badges and so forth. This is from Lil's account.

By the time I got here, all the unis were gone, thank God, and the Xanax had taken hold. Lil, well sedated, told me that the English-speaking cop had apologized a lot and said *noh-koh-tics* about a thousand times while the other men turned the apartment inside out. The headmaster of the school showed up with a few unis of his own, and there was a lot of shouting and finger-pointing.

In the end, they found nothing. Not even a dirty ashtray. Lil said the cops looked genuinely bewildered. Deep bows. Lots of groveling. The headmaster followed them all the way to the gate, shouting insults for the benefit of the hundreds of employees gathered around.

That happened on a Friday. Lillian refused to leave her apartment till Monday, on which day she was openly stared at by everyone, down to the gardeners. Same thing Tuesday. Wednesday she was old news. So it goes.

That sentence appears in *Slaughterhouse Five* one hundred four times.

On Thursday, Madam Wu brought Lil a pan of boiled dumplings and a shopping bag containing something she'd found in her linen drawer. A plastic bag containing roughly two ounces of marijuana.

They flushed it.

All of it.

My sister badly wanted to blame the entire episode on me but couldn't quite construct how. Finally I was able to persuade her that some impaired Chinese detective was trying to make a name for himself. What better bust than a busty blond who stands twice the desk sergeant's height? Tragically for him, when it came time to plant the evidence, there was a mix-up and why *don't* they number the floors in this building?

Could be true for all I know. I don't think so. I think somebody wants us out of China. I've narrowed it down to the US Department of Defense and a nine-headed serpent in need of a breath mint, neither of which should constitute much of a problem, as I see it.

I asked Tree to accompany me to tonight's Spring Festival Celebration, but the girl's booked solid. One family's taking her to the flower market this morning, another has her booked for lunch, and tonight she sings "Rock of Ages" onstage at a gala for school administrators and displaced Mongolian yak breeders. You should hear Tree sing. Really. Girl's as *fortissimo* as she looks.

Moose wasn't a bad year for Tree Carter. To begin with, she resembles one. She's let her hair grow out, and it's, like, forming stray antlers and standing stones and such. To no one's surprise, it didn't take Our Tree-ness long to win over

her headmaster, the faculty, the kids, the displaced yak breeders, just generally everyone west of Puget Sound. Teachers
from all over the province are visiting Tree's first-grade classroom. She's been on the evening news twice. Of course she's
also pumping out her weekly radio show via the portable personal medical device. "China is *filled*," she trumpets to the
world, "with the most amazing Indigo children. I've never
seen such beautiful and intuitive children in all my life. They're
teaching *me*."

Meanwhile I teach myself how to eat unsalted egg-drop
oatmeal from a rice cooker while plotting the murder of a very
young yeti. Get well soon, Mom. And Happy New Year, though
not the real one.

14

"You know this thing, Yellow Fever?" asks Phoebe, her perfect features glowing in the dash lights.

"Yellow Fever?" I say innocently.

"Is get some Chinese woman. Every man have this fever when come to China."

I give a glance to the woman behind the wheel, dazzlingly demure in her black silk dress and silver earrings. Phoebe Sternbaum, born Lian Li Hsu, returns the glance and her eyes hold mine for a moment, seemingly soaking up my admiration. I do love a woman who can enjoy her own beauty.

"Why you no date some Chinese girl? You no *like*?"

Phoebe likes to flip the ends of her questions tauntingly. Before I can reply, she continues, "I tell my friends better just marry some poor Chinese man. Americans so *charming*, take you so good *places*, have so much money you think why not just marry him but then you find out the problems. If he is Chinese, you just do something, just argue or you change it but if he is American—"

Phoebe doesn't finish her sentence. Just as well. I massage the smallest finger of my right hand, which aches in the predawn chill. I don't think the bone was set right.

I hope all this vehicular bonding time won't be wholly given over to discussion of Phoebe's foundering marriage. Hubby is an East Coast biz-wiz by the name of Harold—she calls him *Hah-row*—who it would seem is making a rather poor show of it.

"We eat something Guangzhou," Phoebe says listlessly. "Banquet is two o'clock, so we eat something now, buy you beef and noodles, make you strong like Chinese farmer."

Beef and noodles before dawn. Such a good idea.

She seems to read my mind. "I think you just like my husband, eat only American breakfast, don't like how I cook it, hire some woman make his eggs and toast so expensive."

I wait, expecting more.

At last Phoebe sighs and says, "When I meet Hah-row, we just dance all the time, always go out somewhere, go Vermont see the leaves so beautiful, go everywhere, I think how can I be so happy. And he is also believe this too, so he say marry me, marry me."

Phoebe shoots me a cool look. "Later American husband just unhappy, go back America, leave her look like stupid idiot. Hah-row say, no, no, never leave you, never leave you. I tell him if we have some baby, I never give him the divorce. He say okay. Chinese boy or girl look so white don't have American father here always have the terrible life, is why I ask you Yellow Fever. American man get this so bad, every Chinese woman know."

Again I find it safest to say nothing at all. Meanwhile the Buick seems to be entering the ragged outskirts of Guangzhou. The eastern sky is taking on a vague off-green, or maybe it's just me. I made it to bed around two o'clock.

"Two years after we marry," continues Phoebe, "I get phone call some girl want speak Hah-row say she his fiancé, who *you*. I tell Harold just get out, but he wait until I am weak so stupid tell me all of these stories, so many promises, so *charming* like before so I believe him. Then I am pregnant. My husband so angry, say I do on purpose don't speak to me for a month. When our daughter born, Hah-row *so* happy love her *so* much buy everything get American papers for our daughter, take her everywhere, don't even care about me, just have the girlfriends make me so goddamn crazy."

With a jolt, the Buick stops before a rough-looking roadside café. Phoebe switches off the engine and gazes at me. "So many things I don't understand. You American man, maybe you understand for me." Her eyes search mine for a moment. I hope they don't see just how well I do understand.

Back in the Year of the Moose—I think it was actually the Horse—I encountered a tribe of Sino-Tibetans, the Mosou, with the good sense never to entrust a man with anything more ethically complicated than operating a shovel. Mosou women own everything, make all the decisions, and rear the children collectively. Men play musical instruments and lift heavy objects. There's an important yearly festival among the Mosou when the women pray for good health for the men and the livestock. I don't know why that comes to me just now.

Inside the café, a woman in a gauze mask swipes at our table with a dirty rag. When she walks away, Phoebe says, "That girl worry about all the sick people Guangzhou. You know this? Everybody talk about this, so many sick people nobody know why."

The waitress returns with molten chrysanthemum tea. Just behind her, a sizable rat squeezes its belly beneath the buffet counter. Guangdong Province, of which Guangzhou and Shenzhen are a part, is nothing so much as a squalid tropical soup with eighty-eight million people and as many pigs and domestic fowl standing in their own shit, and nobody knows why so many people are sick.

"Those men Japanese," Phoebe whispers, her eyes sharpening. "*Hate* Japanese."

I wait until Phoebe has ceased staring before turning casually to view four well-dressed men at a booth, obviously capping a long night of drinking. One of the three is lighting the wrong end of his cigarette. His friends try to notify him, but the man thinks they're pointing toward our table. His filter ablaze, he turns to give Phoebe a long, curious gape, and his friends laugh merrily.

"In Nanchang," Phoebe tells me through her teeth, "Japanese kill fifteen thousand Chinese, no reason why they do this, rape the women then kill them, now same men come back here for the vacation, buy some poor Chinese girl beat her kill her have the good time again."

I take the smallest possible sip of my molten chrysanthemum tea. Phoebe's Han ancestors slaughtered eleven million people when they took over Beijing. I decide not to mention that just now.

The beef and noodles arrives in a steaming broth reeking of MSG and wild onions. I push it as far away as possible and reach into my shirt pocket for a fresh installment of ma huang. I think I downed eight caps when my alarm sounded this morning at four. Again, I'd retired at two. Chinese New Year, it turns out, is a quarter of the world's population milling about pointlessly while vendors hawk paper-maché rams and a PA system plays "Old MacDonald Had a Farm."

"Need eat very fast," says Phoebe, checking the time on her phone. "Go meet groom's party at nine, go steal the bride."

"Steal the bride?"

She smiles. "Is the Chinese country wedding. All the men beat on the door, say give her to us but the mother just say go away, groom say *oh* I love her so much always be good to her, he put some money under the door but not enough, this go on for long time. The family just say okay too quick mean they don't love the daughter, always make it hard, he have to answer ninety-nine questions. Groom have to say what her favorite song, favorite color, name of her first doll, so many questions, other men try help him but nobody know, all the women just laugh."

I'm thinking I would have taken fewer wives under this arrangement.

Phoebe's eyes go to my face. "You think Chinese people so silly. I think American people so serious. *You* so serious," she scolds. "Always think about something, never call me on the phone, why?"

I shift uncomfortably.

"You need buy phone," says Phoebe. "You have some problem, you can just call me. I tell you this before, why you no do this?"

I pretend not to hear.

"You just like make me angry," says Phoebe. "What if I so angry just leave you here Guangzhou?"

She stares, waiting.

I massage my crooked finger once more. Women enjoy going after me from time to time, preferably with the aid of a lawyer. Phoebe likes to make me smile, or imagine she has, then jeer, calling me a big important man who doesn't like to be seen smiling.

"You need see doctor, break this again," says Phoebe, frowning at my misshapen finger. With a sigh, she returns her attention to her beef and noodles. I'm keeping a wary eye on mine. I think it may be inching closer. My other eye meanwhile enjoys the sight of Phoebe Sternbaum cooling her broth by blowing across the trough of her ceramic spoon. Hers are strong artist's features, lips full and poetic with little upward arrows at the philthrum. The four Japanese men are staring at her as well. I wonder for a moment at how deftly Asians sort out nationality at a glance, identifying Koreans, Japanese, and Thais as readily as I might Swedes, Turks, and Irishmen.

"How much you pay?" asks Phoebe, examining the jade ring on my left pinkie. It doesn't represent world peace. Actually I got a very good deal on the ring, and I tell her the price.

She shakes her head. "Is terrible price. Is not real jade. You no want beef and noodles?"

"I'm letting it cool."

Phoebe checks the time on her phone again. "I call my daughter six-thirty tell her I love her, she so funny all the time tell me Mommy Mommy I love you I love you."

Her eyes seize mine for an instant. "My husband make all the papers our daughter American citizen and this make me worry something, maybe he just take her. American men do this. I tell Hah-row something so true: 'You do this me, you take our daughter I know some people and they find you, some people Beijing find you make you so sorry you do this to me.'"

I gaze at my beef and noodles. I'm so in the mood for a wedding.

Phoebe has, at least, promised an interview with an uncle of the bride. He was a famous conductor before the Red Guard imprisoned him for playing Western music. Which if it was Schoenberg I can understand.

Outside is a loud *karump* followed by howls of laughter. Phoebe and I look through the front window to see the underside of a three-wheel taxi, its wheels spinning. The driver must have whipped the steering wheel too quickly, and now his buggy is upside down in the middle of the street. Several four-wheel cabbies, standing and smoking nearby, are in hysterics, pointing and applauding. After a moment the driver crawls out and rubs his head. Now a passenger emerges from the other end of the taxi and does the same.

"Why don't those men help?" I ask Phoebe.

She shakes her head in disgust. "So many Chinese act like this, just make me crazy." She checks for messages on her phone, and I watch the driver and his fare try to right the taxi.

There's an old story about a naughty little boy whose family lived near a ferry landing. The boy passed his time jeering at travelers as they struggled to load their donkeys and cargo onto the unstable ferry. One day the boy's mother fell into the cooking fire and four days later died. Following the funeral, the boy's family packed their belongings to start over in another province. At the landing, their donkey balked at stepping onto the ferry, and the boy was enlisted to help. As he did so, he peered at the empty spot where he'd so often stood laughing.

That story is the origin of the saying, "He who loves his mother laughs not at his neighbor's ass."

Phoebe switches off her phone, and we watch the driver and his passenger climb into the righted mini-taxi and putter away. Now she looks down at her soup bowl and mutters something in street Cantonese as the drunkest of the four Japanese men wobbles toward our table with a bottle of maotai and a grin.

"A drink for friends," the man says to me.

I gesture toward my half-full cellophane teacup. "Thanks just the same."

Unfazed, the stranger lifts my cup and dumps my remaining tea into Phoebe's. At this, Phoebe rises and stalks toward the restrooms. The man's friends shouting encouragement, he all but fills my cup with Chinese jet fuel and pushes the drink on me before spreading his feet, lifting his glass, and announcing a toast in Japanese.

Oh what the hell.

"May your seventh generation have facial hair," I say.

We bottoms-up as the other Japanese cheer loudly. The shudder is five seconds in coming but it registers on the Richter scale.

Pleased, the man pours us a second drink while proposing a toast having something to do, I think, with baseball, four-stroke engines, and seaweed soup.

I lift my cup. "To international incompetence."

We down the maotai, to more cheers and laughter. At this delicate moment, Phoebe steps out of the restroom and walks straight for the door.

Oops.

I fumble for my wallet and my last hundred-yuan note. The Japanese man meanwhile grabs my wrists and says, loudly enough for Phoebe to hear, "Yellow Fever very good, *hah*?"

I yank free, drop the note on the table, and barely manage to throw myself inside the Buick before it backs out of the parking space.

Neither Phoebe nor I speak for quite some time. I contemplate spending a long day in the company of yet another woman who understands me rather too well. Hopefully, after the theft of the bride, wine will flow like water and maotai like wine.

Guangzhou falling behind us, I'm left with one indelible image of the city once called Canton: downtown traffic at a standstill, a sandaled man weaving through twelve lanes of idling cars on a flat-bed tricycle bearing a Queen Anne chair and a stack of cardboard boxes topped by a Shi Tzu in a bird cage. Steadying the load is an older man, seated in the Queen Anne chair, his legs crossed, placidly smoking a cigarette.

Phoebe breaks the silence listlessly, as though no one is listening. "Hah-row tell me he want divorce go back America with girlfriend take our daughter, just give me some money. I say no."

I say nothing.

"I don't care this," says Phoebe. "I go my aerobics class every morning, do my oil painting, play with my daughter, I don't care Hah-row."

"If he wants a divorce," I say, "give it to him. Make him pay through his big Jewish nose. It's the American way."

Her eyes flare. "American way *buy* my daughter? Chinese way the daughter stay with her mother until she marry."

Again the car is silent. Gradually a featureless bank of grey overtakes the sun. The whole sky is overcast by the time the Buick enters the village of Fuling, a sagging sorrow of dirty masonry and parked motorcycles. We turn onto a narrow cobbled lane and stop in front of a modern apartment building where the groom's party, each man white-shirted and neck-tied, is forming ranks beside five highly polished luxury cars. You can smell the money.

A somber young man notices our Buick and flings a just-lit cigarette as he hurries toward us. Phoebe motors down her window and introduces me to the best man—in China, it's he who makes all the wedding arrangements—who smiles as he greets Phoebe, revealing a jumble of over-long teeth. As the two jabber, I see him check his watch three times.

The bride and groom, Phoebe has told me, are upscale professionals who share a trendy Beijing apartment. They decided to honor their families by marrying in the old way, even consulting a Taoist priest for an auspicious date.

After a moment the happy groom ambles over to the Buick. He is handsome and excited, two red roses in his lapel and a dozen more in his hand. In all, I count eighteen men here, each as young and winning as the next. Maybe I should have given my clothing a little more thought. I think I've slept in these two nights in a row.

Checking his watch again, the best man shouts a command and everyone dives into the highly polished cars. With a squealing of tires, the motorcade, our Buick last of all, begins to move along a narrow street littered with bits of red paper from spent fireworks. The sun peeks through the clouds then vanishes once more, and I gather my jacket a little closer to my throat.

Phoebe says cheerfully, "I think Hah-row just tell somebody kill me."

Her eyes turn to meet mine for a moment. "So easy do this, you have money, make some connection, nobody care."

"Has he threatened you?"

Phoebe doesn't answer. A long minute later, the motorcade stops before a rust-streaked tenement overlooking the currentless Luxi River. Phoebe kills the engine and we both gaze at a lone fisherman standing and poling a flatboat. The groom's party assembles along the sidewalk and gazes up at a third-floor balcony. One young man throws a pebble through the open balcony door and the others cheer.

Combing her hair with her fingers, Phoebe tells the windshield, "Hah-row girlfriend call me on the phone, not same girlfriend, some different girlfriend, say you give Hah-row divorce very quick or something bad happen."

"Hire some protection," I say. "You have access to Harold's money. Use it."

She shrugs. "I know some people Beijing. Maybe I go there." She turns to me. "You want go there?"

I stiffen. "To Beijing? Now?"

"Never mind this," she says curtly, turning away.

"Phoebe—"

"Never mind this."

"Phoebe, I can't just drop everything and—"

My voice trails off. Crap. I'd hoped this woman's troubles might result in some kind of personal windfall. It's looking more and more like a deadfall.

I open my mouth, but nothing comes out. I'm stopped by the sight of Phoebe Sternbaum, her thin fingers playing in her hair. A shaft of light has knifed through the clouds and now touches the edges of her features with the palest possible gold. Her black silk flowing, strong artist's features set in a pout, this woman is as arresting a sight as I can presently recall.

With a raucous cry, the groom's party assaults the stairs of the tenement. I'm still staring at Phoebe Sternbaum, who turns to look at me, the pout still in place. As I watch, her eyes take in all my admiration.

I do love a woman who can enjoy her own beauty.

15

I answer the phone on about the ninth ring, which is how long it takes for me to realize I am asleep amid my sister's lavender-scented pillows and not being chased through a penis farm by Bo Diddley astride a camo-painted ATV. It's a relief, actually, as Bo was wielding that X-shaped guitar like an M-16 and the cash crop was starting up with that one-eyed *gape* that most days of the week indicates one hell of a screwing.

A bit blearily, I place the American Teacher's Phone against my good left ear while Lillian's voice explains why she once more won't be making her flight from Memphis. It seems that Mom had a really rough night. Quite the coincidence. I myself stayed very late at that Triad bar Arnie's been telling me about. They *do* teach macramé in the back. I made half a sock.

"Listen," says Lil, "you have to call my boss, Joe, and tell him I can't make the faculty meeting tomorrow but will *absolutely* be back Monday for the first day of classes. His number's there by the phone."

"Nnngh," I mutter, groping for the ibuprofen. That was a really close call at the penis farm. I still don't feel entirely safe so near Lillian's sex toys, especially the long black one.

"No, this isn't *nnngh*," says Lillian. "This is my job. Call him."

Nnngh.

"Don't you even want to hear about Mom? You never ask about her."

"How's Mom?" I ask, locating the ibuprofen beside the bottle of ma huang. I dump an unknown quantity of each into my mouth. I think something went down a nostril.

"You never ask about me, either," says Lil.

"How are you?"

"*God*, I don't know," she sighs. "Just being back in Memphis is weird enough. I'm still jet lagged and it *never* stops raining and Mom's vital signs are all over the place. The doctor's putting her on two new meds. He says—"

"What?" I say, reaching for my notes. "Our mother is already taking fourteen medications. Rush Limbaugh doesn't take fourteen medications."

"You sound hung over," says Lil.

"I don't yet qualify for hung over. Technically, I think I'm still drunk. I checked online, and the levothyroxine is probably screwing with the pioglitazone and the—"

"Levo-what?" she asks.

"Are you looking at the list? Levothyroxine. It's her hormone replacement. Regis Labs, five hundred mils, morning and night."

"Regis Labs," says Lil. "That's funny."

"Why would Regis Labs be funny?"

"They're a client," says Lil. "Stuart has them on retainer. I don't think he ever does a thing."

"Ask the doctor about the celecoxib. The paroxetine, too. Both of those are way over-prescribed."

"Celecoxib . . . and . . . paroxetine," says Lil. "You know, this is bringing up all your Mom stuff."

"This is not a good moment for discussing my Mom stuff."

"Name me one moment that ever was."

Falling back on the pillows, I toss the notebook, missing the table.

"Mom was an asshole," I tell my sister. "Doesn't make for much of a conversation, does it?"

She never did anything you could actually point to. The courts do not remove children from the home because of the plastic covers on the living-room furniture. You don't go on SSI because your mother failed to make eye contact before your twenty-seventh birthday.

"I thought you were over it," says Lil.

"I'm over it. I just don't understand it."

After a moment she says, "I understand it. I'm just not over it."

There were plastic covers on our mattresses and pillows, too. I was a college senior before I could sleep on a bed that didn't go crinkle-crinkle in the night. As an underclassman I kept a Wonder Bread wrapper under my pillow.

"How's it going with that animal in my kitchen?" says Lil.

"I'm studying its habits."

"You're what?"

"Before you take an animal out," I say, "you study its habits."

"Doo, buy a goddamn trap."

"What size? Baited with what? Placed where? And while you're waxing eloquent on the subject of wild-game management, *dearest* dear, you might suggest a blunt object to place beside the bed with which to, stark naked, beat its brains out when the trap that *you* would have me buy catches it by a forepaw."

Actually, everything I need to know was written in the flour I scattered on the kitchen floor that first night. I need to buy a goddamn trap.

"I'm going to come back there," says Lil, "and you're going to have a bound-and-indexed dissertation on the rat in my kitchen, and—"

"I'll take care of it," I tell her.

"Today?"

"Very, very soon."

The *soon* whistles slightly because of my missing maxillary first premolar crown. I was eating at the school lunchroom yesterday—mistake number one—and chewing a mouthful of rice—mistake number two; no one chews rice in this country—when a small pebble turned my gold maxillary first premolar crown into a mortar round. Which is to say it *come out.* I now have an appointment with a dentist whose name sounds like something a xylophone would say. Let's just hope that's not mistake number three.

"I found that guy's business card," says Lil. "The debt-collector guy? He's with a company in Kansas City called International Wholesale Distributors."

"It's taken care of," I say. "Gotta go. Time to seize the day, or at least go hug the toilet for a while."

"Doo, when are you going to start taking care of yourself?"

"We have strong constitutions, Lillian. We don't need to take care of ourselves."

"Yes, we do," says Lil. "You'll call Joe for me? Without fail?"

"What does *syzygy* mean?" I ask.

"What?"

"Never mind," I say. "I'll call him."

Making local calls from the American Teacher's Apartment is straightforward enough, if I admitted it. Just pick up and dial. Two days ago I picked up and dialed Phoebe's penthouse. She hasn't returned my message. I suppose it would have been a small miracle if she had, though we may have achieved a small reconciliation during the wee hours of the wedding party. I think I blundered into her on the dance floor. What we did next seemed to be dancing. I was dancing anyway.

"This makes me *so* nuts," says Lil, "trying to be on both sides of the world at the same time. There's something, like, really important going on in China right now. It's killing me. You know what I mean?"

I never know what she means. "Yeah."

"Seriously," says Lil.

"You're talking about completion," I say.

"How did you know that? That's exactly what it is. The Three-three-three's almost here. Tree says she doesn't know if we'll get a window. Do you feel like we'll get a window? I'm not feeling like we'll get a window."

"Have a nice day, Lil."

"Can't. It's night here."

"Then have a nice one of those," I say.

"Love you. Call Joe. And buy a trap."

With a groan, I recover my notebook from the floor and shake off a couple of dust bunnies. Again I see the words: Regis Labs. I know I've seen that name before.

Shivering a little from the morning chill, I rise to switch on Lil's computer, then the kitchen hot plate before stumbling into the bathroom to hear the American Teacher's Computer wheedle and squawk like some kind of rheumatic prehistoric bird. Not to say this computer is old, but the keyboard's a manual. I swing back through the front room to hit the dial-up before returning to the kitchen to start tea and egg-drop oatmeal. No hurry. I could create an alcoholic beverage in the time it takes for Lil's homepage to load.

So. International Wholesale Distributors, is it? That's exactly the kind of name you'd choose for a business that fronts for narcotics, prostitution, and all-occasion nose-cropping. I still can't believe I dropped forty-seven thousand dollars in less than three hours, let alone to a guy named Louie the Snail. That's probably how he's known in KC. He has two sons named Bugsy and Vinnie.

As I load the rice cooker, I replay my swaggering entrance to the party, the nearness of the gaming table clearly palpable and slightly salty on the tongue as I bore my wine goblet from room to room, pool to patio, overburdened white tablecloth to overstocked bar, noting as I strode through the blasé and over-tanned crowd the video surveillance cameras tucked into this nook and that fern; noting too on the faces of the minglers little glances that said *who's that?* I held myself even taller than usual, towering above the torpid rich in their surrendering skin, their shedding scales. *Isn't that Julian Mancer?* I flowed past them like a wind, black-out shades in place, magnificent platinum mane *sailing* around my ears as I followed the unmistakable scent of money.

Clearly there was a lot of it.

Gambling is a vice and an addiction and an abomination and a very Marxist institution for the redistribution of wealth. I felt a major wealth adjustment coming as I crossed yet another patio and entered a formal antechamber attended by more gym rats in black-out shades of their own, plus little wires in their ears. They mutely scanned the stream of people passing through the antechamber into a larger, dimly lit room emitting early Miles.

I sauntered through the antechamber as though I owned the place and immediately wished it were true, as the dimly lit room was adorned with eight tastefully posed women elevated on separate black rectangular boxes. They weren't wearing clothes. For each, strategically placed spotlights illuminated this dangerous curve, that fine-pored meadow.

Slowing my gait to observe, I found that each of the boxes rotated slowly on an unseen turntable, which effected an ever-changing landscape of warm light and dramatic shadow. Security guards stood quite nearby, there being no velvet restraining ropes, and I was happy to join the unruly gaggle, male and female alike, pressing close enough to the nearest model to, had we dared, lean ever so slightly and kiss her sainted thigh.

The first woman on display, her brown hair cropped very short, was a tanner, which made of the pale green eyes headlights. I stood close enough to examine each eye quite closely and found tiny flames of gold and peach in the translucent irises. The woman's body was aware of being desired. You could see it in the rise and fall of the paramilitary belly, its breath shallow and rapid. I imagined hearing the heart beneath the nearly flat chest.

There's something about a flat-chested woman. Something simple and inescapable in her design. The note that her instrument plays is somehow deeper and more resonant than that of others, and a short haircut brings that forward somehow. She is a tomboy in her seventeenth summer. All she has to do is wear a plunging neckline, and everyone is in love with her. One wants to know *just* a little bit more. We want the whole story in two precise words. And no woman is completely flat. Her two little brown hi-there's tip forward to meet your lips. They speak to the exact centers of your palms. Model number one was exactly that creature, and I removed my shades to enjoy her all the more. Maybe it had been Twenty-*One* Mule Team Borax.

And this is two-burro bad tea, I reflect, carrying my sister's smiley-face mug into the front room. I think I may now be turning the corner from drunk to hung over, and frankly it isn't working for me. But the screen of the American Teacher's Computer now displays a snarling young Elvis in a black cowboy shirt. This would be Lil's homepage. I take a seat and turn Lillian's mug around, avoiding the smile. Here's a fresh all-caps email from Jeremy. I delete it unopened. I'm growing less and less patient with this man's inability to handle delayed gratification. And here we have a fresh email from Ralpho with a link to his latest findings on Chinese moon bases.

The idea of colonizing the moon, he has already divulged, arose from China's worsening environmental pollution along with their commitment to burn Manchuria's entire vast coal belt. Thus, it can only be a matter of time before people are falling dead on China's streets. Ralpho says a twenty-person test pod has dwelled on the surface of the moon for some time now. Things have gone well enough, except that the twenty have nothing and nowhere to spit. The government is having to shuttle canisters of bus fumes—and saxophone music, of course—to the base while they figure this one out.

I click on a link where Ralpho writes, "I have uncovered that Bejing [*sic*] was the first point of human-alien contact somewhere around 3,000 BC. The Intrudors [*sic*] made a deal with the Chinese Emprer [*sic*] that provided them with secure living quarters inside the Forbiden [*sic*] City while they made repairs on their spaceship. That was the real reason for the giant walls and all the secrecy." In return, reveals Ralpho, the emperor received instruction in an arcane system of medical intervention known today as Traditional Chinese Medicine.

And the recipe for Twice Cook Pork. Nothing in the current article concerns gun control, vegetarianism, or gas retention.

Ralpho says the ETs bear a striking resemblance to us, the explanation being that they long ago seeded our planet with crosses between themselves and one of the more promising of the local primates, returning from time to time to see how the experiment is coming.

Not well, I take it.

Ralpho should really sit down with Tree, who maintains that the Great Pyramid was constructed as a blocking diode by a do-gooder extraterrestrial race endeavoring to halt further intergalactic interference with human evolution on the plains of Africa. Eventually, of course, our race sallied forth to other geographical parts, leaving the protection of the Pyramid behind and, well, Tammy Fae Bakker is the direct result.

I'm a fundamentalist. I maintain that God created the world in six days and watched pro football on the seventh. Still, I'm beginning to warm to some of Ralpho's theories. I particularly enjoy his argument linking ankle tattoos, sushi consumption, and lesbianism.

Think about it.

I close out the email account and open a search engine. I still can't get that pharmaceutical company out of my head. Tossing down a swig of two-burro tea, I enter two words into search: Regis and Laboratories.

16

"Tell me something, Tree. Do you love your mother?"

She gives me one of her sideways looks. Tree Carter and I are seated at her kitchen table eating inscrutable pink Chinese ice cream. Beyond the kitchen window is a view of the green-and orange-tiled building where Tree provides English to Shenzhen's most out-of-body first-graders. Her refrigerator is covered with examples of their crayon art.

"Of course," she replies. "She drives me crazy, but I love her. Why?"

"Just curious. Do people love their mothers in some kind of predetermined, preverbal, pre-vertebrate way, or is there a moment of choice at some juncture? Either way, I seem to be in need of reinstalling the software."

"Talk," says Tree.

Not easily done, actually. The space that my maxillary first premolar crown once filled seems enormous. Even my vowels are beginning to whistle. Unfortunately, I slept through this morning's appointment with Dr. Xylophone, now rescheduled for the day after tomorrow. Bellamy's busy that day but he promises to send his secretary, Ursula, whose hairline and upper lip are about a quarter-inch apart. That would be roughly five millimeters.

I'm going metric.

"Lil says I am defined by my Mom issues," I tell Tree, dabbing at the pink ice cream at the bottom of my porcelain teacup.

"And what do you say?"

"I think I'm defined by a lot more issues than that. But Lillian always goes straight for the reductionism, projection, and self-justification. Not to mention the family mean streak. And she's probably right."

Tree waits for more.

I gaze at my ice cream. As with most of the prepared foods in this country, the color, scent, and tang are at sharp odds with each other. This particular flavor, I think, is called Bubblegum Hotdog Surprise.

"The first time I encountered the word *adopted*," I tell Tree, "I said, oh that's what I am." I turn to her. "Why do I suddenly have the urge to call you Oprah?"

"You loved your mother, Jules. You still do. You're no different from the rest of us. You just have to pass through the pain and the anger. Then you'll find the love. You know why this is coming up for you now?"

I force myself not to squirm in my chair.

"Everything that is destined to be," says Tree, her brown eyes softening, "already is. The work we came here to do is already complete, Julian. It's calling back to us through time, guiding us in. When we feel that *pull*, that discomfort, that emotional wound crying out for healing, it means we're being prepared for something that can no longer be postponed. Our job is just to *be* with all that. To feel it all, whatever it is."

"Feel?" I say.

Tree nods.

Frowning, I place another spoonful of inscrutable Chinese ice cream on the left side of my mouth. Since losing the premolar crown, I eat everything on the left side, which leaves me feeling curiously half-fed. The crown, a small fortune in jewelers' gold actually, now rides in my left shirt pocket. How nice to be falling apart both emotionally and physically. Maybe I'm spending too much time in Lillian's bed. I keep having the urge to turn on all her sex toys just to see what they'll do to each other.

Tree tilts her head slightly, as though seeing me for the first time. "It's people like you who have the hardest time, you know. Smart people? You learn how to go inside your head, and after a while you forget how to come back out. The important thing is, Jules, you're asking the right questions now. You're starting to take a look at yourself and that's very, very encouraging. I never thought I'd live to see the day when you'd come to me about your feelings for your mother."

"I didn't come for *that*," I protest. "And while we're asking all the right questions, what exactly is supposed to happen on the Three-three-three?"

"I don't know."

"Want to memo me when you figure it out? It's February, you know. To be honest, I have enough on my plate just now without all your little veiled references to things we're supposed to do on behalf of God Almighty Jesus Jerusalem Hogwaller. Between you and that big blond you hang around with, I feel out of sync with inner processes I probably don't even have."

Tree's eyes are steady. "What's going on with you, Julian?"

I set down my spoon and share her gaze. "My publishing deal is dead, my novel is as unfinished as ever, you won't even *talk* about bringing in Truman for me—"

"He said you have to prove yourself."

"—I have to *prove* myself, the Shenzhen Textbook Publishing Company is stiffing me, my teeth are falling out, Lillian can't seem to get out of Memphis, and I can't seem to get out of China. And this ice cream is offensively bad."

"Only if you're expecting something different," says Tree, lifting a spoonful. "You know, you might try enjoying China. It's a pretty special place, you know."

"And I haven't been laid since the Year of the Pterodactyl," I add. "And you can't buy a decent number-two pencil anywhere in this country. Other than that, life couldn't be much sweeter, now could it?"

I avoid mentioning the spot of worry that accompanied this morning's web search. Not only does Regis Laboratories manufacture plastic hormones for old ladies, they also do a lot of hands-on genetics. That's how I'd encountered their name before, years before while trying to uncover Lil's and my birth records. In the end, the only solid fact I managed to unearth was that the artificial insemination of our mother had been conducted in Chicago, Illinois, by one Regis Laboratories. Which I'd call ironic at the very least.

The same company that once horsed around with this woman's ovaries is now managing their tour of obsolescence *while* cutting a monthly check for the attorney who hired her daughter at an obscure Memphis law firm whose usual clientele runs more to multiple-amputees than multinational pharmaceutical trolls. In fact, I'm not sure whether *ironic* quite covers it.

Tree's smile spreads effortlessly. "Julian, everything you're looking for is at the centermost of your heart."

I wait for a little more information. When it doesn't come, I say, "That's really special to know, Tree. And why have you hidden this little nugget from me for so long? Listen. Seriously. How can I convince you to bring Truman in for me? Just once? This material is good for a Pulitzer at *least*. Do you know how few people get the Pulitzer?"

"Everything you need is inside your own heart," says Tree, unfazed. "Ask. That's all you have to do. There are guides, lots of them, whose whole business is to take you where you need to go."

"You mean Jesus, Krishna, Buddha . . . ?"

She nods. "Mother Mary, Guan Yin, Meher Baba, the archangels, on and on."

"Are you going to sing 'Rock of Ages' now?"

"They're codes, Julian, that's all. They're codes that work."

I try to give Tree's proposition serious consideration. I don't get very far. I tried *om*-ing once. It made my nose hairs itch.

"There's one other thing you should know," says Tree, pushing her empty teacup away. "When you ask, you receive. Don't think it won't happen. And don't think this is just about you and your mother. It is, of course. But this stuff is *old*, Julian. It's very old. It's why we came into these bodies. It's why we're in this country, sitting at this table, having this conversation. It's why this solar system is here, as a safe house, a hypothetical learning space for working out exactly these issues."

I scowl at the word *hypothetical*. "What exactly do you mean by 'when you ask, you receive?'"

"It's too late to take it back now."

"Take back what?"

"You signed on for this a long, long time ago, baby. Just pay attention. The universe will send you situations that will take you to your centermost heart. Some people call these kinds of things tests. Some say they're punishments. But they're all blessings, Julian, and I'll tell you why. Each one gives us another chance to love what we could not love before."

"I may need a few more chances with this ice cream," I say.

Tree leans forward. "It has nothing to do with ice cream, or your mother, or your sister, *or* your novel, Julian, and I'll tell you why. What you could never love before is yourself. That's the battle you are fighting. All that adolescent behavior of yours, all that denial you like to wrap yourself up in—that will soon fall away, revealing the warrior within. Once that happens, our work truly begins. Until that happens, it doesn't matter how many Three-three-threes come and go. You're asking the right questions now. That's what's important. That means the answers can't be too far away. Believe me when I say they are coming at you at the speed of light. *Hear* me when I tell you this. There will soon come a time when denial will no longer be a possibility."

I give her a blank look. Go ahead, I'm thinking. Underestimate me.

17

I try to be as cynical as possible. It makes for fewer surprises. So it really pisses me off that I didn't see this coming. Lillian will be delayed for just a few more days, and will I please *please* please sub for her until she makes it in? Me. A substitute schoolteacher. In China.

I said absolutely not, but my sister is a courtroom attorney and had all her arguments queued. The final argument was to burst into horrific sobs when I paid no heed whatsoever to arguments one through whatever, and the rest of the conversation was just an unhappy blur. I was had, and I knew I was had. Here I am lying against my sister's nested pillows watching her pirated sex DVDs on the school's computer while she attends our dying green mother.

So, at ten past eight on Monday morning, here I am climbing three flights of concrete stairs amid a surging sea of white-over-blue uniforms and querulous gazes en route to Lillian's first class of spring semester at Shenzhen High School of Electronic Excellence.

Life is so whatever.

At least I know how to fake it. I stroll into Room 403 with such nonchalance, tossing Lil's clipboard onto the desk and turning to erase the board with such aplomb, even *I* believe I'm a teacher. Behind me, the classroom is a riot of hoots, shoves, pseudo-laughs, and slammed textbooks, altogether equal in volume to any American public school that comes to mind.

No problem, I tell myself, writing my name on the board in a patient wavering line. I spent three hours online last night learning how to manage a classroom. That's what it's called now. Teaching, you no longer even attempt. It comes down to three things, they say. Talk loud, show no fear, and continue with the lesson no matter what.

I can do that.

For about two and a half days.

As I await the late bell, I survey Room 403, which is all windows left side and right. Fore and aft are nothing but old-fashioned green chalkboards. A few rags remain at this or that window where the curtains have rotted away. A few cheap plastic ventilation fans dangle miserably from the walls.

It's a somewhat chill February morning. Many of the windows don't close. All the girls are heavily bundled, arms wrapped around themselves, shivering. The boys, fresh from pre-school basketball, are sleeveless and frisky. One boy torments the girls by throwing all the windows open, and they reward him with high wails. I watch as the nearest girl struggles to close the windows behind him. As soon as she takes her seat, the same boy throws them all open again.

This is going to be interesting.

The students' wooden desks, sixty or more in number, are packed so tight that walking among them would require turning sideways. We won't be doing that.

My desk, actually the common desk of all Room 403 teachers, is a disaster of broken chalk-bits, scraps of filthy rags, a few blunt, eraser-less pencils, and now Lillian's clipboard and my bottle of Binihana purified water. I'm standing on a ten-inch wooden stage, beneath the framed blood-red flag of the People's Republic of China, trying to look gun-boat authoritative.

"They're mostly sweet kids," Lillian has told me, "but not necessarily all that bright, okay? This is a vo-tech high school, remember. Just keep it simple and you'll be fine."

Mostly sweet, I'm thinking. Lillian has never had these particular students. We may have Wang the Ripper right here on row three.

As mentioned, this school is wholly funded by the government-owned telephone company, which finds itself in regular need of warm bodies with opposable thumbs and not too much upstairs. These kids are certifiably dumb, but they know the score. Their futures are already written, and it doesn't make much of a read. They have fallen to the lowest rung of a ladder leading nowhere. Of course their attitudes are going to stink.

Finally, the bell rings for what seems a full minute. As soon as it ceases, I bellow, "Good morning, class."

It doesn't come out *clath* because yesterday a dentist with crooked teeth reattached my crown, I think with Krazy Glue. Dr. Xylophone's office is in the dental wing of an enormous government hospital where Ursula and I stood in line at three consecutive windows before sitting on our hands for an hour. Finally we arrived at a tiny cubicle where Dr. Xylophone smiled broadly with jumbled teeth. During the entire procedure, an unidentified woman stood just behind his shoulder and stared into my mouth. Afterward, I asked Ursula who that woman was. "Next customer," she said.

Now, with an awful extended groan of wooden chairs against careworn tile, all fifty-odd students rise to their feet. "G-o-o-o-m-o-r-r-r-y-y-y-t-e-a-c-h-u-u-u-h," they reply in slow-motion then remain standing, awaiting my instruction.

"Sit," I say, gesturing.

They sit.

Ah. Piece of cake.

Now I spend fifty minutes speaking with exaggerated volume and clarity, drawing maps and pictures on the chalkboard, miming and telling amusing stories with words of one syllable or less, students meanwhile staring perplexedly or else sleeping on their arms. Lil has said they all have had three to five years of English. I'm not sure they've had three to five years of Mandarin. Later on, I get the same impression of students in Rooms 406 and 301. It's somewhat freeing, actually, as I can say anything I want. At one point, I find myself reciting the Gettysburg Address.

Finally, a bit dizzy from the exertion, I carry Lil's clipboard back to the office she shares with the other four English teachers, all of them Chinese, and sprawl in her tiny chair.

Joe looks up from his computer screen, a cigarette going in the ashtray. "Julian, the students say you look very like your sister."

I stare at Joe for a moment. "I'm pleased to hear that."

Joe likes this reply. He goes back to his emails.

Head spinning, I fiddle with Lil's papers for a few minutes, stealing occasional glances at the real teachers to see what they're doing. Bobby is humming along with a DVD of the Peking Opera. Jeff is keying something into his computer. Trish's chair is empty. Joe is stubbing out a cigarette in an ashtray crowded with butts.

Lil has no Monday afternoon classes, which means I've basically survived day one. On reflection, it could have gone considerably worse. My best moment may have come during the morning's third class, when I ran out of memorized speeches and extemporized insults.

"Very well," I said, clapping my hands together. "Let's *rumba*." I began to dance in a little circle, right hand on my belly, left held aloft, gyrating beneath the blood-red flag. Perhaps expectedly, the room exploded into astonished shrieks and howls. One of the boys leapt flatfooted onto his desk and began to gyrate, tossing his head so that his comb-over reached his shoulder. The girls mostly screamed and covered their mouths. Two other boys jumped onto their desks.

Those kids couldn't rumba worth a damn.

"Julian," teacher Bobby says now, switching off the Peking Opera, "it's time for lunch. You can go with Trish and me to the school lunchroom. Very economical."

"Also very chip," says Trish, lifting her purse.

Seconds later, Joe is locking the English faculty office behind us and I'm trying to keep up with Bobby and Trish, who are all but sprinting across the palm-lined campus, seeking every possible advantage over the white-over-blue herd moving clumsily in the same direction, every nostril filled with scents of cooked meats and simmering sauces. Even I'm getting excited. Trish slows a step to say, "Julian, please, how is your mother?"

"Senile," I reply, beginning to pant, "but she'll probably die soon."

"Ah," says Trish appreciatively. "Is also alive your father, too?"

I tell her I've no idea who, where, or if.

Trish wags her head sincerely. "You are so lucky have the beautiful sister like Lillian, always take care of your mother and father. Also very tall and fat."

And chip, I want to say, as the crowd slows to squeeze itself through the double doors of the lunchroom. The aromas are so palpable now you could weigh them on a postal scale. Ahead of us, students are grabbing trays, soup spoons, and chopsticks before hurrying toward whatever food station that beckons, there to turn sideways and reach past the others to grab this entree and that.

The rice station catches my attention. It is an enormous barrel with several enormous metal serving spoons stuck like shovels into snow. It's very white of course. Don't bring up brown rice with the Chinese. They look at you as though you're tragically ill-informed and not a little rude. Rice grows fluffy and white, just as you see it on the plate, and everyone knows it.

For a moment I watch the boys heap mountains of the white, semi-congealed goo onto their melamine platters, piling up *far* more rice than I'd ever imagined a single person could eat at a sitting. A glance at the tables shows boys raking rice into their mouths with both hands, a spoon in one and chopsticks in the other, their faces lowered to plate level. I've seen this same thing on the street, where grunt laborers unable to afford anything more substantial sit along the sidewalk at lunchtime forcing down billowing clouds of the stuff.

I decide to pass on the rice. I also give the soup station a wide berth, though both Bobby and Trish are as happy as lottery winners to come away with brimming bowls of the stuff.

I'm sorry. Soup is a woman's idea of something to eat. Watered-down food. Oh give *me* some. I also pass on the slippery plastic chopsticks standing upright in a pail, preferring the wooden pair in my pants pocket. I end up with a plate of something resembling Chinese cabbage, a pasta dish with a beefy red sauce, and the main course which I think is a pork and spinach casserole. With cheese. And mayonnaise.

"You no get the soup?" says Trish, alarmed, as I join her and Bobby at the table.

"I no want the soup," I reply.

"No?" asks Bobby, equally surprised. "In China, we say soup is wonderful for the health. I will get you some."

"I don't want any," I say as Bobby hurries away.

"How was your first day of teach the Chinese students?" Trish asks with a bright smile.

"Like shooting fish in a barrel," I tell her, removing the plates from my tray. "Tell me something. Do any of these kids know a single English word?"

"I don't know," Trish says happily, blowing across her soup spoon.

I look around. This lunchroom seems more or less identical to its American counterpart, minus the circulating armed security guards and drug-sniffing canines. I notice a refrigerator near the milk station—the Chinese are religious about milk consumption, though most of them are lactose-intolerant—whose glass door reveals ranks and files of chilled longneck Kingway beers.

That's different.

Bobby returns with my soup. "Here you are, Julian. I also brought for you a spoon."

"You really shouldn't have."

The spinach turns out to be some kind of seaweed, but the ground beef could actually *be* ground beef, however fortified with equal parts powdered duck's egg and unfortunate neighborhood dog.

I learn from Bobby that he was a farmer before becoming an English teacher. "I was the first person in my family to have a real education. Really I was extremely lucky. Most farmers never have a chance to change their life."

Trish gushes, "Bobby is very special teacher. Always have the highest—" She confers with her colleague for a moment. They decide on the word *evaluations*. She continues, "I think that Bobby can be very good government official."

Bobby laughs modestly. "I'm not a member of the Chinese Communist Party, so there's no possibility of that. I don't care. I have a good career teaching in the school, and soon I will retire."

According to Lil, most Chinese schoolteachers are in it for the little incentives doled out regularly by headmasters. Corruption, I think it's called. At the better Chinese schools—this is not one of them—before grades go out, teachers are inundated with fat red envelopes full of cash from parents. Tucked inside are gushy thank-you notes carefully spelling out the name of the little tyke in question.

Not that the American Teacher is entitled to any such perks; still, one can only intuit that there could be the occasional little cutie just *really* in need of an A. Though how one might know she is both female and a cutie is a question unto itself, given the identical parachutes the students wear, and the fact that the girls employ not the least trace of make-up. Theoretically, the short ones are the boys. The shorter ones, the girls.

Bobby and Trish top off their meal with fresh apples, Bobby using a folding knife from his pocket to carefully remove their skins. Afterward we place our trays on a wet conveyor belt and stroll back toward the English faculty office, for which Bobby possesses a personal key. I take a seat at Lil's desk and watch Trish and Bobby pull folding cots from behind their desks and pop them open. Within five minutes, each is snoring. I take a look at my watch. Quarter of one.

Miller time.

As I tiptoe away from the English faculty office, I encounter Joe walking the other way, keys in hand.

"Julian," he says blandly, "tonight there is a dinner in your honor. I will call your room at six o'clock."

"Uh, actually, I always take a nap at six o'clock."

"I will wake you up," he says pertly.

"How . . . perfect."

Joe likes this reply.

I return to Lillian's apartment with a massive frontal headache and a whole new appreciation for solitude.

She has till Wednesday.

18

"Tonight you will eat a *real* Chinese meal," says Joe.

You worry when you hear this.

Joe translates his words for the five others gathered on the busy sidewalk in front of Shenzhen High School of Electronic Excellence. They all look at me and laugh.

"In your honor," adds Joe, grinning, and I do my best to blush.

Beyond his proficiency in English, what distinguishes Joe from the sea of other five-foot-four Chinese men is hair count. You couldn't part the man's hair with a howitzer round. Interestingly, Joe is the *head* of the English Department. I thought you'd like that. I had an opportunity earlier today to study his teaching methodology. Joe assigns sentences for the students to copy from the chalkboard then stands outside the open door to smoke cigarettes and talk on his phone.

On the sidewalk before us, two women walk by in gauze masks and surgical gloves, and the dinner party murmurs uneasily for a couple of minutes before Joe turns to me importantly and says, "Those women were wearing something to protect themselves. There is a rumor of some kind of bad disease in Guangzhou, but the government says there is no danger." Now he beams for me.

Color me reassured.

Outside China's Great Wall of disinformation, the disease that doesn't exist is called atypical pneumonia. It's all over the internet. Sudden onset, acute pulmonary crisis, and according to the latest round-up of neighborhood rumors, shockingly high mortality. In this country where straight information can be scarce, rumor is a palpable thing. You feel it moving through the city like a wind. With the close of Spring Festival, a hundred million Chinese are freshly returned from family visits in crowded filthy trains, bringing atypical God-knows-what with them. But there's nothing to worry about.

The dinner party continues to stand on the busy sidewalk, gawking nowhere in particular, evidently awaiting someone.

Ralpho emailed me today. He's coming for a visit. He says he wants to look for a job. And probably sniff around for vegetarians. He promises to treat me to as much *dim sum* and beer as I can reasonably handle. Still I don't know. That guy has got to snore.

"Ju-wen?"

I turn to view the timid approach of Marilyn, a divorcée who teaches night courses in English to phone-company employees in the high-rise office building.

"Ju-wen, so nice I *see* you," Marilyn sings through her nose. "Is your first day of classes. You no have the problem?"

"No have the single one. And how was your day, Marilyn?"

She thinks for a moment and her eyelids flutter. "I think also very good. I go see my son now, cook the dinner. Here, I give you my telephone number so if you have the problem." She begins scrawling.

"You already gave me your telephone number."

"But you no call me."

"That's because you gave it to me an hour ago."

Marilyn's eyes all but close as she giggles. "Ju-wen, you so *naughty*. Also you so fat like your sister." Handing me the note, she says, "Please, thank you very much."

"Also you as well, too."

Marilyn departs, and the men follow her with their eyes and guffaw discreetly. Finally the last couple arrives, late and perspiring. It turns out they, like the others Joe has selected for this dinner party in my *honor*, originate from his home province, speak no English, and have no idea who the white giant is.

"Let's go," says Joe, tossing a cigarette and herding us toward the maw of a nearby alley.

Tree was recently treated to a real Chinese meal. The menu featured, among other things, pigeon, cockroach, civet cat—think mongoose with severe ADD—and a delicacy known as Three Screams. That would be a living, tightly bound, skinless rat. The rat, it's said, screams once when lifted with the chopsticks, again when dipped in vinegar, and a third time when bitten into.

Which seems reasonable enough to me. I hope we are not en route to that particular variety of real Chinese meal. I've heard, as well, about a Shenzhen restaurant that specializes in *yewei*, or exotic meats. The more endangered the species, the higher the price. Crocodile, sturgeon, anteater, barking deer, it's all on the menu. Along with, I think, forearm of Panchen Lama.

The dinner party trails Joe through a maze of crumbling masonry, past an assemblage of Astroturf-topped billiard tables. The latter are surrounded by the dead-eyed pupils of our fine school. Other white-over-blue youths sit at poker, cigarettes dripping from their faces. Joe pretends not to see the students as he leads us into an even drearier alley of parked motorcycles, wandering chickens, a balding cat, and two or three shirtless old men. And isn't that someone asleep on that pile of lumber? Wherever you go in China, there's someone asleep with his mouth open.

Joe stops at what seems a totally random spot. Nothing anywhere suggests that we've arrived at an eating establishment, but the women of the party begin haranguing two disheveled men, who after a short while drag a table out of an anonymous door. Another table is jammed against it, followed by ten un-matching chairs. The two workmen seem disoriented and disgruntled, as though they've never had to do anything like this before.

Just bring the beer.

Is it just me, or are pleasures spaced rather far apart in this country? Either you're really into food, or there's basically nothing for you here. I'm told that gambling, vice, addiction, abomination—the whole good list—is readily available at near-by Macao, a British/Chinese attempt to concoct a Monaco of the Pacific. My own personal tastes favor revolving women. You can have the revolving wheels.

The dinner party in my honor at last takes its seats, myself first. The ground is hopelessly uneven, and none of the chairs sit level. A young waitress appears, and instantly she is set upon by the women of the party who begin to dictate every detail of the dishes we are to receive, including when and how each is to appear at table. This goes on for ten minutes, fifteen minutes, eyes and voices sharpening until it appears that the young tramp of a waitress will be seized and tied with her own hair and forced to sing like Freddie Fender.

That would be nice.

I tune out, setting my elbows on the table and watching various neighbors straggle past, cigarettes hanging from their mouths at the Chinese sixty-degree cant. They're staring at us like *this is no restaurant, man, this is a dirty-ass alley.*

Just bring the beer.

Meanwhile I revisit certain visual memories of that money-scented Memphis night, that single-night Satyricon. How truly delightful: a secret gaming society that conducts a hundred percent of its nefarious activities within the exclusive and securely gated compounds of its members. This month, Boulder. Next month, Barbados. Or perhaps Shenzhen?

My mind settles on what could be my favorite memory of all: rotating box number two. Rocking back in my plastic chair, I let go a sigh and recall the sight of a dirty blond who'd never gone anywhere near the sun in her life, nor the gym, nor should she have, for here was a woman who under no circumstance should ever leave the bedroom. Her full lips begged for red lipstick. The two breasts were certainly showy enough, but my eyes chose to follow a vector between the semi-parted thighs to a shadowed space, a disappearing depth, an inward-plunging center line quite soon to deliver inquiring minds to the *crux* of the matter. As she slowly revolved, the spotlights increasingly threatened to violate that shadowed space, that nest of tawny hairs, and though they never fully succeeded, my eyes were rewarded with a cogent visual understanding of how and, I thought, *why* a woman's central contours cling ever more urgently to their own plummeting depths.

It's awful, this work. Being the narrator. Captive to each terrible detail.

There were two black models that warm Memphis night, and I particularly enjoyed how the honeyed light met their skin, flattening the sheen and lifting each pore for my personal inspection. There is no skin like African-American skin, especially that milk-chocolate mid-tone between high and low yaller, the texture practically mythical in its perfection. The first of those women summoned First Dynasty Egypt with her sharp bones, owlish eyes, and sanguine glow.

The second had abs like a waffle-iron, yet despite all the crunches, her belly was feverishly feminine, its dipping lines grabbing the eye and funneling it along past the tidy, vertical navel. Every visual artist is taught to do this, yet few learn to *pull* the eye along an inexorable course to a compelling singularity that at the same moment absorbs the rapt attention and recycles it along emerging lines that shoot you out only to circle you back in again exactly as do a woman's hips.

You don't find a lot of installations like that in Memphis, naked women on rotating boxes. Though, of course, this was just the antechamber, the warm-up act, the appetizer. The real attraction lay not in the Miles Room at all but in a far more lavishly turned-out space just beyond.

Joe turns to me. "Do you want some fish?"

Sure. Why not?

"Do you want some chicken?"

Okay. Whatever.

"Do you want some pork?"

I stare at him. I'm trying to be agreeable here. Just bring me something to eat.

A few minutes later, "Do you want some beef?"

I tell him I want some beer.

"Okay," says Joe.

A few minutes later, "Do you want some beef?"

The other men sit dejectedly, staring nowhere in particular. My fantasy obliterated, I follow their lead, retreating to my chair back to watch a chicken neck-walk up and down the alley. I do my best not to think about Regis Labs. What's to think about? Here's a legitimate tax-paying American enterprise that manufactures human hormone replacement, does cutting-edge genetic research, and twots young women with the sperm of total strangers. What's offensive about that?

I did a little more research last night, and Regis Labs has stranger bedfellows than Dennis Rodman knows anything about. After half a night tracing a labyrinth of links from the Regis homepage, I arrived at a site where a large lavender logo laboriously loaded, top to bottom, as I waited impatiently then felt the floor disappear from beneath my feet.

I found myself looking at a huge lavender hydrangea.

Not only had Regis conducted the genesis of my and my sister's lives. Not only do they now pad the income of my sister's sleepy-headed employer, Stuart. Not only do they spice our failing mother's bloodstream with God only knows what—Regis Labs is an incorporated subsidiary of Hydrangea Laboratories. Which I'm not going to think about just now.

I've already done what little I can think to do, namely fire off two emails, the first to my sister—"Lil, I need you to send me one of Mom's hormone replacements. Put it in an envelope ASAP. I'll explain later." The second went to my editor at *Magazine Mariposa*—"Miriam, I have a conflict-of-interest question. Are any of the following companies advertisers?" I listed Hydrangea, Regis, and seven other firms within the same corporate umbrella.

Then my fingers froze on the keypad. Nine heads of the Hydra. Nine companies within Hydrangea. I'm definitely not going to think about that just now.

"Do you want some soup?" asks Joe.

"Absolutely not."

Beer arrives, tap-water warm. I use it to wash down four doses of ma huang, then three more. Meanwhile, an old lady squats near a water faucet, dumps some red and green peppers onto the concrete and begins preparing our dinner amid the chicken droppings.

"I ordered Red and Green Peppers with Bloody Duck," says Joe, "especially for you. Have you eaten this before?"

Not recently.

"Very special dish from my home province," he says, smiling.

I can also look forward to brain of pig, liver of swine, and I think pinky finger of sow. I wonder why Joe bothered asking me all those questions if he was just going to order from *Oinker Anatomy*.

I lean on my elbows and pretend to be having the time of my life as these strangers talk among themselves in Mandarin. Chinese etiquette requires that everyone acknowledge me with a silent toast each time he takes a sip of beer, which quickly becomes obnoxious. Last semester Lillian was treated to a dinner in her honor, as well. Evidently an unending series of American teachers to *honor* provides Joe with welcome opportunities to slop his homeys on the school's tab. But I always try to be as cynical as possible.

Which perhaps explains why I'd like to take a close look at Mom's hormone replacement. Actually, what I'm going to do is pass it along to Bellamy, whose brother is a forensic pathologist. As the handgun-impoverished Chinese poison each other with great enthusiasm, there are more forensic pathologists in this country than noodle vendors.

The old lady bends to rinse her hands at the outdoor faucet. Behind her, a balding cat approaches the pile of peppers and gives them a sniff. Meanwhile through the open window of the kitchen, I see flames shoot to the ceiling. Course one will soon be on its way.

"I ordered some soup for you," smiles Joe.

"Perfect," I smile back.

Actually, I'm going to pour it onto the cat. But Joe likes this answer.

19

Ralpho looks good. I ask him where he got the tan and he says, "Dalian. Over in Liaoning Province. Great beaches."

China. Great beaches. I try to force those two concepts together in my head. I have to stop.

"Nice apartment," says Ralpho.

"It's my sister's."

I spit out the word *sister* as one might a bad wad of chaw. Lillian called before school this morning to say that not only can she not make it back here by tomorrow/Wednesday, it's now looking like this weekend/whenever. They've put our mother in ICU. I think that stands for Insufficiently Continent Ungulates.

"You can have the box springs or the mattress," I tell Ralpho.

"Mattress," he says.

Men are so easy. We toss the mattress onto the floor and we're done. Now we can go drink beer.

Except that Ralpho wants a quick shower first. I show him how to activate the pint-sized water heater at the ceiling of the bathroom, always good for a three-minute shower on short notice. I return to the American Teacher's Computer and my pet research project.

Drugs that don't make you high.

It's one more way for the oil-rich to extinguish the last of our lights in as direct a manner as possible while charging us for it. Our mother is on four blood-pressure medications, three of which are guaranteed, given time, to turn her kidneys into kidney beans. And her blood pressure is still fucked. But the important thing is, the oil-rich are a hundred-plus dollars a month oil-richer from one woman's blood alone, having expended nothing more than the trash from their refineries.

The sweetest irony, of course, is that most of the illnesses these pills supposedly cure are *caused* by petro-pollution. Not to drop any bombs here, but you and I drive plastic cars to and from plastic homes, carrying plastic grocery bags filled with plastic-packaged and plastic-enriched foods that we've paid for with plastic. And you wonder why I'm so careful to maintain a healthy level of apathy.

Lil tells me, by the way, that she's unable to provide a sample of Mom's hormone replacement. "Her doctor's a jerk. He says he'll stop the paroxetine but won't change anything else without written authorization."

"What kind of written authorization?" I asked.

"Declaring Mom insane," she replied. "I asked Stuart about it. He says it's doable. I don't know, man. That shit's scary."

I thought about Stuart's handsome little retainer from Regis Labs and wondered what else he finds doable.

"Steal one," I told my sister.

"Steal what? One of her meds? What the hell do you want with one of Mom's blood-pressure meds?"

I finally convinced Lil of a contamination scare with another Regis product. Why not be on the safe side? It's the same basic lie I'll tell Bellamy's forensic brother. Might Regis Labs actually be lacing our mother's blood-pressure med with a subtle and cumulative toxin? Just to force the twins out of China? Highly doubtful. Just like every other truth in my life just about now.

"*God*, I'm missing China," wailed Lil through her bunny phone.

"You're what?" I replied.

"It's the smells," said Lil. "I don't know. There's something about the scents there. When that's taken away, it breaks your heart."

I suggested she find a dumpster to suck on.

After hanging up I spent half the night online trying to map myself and my sister onto whatever this multi-headed floral/chemical conglomerate is up to. I still can't say what that might be. Hydrangea Labs has been investigated thrice for patent theft, each time inconclusively. A series of CEOs have come and gone, none of them leaving much of a mark. The company is consistently in the black while lagging considerably behind the obscene profits of the industry as a whole. Whatever Hydrangea's game, good old American greed doesn't seem to be much of a part of it. Which is suspicious if anything is.

Ralpho emerges from the bathroom reeking of Old Spice, his hair slicked back. He looks at me as though expecting a compliment.

"Your shower okay?" I ask.

"While it lasted," says Ralpho. "I couldn't do my cream rinse."

"You ready to do some *dim sum*?"

"Yeah. Let me get dressed."

It takes him thirty minutes. Finally Ralpho steps into his shoes and I grab my empty wallet—just in time to notice that a Chinese man is standing in the open doorway.

I gaze inquiringly at a perishingly thin man of at least seventy years, dressed in white leather loafers and an electric-blue three-piece suit with white piping. And a white fedora. No feather. He's smiling at me.

"You'll find Madam Wu downstairs," I announce. "Please give her my regards and ask whether she's checked the linen closet lately."

"Mistuh Man-suh?" comes the reply. "I Mistuh Piao Pin Tian. Correct deds."

"I'm sorry?"

"Correct deds," he repeats. "Get the money." Piao steps close enough to hand me a business card featuring purple Chinese characters against the lurid Kowloon skyline. There's exactly one English word, in bright red. Collections.

"Correct deds some gentlemen USA," says Piao. "Please pay money eighty-seven thousand dollar. You got?"

I look up at the frozen smile. There's one tooth missing. "Eighty-seven thousand? Really?"

"Small correction fee."

"You charge a *forty*-thousand-dollar collection fee?" I say, impressed.

Ralpho tosses Lil's towel onto a chair. "Who's the asshole?"

"Little misunderstanding," I say.

Piao says, "You please pay money eighty-seven thousand dollar."

"You please get the fuck out of here," says Ralpho, bouncing on the balls of his feet.

My tongue plays nervously with the newly re-installed maxillary first premolar crown. It doesn't feel exactly right. I think Dr. Xylophone put it in sideways.

"Look, Mister, uh—" I say, "I'll call my friends back in the States and straighten this out. Understand? Make call? Tele-tele?"

"No more call," says Piao, still smiling rigidly. "I correct ded."

Ralpho steps forward and places his right palm over Piao Pin Tian's smile. As I watch stupified, Ralpho backs the old man out of Lillian's apartment and onto the balcony. No longer smiling, Piao grabs his now-crooked fedora with both hands and turns to run awkwardly in the direction of the stairs.

"You come here again," Ralpho shouts after him, "I'll throw you off the fucking balcony—and your cunt of a wife with you."

Only now do I see the old woman waiting at the head of the stairs, a gauze mask over her face and a briefcase in each hand. Her eyes look frightened.

"Uh . . . ," I say to no one in particular.

Ralpho dusts his hands. "Listen, man, I been through that collection shit. There's stuff you just can't put up with. You ready?"

Again I look in the direction of the stairs. Both deds-corrector and wife are gone. Suddenly I'm no longer so worried about the sideways maxillary first premolar crown.

On the bus, Ralpho is moody. After posing a few questions, I learn that he is freshly married. Ralpho says it like it's a medical condition. The new wife is Chinese, twenty-nine years of age, a good speaker of English, and a salaried government employee. Altogether not a bad catch at all.

"And you're looking for work down here?" I ask, surprised.

Ralpho fidgets uncomfortably. "If I find something here, she can put in for a transfer."

Maybe I should put in for a transfer. It's been my experience that debt collectors, like social diseases, have a way of coming back in ever more alarming forms. Could be I should meet Lillian's plane with luggage in hand. I can tell her I feel a *call* to be at our mother's bedside, so could she put my airfare on one of her credit cards for now? It'll be a month before she discovers that my flight was to Amsterdam.

Arriving at one of Dongmen's trendier *dim sum* restaurants, Ralpho and I claim a balcony table overlooking the street, and he nods approvingly at the view of the busy plaza below. "I didn't expect to see so many people out," he says. "From what you hear in Beijing, that pneumonia stuff has this whole province shut down."

"I'm hearing the same thing about Beijing," I say.

"Rumors," replies Ralpho. "New one every day."

"The big pastime around here is boiling vinegar. It's supposed to disinfect the air in your apartment. If you don't die from the fumes first."

"Die?" asks Ralpho.

"Three so far," I say. "People are sticking their heads into the pan and inhaling for ten minutes at a time."

"Stupid fucking Chinese," says Ralpho.

We select a few dishes from a rolling cart, and I pull out my personal wooden chopsticks.

Ralpho stares at them. "You carry your own?"

"Don't you?" I say.

"Don't they get . . . dirty?"

"I put them through the clothes washer every now and then," I tell him.

Ralpho's still staring. "That should work."

"It has to work at least as well as whatever they're doing in the kitchen."

Ralpho examines his plastic chopsticks unhappily for a moment then shrugs and digs in. "How's the novel coming?" he asks.

"Great," I reply.

Bernie just asked me to send him another copy of the manuscript. He'd left his copy in the back seat of a Going Downtown? Taxi. Actually I'm surprised that he left the office with it at all, unless he's using it to wrap fish.

The first round of *dim sum* is pickled something or other with something raw on top. The second round is boiled something or other with something fried on top. I'm learning about Chinese cuisine.

"How's it going with the ETs and gun control?" I ask Ralpho.

He doesn't look up from his *dim sum*. Wrong question.

A young woman passes our table in a sheer black dress, and Phoebe Sternbaum flashes through my mind. She did finally return my phone call. Twice. Now I'm the one not returning hers. After the wedding thing, we met once for lunch, but I don't know. All she wants to do is rant about Hah-row and I haven't been able to redirect her. I no longer attend Happy Learner English Salon. They're slow payers and anyway I'm ineligible for the door prizes.

"You ever read the news?" asks Ralpho. There's a little sauce on his moustache.

I shake my head.

"Saddam met a UN deadline today," I'm told. "The White House was hoping he'd miss it. We want to stomp the living shit out of him, which I suppose we will anyhow."

I refill Ralpho's glass with Hsingtao before my own, following local custom, and ask, "Do you really think we're securing the oil reserves to go after China and North Korea?"

Ralpho's pale blue eyes grab mine. "Did I say that?"

"You wrote it in an email."

He looks stunned. After a moment, he adjusts his glasses and shrugs. "That must've been before I found out it's true."

"So it's true?" I say.

Ralpho sets down his chopsticks and lights a cigarette with dramatic lethargy. "You know me. I like to have a beer and bat the breeze. Sometimes I talk to somebody who knows a few things. Sometimes that somebody gives me a message to pass along to somebody else. I'm not here looking for a job, okay? My wife's terrified of that pneumonia shit. I'd have to knock her out to get her on the plane."

I gaze at Ralpho uncertainly.

"What I'm about to tell you," says Ralpho, "stays here, at this restaurant. Don't ask me about it later, especially at your apartment. Okay?"

"Someone's sending me a message?"

Ralpho taps a nonexistent ash. "He's an okay guy. If he says he's doing you a favor, he's probably doing you a favor. It's kind of cool, actually. The Chinese are terrified of you. It has to do with the ESP stuff. Ever since you and your sister got here, China's remote viewing program has been down. Can't receive, can't send. They're trying to figure out what you two are doing."

I'm still gazing uncertainly. "We aren't doing anything."

Ralpho nods. "We know that, but they don't. Neither do the North Koreans. Here's the thing. Everybody and his dog knows that you guys worked for that lab with the NSA connections. When they scanned your passports in Beijing, flags went up. Now suddenly China's RV protocols aren't working. You connect the dots."

"I think that's called jumping to conclusions."

"They're taking it pretty seriously."

"Shit," I say, falling back in my chair. "Good thing Lillian's in Memphis."

"That's the other part," says Ralpho. "When your sister left and you stayed, that kind of worried them a little. Maybe you two are constructing some kind of information pipeline. They're trying to hack in now."

I blink thoughtfully. "This is some truly amazing, paranoid . . . harebrained . . ."

"It's the most bizarre thing," says Ralpho a bit too happily.

"So what are we supposed to do?"

Ralpho sharpens the end of his cigarette against the ashtray. "Nothing. Stay put. Where you live is good 'cause you're surrounded by people and there's guards. Don't go anywhere alone. Don't trust new people. Just hang tight for now. Our guys are keeping an eye on things."

"Would you like to define 'our guys?'"

"I'm telling you everything I can tell you. Just keep a low profile, okay? Especially for the next few weeks."

"Why the next few weeks?"

"That's the other, other part." Ralpho shifts forward in his chair and lowers his voice. "There's a lot of political shit going on in Beijing. It looks like a regime change. Three guys are jockeying for prime minister and party chairman. The smart money's on Wen Jiabao, but it could shift in a second. The point is, everybody's on edge. All the cliques suspect you and your sister of working against them because they know you aren't working for them.

"When everybody's on edge," says Ralpho, pausing for effect, "people can get hurt. So, no sudden changes in habits. No plane tickets. No phone calls. Just sit tight till this thing blows over."

"How long should that be?" I ask.

"However long it takes for China to get a new leader. And watch what you say, okay? You never know who you're talking to." Ralpho toys with his cigarette for a moment. "Like when some stranger steps forward and offers you a job, for instance. Don't you wonder why?"

I give him a stare. "You're talking about Bellamy."

Ralpho doesn't reply.

"Little round glasses?" I say. "Hooked nose?"

Ralpho nods. "He uses lots of names. I'd be careful around him. Belongs to Wen Jiabao. Everything you say goes into a report."

As Ralpho finishes his cigarette, I try to think of a sensible question. I can't say I'm entirely surprised about Bellamy. Lately he's been pressuring me to move back to my dumpster's-hiney apartment, whatever that's about. Probably so his faction-mates can rummage through my underwear drawer every time I leave the place. I'm increasingly curious as to what Ralpho might know about a certain little corner drugstore called Hydrangea Laboratories, but my mouth can't quite form the words. How do I know that Ralpho doesn't report to the Venusians?

The lonely life of a pawn. Monitored. Coveted. Just generally fussed over until things become tedious and it's time to simplify the board.

"So that's it?" I say.

"That's it."

"What about Lillian?"

Ralpho looks at me in surprise. "Don't tell her. Don't tell anybody. And for the love of God, don't let your sister get on a plane to Beijing."

"I don't feel so good," I tell my glass of Hsingtao.

"I'm not surprised," says Ralpho. "They've been throwing everything they've got at you, pal. I have no idea what that means, exactly. Do you?"

"How the hell would I know? I'm not trained in psychic warfare."

Ralpho eyes me appraisingly. "If I were you, I'd talk to somebody who is."

20

To my credit, I have refused all invitations from door-rapping chauffeurs, formally attired or no, since that mythical warm Memphis night. And I *never* proceed past the room of rotating boxes, no matter the wealth redistribution that beckons from beyond.

Still I often find myself roiling once more within the smoldering Miles, those shadowy depths, the tastefully placed spotlights of that self-contained Eden that seemed to belong so fully and exclusively to me. I'm grateful those beautiful women had not been covered with coy metallic paint or pop-art images. No apologies whatsoever to *art*, whatever that is and whatever it's worth. There is no meaningful aesthetic beyond a single woman at a single moment. Just put a light on her and shut the fuck up.

The unmistakable star that night was a tight rosebud of a redhead with raging blue eyes. A breathless crowd stood as near as possible to the deeply-shadowed spot where this beauty, lit by two *very* thin beams of amber light, revolved slowly, her curves rising and falling seemingly of their own volition as successive wan meadows passed gracefully into and out of the light.

Her folded white legs were short and shapely, one knee raised near the chest, the other turned out, her inner thighs spread as generously as a late-night banquet, emphasizing the broad, taut groin muscles and the rare delicacy they framed. When *that* platter rolled into view, soft oohs and aahs broke out, for, as the light swept across the red-haired woman, it was gradually revealed that hers was a lovely, full yet virginal vulva, its smile demurely closed within a fine auburn mist. One rotation of the box required three minutes. I stayed for fourteen rotations.

I should have stayed all night.

I received a reply from Miriam. Yes, one of the companies I mentioned, Harcourt Pharmaceuticals, does advertise in *Magazine Mariposa*. Heavily. I no longer know what's worse, being paranoid or having actual evil plotters out to get me, but it seems we're looking at one or the other.

There's a fresh email from Lillian. She's going ahead with declaring our mother insane. "There's no real alternative. Stuart says we can have everything signed in a few days. Then I'll be on the plane as fast as I can. Promise, promise, promise!"

I decided it wouldn't hurt to ask Bernie to overnight me a bottle of meds. I can't pay for it, but he and I go back a long way. Maybe he could also throw in a decent German-made pencil. Meanwhile, I'm writing with a bad gel pen and doing a Chinese herbal remedy for "the nervous of mind and disorder."

"Oh, Ju-wen, it's you."

Marilyn stands before me, an over-full tray in her hands. I should have known better than to sit alone in the lunchroom. I've been going over my notes concerning a certain corporation with nine ugly heads and at least as many agendas.

"Why, Marilyn. Won't you please *join* me?"

"Oh, I don't want disturb," she says, staring at my journal.

"Not at all," I say, flipping it closed.

Marilyn places her tray opposite mine but refuses to sit. "You don't have soup. I go get for you."

"I don't want any."

"In China, we believe—"

"I don't *want* any."

Reluctantly she takes a seat. "Here, you can have mine."

"Marilyn, just eat your goddamn lunch."

"Ju-wen," she giggles, "I think you always so naughty. Why you always so naughty?"

"It's my contribution."

The final word whistles handsomely, as my maxillary first premolar crown is once more out. Last night I was taking a bite from the tar-baby of all chocolate Buddhas—made in North Korea, if that tells you anything—and before I understood what was happening to me, Tar Buddha had yanked out the crown and it had fallen down my throat. Furious, I threw the remainder of the Buddha out the kitchen window. There's now four hundred *plus* dollars in jewelers' gold touring my upper intestine. The next few days will be existential, to say the least. I now carry a folded plastic bag in my pants pocket alongside my personal wooden chopsticks.

I watch Marilyn lift a spoonful of soup and give it a timid taste, eyelids fluttering. Her face seems a little puffy today, beginning somewhere around the sandal straps. Her mouth looks like it's worried about something. Marilyn's upper lip makes a kind of beak when she's worried.

"Today my throat so *hurt*," she complains. "Last night I have the window open. This I think make me very ill."

I watch her take a handful of hair and throw it behind her. Chinese women haven't yet learned the toss-the-hair. "My son never like the soup, too, always fight so much with me, make me so angry. Don't want to study the school, just watch the TV, go play with some boys. I think he just hate me."

Her eyes narrow. "I tell him I no make divorce, father make divorce, but he love his father so much. I wish go back my home Guangzhou, but just have the job here Shenzhen."

"You're from Guangzhou?" I ask, re-opening my journal. "Have you ever heard of the Many Flavours Company?"

Marilyn brightens. "Is make the cigarette. Everybody Guangzhou know this."

"Do they offer tours?" I ask.

She looks puzzled.

"Tours," I say. "Tourists? Exit through the gift shop?"

"Is just make the cigarette. Why you ask me this?"

"I'm considering taking up smoking. Do you know anyone who works at Many Flavours?"

Marilyn doesn't, but I write down the name and number of a friend of hers, a Guangzhou manpower consultant who calls herself Eisenhower. "She went to school with me together," Marilyn smiles, "is know everything about the factory Guangzhou."

I close the journal and watch Marilyn suck down her steel-belted Chinese cabbage. That's more than I could do. I'm not looking forward to the afternoon. I have only one class remaining, but it's on the dreaded fifth floor. Lillian was shocked to learn that she/we have classes on the top floor. "Oh, my God," she gasped on her bunny phone. "They keep all the worst kids on the fifth floor. It's like they're trying to hide them. You better talk to Tree."

"I'm talking to Tree hourly," I answered, not that it's helping much. Mostly I get lectures on how poignant is my every moment with these precious and impressionable little divine masters in training. I don't think Tree's kids are passing one-liter cans of toluene along the back row. The afternoon class was so bad yesterday I asked Joe about the school's disciplinary policy. He smiled brightly and said, "You can do whatever you like."

The Splendid Make Vague Articulation of Inscrutable and Authority.

I told Joe I'd just do whatever I liked.

He liked this answer.

"That means he doesn't give a shit what you do," said Lil, "so long as he doesn't have to deal with it. Listen, there's no disciplinary policy at that school. Everyone pretends there's no problem, just like they pretend the students are learning. It's a joke, Julian. You can't take it seriously. Relax. Enjoy it."

Relax. Enjoy.

Eisenhower's phone number comes at a price. Before Marilyn leaves the lunchroom table, I find myself hooked into accompanying her on a shopping mission after school Friday. But she did supply me with one additional piece of information: the Many Flavours Company is rumored to conduct genetic experiments with tobacco strains more addictive than opium. I know a few hundred high-school students who'd like to volunteer as research subjects. When probed for more, Marilyn batted her eyelashes and bore her empty tray away with as much pelvic sway as she could muster.

Throwing good time after bad, I waste another ten minutes staring at my scribbled, hatched, and crosshatched notes, whose lines and arrows describe a corporate structure not very unlike a Hydra in appearance. Eight affiliated companies—one of them the Many Flavours Company—encircle and feed into a central entity, Hydrangea Laboratories Inc., which one assumes is the head that does not die but only mopes somewhere beneath an igneous stone.

I try to make all this add up to something, but it neither adds nor subtracts. Hopefully it doesn't multiply. The lunchroom is practically empty when I rise to mope my way toward Lil's lone afternoon class.

At least I get to share an office with Bobby, who passes time between classes singing along with DVDs of the Peking Opera. His hands are flying around, his reading glasses sliding down his nose, his eyes pleading with the totally queened-out transvestite on the computer screen. The other teachers meanwhile pretend to prepare lesson plans, eyelids drooping as Bobby rises to his feet, issuing a mournful lament equal parts Lord Byron and Tammy Wynette. "Bobby I think is very happy today," Trish deadpanned this morning. "Is almost destroy the light bulb."

It was Bobby who explained to me the school's no-smoking policy. If you can call it that. Between classes, clouds of white smoke *billow* from the windows of the boys' room on each floor. The corridors are open-air, so everybody can see it. The staff's response? To never go near the boys' rooms. By unspoken agreement, the male teachers use the john on the first floor exclusively, where students never go. It took some prodding to get this out of Bobby. No one else was present in the office, but he still lowered his voice to tell me, "Students are not allowed to smoke at the school.

It's a very serious offense. After only one violation, the student will be sent away permanently. Well, no teacher wants to have this kind of trouble. You will destroy his whole future. Maybe there's bad trouble with the whole family because of this. And *all* the boys smoke, so what can anyone do? Already you cannot teach them. If you do not let them have their cigarette every one hour, maybe they will throw you out of the window of the school."

Made sense to me.

Personally, I pee wherever I like, including on Joe's desk. The first time I walked into an upper-story john, something like twenty-five cigarettes went flying into squat toilets, some of which were occupied. It didn't take the students long to figure out the American Teacher doesn't give a sweet-and-sour damn. Now they make jokes about me as I wizzle. I can tell.

I suppose I'm in a mood. Not only is my life in jeopardy in more ways than Wiley E. Coyote knows anything about. Not only are Lil's four and five daily English Conversation classes heading south like Sherman in early spring—the boys at the rear of the class are no longer even pretending; they're playing cards and swapping Game Boys and I think toying with their little yellow give-the-happiness.

Not only am I reduced to playing a daily round of Go Fish if I ever wish to see my maxillary premolar crown again. Not only is Marilyn clearly stalking me *and* I've agreed to accompany her shopping. Not only am I rationing my meds so severely I no longer remember why I'm taking them. Now Bellamy is threatening to take back my key to the dumpster's-hiney apartment unless I return there.

And then there's the Ralpho material. Yesterday, as I put him on his plane, Ralpho leaned toward me and whispered, "They're watching us right now, you know." I think they were also smelling us right now. Ralpho was wearing an entire bottle of Old Spice.

At the last moment, he asked me whether I might be able to hook him up with Tree. "Just to meet her," he said bashfully. "I've listened to Shatrina forever, man. She was the one who first turned me onto how second-matrix birth issues tie into crude-oil prices. I'd never have made that connection myself."

"How did you know that Tree is Shatrina?" I asked.

"The voice. There's only one voice like that, dude."

I frowned, trying to recall a moment when Ralpho and Tree were in the same room. "Shatrina's very busy," I told him. True, actually. A Chinese friend is helping her upgrade her website, making all her old shows available for download.

Also, Ralpho snores. Big surprise there. All things being equal, though, he left me with some Vietnamese mushroom spores that he described as *really* interesting.

And then there's the Lillian material. This morning she told me on the phone, "I'm kind of seeing somebody. We've gone out three times. He's a tax accountant."

"How tall is he?" I asked.

"*Why* is that always the first thing you want to know? Adrian is very sweet, and we're having a very nice time together."

And stepladders are inexpensive.

"Doo, what's going on with you?" my sister asked before hanging up. "I know there's something you're not telling me."

"There's always something I'm not telling you, Lillian. It's called healthy boundaries. You might look into that sometime."

I wanted to tell her to stop fooling around with lower story bean-counters and get her ample bee-hind back to Shenzhen, but I can't quite dismiss the possibility that Ralpho could be right about not booking any flights right now. Even a broken clock is right twice a day.

She says one of Mom's blood-pressure meds is in the mail.

Entering Room 506, I toss the clipboard onto the desk and watch my afternoon class congeal before me like so much sleep-deprived yellow goo. Tree says the toughest time of the day is right after lunch. Personally, I'm ready, having recently downed enough ma huang to incapacitate a rhino, or at least help him burn off those unsightly love handles.

Awaiting the bell, I watch one of the major fifth-floor warlords swagger into the room and drop into a chair at the rear of the room. I've learned this fellow's given name is Bang, which rhymes with *bang*. He's tall for a Chinese, maybe five-ten, which could explain the preoccupation with lunch-period basketball. Like most fifth-floor boys, Bang comes to class pumping so much adrenaline you could use him for a right-wing radio host. He seems to be going for the Japanese toy-boy look, with orange-tinted hair that flirts with his collar and describes little arrows before each ear.

Today Bang occupies himself by flicking his fingers into the purse of the girl seated in front of him. She moves it to some other place, and Bang reacquires it, despite her best sullen efforts. Actually, the purse in question is the first I've seen on this campus. I'd assumed they'd long ago been banned, right along with lipstick, original thought, and B.O. There is no B. O. in this country. Thought you'd want to know. You can't buy a stick of underarm deodorant anywhere in China. The girl with the purse is *itsy* small and quite possibly sultry beneath the baggy uniform. I'm surprised not to have noticed before.

Finally the bell sounds, or rather begins. In China, school bells set in like a spell of weather. As I wait it out, Nancy Drew smiles toothily up at me from the front row. That would be Lillian's pie-faced private student, now my very own. At our recent tutoring session, Nancy Drew informed me that my country of origin is going to war with Iraq because our citizenry is too fat for the present continent. "Ev'ybody my school know this," she said happily, grabbing my middle and giving it a few shakes.

If she touches me again, I'm going to sit on her head till I hear it crack.

Finally the late bell ceases and I draw a breath, but before *good morning class* can leave my lips, I hear these words snarled in perfect African American dialect:

"You keep your *fucking* hands off my shit or I be on your ass like green on grass, you evil rice-eating motherfucker!"

Everyone in the room turns to stare at the itsy girl seated in front of student Bang, whose eyes now regard her with astonishment. Itsy, fully turned in her chair, has morphed into something truly menacing, her mini-ass lifted off the seat as though she's about to spring for Bang's left-frontal inguinal node. As suddenly, this girl, fully Chinese in appearance, is back in her chair facing forward, eyes demurely down. The whole class gives her an elongated and approving, "OoooOOO-OOOoooooooooooh."

"Good morning, class," I say, and everyone stands.

I think I'm in love.

21

In this morning's foggy, foggy dew, two packages arrived from the States. One, quite small, contained a sample of Mom's blood-pressure medication. I gave it a sniff (no odor) and placed it on top of the TV to later pass along to Bellamy. The other package was from Bernie. Inside were ten free-sample packets of my medication. Cheap-ass Bernie wouldn't put a bottle on my tab. Enclosed as well was a very nice letter on Bernie's agency letterhead saying how much he's enjoyed our professional relationship but he feels the need to yada-yada-yada.

Who needs him.

Funny thing. I'd never noticed before but each of the free samples has an H punched into it. Reading the packaging, I learn that my medication is manufactured by Harcourt Pharmaceuticals. Or maybe that isn't a funny thing. I couldn't quite bring myself to place one of them in my mouth. Instead I took another nervous and disorder capsule and a handful of ma huangs. The sample meds I tossed into a kitchen drawer except for one, which I placed on the TV beside Mom's blood-pressure med. I'm going to pass both of them along to Bellamy's brother.

So began the day.

For some reason, at mid-afternoon I'm following Marilyn up a stack of escalators to the sixth floor of Women's World and into a three-acre wood of brassieres. I'm instantly on guard. There's nothing a man can say in the brassiere section of a department store that isn't exactly wrong. At least there's no saxophone music. Yet. A saleswoman comes forward, and she and Marilyn speak at length while I pretend to be invisible, idly browsing the complete line of ladies' undergarments in University of Alabama crimson.

Roll Tide.

According to Chinese thinking, there's an increased susceptibility to ill fortune during one's birth year. It helps to wear something red. Want to guess the age of your favorite Chinese human? When you see red undies on the clothesline, round your best guess to the nearest twelve.

Two college-aged women walk past, and I'm surprised to see a "Peace" button pinned to the lapel of each. Lil tells me anti-war protests are worldwide this week. "Isn't it amazing?" says Lil. "Eleven million people demonstrate for peace, and we're just totally fucking ignoring it. We've become a nation so obsessed with vengeance that it doesn't even matter who anymore. Did Iraq do Nine Eleven? Who cares? They're brown people with their asses in the air. Go get 'em. I have to really wonder how long before we go get China. They're like this huge red vacuum-cleaner sucking up American jobs, and you *know* we've got to be fucking with them somehow. Remember the tobacco fungus in Cuba? That was us."

Actually, at the time I was remembering the raised ass of that *itsy* Chinese schoolgirl. I liked how her little pelvis tilted back as she dog-cussed that evil rice-eating motherfucker behind her. I also enjoyed how her upper lip flared at two precise points when she timidly approached my desk after this morning's class as the other students swarmed the doors. "Can I talk to you?" she said. "God, I'm sorry. I guess I picked up that whole bad-mouth thing back in Westmont."

"You're from Westmont?"

That's a suburb of LA. Not the best one.

"Born in Westmont, lived my whole life in Westmont," she replied, oozing gritty inner-city charm. "I been in China less than a month and this place is, like, playing with my *head*, man—I mean, Mr. Mancer. My daddy don't speak a word of English, and I most definitely don't speak no Chinese. Ain't *nobody* I can talk to."

Her eyes reached out to me. Asian eyes. From a one-hundred-percent Asian face.

"Who the hell are you?" I said.

"Rui Long. That's my name from my daddy's side."

Rhymes with everyone's favorite governor of Louisiana.

"What are you doing here?"

"My mama sent me here to live with my daddy. Ain't seen him since I was six months old. So now I'm supposed to live with him. Whatever. Ain't nothing I can do about it."

I think that would make Rui Long, while clearly underage in the United States, fully adult in China.

I love numbers.

The two women with the Peace buttons head for the escalators, and I note that neither is wearing a bra. Wrong floor, girls.

Memphis's big peace vigil is tonight. "We're going to burn candles," Lil told me this morning, "and envision a world where we can all sit down and discuss chemical warfare and genocide like civilized people."

"Burn one for me," I told her.

Actually I have my own little heart-project. Counseling displaced American schoolchildren IHW. In Harm's Way. I told Itsy she can visit me at the American Teacher's Apartment anytime she feels troubled. And it's after dark. And that little purse of hers has a photo ID.

The Women's World saleswoman hurries forward with a boxed brassiere in bone white, and Marilyn fingers it with distaste. I'm keeping an eye on the escalator. When you think about it, what better place for a man to learn if he's being tailed than on the sixth floor of Women's World? If even one man dismounts the escalator and begins browsing the merchandise—see what I'm saying? Of course, Ralph O'Malley has more conspiracy theories than a flea has knees. And he uses *there* for *their*.

The saleswoman runs for another bra and Marilyn checks her phone for messages. Bored, I lean against a counter of boxed pantyhose and try to recall the last time I slid a pair down a fair lady's legs. Nothing comes readily to mind. My brand of woman goes in more for wool hiking socks. I sigh and loose my imagination, letting it settle once more on a warm Memphis night and a room full of my favorite rotating rockettes.

It's almost as though I were there in the Miles once more, browsing lurid limbs beneath the unhurried ooze of a muted trumpet. Even in my trance of the fourteen full rotations, I was more than aware of the purple light spilling through an open door at the rear of the room. Beyond that door lay the real attraction. Reluctantly I blew a kiss to the rosebud smile and sauntered toward the purple threshold.

The dark silhouette of a man blocked my path. "Mr. Mancer," I heard, "we weren't expecting you."

"I wasn't expecting myself," I replied cheerfully, "but it's awfully nice to be here."

"Do you intend to play?" asked the same voice.

"Of course."

Always say of course.

After a moment, the silhouette said, "This evening's activities are underwritten by a Mr. Vionetti. He would like to know whether your . . . unique talents would place you at any unfair advantage. Of course, he trusts your candor completely."

Returning the black-out shades to my face, I said, "Please tell Mr. Vi—, uh—"

"Vionetti."

"—Mr. Vionetti that my talents are far more meager than he supposes."

Bowing slightly, the silhouette stepped to one side. "You'll find chips at the bar. Please take as many as you'd like."

"Thank you," I said, hurrying on my way.

As many as I'd like. I was once told I could take as many white-frosted cupcakes as I liked. I was eleven years old, and it was Jeremy Simmons's birthday party. Yes, the same Jeremy. I liked twenty-seven white-frosted cupcakes. I could have stopped at liking fourteen or nineteen, but I didn't particularly like either one of those number. Twenty-one was a fairly decent option, but it held resonances of both three and seven, each of them a prime that, when combined with my age at the time, formed further monsters. Twenty-two was even worse, and so it went. They pumped my stomach four times. I wasn't crazy about that number, either.

Suddenly Marilyn announces, "We can go," and dashes past me. Following her toward the escalators, I note Marilyn's not-altogether-bad legs. Solid. Functional. Blue veins clearly visible behind the knees.

This morning I gave a call to Eisenhower, Marilyn's old college roomie. Calls, actually. Dialing long distance is complicated here. Before finally connecting to Guangzhou, I roused a man out of bed in Bucharest. In the end, Eisenhower wasn't able to offer much illumination vis-à-vis the Many Flavours Company. Foreign investors are buying into everything. Why not tobacco? "Is make money," as she put it. And the rumors about naughty genetic experiments? "Everybody hear this, too," said Eisenhower. "I don't know."

I don't know, either. Before hanging up, Eisenhower asked if I was "very love" Marilyn. When I replied in the polite negative, she said, "You come visit Guangzhou, I show you the good place eat sheep intestines."

But can I call her Ike?

Marilyn stops suddenly to pinch a blouse, and I practically collide with her. The blouse, I note, is identical to the one she's wearing. Conservative to the point of nonexistent. Now something in a silky fire-engine red catches her eye, and Marilyn lifts the price tag then flings it.

"So expensive," she complains, heading toward the exit. "I too old buy beautiful clothes like some girl. I have the son, have to worry about everything."

Marilyn stops just short of the automatic glass doors and turns to stare at me. "You have son?" she demands.

"No."

"Daughter?"

I shake my head.

Marilyn says, "You marry four times, no children?"

"There are lots of Americans," I tell her, "with four children and no marriages. It evens out."

We reenter the heat and glare of midday. Over her shoulder, Marilyn says, "I know what you mean, Ju-wen. Chinese have the expression, is like teach your grandmother drink eggs.'"

"Nicely put," I tell the blue veins.

Marilyn and I round a corner, and a small shop comes into view. Inside, a teenage boy slouches in a folding chair. Above him is a sign I've seen all over Shenzhen. A drawing of a human face is dotted with red acupuncture points. I ask Marilyn about it.

"Oh, this can take away," says Marilyn, stopping to point out a mole on her right cheek. "Also take away the . . ." she points to her behind. "Something there hurt very bad. You have this?"

I shake my head a bit too emphatically.

Marilyn fires a series of questions at the young man. He answers listlessly. Again she points out the mole on her cheek. "He say this mean somebody want me be very unhappy," she says. "I know is my husband." Marilyn indicates a smaller mole beside her left eyebrow and says, "This one mean maybe some problem with health. This one good luck," she says, pointing out a dot on the bridge of her nose. "He take off other two, forty yuan. You want ask him something?"

"Something what?" I say.

Marilyn speaks to the young man, who examines me from a distance. Now he's speaking to Marilyn. I don't care what he says. My face is spotless.

"He say," she reports, "you have the much trouble from women. Also somebody want steal your brain."

"I'm sorry?"

"How you say? Steal something inside. We say *nao zi*."

"Someone wants to steal my mind?"

She nods. "He fix this for you. Fix the women too. Sixty yuan."

I look at the slouching teenager. That sounds like a lot of fixing for four bucks.

I watch Marilyn take a seat. The sidewalk surgeon opens a tiny bottle filled with clear liquid, pulls a hooked needle from inside, wipes it once on a cotton ball and now sticks it into Marilyn's face. She's in agony. The boy pulls out the mole in about two seconds, wipes the needle on the same cotton ball, and goes after the second one. As Marilyn whimpers, he dabs something pale yellow—wood putty by the look of it—into the holes he's made in Marilyn's face. The whole procedure takes less than a minute. Before we're out of there, another woman is in the chair. I watch the boy pick up the same needle, same bottle, same everything. All he changes is the cotton ball. I ask myself how many bits and pieces of other peoples' moles are now inside Marilyn's head. To say nothing of something-there-hurt-very-much.

Really *is* like teach your grandmother drink eggs.

As Marilyn convalesces dizzily, I buy us each an ice-cream sandwich, and she and I stand in the shadow of an florescent-orange skyscraper to eat them. Though we're barely into the Year of the Ram, Shenzhen feels like midsummer Memphis.

I gaze into the window of a pet shop and spot a stack of empty aquariums. I ask myself whether I might be able to persuade Ralpho's mushroom spores to get happy in one of those things. All I really need is a dark corner, a little rice flour and a few weeks of wet weather. Failing the wet weather, I could just leave the top off the water-boiler for a few days. As I recall, the last time I ate a mushroom I became convinced I was a wealthy Republican philanthropist. I wrote a string of checks to front organizations for paramilitary groups I couldn't possibly have known anything about. Fortunately, I later found out I'd written them all with my forefinger.

I finish my ice-cream sandwich and use my bottle of Bini-hana purified water to wash it down. While I'm at it, I toss down three ma huangs and two nervous-and-disorder capsules.

"You take some Chinese medicine?" asks Marilyn, still eating.

"Relaxes me," I tell her.

"Only think too much," she says. "Think all the time not good for health."

I nod. I visited Bellamy's office yesterday and handed him the two recently arrived tablets, one marked R and the other H. I think way too much.

Before I could get away from Bellamy, he reminded me that his company had provided me with a *very* fine dumpster's-hiney apartment now going to waste. I reminded him that his company owes me a considerable amount of money. Now we're both reminded.

Oh. Word came this morning from New York. Someone has read *The End of Day*. Including my new final chapter. And has received it with some excitement. His name is Ahmed Massoud Monzur, and he represents the Going Downtown? Taxi Company. "I found the story lost inside of my cab," Monzur emailed me last night. "At first I decide to just wait until somebody will call me first, then I open and read it. I can not [*sic*] stop. I think you are great writer and also very much disturb. Unless you don't mind my say this to you, I'm so sorry but please to come get this very soon or eels [*sic*] I am afraid my family reads it too. That is all. Ahmed Massoud Monzur."

I have my blurb for the back cover.

"We go Kuang now," says Marilyn, tossing her ice cream wrapper onto the sidewalk. I try not to stare at it.

Approaching the nearest escalator of the teeming five-story anthill called Kuang Electronic Emporium, Marilyn and I are instantly surrounded by five young men who whisper urgently, "DVD." At the top of the escalator, we melt into a densely packed labyrinth of tiny overflowing kiosks. Marilyn, both arms wrapped tightly around her purse, bulls her way toward the second escalator. I follow, clutching the wallet inside my pocket. Three escalators later, we arrive at a tiny kiosk with a curtained rear chamber. There behind the curtain, Marilyn negotiating, I purchase two thousand dollars' worth of software for roughly four and a half bucks.

Screw Bill Gates. And his foundation.

I also come away with a copy of the movie *Cast Away.* Here's Tom Hanks stranded half a globe away from Memphis chatting with a volleyball. Ask me if I can relate.

"Follow my blue veins," says Marilyn, heading back toward the escalator. Or words to that effect.

There are no privacy walls separating the squat toilets at Shenzhen High School of Electronic Excellence. Just by the way. I'm doubtless giving rise to a whole new round of speculation concerning the personal habits of Westerners. *Do they all do it in plastic bags and carry it home?* Why yes, we do. Thanks for inquiring.

Morale seems to be tanking back at the English Department. The school has a new headmaster who, according to the latest roundup of murmurs, is not coming across with the little incentives the previous headmaster had dispensed rather freely. The new guy, Bobby has confided, seems to be a legitimately high-minded administrator, but what mere man can accomplish great things alone? Bobby didn't answer his own question but only arched his graying eyebrows. Think all the grand thoughts you want, seemed to be the drift, but neglect your people and sooner or later your tofu is left out in the wind.

As Marilyn and I ride the escalator back down to the street, I survey the multitude on their way up. In a moments' time, I've count fourteen people wearing gauze masks. The government of this country has no clue what to do about atypical pneumonia, and nobody wants to be the one who says it.

This stuff has spread to Thailand and Canada, and Beijing still hasn't acknowledged that it exists. The World Health Organization is starting to really raise a stinky about it.

Ana Manguella comes to mind. "Viruses are less living things," she said on a moving train, "than self-replicating codes that lack a braking mechanism. They just go on doing what they do, regardless of the consequences."

That tousled woman is *just* across the Sham Chun River in Hong Kong. I can't believe I came away without her email address.

"Oh, my God, it's Julian!"

Oh, my God, it's Tree Carter! Beside her is a nondescript Chinese man bearing two shopping bags. After the usual preposterous hugging demonstration that Tree requires, I introduce Marilyn and greet Cangming Xu, whom Tree has briefly mentioned. Xu (sounds like *shoe*) helps with her website. We shake hands, and I notice his cheap plastic watch. Practically the same as mine, actually.

You don't find dime-store timepieces on Asian men. I also note his khaki trousers and cotton shirt, the sleeves rolled to just below the elbows. Add a loosened tie, and this man could be running for office in Nantucket. Xu's accent is both Chinese and Australian. Tree has told me he's a Shanghai native who spends his free time Out Back conferring with native seers.

"We're on our way to Kuang's," says Tree. "We need some software for the website. You wouldn't believe what Mr. Xu is doing for my page, Julian. It's incredible."

"How incredible," I say.

Actually, I'm not thinking very clearly. I may have done too much ma huang this time. My knees seem to be speaking to each other in Brazilian Portuguese.

Marilyn poses a question to Xu in Mandarin. As he replies, Tree leans toward me and says, "We need to get Lillian back here as fast as we can, Jules. Something big's going down."

"Tell Mom," I say.

"I think you know this is not about your mother," says Tree.

"Tell Lil."

"I'm telling Julian because Julian is the one who needs to hear it," says Tree, fanning her smile with one hand. "It's starting, okay? Whatever it is, it's starting."

I separate my knees a little to cut down on the chatter.

"You can count on me," I tell Tree.

"Listen, you need to sit down with this Mr. Xu. The man is amazing."

"How amazing."

Maybe it's not in fact the ma huang. Maybe my nervous and disorder medication is finally kicking in.

Tree tugs on Xu's sleeve. "I got to get out of the sun, sweetie. Nice to meet you, Marilyn. You take care of yourself, Julian—and remember what I said."

Xu and I share a handshake. As he turns away, I notice a slight limp and recall being told that Xu has a wooden leg. Not a flesh-tone plastic prosthesis. No, an old-fashioned Captain Ahab wooden leg from the right knee down. Australian Eucalyptus. Which I suppose is admirable in its way.

"Your friend so *fat!*" Marilyn cries happily as we turn toward the bus stop. "Why is she so fat? I cannot believe. You and your sister so fat too, but she *so* fat."

"You have an excellent eye," I tell Marilyn. "Too bad it's at the center of your forehead."

"For what?" she asks.

"Foreskin. Forefather. Four gates to the city, halleloo. I think that's our bus."

Marilyn and I hurry to join some dozen others wedging themselves inside an already full city bus. I don't quite make it inside, and the door doesn't quite close, but we're underway. I think my ass is signaling for a right turn. A couple minutes of this and Marilyn and I change buses. Finally we stagger half-dead through the gate of Shenzhen High School of Electronic Excellence. For a change, the guard isn't asleep. He's playing sol. At her door, I thank Marilyn for the afternoon, and she giggles girlishly. "We go eat dinner sometime. What you like to eat?"

Involuntarily my eyes tip to the two swells beneath her blouse. "All of it."

"Okay," smiles Marilyn, looking away. "We do later."

22

Itsy's passport is somewhat reassuring. The official stamps on its pages corroborate her story of travel and travail. More to the point, she is precisely sixteen years old and so a consenting Chinese adult.

Returning the passport to Rui Long's small hands, I say, "The photo does you little justice, but what camera can capture the torment of the human heart or the lightning from a young woman's eyes? Have a seat."

Upon Itsy's arrival at this apartment scarcely a minute ago, I closed the door behind her and peered through Lillian's emerald curtains long enough to conclude that no one had noticed her arrival or else had not cared. And why should they? Many students live with their families in this dormitory and so come and go in their white-over-blues as a matter of course.

Rui Long drops her small amber body into the nearer settee chair and tosses her mane. "I *so* appreciate your letting me just show up like this, Mr. Mancer," she says. "I am seriously going out of my head."

"Call me Julian," I say, settling into the other chair.

The schoolgirl winces. "I don't know if I can call you that."

"Try it. Juuuuuuulian."

"Julian." She rolls her eyes. "Whatever. I told my father I was going to the supermarket. You know how I talk to him? I hold up something. So I hold up a grocery bag and say *go supermarket me now okay* and split before he can start with all his evil-ass—aw, man, I don't even know. My dad's just so totally disapproving. His whole family just does not get that I am not a little Chinaman or whatever. My mom's half-black and half-Thai, and my dad's totally Chinese. I just got my dad's side, and so what? They're like giving me stuff to eat I can't even recognize as food."

"Why'd your mother send you here?" I ask.

"She couldn't deal with me. I was always in some kind of mess. Finally she says my daddy sent for me. My daddy ain't sent for nobody or nothing. He *hates* my yellow ass. I'm sorry but it's true. Now I'm like, '*How* am I supposed to go to a Chinese school when I don't speak no Chinese?' But the guy at the embassy said my dad must've paid a huge bribe to get me in this school, so whatever."

I've learned already that Chinese-Americans are roundly scorned in this country, especially the young women. If you're not expert in Chinese culture, do not come over here in a yellow skin.

Rui Long's school jacket sags open, and I try not to stare at the contours of the thin white blouse, assuming there's anything there to see. Her dark eyes are blinking and darting every moment. When they hold my face for an instant, I feel as though neither eye is looking at me but at something just behind me. I almost want to turn around.

"What do your friends call you, Rui Long?"

"Back in Westmont, I'm Doo."

I stare at her. "Doo?"

"Short for Doodle. I'm all the time doodling on something. Nervous energy, I guess."

I'm still staring. "Does your father have a room for you?"

"I stay in his auntie's bedroom, or great auntie, or whatever in the world that woman is. In the same *bed* with her. I put my sleeping bag on the floor. I have to keep everything shut up inside my suitcase 'cause this Chinese lady's going through it every time I leave the room. I'm like *shit*, the winos back in Westmont live better than this."

Rui Long wilts. "Mr. Mancer, I'm really so sorry. I swear if I had anybody else to talk to—but from the first time I saw you, I don't know, I just felt like you were somebody I could trust."

The schoolgirl's sorrowful eyes rise to meet mine, and I go for a comforting smile. Hopefully she doesn't spot the fangs.

It's certain that Rui Long doesn't spot the gap where my missing gold maxillary first premolar crown should be. I now have a temporary. Tomorrow I re-visit Dr. Xylophone for my first fitting. There comes a time when you stop panning for gold in your rectum. A time when you by God break down and get fitted for a new crown. I can more or less afford one, as the Shenzhen Textbook Publishing Company has actually paid me in full. Just like Lil's school, they pay out in bright new bank notes so salmon-belly pink that Mao Zedong looks occidental.

Still, after all the dental work I'll be left a weensie bit short of the eighty-seven thou' I owe that debt collector. But he looked like a fellow with a good sense of humor.

"All this is my fault," moans Rui Long. "I *so* know that. But now what am I supposed to do? My momma won't take me back, and my daddy can't even talk to me. I don't even have no clothes. I got two pants and one . . ."

I let Rui Long ramble on, enjoying the small gravelly voice as it slides from dialect to dialect, Little Miss Valley Girl for a few lines, the Channel 6 news reporter for a bar or two, then she's back to the palm-lined bullet-riddled streets of LA. To witness *that* buffalo-wing jive coming from this perfect Chinese face is a novelty I'm not sure I'll ever quite get past.

" . . . I don't know, man," she concludes. "Like, I pulled a rune this morning—you know the runes?"

I nod.

"I have the Barbie deck. Sounds really dumb, I know, but sometimes it's just *so* right. I got the Mall Closed card. It's like I can't go forward, so I have to go back only I don't know if that means back to Westmont or—"

"I think your rune is telling you to focus inward on the native magic of your unique artistic voice," I reply authoritatively.

Rui Long's mouth sags opens, the lips sticking together momentarily. "That's *it*," she whispers. "Focus *inward*."

"Personally I use the GQ deck," I say. "Whatever works for you."

"My God," breathes Rui Long. "Mr. Mancer, you are just such a powerful finger pointing to the moon, if you know what I mean."

"I think you listen to *Shatrina*," I say dryly.

"Totally. Till my momma took away my radio, Shatrina was like my guiding light and shit."

"You know?" I say thoughtfully. "I think you're really stressed just now. *Doo*. I can see it in your aura. Lots of red and burnt-orange and just the slightest touch of mocha near the right earlobe."

"You read auras? Really?"

"I'm a ninth-degree master of a little-known school of Nepalese Foot Reiki. I don't accept students."

Shoving aside the small table, I say, "Give me your syzygy, I mean your left foot. Don't worry. I'm a professional."

"Geez, I've never had Reiki," Itsy says giddily, raising her foot. She's wearing heavy white sneakers with a wad of purple bubble gum on the left sole. Placing the heel between my knees, I begin to loosen the broad violet lacing, fully enjoying this now. Itsy's nylon socks are eggshell-thin. I force myself not to speculate on her taste in undergarments.

This is a client.

The laces thoroughly loose, the shoe surrenders to my hands and I toss it. An oaken smell rises, that of dried leaves on a November day. Grasping the toe of the sock, I slide it off the tiny foot, place my palm beneath the sole, close my eyes, and announce, "You are a very old soul."

I always start with you-are-a-very-old-soul.

Before I can say, "You have lived many lifetimes," I'm jolted by something quite unexpected. Though my eyes are closed, I clearly see the person seated before me. Not her exterior, but a vast constellation of glowing pinpoints of light.

Puzzled, I open my eyes. When I close them again, the array is still there. Before I can file this experience away under Strange But Not Presently Pertinent, I realize that the light display is richly embedded with information. Curious now, I focus for a moment on the inflow of what I can only describe as an *emanation* from the person before me. Suddenly the thought registers: this is a very old soul who has lived many lifetimes.

Stop it.

"You have lived many lifetimes," I say gravely but before I can continue, another realization intrudes, one less prescient than present. I know that the essence of this creature is severe and magnificent and not to be trifled with.

I file this information away under Stranger and Even Less Pertinent.

"Hold the arms of the chair," I order Rui Long.

She complies and I pull foot, chair and all, toward me. Itsy's naked heel now rests a scant inch away from something else severe and magnificent and not to be trifled with.

Rui Long giggles, enjoying this. "What else do you see in my aura?"

"Shhhh."

My fingers search for a pressure point along the second metatarsal, generally effective for stimulating the right nipple. I still can't say exactly what slumbers beneath that white poly-cotton blouse of hers, or rather how much of it. But I'm always willing to learn. Ah. Here's the pressure point. My fingertip circles it soothingly, imagining the supple corona of a rising nipple.

"Close your eyes," I command, "and take a deep breath."

The two almond eyes roll closed.

"Deeper. The biggest breath you can take."

Rui Long inhales and the open jacket parts a bit more. *Two* rising nipples appear through the thin poly-cotton. They are lower on her chest than expected. Pleasant discovery.

"Wow," she says. "I've never felt so . . ."

"Shhh," I say, pulling Itsy's foot slightly closer.

Oops. Too close.

The almond eyes open and blink, and the foot vanishes from my lap. "I gotta go."

"What? In the middle of your Nepalese Foot Reiki session?"

"I think my dad's looking for me. I mean, I know he is."

Quickly pulling on her sock and shoe, Rui Long bends to tie a violet shoelace, her thick hair nearly reaching the floor. I fight the urge to reach out and touch the glossy tresses. This is a very beautiful girl. Too bad she's sprinting for the American Teacher's Door.

"Thanks for the Reiki and everything, Mr. Mancer. I just— see you in class, okay? And I'll remember what you said about the native magic and stuff."

"Feel free to come again any time you feel—"

The door slams behind the itsy schoolgirl.

"—troubled."

23

When I left campus at lunch today, Phoebe's Buick was at the curb. The driver's window motored down, and Phoebe said, "Why you don't call me? I leave you two messages." The dark shades concealed her eyes but not her implacability. I muttered an excuse, not a very good one even by my standards.

"I want to tell you something," said Phoebe, "but not chase you around like some schoolgirl. You want talk to me, I eat dinner at Shanghai Hotel tonight. You come, you don't come, I don't care."

Up went the window and off she drove.

Women. What can I say. Listen politely to one or two of their hard-luck stories, and you see what it gets you. Besides, I have plans tonight.

I'm standing outside the open doorway of the American Teacher's Apartment, coddling my fourth gin sour of the evening and watching the sun put itself to bed in the pink hydrogen sulfide soup of the west. It's been a day. After Lil's four English Conversation classes—and my brush with Mrs. Sternbaum—I bused over to Primary School Focus Youth Shenzhen to help Tree with her balky satellite uplink. I carried along a few common fuses, which turned out to be all the situation required.

"Buy yourself a good voltage regulator," I told Tree. "Chinese voltage is all over the place."

"Praise Jesus Janus Aphrodite," she cried. "I could see myself walking into the hardware store and asking for a satellite uplink. Sit yourself down. I'll pour you some iced tea."

I willingly pulled back a chair. Tree's iced tea is not the typical exercise in prudery one encounters in restaurants these days but a liberally sugared and lemon-wedged delight of rattling ice cubes and wistful dreams of Old South front porches in late June. "I can only stay for a few minutes," I told her. "I'm working on a little project in Lil's kitchen. Making better use of the space."

Much better, in fact. Last night I'd walked home from Studebaker Supermarket with a small aquarium, a pair of disposable latex gloves, some stainless-steel tweezers, a veterinary syringe, five glass jars with lids and a package of freshly milled rice flour. This evening's plan involves hanging my strongest reading glasses on my nose, pulling the latex gloves onto my hands, lifting Ralpho's spore-print *delicately* from its envelope with the stainless-steel tweezers, and injecting myself with the rice flour.

Actually I need to check the online instructions once more, but with spring fast approaching with its daily thundershowers, how long can it be before mushrooms are sprouting from beneath my underarms? More than the usual number, I mean?

Tree took a seat at the table and I said, "So what's the story with you and that Xu guy?"

"*Mister* Xu," she replied crisply (still sounds like *shoe*), "has put my entire library of broadcasts on the website. You can listen, you can download, you can do anything you want. I'm extremely indebted to him."

"I'd say," I said, rattling my ice cubes, "that either the faint scent of romance is in the air or someone's burning a truck tire. Tell me, dear. Does that wooden leg have any common household uses?"

"Mr. Xu," said Tree, "may be the world's number one authority on Chinese astrology and numerology. And he knows a great deal about the Fibonacci sequence—more, in fact, than you. You owe it to yourself to talk to him."

"Ah," I said, "Mr. Xu and Mr. Fibonacci have met."

Fibonacci, for the uninitiated, actually Leonardo Pisano Bogollo, was the first modern thinker to notice that nature moves in predictable lurches. A typical seedling, for example, begins by making one leaf, then two, then three, then five, then eight, and so on, exactly the same sequence every time. What fascinated Fibonacci was that the next number always equals the sum of the previous two. This remains perfectly constant, even when the numbers reach into the hundreds of thousands. Not rocket science, perhaps, but pretty cool for thirteenth-century Italy.

Tree continued, "Our Mr. Xu has established absolute correlations between the Sequence and the development of human intelligence. His work shows that we are at the brink of a huge step forward. You know how when you plot the Sequence on the number grid, it makes a spiral?"

"I do."

"And that the spiral exactly matches the growth pattern of a nautilus shell?"

"And a sunflower," I said, "and planetary motions, and I think the national debt."

"Well, Mr. Xu says there are *very* clear numerical landmarks that show where we are right now, and—"

"Which is where?" I interrupt.

"You know exactly where," said Tree, feigning astonishment. "We are at the Three-three-three."

I set down my frosted glass. "Tree. Listen to me. There is no Three-three-three in the Fibonacci sequence. I don't know where you got that whole big wad of goo, but it's something less than fully baked, if you don't mind my saying. Besides which, Lillian is on the other side of the world and there's not one thing we can do about it."

"The devil may be in the details," said Tree, smiling, "but the angel is in the intention."

"I love all these little slip-joints in your theories," I complain. "If something doesn't tie together—hey, just insert a little Uncle Remus or nose hair of Nebuchadnezzar. Or better yet, conduct a little more in-*depth* research with our Mr. Xu and his wooden—what body part was it?"

Tree has another Mister back in Memphis, should you care to know it. Mr. *Carter*. I've never met the man, but Lil swears he's a mortician. "Let the dead bury the dead," Tree is said to have declared some years back when she picked up her purse and walked out on him. Evidently neither of the two seems capable of divorcing the other. Lil tells me they're actually very close in their way.

I'm a senior Assumptionist nun in my way.

I throw down the last of my fifth gin sour, gazing at the grey-brown goo of a western sky that recently promised me a sunset. Hurrying to set the empty glass in the sink, I wheel and grab my keys. Darkness is setting in and I need to make one more run to Studebaker Supermarket. I'm a bit low on gin. And ma huang. And vermiculite, which is supposed to be good for really frisky mycelium growth.

Exiting the gate, I wave to the two guards—both of them are awake and wearing pants—and walk past the spot where Phoebe's Buick intercepted me earlier today. I can't help but skirt around it. I don't know what's with that woman. Or with me. The ground seems to have subtly shifted beneath my feet. I find myself wondering why men put up with the negativity of a Phoebe Sternbaum.

It's hard to say, but something seems to happen to a woman when she hits that spot around thirty-two, thirty-three, somewhere in that faded and jaded spot. She's pissed about it and now her needle-like eyes are surveying the room in search of a man to blame it on. God help you if you happen to be sitting there. I don't think I was really *seeing* that before I looked up to discover that lively little sprout of a Rui Long perched on the edge of the American Teacher's Settee Chair.

So open. So pliant.

Not that I would place a mere teenager above a fully formed and self-arrived woman. What fully formed and self-arrived *man* would favor a sprig to a completely opened jasmine? A half-formed idea to a master's thesis? A giggle-box to a fine cello?

I'll let you know once I've thoroughly sampled each.

There was an article in a recent English edition of the *Beijing Daily*. A schoolteacher in Shaanxi Province was convicted of behaving in an untoward manner with one of his female students. The verdict came two days ago. They executed him this morning. I don't know why that comes to me just now.

As usual, I avoid the busy intersection approaching Studebaker Supermarket, turning instead onto a narrow side street. The unceasing noises of the inner city retreat as I'm closed in by the small sounds of apartment life drifting from open windows. On weekend nights, there's at least one major mah-jongg game in progress here, the tinkle of the tiles rising above the laughter of unseen women, their husbands away drinking beer at a neighborhood café. On this weeknight, aromas of dinner mingle with soft television sounds. As I turn a dogleg in the little lane, I'm surprised by the appearance of a surprisingly full moon between two high-rises. Asked Li Bai:

> The bright moon, how long has it shone,
> I ask the great sky, while lifting my cup.
> I cannot name where in the Heavenly Palace
> To place this miraculous night . . .

Or this untimely hard-on. I should never contemplate Rui Long as the moon is rising. Such a *gem* of a young woman and so in need of guidance. I admit I may have pushed things a tad during her first visit. In class today, Rui Long didn't so much as make eye contact. Well, give her a few days to digest everything she's going through just now. Soon enough, she'll heliotrope back in the direction of her true support.

Suddenly behind me is the roar of an eight-cylinder engine, and I move to the right as garish high-beams flood the little lane. Beside me, a police car abruptly stops and a uniformed officer steps out of the passenger door to block my way. I look upon a stocky middle-aged man with an arrogant smirk and a stump for a right arm. He uses his left hand to open the rear door of the cruiser and motion me to get inside.

"English teacher," I say, my thumb pointing toward Lil's school. "Diplomatic Immunity. Facial hair."

Ignoring my words, the officer spreads his feet, grabs me by the shirt collar, and yanks me forward while kneeing me in the groin. I bend forward with an *ooof* and he shoves me into the rear seat of the cruiser.

"American citizen!" I howl. "*Magazine Mariposa*! Best Southern Novel of 1999!"

The one-armed policeman seats himself beside me in the back seat, his dark eyes gleaming with menace.

"I swear to God," I tell him, "I haven't touched a hair on her head."

"Put inside your arm," says the officer.

"Put what inside my arm? Did you hear what I just said?"

He's holding a plastic leaf-and-garden bag. "Put inside your arm."

"Listen to me. Call Miriam Goldfarb at—"

The officer behind the wheel turns to backhand me hard across the face. Stunned, I don't put up much of a fight as the one-armed man covers my right arm with the plastic bag, seizes my right hand with his unexpectedly powerful left, and forces it the wrong way. I bay like an adolescent Beagle hound.

"Is courtesy Mr. Piao Pin Tian," he growls. "Correct ded."

With a sudden and horrific yank, the policeman forces my arm even farther in the worst of all possible directions. I think I hear the tendon pop. Just as suddenly, he reverses direction and I hear both bones of the lower arm snap. One more jerk, and I feel the jagged bones rip through the skin.

The last thing I hear before passing out are the words: "Fourteen day you pay ded or fix other fucking arm, too."

24

I'd like to make it up the stairs to Lil's apartment without being noticed, but at least half the population of China is out on their balconies today hanging wash, and each of them pauses to give me a stare. Obviously word has gotten around that the Substitute American Teacher presented himself to the portal guardian three nights ago semi-coherent, bleeding from the mouth and holding the splintered remains of a bloody right arm in a heavy-duty leaf-and-garden bag. Not as impressive as the discovery of the shot-dead red-stockinged man in the Year of the Horse perhaps but reasonably close.

Making this procession to Lillian's apartment all the more maudlin are the white-clad school nurse who leads the way, the security guards who support me at either side, and Joe and the headmaster, trailing soberly behind. My guess is the marching band had a scheduling conflict.

As we arrive at the first landing, Marilyn appears before me and gushes an unintelligible lament. One of the guards brushes her aside, but not before she has handed me a slip of paper bearing, one fully assumes, her phone number.

Again I admonish the guards that I don't really require their assistance, but I'm practically losing consciousness. One reason is the *prodigious* needle the nurse hit me with before I was released from the hospital. It was my fourth injection in a span of thirty-six hours of hospitalization that included four in surgery.

I'm telling everyone I was mugged. I fought back heroically and they—three, four, or nine hoodlums, depending on the audience—punished me accordingly. "So foo-rish," everyone tells me.

The headmaster wanted to keep me in the hospital for a few more days, which was tempting actually, as Wa Bell was picking up the tab and the drugs weren't entirely bad. But only eleven days remain before my other arm is due to be *fixed*, and I'd kind of like to prevent that.

I wonder if he meant fourteen business days.

Finally the procession arrives at Lil's door, which my key doesn't seem to fit. Everyone huddles importantly around the metal door, which finally pops open to reveal the face of Madam Wu. She points up and yammers excitedly and the procession turns back toward the stairs.

"So foo-rish!" wails Madam Wu as we scuttle away.

And so painful. The doctor initially offered acupuncture instead of opiates, and I offered to chew off my own tongue. When finally the doctor relented, I reminded him and every nurse thereafter that a man my size requires twice the usual dosage of any and all medications. I think they're probably glad to be rid of me, quite honestly, especially after the incident in the bath. I accept my fair share of responsibility. I was woozy at the time. Besides, the nurse's right breast imposed itself on *my* good left hand, not the other way around. I've decided not to file patient-abuse charges.

Halfway up the final flight of stairs, I halt the procession to catch a bit of my breath. As I curl forward, a salty taste spreads through my mouth, and I fight the urge to distribute beef and noodles on the upturned faces of the gardeners below.

Four Phillip's-head screws now hold my right arm together, with a little help from thirty-seven sutures, a plaster cast that runs mid-palm to my right armpit, and Kangaroo Glue. Along the forearm of the cast are the words "Ready to be present now, Julian?" penned by Tree while I was unconscious. And a smiley face.

The procession begins to move. The door to Lil's apartment, fully open, emits impossible aromas of cornbread, turnip greens, and black-eyed peas. Tree appears in the doorway. "I'll take care of things from here, gentlemen," she says.

"No, the bed, the bed," I cry as Tree begins to deposit me at the settee. I am placed down among Lil's nest of lavender-scented pillows. Instantly I vanish into the inner architecture of opiate rest. No longer in Shenzhen and its drifting cascades of tinkling mahjongg tiles and popping tendons, I stand in a dark gardenia-perfumed corridor where a bowing silhouette says, "Take as many as you'd like." Those happen to be my favorite words, along with "would you like me to do something?" in a timid feminine voice.

Always say yes.

Go toward the light. In this case, the blue-ish light issuing from the far end of a gently twisting corridor of purple blooms. A moment later, I stand inside what could be Memphis's grandest ballroom, its three ornate chandeliers tied back for this evening's activities. A three-level observation terrace has been constructed on each side of the room, looking down onto a brightly lit space at the center. The uppermost tier of each terrace is enclosed in heavy tent fabric, creating more private spaces. The lower tiers are carpeted in a royal-blue canvas topped by leather sofas and loveseats, richly uphol-stered divans, rubbery potted plants and teak coffeetables overflowing with finger-foods and wine.

I'd say that well over a hundred people populate these ob-servation terraces, most of them leaning together to murmur in excited expectation as white-jacketed waiters scurry about. Mounted high on the walls at each end of the ballroom are large video screens that proffer detailed close-up views of the activities soon to begin below in the center of the room.

Nestled at its center of this elaborate frame is what ap-pears to be a movie set conjuring a rural general store from a century ago. An iron potbellied stove sends a rusty stovepipe into the air. A few sagging wooden shelves offer canned meats, beans, and peaches. Along a counter are jars of pickled pig's feet, sow's ears, and boiled eggs. The floor is unfinished wooden planks. At the center of this incongruous setting are three un-matching card tables jammed together and surrounded by an assortment of stools, rockers, and one squat wooden barrel topped by a lumpy feather pillow.

My breath stops as my eyes take in what defines the exact center of the conjoined card tables. It is a worn set of double dominos.

I clamp my urinary sphincter just in the nick of time.

"Five minutes," announces an amplified voice. "The players will please make themselves ready."

Rudely I push through the crowd until I discover a wet bar with neatly stacked chips of white, red, blue, and gold.

"Fifty of each," I say to the nearest of four ebony faces manning the bar.

All four turn to stare at me.

"You want fifty of *each*?" asks the nearest bartender, his accent Jamaican.

"Unless that's a problem."

The barkeep smiles, exposing a set of impossibly white teeth. "Give Mister Tall Man his chips. And something more presentable to put hisself in. Good luck, Mister Tall Man."

"And a gin sour," I add, setting down the wine goblet. "Light on the sugar, heavy on the gin."

Minutes later, I'm stepping barefoot onto the rough plank floor of the movie-set general store, clad in clownish bib overalls and a red-checkered shirt. My black-out shades have been confiscated and my hair braided into long pigtails. I carry my gin sour in a stained coffee cup. I am the final player to take his seat, a wooden crate in this case, at the long table. Three colors of chips, fifty in each stack, are arrayed before me. At the head of the long table is a swarthy man in a faded denim shirt, his face pitted by acne scars. He gestures to me with his own coffee cup, and an unseen microphone picks up his words, amplified for the audience.

"I think everybody here knows Julian Mancer. Hey, Julian, how come you stopped doing Hollywood Squares?"

After a scattering of applause, I reply, my voice amplified, "Paul Lynde was goosing me under the table."

Over the tittering of the crowd, the scarred man shouts, "We'll have none of that here! Understand! Okay, let me explain the rules. . . ."

The man—I will later learn that his name is Louis Vionetti, or more winningly Louie the Snail—goes into the standard rules for enhanced double dominos, Vienna version, Prudhomme variation, while I scan the faces around the table. We are nine in number and all male. I carefully read each pair of eyes. While you can never trust a facial expression at the gaming table, I have learned that eyes are incapable of deceit in two crucial ways, the first being intelligence. I can read it at a glance. The second is self-control.

Chinese physiognomists speak of the difference between controlled and uncontrolled glitter. Moist, twinkling eyes that send off smooth, oblong beams—this is controlled glitter, and it means you're capable of holding your impulses in check. Wildly glittering eyes that send off sharply pointed rapid-fire spikes, on the other hand, indicate a man quite apt to make a mistake under duress. After surveying all pairs of eyes, I am roundly pleased.

First, none of the other participants is scanning *me*. That already means they're in over their heads. I'm also gratified to note that none of the other players registers an unusual measure of intelligence, Vionetti being a borderline exception. I'd almost worry about him if not for his serious glitter challenge. When the man makes eye contact, you want to duck.

Perfect. I know exactly how to play a man like this. As Vionetti closes his introductory remarks, it requires an effort not to smirk.

Famous last concealed smirks.

The fly in the ointment, I can now tell you quite authoritatively, was my failure to gauge one very crucial pair of eyes. My own.

Something jostles me. With difficulty, I return to the American Teacher's Apartment and an inordinate amount of pain. Tree has taken a seat on the side of Lillian's bed. A large platter rests on her lap. Steamy scents rise from boiled turnip greens and black-eyed peas with soggy strips of bacon. Soaking up the juices is a wedge of generously buttered cornbread. Completely gone is the sunlight that but a moment ago illuminated Lil's curtains.

"Suppertime," says Tree.

I gaze longingly at the food, unsure whether I can operate my mouth. At length, I manage to get it half open.

"Did you know there's a rat up in here?" asks Tree.

"Nnnng."

"Have you ever thought about cleaning this place?"

I croak, "What have you told Lillian?"

"About your arm? You told her. Open your mouth."

Tree's dark fingers break off a piece of golden-brown cornbread and place it at my lips. Sweet. Soft. Brown and crisp at the edges. It's heaven at the very least.

"What did I tell her?" I ask. "Peas."

Tree chortles as she loads the fork with glistening black-eyed peas. "It depended a little on the day. You enjoy this spoon-feeding while it lasts, okay? Tomorrow you feed yourself, and the day after that you're on your own. Now. Tell me what happened to you the other night, and tell me the truth or else don't say nothing at all."

"Nothing at all then," I reply, watching Tree re-load the fork with drooping, darkly fragrant greens. Suddenly I am aware that the walls of Lil's apartment are covered with brightly colored poster art. Done by kids, judging from the materials. Several compositions feature a tall, chalky-white man with a serious arm problem.

"What's that on the walls?" I croak.

"Get-well cards," says Tree. "Your students made them for you."

Despite the dense opiates, I experience a moment of shock. These were made by *my* students. I hadn't realized I had students. For a moment I wonder which of the surrounding images flowed from a certain *itsy* yellow hand. Now I see that the settee is completely obscured by vases of flowers and boxes of candy, each adorned with a bright red ribbon. Other vases are jammed together all along the walls.

"There's more flowers in the kitchen," says Tree, "and the refrigerator's full of dishes these people cooked for you. Everyone here is *very* upset about what happened to you, Julian. Probably every family in this building has come up here with something. They all give a little speech before they go. They can't help it, baby. Same way I can't. We love you."

Tree places a warm piece of cornbread against my lips, and I open my mouth without comprehension. Now she smiles and lowers her face to mine. "What did I tell you? That events would conspire to take you to your centermost heart? Here you are, baby. All you have to do now is feel it. Feel it all, Jules."

Wearily, my eyes roll closed. I can't possibly feel all this and survive.

"Now that you've got some time for reflection," says Tree, "you might give a little thought to why you're drawing all this violent energy to yourself. Open your mouth."

Instead, I open my eyes. "Tree. I may have to go away for a while."

"You can't even lift your head, and you're going away for a while. Go where? Open your mouth."

I accept a forkful of black-eyed peas. "I haven't figured that part out yet."

"Your headmaster doesn't expect you back at work for two weeks at the earliest," says Tree. "I'd take that time to get myself back on-center. Chew."

"Did Lil call today?"

"She's supposed to call around eight o'clock."

"What time is it?"

"Around eight o'clock."

"Would you talk to her?" I beg. "I have no idea what to say."

"You don't have to say a word, baby, to her or to me. We both know exactly what's going on with you. A seven-year-old could see it."

"Then why don't I see it?"

Tree lowers the warm plate to her lap. "Your decisions are catching up with you, Jules, and that's *exactly* as it should be. All these old issues are coming up for healing so you can enter the future completely unencumbered."

"I'm feeling pretty unencumbered right now," I say, voice trembling. "Tree, this is too much now. I can't go on with this."

"I'm here to help you, baby. Chew."

"The story's too out of control."

"It's never been anything else," says Tree.

"No. I mean it's way out of control. I can't narrate this."

"You signed on for exactly this," says Tree. "Exactly what you're going through right now. You knew you could handle it."

The phone rings. I look imploringly at Tree. She sets down the platter and lifts the receiver.

"Hello? Hey, sugar. Yeah, he's awake. He's eating something. Of course he wants to talk to you."

Her eyes on mine, Tree presses the phone against my left palm.

I can scarcely lift it. "Tree says I don't have to tell you a word," I mutter into the phone, "because you already know exactly what's happening with me. Greens."

"Greens?" says Lil's voice.

"That was for Tree. How's the peace movement?"

"Peaceful," says Lil. "And I have *zero* idea what's happening with you, so you can start explaining now."

"How's it going with Stumpy?" I ask her. "I mean, Adrian?"

"Doo, what happened to you?"

"Well, Lillian," I sigh, "I'm not entirely clear on that. I got beat the fuck up. That much seems pretty certain."

"Who did it?" asks Lil. "Why?"

"I didn't get their business card. My wallet's gone. I think that means I was mugged."

"How's your arm?"

"Broken," I say. "Listen, this has been a big day for—"

"Have the police done anything at all?"

"More than you can imagine. We'll talk about it sometime real soon."

"Why won't you talk to me?" says Lil. "Why won't you *ever* talk to me? What's going on over there, Julian?"

"What? I'm supposed to know? I'm on more drugs than the whole First Family. Peas."

"I cannot believe that you—just a minute."

I hear my sister punching numbers into her cell phone and murmuring. After a minute, she says to me, "If you're as ignorant as you claim to be, how do you always know exactly what to conceal?"

Damn, that was a good comeback.

"Did you just call Arnie?" I ask. "You did, didn't you?"

"He provides a very useful service," says Lil.

"Jesus. I can't believe it."

"Look, if you're not even going to try to communicate with me, just give the fucking phone to Tree."

"Peace. Love."

Cornbread.

25

There's no trace of toxic material in either of the two pharmaceuticals recently passed along to Bellamy's splendid forensic brother. Or so Bellamy tells me. I received this report by phone sometime yesterday—either that or I imagined it. It actually occurred, I believe, as I recall an announcement that a cleaning lady has just gone through my dumpster's hiney apartment so it's especially splendid now for go return that place at once please thank you.

I told him to go suck on a mop. Actually I'm not sure what I told Bellamy. I've other things to grouse about just now, chief among them the spirited rapping now occurring at the American Teacher's Door. I don't like the sound of it this early in the day. Nothing good ever happens before eight a.m.

"That would be Mr. Xu," says Tree, setting down Lil's smiley mug and rising from the settee chair.

"You didn't tell me that somebody's coming over," I complain from my sister's pillows.

Tree turns to fix me with her golden-browns. "It's *time*, Jules, and you know it. That's why your whole body just tensed up when you heard that knock. Now I am going to go answer the door, and you are going to breathe, okay?"

I avoid the golden-browns. It's not breathing that has me worried. It's being double-teamed by fanatical millennialists while lying helpless in my underpants. That last morphine shot was an awful long time ago.

Tree shows Xu into the apartment. After the whole hugging thing, he approaches Lil's bed. "Julian! How's the arm?"

"Great," I reply. "How's the leg?"

Xu titters. "About the same."

"You'll get used to Julian's sense of humor, Mr. Xu," says Tree. "May I get you some tea?"

"Please," he says, pulling the computer chair nearer the bed and taking a seat.

"So, Mr. Xu," I say, eyes narrowing, "I'm told that you have *delved* into Fibonacci. I can't wait to learn what treasures you have unearthed."

"Easy, Jules," calls Tree from the kitchen.

"Actually, I haven't found much of anything," replies Xu, surprising me once more with the flippant Aussie/Chinese accent. "But I'm enjoying the chase."

"Are you now?"

He nods happily. "That's all it is, really. A chase. An open inquiry. I don't think you ever get closure with the Sequence. But people have always studied the patterns of nature, right? The cycles of the moon and the turning of the seasons. Eventually every civilization evolves a system of math and encounters this same strange sequence of numbers: zero, one, one, two, three, five . . . , each number the sum of the previous two. The Mayans were working with the Sequence two thousand years ago. What fascinates me about the Sequence is that it never cycles back, making it evolutional rather than cyclical. How amazing that you can have something in motion along a vector completely beyond its own parameters. It wasn't until Descartes's number grid that we had a lens to even see that through."

"Ah," I say, adjusting the position of my right arm, "little René."

"Don't you get me started on that man," calls Tree from the kitchen.

"Descartes was not the devil incarnate, Mrs. Carter," Xu calls to her. "His first big breakthrough was given to him by an angel, you know."

"*Which* angel?" replies Tree's voice.

Xu leans forward. "As soon as we charted the Sequence on Descartes's grid, we could see sunflowers, seashells, pine cones, *everything* in nature."

"Then came your own lovely breakthrough," I say, straining to remember what Tree has told me. "You overlaid the spiral with the arc of human history. I'm very curious as to how you arrived at that notion."

"I love this part," says Tree, arriving with a teapot.

"My Taiji showed me," says Xu with a giggle. "I didn't use a rational process at all. To understand how nature expresses through time—to understand, let's say, the currents of a river—we can stand on the bank and observe, or we can throw ourselves in and become one with those currents. Not swimming forward, not holding back, just letting every part of the body be arranged and shaped by the river. If the body can be that supple, the mind that supple—"

"You drown," I say.

"But," says Xu, raising a finger, "before you die, you know a lot about that river. I think that's one description of Taiji. Allowing the body and mind to be shaped by the currents of the moment. I find that can lead to certain understandings."

Xu cools his tea by blowing across the top of the cup, and I notice a bit of grey where the black-framed glasses meet his temples. That would make him the only middle-aged Chinese on the planet who does not color his hair.

"What certain understandings?" I ask, remaining on the offensive.

"Nonverbal ones, usually. But sometimes an idea just appears fully formed in my mind."

With a sudden burst of enthusiasm, Xu springs from his chair, adjusts his glasses, and begins to move slowly as though conducting an unheard adagio. I watch with unexpected interest, noting how his body seems to swell and deflate moment by moment, his face relaxed and listening, the glistening eyes seemingly turned inward, or perhaps reading the code of the moment. Xu's attention seems focused yet diffuse enough at the edges to allow the moment to surprise him, to evade its own comprehension, and I'm surprised to see all that at a glance. For a moment it seems that his body and its tempo are not overlaid upon the air but have somehow slipped beneath it, to describe its inner architecture, its nuances and micro-currents, from within their midst. One arrives at certain understandings, Xu has said. What he hasn't said is that just watching can deliver one to certain understandings.

Maybe that last shot hasn't quite worn off.

As though hearing the thought, Xu is suddenly stone-still, seemingly spellbound by his own one-pointed attention. A moment later, he is animated and grinning, returning to the computer chair. "I've found Taiji to be very instructional," he says, slurping his tea. "Each moment tells you something. Each posture tells you something. That's been the function of these postures for generations. Carrying forward nonverbal information."

Tree says, "Mr. Xu tells me the communists banned Taiji when they took over the country. It was too spiritual for them."

"Mmm," says Xu, "yes. They later brought Taiji back but in a very simplified form. Now it's just a way to keep the body healthy. When the government ordered the old masters to teach Taiji this way, they refused but the government was very firm. They said, 'Okay, we'll kill everyone in your family.' So the masters had no choice. To this day, you cannot teach real Taiji or Qigong anywhere in China. Have you heard about Falun Gong?"

I nod. There's been an international hue and cry about Beijing's ongoing oppression of practitioners of this popular form of Qigong. Thousands have been imprisoned and tortured, executed, all the usual.

"They took their practice too far," says Xu. "They were discovering powers within themselves that no government wants its people to know about. Those people will never be seen again."

"You're saying today's Taiji isn't authentic?" asks Tree.

"Oh, it's very authentic!" he says after another loud slurp of tea. "The truth of Taiji can never be obscured because it's encoded in the postures. Anyone who performs the postures with an open mind and an open body will absorb their meaning. The postures tell you what they are and what they are for, and that is the truth. I'm not saying that the postures themselves are magical. They accentuate certain—"

"I think it's we who are magical," says Tree.

Xu practically falls out of his chair in agreement. "Yes! We bring the magic! Truly, everything a human being does is magical. It's just a matter of bringing all that potential into focus, arraying our awareness so that the information around us becomes an absorbable field. Taiji does that, and I don't think anyone can say how it does that, but it's the basis of everything I think I know."

I gaze at Xu's suddenly sober face. I'm unexpectedly struck by the near-perfect symmetry and the bright controlled glitter of the dark eyes. Here is a face easily overlooked in a crowd, yet there comes a moment when you realize he has drawn you in.

"And all this relates somehow to Fibonacci?" I say.

Xu and Tree look at each other and blink.

"Yes, actually," says Xu.

Unselfconsciously he begins to perform Taiji in his chair, shoulders rolling unhurriedly, his tempo comfortable and un-forced. One of his hands makes a broad sweeping gesture along a horizontal plane while the other describes a tightening spiral. "I was doing this movement one day and I noticed how it feels to be an object moving through space and time, and I thought *wow*, we always think of time as moving but maybe it's *we* who are moving.

Remember Einstein's analogy of a train? If we are passengers on Einstein's train, watching the countryside move past the windows, it seems that the landscape occurs sequentially. We see it as a narrative because of our method of observation. But all we'd have to do is step off the train to see that all the scenery was there the whole time. What if time is that way?

We see it as sequential, but is it? Quantum physicists say that every possible event is stored end-to-end on long spirals coiled up in space/time points, waiting to be experienced.

None of those events actually *occurs* until consciousness touches it. So there's this huge field of possibilities out there, like an endless field of wildflowers, each flower containing within itself other huge fields of wildflowers, and then others beneath that, level after level, out to infinity, no end to it—and we're like this big swarm of bees going from one experience to another, opening up reality one packet at a time."

"Whew," says Tree.

Xu thinks for a moment. "It's like when we read a book. We're seeing one word at a time, right? One page at a time, but the whole book is there all the while. We experience things this way, all strung out in a line, because that's the kind of creatures we are. Or, I don't know, maybe that's just how it comes off the coils."

Tree says, "I think I'm starting to get it."

I hope it isn't contagious. The last time I visited this particular packet of ideas, I think I was seated at a Boy Scout campfire. And my arm is really beginning to hurt.

"Then," says Xu, "I asked myself, what if Einstein's train tracks were riding those unwinding coils, riding the curve of a Fibonacci spiral? What would that look like? I think it would look a lot like this." Xu looks around the apartment. "That got me wondering how the timeline of history might describe a Fibonacci spiral, and whether we could chart that and find out where we are right now. That would be interesting to know because we'd know what's coming next."

Xu finishes his tea, and Tree pours more from the teacup.

Xu continues eagerly, "I started reading everything I could find and writing computer programs that laid the Sequence over various historical spreads, just to see if things would line up. The whole time, I'm thinking why *shouldn't* it? If the Sequence can predict the way a plant or a nautilus develops, why wouldn't it predict the development of human civilization? It absolutely should."

"So everything lined up?" I ask.

"Nope," he says.

"Mr. Xu is being modest," says Tree. "I think his work is absolutely crucial to our understanding of the human adventure, especially as it relates to evolutionary timing. Like that movie, *A Room of Eyes*. Seriously, Julian, you should see that movie. It shows how everything is relative except consciousness. That's the one thing that doesn't reduce to something else. Everything else is experiential, and its structure shows us that."

Xu smiles. "I'm learning a great deal from Mrs. Carter. The Three-three-three, for example. That's something I never would have considered because it has no basis in classical numerology. Yet I see the obvious correlations. The third day of the third month of the third year of the millennium. Certainly there could be some kind of penetration on such a day."

"Ah," I say. "We're finally talking dirty."

Tree says, "In the sense of a new idea pressing in from the outside."

Xu nods. "Sometimes an idea just appears from nowhere. Like when Newton saw that apple fall. How many people had seen an apple fall before that moment? Think about it. How many times had Newton himself seen things fall to the ground? But suddenly, at that precise moment, it was obvious that there's a force pulling things toward the center of the planet. People have been talking about gravity ever since, but before that day *nobody* saw gravity. That's what I call a penetration, and my work is about discovering the patterns—if there are patterns—of the penetrations that move across human consciousness and pull us forward along our evolutionary course."

Xu smiles at me timidly. "Actually I was hoping you might be able to help me with the math, Julian. I feel that math is very bound up in this whole process, either as the engine or its reflection."

"Math has no meaning beyond its own music," I argue comfortably, closing my eyes. "It's a closed system. Our interpretations have absolutely nothing to do with it. Nor," I add, opening my eyes and turning to Tree, "does the day of the week, the month of the year, nor where we are in our personal moon cycle. You want me to spare you both a lot of unnecessary suspense? The world's going to be exactly the same after March third—about half a quart low."

"Thanks, Julian," says Tree.

"No, thank *you*."

"Actually," says Xu, "I can appreciate what you're saying, Julian. What science most essentially is, is a system of eliminating faulty theories, and every scientist should be reminded of that from time to time. Science is supposed to hold no beliefs whatsoever. There are no truths but only theories yet to be disproven. The assumption has to be that all of them will eventually be disproven."

"We *have* to believe in something," says Tree.

I groan. "That's a psychological need having nothing to do with truth."

Tree says to Xu, "You see what I have to deal with? It's like dragging around an anvil."

"I just believe in the integrity of the system," I say.

At this, Xu practically jumps out of the computer chair. "Yes! The integrity of the system! Julian is more of a purist than either of us, Mrs. Carter. The only difference between your view and mine, Julian, is very simple. Permeability. You seem to recognize no creative interplay between the world of ideas and that of physicality. You really should read mythology."

I give Xu an unhappy glance.

"Mythology," says Xu, "is all about the interplay between the gods and mortals. Until that interplay begins, nothing of interest happens. After that interplay, you have *everything*."

"Lots of penetration," I say.

"Let me tell you about penetration," he continues. "I have a random number generator, and it's always turned on. You've seen it, Tree. I wrote software that combs the numbers looking for patterns. An alarm sounds every time an anomalous pattern comes up. I call it my Serendipitometer. Every time the alarm goes off, I pay careful attention to whatever I'm thinking or seeing at that moment, or to what someone is saying to me. Just whatever's happening. I know that at that instant there's a penetration of order into randomness—or randomness into order, which can be just as significant. Either way, something new is coming in. Maybe it's a mental construct like the theory of gravitation. Maybe it's a new organizing principle. Maybe it's a re-crystallization of what's actually possible on this planet."

"Ding!" says Tree. "That was the alarm going off."

The two love-birds giggle, and Tree turns to me. "Julian, this is exactly why I wanted you to sit down with this man—and *how* I wish Lillian were here. Mr. Xu has his finger on the pulse of what's happening on this planet, and he senses, just as we all do, that we are at the tipping point of something absolutely incredible. We have to be. Either we all grow out of our childish ways in a hurry or we're history."

"Ding, ding!" says Xu.

I think our Mr. Xu may have his finger elsewhere, anatomically speaking, but I let it pass. I'm experiencing some serious pain over here. I loose a theatrical groan, and Xu stands abruptly.

"I should go. It was a pleasure to talk to you at last, Julian. I really admire your work on Lindenmayer grammars. Maybe someday you can explain the subject to me in language a novice can understand."

"Next time," I say.

"I'll walk you out," offers Tree.

"No, no, I'll be fine. Goodbye, Julian."

"Have a pleasant day," I reply.

Careful of termites.

26

At dusk, eight red taxis are cued in front of Studebaker Supermarket. I sit next door at the Sidewalk Fish Brains Café, attending the remains of a Japanese baked flounder. All eight taxi drivers are asleep or very near it, their feet either on the dash or hanging out the passenger window. Fares are hard to come by these days, as the latest round of rumors links cabbies to the spread of atypical pneumonia. In Beijing meanwhile the word is that household pets are responsible for spreading the blight. In response, people are flushing songbirds down toilets and flinging lapdogs and tabbies from upper-story windows. Those Chinese. Such sentimentalists.

I've picked my way, single-handed as it were, through most of today's *China Daily* and all of tonight's baked flounder, yet I can't quite make myself rise and return to Lil's apartment, where Tree no longer dutifully waits, nor does much of anything else but a slow dial-up and a lot of wilting flowers. I'm running a three point one, possibly three point one five. The coping mechanisms kicked in at two, what little aid they provided. Here I am less than a week away from another close encounter with a rabid one-armed policeman, and there doesn't seem to be a whole lot I can do about it.

A waiter approaches to offer me a fresh Hsingtao, but I'm growing increasingly fond of the old one. I pull my glass and its three fingers of flat beer a little closer, and he gathers up the remains of the flounder. This place I call the Sidewalk Fish Brains Café because once you select a live fish from the tank, a young man in a dirty apron flips it onto the sidewalk and stomps its brains out. You can arrange for yourself how the sidewalk smells. I selected this particular fish on this particular night because I enjoyed the unexpected flashes of blue along his flanks as he—presumably he—coasted effortlessly around the huge tank. As soon as he was out of the water and struggling on the sidewalk, there were no more flashes of blue.

So it goes.

Before Tree returned to her school two days ago, she swept, mopped, and dusted every square centimeter of the American Teacher's Apartment. It now smells like the school lunchroom. Lil's resident rat doesn't seem very impressed. He hasn't been back since.

As Her Treeness cleaned, she lectured me relentlessly about my wounded warrior issues. Actually, I prefer Tree's story to that of just being a fuck-up from Memphis.

This morning, Joe and the headmaster knocked at the door to check on me, usual big smiles in place. The police, they informed me, have made little progress in solving my case. Big surprise there. Joe did think to bring along an envelope full of cash, though, which was a nice touch. Turns out I get to collect all of Lillian's salary, despite all the sick days. I told them to expect me back in the classroom Monday morning. Truth is, I need something to focus my mind on. The plan for the weekend, meanwhile, is to take a fast train to the casinos in Macao and get lucky to the tune of eighty-seven thousand dollars. Actually, I'm shooting for eighty-eight. I'd like to buy myself a set of silk threads before returning to Memphis. Never come dragging back into town looking like a substitute teacher.

I'd consider running from these ill-mannered people if I had some faint notion of where to. The world only has only so many sides, geographically speaking. Meanwhile I'm down to five days and one arm.

I tried making a call to the States last night, but it required the use of two hands plus sundry phone cards, the patience of Job's housecat, and half a liter of blood. I managed to connect to the Western hemisphere once, I think. I also think the brassy whiskey-voiced woman is coming on to me. She must have located her placemats. Now she phones me for no reason and talks about her day as though I'm listening. I think she imagines she's cheering me up.

Yesterday Marilyn and Madam Wu each brought me a pan of chicken soup. Marilyn's looked the better of the two, so I poured off the broth, mixed in some rice and barbeque sauce and ate it for dinner. Madam Wu's went into the toilet. It wouldn't flush. I ended up on my knees *raking* grey hunks of chicken back into Madam Wu's pan. Now what was I was supposed to do with it? The answer seemed to be: open the kitchen window, rear back, and fling it into the trees below. I kind of missed the window. Now toilet-flavored chicken was dribbling down the wall. That's when I noticed something.

Beyond that same kitchen window, on a masonry ledge—actually the ledge of another wing of the building, if you're tracking—was a careworn but still recognizable North Korean chocolate Buddha, one bite missing from the globe of his head. Even the insects hadn't been able to deal with the goddamn thing. The chocolate wasn't even melted. Here was North Korea's answer to mortality. *And*. Embedded in the still-laughing chocolate head, at the exact spot of the third eye and gleaming quite brightly in the direct afternoon sun, was a small but unmistakable nugget of jeweler's gold. My maxillary first premolar crown.

I ran my tongue around the replacement recently installed by Dr. Xylophone, formed entirely I believe of JB Weld, and tried to picture myself crawling out onto that ledge, negotiating the ninety-degree turn, and returning ass-first back to this window. I shuddered at the thought. As toilet-flavored chicken dribbled down the wall. But it was my maxillary first premolar *crown*. And it was worth *money*. Maybe if I could get my hands on a length of bamboo and a decent wad of bubble gum . . .

"Excuse me. Are you Julian Mancer?"

With a start, I return to the Sidewalk Fish Brains Cafe to look up, and up, at a very tall Westerner in new khakis and a comical safari hat. In his right hand is a shopping bag. From the slightly dazed expression, I'd say he's less than five hours off the plane. But I'm wrong a lot.

"Do you have any drugs?" I reply. "Or a decent wad of American bubble gum?"

"You're Julian, all right," says a husky American voice. "I'm Tim Dobbins from Chicago. Do you mind if I join you?"

"Won't you please do," I answer, my mind suddenly reeling. Tim Dobbins. Chicago. Timothy Dobbins. Director of Research. Hydrangea Laboratories.

Dobbins remains standing. "Could we possibly move to another table?"

Mind still churning, I pour the last of the Hsingtao from the bottle into my glass and follow Tim Dobbins to a table deeper in shadow.

"I hope you don't mind if I call you Julian," he says, struggling to fit his knees beneath the table. I notice that he's wearing suede desert boots with checkered laces. Though his erect bearing puts this man's age at little more than fifty, Dobbins has the thin, wrinkled arms of an octogenarian. I watch him place the plastic shopping bag on his lap, pull out an antiseptic wipe, and clean a spot on the table before placing his reedy arms there and leaning forward. "I've followed your writing career for some time," he tells me. "Your recent pieces in *Magazine Mariposa* have been nothing less than spellbinding. I'd give anything to visit the Lu Shoukun scrolls before leaving South China, but I'm afraid that will be impossible."

"You've had me followed," I say bluntly.

Dobbins's smile thins just a little. "True."

"You tried to have Lillian arrested."

"Not arrested," says Dobbins. "Deported. Sent away from here."

"Why?"

"Because China's not a safe place for her. Nor is it for you, Julian."

We share an unblinking gaze.

"Someone was killed," I tell him, "in front of Lillian's school."

Dobbins says, "We had nothing to do with that. We are a pharmaceutical company."

"Who was responsible?" I ask.

"I don't know, Julian. Many people are watching you. They're probably watching us right now, which is why I can only meet you this once."

Dobbins's eyes tip down to my prodigious cast and sling. "Sorry about the incident the other night. It happened so quickly, there was nothing to be done. But steps have been taken. You won't be bothered by that collection agency again." The cool green eyes almost smile. "But I think I would steer clear of secret domino societies for a while."

I stare.

"I'm going to leave this table in thirteen minutes," says Dobbins, placing his wristwatch on the table. "Here's my proposition. I'll tell you everything I'm at liberty to share. All I ask in return is that you listen. Agreed?"

Before I can answer, Dobbins says, "I'm here because someone in the States is very concerned about you. I can't tell you this person's identity but—"

"Excuse me," I interrupt, "*Tim*. Someone seems to be horsing around with my life and, if it's not too much trouble, I'd kind of like to know who it is. And those articles in *Mariposa* are horseshit, and you know it. And I'd rethink the hat if I were you."

Dobbins folds his long, thin arms. "Why don't I just come to the point then? I don't know how closely you're following this atypical pneumonia thing, but it appears that China is in for a rough ride. At this juncture, they don't really know what they're up against, and once they figure it out—what are they supposed to do about it? With the population density and the lack of sanitation, what could anyone do? No one controls China. Not the Chinese, not anyone."

"Oh," I say, "I get it. You're here to save my big white American ass from certain death. By the way, did you just tell me, or did I imagine it, that our otherly-abled policeman will never disturb me again?"

"Yes and yes."

"Thanks and thanks. I'm quite sure no strings are attached. Or could this outpouring of benevolence have something to do with current research projects at Hydrangea Laboratories?"

"Not really," says Dobbins.

"Oh?" I set down my empty glass. "Here's where you lose me, *Tim*. I distinctly remember hearing a very different story from a certain latter-day Charlestown attorney."

Dobbins shakes his head. "That was a hoax."

"I'm sorry?"

"There is no research project," says Dobbins. "The focus all along has been getting the two of you out of China. The timing's wrong. It's very wrong."

"Oh," I say.

"Sorry about that," he half-grins.

My ears are starting to ring. "Well, you managed to get Lillian out. That makes your job half-done, doesn't it?"

"That wasn't my doing," says Dobbins.

"What wasn't?"

"Lillian."

"Oh. Then you *didn't* poison our mother?"

Dobbins's eyes dull. "I don't know what you're talking about, Julian."

"I mean did you poison our mother? It's a simple question."

"Of course not."

"I think you're a lying sack of shit," I say.

"Julian, I need you to be calm right now."

"I don't know or *care* whether you and your hunchbacked friends are DIA, or CIA, or Monty fucking Python—"

"Your sister will very likely die unless you calm down and listen to me," says Dobbins.

We glare at each other across the table. Gradually the sounds of the street return.

"Lillian can't come back here," says Dobbins. "It's that simple. The only way we can ensure that is for you to go to Memphis and tell her what I'm telling you. And there's something else." He places the shopping bag on the table.

"I'm very glad to hear there's something else," I reply.

"Don't talk, Julian. Listen."

"Because there's a small problem with your story, Tim. Atypical pneumonia was unheard of before February. It was nonexistent before November. Yet you've had your nose up my ass since August of the Year of the Horse. You see my problem?"

I watch the face across the table soften into a rueful smile. "I knew you'd be a hard nut to crack. I don't suppose I can ask you to take my word for it?"

"Your word?" I reply. "Want to give me your word that Hydrangea did not arrange Lillian's hiring at Stuebans and Rehnquist? Or my little job at *Magazine Mariposa*?"

Dobbins shifts in his chair.

"And before that, Tim, back in our college years. Wasn't it Hydrangea that suckered us into that lab so we could be measured and earmarked like a couple of white mice—and then sold to Defense?"

"Julian."

"And what about our *births*, Tim? What about Lil's and my immaculate conception? Whose work was that? Why do our whole *lives* seem to be one continuous hoax written, produced, and directed by Hydrangea Laboratories—except for one thing, that is. Our coming to China. That really seems to have you peed, Tim, and I'll tell you something. That kind of makes me want to stay here."

"It's about Lillian," Dobbins says dryly. "Think about Lillian."

"Okay." I nod. "I'll think about Lillian. I'll get on a plane. I'll do anything you ask if you'll just tell me one thing. Why? Why would an international chemical conglomerate be so invested in two tiny lives?"

Dobbins closes his eyes. "Julian, I know it's hard but you've got to focus right now. I have to leave this table in"—he checks his watch—"seven minutes. There won't be another chance."

His long fingers push the shopping bag a little closer to me. "There's a vaccine, Julian."

"Get away from my table."

"*Listen* to me," hisses Dobbins. "Just getting you out of China isn't enough anymore. This thing is everywhere now. You could be infected in a taxi, at the airport, even back in the States."

"And wouldn't that play hell with your little science project?"

Dobbins shoves the shopping bag across the table. "Just take it. There are two doses. I included the syringes."

"Another lie," I reply. "A vaccine will take at least two years to develop. Read the fucking newspapers."

Dobbins's face flares purple-red. "Will you come out of the *fog*, Julian? I have the vaccine because I *developed* it, just as I developed the—"

The stranger falls panting against his chair. After a long moment, he gasps, "It was all hypothetical. Hypothetical. Just a scenario. There are thousands of scenarios. Thousands . . . "

I'm suddenly transfixed by something in this man's breathing, in the way the words chase each other between gasps.

"High population. Low sanitation. Holiday travel. Move up delivery. Increase security." Two bleary eyes search mine. "I didn't want to believe it. I tried not to believe it. That they were actually going to use this thing."

"Who are you?" my voice asks.

"They're onto me," says Dobbins. "They know I've tried to get to you. They've followed everything back to me. That's why I have to disappear. I'm running, Julian. You have to listen."

"Who *are* you?"

"It's more dangerous than they know. It's mutating. No one knows what happens next. No one."

"Why wouldn't you meet us?" I ask the man across the table. "Why?"

Dobbins's green eyes meet mine uncertainly before turning away. "Your mother had an excellent IQ, good health, good bone structure. Why not? Why not see what would come of it? It was easy to do, to switch the specimen, to use my own genetics. When I learned that you were a mixed-twin pair—I don't know. For some reason I couldn't stop thinking about you. Vanity, I suppose."

"But you refused to meet us. Why?"

Dobbins pulls out a handkerchief and dabs surgically at one eye. "Everything was exactly as I wanted it. I could enjoy your successes. I could reach out and help you when necessary. Why change things?"

"Because we needed a *father*?" I reply.

"Don't judge me, Julian. I've helped you more times than you know. I've given up everything to come here. I couldn't stand by and watch you and your sister be harmed, not by something I myself . . ."

His eyes lose focus for a moment. "You've no idea the things I've created, Julian. I'm approaching the end of my life, and I realize that I've created nothing of value. Nothing except—"

He looks at me. "Take the vaccine. Give it to Lillian. Don't wait. Another mutation or two, and it may no longer work."

"I'd sooner die," I tell him.

A sneer crosses Dobbins's expression. "Don't be melodramatic. Not when your sister's life is at stake."

I lean forward. "Listen to me very carefully. My sister's life, *both* our lives, begin at the precise point where"—I shove the shopping bag onto his lap—"your help ends."

I stand up.

"Sit down," says Dobbins.

Leaning, I say, "You want to be a big help to me? Fine. You can buy dinner."

I leave him sitting there.

27

When I was young, there was a room where I had a father. I visited him there sometimes when the house was too still for sleep. He'd return from work by twilight in a long, polished car. The tires made a popping sound in the gravel. I'd watch him close the car door with a flick of his wrist and toss me a quick smile. Then my father would squat on springy legs and open his arms for me.

He didn't look at all like Timothy Dobbins.

The last time I saw that father of the long, polished car, there was someone with him. I could only see the top of her head on the passenger side. On that final day, my unsmiling father held the door open as this second person climbed out of the driver's side and walked to where I stood. "Don't do this anymore," my sister told me evenly. "It hurts your head and mine, too."

I pace along the dark, clothesline-strewn balcony, wishing I could open my fly and pee into the honest black earth as did Li Bai among his peonies and Mao Zedong among heads of state. I wish a lot of things. It still doesn't quite register. It's a bad nickel that won't quite drop. I have met our—

The power went off more than an hour ago. I was pacing this same balcony, less drunk than now but every bit as hollow, every bit as shattered, asking the warm, starless, and godless sky my too-open question, when all at once every electric light within view dimmed, flickered twice, then perished. So it goes. My too-open question concerns what happens now if powers-that-be really are after Timothy Dobbins and someone really was snapping photos of our *tête-à-tête* at the Sidewalk Fish Brains Café? When the time comes for my debriefing, let's hope I won't be tied to the chair. And that no one assumes that my highly psychic sister knows everything her brother knows.

Lil hasn't phoned since Tree was staying here. I'm told my sister has tired of the psychic distance between us. "He outright lies," she said to Tree. I asked Tree for the exact quote, since with my sister there is a qualitative difference between, "He's a disinformation campaign," "He fucking lied to me," and "He outright lies."

She's always felt his presence. She's felt him all along.

Before tonight's power failure, I went online and skimmed *Rebuilding America's Defenses: Strategies, Forces and Resources for a New Century.* It's everything that Beijing professor said it is. A bald-faced declaration of war against any society whose prosperity rivals that of the United States. The affixed names are those chanted nightly on the evening news, the men who currently run God's Country, not that they're essentially different from those running it before. We were overturning governments and installing dictators when Howdy Doody was a stave of wood. If anything is different in the current regime, it's the hubris. No one sees the need to conceal it much anymore.

Then I rose from the computer, gin in hand, to pace barefoot here on the balcony in ever more ragged circles, recollecting rumors recently flowing through the neighborhood. That atypical pneumonia is a bio-weapon created and released by the dear hearts and gentle people of Dubuque and Bloomington and Tallahassee, the same crowd that gave us HIV two decades ago, and who am *I* to dismiss such suspicions, having already read Memorandum 200?

You remember Memorandum 200, wherein our seated secretary of state announced that no more important goal exists for the US government than the depopulation of the third world. Depopulation. Such a better word than genocide.

Evidently, not only do my darkest intuitions concerning my country of origin appear to be reasonably accurate, my worst premonitions about Hydrangea Corporation may in fact be badly understated. Then there's the matter of my whole life. As in, maybe I've never had one. Every significant turn in both Lil's and my life seems now to have been a case of fraud.

Worse, there's no reason to suppose that I've reached the bottom of it. What if there's more, much more, surrounding the matter of Lil's and my inception? What if we are *purposeful*? If so, whose purpose might that be? A doting asshole father would be bad enough. What if it's the people he works for? One thing seems to be certain. Someone's going to an awful lot of trouble.

Turning to pace once more toward the shadowed staircase, I'm startled by an unexpected sight. A soundless silhouette seems to be gliding directly toward me. The silhouette is small in stature and seems possessed of a long trail of hair. The figure stops.

"Mr. Mancer?" asks a young woman's voice.

"Rui Long?"

"Thank God you're awake. I totally need to talk to you. I mean, I know it's late and you're injured and everything—how are you?"

Unexpectedly warmed, I say, "I'm better. I'm much better. Come inside. There's no power, but Lil has candles."

"Lil?" asks the schoolgirl, following me into the cave of the apartment.

As I fumble for candles and matches, I relate the short version of my sister's aborted year abroad, concluding, "Our mother was just moved out of ICU. I suppose that's a good sign. But realistically I don't expect my sister to return here at all."

No sooner do I speak the words than I know they are wrong. Lillian is coming back. She has to.

"So you're stuck in Shenzhen, same as me?" says Rui Long. I turn to see her ironic face in the candlelight. There are twin glitters in the two dark eyes. Wildly uncontrolled.

"With the Memphis blues again," I reply. "I'm going to make myself another gin sour. I don't suppose you ever have a nippity-nip?"

"Double," she says. "No sugar, no ice."

"Get out of town."

Rui Long giggles and her voice goes raspy. "You grow up fast in Westmont, man. Really, Mr. Mancer, I have had *such* a day. My crazy-ass father has decided—"

"Hold that thought. I'll be right back with medicine for the soul."

Even from the other room, Lil's three candles half-illuminate the kitchen, where it's soon clear that the gin is getting really low. I manage to squeeze two more sours out of the bottle, one finger remaining for a nightcap. Then I'm down to a Guangzhou vodka I was really hoping to avoid.

Returning with drinks, I'm greeted by a soft breeze from the open doorway. The three fluttering candles on the settee table form a seeming shrine to the young goddess whose soft smile they illuminate.

Rui Long goes back to her rant, and I make an effort to listen. Truth is, I'm taken utterly away by the pale, candlelit face, its color stolen by the dancing yellow light. A strand of hair casts a threefold shadow across Rui Long's forehead, which lurches as she speaks. Because a candle does not know how to drink gin, I watch the colorless ingénue speak, ignoring the words, absorbing the raging pheromones, the lush art-deco lips describing every contour of my longing, my crushing need to escape my own thoughts .

The almond eyes dart unselfconsciously as Rui Long speaks. I see the petty rebelliousness, the deeply caked melodrama, the sad naiveté beneath the failed swagger. These I know are footnotes to a text that I can but imagine. Flowing meanwhile like an underground river beneath the visual delights roils the same unmistakable preponderance I noticed when last Rui Long warmed that settee chair. That knowing should counsel me to hold my distance. Instead, it draws me in all the more. I want to know how the ascending arc of that gravelly voice might taste inside my own mouth. I want to know the scent of those swollen lips moistened by my own meager tongue.

" . . . so I ran out the door and came here," says Rui Long, perched on the very edge of the chair. "Can I use your bathroom?"

"Turn left at the kitchen."

She sighs loudly. "Thanks for letting me vent like this. I know there's like nothing you can do and everything, but just having somebody who can listen—you know, I pulled a Barbie rune about you. I got the Free Extra Minutes card, which is like the best card in the deck. It's about open communication. I think I'm supposed to trust you."

"Rui Long," I say, "you're talking to a sinister man. I destroy everything and everyone I come near. You might bear that in mind."

She smiles happily. "See? Would you say something like that if I couldn't trust you? Anyway I checked you out online. I didn't know you were like famous and shit. Anyway I feel like I already know you from somewhere."

"You don't know me, Rui Long."

"Hold that thought?"

She springs up and bounces from the room, taking all the magic with her. I'm left once more with the grotesques of my mind. I try not to anticipate the return of the young schoolgirl with every cell in my body. I try not to see my own adolescent melodramas, my own petty authority issues. I try not to see quite so clearly the childishness beneath my own failed swagger, the easily traceable arc of moral degeneration that accompanies my ever-more-pitiful flight from myself.

Rattling the ice cubes in my glass one final time, I drain the last drop of gin onto my tongue. Maybe I should be literally running. Hauling ass down the darkened stairway, taking four steps at a time. How does one *know* anything anymore?

Post-medication. Pre-comprehension. Transdermal. Sublingual. Semi-imprisonable.

"What's all this?" calls Rui Long from the kitchen.

Rising, I enter the dark kitchen to stand behind Rui Long. She's gawking at my aquarium/spore-incubator and its various bells, whistles, and three-eyed toads.

"A futile attempt to breed rare tropical fish," I say. "I foolishly forgot to add water."

She laughs. "Mr. Mancer, you are so totally 'shroom-farming."

"Am not."

"Are too. You've got the vermiculite and everything. I hope you'll let me know when it's harvest time."

As Rui Long speaks, the back of my good left hand describes the faintest outline of her pert bottom. The two taut swells are as high and tight as a gymnast's.

"Umm, are you sure this is completely ethical?" asks the schoolgirl, a hint of a smile in her voice.

"I'm certain of it," I say, left hand now rising from the dip of her waist to a tiny shoulder blade. A moment later, my fingers have outlined her left breast.

The gravelly voice drops to an ironic register. "Mr. Mancer, I don't suppose you'd have any dope to smoke?"

"Hard to come by," I whisper, my hand now arriving on the firm belly. "Join me in the front room?"

"First make me a real drink."

"Gladly."

"And don't put your hands on me again unless I tell you."

My left hand freezes and withdraws. "No sugar, no ice, right?"

"And more gin this time," says Rui Long, exiting the kitchen in a saunter.

I give her the Guangzhou vodka. Like I said, never trust me. I pour myself one, as well. Now I'm lurching into the candlelit front room where Rui Long is seated imperiously, one blue-uniformed knee crossed smartly over the other. Her school jacket is hanging on the back of the chair.

"Let's get something straight," she says. "You're world-famous and everything, and I'm just nobody, but you keep your hands off my body. Understand? If it weren't for that rune, I wouldn't even be here."

"Got it," I say, holding out her drink.

After a moment's reflection, Rui Long accepts the drink. "My mama's boyfriends used to do that shit. I hated it. Old men putting their hands on me. *Mister* Mancer. Julian. Whoever the fuck you are."

The itsy schoolgirl gives me a stare as she takes a long drink. "Maybe you have some kind of answer for me, and maybe you don't. The thing is, I don't think I've ever met anybody like you, okay? What you don't know is, you've never met anybody like me."

There is a challenge in the stare.

"Actually," I reply, "I'm developing a rather clear sense of that."

We drink in silence for a minute, watching the three flames sway in the breeze from the open door. Tree's theories on Indigo children come to mind. Special kids, she calls them. Curtain-climbers for God. Knee-huggers for Jesus. Highly advanced spiritual entities that crap their pants thrice a day. Tree says those children have to deal with the same growing pains as everyone else only more so, as they never quite fit in, never quite see the world through the same half-lidded eyes as those around them.

Curious, I close my own eyes to see whether I might still catch sight of that constellation of lights I once viewed in Rui Long's presence. There's nothing now. Nothing to feel beyond that bothersome background hum, that odd sense that I am in the presence of—what? Something well beyond my estimation and easily within my grasp? I find that quite alluring. Here is a bright-eyed ravaged angel, her wings not yet fully open, who imagines she can get away with toying with me. I've given fair warning.

"I'm not an Indigo," says Rui Long. "That's what you're thinking, isn't it? I used to think that was my problem. I wasn't inferior to everybody else—I was superior. Now I think I'm just different."

Ding.

I hear a small sound on the balcony. A cat, most likely. Still I rise and close the door. No sense advertising the fact that a female student is drinking bad vodka in the American Teacher's Apartment in the middle of the night. I turn to Rui Long. "How did you manage to get past the gate guard?"

"Waited till he took a pee," she says.

I nod. Ralpho said the presence of the guards makes me relatively safe here. I'd say *relatively* is the key word.

The second drink seems to have hit our little schoolgirl. She launches into a rant about her messed-up childhood. I let her talk, glad to not be alone, comforted by the soft light from my sister's too-scented candles. They make of this shabby collection of angles and absurdities a nearly enchanted space— but it's Rui Long who brings the magic. I would be so desperate if she weren't here with me.

"Do you ever tell the truth?" asks Rui Long, clumsily setting her empty glass on the table. "I mean, really? I don't think there's anything more important than the truth. It doesn't matter what we do 'cause nobody's watching, but it matters a lot what we say because the universe is always listening. Do you, like, get that?"

"I, like, get that you'd better stay here tonight."

"There's a lot of truth in lies, though," says Rui Long, rubbing her eyes tiredly. "And there's a little lie inside every truth. It gets soooo complicated."

"You can have the mattress or the box springs," I tell her, standing, "but you've got to be out of here before dawn. You can hang around the basketball courts till the other students start showing up. Then my advice is to go back to your father's."

"I'm not going back there."

"As a matter of fact, you are. I'll take the mattress. Help me move it."

Rui Long's eyes search mine. "Can I ask you something?"

"Ask."

"But you're standing up."

"I listen very well standing up," I say.

She waits.

Sighing, I drop into the settee chair. My arm hurts more when I'm tired.

"There was something on your webpage," says Rui Long, "Julian. God, it's weird calling you that."

"Call me Doo," I say.

She stares, uncomprehending.

"I've been called Doo my whole life," I tell her.

In mock slow-motion, Rui Long grabs her head with both hands. "Oh, my Goddddddd! We're Doo and Doo! See what I mean? There's something about—I don't even know but *shit*, here's the thing. I saw something on your website. You said there's an inverse relationship between emerging truths and devolving—what was it?"

"Devolving systems based on subtractive processes."

"But why *inverse*?" asks Rui Long. "To me, it's like the exact opposite of inverse."

I rise. "I've already reached my conversation quota for the day. Help me with the mattress."

"You know," says Rui Long, rising, "I think you're telling the truth when you don't even know it. It's when you think you're really saying something that you're just making shit up. You *know*?"

"Have you been talking to my sister? Help me with this. I only have one arm."

Clumsily, we each grab one corner of the American Teacher's Mattress and yank. The mattress doesn't budge.

"You're going to have to really pull," I say.

Nimbly, Rui Long drops to the floor and places both feet against the side of the bed. Again we give a mighty pull, and the mattress slides onto the floor. One of the candles goes out.

I hear Rui Long laughing.

"Where are you?" I say.

"Help!" she cries.

I lift a corner of the mattress, and Rui Long crawls out, laughing. I watch her jack her little ass before rising to her feet. That was for me, I muse. Rui Long, still turned away, combs her hair with the fingers of both hands.

"You want to know what's really true?" she asks the wall.

The itsy schoolgirl turns to face me. "Sit down."

There's something new in the scratchy voice. I let myself fall into the settee chair.

Her eyes fixed on mine, Rui Long begins to unbutton the white school blouse. I watch the small fingers do their work, beginning at the tiny throat where dangles a silver butterfly pendant. The blouse falls partially open, and I see the bony notch of her sternum. In the candle light, Rui Long's skin is Chinese-perfect.

A shake of her small shoulders, and the blouse cascades to the floor. The two breasts are small but oddly heavy, their broad bases surrendering against the thin bones of her chest before suddenly and dramatically presenting the dark nipples straight forward. It's as though my eyes are pulling at them. I notice with satisfaction that the right breast is slightly larger than the left and a bit turned out.

The almond eyes blink slowly as Rui Long's hands reach down, sliding beneath the elasticized waistband to ease the uniform pants past the swell of her hips. Rui Long's thumbs hook her panties, as well, and a moment later both pants and panties are pooled at her ankles. Another surprise. A modest patch of hair marks the spot where Rui Long's thighs meet, and emerging from that small, dark patch is a diminutive and partially erect penis.

There's always a catch.

"Umm . . . ," I begin.

"It's not what you think," whispers Rui Long.

"You can put your pants back on now, *Roy* Long."

"Julian. Doo. Listen. I'm something new."

"Nice breast job, by the way. You really had me going for a—"

"*Look* at me," says Rui Long.

With difficulty, I return my eyes to the slight youth before me who, I cannot deny, cuts a splendid figure in the gently swaying candlelight.

"Look at my hips," instructs Rui Long. "Could a surgeon give me hips like these? Look at my shoulders. Are these the shoulders of a man?"

Frowning at Rui Long's round hips and the birdlike bones of her upper body, I say, "Hormone pills. Whatever. Really, why don't you put your pants back—"

"Not until you look at me."

"I've looked, thanks a million."

Rui Long drops to the mattress and raises one knee. One hand lifts the half-awake penis. Even in the candlelight, I can see that beneath it smile the lips of a very familiar opening.

I blink. "You're a hermaphrodite?"

"I'm something new," whispers Rui Long.

Color me impressed, hermaphrodites being both somewhat rare and at least as intriguing as the odd two-headed calf. Every human fetus, you may know, starts out female. In roughly half the cases, the hormones shift at a certain point and the clitoris becomes a penis. In some cases, the change is more or less inconclusive, which is information easily gleaned from books, but here spread disturbingly before me is a compelling case in point, a golden pubis aswirl with a fine mist of hairs and a two edged sword. *Rising* from that mist like the head of a young cobra is something for which I lack a ready frame of reference.

I'm beginning to perspire.

"You're not something new, Rui Long," I say carefully. "And there's nothing wrong with you. There have always been—"

"Come here," is the reply.

28

"Hermaphroditus was the daughter of Aphrodite and Hermes," says Rui Long, her mouth busy with take-out from the Sidewalk Fish Brains Café. Outside is bright midday. "Hermaphroditus was a female with a dick. That's where the name comes from, but *hermaphrodite* is like—it's a terrible word. Now people just say *intersex*. That's what I am."

"Intersex," I repeat, tasting the word in my mouth. It mixes well with General Tso's Chicken and Broccoli. "Is that kind of like being differentially sexed?"

"It's like being *fully* sexed," Rui Long corrects me. "I can make a girl pregnant if I want."

I give her a doubting look.

"I can have a baby, too," she continues. "I'm the whole package. That's why I say I'm something new."

I clear my throat. "Rui Long, what you're talking about is not new at all. Sometimes the genetics just work out that way. It's—"

"That's what everybody says, and it's bullshit," she replies, still eating heartily. "Everybody acts like it's some kind of birth defect, and it's not. *Every* intersex kid is butchered before she's old enough to understand what's going on. Butchered! Involuntary surgery. It's horrible. After we've been mutilated, we're put on hormone pills and told to act like a boy, or act like a girl, because anything else is too embarrassing for the family. That same shit would've happened to me if my momma'd been halfway right. She's a crack ho, so I just learned to hide it. I went all the way through school without anybody knowing. You think that shit was easy?"

"I'm not saying it was—"

"It still ain't. Nobody understands, including you." Her eyes pin me in place. "I didn't understand either until I heard Shatrina talking about polarity. Everything has gotten so polarized that nobody can communicate anymore. Everything is us against them. Shatrina said what we need now is something new, some kind of third alternative that breaks the stalemate. I was listening to this shit, and suddenly I'm like: that's *me*. I'm the something new. I'm the third alternative. Can I have another hit that chicken and broccoli?"

"Help yourself."

"So anyway, I went online and read everything I could find about biology and reproduction and—man, this chicken is some kind of good. Say whatever you want about these motherfucking Chinese, man, they can forevermore burn."

Ricky Ricardo Syndrome, Tree calls it, the tendency of multi-lingual and multi-dialectal people to revert to the mother tongue at moments of strong feeling. I'm not sure Rui Long has any other kind of moment.

"What did you find out?" I ask.

Rui Long reaches into her blouse and extracts the silver butterfly pendant. "This. We're caterpillars becoming butterflies, and I don't mean just us intersex people. All of us. We're at the dawn of a new human."

I recognize Tree's terminology. Clearly this Westmont girl has spent a lot of time alone in her room with a radio and a tube of airplane glue. But I let her continue.

"Most humans are gonochoristic," explains Rui Long. "Male, female. Polarized. Everybody's limited to being just half the picture. Butterflies are gynandromorphous. Sexually complete. They don't lack nothing."

Rui Long gives me a slightly superior glance before pointing to one of the get-well pictures on the wall. Prominently featured is the yin-yang circle of cavorting fish. "It's like that symbol. Masculine and feminine in one package. With just one fish, you got zip."

"Well," I say defensively, "the whole appeal of polarized sexuality is that singular moment when black fish and white meet. That can make for quite a party."

The teenager looks at me. "You're telling me we didn't have a party last night?"

Point well taken. It was certainly unlike any party I'd ever been party to. At first I had trouble getting around, quite literally, being in bed with an Uncle Wiggly not my own. Finally Rui Long propped herself up on a couple of pillows and said, "Look at it. Look at it good."

With an unhappy sigh, I turned my full attention to this young woman's wee-wee. In the flickering candlelight, it was as pale as the rest of her, its skin seemingly quite smooth. The head was not nearly as reddish-purple as I might have imagined and little larger than my thumb pad. It looked immature, in fact, altogether a relatively wan presence within its abbreviated collar of foreskin. I was almost looking at a tender young shoot, a *bud* awaiting permission to open.

And it was a goddamn dick.

"Encountering our sexual issues, are we?" taunted Rui Long, watching me with interest.

"Give me a minute," I sighed.

"Take all the time you want," she said. "I'll tell you what I finally decided. It's mine. Everything I got is mine, and it's *all* for playing with. I play with it all the time. You want to play with it?"

"I said give me a minute."

Deciding to get it over with, I inched closer to Rui Long's crotch and studied the underside of the small animal unaccountably nestled there. As I drew still closer, Rui Long inhaled sharply. Evidently my breath had touched the tender underside of that young shoot. For a moment it trembled and seemed to struggle against itself. At the same moment, Rui Long raised her hips slightly, and I examined the taut smile of the opening of the glans, quite familiar yet somehow different, and I strained to understand what that something was. And then I knew.

"It looks . . . feminine," I said, surprised.

"Of course it's feminine," whispered Rui Long. "It's me."

And it *was* her. Rui Long's flesh. Rui Long's blood. Her own coiled pleasure. Her own jittery breath. Her tiny fingertips, her raspy voice, every part was exactly her, exactly hers, precisely feminine. At that thought, a smile crossed my lips. I pursed them and blew warm air across, then around, the tender shoot, and Rui Long's back arched. I blew into that small patch of hair, and she giggled.

What is a female? A human whose warm body-core harbors new life. A human whose breasts enlarge and fill with milk, and whose rhythms and moods are circumscribed by cycles beyond easy measure. A woman, in short. The most alive and sensuous of all earthly creatures. I gazed at the lazy spread of Rui Long's hips and breasts. Clearly, here was a woman.

And more.

Timidly at first, the back of my hand stroked Rui Long's belly, each stroke a little longer than the previous until I brushed that dark patch of hair and she moaned. Then my hand brushed against Rui Long's most electric place, and in response her ribcage rose and fell. Then her eyes closed and her hand fumbled for the buckle of my belt.

From the first moment, I enjoyed the easy access I had to Rui Long's pleasure. Even my brutish fingers were able to articulate each moment of her super-clitoris. I traced unhurried circles along its warm throat and with each little variation, Rui Long gasped, completely present with my tiniest gesture.

She was utterly young, utterly transparent. I was easily able to take her to the brink of orgasm—and then stop her there, enjoying the control I held over the over-amped young body. Meanwhile Rui Long proved to be marvelously adept at touching me. Her hands knew the contours of my delight quite well. At times, our touches mirrored each other's, listening with our hands, responding to the simultaneous inner rages of fire and blood and want.

Increasingly delirious with pleasure, I touched and was touched, became wet and made wet, probably drooling generously all the while, my eyes on Rui Long's outturned right breast as it rose and fell in the flickering light. Finally overcome by curiosity, I lowered my head and nosed aside the prodigious clit to bury my face in her scent. I remained there for some time, breathing her in. I think I can authoritatively report that Rui Long is unquestionably a woman.

Still, I was a bit daunted by the question of positions, which Rui Long found amusing. At last, I adopted a modified missionary, one knee forward and the other back, allowing my plaster cast to rest safely to one side. Suddenly a packaged condom was held up before my face.

Even so, Rui Long's interior was shockingly warm.

I found myself easily capable of pressing my body against the underside of her prodigious clitoris. It was mere seconds before her voice erupted in delicious nonsense. Her orgasm was violent and seemingly painful, accompanied by a hoarse birdlike cry. I felt both our bellies grow warm. Then Rui Long fell limp as though dead.

About an hour later, I turned her over, enjoying how the super-clit showed between the tight buns. Minutes later, we came simultaneously, our cries hyper-comical. After a moment, we laughed at ourselves. A minute later, we laughed again.

After an hour or so of napping, Rui Long and I talked for most of the night, the difference between my age and hers gone from the flickering room. Around dawn, we began to touch once more, my fear of her body no longer anywhere to be found. She and I laughed and licked and sucked each other, our wet tongues twirling, until we both came with silly little yelps. Then we slept again. Gradually I became aware that

Rui Long was lying behind me, quite close, some specific part of her anatomy nudging me awake.

"Do you mind?" she asked.

What a gal.

"Call it a mutation," Rui Long says now, raking more General Tso's chicken onto her plate. "I don't know what it is. Shatrina talks about something waiting at the end of time, attracting us. All I know is, something's gotta change, so it's changing."

Again she fingers the butterfly pendant, a smile on her lips. "Mosaic gynandromorphs. That's what they call butterflies, and that's the new human, too."

"That particular mutation," I say, "would seem to make men expendable."

I know at least one feminist who would welcome that bit of news. We just spent the night among her scented pillows.

Rui Long's dark eyes fly to mine, the one on the right missing wide-right. Rui Long is slightly cockeyed. "Men *are* obsolete. Where's all the violence and rape and murder and shit coming from? Men. Where's all the wars and bombs and chemical weapons coming from? *Men.* Where do all these new inventions come from that poison the whole motherfucking world? It's coming from the goddamn men, and I think that's exactly what this mutation is about. Getting men out of the picture is *necessary*, fool, if we're going to survive."

"I'm feeling you," I say defensively.

Rui Long calms herself. "Well, I do prefer men in bed. I don't have much of a thing for women personally. Except for Halle Berry. I could like *go* for Halle Berry. Anyway that's the story. We're moving from gonochorists to mosaic gynandromorphs. Freaks like me are the first wave."

"You aren't a freak, Rui Long."

Still chewing, Rui Long takes my one good hand and places it on one side of her head. My fingertips feel something beneath the raven hair. A small, hard lump of some kind.

"What's that?" I ask.

Rui Long moves my hand to the opposite side of her head. I encounter another small, slightly pointed lump. Curious, I part Rui Long's hair and examine what appears to be a bony structure of some kind. Almost a budding—

"Rui Long?"

The schoolgirl bursts into laughter. "If you could see your face. I don't know what they are, but it feels pretty good when you touch them. At least they aren't growing. I can just see myself with fucking antlers."

I draw closer and take a good look. At each side of this child's head are what indeed appear to be vestigial—I can't even think the word. Begins with an *h*.

"Still say I'm not a freak?" asks Rui Long, amused.

"Well . . . ," I begin, hoping something will follow. It doesn't.

Rui Long says tauntingly, "You think you're such hot shit, and you don't know nothing about this world. You want to finish this noodle stuff?"

"I'm stuffed with noodle stuff."

"Me, too."

She surrenders her fork and I my personal wooden chopsticks. We fall side-by-side onto the mattress still sprawled on the floor. This room is post-tornadic. I am post-tornadic.

"How am I supposed to get out of here?" asks Rui Long.

I sigh and lace my fingers behind my head. "You're stuck here for now. You can slip out after dark."

"My dad is having a shit fit."

I glance at Rui Long's half-clothed body in this littered shambles of an American Teacher's Love Shack and ask myself what manner of fit her father would be having if he walked in right now.

At the thought, a loud banging erupts at the metal door, and Rui Long and I turn to gape at each other. A moment later, I'm on my feet and Rui Long is crawling double-time toward the bathroom. Now I crash into the settee table, and Chinese take-out flies through the air, a chair crashes to the floor, and my cast hits the floor lamp. *Shit*. Cradling my right arm, I look down and discover I'm not wearing any pants. All I see on the floor is Rui Long's blue-and-white uniform, wrong side out and sprinkled with herb-seasoned chicken. The loud banging comes again. Now I hear, "Mistuh Maaaaan-suh? Hellllo?"

I recognize the voice of Nancy Drew, whom I tutor twice weekly. I now want to kill her twice weekly.

"What do you want?" I shout through the door.

"Oh. Mistuh Maaansuh. How are you?"

"Fine. Thank you. And you?"

"You vaawy waalcome. Mistuh Maansuh. Want tomaaa-aaaaah-low go see big paint museum with you okay."

"See what?"

"Tomaaah-low go see painting museum four o'clock with you okay."

"See *what* painting museum?"

"Okay, bye bye. Oh. Mistuh Maansuh?"

"Yesss-ssss?"

"USA is have the wahhhhh."

I listen to Nancy Drew's footsteps fade along the balcony. Rui Long's face appears. "She gone?"

"Yes," I say, still cradling my throbbing right arm.

"What did she want?"

"Something about an art museum. And I think World War Three. Can you help me with this mess?"

"Jesus, look at this," says Rui Long, hooking her hair behind her ears.

Before we can begin, another knock comes at the door.

"*What?*" I shout irritably.

"Julian Mancer?" comes a man's voice.

Rui Long scurries away, carrying her chicken-strewn uniform with her.

"Yess-ss?" I say through the door, scanning the apartment once more for my pants.

"Uh, could we talk for a moment?" comes the voice. "I'm Agent Jim Barnes of the US Department of State, and I have Agent Raul Velázquez with me."

That can't possibly be good.

My feet are still bare and my shirt unbuttoned, but both legs are more or less inside a pair of trousers when I yank open the door.

Two thick-necked Westerners in dark suits. Matching moustaches. Matching smiles.

"I have plenty of life insurance already, boys," I tell them.

Both men laugh and hold up shiny gold badges for my inspection.

"I'm Agent Jim Barnes," says the chalky one, "and this is Agent Raul Velázquez."

"Do come in. Sorry about the mess. Bachelor housekeeping and all."

The two agents pick their way through Chinese take-out.

"I can make you some very bad tea," I offer. "Otherwise it's boiled tap water with or without cockroach."

"I'm good," they each say.

"I'm good, too," I tell them, nodding. "Isn't it good to be good?"

"Could we sit for a moment?" asks Barnes.

"Bed or mattress?"

Velázquez rights the overturned settee chair. The two men seat themselves. Barnes looks at my cast and says, "Seems you've had yourself a little accident."

"Seems." I drop into the computer chair. "I hear we are a nation at war."

The two men nod soberly.

"Actually, it's an operation," says Velázquez.

There's a hole in Barnes's left earlobe where a stud should be, and Velázquez's shoes are awfully pointy at the toes. If these guys are from State, I'm a senior auditor for the IRS.

"With or without anesthesia?" I say. "Actually I'm mad as hell about all those weapons of mass destruction, aren't you?"

Clearing his throat, Barnes says, "Mr. Mancer, we'd like to ask you a few questions about—"

There's a knock at the door, and our heads pivot in unison.

"Excuse me," I say.

I open the door to discover Madam Wu in her powder-blue cat's-eye glasses. Between two potholders is a covered dish. "Is General Tso's chicken!" she exudes.

"Wow," I say. "Did you ever read my mind."

Madam Wu trots past me toward the kitchen and the mushroom nursery.

"Uh, actually—" I call after her. "Agents Barnes and Velázquez?" I say as she vanishes into the kitchen. "Madam Wu."

Now someone else is standing in the doorway. It's a broadly smiling uniformed guard. I accept from him a number-ten manila envelope with my name scrawled in purple ink.

"Thank you very much," I say.

The guard gawks at the ruin of an apartment before turning away. Now Madam Wu trots back through.

"Thank you very much," I say.

Before closing the door, I check outside. No other visitors just now. I feel the envelope disappear from my hand. Turning, I stare at Agent Barnes who's walking back to the settee with my delivery.

"I'm *sorry?*"

"Just a precaution," says Velázquez. "Have a seat, Mr. Mancer. We'll explain everything."

Barnes extracts from the envelope a single sheet of spiral-bound notebook paper with an attached sticky note. Frowning, he says, "Do you know someone named Tree?"

Again falling into the computer chair, I reply, "She's closely related to Flowering Shrub, and I'm not saying another word until I know what you two are here for."

I gaze at them, ice water in my veins. I'm not too bad at this.

"Of course," says Velázquez, reaching into his briefcase for a glossy eight-by-ten. "Mr. Mancer, have you seen this man before?"

No safari hat. Otherwise I'm looking at Timothy Dobbins.

I shrug. "I met him two days ago."

"Can you tell us about that meeting?" says Velázquez.

"He said his name was Dobbins, and he seemed to know a lot about my sister and myself. I didn't feel very good about it."

Barnes says, "Tell us about that meeting."

I give them the sanitized version. Some guy walks up and says he's my long-lost dad. He tells me there's undeniable proof in the shopping bag. I refuse to look. That's basically it. "Nutcase as far as I'm concerned," I conclude. "I haven't mentioned this matter to my sister, and I'd appreciate it if you didn't either."

"What else did he say?" asks Barnes.

"I'd like to hear what you can tell me, actually."

"We would appreciate it," Barnes says carefully, "if you'd let us ask the questions."

Velázquez frowns for effect.

"I don't have to talk to you guys at all," I say.

Barnes leans forward. "Mr. Mancer, this is a United States Department of State investigation. It would be in your best interests to cooperate."

I lean forward, too. "If this has something to do with me or my sister, you need to come clean with me right now, and I mean *right* now."

"You want to calm down?" says Barnes.

"I should have gone straight to the Chinese," I snarl. "I should have had his ass thrown out of the country."

"We're working with the Chinese on this," says Barnes.

I fall back against the back of the computer chair, and it rolls a few inches. "Who is this asshole anyway? What's he after?"

Barnes and Velázquez exchange a glance.

Velázquez turns to me and says quietly, "Mr. Mancer, this man is not who he says he is. His name is Jerome Stiles. Stiles has been involved in intelligence and counterintelligence in one way or another since the 1950s. We think we know who he's working for at the present time and, while we cannot reveal that information, I will say this. Jerome Stiles is not friendly to the best interests of the United States of America."

Both men stare.

"Since he has contacted you," continues Velázquez, "it's possible that he will attempt to contact you again."

Barnes pulls out a business card.

"If he does," continues Velázquez, "we ask that you say nothing about this interview, and further that you call us from a pay phone using the number on this card. Should you have any questions or concerns, any at all, call this number and ask for myself or Agent Barnes." Velázquez folds his hands in his lap. "We agree that your sister does not need to know about this matter. In fact, we consider it advisable that you mention neither Mr. Stiles nor Agent Barnes nor myself to anyone."

They search my face.

I wonder what questions I should be asking right now. Finally I say, "But why would he approach me in the first place? What possible . . . ?"

Wrinkled brows.

"Did he show you his so-called proof?" asks Velázquez.

"I refused to look. I guess I was a little worked up."

The men glance at each other, and I ask myself how much they know and how much they're fishing for. I also wonder who they work for, if anyone. Agent Barnes has the look of a county-fair pickpocket.

"Look," I say with a sigh, "this is a little embarrassing. My sister and I have never known our father. A few years ago, I searched very hard for his identity. Could it be," I ask, "that I left a trail that someone, some con artist, somebody like Stiles, could follow back to me?"

"It's possible," says Barnes.

"If you find out anything one way or the other," I tell them, "would you give me a call?"

I busy myself writing down the phone number of the American Teacher's Apartment and Barnes accepts it. We all rise to our feet.

"So, what do you think of this atypical pneumonia thing?" asks Velázquez.

Both men grin icily, awaiting my answer.

"*Most* atypical," I say.

"You don't think it's serious?" asks Velázquez.

"Atypical pneumonia is the least of my worries," I reply. "What about you, Agent Velázquez?"

He says, "It's the least of my worries, too."

I turn to the chalky one. "And you, Agent Barnes? Is atypical pneumonia the least of your worries?"

"Absolutely," he says cheerfully. "Mind if I use your bathroom?"

"Uh—"

Barnes begins walking toward the rear of the apartment.

"Actually," I say, "it isn't working."

"Oh? I'll take a look at it," he says, still walking.

"You really shouldn't," I call but Barnes is already jiggling the doorknob.

He turns to me. "That's funny. This door is locked."

"That's what's not working," I say. "The lock."

Barnes and I share a gaze. Talk loud, show no fear, and continue with the lesson.

"We appreciate your cooperation," says Velázquez, extending his hand.

"Sorry if I got a little hot under the collar," I say, shaking his right hand with my left.

"Quite understandable," says Velázquez.

As I shake Barnes's hand, he says, "You sure about that life insurance? You can never have too much."

We all laugh.

After the two visitors leave, I press my ear against the entrance door. A full minute later, I open it warily. There's only a woman hanging wash. I eye her suspiciously before closing and bolting the door. I'm suddenly aware that my legs are shaking.

"You can come out," I call to Rui Long.

She emerges fully dressed. "Who the great big shit was that?"

"Insurance salesmen," I say. "I didn't want any." Wobbling to the kitchen, I uncap the Guangzhou vodka and turn it up.

"You all right?" asks Rui Long.

I don't reply till I've recovered my breath. In Guangzhou, it is said, vodka is formulated from cigarette butts and previously owned footwear.

"Perfect," I say hoarsely, pushing past her.

Back at the settee table, I lift the document delivered by the gate guard. The attached sticky note reads:

> Julian,
>
> When I woke up this morning, I found this page in my dream notebook. It came through when I was sleeping. Excited???!!
>
> Love, Tree

I examine the spiral-bound page. The handwriting is unfamiliar, but the two words scrawled across the top register pretty clearly. Chapter Thirteen.

29

"Have you heard?" Nancy Drew shouts into my face. "Fief dollars under sis have and haaal the people."

"Say again?"

"Fifty daughters," says Nancy Drew. "Haaal the people. Have you heard thees?"

"Fifty daughters?"

"Doccccctors," says Nancy Drew.

I close my eyes in hopes it may keep my head from exploding. It doesn't help that I'm clinging to the grab-rail of a city bus during peak after-school rush. Children's backpacks assail me from every direction, and the bus driver is playing "The East is Red" at a hundred forty-two decibels, quite possibly shattering my J-B Weld premolar crown.

And this is Nancy Drew speaking.

"Oh," I say. "Doctors. What about them?"

"Yes. Fifty doctors. Have you heard thees?"

"Have I heard *what*?"

"Fifty doctors!" Nancy Drew replies incredulously.

"What are you *telling* me about the fifty doctors?" I inquire through my teeth.

"Fifty doctors and nurses haalp the people. Have you heard thees?"

"No."

"No?" says Nancy Drew. "I very surprise."

I very fatigue. I break eye contact with Nancy Drew. For reasons that presently elude, she and I are en route to Guan Shanyue Art Museum. I've barely completed today's classes, and this vacuum-tube of a girl shows up breathless with two tickets and the grin that ate Shanghai. "We go now paint museum okay!"

People are staring at me. More than the usual number, I mean. I wonder whether it could have anything to do with my country's having spent the previous twenty-four hours bombing Baghdad into the early- to mid-Mesolithic.

Nah.

"Do you like thees?" asks Nancy Drew, pointing through the bus window at an anonymous department store.

I ignore her.

"Tell me a funny story," says Nancy Drew.

I ignore her a little more. I was hoping that an outing might help me clear my head. Here I am rehabbing from perfectly normal police-inflicted trauma when my dad shows up with a syringe, a horned schoolgirl puts her dick up my ass, and I receive a page of not-bad prose from a dead queer.

"Quite understandable," said Agent Velázquez. For him maybe. One has to wonder just a little as to what possessed our little Truman to end his protracted pout exactly now? If I have somehow *proven* myself, I've no idea how, though I did recently violate a mutant, which may have played to his interests.

"Do you theenk my English not very well?" asks Nancy Drew.

"Your English is adorable," I tell her.

"A dull lull?"

"Exactly."

I was also hoping a little outing would provide an opportunity to grow some new skin, as I've none whatsoever between my navel and my knees. Rui Long reports being in more or less the same condition. Girl can't get enough of me. She returned to her father's apartment last night just long enough for a change of clothes and a really fine argument. She was back at the American Teacher's Apartment before midnight. With her toothbrush.

"Uh, Itsy, you can't live here," I said, to which she replied, "I told you not to call me that. And I'll be out of here before morning."

Or that was the plan. The current one, should it manifest and I personally hope it does, is for Rui Long and I to keep our body parts pointed in different directions while she figures out what comes next in the exciting saga of Westmont Girl Seeks Roots, Finds Tuber. This morning she told me I might think about cleaning the bathroom. I informed her that Tree had cleaned the bathroom quite competently scarcely a week ago. "Who's Tree?" asked Rui Long. "Never mind who's Tree," I replied. "Just be out of here by dawn. And stop doodling on the toilet paper."

In truth, I can't help but feel a fresh wave of arousal at the thought of our little Two-Fer. The girl is mad as a hatter, of course, but since when did that constitute a problem in bed? In a little over a day, she and I have added at least three chapters to *The Kama Sutra* and, skin regeneration allowing, may yet be looking at a free-standing Volume Two. I think we'll call it "Two in the Hand, Three in the Bush."

"I theenk you very quietly," says Nancy Drew, inclining her face. "Why you so quietly?"

"I'm always quiet," I say, turning away from a withering gust of garlic breath. Nancy Drew's mother is among the many who believe that a clove a day keeps atypical everything away.

"Oh?" says Nancy Drew. "Whyy-yyyy?"

I let the question pass, knowing that another will come along shortly.

It does.

"How much you pay this shirt?" asks Nancy Drew, tugging on a sleeve.

Eat my calf-length argyle socks.

"Do you like *kai xin gou*?" she asks.

"Do I like what?"

"*Kai xin gou* present I give you," says Nancy Drew.

She must be talking about the bell-pepper-looking thing on the kitchen windowsill. I really should think about watering it.

"This plant is mean your haaa-aaht," says Nancy Drew. "Make your haa-aaht very happy, I think. We go down now."

The bus lurches to a stop, and Nancy Drew darts out the rear exit. I manage to stumble out behind her just before the door hisses to a close. The bus roars away, spewing a brown cloud, and I gaze straight up hoping against hope for a little cheery Mediterranean blue. Instead is the usual East Hudson pewter.

"What do you see?" asks Nancy Drew.

"I was looking," I reply irritably, "at the sky."

"Ohhhh?" She gazes up and blinks, seeing nothing.

Nancy Drew's going through an awkward year.

As we approach the steps of Guan Shanyue Art Museum, several uniformed kids saunter past and one glares at me and imitates the whistling sound of a bomb. The others follow suit.

I haven't heard a single word from Lillian. I suppose she's busy venting about the war to that mutt boyfriend of hers, though I suspect most of it is over his head. Tree keeps saying I should call Lil, and I suppose I should but that means first preparing an itemized list of what I'm apologizing for. Women want the details, and they want them right.

Nancy Drew leads me into the art museum, a smugly modern building with vaulted ceilings and stepped echoes. She has promised, if I understood correctly, a nice collection of neoclassical nature paintings. Which could fit right in, career-wise. "Do you write for this magazine?" Miriam recently asked me on the phone. "No pressure or anything. I'd just like to know."

Never work for a woman with her hair in a bun.

Actually Chinese painters as a whole are a surprise. They take far greater trouble than their Western counterparts, which I expected—but without forfeiting expression, which I didn't.

And they do everything. Every style, every approach. Nancy Drew and I enter the first exhibit room, and out comes my journal, which I've learned to balance on my cast. Next to Tree's smiley face.

"What do you wiiiite?" asks Nancy Drew.

"Notes."

I may have to write a real article this time. I move a little closer to a very old scroll—too close, it appears, for an alarm sounds. A moment later, a uniformed guard attaches to me, but I scarcely notice, occupied as I am by a cluster of ghostly images from Huang Ge, whose one foot is in traditional Chinese landscape painting with its insistence on line and discipline, and the other in French Impressionism. When this country opened its doors to the outside world in the seventies, nothing astonished Chinese artists quite so much as the Impressionists. Unless it was the Carpenters.

The guard is still attached to my hip, and I turn to give him an evil stare. He is flat-nosed, crew-cut, and it would appear determined to lose as few pieces of neo-traditional Chinese art to colorless Westerners as possible.

"Do you like theees?" Nancy Drew calls from the next room.

I tell the guard's flat nose, "Nancy Drew is calling me."

I now stand before a large and airy landscape by Yuan Rong Cueng, whose soft grayscale touches make of each mountain crag a billowing cloud yet an inescapable singularity. Next are the tiny, meticulous fan-shaped landscapes of Song Dai. In one of his images, a tiny traveler gazes straight up at a sun-paled moon, ignoring the lush landscape of forested slopes, austere cliffs, and frothing streams that tumble all about him.

Nancy Drew and I enter a room of lurid nature paintings in the Palace style, including several by Muo Xiao Suong, known for his dragonfly-festooned idealizations of nature, each impossibly bright. You can almost smell the thunderstorm that just passed through. The guard has wandered off somewhere, and I'm tempted to inch a bit closer to a particularly vivid Muo but think better of it. Instead I follow Nancy Drew through another four rooms of traditional landscapes and dentist's office crap and cock-obvious Commie propaganda, and it's all pretty decent. Especially to a Westerner accustomed to posture-ism as art. Take *that*, Cy Twombly.

Actually, I may have overdone the ma huang today. But I say that every day.

"Hmmm." At eye level between two canvasses is a rectangular air-return vent. "Very interesting," I say, stepping closer to study the vent, and Nancy Drew stares at me.

"No, not this," she scolds, pulling me along.

A good eye for art, that girl. In the States, the air-return grate would carry a title *and* a price tag. In the USA, if your local art museum doesn't have a porcelain toilet suspended by a wire, the only possible question is why.

We enter a room of mawkish comrade paintings. Tacked onto otherwise proto-traditional landscapes are rows of handsome, smiling soldiers marching along in well-fitting unis. I begin to move toward the exit—when I hear the sound of spoken English.

I turn to see three women huddled before a large still life. One is a blond Westerner who tans too much, the second a Chinese in a crisp business suit, and the third a pale foreigner with abundant dark-brown tresses. I begin to walk zombie-like toward this third woman as though drawn by a silken thread. When I reach the spot where she stands, she turns upon me an eye of blue and an eye of green.

"Ana," I say.

"Oh," she gasps. "I'm sorry . . . "

"Julian," I prompt. "We met on a train."

"Of course. Julian, what a surprise. These are my friends, Lian and Heather."

I greet the two women without taking my eyes off Ana Manguella.

"Somehow," she teases, "I didn't figure you for a connoisseur of revolutionist art."

"More of an aficionado."

We were put together once, I was told on a southbound train. It can happen again.

"What has befallen your poor arm?" asks Ana.

"Newtonian physics. Meet my chaperon, Nancy Drew."

Another round of introductions. The three women make much of the fact that they'd stopped at the museum on impulse after getting lost in Shenzhen traffic. Lian, the woman in the business suit, takes a high-heeled step toward me and announces, "Excuse me for asking, please, but what do you think of the war?"

Heather, the overtanner, tosses her mane and says, "That's all I've heard all day. War, war, war. Nobody asked *me* if we should start a stupid war."

Ana nods. "I'm getting it, too. Unfortunately we Brits are as deep in this business as anyone, and of course it's utterly senseless."

I gesture toward the nearest wall. "It's like these paintings. Happy, healthy soldiers in neat rows, marching off somewhere to right the world's wrongs. This war will end up being the same basic catastrophe as the Chinese Revolution."

I glance at Lian, wondering whether I might have couched that a little differently.

Ana rescues me. "Mass bloodshed never has been much of a solution, has it? But I'd like to know what Nancy and her classmates think of all this."

All eyes turn to Nancy Drew, who grins hugely, her eyes becoming slits. "I think is very *excite*. Everybody think this so good because USA spend all the money fight the wahhh become poor like Chinese."

Lian speaks sharply in Mandarin to Nancy Drew, and the grin fades.

"Well," says Ana, "that puts a dot at the end of it. Anyone want tea? I saw a little shop at the entrance."

Moments later we're seating ourselves at a lacquered black table covered by a split bamboo mat. When the waitress takes our order, she is wearing a gauze mask and a pair of clear surgical gloves.

"I hear they've brought in fifty doctors from somewhere," says Heather. "The government won't admit it, but this pneumonia thing's way out of control. *Way.*"

Lian knits her brow. "My mother's friend is work in Guangzhou, and she say all the hospitals have a big problem. The nurses get this atypical pneumonia, and now nobody want to come to work."

"It has a new name," I announce, and everyone turns to look. "The World Health Organization says it's now SARS: Severe Acute Respiratory Syndrome."

Ana says, "That solves the problem. Just give it a winning name. Like Operation Iraqi Freedom. Has such a nice ring, don't you think?"

"To nice rings," I say, lifting my teacup.

"To freedom," says Ana, lifting hers.

Heather thinks for a moment. "To being atypical."

"Cheers," says Lian.

Nancy Drew, scanning her cell phone screen, misses the toast.

The black tea finds the ma huang. Suddenly I'm lecturing the table on Chinese art. " . . . And I've never seen color used quite this way. And the *brushstrokes*. The Chinese don't load the brush like the Western Impressionists, but still there's this—"

Everyone is staring.

"I'm sorry," I say. "I shouldn't be allowed to drink tea."

"I'm totally into Andrew Wyeth," says Heather. "You can't tell him from a photograph."

"Please go on," Ana encourages me, and I give her my most winning smile.

Ouch. Something just stirred that doesn't have skin. My entire being cries out for this snowy woman with the trailing tresses. No matter the two-in-one schoolgirl waiting at home.

My sister is fond of telling me that I don't have a prayer against a pair of tits. "All a woman has to do is inhale and she owns half your portfolio, and you don't seem to be getting any smarter about it." My sister meanwhile is still dating the lower-story accountant. The last time Lil dated someone who came to her shoulder—he was a ballroom dancer whose favorite move was to twirl his partner beneath his arm—the relationship lasted through about nine bars of "Mood Indigo."

She doesn't seem to be getting any smarter about it.

Our little group decides to leave a tip for surgical-waitress, hiding it beneath a saucer and scurrying away before she notices. Outside, dusk has set in and we're rewarded with a hint of pink at the farthest edge of the sky. I bid the three women farewell, saving my warmest handshake for Ana Manguella.

"We've been put together a second time," I tell her. "Surely you won't deny me your email address now."

"You can give me yours," says Ana. "I'm terribly busy just now, but I might show you around Kowloon when I've the time."

After the women depart, Nancy Drew and I decide it's a nice evening for a walk. Though we're well into spring, a cool snap seems to have appeared from nowhere, adding a little zip to everyone's gait. It's as though something very good waits at home.

Which happily should be the case. If only I possessed the requisite epidermal sheath. During the long stroll back to campus, Nancy Drew babbles nonstop and I ignore her, enjoying instead the pleasant tugs of simultaneous yearnings, one *itsy* golden hand pulling tauntingly at one ear, a cool white hand teasing the other. I'd love nothing more than to take those two hands into mine—and place them on each other.

That would be a party.

Nancy Drew and I approach a corner where an old man with a stringy beard squats in front of an open-face shop, lighting an upright tobacco pipe cut from giant bamboo. Behind him, a whole family gnaws lengths of sugar cane amid the general clutter of bicycle repair. Nancy Drew and I pass one after another of the voracious and encyclopedic shops that line every Chinese sidewalk, everything open to view, families wielding chopsticks, men sitting at cards, children poring over homework, faces inclined to upper-shelf TVs and lofty altars to Guan Yin, Goddess of Mercy and Rapid Skin Regeneration.

Suddenly, my eyes register something unexpected. I stop walking.

Nancy Drew stops as well. "What do you see?"

I see an untended spot of ground between two buildings where an exuberant eruption of plant life has welcomed itself to thrive. Bamboo specifically. A lot of it.

"A premolar crown retrieval device," I reply.

"Oh," says Nancy Drew, studying her phone again.

The longer canes I judge to be some four meters in length. More than enough. I turn to follow Nancy Drew. All I'd need is a reasonably sharp machete—readily available, I'm quite sure, at the neighborhood hardware and prophylactic emporium—and a nice wad of pink bubblegum, preferably not of North Korean origin. And the phone number of a reliable bail bondsman, depending on the exact wording of Chinese environmental statutes.

It's wonderful how everything's coming together for me just now. Not only have I discovered bamboo, Ana Manguella has re-appeared in my life, and an amber sixteen-year-old awaits me at Lil's apartment in nothing but an unbuttoned dress shirt from Lil's closet and a dangerous cock-eyed smirk.

I think I may have grown a little skin at the art museum.

Earlier this afternoon, I returned from a shopping trip loaded down with booze and steaming carry-out. Rui Long didn't give me a chance to get out of my shoes. The moment the door closed behind me, she fell onto her knees on the mattress, threw her hair behind her shoulders, unbuttoned the dress shirt, and summoned me with a forefinger.

I've always said you gotta have one to know how to do one.

"Thanks for the museum," I tell Nancy Drew at the stoop of her dormitory.

"You vaawy waalcome," she says toothily. "Goo night."

The white-over-blue uniform trots the stairs.

I return to Lil's dorm a bit more eagerly than usual. But when I unlock the steel door, no one greets me. I turn on the light to discover that the room has been straightened. At the center of the mattress is a note beneath a small pink box.

> Dearest Doo,
>
> I decided to go before it's dark. Don't worry. I'm an expert at blending in, remember?? I really don't know how to thank you for last night and also today. I can't believe it was less than 24 hrs can you??? Anyway I am leaving you this tokin [*sic*] of my thanks, and I hope you will except [*sic*] it.
>
> Love always and always,
>
> Your Doo.
>
> P.S. Did you know there's a big rat in here!?!!

The small pink box is wrapped with a ribbon cut from a sheet of printer paper. Inside the box is Rui Long's deck of Barbie runes. There's an inscription on the cover of the box, written in the same loopy, feminine hand:

> Light will someday split you open
> Even if your life is now a cage,
> For a divine seed, the crown of destiny
> Is hidden and sown on an ancient
> And fertile plain you hold title to.
>
> — Rumi

I close the box once more and toss it onto the mattress. Rumi. I'll bet he's a big hit in Westmont. I walk into the kitchen and begin to wash China off my hands, challenge enough even without a plaster cast. Gazing at the bell-pepper plant on the windowsill, I ask myself which of Ana Manguella's eyes is my favorite. The green one has a kind of cool, playful sparkle that summons early May and the year's first tall glass of iced tea topped with a sprig of mint. But the *blue*.

Oh definitely the blue.

Drying my hands, I notice a nasty crack running along the top of the bell-pepper thing. Guiltily, I pour a little tap water into the pot. What was it Nancy Drew called this thing? *Kai xin gou*? She said it symbolizes the heart. Before, she'd told me it represents the world. I turn the pot a little, and the bulb takes on a definite heart shape. I turn it a little more, and there's the world. Tossing the hand towel, I ask myself whether we're looking at a world splitting wide open, or one lumpy green heart just about to break.

30

"The people who were big and strong," says Bobby, "were the first ones to die."

Bobby and I are alone in the English faculty office. His voice is muted. No Peking Opera just now.

"Everyone was given the same amount of food, you see," says Bobby. "If you were very small, very thin, you could survive. That's all, just survive. Everyone had a very difficult time."

I squirm in my chair. I love Chinese-y as much as the next guy, but this is my first day back.

"All the books say the Great Famine was caused by drought," continues Bobby, "but that's not true. Those people starved because of Mao Zedong. My father was one of those people. I dug the hole to bury him."

I know already that Bobby's was a family of semi-literate Gansu Province farmers who'd never had much of anything. They'd always managed, but that changed dramatically when Mao decided to inflate rice production numbers so he could go down in history as an all-around genius. He did go down in history, having put to needless death more of his own people than Stalin ever thought about.

"There was a lot of pressure," says Bobby, "to have very big harvests. There was no reason for it, but you had no choice. If the soil and the weather in your area only make so much rice for every *wu*, well, that's all it can make. People know because they have been on that land for many generations. But now you were expected to double or triple that amount."

Farmers were forced to use their rice reserves as seeds planted very close together. The result was a lot of weak plants that couldn't hold their heads above water. At the same moment, Mao was pressuring farmers to neglect their fields in favor of producing crap-quality pig iron, to inflate iron production numbers. Mao's ego tantrum, called the Great Leap Forward, starved thirty million people.

"In my own family," says Bobby, pushing his glasses higher on his nose, "my mother gave up some of her food for the children. Some days she couldn't get out of the bed. My father was a big man, so he could never get enough to eat. He became very sick."

I squirm a little more, but Bobby continues with accounts of people dying from colds and minor infections. No one wanted to use the word *starvation*, least of all the local officials held accountable by Beijing. The extent of the catastrophe was severely undersold.

"Finally the government had to do something, so they said that every family could have a small garden just for themselves. That made a very big difference for us. Really, that is what saved us."

Eighteen-year-old Bobby, head of household now, eagerly planted turnips and pumpkins and cabbage and other vegetables from the family's secret store of seeds, plus a small plot of rice that he worked every evening after laboring in the common fields. The garden thrived and Bobby's remaining family eked by. After several hard years, they were able to store a small cache of grain.

"This was so important to our minds," he says. "It gave us a little feeling of control. One year later, we began to think about having a pig. That was a very frightening idea for us because that pig would eat a lot of our food. We could not imagine giving our food every day to a pig." He laughs at the recollection. "After years with no meat, you couldn't really believe that it would ever be on your plate again. When you are in a time, your thinking is just limited to that time."

I nod. I never throw any of my food to a pig.

"Finally," says Bobby, "in 1972, the universities opened again. There were no examinations because no one was able to pass. There had been no schools for many years, you see, except for studying Mao Zedong's writings or singing some patriotic songs. So everything had to begin from nothing. Some officials came around and interviewed young people in every village. I was selected for university and my life completely changed. I was sent to Gansu Foreign Language School to study English. Then I was given a teaching job for one dollar a day. That meant my family would survive. I took care of my sisters and brothers, all five of them, for half of my life."

Bobby leans back in his chair, removes his glasses, and massages his thick eyebrows. "I can't believe it, really. Soon I will retire, and I have enough money to do whatever I want. I remember how to farm. I can hold some earth in my hand and know exactly what to do with it. Maybe I will buy some piece of land in the United States and be a farmer again."

I nod, picturing Bobby somewhere outside Des Moines in a John Deere cap, singing falsetto through his nose as he throws some of his food to a pig. Hey, if I can be a Chinese schoolteacher . . .

Bobby has promised me a personal translation of Li Bai's poem, "Drinking Alone in the Moonlight," which has never been properly rendered in English, says he. Every Chinese character has multiple meanings, thus every Chinese poem has multiple threads running through it, and all but one are lost in translation. Not to worry, though. Bobby's on it.

After the final class of the day, I labor up the stairs to Lil's apartment. My first day back on the job went well enough. The kids all stared at me, but at least they were paying attention for once. For my own part, I had trouble not staring at Itsy, who kept those spooky eyes of hers demurely down. Once I thought I saw a sly smile at the edges of her pout, or so I congratulated myself. It was the smile of a cat who'd just passed a *wonderful* night with the canary.

"How'd it go with your father?" I asked her after class.

Rui Long shrugged her bird-like shoulders. "I think I'm grounded. That auntie woman walked me to school this morning. I guess she'll be walking me home, too."

That could actually be a good arrangement. Not only does my body need a little rehab, but this is China, where the top three national pastimes are gossiping over rice, gossiping over noodles, and gossiping over Twice Cook Pork. *No* one keeps this kind of nugget secret for long here, if indeed it's a secret now.

At the top of the stairs, I pant my way beneath and around the neighbors' wash. Never walk beneath a pair of trousers, I'm told. Especially if you're wearing them. I push open the door of the apartment and hear a scraping sound. Looking down, I find that a manila envelope was slipped beneath the door while I was away.

Inside the envelope is a fresh raggedy page from Tree's dream journal. This would be page two of Chapter Thirteen. I decide to make myself a drink before reading it. Dropping the page next to the computer, I hit the on button and walk into the postage-stamp kitchen.

Ah. As I roll up my one shirt sleeve to wash, I'm pleased to see the tiny beginnings of a forest of mushrooms erupting from the vermiculite in the aquarium. Their color, a menacing dark red, is beginning to show. The *kai xin gou*, on the other hand, could be in a spot of trouble. That nasty crack has grown in size, all but cutting the bell-pepper thing in half. As I wash my hands, I give it a bit more toxic Chinese tap water. That'll help.

I lean forward over the kitchen sink to check the status of my gold maxillary first premolar crown out on the ledge. It's still there, dotting the third eye of Immortal Korean Chocolate Buddha. He's still laughing. At me, I think.

As I wash my hands, I wonder what that little nugget of gold might actually bring. I also wonder how, in the middle of a city of eleven million Chinese, a six-foot-four near-albino with a machete might go about harvesting a three-meter length of bamboo without being *noticed*. But a helicopter and rope-ladder seems out of the question.

Tree phoned me this morning to crow about the new pages, and of course I said I was gratified. She apologized for not delivering them herself, but she and her Mr. Xu are up to their *mmmm's* just now. "Julian," she said on the phone, "this Fibonacci stuff is the most exciting information I've ever encountered. I'm doing my whole show on it this week."

The last time Tree stumbled onto something really exciting, she and Lillian and I wound up inside a refrigerator carton with a candle, the Kabbalah, and a double-terminated Herkimer quartz crystal. Naked.

The first page is good, by the way. No, it's really good. I went over it several times last night, more than a little jealous at how deftly the conclusion is turning in a direction I'd totally failed to anticipate. Odd, though. Truman is talking *dip slopes* and other obscure geologists' terms that can't have very much to do with Southern Noir. I'm more than a little curious about this second page.

I seize the gin bottle by the neck and suck on it for a little while. My definition of making myself a drink these days. There's a popping sound as my lips come away. Shuddering, I return to the front room and the American Teacher's Computer and say hi to Cowboy Shirt Elvis. He doesn't reply. I decide to make a quick check of my email and there encounter the usual spams, chain forwards, too-little too-late petitions against the Iraqi war—uh, operation—and another all-caps message from Jeremy, which I delete unopened. Sore loser.

Now my eyes register a name I've never before seen in print, let alone in my personal inbox: Ana Manguella. I open the message.

Dear Julian,

What a surprise to encounter you at the museum! It was quite a chain of improbable circumstances that put me there that day, and I've reflected on what that could mean. Still don't know! But, recalling our conversation on the train, I thought you might be interested in the link below. Happy reading.

All the best,

Ana

The link takes me to a highly academic site on European mythology that features an article on Heracles. Above the article is an old drawing of our superhero, club in hand and lion skin adorning his head. With the aid of his cousin, Iolaus, Heracles is battling the wicked Hydra. He/they don't seem to be making much headway.

Deciding to put off reading the article till I've savored Truman's latest page—and *made* myself another drink—I thank Ana for the information and ask whether she might be able to free up some time for an afternoon stroll along Kowloon Bay. No woman can resist being walked beside a body of water. It can be a sewage treatment lagoon. Doesn't matter.

After mailing and downing drink number two, I break out Page Two. Nothing earth-shattering. More wacky handwriting. More geological peculiarity. *Here's* something strange. The first paragraph of the new page ends with the word "blue." There's only one other paragraph on the page, and it ends with "green." Curious, I go back to the first page of Chapter Thirteen, which too is composed of exactly two paragraphs, the first concluding with the word "beware," the other "sheen."

We won't think about that just now.

31

"It's been a very strange year," I say to Ana Manguella.

Very close by, a cruise ship glides soundlessly along Hong Kong's Victoria Harbour.

"Everyone I know says the same thing," replies Ana, strolling beside me in a long tan raincoat. "Let me guess," she continues. "You're experiencing one unexpected turn after another, you're frustrated and stressed to the limit, yet there are more opportunities than ever. Am I right?"

"Except for the opportunities part," I say.

"Oh, the opportunities are there, I assure you," says Ana. "It's the outer planets. Things won't settle down till after the eclipse in May. Think you can last that long?"

"That's the plan," I tell her.

"I'm sure you'll be tucked back into your Memphis well before then, and that *nasty* break will be fully mended."

Ana raps lightly on my cast, now adorned with a complex ball-point doodle by Rui Long.

"Can it be somebody else's Memphis?" I inquire. "I keep moving away, but I always wind up back there. It's probably the food. Hard to beat barbequed pork on white buns with sugared coleslaw and cold beer. My favorite breakfast actually."

"Didn't Memphis recently erect an enormous pyramid?" asks Ana.

"In the middle of downtown. Fits right in."

"Wouldn't that change things enormously? In the energy sense, I mean?"

"Hard to say," I reply, "but the winos are now asking for spare *deshrets*. What's that strange smell?"

"Smell?"

"I think it's oxygen. Actually I think spring has come to the mainland. The way you know is, the public restrooms come to *you*."

Ana pauses to pull a small bud from a tree. With a bow, she delivers it to the palm of my hand. There's a hint of purple at one end. "The way you know that spring has come to Earth," says Ana, "is the emergence of flowers."

I place the bud in a shirt pocket and we step onto a wooden pier. Before us, the breathtaking blue of the bay reflects the white skyline of Kowloon. Reaching the farthest end of the pier, we lean against a sun-warmed iron railing.

"So you're planning to return to Memphis yet again?" asks Ana.

"If I can just get out of China," I answer. "But I never stay any one place for very long. This guy I work with, Bobby, asked me how many times I've moved in my life. He said he'd moved four times, which for a Chinese is practically nomadic."

"And you?" asks Ana.

"Fifty-four, so far. Living somewhere is intolerable, if you want to know the truth. Have you ever put off going home because you can't stand the thought of being there? Yet you end up home anyway because every other place you can think of is worse?"

Ana blinks. "Have you ever been treated for depression, Julian?"

"Successfully? No."

"Go on," she says.

"What better way to shake things up than to move? Suddenly you're in survival mode. You're living out of unmarked boxes. Even brushing your teeth requires creative thought. You're eighteen years old again. You're setting up your first apartment."

"I never looked at it quite that way," says Ana. "To me, moving is simply hell."

"Of course it's hell. It may be six months before you get your life back online. Finally you establish these little rhythms.

You're back. Which is the problem, of course." I look at her. "You. Or me, as the case may be."

"I had no idea," says Ana, "you were this fucked up."

"I'm at least this fucked up," I tell her.

"Here you are being so *transparent* with me," adds Ana. "Frankly, you were just awful on the train. I'd say China has been good to you, Julian."

"Tree says I'm changing."

"And what are you changing into?"

"I think I'm just changing out-of," I reply.

Ana gives me a questioning gaze. I watch the breeze toy with her hair. I'm becoming somewhat fond of the fine hairs around her ears.

Stepping off the pier, she and I pass a sidewalk poet with long chin whiskers and a longer paintbrush. He's doing calligraphy on the sidewalk using water, onlookers admiring each stroke. Before he reaches the end of the poem, the beginning has evaporated.

Escaping campus today wasn't easy. The moment my final class dismissed, I hurried to the English office to drop off the clipboard, which usually entails dodging Marilyn, who has taken to haunting the patio just outside the English office. *Oh Ju-wen, it's you.* I did manage to skirt around her, only to discover a familiar hiney in Lil's desk chair. At least she didn't have her feet on the desk.

"I have a question about the homework," said Rui Long imperiously.

"I didn't assign any homework," I replied.

"Then I have a question about today's *class*."

The other English teachers pretended to be very busy at their desks.

"Could we step outside?" I suggested with an icy smile.

Beyond the door, I wedged my hands as deeply into my pockets as I could manage, so as to keep them off Rui Long's little throat. "I thought you were an expert at blending in.

What you're doing right now is the blending equivalent of a Falun Gong demonstration."

"You're just going to criticize me?" said Rui Long. "Somehow I expected more than that from you."

"Oh Ju-wen, it's *you*."

"Why hello, Marilyn."

I managed to get away with the greater part of my skin and very little in the way of dignity. I'm not sure just what's going on in my personal life right now. It's the outer planets, no doubt.

"So," says Ana, "what do you intend to do?"

"Do?"

"About your problem," she says.

"I have a problem?"

"You're all fucked up."

"Oh," I say, "that's not a problem."

"You might think about moving on to the second Noble Truth," she suggests. "There's little fun to be had in the first, you know."

I shake my head. "I'm way ahead of you. I'm at Noble Truth Number Four, which is 'Ignore Truths One through Three.' Would you like to hear my technique for turning a grade-three depression into a grade-two?"

"You have grades?"

"It helps to objectify. I assign three grades. There's a grade four, as well, but I stay away from it. If there's a grade five, I think one simply loses consciousness. Do you know what *syzygy* means?"

"Sy- what?"

"Never mind. Most people only know about grade-one depression. That's the blahs. You're not in the mood for anything. For me, that would be a pretty good day."

Ana bursts into laughter before catching herself. "I'm sorry."

"Grade two," I continue, "is actual suffering. You're burning calories. You're practically aerobic. When you hit grade two, you're reaching for the coping mechanisms. You're sitting in the bath eating from the one-gallon tub of Rocky Road with a spoon. You're doing everything you can think of. Still, grade two is common enough." I turn to her. "What's broadly misunderstood is grade three. You're suffering about suffering. You're suffering about *suffering* about suffering. It's a pain feedback loop so intense that it leads to thoughts of death. Not that death is an actual remedy. All depressed people believe in an afterlife because it's the most depressing thing imaginable."

Ana studies the paving stones before us. "And your technique?"

"Technique?"

"For turning a grade three into a—?"

"Oh. Very simple, really. You stop wanting to feel better."

"That's it?" she says.

"You think that's easy?"

"I didn't say—"

"You're surrendering your last vestige of *hope*," I say grandly, throwing my hands. "You're giving up the only thing that could possibly matter to you, which is finding a way out of the pain. There's nothing harder."

We walk in silence for a moment, and with a start I cognize what I've just said to this alabaster woman. I suppose it's a little late to take it all back.

"I suppose I've never thought about it," says Ana. "I'm a very work-oriented person—not career-oriented, mind you. But extremely focused on what I do. I suppose I never take the time to think about being happy."

"Have you heard the story of the horse that forgot how to walk?" I reply. "Someone asked him which leg moved first, and which second, and so on. Once the horse thought about it, he couldn't move at all." I look at her. "Don't think about being happy."

Ana places her right hand in mine. It's lighter than expected. Slightly cool to the touch.

"I've never told anyone that before," I admit.

"About the horse?" she asks.

"The other part."

"Not even your sister?"

"My sister and I don't really talk," I say. "She self-discloses. I smart off."

Actually, we don't even do that anymore. I suppose I should call her.

Ana says, "Actually your method isn't exactly Buddhist. Very few people realize that Buddhism is, in fact, a psychological system—just as Celtic spirituality is, once you unpack it. But all the wisdom traditions converge at a certain point, don't you think?"

I nod. "You give up the struggle, then you realize that it was the struggle that was driving you crazy. In Buddhism, when you finally get that, you're enlightened. In Taoism, you just get an erection."

Ana laughs before catching herself. "And in Christianity?"

"In Christianity, you get a little wafer. Listen, I don't have this hand-holding thing down exactly. When are we supposed to let go? And am I supposed to be making little *squeezes* or something?"

"You've never held a woman's hand before?"

"Only long enough to get the handcuffs on her."

"You can let go anytime you'd like."

"But how do you know it's *time*? And since you initiated it, if I let go first, wouldn't that constitute some kind of message? But I can't hold on forever, both of us perspiring heavily—why are you laughing? This is serious stuff."

"Julian, you just need to relax a little."

"Oh, is *that* all?"

"Let's try an experiment," says Ana. "Instead of thinking of my response, just make yourself completely comfortable with my hand. You can pretend I'm sleeping, or in some other way completely insensate. Do you see?"

I consider this dangerous proposal for a moment. "What I'm hearing is, I'm supposed to be totally myself with your snowy right hand?"

"Exactly."

I stop Ana Manguella in a patch of shadow. Slowly I lift her right hand with both of mine and marvel at the delicate white fingers. Ana's nails are short and tidy, almost boyish. Before I realize it, I have kissed each nail in turn. Now we're walking again, quite slowly now.

"How would you rate your mood just now?" asks Ana, smiling.

"Point eight and dropping."

"Dropping? Is that good or bad?"

"There's no good or bad," I tell her. "As soon as you establish a preference, you've lost the round. Actually point eight is quite low, considering the time of day. After lunch, I'm usually well into the twos."

Ana looks puzzled. "Is that what it's like inside a man's head? Are there just little numbers stacked in there? I don't think it would occur to a woman to assign a number to a feeling."

I glance at her face. "You know what's funny?"

"What?" says Ana.

"I just realized that my arm is wrapped around yours."

"It's nice, don't you think?" asks Ana, studying my face. "Are you Jewish? You are, aren't you?"

"Being fucked up doesn't make you Jewish."

"I have a Jewish grandmother," says Ana. "I'm one-fourth Goodblat."

"Would that be the fourth I'm holding?" I ask. "Feels Goodblatian. The Chinese think I'm British, you know."

"Do they?"

"I suppose I'm a little reserved. Do you think?"

Ana seems to let her mind drift for a moment. "I think that thinking's over-rated," she says at last.

We walk in silence, and I steal a long glance at the woman in the open tan raincoat. I'm genuinely curious. How exactly does this human draw me in so utterly? She's easy enough to look at, obviously, in her fair brunette kind of way. But there's something else. Something neither blue, nor green, nor . . .

The two new pages from Tree come to mind. However much I'd rather not think about it, Truman seems to have been warning me away from this particular woman's *sheen* since before I was last sodomized in jail. Or was it the time before? Either way, I see no reason to worry, as Truman's taste in women would have to be the equivalent of no taste at all. Anyway I'm not sure whether I can ever fully trust a disincarnate Pulitzer laureate who begins a chapter with instructions on how to prevaricate syncline and anticline of concurrent tectonic vectors by means of reverse analysis, past-life regression, and used rubber bands.

Ana and I come to a stop at the entrance of a subway station, where we turn to look at one another. She seems as unsure as I how we have arrived here. Kowloon Bay is presently nowhere in sight.

"We're at the train," I tell her.

Again the warm wind plays with the fine hairs at Ana Manguella's ears. "Yes, we are."

"Might we be moving to Crime Scene B?"

The blue and the green seem to confer. "Does seem. But I really must ask a question."

I wait in suspended animation.

"On the train you said something about being a narrator."

"*The* narrator," I correct her. "And?"

"Does that mean you're narrating this? This moment, I mean? I do prefer to keep a low profile."

With a smile I say, "My lips are sealed."

32

Ana's vast unscreened windows are open to the night, admitting the low murmur of traffic sounds from the street below. Like most of Hong Kong, Sheung Wan is a cramped, vertical neighborhood with colorful signage draped across the narrow streets. Walk-up apartments are catacombed atop storefronts, delis, and restaurants nearly impossible to enter without turning sideways. I'm not sure how we negotiated the three or four blocks from Ana's favorite Italian mini-restaurant to this second-floor flat. Something to do with ethanol receptors in the lower rear region of the brain.

"I can't believe I'm pouring us another drink," says Ana, kicking off her sandals and handing me a brandy. "What kind of music would you like?"

"I don't do recorded music," I reply.

She blinks. "I, um, don't think I have any unrecorded music."

"Then you don't have any music," I say. "I'll make an exception if you'll agree to dance with me."

Ana blinks again.

"Was that an apprehensive blink?" I ask.

"I'm a bit challenged that way," says Ana. "I am British."

I step a little closer. "I don't mean that kind of dancing."

"Then I'm not sure what kind you mean."

"I mean the kind," I reply, stepping closer still, "where we lean against one another. And I kiss the back of your neck. And every now and then we move our feet a little."

The two eyes glisten. "Which way?"

"Which way what?"

"Which way . . . do we move our feet?"

"Just nearby."

"Nearby," she whispers. "I think I can do that. Why don't I go find some . . . nearby music."

"No vocals. No saxophones."

"Got you."

Ana's bare feet pad into the bedroom. A moment later comes a strain that includes neither vocal nor saxophone. But the trumpet is a little flat.

Tonight's spaghetti wasn't half bad. The accompanying Chardonnay, meanwhile, gradually softened Ana's crisp reserve until she was dangling modifiers like a deck hand. I spent my own time smiling idiotically, more than pleased to have all this woman's attention to myself. When she retreated to the loo, I very nearly followed her there.

Then we were feeling our way along the walls of Sheung Wan and making stranger conversation by the moment. "You're quite the odd duck then, aren't you?" Ana queried at one point. Before I could reply, she continued, "Every time I think I've finally seen into you—actually *found* Julian Mancer—I learn there's considerably more. And a good deal less."

"You're far too kind," I replied. "And pitiless."

We were nearly to her door when Ana stopped stock-still and her voice surrendered to a minor key. "Is it all right if we just keep a loose hold on things? I mean, it could change quickly, you know. To tell you the truth, I'm not sure whether we are friends or foes, Julian. It could be a little of both at the same moment, but I'm willing to just let that be, if I'm making the least sense."

I nodded. The *I'm willing* made a great deal of sense.

Then what's keeping her?

Dully, I look around Ana's Spartan apartment. Two unfussed-over rooms. A turquoise leather sofa. A coffee table. A busy altar with crystals of various hues, along with a litter of spent candles. Above the altar is an unframed canvas displaying a yantra I haven't seen before. A red square encloses a golden triangle that in turn embraces a blue circle. On the coffee table are stacks of paperbacks, among them *In Cold Blood*. There's even a yellowing *Breakfast at Tiffany's*. Nothing by Gore Vidal.

Nothing by me.

Stacked on the floor meanwhile are a few dozen books on mythology. I finally did go through that article on Heracles. He turns out to have been the son of Zeus and a mortal named Alcmena—rhymes with Purina. It was an immaculate conception, if you believe in that kind of thing. I wonder for a moment whether artificial insemination might be thought of as immaculate. There seems to be roughly the same amount of fun involved. Moot point, of course, unless Timothy Dobbins turns out to be God, which personally I'm betting against.

My eyes catch sight of a worn book of runes. This morning, apropos of nothing, I pulled a card from Rui Long's Barbie deck. Actually I suppose it's my Barbie deck. Anyway I got the Ken's Mad card. I should be, like, really careful with decisions about people right now.

Check.

Okay, I may have gotten in a little deep with the itsy two-in-one schoolgirl, who's turning out to be about as self-possessed as Paul Reubens at a Saturday matinee. The last thing Rui Long said today outside the English office was, "Fine. You just do your own thang, Mister 'Shroom Man. Ain't nobody here but you." As she sauntered away, I noticed three students staring at her then me. Not that it matters a whit, of course. As soon as this country has a new political figurehead and I have the final page of that chapter, I'm back in Memphis before you can say Lorraine Motel. Until then, it's about keeping my head low.

All at once a barefoot Ana Manguella materializes before me, her bright eyes inclined to mine. She has changed into an azure silk blouse with a string-tie at the throat, a wooden bead at each end. Below are loose cotton pantaloons, their droopy sash nearly reaching the floor. Another tentative step, and two breasts press themselves against my ribs. Our fingers interlace. My plaster cast hooks her waist and my nostrils fill with the scent of her hair.

> . . . I dance and the shadow lurches grotesquely.
> While I'm still awake, let us rejoice together.
> Soon each will go its separate way . . .

"Do you read Li Bai?" I hear myself murmur.

"Mmm?" Ana replies sleepily.

"I said, you dance well nearby."

"Mmmm."

"Your hair," I whisper, "is a rainforest."

"No," she whispers back. "It's a rainforest."

Good. She's as drunk as I.

Pulling the ivory woman closer, I bend to snuffle at her left ear like a Dalmatian. My right hand struggles in vain against the cast, meanwhile, wanting to slide down her waist a bit farther. And are those fingernails digging into my back? Just asking.

"Marry me," I command.

"No," says Ana.

"Yes. Tomorrow."

"No," she sings. "Never."

"Okay."

We whirl drunkenly, the music pulling this way and that. Now we seem to be whirling a little closer to the bedroom, and my left hand discovers the warm dip of a waist. Ana's hands meanwhile are inside my shirt, exploring hungrily. I think we just whirled through the bedroom door. Ana's chin digs into my chest. Slipping beneath the waistband of the pantaloons, my fingertips discover a mute tailbone. There they rest, enjoying the nudge of first one white bun and then the other as our dance dips between the dip slopes to drop us—

Onto the satiny plain of Ana's bed.

I pull at the two wooden beads and Ana's breasts spill out, their broad auroras a rich auburn brown. I bury myself in that abundance, roiling my face happily in the plenty, and the two nipples sharpen against my cheeks. I coax one of them to my lips, wetting its edges by tauntingly slow degrees, and Ana's chest rises. I feel her whole body stretch as the nipples harden. Ana's sounds move from the *aa-aahs* to the *oo-oohs*. I love the *oo-oohs*.

"I'll marry you," she says breathlessly. "I'll marry you."

My hand glides beneath the silk pantaloons and discover a place of extraordinary warmth. I press lightly. She presses back. Ana's breath catches, and a ragged howl becomes something like *ooo-ONNNG-gggdkttrq*. After a moment Ana falls spent against the bed.

Neither of us moves for a moment.

A giggle erupts in Ana's throat. "Sorry. I guess I was a little keyed up."

I draw away for an avaricious gape at the heaving white chest. "Sorry, is it?" I say. "I'll make you sorry."

My left hand yanks at the sash. Again Ana giggles. Another great yank, and the pantaloons are at her ankles. With my good left hand, I unhurriedly begin to open my pants. Ana begins to pant. Her eyes flare with what seems rage.

"You *shit*," she hisses, her head falling back against the bed. "You fucking *shit*."

As one, we wet our fingers. Suddenly we're not quite sure now who touches whom, warm saliva mixing, bodies pressing into a delicious snarl of pleasure. A rough shove from her hips, and Ana Manguella has captured me into her depths. Her free leg locks me tightly against her. There is no longer any possibility of escape.

33

Shards of morning dapple a room wrapped in the scent of freshly ground coffee.

"Kona," Ana tells me, playfully throwing her hip against mine as she takes a seat on the sun-warmed turquoise sofa. "It's Hawaiian."

Her red silk robe is not quite closed. My eyes coax it open a bit more.

"What grade would that be?" she teases.

"Grade?" I ask.

"That smile of yours."

"That smile," I reply, "would be a minus one."

She laughs. "You get a *minus* one for being happy?"

"No. Happy is extreme. Happy would be a minus two."

Ana laughs again, touching a higher note, before grabbing her head. "Don't make me laugh. It hurts. But I do love this number system of yours. Cuts straight to it."

"You're mocking me."

"I'm *mocking*-mocking you," says Ana, leaning to kiss my lips. "Tell me about your writing. Are you fiction or non-fiction?"

"Interesting how you put it," I reply, my fingertips finding the earliest beginnings of her left breast.

Ana closes her robe. "We're having a discussion. Do you write fiction or don't you?"

I pull myself a bit straighter on the sofa, adjust my white robe, and look around for my coffee cup. It's only mildly troubling that Ana keeps a man's bathrobe in her closet.

3X.

"It's a tackier question than you might imagine," I tell her. "Fiction contains a great deal of truth, and *vice versa*. Where did I put my splendid Hawaiian coffee cup?"

Ana hands me the ceramic mug, still warm to the touch.

"Place ten writers in a room," I say. "A woman in a raincoat walks in, pulls the petals from a rose, and walks out. Now ask each writer to describe what he or she has just seen."

"And you get ten different stories," says Ana.

"Every time."

"Like still-life painting," says Ana. "Thirty art students all painting the same bowl of oranges, and no two paintings alike."

I shrug. "I can't imagine who would want to paint a bowl of oranges in the first place. Especially with someone looking over your shoulder saying, '*Zees* orange, he's not look happy.' Same with piano lessons. At a given moment, half a million students are banging away at the Moonlight Sonata. Same bowl of oranges. You know how many people have given up piano on the twelfth bar of the Moonlight Sonata? It's not a musical piece. It's a graveyard."

"That's what you write about, isn't it?" Ana turns her head slightly and the green eye measures me. "The fine arts?"

"What's so fine about them?" I reply, sipping my coffee. "Actually I'm not that kind of writer. I'd much rather hear about your own breathless pursuits."

Ana lights a Gaulois with the dry scratch of a wooden match. "I consult."

"And study myths," I add.

"What's so mythological about them?" replies Ana. "There is nothing we are that myth is not. Myth is a schematic of who we are at the deepest of levels. The complexity and perversity of myth *exactly* reflects our own."

"I read that Heracles article you sent me."

"Did it answer your questions about the Hydra?" she asks.

"The Hydra was known as the Guardian of the Underworld. What's that supposed to mean?"

"Give it some thought," says Ana. "Give it some serious thought. There's no way to accomplish anything of importance without entering the mythical."

"How does one go about that?" I ask.

She dusts an ash. "One finds a doorway, a metaphor of some kind. You're into music, right?"

I gaze at her neutrally.

"You don't have to answer," Ana continues. "It really couldn't be much more obvious. You're so fussy about music."

I shrug. "Tree tells me I'm a born singer. I tell her she's a born lunatic. Tell me about your soul group."

Ana looks surprised. "Did I say something about my group?"

"On the train. There are four of you. You manage things."

She rolls her eyes. "You made me drink too much wine. I think I scolded you."

"Scold me again."

"I should," says Ana. "Where did you say you're from? Cetus? Aren't you all bearish-looking creatures with lots of fur?"

"We shed like crazy every summer. And where are your own counterparts? Glastonbury?"

"They don't have bodies just now. We tag-team. One incarnates and the other three assist."

"From the other *side*?" I say.

"Do you find that amusing?"

"I find everything amusing. I'm a very amused person."

Ana turns the blue eye on me. "What would you say if I told you I was there when the earth formed? That I watched the gasses cool? That I exist because of this planet, and it exists because of me? And others like me, of course."

"Of course," I say. "And what would you say if I told you neither my sister nor myself has ever been ill, that we're twenty years older than we look, and that we are impervious to the sun's rays though our complexions are roughly that of a bedsheet? If you must know, our intelligence quotients cannot be charted except by the Bernard-Baugh method."

"I'd say you're being modest," replies Ana evenly. "I'm very well aware of who you are, Julian."

We share a long, unblinking gaze.

Ana exhales smoke forcefully. "This is a very trying time for this planet. Entities are coming in from civilizations that haven't begun yet, back-shifting millions of years to help with the evolution of their own ancestors. Think about that for a moment."

"I'd rather not," I say, squirming a bit in the white silk robe. I wonder if she has anything in a 4X.

"Of course, when they arrive," says Ana, "they're a total muddle. All those filthy schizophrenics you see wandering the streets? Back-shifters. Just how much help would you say they're providing?" She glances at me. "At least you're functional."

"Thank you," I say. My eyes stop on the image above the altar, the triangle within the square. I don't like it. "What's that image supposed to be?" I ask.

"A yantra," says Ana. "And then there are the *tourists*, the extra-dimensionals who drop in just to rubberneck and add to the general confusion. You'd think a planet never went through a shift before. Then again, I suppose it must be interesting to watch. What do you know about the timetable?"

"Timetable?"

"For the shift. You said your group is focused on the Three-three-three."

"If we manage to get it together," I say.

"That's always the question, isn't it?"

The sun has moved imperceptibly across the uncurtained window. It now bathes Ana Manguella in a brilliant yellow-white, backlighting the smoke from her cigarette. "Didn't you say your soul group is constitutionally opposed to polarity or some such?" asks Ana.

"I'll answer your question if you'll answer mine."

She eyes me suspiciously. "What's yours?"

I finish my coffee and set down the cup. "This totally boring consulting thing you do—you work in security, don't you?"

Ana gazes at me. "I am in charge of security. Now you can answer my question."

"You're in *charge* of security?" I repeat.

"Don't be coy, Julian. You've known all along."

"Might that explain why you said you're in China to meet me?" I ask.

An ash falls from Ana's cigarette. "Did my duties summon me here? Yes, but that involves far more than you, Julian. And it has nothing at all to do with our little dalliance last night, if that's what you're wondering. Now I'd like for you to answer my question."

I stare.

"Soul group?" she reminds me. "Polarity?"

"Ah. Yes. Tree says we're stuck in polarity, globally speaking. The good news is, when you introduce a third element, it opens a dimensional door. Either that or your digital pedometer stops working. Can I get some more of this coffee?"

"And then?" asks Ana, appraising me.

"What? You mean that's not enough?"

Ana taps her cigarette impatiently. "Before you go opening dimensional doors, Julian, you might give the resultant *effects* some little thought. You might also consider that polarity is not a problem in need of repair but the engine that drives this planet. Without polarity, there's no positive and negative, no masculine and feminine. Only a muddy grey."

"Actually, grey would be the fusion of two opposites," I correct her, "which is not the idea at all. And I could use another cup of that Hawaiian coffee."

"Make it yourself. And stop defending a hypothesis that you don't subscribe to."

"I subscribe. I always subscribe."

"And that temple you mentioned?" asks Ana.

"The Temple of Heaven? Well, it certainly seems intentional. Especially the Circular Mound Altar, which is laid out in concentric circles of—"

"Nine. I remember."

"Yes. Eighty-one stones around the outside, then seventy-two, then—"

"And the connotation . . . ?" asks Ana.

"Among the Chinese, Nine connotes fruition, completion, that kind of thing."

The green eye measures me. "And what would be your interpretation of this word *completion*? And why is it you're so concerned with temples?"

"Are you grilling me?"

Ana smiles coolly. "What if I suddenly showed up in your Cetus galaxy and announced that I was going to solve all its problems? This is the planet of free will, Julian. You have to begin by respecting the process that's going on here."

I pick up my empty coffee cup. "Didn't I once tell you that? Maybe you should consider *traveling* a bit more? Maybe see what the rest of the universe is about? Where do you keep the coffee?"

"In the kitchen."

I lower my coffee cup. "I don't suppose you could be taking all this a bit too personally?"

"*Personally*?" Ana stabs out her cigarette a little too hard, breaking it. "I'm taking the fate of this planet too personally?"

"I think there's a point where one acknowledges there's more going here than her own little private tea party. It's called humility, Ana. You'll find it in the h's."

"A fucking lot you know," snaps Ana. "You've been here half a lifetime, and for most of it you've been tanked."

I give her a stare. All this aggression is starting to turn me on. "Would you care to repeat that?"

"Why? Are you going to call me outside?"

"It's a thought."

With a sudden burst of animal energy, Ana springs to her knees on the sofa and kisses my mouth very hard, pulling away with a loud smack. She draws herself tall and the red silk parts a bit more, revealing the dimple of her navel.

"Let's get dressed," she says. "You can buy me a glorious Cantonese breakfast, and I'll lord it over all the women sitting with uninteresting men."

"Oh, I'm interesting now. A moment ago, I was a furry interloper and not a very bright one."

"But you kiss well," says Ana.

"And you're amazing in red," I observe.

I give her a rough shove. Surprised, Ana lands with a soft thump against the sun-warmed leather. The silk robe surrenders to each side, leaving only the red sash at her waist. With a defiant glare, Ana parts her knees a little more and the direct sun reveals that she, too, is aroused. Last night, this woman was a moonlit snowfield. In the direct sun, she is a hallucination of haughty splendor.

I lean forward to lick a long line along a luminescent leg, finally forcing my face into the very crux of the matter, enjoying the woman-scents there, teasing them out one by one. Ana's fingertips dig into my scalp. Moments later, her belly swells and I know she is mine. I have known this woman's alpine snowfields. Now I will learn of her equatorial jungles.

Unexpectedly, though, the white belly deflates. Ana Manguella is a fallen cake. Did I miss something here? Ana gives off a post-orgasmic glow, yet I don't remember any orgasms. Eager to rekindle the blaze, I apply the Unfailing Tongue. It's mere seconds before the white belly swells again, and Ana presses against me with an "*ooo*-ooh."

Got her.

At the very last moment, Ana pulls away. Unwilling to let her go, I follow, pressing adamantly. I hear a throaty sound almost like mourning—but again she backs away. I follow hungrily, only to learn that two bare feet are pressed against my shoulders. Those feet now give me a savage shove, and I find myself sprawled on the opposite end of the sofa.

Lifting my head, I stare dumbfounded at the woman of the tousled tresses.

Ana sits up, crosses her legs, tidies her robe, throws her hair behind her shoulders, and says, "*I* decide when I come."

I stare a little more.

"I had multiples last night," she tells me calmly, combing her unruly hair with her fingers. "It was a wonderful release, but another right now wouldn't be the best of ideas, so I circulated."

"Circulated," I repeat.

"Really, Julian, you're old enough to understand how sex works by now. It's an energy pump. You use it to accumulate and discharge energy. Personally I find that being a little overcharged has its uses. It keeps me primed. Being blown all to hell, on the other hand, is quite limiting. Like I told you about polarity, maintaining a little tension between positive and negative is the engine that drives everything."

With an effort, I pull myself upright. I still want that cup of coffee.

Ana says, "Sex is fun and it's also a technology. I woke up with a headache, so when you started feeding me energy, I received it and circulated it. The headache's gone. Simple as that." She tilts her head. "How are you feeling?"

"Feeling?" I repeat blurrily.

"You'll find it in the f's. I think you're totally out of focus, Julian. Lie down." Ana pats the spot beside her. "On your back. Get comfortable."

I fuss about for a minute, fighting the undersized bathrobe. Finally, I'm more or less situated.

"I said comfortable," says Ana. " Look at how your leg is twisted. And this shoulder is high. Do something with yourself." She begins yanking at me, jamming cushions under this spot and that until I am very comfortably arranged on the ultra-warm leather, my knees bent and supported by cushions. Ana pulls at both my knees now, shaking them until they release their customary tension. Sighing, I feel my lower body surrender, one knee falling against the back of the sofa, the other against Ana's breasts. "Good," she says. "Hold that spot."

Slowly Ana's hands part my robe, dragging its smooth silk across the delicate skin of my thighs. The sunlight now pours deliciously onto something that stirs expectantly. All of Ana's fingertips go to the beginnings of my scrotum, making tiny unhurried circles there. "You have nice balls," she says without emphasis. "It's a secret pleasure among women, stealing glances at men's balls. Handsome ones, anyway." The fingers arrive at the base of my pleasure, pulling at it, exposing more and more of the rising serpent's head.

"Mmmph," says someone. It might have been me.

"Is it good?" asks Ana curiously.

I open one eye. Ana doesn't notice. Her smile is tipping forward, drawing ever nearer the serpent's head. I feel her busy fingertips glide further along the sensitive shaft.

"*Oooh,*" says someone.

My one eye watches Ana lick her lips. I feel her warm breath touching me. The warm finger pads reach the hypersensitive throat of my pleasure, and I cry out as her right hand grips that throat and gives it a punitive twist.

"Slow your breath," she says, and I feel her hot breath again. "Let the energy build."

I try to locate my breath. I can't find it.

"Focus," says Ana.

Closing both eyes, I find my breath and force it to expand. Instantly the excitement fades a bit and with it the erection.

"Breathe," she says, her hand pumping now, teasing the phallus back to life. I only manage a couple more deep breaths before I'm approaching my limits.

"Orrurrgh."

"Breathe," orders Ana, stilling her hand.

My nervous system skids to a rough halt.

The hand disappears. "Julian, you aren't breathing. You have to move back and forth between the sensations and the breath. The sensations are the accelerator. The breath is the brake. Between the two, you can fill your whole body with light. But you have to try."

"Light," I say dizzily.

The warm hand reappears at my groin. "I'm going to massage you some more. First just enjoy it on the most basic level. When the energy begins to build, shift your focus from external to internal and work with the breath. Accelerator and brake."

I close my eyes and lace my hands behind my head. "Got it."

Fuck her. I'm going to come.

"As you breathe," says Ana, "picture a bright yellow-orange light building in your second chakra, flooding your whole body. It builds on the inhale and circulates on the exhale."

Suddenly I'm aware that Ana's other hand has closed around my balls. My eyes jerk open.

"If you come," she says, "I'm going to squeeze until you're unconscious, drag your ass out on the street, and leave you there."

"Uh, no real need."

"If you're getting close, just say stop, and I'll stop."

I nod obediently.

Might actually be worth it. Ana's right hand moves slowly and affectionately now, as though behind the ears of a beloved pet. This is pure mammalian touch, I realize. Something due every one of us. Basic to our membership. Foundational to our wellbeing. I can't complete the thought. The back of Ana's right hand is now twirling against the reawakening penis. Quite unexpectedly I laugh.

I'm laughing, stretching, yawning, and shuddering at the same moment, as well as pressing quite rudely against the back of the friendly hand, pressing as might a greedy cat demanding more. The warm hand matches my pressure exactly, pushing back, now turning, thumb and forefinger closing around my dick to tug and twist. The tip of Ana's smallest finger appears lightly at the edge of my anus, and the energy builds dizzily.

"Brake," says Ana, and the fingertip disappears.

Desperately I shift my attention to the breath, trying to envision a yellow-orange light at my center. I'm too distracted by the burn of pleasure. Or. Maybe it's the burn itself that she's talking about. Curious, I slow my breath to more closely observe. A few moments later, I'm surprised to discover that the center of my pleasure is located deep within my body's core. The skin-sensations feed energy to that central burn as would dry sticks tossed onto a fire. But it's the enduring coals beneath the flames that provide the deepest undercurrents of pleasure.

I focus on that deep, slow burn and find it not at all featureless but composed of tiny, bubbling cells of translucence. I try to discern a color. Ana's hand begins to move, and more bubbles appear, welling, brimming, colliding one against another, a golden white when first appearing. As they tumble faster, the color becomes yellow-orange. I find I can rest my point of perception in their midst and let them carry me up, boiling up from the center of the cradle of the pelvis.

Oooh.

Ana has gripped me quite firmly, the flat of her thumb pressing into the underside of the cobra's head. Now her hand begins to tremble spastically, and the tip of her smallest finger re-appears at my anus. My mouth falls open a little wider. I think I'm drooling. I don't care. I also don't care if I spend the remainder of the day unconscious in a gutter.

Deftly, Ana holds me teetering at the edge, reading my micro-moments. Time ceases moving. The erection rages, the glistening bubbles boiling furiously until they threaten to burst their container, and my breath catches. Instantly Ana's hand becomes still. Belatedly I remember to use the breath to distribute the glow throughout my body. A moment later, the bubbles die down but the undercurrents continue to radiate warmth to my whole body.

I realize that each of Ana's little tugs and squeezes is intended to stoke that inner glow deep at my center. Is that what she means by shifting my focus from external to internal? Ana's fingers begin to move, and the bubbles stir once more. Soon I'm again teetering at the edge.

Ana stills her hand.

"Is it too much?" she whispers. "Too much stimulation?"

I nod helplessly, and the hand glides to the underside of my balls.

"Just breathe," she says. "Let yourself relax into it."

The flat of her thumb presses into the perineum and slowly circles there. I loose a contented sigh.

"Good," says Ana. "Good."

Her massage is soothing. I fall forward into the sensation, melting into the glow as does my skin into the sunlight from the window. I realize that I am in the presence of orgasm. Not as an approaching event. As a present reality. Not as a sneeze of the loins but as a surrender of the entire organism. But unto what? I feel a strange sense of completion, strange because I'm not sure I've ever felt it before. Not like this. No need to reach for something further. Everything I want is present and basking in its own light. This can't be possible. Following Ana's instruction, I relax farther into that sensation, becoming a tumbling point of acceptance within an undifferentiated sphere of self-pleasure that—

"Is it good?" asks Ana.

My eyelids part for a bleary glance at her face. If only she knew how good. Then again, I suppose she does. My eyes roll closed. Again I fall forward into the glow, surprised at its depth. I recall what I've read about the second chakra, about all the chakras, how they're capable of opening astonishingly wide when cultivated. Yoga-speak. Whatever. But now I am an unknown creature coiled at the center of that truth, gazing serenely out. I am within orgasm, within its warmest and safest chambers.

Ana's hand grips me very tightly, and the coal at my center sends forth a flare. I realize that in an instant all will flash white-hot, consuming itself. I deepen my breathing, using the exhalation to dissipate as much of the yellow-orange fire as I can until the moment of danger has passed.

"*Very* good," says Ana, her hand becoming still.

I rest for a long moment, opening my eyes to check whether my body is emitting light. No, yet I'm quite certain of something. Each cell of my body is a tiny engine of ecstasy that feeds the collective flame that feeds it in turn, conjuring an arrival in self without boundaries or purpose beyond its own micro-cellular brilliance.

"Very, very good," says Ana, her palms spreading across my lower belly. I feel them glide up to my chest then down along my thighs, as though helping me spread the glow from my center to every part of my body. My erection slowly descends to a place of rest at my thighs. The session is coming to a close, yet there is no sense of anticlimax. No sense of deprivation. I feel only that same unexpected sense of completion. I can't quite find my edges.

"How do you feel?" asks Ana.

"Bnrrrgh."

"You see how it works?" she says. Ana Manguella's hands grab fistfuls of my pubic hair and give it a playful tug. "Breakfast!" she cries.

34

"Death to all Americans!"

Those words were heard on a Baghdad street yesterday. We bomb their cities, we kill their sons, we depose their government, we destroy their infrastructure, we tell them what their religion can and can't do, and still they're not satisfied.

I woke up alone this morning among my sister's scented pillows. Which is not the first line of any existing twelve-bar blues. On my way to the American Teacher's Bathroom, I discovered Lillian's rat inside my aquarium leaning against one glass wall, a dazed expression on its face. I did a double-take. All the promising menacing dark red mushroom sprouts had been mowed as level to the ground as the eighteenth green at Augusta. "You *didn't*," I growled, lurching toward the aquarium.

At which point, the rat startled and crouched. Then there was something like a silent explosion of light at the center of the aquarium, and the rat was no more. I mean. Literally. I blinked and looked again. I even brought my face down to the level of the aquarium and gave its interior a really good examination. No 'shrooms. No rat. No explanation.

> Woke up this morning
> Rat inside my mushroom farm
> Yes I
> Woke up this morning
> Rat up inside my mushroom farm
> Reckon dematerialization
> Never done no rat no harm

That's how the day began. Then, before I could get my shirt buttoned, Rui Long was knocking at the door. Below is a transcript of our conversation.

Why, Rui Long.

Why not Rui Long? Aren't you going to invite me in?

Invite you in. In broad daylight. With or without a film crew?

Then when can I see you?

Before or after class. You'll find me at the front of the classroom, quite near the chalkboard.

That's not enough, and you know it.

Rui Long. You can't come here anymore. You know that.

That stupid Chinese girl comes here anytime she wants.

That stupid Chinese girl is sent here by her parents. And I leave the door open.

You're fucking dropping me.

I think that would require first having a relationship.

I can't believe you said that to me. I've told you things I've never said before in my life.

I've heard things I've never heard before in my life. Still in all.

You are one sorry-assed motherfucker and a fat-assed one at that.

Rui Long. We can't go on meeting like this. And my ass is no fatter than the rest of me.

Yes it is, you lard-assed pussy-assed motherfucker. I'm gonna tell every goddamn person at this school what you did to me. And the po-lice. And a lawyer.

Rui Long? Itsy? *Doo?*

So it goes with counseling displaced American schoolgirls IHW. You see what it gets you.

Found me a little schoolgirl
Yellow as moonlight in the pines
Whoa I
Found me a little schoolgirl
Yellow as moonlight in the pines
She had a protuberation
But not nearly big as mine's

True is true.

Anyway, who would prefer a sprig to a fully opened jasmine, a half-formed idea to a master's thesis, a giggle-box to a fine cello?

Now, at mid-morning I am en route to Studebaker Supermarket, hurrying somewhat, as it's Saturday and I'd like to beat the worst of the crowds. I stick to the busy streets these days, no more charming little alleyways with differently abled po-lice, though hypothetically I am now entirely safe from the latter. How does one really *know* without testing the theory? I'm not really into testing right now. All I'm into just this moment is a dozen large eggs that have never been anywhere near a duck and an un-previously-owned wad of bubblegum.

I also feel an unaccountable urge to purchase flowers. Ever since yesterday morning's little lewdness with Ana Manguella,

I have felt practically romantic. I don't, in fact, think I've pass-ed five consecutive minutes all morning without thinking of one particular warm-leather love session, as I'm quite certain I have never been touched like that in any recent lifetime. I've certainly never experienced so much sensation at my inner core.

It was at the same time exquisitely sexual and nothing of the kind. And both. And quite possibly neither. I'm no longer sure whether anything lies outside pleasure. I seem to have penetrated levels of experience that up to now I've taken con-siderable trouble to avoid. I hate to acknowledge it. Then again, I'll acknowledge pretty much anything you want if you play with my dick long enough. Rooms. Levels of experience. Faux bubbles. Whatever you got.

Crossing a busy intersection, I encounter three teenage girls, each in tight jeans and a tighter blouse, their dead hair teased, their faces painted on. All three are chewing gum. All three gaze listlessly at cell phones. Two days ago, I would have stolen at least one glance at certain of their body parts, filing away snapshots as future sexual capital. Now I am only struck by how tragically clueless those girls are.

Again Rui Long comes to mind, and I sigh uncomfortably. Without a doubt, our little sex parties were marvelously in-tense. Truthfully she and I are at the same level of maturity, sexually, emotionally, whatever you got, everything fantasy-driven, excitement-driven, *driven*-driven. Danger. Predation. Taboo-busting. Giving it to her *there*. Getting it from her *here*. Practically checking items off a list. The more items you check off, the better the encounter, right?

Right?

Tree says I'm maturing. Scary thought.

I wonder why Tree hasn't sent over any new pages this week. Three pages last week. This week, nothing. Have I un-proven myself?

I approach Studebaker Supermarket, its car-less parking lot frantic with fruit vendors and beggars and idle adults lounging and smoking as their children animate plastic trikes. I thread my way through the mob and past the automatic doors, clawing my way through the manic crowd to the files of waiting shopping carts.

The first floor of Studebaker Supermarket is groceries only. The second offers stylish clothing for the entire family plus a complete line of poodle-eating vacuum cleaners. On the third floor you find electronics, home furnishings, and two hopelessly trashed restrooms as far from the escalators as could be architecturally arranged.

Chinese shopping carts require getting used to. They are perhaps one-third the usual length, and all four wheels swivel witlessly, making it quite easy to spin out into the Charmin. The idea is to have carts capable of maneuvering in impossibly tight throngs such as today's. Though I'm early, I don't think there's any possibility of getting into the fish market or the produce section.

Stationed at the entrance of each isle is a uniformed young woman with a megaphone set on *stun*. Then there are the pickpockets and the bad-asses who work with them. Chinese pickpockets work in twos. If you detect your wallet being lifted, don't put up a fight. The second guy is never more than a couple steps away, and he's got a razor. Personally I'm not too concerned about my wallet, which seldom bears anything beyond a few moldering phone numbers and a Guan Yin wish card. Far more important is my journal, safely tucked into a twisted front pocket.

My snub-nosed shopping cart hangs a haughty left against the traffic and barely makes it into the MSG section without provoking a five-cart pileup. There's a whole aisle of MSG here. You can buy it in ten-kilo bags—enough for an entire week—but I'm just cutting through on my way to the candy section, where I now discover a perplexing array of bubble gum in various shades and hues, including pink, purple, and canary.

Yesterday I stopped into the neighborhood hardware and condom emporium, the characters for *machete* scrawled on a scrap of paper. I have a picture dictionary. You leaf through the various sections until you find an illustration of what you'd like to buy. Beside each drawing are the appropriate characters. The hardware guy scowled at my note then at me. With the various oddities recently purchased for my 'shroomery, I may have shown myself to be far too grave a danger to society already without a machete. He gave me a hatchet and a sharpening stone. Fine with me.

After selecting a pack of chewing gum in a nice shade of lavender, I turn my cart toward the produce section, managing to squeeze into the crowd surrounding the banana bin. I begin scouting for something in a nice dappled yellow when my ears register an appalling English sentence.

"I hope you don't believe all that horseshit Dobbins told you."

I turn to encounter Agent Barnes in a pair of white sneakers and a sun visor. He's shorter than I remember.

"That he invented SARS?" says Barnes, an ironic smile twisting his moustache. "That's what he told you, right?"

I'm not sure how to respond, so I don't.

"Tim Dobbins didn't invent SARS," says Barnes. "Dobbins doesn't invent much of anything. He steals what other people invent. He raids other companies' R and D and beats them to the patents. Then he leverages the companies for cash for his fucked-up genetic experiments. Oops. Didn't mean to get personal." The grin stretches wider. Barnes is wearing the ear stud today.

I place four dappled bananas into my cart. "I thought you said his name was Stiles."

"Velázquez told you that. You're talking to me now. I'm the truth guy."

I gaze for a moment at Agent Barnes. There's something stuck between the truth guy's teeth. Possibly an entire head of Swiss chard.

"You don't work for the State Department," I tell him, turning my attention to the navel oranges.

"And you don't write worth a shit," says Barnes. "Dobbins pays that magazine to keep you around. Did you know that?"

Rising a little taller, I say, "Did you know that men with both a moustache and an ear stud have more than double the probability of being under five foot eight?"

A shadow crosses Barnes's smile. "Yeah, you're smart, Julian. Big word guy. Big IQ guy. But guess what? Everybody's fucking you, and you don't even know it. I'm the one who's willing to bring you into the loop." He glances around the fruit section. "I know what was in that shopping bag Dobbins tried to give you. He wanted to inject you with something, didn't he?"

I don't answer.

Barnes laughs and shakes his head. "I'm with you, big guy. I wouldn't let that man near me with a needle. You wouldn't believe the shit he has access to. Know something? I think the old fuck kind of likes you. More than the others, anyway."

I continue to stare.

"Did you really think you and your sister were the only ones? Dobbins had a regular little puppy mill there at Regis Labs. He did about a hundred artificial inseminations before the government shut him down. They said there were 'insufficient controls.' Shit, I'll say. Nobody but Dobbins knows what really happened in those procedures. I'd say it's a safe bet that he used his own cum in pretty near every one."

Lifting a green bunch of bananas, Barnes says, "God only knows what that man is up to, but I can tell you this. He's tracking every one of you. You can't eat a taco without Tim Dobbins knowing if you used hot or mild.

Barnes tosses the bananas. "Now that I have your attention, there's something you need to hear, Julian Mancer, smart guy, and if I were you I'd pay very close fucking attention. When Dobbins sat down with you for that little chat the other night, he sentenced you to death and not a very pretty one. The only reason you're alive right now is that Dobbins is alive.

You're bait. Once we get him, you're next. And then your sister."

The truth guy and I share a silent gaze.

"Dobbins stole something that nobody was supposed to know about," he continues. "That's why he's running. I don't know what he told you, but that man is first and foremost one huge motherfucking liar."

Barnes leans back against the navel orange bin. "Of course, he's also a genius in his twisted-ass way. He was doing genetic engineering back before anybody knew what genetic engineering was. Before he worked for us, he worked for the Chinese. The *Imperial* Chinese. When Mao took ever, Dobbins came over to the US. His deal was: I help you make your little biological stink-bombs, and you leave me and my personal projects alone.

So Dobbins gets to do his own thing—or did, before he stole the wrong thing from the wrong people. Let's just say he stumbled onto a very dirty little secret. He not only got the smoking gun but the documents that show who gave the orders. Release date, point of release, projected casualties, everything."

I steady myself against the shopping cart. On a certain level I've always known that the Mancer twins were never the MacGuffin. Not in and of ourselves. A question comes to me. "What's the connection between Dobbins and Iraq?"

"I never said there was a connection."

"Call me psychic."

Barnes picks up a navel orange and gives it a sniff. "You're a smart guy. You figure it out."

It's not very hard. Given the current leadership in Washington and their sudden urge to station 170,000 soldiers on top of the world's richest oilfields, it's not much of a leap to conclude that somebody's readying themselves for one very high-octane war. Uh, operation. And when you think about it, who's out there to fight against anymore but the Chinese?

So you keep this awakening giant busy slapping at micro-organisms while you vouchsafe your oil reserves for the next twenty years. And what if, in the midst of all this fevered jockeying about, the front page of the *Post* reports a secret dirty enough to send the current administration to the bottom of the Potomac—blue suits, power ties, operation, and all? If Barnes is even half right, those people are ready to do absolutely anything to absolutely anyone to keep that from happening.

"You have to understand," Barnes says carefully, "that we are talking about individuals without a well-developed sense of humor. Anyone even marginally close to this mess is going down, and that very probably includes me. It definitely includes you. So we may as well work together."

"Meaning?" I ask, dropping a bunch of bananas into my cart.

"Meaning you deliver Dobbins to me. I don't want to kill him. I want to broker a deal between him and the people he worked for. If everything works out, I get a payday, he gets to continue his research, and the powers-that-be still get to be. Most important, everybody stays alive. For the time being, anyway."

"Including my sister?"

"You deliver Dobbins?" says Barnes. "You and your sister are golden."

"And you're in a position to guarantee that?"

Barnes grins. "I'll even throw in the ape."

"Ape?"

"Shatrina Carter. She's dead too." He slides a business card into my shirt pocket. "Sooner or later, Dobbins will contact you. When he does, you contact me. Not Velázquez. Me."

"Would it be all right to just dial the International Intrigue Hotline?" I ask.

Barnes extracts a pair of sunshades from the placket of his shirt. "Know what's interesting, Julian? They all look just like you. Tall. Blond. Eyes either blue or green. IQs off the chart. And why not? The man's a genius. Too bad he's also a fucking freak."

Barnes leans toward me. "Here's the kicker. The ones he doesn't like? The ones whose eyes are a little too close together, or who didn't make an A in Algebra? They come down with a mysterious tropical illness. Always fatal."

Barnes slides the shades over his eyes. "Your family keeps getting smaller, Julian. I'd say there's only a dozen or so of you geniuses still around. Kind of gives you the creeps, doesn't it?"

As I stare, the truth guy disappears into the frozen foods.

35

The moment the bell signals the end of Monday's final class, I hurry to the train station and through customs to throw myself into a taxi—then into the arms of a *glowing* Ana Manguella.

"Come in, Ju—" she begins, before being pancaked against the excellent turquoise sofa.

"Julian," laughs Ana, "I'm cooking."

"Let it burn," I say.

"But it's fresh squid. I paid a fortune."

"We'll move the sofa into the kitchen."

"Did you bring wine?" she says.

"I fully intended to."

"There's a wine store on the corner," says Ana. "That can occupy you while I start the rice and scallions."

"White or red?" I say.

"A Sauvignon Blanc would be perfect."

I kiss Ana's white throat before pocketing her keys and cascading down the stairs. It's oddly satisfying to take possession of someone else's keys, which are never anything like one's own. Ana's three unmatching ones, each seemingly from a different decade, are attached to a worn leather fob imprinted with a rune. Algiz, if memory serves. The Rune of Protection.

She'll need all she can get tonight.

The evening sidewalk is busy, practically Christmas-y in a tilted Hong Kong kind of way. Crowds have the effect of reducing the per-capita number of jackals at my heels, imparting a false sense of security, the only kind I ever feel. But here's the thing. Whomever is assigned to tail me this practically

Xmas-y night will spend several hours shifting from foot to foot in the shadows of a windy street, while I shall dine on squid and white-throated woman. Who would you say is winning this game?

I duck into the corner store, where a daunting line waits at the check-out. The clerk, I note, is wearing a gas mask. That's nearly always a sign of a bad news day. This morning the USA and Singapore announced their first documented cases of SARS, and Hong Kong their 327th. Meanwhile, construction crews are working around the clock to complete a humorless ten-thousand-bed quarantine hospital / concentration camp north of Beijing. To comfort the afflicted / medically incorrect.

I locate two acceptable Australian Blancs and decide on the one with the sober white label and cursive font—I know how to pick a wine—plus a small bottle of English gin, while I'm at it. I take my place in the queue.

Did you think you could get rid of me so easily? That's what Truman said to me last night in a particularly low-rent lucid dream. He was wearing Bermuda shorts and a Panama. I think he may also have been wearing cowboy boots. With spurs. The bad thing about cogent dreaming is that you don't get to choose whom you cogent-dream about.

I probably need to call Tree. When I blew through Lil's apartment this afternoon, pausing only to change shirts and grab a windbreaker, I noticed four new messages on the American Teacher's Phone, all from Tree, and all, I've little doubt, imploring me to call the pouting one. Fine. There'll be plenty of time for sulking sisters during the refractory period.

Moving forward in the queue, I feel almost cheery. I've no trouble at all imagining that the dog-faced customers ahead of me are bearing their *own* keys in hand and fully envying me and my expectant smile.

Back on the sidewalk, I pass a small bespectacled boy in a blue-over-white school uniform, and my spirits sink a notch as I recall the recent spew of threats from Rui Long. As though I should worry. Even if that little runt of a hellion were to come forward with some kind of tiresome nitpicking *and* were capable of mustering the requisite Mandarin or Cantonese to do so, why should the authorities so much as give her the time of day? Every young woman in this country is perped, and everybody knows it. Besides which, Rui Long is an American, which by the way so am I. Not. Their. Problem.

Besides besides which, it always comes down to *guanxi* here. My own, feeble though it may be, certainly trumps that of a Chinese girl with really bad manners. End of funky-ass story, or so I certainly hope. As malodorous as this teaching job is fast becoming, I need to keep hold of it just a bit longer. China has just named a new premier, Wen Jiabao—Bellamy must be very happy—which supposedly means a more settled political climate. Still, with all the diseases and agents and mad scientists and one-armed policemen crashing about, I don't quite see re-inserting Lillian into this anytime soon.

Bounding up the stairs, I unlock Ana's door as though it were my own. Warm aromas of seafood and scallops enfold me—as does the sight of Ana Manguella, barefoot in a freshly donned black kimono, her abundant hair fixed loosely atop her head with a pair of ivory chopsticks.

"Are *you* a sight?" I say, and Ana replies with a demure bow.

The stacks of books are gone from the coffee table, replaced by two wine glasses and a corkscrew.

"The clerk at the corner store was wearing a gas mask," I announce, beginning to work on the wine bottle.

Ana says, "The subway stations were passing out free surgical masks this morning. Your choice, white or blue."

"And you chose . . . ?"

"I chose not to choose. SARS isn't airborne. You get it from doorknobs."

"Shhhh," I say. "You'll ruin the placebo effect."

"Where I work," she continues, "the elevator operator wears a surgical mask every day of the week. It's completely dirty and so loose you can see his mouth. But he's protected. That's the important thing."

Filling the two wine glasses, I say, "Last night, Hong Kong TV showed film of the plumbing at Amoy Gardens. You wouldn't believe—"

"Is that the high-rise with all the SARS cases?"

"Over two hundred, so far, and little wonder. The sewage pipes leak. They have footage of this brown *dribble* coming out of the pipes and roaches and rats running happily through it."

"Julian, I'm cooking."

I offer Ana her glass of wine. I added a little English gin to mine.

"This is *so* how I like my women," I say, squeezing a bun through her kimono. "Barefoot and in the kitchen."

"Would you be a dear and set out the yellow plates?"

Fortunate choice, actually. Accompanying the chopped red peppers, I now learn, will be green scallops on a bed of cabbage that's practically blue. There's also a fragrant rice dish dotted with chopped almonds and ringed by sliced cucumber. I'm not sure that I can digest this many colors at once, but I'm certainly going to try. Ana arrives with two hot pans and each of us seizes a plate. Now we're sprawled half on top of each other to serve ourselves, barely mumbling *bon appétit* before beginning. We're practically finished before remembering to make conversation.

"How's school?" Ana says at last.

"I've identified the warlords," I tell her, my mouth full. "It's a step. Now I know who to negotiate with."

"I'm sure they all love you."

"Mmm. Except for the dead guy."

"Dead guy?"

I nod. "No one bothered to tell me. One of my students dropped dead at school last month sometime. I called on him yesterday, and the other kids made gestures at their throats. I'm flunking him. I don't care."

"Julian."

"Class participation is important to me, okay? And how is the security business these days?

"Insecure," says Ana. "I've gotten one full night of sleep this week, if that tells you anything."

"Here's hoping they don't have you on straight salary," I say.

"We won't even go into my compensation package."

"What, they don't pay you? You just receive compensation?"

She nods. "In a package."

"Beastly."

Ana lifts her wine glass. "If I didn't find the work important, I wouldn't dream of doing it. Not for all the rugs in Persia."

"It's called Iraq these days," I correct her, "what little remains of it. So the work's important now? Before, you called it boring."

"Important. Boring." She shrugs. "It is what it is."

Ana and I reload our plates and my mind flits from worry to worry, finally settling on the telegram handed to me in the English faculty office today. Unless you are a finalist for an Oscar, the chances of receiving good news by telegram are something like one in twenty-three. This one didn't beat the odds. It was from my old drinking buddy, Jeremy: "CONTACT ME IMMEDIATELY CONCERNING DEBT."

I don't know why telegrams don't say *stop* anymore.

"I hope you can finish the squid," says Ana, surrendering her fork and plate. "I'm done."

"More wine?" I say. "There's gin, as well."

"You're not getting me drunk again."

"No? Last time, you agreed to marry me. I thought this time we might decide on the silver."

"I did not agree to marry you," says Ana, falling back against the cushions and pressing her bare feet against my thigh. Her feet are slightly cold, and I set down my fork to warm them with my hands.

"Julian, Julian, *Julian*," she sings, stretching languorously. "What am I doing spending my precious free hours with you? If you and I are a logical match, I'm Ann Boleyn's hand maiden."

"It is a bit surprising," I admit, surveying the curves beneath the black kimono. "But it feels pretty good, wouldn't you say?"

She smiles. "Did you like our little morning tantra session?"

"If that's what it was."

"Call it what you like," says Ana. "We were paying attention to what we were doing, that's all."

I slide one hand beneath the kimono. "It was considerably more than *that's all*. It seemed almost . . . I felt that I'd encountered an information source."

Ana looks at me in surprise.

"Or not," I say. "No, definitely not."

"What kind of information?" she demands.

"I just felt that I was in the presence of knowledge. Nothing specific. I just couldn't find my ignorance anymore."

I glance at Ana. "Or not."

"Julian! You found the Library? In your very first session, you found the *Library*?" She laughs. "You continually surprise me. My God, if you ever harness all that random devilment roiling around inside you—really, you've no idea."

I can't resist hiking the hem of the black kimono just a tad. Her panties, too, are black.

"So," says Ana, smiling. "Whatever will you do? You've been addicted to chaos and failure your entire life, at the very least. Now suddenly you're invited to the dance. You're invited to ecstasy. Will you accept?"

I begin to reply but Ana interrupts, "Don't answer too quickly. Ecstasy comes at a terrible price, Julian. You have to sacrifice everything. All your clever little neuroses. All your comforting self-sabotaging behaviors. Your favorite stories about yourself. Everything that keeps your notions of reality propped up—it all goes. You are being called to utter transformation, Julian, and quite honestly—what *are* you doing with my foot?"

"Sacrificing everything to ecstasy."

Having lifted one of Ana Manguella's lily-white feet, I'm now making proper use of it.

"Relax," I tell her. "I'm a ninth-degree master of Nepalese Foot Reiki. I don't accept students."

Ana giggles. "Let me."

I release my hold on Ana's foot, and her toes begin to explore my mid-body in more minute detail. "Is this it?" she asks.

"It depends on what you're looking for. If you can manage the zipper with your toes, I'll be forever in your debt."

"You're already forever in my debt," replies Ana. "And I'm telling you something important. You. Julian Mancer. Are being called to ecstasy, and it's not an easy calling. Just pay attention. That's all anyone can say. You'll figure it out. Or else you won't."

Her toes fail the zipper-pull contest, but the effort parts her kimono. My hand slips beneath the black undies. Ana surrenders her legs, letting them sprawl. I enjoy watching the broad face relax into an absent smile as my fingertips describe the beginnings of my favorite mound. Careless minutes pass, my fingers neither provoking nor seducing, not hurrying toward an outcome of some kind, nor going straight for the crux of the matter but only referring to it ever so indirectly.

"The dishes . . . ," says Ana weakly.

"Let them wash each other."

Ana releases a sigh and the cares of the day, and her hand reaches lazily for me. I move closer, letting the white fingers discover the contours of my pleasure. Searching blindly for the zipper-pull, Ana's fingers find it. Now her fingertips are in my hair, probing without hurry. I track the arcs of their tiny explorations, their unhurried discovery of the beginnings of my arousal. My eyes meanwhile enjoy the subtle change in Ana's expression as her finger pads squeeze those stirrings, release them, squeeze them again. Almost imperceptibly, Ana tilts her pelvis, and I feel the warm, sharp tip of her pleasure against my middle finger.

"Softly," she whispers, and I realize that excitement has gotten the better of me. I refocus. By tender degrees the moment re-opens. Again my lover and I are adrift. My eyes close, and I imagine the balmy sun at the window once more, but the warmth I feel is within, pulsing from my awaking center. The left-hand path, tantrists call it, letting the fire of pleasure burn away all else until you are present with truth alone. If you can be fully transparent, it's said, you pass through its single eye into the vast non-differentiation.

Ana Manguella's knowing fingers reach a bit farther to tug at my attention until I'm no longer sure what I was thinking about. I watch the white hand reach greedily into my trousers as the black kimono parts a little more to reveal a sleepy nipple. Ana stretches, and for a moment her whole body shudders. Her hand, meanwhile, closes around the shaft of my pleasure and roughly pulls it through the teeth of the zipper, evoking from me an involuntary ahh-*rrrgggh*-hhhh. She snuggles into a more comfortable position, and the circle of her fingers and thumb tighten around me tauntingly. "Mmmm," she murmurs. "Adult pleasure. Don't you love it?"

I'm too engaged to presently reply. What we are doing is, I believe, called *petting*, widely considered the province of hyperventilating teens and doddering seniors. *Zipper* moment aside, however, I must report that I find this activity completely enjoyable if not debased. Maybe it's just the abundant and adamant presence of Ana Manguella that makes of the simplest crumb a full banquet. As though on cue, she and I bring our fingertips to our mouths, wetting them generously. A moment later, we are both *ahhh*-ing at the glow building brighter at our pelvic centers. Or center. I'm not sure I can separate that out just now.

"Slowly," she whispers, and I realize I've gotten carried away again. We each let our hands rest for a moment, and I refocus, letting my erection slowly fade. Again I am aware of a warm glow at my center. The mere act of noticing, I note, has the effect of blowing gently on that coal. Intrigued, I focus on the friendly orange-tinted warmth within my, within our, pelvic cradle whose center seems less an endpoint than a beginning. But of what, exactly?

"Grrd," says Ana.

She's right.

And I was wrong. About everything, basically.

"Congratulations," I say weakly. "You've disproven it."

"Disproven what?" she mutters.

"It."

"Ah. *It.*"

We resume our gentle probings, and again I'm dissociated from thought, from self, I'm rescued, *pulled* from the wreckage by Ana's small white fingers. I know quite well that the moment of climax likely waiting some half-hour in the future will in no way be superior to this moment, the two of us sprawled here on the sofa, smelling highly of squid, just petting away. By that time, that future moment, all the tasty little thresholds will have been savored and eclipsed, and it's these, the little thresholds, that deliver us into the hands of sweetest of surrenders. Very soon we'll be hammering away like a couple of power tools, but will the experience have this same broad *edge*?

We'll see.

Certainly Ana Manguella is right about one thing. I am summoned to something beyond what I've thus far known, something with no interest in my excuses. Perhaps this should concern me, but Ana's fingers are working magic. A fitful erection now heliotropes toward her like a rhododendron. But wait. Now fighting the impulse to turn my whole body toward hers, I open my breath and let my awareness plummet into the glowing warmth at my center, curious as to what that inner portal might open unto. I can't quite make my way there.

Finally I admit that I've left my body in an awkward posture. The growing discomfort is draining off bits of my attention. Reluctantly I take a moment to rearrange myself, at the same time loosening my pants.

"Take them off," says Ana, reaching clumsily to unbutton my shirt. I find my movements slow and awkward. Finally the last of my clothing is jettisoned, and I see that Ana's kimono has vanished as well. Our limbs re-entangle on the leather sofa, our hungry flesh soaking up every detail of the other.

Suddenly. Inexplicably.

A deep pang of vulnerability convulses me. I find myself gasping. I've never felt so open before. So exposed to what I most fearfully want.

What if she just leaves me here? Splayed in my wantingness?

Really. What does happen to me if the clock strikes twelve and this *flaming* chariot becomes a pumpkin and a disappearing swarm of mice? Could I survive losing this? Innocent of answers, I let the questions ring in my bones. I let them course through me like a quavering sob, and I realize that ecstasy requires more courage than I might have supposed. I open even wider, my mouth hungrily reaching for more, *more* of myself, more of Ana Manguella, more of this scent, this terror, this deadly secret craving. Maybe if I can just *be* with these terrible questions, just feed this nakedness, my horrid wantingness one more moment . . .

Ana's ragged breath takes on a slightly guttural sound. Her one hand still grips me. The other directs my fingertips to exactly where she wants them, at the same time offering darting touches to her own pleasure. I surrender, roll onto my side, bring my middle closer to hers, and she makes a desperate sound.

I watch the white fingers go again to her mouth, and my anticipation builds as her wet hand sleepily seeks me out. I re-wet my own hand, summoning the thicker saliva at the back of my mouth, and both our hands return to their touching. My moan becomes a giggle, and hers replies. We're kissing each other sloppily. For a magical moment I'm not entirely sure which one I am, whose body I touch, which of the tangled hands is mine, to whom this hot breath belongs.

"Bed," gasps Ana.

"Bed."

It takes us a while. Each of us falling-down drunk on our own endorphins, we half walk, half roll toward the bedroom. Finally Ana throws back the covers. I'm only partially on the bed when she wraps her upper body around one of my legs and begins circling her chin against my scrotum, inhaling my scents. I feel the peppery warmth of her breath as Ana wolfs down my body's every secret, half-kissing, half-licking the outline of my balls—and not for my pleasure, I note. This is her own little indulgence, her own brute theft. In reply I press against the soft white face aggressively, shivering with excitement from the random touches of her tangled hair. Still nuzzling, Ana wets her tongue and pulls it slowly along the underside of my penis until her mouth has captured me.

"Ooh-*ooo*-ooh."

I enjoy the warm wet embrace of the small mouth, the fine-textured details of its arriving and departing, arriving and departing. Maddened, I shove Ana Manguella against the bed and fall on her like a ravening wolf, attacking her mouth with mine. Almost violently, her hand seizes my penis and throws her body against it. I thrust rhythmically but not yet deeply, letting Ana place me here, there, now at the center of her pleasure, now just above it, now at the warm opening of her body, now in the forest of hairs at one side.

"*Nnn*-mmf," moans Ana, and I kiss the moan. She shifts her weight to one hip then the other then tosses me to one side long enough to lift one of her knees, exposing her ass. Ana's hand shoves me against the tight ring of her anus, her wet mouth smothering mine with hungry kisses as the grip of her anus softens at the center. I begin to press against that soft opening, but her hand moves me.

Now I am at the wet mouth of her vagina. Forest of hairs. Clitoris. Ring of the anus. Clitoris. Vagina. Clitoris. My thrusts become more savage, demanding the warmest depths of her. Mocking me with a laugh, Ana deflects my thrusts to one side then the other. I insist. She pants. It is a honey-dripping eternity before the hand places me at her exact center. I stab deeply, pitilessly, using my hips to penetrate deeper, and Ana's mouth emits a voiceless yelp. Both her hands rise trembling into the air, palms open and imploring.

I've got her now.

I unleash the Unphailing Phallus, rolling my hips devilishly from side to side, twirling the head inside her. Ana's chin rises toward the ceiling, her neck muscles bulging. I exaggerate the twirling motion, and a gargling sound erupts from her throat. All at once, her body spasms, contorts, and flails, the white breasts spilling this way and that. At this sight, I discover another three-quarter inch of erection and use all my weight to drive it into the unknown depths of Ana Manguella. At this, her eyes pop open in surprise and she ceases breathing altogether.

A timeless moment.

As I watch, spellbound, Ana's fingers, still spread in the air, describe unknown mudras of transfiguration. Still not breathing, her face opens in a smile I've never before seen. The white teeth are lovely, and I suck on them furiously, the innermost chamber of Ana Manguella gripping me ever tighter until, at the last possible moment, her deepest recesses open to admit me to an even deeper warmth. Into that bright inner space I tumble.

Everything vanishes in yellow-white brilliance. I hear the distant baying of a curly-coated retriever. I think that's me. A higher voice replies in a perfect fifth. Now all hell truly breaks loose. Desperately my knees grip the bucking body beneath me. Ana, her eyes raging, is trying to throw me into the sky. The yellow-white brilliance throbs ever brighter until a blinding flash erases pretty much everything.

I try to ignore the gently fluttering intrusions of the photon belt. Or is the bedsheet tickling my nose? Soon I know I must send out emissaries. In such a sprawling and uniformly luminescent reality, its farthest edges just vaguely sketched in, one arrives only gradually at the true comportment of things. Yet one *does* sense within the general tumult a sensation quite alike unto fluttering.

It has taken me quite some time to arrive at this plateau of comprehension, my senses having recently been blown to the farthest reaches of the Schnoid Belt by a relentless force loosely termed *woman*.

"Aaay gawder someep," utters Ana Manguella, semi-conscious beneath me.

"Mnnn," I reply.

I know exactly what she's trying to say but am presently no more capable than she of arranging it. Clearly something must be done. There seems to be a colorless fully opened eye at my center now, viewing me from every perspective at once, which I find somewhat bothersome. Then there's the matter of the emissaries. The trouble with sending out emissaries, as you know, is that they seldom return and if they do, they never look quite the same as before, their beards coarse and sun-bleached, their eyes pleading as you try to understand who they have become and to what end. Not to mention how to *glean* from the oh-so-gentle flutterings exactly what it is they mean to say.

Ana tries again. "Aay gotta eh sommeep."

Clearly, she too has noticed the intrusions. Ana lifts her head off the pillow long enough to groan, "Julian. I've got to get some sleep. Do you mind terribly?"

"What? I have to *leave*?"

"Glrrn," she says. Fumbling for the bedside clock, Ana activates her alarm. A moment later, she's out.

"In this condition," I say to myself, "I am supposed to cross an international border?"

With a sigh, I pull the covers around the white shoulders of Ana Manguella, kissing each in turn. Actually I think I kissed the left one twice. I give the right shoulder one more, and the world lines up more or less straight again. Now to see if I can get myself into my clothing with a minimum of blood loss. It's a situation.

After a shot of straight gin and an unsteady trip the bathroom, I discover myself badly dressed in the center of a lamplit street. A nippy wind has appeared from nowhere. I should have made it two shots of straight gin. Clutching my shirt collar, I make my wending way to the corner to flag an approaching taxi—or am I writing my name in the air? The taxi stops nonetheless.

"Train station," I tell the driver. "Careful of the fluttering."

Minutes later, I am aboard an empty train hell-bent for the nearest raw edge of the Chinese mainland, where I soon discover that the Immigration turnstiles are padlocked for the night. A bilingual sign informs me that they will re-open at five. It's not quite four. Blearily I take a seat in the florescent-lit waiting room where four Chinese men sprawl in plastic chairs, nearly horizontal. Two are trying to sleep and smoke at the same time.

Mechanically my left hand goes into a pocket and comes out with my journal. I am just lifting my semi-sharpened number-two pencil when a man chooses the seat at my left. I look up to discover a face at once familiar and unwelcome.

"Please allow me to join you for a moment," says Agent Raul Velázquez. "I think you may remember me."

I close the journal. "Where's the shiny gold badge? No, don't tell me. You're off-duty."

Velázquez nods humorlessly. He is dressed in jeans, a navy polo shirt, and a spotless denim jacket. "Mr. Mancer," he says, "I need to discuss something with you that has no connection to any matter concerning the US State Department. It's completely off the record, in fact, and must remain so. Yet it does concern the security of our country and the safety of your own person. May I continue?"

"I'll continue for you," I say. "You want me to deliver Jerome Stiles to you. You're just about to hand me a card with a private phone number that is not to be shared around."

Velázquez blinks, surprised.

"I *am* psychic," I tell him.

After a dry chuckle, Velázquez continues, "Please understand, this is no ordinary situation. We're not talking about an ordinary man. Jerome Stiles's knowledge goes beyond that of anyone else we're aware of. His value to our country is enormous. Unfortunately his sense of loyalty does not seem to extend beyond himself."

Velázquez pauses to deliver a steely gaze. "Are you aware that Stiles has followed every detail of your life and your sister's, since birth?"

"And before," I reply. "What I don't know is why."

"No one knows that," says Velázquez, cold-eyed. "Stiles works almost entirely alone and keeps no written records. He has neither family nor friends. What we do know is that Jerome Stiles—"

"Cut the crap," I interrupt. "His name isn't Stiles, just as yours isn't Velázquez. All I want to know is, how many others are out there? Others like myself and my sister? And I want to know *why*. If you can't tell me that, I've absolutely no reason to talk to you."

Velázquez leans slightly toward me. "Where there are no written records, there can be no certainty. But it appears there were originally some sixty or seventy others. When—"

"Sixty or *seventy*?" I say, disturbing the sleepers/smokers.

"That's what we believe."

"You said *were*," I press. "Why were?"

"I'm afraid that the number has dropped quite dramatically over the years," says Velázquez. "We believe that he is culling genotypes."

"Culling genotypes," I repeat. "I think you mean he is murdering his own children."

Velázquez gazes at me neutrally.

"Tell me about Regis Labs," I say.

"Regis Labs conducted a very early pilot program in human artificial insemination, funded in part by the US government. Stiles—Dobbins, if you prefer—extended invitations to some of the most prominent academicians of that time, including of course your own mother. He screened both male and female candidates, but with the males it seems to have been an empty gesture. From the beginning, Dobbins's interest was the propagation of his own DNA."

"Why?"

"No one knows. There's very little information about Tim Dobbins. Not even his age. I've seen photos of him taken in 1950, and I've seen photos taken of him last week, and there's not much difference. But time's got to be running out for him. He's behaving erratically. The people who've worked with him in the past are very uneasy."

Velázquez looks around before continuing, "Stiles has something very specific in mind for you and your sister, Mr. Mancer. Don't ask me what because I don't know—but he's certainly taken a lot of trouble on your behalves. That's why you're being watched so closely now, by all the parties involved. May I ask you something?"

"Ask."

"Why China? What brought you and your sister here?"

"Happenstance," I reply. "A friend of ours signed up for a teaching program. My sister followed suit."

"Interesting," says Velázquez. "The reason I say 'interesting' is that all your remaining siblings are now on their way here."

I gaze at him questioningly.

"Those not already in China," continues Velázquez, "are preparing to come, all for different reasons. We're certain there has been no communication among any of the parties. Curious, don't you think?"

I sink a little deeper into my seat, recalling a rainy day in Kunming and an encounter with myself in epaulets. I'm not sure that *curious* covers it. China's the endgame all right. I'm no clearer than before as to what game we're talking about. But it ends here in China.

"How many of us are left?" I mutter.

"Nine. There were six sets of twins in your peer group. You and your sister are the only pair remaining. Only one week ago, there was a murder-suicide involving the last remaining fraternals. We believe it to be an actual murder-suicide. This may be a little disturbing to hear," says Velázquez, "but there is a very high incidence of violence in your group. Nineteen have been charged with domestic violence. Six have murdered a family member."

Perfect. Everyone is either dead or en route to China with murder in their hearts for the kinfolk.

At least I know that Timothy Dobbins had nothing to do with luring the Mancer twins to this country. If anything, he worked overtime to get us out of here. Maybe it was a case of bad timing, I consider. Lil and I may have come earlier than expected and gotten tangled up in someone-or-other's depopulation program. That time seems now to have passed. But why here, why now? Could it be that the Communist takeover a half-century ago interrupted a pet Timothy Dobbins project that now requires . . . completion?

"What's in this for you?" I ask Velázquez. "Why do you want Dobbins all to yourself?"

The man seated next to me takes his time formulating an answer. Finally he says, "Forgive me, but I must answer your question thoughtfully. There's no point in further complicating your situation with information that can't help you. Let me just say that Dobbins is in serious trouble, and so is anyone in whom he has confided. It's believed that he has confided in you, Mr. Mancer, and it is further supposed that you have confided in me. We must both, therefore, play our cards very carefully. If I may say so, you yourself are in no position to bargain with any of the players involved. I believe that I am. Unfortunately the only thing that either of us can possibly use for leverage at this point is Dobbins himself. Either we gain possession of Timothy Dobbins, or soon we will have no place to stand."

"And Agent Barnes?" I ask.

"Unfortunately Agent Barnes is not to be trusted."

At last, a rational statement.

I extend my hand. "I think this is where you hand me a phone number and wish me a lot of luck."

"It's written backward," says Velázquez, producing a small scrap of paper. "A primitive device, I know, but we do what we can. And I do wish you luck."

Rising, Raul Velázquez walks away into the night.

I gaze unhappily at the backward phone number for a moment before tucking the card into my wallet. Right beside the one received from Agent Truth Guy, along with various other numbers I'll never dial.

Life is so whatever.

Re-opening my ironclad journal with a sigh, I record the date at the top of a fresh page—and now I stare at that date.

March fourth, 2003.

Hmmm. I'm pretty sure that makes yesterday March *third*, 2003, also known in some circles as New Age Groundhog Day. The Three-three-three. My eyes roll listlessly as I recall Tree's four unheard messages on the American Teacher's Telephone. I may have let something slip my mind.

36

Below Lil's balcony, the basketball courts glisten with the day's third rain. I've spent this entire Sunday in Lil's bathrobe, sitting unshaven at the American Teacher's Computer, a pilled acrylic blanket wrapped around my legs. In early March, we have back-tracked to midwinter.

"It wasn't our time yet." That's what Tree said about the Three-three-three.

I told her that was my feeling, too.

"I tried to find your energy," she told me yesterday over Korean barbeque, "but I hit a firewall. I saw you surrounded by—I don't know what it was. Almost like an electrified fence. I never did find you."

"Mmm," I replied. It was something to say.

"We were met," said Tree. "Every time you attempt to do something powerful, you are met by the Opponent, and we were *met*. Don't worry about it. Another day's coming, and we'll be ready. Four-four-four, Five-five-five, whenever it is."

I told her that was my feeling, too.

If not for the rain, I'd have run a load of laundry through Lil's refrigerator/clothes-washer this morning. The first and only time I've felt practically Chinese was when I hung my first load of wash on the balcony. There are metal pipes along the ceiling over which you hook your clothes-hangers with the aid of this odd broomstick-looking thing. My above-dumpster flat has one, too. I asked Bellamy what it was for. He could've really sent me up. *Ah, this Chinese rectum device.* Wow. Really?

These people hang their wash everywhere—trees, street signs, fences. Stand still long enough, and they'll hang it on you. But they're at their best decorating balconies. On a windy day, you can go through the bushes beneath the tenements and find anything you want. Never have to buy clothes in this country.

Hong Kong just passed an ordinance against attaching aluminum clotheslines to your windowsill. You buy them at the supermarket. They unfold and unfold till you say *wow* I can hang everything I own on this thing. Problem is, wet clothes are heavy, so, with the aid of a gust of wind, they tend to break away and start laundry avalanches that can take out a city block. Here's poor Chen Chan Chang walking along the *lu*, evening paper beneath his arm, and—what's that curious sound? Chen's final worldly act is to look up into the maw of fifty-seven floors of poly-cotton. All of which is a way of not saying what's really on my mind.

Ana called to say she's tired, so let's not do anything tonight after all. For this I've waited four days. She wouldn't even book our next date. *I'll call you*, she said.

I'd really like to check another book out of the library.

My hand goes to my throat where the moldavite pendant should be. I guess somewhere between the fracas on the turquoise sofa and the fray on the satiny bed, it came off my neck. I'll do well to get that little green stone back before Tree finds out. Anyway you measure a good sexual experience by how long it takes to find everything you'd been wearing. If it's four days before you have both your shoes, you know you probably had a really swell time.

I wish I could stop thinking about just how swell. That blue/green-eyed woman has got me so tore open that I keep checking to see if I still have my entire transverse colon. It's probably all this newly discovered emotional *availability* that's got me spooked. Whatever, there's not one hell of a lot I can do about it except wait until Ana Manguella decides to pick up the phone. Four-four-four, Five-five-five, whenever.

Tree won't admit it, but she's really shook about the Three-three-three. Girl had her head loaded all wrong. Absolutely nothing happened on March third, and now she's saying she can't trust her intuition. Hell, I knew that all along. "I feel the need for a serious retreat," she said as we finished the last of yesterday's barbeque. "I need to get out of my apartment, out of this city, just get out of my *head* for a while. I've asked my school for two weeks off, and I think they're going to give it to me."

"And go where?" I asked.

She smiled dimly. "Mr. Xu has been telling me about China's seven sacred mountains. I'm reading about them online. Any one of them would be great. What I'd really like to do is make a pilgrimage to all seven."

You might want to stick with one, Tree. Pilgrims *walk* up China's sacred mountains.

Meanwhile I needn't expect any fresh pages from Truman/whomever. Tree is burning them as fast as they come.

"I can't trust anything I'm getting anymore," said Tree. "I've gotten off-track somehow."

"Tree," I said, "I think you can, like, *really* trust these pages."

I'm, like, really starting to talk like Itsy.

Tree shook her head. "I took a close look at the last page that came through. I sat down and traced the handwriting with my finger and let that guide me back to the mind that created it and—Julian, that novel is *not* from who we thought."

I blinked, waiting.

"I followed that handwriting back to an old friend of ours."

"What's so bad about an old friend?" I said. "I've never been all that attached to Truman, if you really—"

She shook her head again. "This is an old friend I was really hoping not to see again anytime soon, least of all now."

"Could have been something you ate," I suggested.

"I burned the page," said Tree, "and I burned the two that came after it. If another one comes tonight, I'll burn that, too."

"You're burning my Pulitzer," I informed her calmly.

"Jules. If you have a Pulitzer in you, it will come out. You do not have to bring it in from some other galaxy, and I *will* not jeopardize our work for the sake of your vanity."

Girl's right. She has gotten off-track. I'm not sure all seven sacred mountains will do it. Then again, that last page from Truman was a bit odd. Maybe he's finally figured out how to order martinis up there.

My hand keeps going to my throat. I never realized how much I've depended on that ugly interstellar road-kill for . . . whatever I'm depending on it for. My abiding sense of the absurd, I suppose. Isn't much of a neck-warmer.

Here on Lil's computer is an article that says Operation Iraqi Freedom has already cost us twenty-five million gallons of jet fuel and sixty-five million gallons of gasoline. All I can say is, if we didn't go over there to grab their oil, we might begin to give it some little thought. Otherwise it may be necessary to borrow a gallon-can to get back home.

China's operation against the deadly SARS virus, meanwhile, is going as one might reasonably expect. Rumors have people dropping like flies on city streets, especially here in Guangdong Province where the disease first emerged. The Chinese government is still completely mum despite growing protests from the World Health Organization. Here at Shenzhen High School of Electronic Excellence, they're swabbing everything in sight. All day Friday, there was a huge cauldron of black medicinal tea simmering in the courtyard, beside it a ladle and a stack of nested cellophane cups. I even saw a bar of soap in one of the boys' restrooms. Next thing you know, they'll have toilet paper.

I also found a couple of articles about ma huang this morning. Seems it's very, very, very bad for you, and what isn't that's even remotely enjoyable? The article calls it ephedra, labels it "herbal speed," and cautions chubby Americans not to get strung out on the stuff or they may find their knees speaking to each other in Brazilian Portuguese. A word to the wise is sufficient.

The rest of us will require a little more information.

Lil paid me a visit last night. I was lucid dreaming that I was sitting atop the pyramid in downtown Memphis—it's not as sharp as you might imagine—when Lil appeared mid-air with angel wings. She was wearing all white. "You totally blew the Three-three-three," she said.

"I really like the little harp," I replied. "Do you take requests at all?"

"Do you have any fucking idea," said Lil, fluttering furiously, "of the enormity of what you have just undone?"

"Tree says it wasn't our time."

"It wasn't our time because you were too busy getting your brains fucked out by that woman. Who is she anyway?"

"Taller than Adrian, for one thing," I replied. "Beyond that, she's none of your business."

"Does she know about our work?" demanded Lil. "She does, doesn't she?"

"What work, Lillian? *Nothing* happened on the Three-three-three."

"And why was that, Julian? I'd really like to know. I'd also like to hear how you intend to make up for this."

"I've had enough of your abuse. I'm waking up."

"Don't you dare. How else am I supposed to talk to you? You never meet me in the glow anymore."

I adjusted my posture. The point of the pyramid *was* a little sharp.

Fluttering a little closer, Lil said, "Tell me if this sounds the least bit strange to you. A beautiful young woman suddenly appears in your life and *throws* herself at your dick—"

"It was more of a soft lob."

"—*just* before the Three-three-three."

"That was a coincidence."

"Right," said Lillian. "I suppose it was also a coincidence that she snatched your moldavite?"

My hand went to my throat. "It fell off."

"And now that we've missed the Three-three-three, she's suddenly dropping you."

My voice became a growl. "You have *never* been able to deal with my relationships."

"That woman is working for the other fucking side, Julian."

"It's been so nice talking to you, dearest."

"You get that moldavite back. You hear me?"

"I'm waking up."

Lil fluttered to within an inch of my nose. "Do, Julian. Do wake up. That would be really swell for Tree and me because we're just a little bit tired of cleaning up behind you."

A burst of sunlight knifes though the gap in Lillian's curtains. I think the rain has stopped again. I don't know what this spell of damp weather is about, but I can tell you it plays hell with knitting bones. There's an outbreak of black mold on the ceiling of the American Teacher's Bathroom that's threatening to make SARS look like a fingernail fungus. Thought you'd want to know. At least my menacing little red mushrooms are regenerating. They've grown two inches the past two days. Meanwhile I'm covering the top of the aquarium with a grill of hardware cloth topped by a sauce pan. Rodent extrusion device.

Unable to bear this chair a moment longer, I rise and the acrylic blanket pools at my ankles, causing electric sparks all about the groin area. I needed that. Stepping around the American Teacher's Mattress, I throw open the door to the balcony and gaze out at the fracturing cloud cover.

Marilyn caught me yesterday weaving in the general direction of Studebaker Supermarket. It was a straightforward conversation as I reconstruct it. Nothing at all about armpit sex or German-made number-two pencils—I've found a stationer in Hong Kong who carries them. Afterward I walked away with the troubling realization that I'd just agreed to have dinner with Marilyn tomorrow night in Shikou. Whatever. She's paying.

The sky does seem to be clearing a bit. I decide to leave the balcony door open to gather a bit of cheer. Taking a deep breath, I head for the bathroom to duck beneath the black mold and pee in the general vicinity of the toilet. It's the intention that counts.

Lil has always maintained that I should have a housekeeper, but I've never quite seen the advantage in paying a stranger to wander through my apartment with a vacant stare and a squirt-bottle of chlorine. Lil's maid is a Honduran immigrant with multiple personality disorder. Her name is Rosita. And Lupe. And Maria Luisa. I tried her at my place for one week, at Lil's insistence. But on Friday all three wanted to be paid.

I use my left foot to flush the toilet. Returning to the front room, I'm surprised to discover that the balcony door I left open is now closed. Even more surprising is the presence of a petite amber-hued human kneeling on the mattress. She is facing away, her blue trousers and pink panties down around her ankles and her face buried in the covers.

"Rui Long," I say. "So nice to *see* you."

"Come fuck my crack," she says.

I sigh. "Exactly how many people saw you walk into this apartment?"

"Nobody noticed," Rui Long's voice replies. "Anyway, it's done. You might as well get the good out of it." A small hand appears between the two thighs, palm up, fingers imploring.

A jolt of greed shoots through me. I can't quite pull my eyes away from those honeyed little hams. Rui Long hikes her hiney a little higher, and the perfect dot at its center beckons. Someone has been reading my fantasies.

Or. Maybe she's been reading the letter of the law. Didn't this sweet child recently offer to obtain the services of an attorney? And might this little conjugal visit be, in fact, a forensic-evidence-gathering foray? Helpless schoolgirl sodomized on school grounds by substitute teacher. Actually I kind of like the ring of it.

"Pull your pants up, Rui Long," I say, despite the ring of it. "I'm not buying. And just for the record, I require a little more foreplay than this."

The young woman spins around, and her long hair flies. "What? You're turning *this* down?"

I'm reconsidering, in point of fact. But Rui Long is now on her feet, kicking her trousers and panties into my face. Now she's throwing Lillian's smiley-face mug at my head, and I'm doing my best to duck.

"Uh . . . ?" I say.

Rui Long lifts a ceramic ashtray but before she can hurl it, her face closes in a tight grimace. The ashtray slips from her fingers onto the mattress, where Rui Long now falls to her knees. Lifting her face to the ceiling, she begins to howl like an adolescent Norwegian elkhound.

"Noo-ooOOOoo-body wants me," she cries.

"Uh . . . ?" I say.

"My life is *over*," howls Rui Long. "I'm going to spend the rest of my life cleaning ashtrays at the Chinese phone company. I'll never find anyone who loves me."

Rui Long crawls forward to hug my ankles. "Doo, you're the only person I can talk to. Please, *please* don't send me away."

"Uh . . . ?" I say, as a wet little face burrows into the opening of Lil's bathrobe. "Rui Lon-*NNNNN*-nng?"

By the time I'm able to pull away, her blouse is unbuttoned. She shakes free of it. "We can run away together," she says.

"You're completely insane," I tell the slightly outturned right breast.

"We'll start a new life," she pants. "No one can stop us."

With this, Rui Long spins around, jacking her ass again. "I'll give you anything you want."

"Jesus," I say miserably. We're getting really close to enough foreplay now. Unable to resist the itsy golden body an instant longer, I turn and flee into the bathroom, locking the door behind me. "Rui Long?" I shout through the door, glancing uneasily at the killer black mold above my head. "You have to leave. Do you hear me?"

Silence.

"Rui Long?"

More silence. I'm just about to place my ear against the door to listen when I hear a throaty scream that approximates the distress call of a wounded civet cat. The blade of my newly purchased hatchet crashes through the hollow wooden door and stops an inch from my face. I fall backward over the toilet seat and land with my feet in the air.

"Rui *Long*?"

After three yanks, the hatchet comes free and a dark eye appears in the ragged hole. "*Herrrre's* Itsy."

A moment later I hear a dull thud against the door followed by a loud clatter on the kitchen floor. "Oww-ww," sobs Rui Long.

"Doo? Are you okay?" I ask, trying to rise from the floor.

I hear breaking glass followed by more breaking glass. Rui Long is smashing everything in the kitchen. I think that last crash was the gin bottle, nearly full.

"I can't stan-*nnHHHnnn*-nd it any longer!" comes a shuddering cry.

I think I just heard the sound of a window sliding open. Struggling to my feet, I open the door just in time to see a naked bottom exiting the kitchen window. I lurch forward to grab Rui Long around the ankles, but she yanks free and kicks me squarely on the bridge of the nose. There's a terrible cracking sound, and I slip in the puddle of gin.

"God in heaven," I say to myself, seated on the floor holding my shattered nose. An instant later, I'm screaming and scrambling to my feet, as the shards of broken glass beneath me are soaked in alcohol. The moment I'm back on my feet, both my nostrils begin gushing blood.

"God in hea-*ggggh*-ven," I say, leaning over the sink, blood bubbling from my nose. I catch sight, meanwhile, of Rui Long's naked body standing on the narrow ledge.

"Rui Long-*ggggh*?" I say.

"I can't stand it any longer," she gasps, looking down terrified. The excitement is giving her a woody.

I hear the sound, four stories below, of a woman's scream. The itsy schoolgirl was right. I should have gotten the good out of it.

"Don't do it, Rui Long-*ggggh*," I bubble. "You've got your whole life ahead of yo-*ggggh*."

"With a dick," she whimpers, "and a crack ho mama, and a daddy who hates me."

More screams erupt. People in neighboring buildings are coming out onto their balconies and pointing.

"But you're the new *human*," I say, my eyes going to the chocolate Buddha at Rui Long's feet.

"It's too much," she gasps. "I can't deal with it."

I'm still looking at the chocolate Buddha. "Actually, since you're out there . . ."

Rui Long teeters for a moment. Panicking, she tries to right herself but overcompensates. The next thing I know, she has launched herself through the air, screaming as she executes a near perfect flip and crashes through the fiberglass roof of Madam Wu's balcony below.

I stick my head out the window. Through the shattered fiberglass, I see that Rui Long has landed on her back on a deck lounger. The chocolate Buddha, spinning through the air, comes to rest seated on her belly, his silent laugh directed at her groin.

I think this may be a good day to give my two weeks' notice.

37

The setting sun framing her small shoulders, Marilyn awaits me on the rough boards of Shikou Pier. At the sight of her expectant smile, I almost turn around. If I'd been able to pick up the phone, I'd have cancelled. "Why, Marilyn," I manage to say, forcing myself onto the pier, "don't you look wonderful?"

True actually. This woman's freshly blow-dried hair is almost feathery. And below her short skirt, the two legs are golden-perfect. And the red blouse . . .

"You bought the blouse," I say, surprised.

Marilyn laughs triumphantly. She knows she looks good. "Ju-wen, your face look *so* terrible."

The bandages cover the worst of it. Beneath the elaborate gauze and aluminum muzzle, my nose is at least as colorful as a *piñata* and roughly the same size. It's a nice match for the cast on my arm, actually. There's no need to go into the nine stitches in my rear.

"Is terrible," says Marilyn, shaking her head, "this very crazy girl attack you so bad."

"I don't want to discuss it."

"Everybody the school so surprise," she says. "This crazy girl have the—" Marilyn makes a gesture at her groin. "How you say? The dcc-*eee*-eek?"

"I said I don't want to discuss it. Where are we eating?"

"What restaurant you want go?" asks Marilyn. "You choose."

"You're choosing. I'm drinking."

Marilyn shifts into worry mode and the beak appears. "Chinese or Western?"

"Chinese," I say. That narrows it down.

"Cantonese or Sichuan?"

"I don't care," I say.

We begin walking along the rusting waterfront, Marilyn peppering me with questions. Large restaurant or small? Outside or in? Balcony or downstairs? Fish or no fish? How I want it cook? I keep telling her I don't care but Marilyn isn't listening. By the time we take our seats at a Cantonese place near the ferry, I'm ready to OJ her with the waitress's ballpoint pen.

"Beer," I say pointedly.

"What kind?" asks Marilyn.

"I don't—Hsingtao."

"Light or dark?"

"I—dark."

"Warm or cold?"

"Cold."

"Large or small?"

"Quick."

That last part is in vain, of course. The waitress stands there taking down the entire order, meaning at least ten minutes of increasingly heated discussion.

"You want fish?" begins Marilyn, and I push away from the table.

Near the kitchen door is a cooler filled with beer bottles, and I yank a longneck free. There's no opener. Grimfaced, I enter the kitchen where three aproned men look at me in horror.

"You should see the other guy," I tell them, setting down the longneck and using my one good hand to mime a bottle-opener. Still staring, the youngest chef walks over, takes the chilled bottle from my hand and pops off the cap on the edge of the counter.

"*Shi shi*," I thank him and turn it up.

As the three watch, I drain the beer, set down the empty bottle and exit the kitchen with a muffled belch. On my way back to the table, I pull two more bottles from the cooler.

"Fish will be fine," I tell Marilyn, seating myself.

She asks, "How you want cook?"

"Yes," I reply, handing one of the bottles to the waitress. "Cooked."

By the time our order is a matter of public record, I'm well into beer number three.

"I order you soup," says Marilyn.

"Perfect." I smile and my muzzle flexes.

Marilyn's phone rings. It's her fourth incoming call. Marilyn's ring tone is "Listen to the Rhythm of the Falling Rain," one note nearly a full half-step flat. As she answers, I glance at the next table where four men hunch forward, sucking down noodles. One of them has chopsticks in one hand and a lit cigarette in the other. At least most of the people here have stopped staring at me. Marilyn's voice is hushed and urgent as she speaks into her phone. I've no doubt she's providing her friends with regular news updates.

The moment she hangs up, Marilyn leans forward and begins grilling me. Why this crazy American girl attack me in my apartment? Why she jump off the building without the school uniform? Why she have the dee-*eee*-eek? There's no putting Marilyn off. Now that my three point five Hsingtaos have met the pain medication that preceded them, I'm willing to humor her, going through the same story I've already laid out for Joe and the headmaster.

This neurotic Western devil of a defective Chinese girl seems to have developed an unhealthy attraction to me. All too common, unfortunately, as I *am* somewhat famous in the States. (At this, Joe turned to the headmaster and said, "Horrywood Squares," and the headmaster looked at me with new eyes.) What could I do but try to avoid her primitive advances and—well, the splintered bathroom door tells the tale. When it was finally clear to the deranged young woman that her affections would never be returned, she decided to end it all.

So foo-rish.

As for the dee-*eee*-eek, I'm as much in the dark as everyone else. But delicate young girls who take too many strong American street drugs—what are they to expect? At this, Joe and the headmaster nodded in unison like dashboard dogs, and now Marilyn gasps and wags her head. Before she can come up with another question, her phone chimes again and she answers eagerly. I wave to the waitress for another beer. I was right about the whole *guanxi* thing. At the conclusion of my debriefing, the headmaster asked for my autograph, and not long thereafter Rui Long was inexorably exorcized from Shenzhen High School of Electronic Excellence and turned over for prompt deportation.

Best thing all around.

My hand goes to my throat for the eighty-first time today. I try not to remember a certain recent lucid dream.

Marilyn sets down her phone just as the soup course arrives. There's a chicken's foot in each bowl, claws and all.

Marilyn stirs her chicken's foot around with a ceramic spoon. "When a girl is older," she tells me, only it comes out *odor*, "sometimes she must do something. I don't know how you say. One time every month, she must do this. I think mah-hhn-, mehhhnnn-. . . ."

I'm not saying it for her.

"Mehhhhnnnnn-. Mehn-something. Do you know this?" asks Marilyn.

I know this.

"After this time every month, she eat this soup to build her up. I just finish this time, so I eat this soup."

I gaze down at my chicken's foot.

"How much you pay?" asks Marilyn, pointing to the fake jade ring on my left pinkie. It still doesn't symbolize world peace.

"I'm not telling you," I say, hiding my hands beneath the table.

"Is not real jade, this one," she says. "Just somebody make this Guangzhou. Next time I go with you, get the real jade."

"Thanks. So much. Marilyn."

After the soup comes steaming tofu stuffed with ground pork in an MSG-free brown sauce. I'm surprised at the flavor, which is almost northern Italian. There's also a leafy vegetable of an almost emerald green in a kuzu sauce, followed in short order by a flaky herb-roasted sunfish. This place isn't bad.

Halfway through the tofu, Marilyn locks her eyes onto mine and asks, "Why you divorce your wife?"

Asians. Indirect. Inscrutable.

"Very difficult to say," I stall. It depends a little on which wife we're discussing. I decide to answer in the global. "Personally I think that marriage isn't the best of ideas."

"You not get married again?" asks Marilyn.

"No."

I can see the wheels turning.

"You only want some girlfriend?" she asks.

"Yes."

"You want sex her?"

"Yes."

How you want cook?

Marilyn also wants to know if I have a Chinese girlfriend, a girlfriend in America, is she beautiful, am I faithful, do I want sex a Chinese woman, all this in exactly the same tone as do you want fish?

Unsteadily I wave for another beer. Why can't they just bring them two at a time? "Yes, no, goddamn right, what's your sign?" I reply.

Marilyn sighs with dismay. "I don't understand so many women have the sex. Just some boyfriend do this, but maybe she get the AIDS. You know about this?"

I nod. Beijing only recently got around to telling the Chinese about HIV, those of them not already dead of it. The government admits to around forty-four thousand fatalities thus far, which should put the actual number somewhere over a hundred thou.

"Always I just stay home," complains Marilyn. "I am so *boring* but have son, can't just go play some fun, some boyfriend. Also this hurt me so bad, my husband divorce. I don't want this again. Better just stay home." She sighs petulantly.

"That's always the choice, isn't it?" I ask, helping myself to more sunfish. "Death of boredom or ritual disembowelment."

"Is what?" asks Marilyn, eyes sharpening.

"Be lonely," I say, "or get hurt."

She nods. "Which answer you choose?"

My thoughts drift to a snowy British woman due to call me five days ago. Nearby Shikou Ferry, it occurs, could have me at her doorstep in less than an hour. I have enough of a buzz to answer Marilyn, "It's better to love even if it kills you, which it undoubtedly will."

Marilyn sighs. "Chinese men go see the American movie, always get some idea just make big problem. Want sex her. Want put it in—what is it?" She's pointing at her rear. "I say, why you want *do* this, so crazy? You like do this?" she asks and awaits my answer.

I set down my personal wooden chopsticks. "Not right now."

Marilyn laughs. "But you like some other time?"

I close my eyes and open them again. "I'm afraid you mistake me," I say measuredly, "for someone of far cruder sensibilities."

Marilyn says, "I think you embarrass. In China everybody just laugh. Don't laugh, nobody know you embarrass, just keep ask you some more."

"To Americans," I inform her, "it's very embarrassing to be embarrassed. You'd rather no one knew."

"Why?"

"Americans are supposed to be cool. Experienced. That sort of thing."

Marilyn shakes her head. "Chinese not cool. Not experience. Nobody care about that."

"What do Chinese care about?" I ask.

She smiles slowly. "Good food."

I raise my glass. "Good food."

Her expression changes. "So hard *find* good food. This restaurant have one good dish. The other place one good dish. Chinese people I think very difficult, understand food too good maybe."

Understand pain medication pretty good too also. I finish my glass of Hsingtao, or maybe I just poured it in my lap.

"When you go back America?" asks Marilyn.

"Tomorrow would be nice," I say.

"Mmm, you miss your family."

I stare at her. The Chinese never tire of proposing this to me, and I never tire of wondering what they could possibly be thinking. Our mother has slipped into a coma, by the way. Tree gave me the news. That's how you say it. She's *slipped* into a coma. One's mother never slithers or lumbers into a coma.

"I don't have a family," I tell Marilyn at last. "I have a twin sister and a turnip mother and a father who steals things and gets caught." I struggle to hold the round face in focus. "You know, Marilyn, you're not a bald looking woman. Bad, I mean. I mean good."

Marilyn glistens for me. Now the beak re-appears. "I think you just go back America, forget about me. I am old-fashioned Chinese woman, need a husband help me. My son need this, too."

Unexpectedly Marilyn's hand crosses the table. I feel two firm pats on my hand. "But I lonely," she says and the hand remains there. "I think you lonely too, Ju-wen. You feel lonely, you can call me."

I gaze at the plump, warm hand. This woman can take me so quickly from attraction to repulsion and back again that I've no idea what to think. The hand disappears. "Where that waiter girl?" says Marilyn vexedly. "Supposed to bring Pineapple Fried Rice same time as fish."

There's an old story about a woman in need of a husband. Early one spring, she went to an enchanted well and said into it, "I want a husband. What should I do?" Her reflection re-plied, "Fill your pockets with gold coins and jasmine flowers." The woman did as instructed but no husband appeared. She returned to the well and said, "I did what you asked. Where's the husband?" Her reflection answered, "He is here!" The re-flection of her face on the water's surface changed to that of a handsome young man. Overjoyed, the woman jumped in. The gold coins took her straight to the bottom, of course, and she drowned. To this day, you'll find coins at the bottom of every well, and early in the spring you can still catch the faint scent of jasmine.

"Ow!" I say.

Marilyn looks at me.

"Glass," I explain, shifting my weight to the other but-tock. "I don't think they got it all."

I reach into my shirt pocket for my pain medication. One tablet every four hours or every four drinks, whichever comes first. My fingers close around something. It turns out to be a withered flower bud. Stricken, I gaze at it. A gift from our lady of tousled tresses. *The way you know that spring has come to Earth is the emergence of flowers.* The bud is drying. Only the faintest blush of purple remains at the tip.

"I need to use your phone," I tell Marilyn decisively. "Can you dial the number for me?"

Marilyn accepts the note from my wallet. "Hong Kong?" she says. "Is very expensive dial this from—"

"I'll pay double," I say, beginning to slur. "I'll pay you in jeweler's gold. I recently came into some."

Marilyn is still looking at the note. "This say some wom-an's name. You want call some woman Ana Hong Kong?"

"A man," I say. "Anabolic Steroid. Old workout partner."

Marilyn dials and hands me the phone. I stumble away from the table. After one ring, I hear a familiar *hello*?

"You always know it's springtime on Earth," I say, "be-cause of all the *flii-iiers*."

"Julian? Are you sloshed?"

Pushing through the men's room door, I say, "My little snowflake. It's just so magical to hear your rather pristine voice in my ear. Especially in the men's room."

"I'm at work," says Ana. "Are you all right?"

I gaze at the dying bud in the palm of my hand. "I need to see you immeeedially if not sooner."

"Um, do you remember that I said I'd call?"

"I can be at your rather pristine door," I say, holding the phone with my shoulder and struggling to open my fly, "in less than an hour."

"Julian, I won't be home in less than an hour."

"Then half than less an hour," I say.

Ana sighs. "I've no idea when I'll be free. That's why I said I'll call you. I have to go now."

"Why? Who are you with?"

"Oh my *God*, Julian. Do grow up before you call me again."

I hear a click.

"Ana?"

Damn. I've just pissed all over my shoes. Wiping them on my trouser legs, I return to the table. Marilyn is not in her chair. At the center of the table is a pile of bills. Fine. I never did care for women with no sense of humor. Turning, I aim myself at the doorway and very nearly miss. Bursting into the humid night, I make a wide left turn and head toward the dock of Shikou Ferry.

Standing shivering on Ana's windblown street in Sheung Wan, I find three things unmistakable. First, I might have given more consideration to passing out on the floor of that men's room, as it turns out to be fully cold in Hong Kong and Ana Manguella's apartment is as dark as a Memphis pawnbroker's heart. Second, I'm not sure I've ever felt quite this alone, as I have not in quite some time detected my sister snooping at the edges of my awareness, and Tree has departed for her pilgrimage to Taishan Mountain, no doubt in the company of a one-legged man in a cheap watch.

Rui Long meanwhile awaits deportation proceedings handcuffed to a snoring great auntie, while Marilyn sits sans cell phone boo-hooing her way across town on a Route 101 bus in a nice red blouse, and Ana Manguella is out on the Pearl of the Orient with God only knows who or what. And here I shiver *devastatingly* alone on a damp and windy street with my sad stories and my disheveled bandages and my oh so reckless heart.

Was that three things?

Anyway, it's certainly true love this time. One knows by the scale of the suffering, or so I was once told in a Beijing lunch-buffet place. I have, at least, stationed myself quite strategically beneath a balcony that offers a bit of protection from the fine mist now issuing from all directions at once. Good thing I thought to wear a jacket tonight, though a watch cap and peacoat might have better served. I've also wedged myself between two large shrubs that cut the wind a bit while making me invisible to whatever pierced and ear-notched hoodlums possess these streets between dusk and dawn. As I am situated directly across the street from Ana's door, I feel reasonably assured of seeing anyone who approaches well before he/she, say nothing of he *and* she, catch sight of me.

I hear the strains of "Listen to the Rhythm of the Falling Rain" for more or less the nineteenth time. Extracting Marilyn's phone from my jacket, I announce, "Marilyn can't talk right now. I tossed her headless and unclothed body into Kowloon Bay. You're next."

I click off the phone and return it to my pocket.

Two men showed up at the American Teacher's Apartment today. I thought you'd want to know. They didn't have brown mustaches or shiny gold badges. They'd come to replace the bathroom door. I covered the 'shroomery with Lil's largest bath towel and busied myself at the computer during the installation process. The new door is fashioned from steel.

Good thinking there. There's no removing the blood stains from my sister's bathrobe nor from the kitchen woodwork. But who wants to pass through this world without leaving some kind of mark?

"Julian. *What* has happened to you?"

I turn to discover Ana Manguella in her tan raincoat. Somehow she has appeared between me and one of my shrubs of concealment.

"Did you think you could get rid of me so easily?" I reply.

"Julian, my God."

"Ana, my goddess. Would you consider making me a small pot of tea?"

"No, I would not," she says. "I've just put in a long day, and I'm going straight to bed."

"Half a pot, then?"

"Julian, I said I'd call you."

"That was five days ago. Exactly what is going on with you?"

She sighs. "I can't go into it right now. There are problems at work and—"

"*You're* having problems at work," I interject. "Why don't we go inside and compare problems at work."

"Dammit, Julian. I should never have gotten involved with you in the first place. I knew you were hopelessly immature. Now I find that you're unstable, to boot."

"But I kiss well," I say.

"Actually you use too much tongue. Good night." She turns away.

I lurch forward to follow the tan raincoat across the street. "No. Don't say good night."

"Goodbye then," says Ana. "My life is far too complicated for this."

"*Goodbye*?" I say, grabbing her by the shoulder. "Did you just tell me—"

All at once I am face-down on the wet cobblestones, my gauze muzzle soaking up a puddle, my cast twisted awkwardly beneath me. Ana's foot is on my shoulder and both her hands are forcing my only functional wrist in the worst possible direction. I'd scream in agony if I could draw the requisite breath. "Don't you *dare*," says she, her voice throaty and dangerous.

After a moment, Ana releases her hold and I hear the tinkling of keys then the sound of a door opening and closing. The rain starts down a little heavier. On cue, Marilyn's phone tinkles its lone forlorn melody then goes silent. I think I'm weeping. Maybe it's only whimpering. Above my head is the sound of an upper-story window opening. Now splashing into a puddle near my face is a moldavite pendant. The window closes again.

PART THREE
THE YEAR OF THE HYDRA

38

"Just how long has it been since you ate something?"

The sight of Shatrina Carter standing perspiring in this funky ruined-ass apartment strikes me as so novel that I can't help but stare. Actually I think she was here last week. Or maybe it was last month. That would depend a little on what month this is.

"Did you even hear me?" asks Tree. "I just spoke to you."

Tree just spoke to me, but "Suzanne" has started up again and I want to listen to the words. The American Teacher's Computer, I've recently learned, will repeat a single song more or less forever if you ask it to. Now each time that nasal whiskey-edged tenor returns to this stark reptilian space, to my horseless and monthless latitudes, I am pinioned once more against an iridescent landscape of sea-foam and seraphim bones. At last I've heard these verses for the first time. And the first time. And the first time.

Dr. Carter has bored of our conversation. She now harrumphs in the kitchen, which I admit needs a little work. My left hand reaches for a nearby pair of khakis to cover the charred hole in the American Teacher's Mattress. Now the hand returns to its customary office of cradling the right wrist, which feels appallingly naked without its customary plaster cast. They wouldn't let me keep it a day longer. Now my eyes re-visit the honey jar on the settee table. Something is unfinished.

"*Lord* have mercy," says Tree from the kitchen.

I hear sirens. Beneath the high arcs of their wails, Leonard Whisper Boy creeps in once more, minor-ing the key and dropping the register to just above the glazed ceramic tiles where the heavy gases accrue, there to rot the grout and distort space/time, syncline and anticline beginning somewhere near the dresser and heading irrevocably this way. I've no idea what will happen when that vector achieves the spot whereon I lie each hour of day and most moments of night, awaiting the singularity that dots the eye of the tigress.

It stalks me, that singularity. But by painfully slow degrees.

Tree returns to the front room where the kiddie art is half-fallen from the walls and I am fully fallen from grace, it would seem.

Gravelly laughter. She tosses her long hair behind her shoulders. Do you want to know what's really true?

As I watch, Tree clears off a settee chair and kicks aside the clutter until she can place the chair opposite my spot on the mattress. Now she tries to wedge herself into the chair, turning a little sideways. This doesn't seem to please her very much. But I don't think much of anything here does. At least the burnt plastic smell is gone. I returned from Studebaker Supermarket to find the apartment filled with acrid black smoke.

I threw open the windows and poured a pan of water onto the corner of the smoldering mattress, a place where nothing at all had been, as far as I could recall. Still, a charred hole penetrated Lillian's fitted sheet and mattress cover and continued all the way through the foam mattress. Whatever had melted down hadn't stopped before charring the floor tiles, leaving a permanent stain. The tarry deposit provided no clue as to what had generated such heat, but some days later *one* item did turn up missing. The moment that something came to mind, I knew exactly where I'd last seen it. That very spot at the corner of the mattress. The Barbie deck.

Ken's mad.

"Lillian tells me that you aren't taking your medication," announces Tree. "Are you, or are you not?"

I gaze at her.

"*Why* are you not?" says Tree. "It came in the mail. What happened to it?"

I try to answer but my voice isn't quite working. I clear my throat. I clear it again, more forcefully. Finally I croak, "How's Lil?"

"Worried sick. The school called her and said you aren't coming to class anymore or even leaving the apartment. They said you aren't eating. I came here to cook something and give you your medication. Where is it?"

I pretend to be considering a reply. In a moment perhaps I'll know what this woman is talking about. The part about not going to class is definitely untrue. I go at least once a week. Anyway, it averages once a week.

"I didn't climb those stairs to talk sweet with you," growls Tree. "*Where* is your medication?"

"Verse three," I whisper hoarsely.

It's all in verse three.

We tried to tame the madwoman, you and I, and thought we had, only to find that beneath the cover of night she'd molted, spawned, come swarming back with tendrils aswirl to swallow civilizations like the jungles of Yucatan at the eleventh minute of the eleventh hour *just* before we'd succeeded in laminating facsimiles of ourselves to the living room furniture and mailing our fingers to the Bureau of Records.

I think we fear only two things, you and I. Being dead and being alive. The closer we get to either, the more attractive the other starts to seem. In truth, we don't like either one very much. You and I.

We left no forwarding address when we disappeared into the night with these terrible dreamers, wrapped in our cloaks of regret and secret oaths to forest nymphs. Whispered and re-whispered in leaf beds of humid and perilous screwing beneath the watching sky. We thought we would arrive somewhere and mythologize our journey, rear strong-boned children who'd help in the fields and become complacent with fire. But something had already shifted beneath our feet, the deer trails become rabbit trails then ant trails. And then the ants were following us, hoping *we* knew where the grasshopper lay dying and which curled leaf held morning's final teardrop. And following behind the ants were the rabbit and the deer.

We disappear again into that forest each time we sleep, *hurl* ourselves once more into that darkness that promised so much, there to dream all of this into possibility that we may again awake as something recognizable, utter words that others may distinguish, eat for breakfast what we couldn't finish at dinner, and scheme to forget what we have suffered so hard to learn.

I don't know how long I can stand to look at these things.

I *am* hearing sirens, the melancholy two-tone kind from old European films. There seem to be three of them, one a bit flat, almost major-seventh-ing the others. They issue from different directions, their vectors seeming to cross very near this very mattress.

"What are you growing in here?" asks Tree's voice. Someone's in the kitchen with the 'shroom farm. Someone's in the kitchen I know.

"My lorr-rrd?" sings Tree.

Could be it's time for the other sandal to fall. To finally bring the other side of the equation, the part that doesn't add up but does multiply. That lives somehow despite every death sentence and failed appeal, that even now delivers fresh messages from the fallow field from which blow the seeds of all possibility *and* the dreaded spores of gnosis. Which is why Leonard Whisper Boy reaps so grimly, his little worm-words eating into both sides of the brain, serving up the horrific alongside the celestial and saying *all* of this is what you are.

All of this is what we are.

Tree returns to stand before me, her hands filled with spent packages of ma huang gathered from the floor. Her eyes hold accusation.

"This is your new health-food diet? Mushrooms and ma huang?"

"Very low in fat," I croak.

It's a good thing I just carried out the gin bottles.

Tree opens her hands. The plastic wrappers fall to the floor. She stares at me for another moment before placing most of herself in the settee chair. As she closes her eyes and takes a deep breath, a crease appears at the center of her forehead.

I think I slept for an hour or so around dawn, awakening with what seemed perfect continuity of thought, though recalling the thoughts themselves proved problematic. The mushroom tends to come in waves. I never know when another swell may appear to suck me down and drag me along the gritty sand at the ocean bottom. My eyes return to the honey jar, nearly empty. Something is unfinished.

Tree begins another deep breath, and I watch her body swell. The crease in her forehead begins to fade, and I wonder whether the sabbatical to the mountain worked for her.

I deleted the novel last night. And told Ahmed Massoud Monzur to burn his copy.

Tree draws another deep breath, and I wait. The suspense is difficult to bear. Soon her eyes will roll open and precisely chosen words will nail these wrists and feet to a mattress in dire need of sweeping, its charred hole beneath a dirty pair of pants. But what day is without its dilemma, what dilemma without its day?

Tree's eyes open. Her voice is calm. "Julian. Your mother has been in a coma for three months. Your sister is fighting a court battle over the living will. She was just arrested at a peace demonstration, and it was . . . messy. There's talk of having her disbarred. This SARS thing is totally out of control—they're quarantining whole airline flights—and now Lillian gets a phone call from Shenzhen saying her brother has flipped out. I told her I'd come and check on the situation. So I come here. And this is what I find."

My eyes roll closed in shame.

"I don't know what's going on with you," continues Tree impassively, "but I know what's going on with Lillian, and she needs to remain exactly where she is. *What* can I do to help you?"

I resist my body's urge to draw in, to curl forward and swallow its own tail, to disappear in the face of this unbearable love. The last time I attended classes, I was overwhelmed by it. I'd never seen it before. Never felt it. Now I was threading bewildered through it, clipboard and water bottle in hand, stairwells swarming, face after face exploding with HULLO, HOW AHHH YOU, WHAT ZAHHHP and MAHN-SUHH-HHHH, so lost in it, spun around in it, so painfully naked and womb-wrapped in it, no longer apart but a *part* somehow, and how now to harbor this private sorrow, this . . .

Annihilation.

The last time I found myself roiling within that slow-mo sea of white-over-blues, their eyeglasses crooked, tits too small and sideburns that won't grow, all of them utterly futureless and *every* last one of them too fucking stupid to not love, I found myself half-buckled over, groping for an exit, a source of air, a means to behold something *anything* but this lingering simpering image of someone somewhere helplessly transfigured.

I'd feared that losing Ana's love would kill me.

Losing love doesn't kill you. Receiving love kills you.

The sirens have stopped. I hear shouts. Tree is no longer here. I am alone, curled on the mattress, cradling my shriveled and too-naked arm. It's another incoming wave. I try to dig deeper into the mattress. I think I know something, and I'll tell you what it is. Either we die completely each moment, or we live a slow death while someone somewhere else carries the note. Maybe Tree's right. Maybe *they* summoned us here. The poker-playing fuck-tragic juvenile delinquents of this country. The fifth-floor boys with the biceps and the stare. The going-nowhere girls asleep on their own forearms. This whole doomed generation of too many, too little, too late, too yellow, too bad. A half-billion voices raised in clueless silence, and no one listening.

The metal door opens and slams. Busy footsteps disappear into the kitchen. Boisterous sounds. Lots of clanging. "Suzanne" returns, its background singers caked in mascara, their little *puffs* of song naively hoping to convince us that they occupy the same time-space continuum as the grave, dark man-whisper they attempt to ornament. Now comes the preposterous and defining stroke, the splaying of Brer Yeshua, not between two thieves but between two verses concerning a crazy rag-picker, hitting the same anomaly at a different octave and birthing a vision that towers even as it sags in surrender.

Whispered into the right brain are weird yet instantly recognizable evolutionary code. Rabbi, rabble-rouser, messiah, martyr. We slip these garments over his head time and again, only to discover that he's escaped through the arm hole and wandered again, barefoot and breathing, into the subcontinent to dream worlds into existence where phantasmagoric creatures rut in moonlit meadows and thirsty scrolls open themselves like the soft hands of a child, stealing into the municipal limits by night to send his snakes into our hearts, destroying our families' hopes for us, sewing shut our futures with cotton twine and a thorn.

He plummets so deep that he comes out the other side where all is reversed and his face Issis's, his body Gaia's, his thoughts Sophia's, and all else, *all* else, the singularity he must now and forever cling to.

Trembling.

I'd give anything for two hours of sleep.

In the end, the patient little mushrooms ate his perfect body—but not before he had tasted theirs. Did I say that out loud? All of this is what you are. All of this, too-yellow children, is what you are.

"Julian."

My eyes are so dry they make a grinding sound as they open. Tree is half-sitting in the settee chair. "How do you feel, baby?" she asks. I whisper that I feel a little weak, and she nods.

"I'm making a big vegetable soup," says Tree. "And there's a bowl of fruit on the counter. May I slice some up for you now?"

I gaze at her blankly.

"May I *slice* some up for you now?" says Tree.

I shake my head.

"Why not?"

"Because the moon," I whisper.

"Julian. Look at me. Why won't you eat something?"

"I don't know. Something's turned wrong, Tree. Something is incomplete."

My voice quavered when I said that.

Tree's brown eyes confer with mine for a moment and then another moment. Now she looks away. "I'm not cleaning this place up for you. You're going to get up and do it yourself. The *way* you're going to get up and do it yourself is by eating the fruit I slice up and then eating a little of that soup. And then you're going to take a hot shower and get a good night's sleep."

The soft brown eyes return to my face. "I flushed those mushrooms down the toilet. And if you so much as *look* at another package of that ma huang . . . It's Saturday. You're teaching Monday morning. In clean clothes. I'll think of something to say to your—"

Tree pauses and closes her eyes. "Somebody's probing us," she says. "Do you feel it?"

I blink.

"How long since you've cleared and sealed this space?" asks Tree.

"I haven't, umm, exactly . . ."

"No wonder you can't sleep," she says, using her arms to push herself up from the chair.

Moving slowly, scanning with the palms of her hands, Tree picks her way through the debris-strewn room, pausing here and there to draw symbols in the air with her fingers, chanting words I can't quite hear. Now she claps her hands three times and spreads her arms. "Lord God," she whispers.

"What?"

Tree doesn't answer. Too exhausted to follow the thread any farther, I let my eyelids fall.

"*Lord* God," mutters Tree, but he's no longer listening. Another wave has come raging in, opening beneath him a space through which he tumbles, spiraling down like a dry leaf, brittle and succumbing. He is a single point of awareness in a vast, cold space, surrounded by silent satellites that orbit obediently, each rotating slowly as it draws near. He sees that the surrounding satellites are rectangular boxes, each bearing a naked woman posed artfully, each curve illuminated by a sunless light. He focuses on one woman, her face freckled and familiar, her silent lips accusing.

I know her. She is a tight rosebud of sixteen. First love. First offense. She is cold and vanishingly thin as though methodically starved, her two brown irises enormous, wan and unfocused. Unwilling to gaze at her a moment longer, I look away only to discover another face I know too well, another young woman. And another. Is it possible that every woman of my tragic and loveless love life circles yet, perishes yet in these interstellar depths, their eyes bearing the same injury that long ago should have dried and hardened?

Trying once more to turn away, I discover that I am surrounded by not one circle of satellites, but countless concentric circles of rotating boxes displaying cold and undernourished women, each orbiting as though around a sightless sun. Weakly I strain to see the farthest circle, but they reach to infinity and beyond, the numberless women, the innumerable generations, all spinning pointlessly in the cold vacuum of periodic lust and undying indifference.

I want to pull in, to swallow my own tail. I am no sun, no source of light nor warmth but only a singularity of self, sucking what remains of each bone, each woman in turn, sucking their still humid marrow until there is none. I want to turn away but there is no direction of escape. I try to close my eyes but they are already closed. I try to open them but they are already open.

Again in front of me is the same freckled face, first love, first offense. Helpless, I watch her features morph into those of the girlfriend who shortly replaced her. Now she is the college coed who sold her Volkswagen to pay for an abortion. Now she is my first wife. Then my first lover on the side. My second lover on the side. Third. I long to turn away, but the two eyes hold me in place as they change their color and shape again and yet again, fragile faces forming and re-forming until I no longer know whom I look upon and whom I do not. And now I know that it doesn't matter.

The same blood pulses through each one.

Suddenly I am startled to encounter the face of my own mother as a young woman, her cheeks high and firm, her green eyes bright with promise. Those eyes arrest me. They ask me whether they are different from the eyes of all the others. As quickly as the question registers, the features surrounding the emerald eyes morph until I am looking into the face of my sister, astonished at her beauty. Now one of the eyes changes, and my breath stops. Glistening before me are blue and green irises I know quite well.

Her lips begin to move.

"We are each the same woman, Julian. Each a failed mother. A failed sister. A failed lover. Each a pair of hands that have touched you with imperfect love. Each a beating heart that came close enough for you to feel and to hold and to harm. And we're more than that. We are no mere extensions of your want."

Ana's gaze holds mine for a long, punishing moment. Gradually the colors of her irises darken to two pools of gold-spattered umber, and it is Shatrina Carter's face that looms before mine. "Say this after me," she says. "I call upon the Masters of Light . . ."

I struggle to understand.

"I *call* upon the Masters of Light . . . ," she repeats.

"Tree?" I say, voice trembling.

"Do it," she says.

"I can't, Tree."

Her hand touches mine. "I call upon the Masters of Light . . . ," she says softly.

My eyes roll closed in surrender. "I call upon the Masters of Light . . ."

"And Archangels Michael and Gabriel," Tree continues, and my voice trails childishly behind, "to assist in clearing away now and forevermore any and all alliances contracts and agreements, accords unions and fraternities, bonds links and attachments, that do not serve my highest good. These I do hereby negate cancel and rescind, dispatch destroy and disambiguate, in all times places dimensions and universes. I hereby release unto their truest destinies all whom I have enslaved usurped or detained, affronted offended foisted or forgotten. With deepest humility and thanks, I send any and all, *each* and every, to their warmest and safest harbors of rest regeneration and refuge, all praise Aphrodite Almighty, be it hereby and forevermore so."

". . . hereby and forevermore so," I warble.

Tree's gaze pierces me.

"I heard you say something about the beloved Master Yeshua Ben Joseph," she says firmly. "Now I'm going to tell you something. There was a gap between the Father and the Son. Yeshua felt this gap, and it hurt his soul very deeply. He knew that he must refuse to be either Father *or* Son as long as either came at the expense of the other. So Yeshua went into the desert. It took him forty terrible days and nights, but he found an answer. *He* was the answer. He became the principle of unifi-cation, the third element that mediated Father and Son. He became something that had never been because someone had to do it, and once he knew that, it became his responsibility."

Tree doesn't blink.

"Yeshua became the Holy Spirit because someone had to. Someone had to bring in the solution, and that's why you and I are here, Julian. That's why we have gone to all this trouble. It's why I have agreed to be this—ridiculous creature. It's why you have agreed to occupy this terrible moment of trial."

Tree looks away. When her eyes return, they are soft with pity. "Jules? Are you hearing me? Are you taking any of this in?"

I nod weakly.

"There's a lot I could tell you about what Mr. Xu and I learned up on that mountain," she says. "A lot, Julian. You aren't ready."

I watch Tree pull herself erect.

"You know what Xu means?" she asks. "It means *allow.* That's Taoism and that's Mr. Xu. The fruit's in the fridge in-side a plastic bowl. Listen, I don't know *who* you made mad, but there was some very strange energy up inside this place tonight. I kept seeing the image of a minotaur with a wom-an's body. You know anything about a female minotaur?"

Someone shakes his head.

"I did what I could. I left a little stone in each corner of the room. Don't move them. They're holding the shield in place. Now . . ."

She gazes at me tenderly. "*May* I bring you your medica-tion?"

"I threw it away."

Her gaze doesn't flicker. "You threw it away."

After a moment, Tree sighs. "I have to trust that you know what you're doing, Julian. That's all anyone can do now. You're in the birth canal. What happens now, happens. God bless you and God bless you. And may God bless you."

Tree limps slightly as she walks to pick up her purse. "Eat something and go to bed."

"I love you, Tree."

She turns to look at me, surprised.

I watch her open the American Teacher's Door. The scent of rain enters the room. "And *do* something about this mess."

The door closes behind Shatrina Carter. I am alone with what must be done.

With a mighty effort, I reach up to the settee table and take hold of the honey jar. Falling back against Lil's folded pillow to catch my breath, I wonder if Tree was really here. I no longer smell the rain. Returning my attention to the jar, I remove its lid and look inside. The earthy scent of chrysanthemum honey fills my nostrils. The jar is almost empty, but enough honey remains to gloss the obscene ochre edges of one very large and very menacing mushroom.

39

How does anyone sleep?

There's too much within a single heartbeat. Especially very late at night when the glass shards of the past are making inroads in the entrails, and unfinished affairs are spinning and spitting hell-heat. How do you put an end to anything, ever? Instead we layer something else over the top, new lovers over old until their accusations are muffled then no longer heard. Until.

One *very* still night.

How long has the plastic jar lain open in my hands? I can no longer tell whether the nasal whiskey-edged tenor still seethes here or it is I who populates the air with this dread, this spider-bristling presence, this multi-ratcheted overlay of unstill ghosts and unmourned ills. Mancer's little penance pills.

Licking the last of the honey off my trembling fingers, I await the assault of the insinuating filaments. Let them come. Even one more day in this old skin is unthinkable. Should the sun touch it again, it will wither and explode into dust with the first breeze, revealing the horror now freefalling into this moldering pillow, this filthy mattress, this moment stolen from a rumored life, a body borrowed from the wrong constellation, the distance between two non-existent points where no one can possibly remain. There is only obliteration now. That and its frail, thin shadow.

Again he hears sirens, more insistent this time. If only he could surrender into death's warm lap, disappear into the folds of forgetting's final ferment. But he knows that no prisoners will be taken tonight.

Someone begins to sing his sorrow. No one hears. Suddenly it is *he* crouching shivering, clinging to a rotating box, spinning pointlessly through cold emptiness. Cruelly placed lights illuminate his sagging flesh, his vast white shame, and he wants to curl forward, to swallow his own tail, to scuttle beneath the fridge—but here is only punishing brightness, painful inquiry, injurious reply.

Did you think you could get rid of me so easily?

It is his mother's cracked voice. Before him lies her withered form. A crone curled like a toenail clipping on a faraway hospital bed, eyes closed never to reopen. Yet she *is*. Why am I standing here? Panting in the kitchen. Gazing into the refrigerator. A plastic container melting dripping plastic down onto the lid of the pan of soup below, my own mouth melting, drooling, my very teeth falling two and three at a time onto the prim tile floor.

Outside, the sound of breaking glass. I lean to look through the window at the improbable reality next door. Its rhy-thmical balconies. Their edges precise. Its eerily mustard streetlight munge. Green smoke is belching. Shirtless men are pointing. It's senseless. Monstrous. Two men scamper across a rooftop, bent at the waist as though chasing a small animal.

Unable to bear it another moment, he stumbles back to his mattress, throws himself beneath the covers, prays for unconsciousness, begs for clemency, applies for an easy death, but the mattress itself writhes beneath him, becoming the warm skin of some awakening animal who tenses, rears, bucks and turns its head to glower, its two horns threatening, the nostrils snorting smoke and flame, the dark unmatching eyes staring, the hot musculature arching, the naked skin glowing.

She is severe. Magnificent. Not to be trifled with. The massive head withdraws, cants and then attacks, goring his tender bowels. A flick of her head and he is launched spinning into the great nothing. Off he tumbles, clawing, kaleidoscope wheeling, bits of glass grinding, hallway of mirrors opening, no image appearing. *We see.* These two words emerge in the foreground of his awareness as though someone has spoken. No one has spoken.

Gradually, fearfully, my eyes open. I am a single point of awareness at the center of a vast room composed entirely of thousands of unblinking eyes, each one alive and moist and self-adjusting. Irises of every shape and color. Of every description. Too much scrutiny. Too much light. *I don't wish to be here.* The thought registers in every eye present, and each shifts minutely in response, absorbing every nuance of my silent utterance without judgment.

We see, is the consensus reply.

A knowing appears at my center, self-elaborating until it is a cogent thought understood an instant before it arrives: *Into this place come those who wish to see what is seen.*

So overpowering is the obvious, the numinous, that my resistance burns itself away the instant it appears.

The thought continues: *You too are welcome to see what is seen, to share what is shared, to fear what is feared, to know what is known. Only this. For consciousness comes here to know itself.*

I am helpless before this truth. Consciousness does come here to know itself. At this, a shudder begins but is as quickly gone. My protest belongs in some other place. I am focused inside a flame that burns at the center of itself. In another moment, everything that I know as me will flash into flame and be gone before it can possibly begin.

I feel myself gravitating toward one particular eye. I let myself be pulled by a single red-orange iris, perfectly round and seemingly feline. Before I can stop myself, I have zipped through its center into a passageway that narrows until I fear I will be crushed—before expanding into a completely articulated environment. I look around myself at a grotesque landscape of blazing colors never before imagined. I recognize nothing. Looking up, I see six or seven luminescent orbs adorning what seems a hazy, swirling sky. The body enclosing me is warm and ravenous and balanced on five legs.

My shaggy head now stretches to nibble at the edges of a very bitter plant. At my center, I feel the churning of several stomachs. Now before me, erupting from a dark patch of pungent vegetation, is the penile shape of a russet mushroom. Beneath it spreads a vast underground webbing of branching white filaments that conduct thoughts and images in every direction at once, acting both as a wired network and an antenna array broadcasting and receiving at the same instant along an unimaginably broad bandwidth. Alarmed, I pull back. Again I am a single point at the center of the room of eyes. Where have I just gone? To where have I returned?

As though in reply, the undulating irises surrounding me flicker minutely, and within my mind appears an understanding. *All is consciousness elaborated into form, into mineral consciousness and gas consciousness and light consciousness and vacuum consciousness and organic consciousness in unending variety, each an orifice of perception through which the all may know itself more completely—and each part may more completely know the all. To complete its awe and pleasure.*

A bit more comfortable now, I examine my surroundings curiously. Instantly I know that this room of eyes is a living thing. Experimentally, I send my attention to its farthest edge and there encounter the inside of a very hard spherical shell. Without knowing how I know, I understand that the room is constructed of interlocking molecules so finely fitted that the resultant sphere is capable of resisting severe outer atmospheric pressures. I know, too, that along the inside of the shell are tiny embedded sensors that monitor outer conditions of moisture and temperature and the presence of certain organic compounds.

The sensors require no energy to operate, as they draw upon the energy of that which they monitor. When the time is right, powerful chemical changes self-occur, increasing the inner barometric pressure until the shell bursts quite easily from within. I actually see this occurring all around me. I'm viewing a hologram of a bursting shell, countless organic compounds now rushing in from the outside, along with molecules of water. Now awakening are slumbering DNA spirals.

I realize that I am witnessing the life cycle of a single mushroom spore, a self-enclosed packet of potential so tiny and weightless that the weakest rising air current can lift it to the scantest outer reaches of any planet's atmosphere, allowing it to escape into space. Yet so incredibly durable and patient that even lengthy interstellar travel scarcely registers. Impossible. Self-obvious. Hypothetical. Occurring before my very eyes.

We scour the galaxies, says a voiceless voice, *waiting opportunities to be devoured, that we may merge our awareness with that of any willing life-form, speeding forward the evolution of gnosis.*

Who is *we?* I wonder.

The reply is instantaneous. *You may call us the Archaic Ones. This mushroom species has agreed to assist us in expanding our sphere of knowledge and influence.*

The room of eyes goes silent. I'm feeling really creeped all of a sudden. This room is totally open, the door ajar to any form of life capable of munching a mushroom. At the thought, I sense the presence of certain eyes that wish to see without being seen. This thought seems to propel me in a certain direction, and I find myself pulled in the direction of a single dark, almond-shaped eye, eerily gold in color, which now opens wider as though in surprise at my approach. An instant later, I am passing along its line of sight, zipping along a corridor that narrows then opens unto a very unexpected scene.

I am inside a cluttered room filled with books and computers. One wall is entirely of glass. Through it I gaze upon a dingy cityscape beneath a blank sky. Atop a tall building across the street is a sign composed of red plastic Chinese characters on rusting balustrades. The penultimate character is missing. I look down at my body. I am seated in a wheelchair. In my lap is a white plastic bowl containing half a dried mushroom.

"Who *are* you?"

I feel these words leave my mouth, but it is not my voice that inquires. Frightened, I dart back into the dark corridor, and the cluttered room closes behind me, but not before I hear the same voice cry, "Wait! Don't go! We are the Hydra! *We* are the Hydra!" Now I am vomiting in the American Teacher's Bathroom, sweat dripping from the tip of my nose, nauseous tears pouring from each of my eyes.

No more. No more waves. No more dreaded spores of gnosis. I've had all I can take.

Again he finds himself stumbling into the kitchen, gazing mindlessly into the gaudily lit refrigerator, mouth parched. Impossible. Slamming the fridge door, he falls back onto the mattress to burrow beneath the covers, hoping against hope there will be no more. There he lies gasping, too sentient, too spent, defenseless before the hard lines, the iodine hate, of the woman's face now towering above him. She is a closed circuit, self-complete, requiring nothing from him except his wrongness, his infallible weakness. Through the pasteboard wall come his sister's sobs, dull, succumbing, and he feels again his horror, his shame at what he is. He hears again the tiny voice that once was his, pathetic, insufficient, wrong before it began.

Compassion opens within him like a terrible lake.

His love is so painful I fear it will kill me. Someone cries out. I sweat and pant and weep and beg for it to stop. No one here can bear it. I give up all my lives in the dark—except for that of the small boy. The underdeveloped, overgrown white worm of a boy who cannot protect his sister. I'm holding him close to me. I'm protecting him and telling him so. I'm sending him every shred of compassion this humid and twisted darkness affords. I strain to believe that need alone can carry these gifts to where he is.

Someone collapses, spent.

No more.

Now the small boy is older. The same woman towers over him, but not as high as before. Nothing she says can reach him now. His eyes are cool. He is a closed circuit, self-complete, requiring nothing from her except her wrongness, her unerring cruelty. Now there's a glint of satisfaction in his pain. Suddenly I realize something else, and as I do, my breathing stops.

There is no sound of sobbing through the wall.

I open my eyes in the dark. All those years. Lillian struggled to keep me focused in sanity. Those same years, I absorbed her pain. Along with mine, I absorbed it deep into some night forest to be forgotten in the tangles of the madness, the willful drunkenness, the numbness and the rage. There was too much pain, too much pain, and once I knew that, it became my responsibility.

"You've got to feel," I hear myself whisper hoarsely, my eyes closing.

The cool-eyed boy isn't listening.

"You've got to carry your own sorrow, Jules, and let Lilly carry hers."

No one hears. I am an infant incapable of lifting its head. I try to conjure my mother's face. Any face at all. But there is no thread to follow. No place to hide. No match between what I am and what the world must be. Yet I feel something. There's some vague something that I now grope toward. A pulsing warmth. Groping my way there, I finally arrive at . . .

A faraway hospital bed, at its center the wan and tortured form of my mother as a crone. I listen to her thin wheezing, and something unexpected begins to fill me. What is it? This foreign impulse? This unaccountable urge? To *touch* the thin skin of the pale forehead, to soothe something there, to offer a measure of rest to someone suddenly *so* like the small boy. Just a somebody. Just an anonymous dying somebody who never got what she wanted. Is this compassion, I wonder? Not for my mother. Just for this . . . person. Whoever she was. Whatever her sad story. Everybody has one. Everyone has one.

And then one day, you never were at all.
I cry and I cry. I cry and I cry and I cry.

Somehow, by unseen degrees, a sense of rest seems to wrap itself around someone's bones. Gradually he understands that he is enclosed. All this time. All this time I feared so that I was loveless. Now I know that love has been in me all along. As yearning. As sorrow. As ceaseless secret *bitter* longing. Driving me forward like . . . a hunger.

Slowly my eyes roll open. I feel a sensation utterly new to me. Something is opening. A primeval sense of . . . want. A decision to grow and to be. A feeling of writhing incompletion that summons: warm breast, cooing voice, *plenty*.

I am hungry.

I run a knife through a fresh apple, my fingers dripping with the juice, my mouth tasting its tartness even before I can lift it to my lips. Even the mist rising off it is a guilty intoxication, a sexual encounter. The first bite is so abrupt, so explosive, that I can't imagine what to do. My teeth know: crush it very quickly. Get its slurry of nutrients as deeply inside as possible. Empty the mouth quickly for the second bite.

In exactly this way, three small green apples find their way inside me. I stand trembling in the kitchen, leaning against the sink, staring at the next bite as I chew the current one, juice dripping from my wrist, no thought in all the world but . . . apple.

The *kai xin gou* plant wilts on its windowsill. I lower my head for a closer look. To my surprise, a sprout has risen from the bottom of the crumpling bell-pepper thing. From the very center of the awful gash, the irreparable wound, the death of all promise—an optimistic two-inch sprout is now uncurling toward the light.

Light will someday split you open
Even if your life is now a cage

I lick my fingers and use a dribble of tap water to rinse them. Gradually I make my way outside to lean against the balcony railing to watch a sourceless pale grey-green spread itself across the sky. Two women and a man are exercising separately on the basketball courts below. Two white-over-blue girls walk, heads down, toward the classroom buildings. Beefy breakfast aromas drift from the dining hall. The fruit is slightly heavy in my stomach, but it has pushed back the mushroom onslaught for now. I may actually feel more grounded than in some time.

The phone begins to ring.

I ask myself whether I can deal with a telephone conversation right now. Deciding I'm most likely up to it, I pick my way carefully through the debris, following the trumpeting ring until I've discovered the phone under a layer of dirty clothes.

"Yes?" I inquire.

"Julian," says my sister's hushed voice. "She's awake."

40

"I stopped in to see her after work, just like always," my sister tells me breathlessly. "I was sitting beside her and telling her about my day—I mean, who knows? People in a coma may hear every word you say. Anyway when I touched her forehead, her eyes opened and looked straight at me. It was so—"

"You touched hggg—" I begin before breaking into a jagged cough. Clearing my throat, I say, "You touched her what?"

"Her forehead. I was caressing her forehead. Why?"

"With your fingertips?" I ask hoarsely.

"Yes," says Lillian.

"When was this?"

"Less than an hour ago. Why?"

After a moment I say, "No reason."

A brief silence.

"Fuck you, too," says Lil. "Listen, I don't even care anymore. I just thought you might want to know. That's all."

"Lil . . . ," I begin, not knowing where the words may take me. "Lil, something's happening to me. I don't really know how to talk about it."

Silence from the bunny phone.

I clear my throat. "I know I haven't been exactly open with you. It's . . . uh . . . I just need some time, okay?"

When Lillian's voice returns, it trembles.

"I can't even begin to tell you how angry I am," she says quietly. "You have shut me out so . . . *totally*. Here I am between my mute mother and my mute brother, talking and talking, and nothing's coming back. You don't want to take your medication? Fine. You want to fucking starve yourself? That's excellent. You want some more time? Take as much as you want. But I'm not holding my breath anymore, okay?"

My turn to be silent.

"Two men came to see me," says Lil.

My breathing stops.

"Exactly how long have you known about this?" she demands.

I lean against the settee table, and it almost tips over. "Uh, what exactly do you mean by 'this?'"

"I cannot believe," says Lil, "that you just said that to me."

I'm suddenly aware of other listening ears besides those of my sister. Many of them. "Oh," I say. "*This*. Everybody knows about *this*."

"Everybody?" she says incredulously. "Everybody knows that you have met our father?"

"Umm . . ."

"Over dinner?"

"More like beers, actually," I say, falling into the settee chair.

"Julian, I can tell from the sound of your voice that you are bullshitting me. Just like always. I am going to listen now, and you are going to talk, and you're going to tell me the whole story about our father. And if you leave anything out—*any-thing*—I'll. Never. Speak. To. You. Again."

A salty taste floods my mouth. She means it. But what can I possibly say over the American Teacher's Telephone? I only understand one thing. I must make it immediately clear that my sister knows nothing of what I know. And never will.

Swallowing hard, I say, "I have met our father, Lillian. And I'm not going to tell you about it. Not now, not ever. There's a reason for that, and I'm not going to tell you that, either. Don't ever ask again."

I cringe. Now comes the sound of a hand being placed over Lil's receiver. Muffled words are spoken. After a moment, I hear a man's voice on the line.

"Julian?"

"Who is this?"

"This is Adrian McPherson, a friend of your sister's. Lil asked me to tell you something."

"*Stumpy?*" I say.

"Uh, Lil says she'll be back there Sunday and will take over her classes Monday morning. If you could just relay that infor—"

"Back?" I interrupt. "Back here? In China?"

"Yes," says the voice on the phone. "Your mother seems to have—"

"Put Lil back on the phone."

"Uh, I was saying that your mother seems to have stabilized to the point—"

"Would you *kindly* put my sister back on the phone?"

"Uh—just a moment."

More muffled words.

"Julian? Lil says that Tree can meet her at the airport. If you could just have your things out of the apartment by noon on Sunday?"

I'm beginning to pant. "You *put* my goddamn sister back on the phone, Adrian."

I hear the receiver settle into the bunny cradle.

41

"It's my fault," I tell Tree, pacing in her kitchen. "I should have leveled with her a long time ago. I should have leveled with both of you. Now . . . I don't even know where to start."

"You can start by sitting down," says Tree, stirring her tea. "You're making me nervous."

I pause in front of the fridge, which displays a new piece of kinder-art. Three crayon orbs are lined up in a row. Beneath them is scrawled, "8 + 9 = 13."

"Monique," says Tree with a smile. "My special little Indigo child."

"Math whiz," I mutter, resuming my pacing.

"Let me make you some of this chamomile tea," says Tree. "It'll calm you down."

"I don't want to calm down."

It's bad enough that Lil's return flight takes her into SARS-riddled Hong Kong. Worse, it takes her there by way of a totally upside-down Beijing.

"You read the *Beijing Daily* this morning?" I ask Tree.

"You know I don't read newspapers."

"Wen Jiabao just finished talks with the USA and North Korea. Now he's—"

"Who's Wen Jiabao?"

"The new Chairman Mao. He's about to meet with the US again. Next it's the Russians. The World Health Organization is demanding a meeting too. Beijing is *very* on edge right now, and I don't like the idea of Lil flying right into the middle of it."

Tree shakes her head. "I can't tell the girl a thing. She just says, 'I finish what I start.' I told her, 'Baby, it's too crazy over here. Let Jules and me finish this up and we'll all go to the Rendezvous and eat some barbeque.' I couldn't make her listen."

My pacing takes me to the kitchen window. I gaze out at nothing. Velázquez said all the robotic little Dobbinses are on their way to China. Lurch, lurch. Maybe Lil's flight will turn out to be entirely kinfolk.

"What's got you so on edge, Julian?" asks Tree. "Sit down and talk to me."

"Why is Xu coming over?" I grouse.

"He's a friend of mine. Friends of mine come over."

"Why now?"

"Mr. Xu is just back from Australia, and there's something very important he wants to share with me."

"Like what?"

"I don't know." Tree sets down her teacup. "Julian, sit down."

"I deleted the novel."

"Why?"

"Who is this 'old friend,' anyway?" I ask. "The guy pretending to be Truman? Why does he decide to send me a Southern Noir novel then decide not to? And then decide to again? Or whatever it is he's currently deciding?"

"I'm not going there."

I grab one of the wooden chairs, spin it around, and sit at the table. Tree's eyes are on mine. "The government's watching us, Tree."

"Which government?" she asks.

"All the governments. It seems to go back to that job Lil and I had with Hydrangea Labs."

"The one with the connections?"

I nod. "Our names went into all the databanks and forgot to come back out again. Yours, too, evidently. You remember what happened in Italy?"

"Remember?" says Tree. "They detained us for eighteen hours."

"And Argentina? And *returning* from Argentina? It's not just the governments, Tree. Or the agencies. Or the cartels. Or the secret societies. Whatever and whoever these people are, they don't seem to like my sister and me very much. Especially when we're around you."

"You don't have to convince me of anything," says Tree, unfazed. "If you can bend a spoon, you can interfere with communications. You can influence negotiations. You can do a lot of things. But what those people don't know is, energy is hierarchical in nature. All that cloak and dagger stuff is very low. Of *course* you and Lillian weren't attracted to that. You came in with a much higher purpose."

"Yes, well," I say wearily.

"There's no *yes well* about it," says Tree. "The three of us came here on a mission, and people can sense that. Fear-based people sense it right away. They are challenged by our very existence."

"Actually it goes a little farther than you know," I tell her. "The Chinese remote viewing program went dark the minute we came here. They think we're responsible."

"We are."

I look at the woman across the table. "What?"

Tree leans toward me. "Julian, the instant the three of us met, something happened. Our energies combined, and something new came about. You remember what we did to people's computers?"

"Fried them."

She nods. "Stereos, TVs, everything we came near. Now that our energy has stabilized, we no longer throw off those spikes—but we do interfere with certain things."

"Such as?" I ask.

"Such as evil."

"Evil?" I reply uncomfortably.

"Spirituality without ethics," says Tree, "and it's very real. All I'm saying, Jules, is that certain energies come apart the moment they enter our field. We don't do anything. They just can't be where we are."

"So you're telling me that we could be blocking Chinese remote viewers without knowing it?"

"Of course we could. Listen, when our feet first touched this soil, something shifted. I knew it then, just as I know it now. China's the place. This is where we're to do our work."

I avert my eyes.

"You talk about shadow governments," says Tree. "Those things are only as real as our *own* shadow, Julian. If our personal and collective shadows are filled with fear and lies, we will definitely see that in the outer world—but the way we deal with that is through our internal work. Doing our healing. Generating a clear signal. Broadcasting a healed energy. Not turning our tails and running. *Never*. No matter what we see. That's our work, Jules, and it's the most revolutionary work anyone can possibly do. You and I and Lillian are the most dangerous people on this planet. And yes, the citadels of power do tremble before us."

"That's kind of what I'm saying, Tree, only the citadels of power aren't limited to just trembling."

"What have I always said?" she says, lifting her teacup with a smile. "Whenever we do something powerful for the good, the Opponent appears. All that tells me, baby, is that we're exactly on message."

I feel Tree's warm hand grip my wrist. "It's the *children*, Jules. They called us here, just as their souls called us to this planet. The real work won't be done by us but by others far greater. We're just preparing the soil. When the time comes for us to do our small part, help will be provided."

I force myself not to fidget.

"I know you don't believe it," says Tree. "That's why I do. One of us has to hold a place for it. One of us has got to see it until everybody can see it. I *know* it's there. I'm looking at it. The time will come when you see it, too."

I lift my face to hers. "Tree. The moment Lil arrives, I'm out of here. Just *out*, okay? You need to understand that."

Tree's cell phone rings. Her eyes still on mine, she says, "I don't understand anything, baby. I just see."

On the phone is Xu. The guards won't let him in.

"I'm on my way," Tree says, closing her phone and hurrying out the door.

For better or worse, so am I. Very soon I'll find out whether *Daddy* was kind enough to clean up all my little debts in Memphis. Miriam meanwhile is sending airfare in return for my promise to produce a series of articles on second-generation Chinese-Americans. Fine with me as long as my research doesn't take me anywhere near Westmont. Meanwhile, I have a lot of housecleaning to do before my sister shows. The literal kind with a bucket and brush. No rat trap will be necessary, at least. It seems to have vaporized for good. Serves it right.

My eyes fall once more on Tree's refrigerator art. 8 + 9 = 13. Or whatever you'd like it to equal, darling. It's the *feeling* that counts. For a moment my eyes linger on the three orbs in a row, and suddenly I remember something. What that word means. Syzygy. It means three orbs lined up in a perfect row. As I consider that, the door pops opens and Tree and Xu enter, laughing.

"They didn't want to let Mr. Xu in," announces Tree breathlessly, "because his ID showed an Australian address."

"So much paranoia!" says Xu, approaching to shake my hand. "At the airport, we weren't allowed off the plane before everyone's temperature was checked."

"Beastly," I say.

"Mrs. Carter tells me you're returning to the United States, Julian."

"That's the plan."

"A going-away gift then," beams Xu, dumping the contents of a small paper sack onto the table. Individually-wrapped chocolate bunnies, each tied with a pink ribbon. Seems I've forgotten Easter again. Tree and Xu seat themselves at the table, and we each open a bunny.

Xu's eyes meet mine. "I hope I can convince you to remain in China for a few more days. I feel that something momentous will occur here in exactly nine days."

"How momentous," I say.

Tree places her warm hand on mine. "Julian, before you go into your turtle routine—just listen, okay? Lillian is about to join us here. Think about that. The three of us coming together *just* in time for one of the most important evolutionary events in history."

"Like the Three-three-three?" I say.

"*Forget* the Three-three-three."

"I'm really trying."

Xu adjusts his glasses. "Actually Mrs. Carter's intuition was very close. She expected a major penetration during the first half of 2003, and she was right. This information just came to me, actually."

"And a Ouija board had absolutely nothing to do with it?"

"Julian," says Tree.

Xu continues, "The Fibonacci sequence does not after all plot the development of human civilization, as I first hypothesized. Why should the universe care about human civilization? What the universe cares about is consciousness. So I began to look at that and—"

"*Everything* goes back to consciousness," interrupts Tree. "It's the one irreducible thing."

"That's what my Taiji tells me," says Xu, smiling. "I was practicing the other day and I realized that movement and consciousness go hand-in-glove. Movement is the way the eye of the body opens. The body is aware on many levels—but the *eye* of the body opens only when it's moving in accord with the body's design and purpose. The question is: what *is* that design and purpose? When that question occurred to me, I didn't go to my head for the answer. I just kept moving, and instantly I knew. The body is designed to be a probe, just like every other living creature here. Everything is designed to, first and foremost, generate experience and transmit every detail of that experience into a central databank."

I fold my arms, recalling something recently passed along to me by a particularly strident mushroom. The same brand of gibberish as Xu's, basically. Minus the rotating boxes, which is fine with me.

"When we're able to relax the thinking process," continues Xu, "and just observe first-hand, the truths just jump out at you. The universe is a vast exercise in self-awareness. It's a methodical, meticulous ongoing self-exploration—a running inventory. The true business of every sentient creature, then, is to upload information to the central databank, the Akashic Records, the mind of God. Just however you want to say it. Here on Earth, our job is to explore the types of organic consciousness that arise from Fibonacci growth spirals. That's how the Sequence can be so accurate in tracking everything—there's nothing else here. Just that and awareness. The Sequence can absolutely predict where consciousness on this planet is going, and when it's going there."

I look at him. "I have a feeling you're just about to tell me."

Giggling, Xu clears a space on Tree's round kitchen table. Placing an individually-wrapped chocolate bunny near his own teacup at the table's edge, he says, "The first number of the Fibonacci sequence is, of course, Zero. That's Wu Chi, the fertile void. Everything is undifferentiated. There was no consciousness at that point because there was no foreground-background. All there was, was a spark of curiosity."

"Why curiosity?" asks Tree.

"See what I mean!" replies Xu. He and Tree share a laugh. "The way we know that is simply by looking around. What I see is a universe intensely interested in examining itself, knowing itself in every possible way. Which leads directly to the next step in the progression . . ."

Xu places a second chocolate bunny several inches from the first and slightly farther from the edge of the table. "The second integer in the Fibonacci sequence is One. Selfhood. The primordial 'I am.' It was like an eye suddenly opening. The problem was, nothing existed except that single eye, so there was nothing to see. So the next step was as inevitable as the first."

Xu sets down a third chocolate bunny, this one nearly midway to the center of the table. "Another One. The mirror image of God looking back at him. The reflection was exact in every way. No difference except that the creative power lay in the original One. The second One is just a reflection. It's what you and I call the universe. The second One was the Big Bang. So now we arrive at the first event that has a date. The Big Bang occurred thirteen point seven billion years ago." Xu pushes his glasses up his nose. "Now all we need is a second verifiable date, and everything lines up."

Xu lifts a fourth chocolate rabbit and holds it aloft. "Now we arrive at the Two. Up until now, everything has been unified. Not anymore." He sets the rabbit down near the center of the table. "Here we have the birth of duality. Original yin and yang. Some say it was the fall from grace because the One and the One looked each other in the eye and said, 'I'm not you. There's a fundamental difference between us.' The Two was the beginning of a great adventure, and it was also the birth of estrangement and alienation and disempowerment—you name the problem, it started right here with the Two."

"The terrible twos," says Tree, grabbing the fertile void and unwrapping it.

Xu says, "I asked myself what date to plug in for the Two. I decided to try ten thousand B.C.E., which is roughly when the human forebrain reached its present state of development. Think about it! For hundreds of thousands of years, we were just these happy, thoughtless hunter-gatherers. I don't mean stupid. I just mean we weren't abstract thinkers. Suddenly this huge forebrain comes online and *wham*, we're seeing everything from this spooky theoretical distance. We're seeing our own lives and our own deaths in abstract terms. We're still channeling that original curiosity, that original 'Who am I?' Only now it's a whole range of questions. Now it's 'Where am I?' and 'How did I get here?' and 'Where am I going?' and 'Why is all this happening to me?' Those questions had never occurred to us before."

Xu leans forward. "We were suddenly at a distance from truths that had always been self-obvious before. Our intuitive grasp was gone. We'd been cast out of the Garden of Eden, or that's how we felt. Now it was up to us to reacquire all our knowledge the hard way, through learning. In a way, the Two was a fall from grace, but it was unavoidable. That's where the Sequence takes you. It has to be explored all the way to the end."

"And we're the ones exploring it," says Tree, turning to me. "I've always said that we volunteered for this. We *asked* to do this dirty work, to explore the darkest and most disorienting place in the multiverse: that place where we experience ourselves as separate from God. We came to bring the light to this place, and we are doing it, Nimbutsu Nimbutsu Nimbutsu."

Xu lifts another chocolate bunny and gives it a shake. "Which brings us to the principle of reconciliation. Again it's an inevitable consequence of what has come before."

With a thump, Xu places the fifth bunny down very near the center of the table. "The Three. The Holy Spirit. The Comforter. This was the dawn of spirituality."

"Halleluiah and amen," says Tree.

"Only it wasn't intended to be worshipful," adds Xu, "or sentimental or anything of the kind. It was a cognitive correction, a way to get the One and the One—"

"Seeing eye to eye?" I suggest.

Xu grins. "Very good, Julian."

"Thank you. And what would be the date on that?"

He sucks his teeth. "If the Two came in twelve thousand years ago, that puts the Three somewhere very near 3,000 B.C.E. There are practically no historical accounts that go back that far, but the Chinese and Indian civilizations have stories that speak to that time. There were sages, very powerful individuals who rewrote what a human is capable of being. They say Fu Xi lived around that time. Fu Xi came up with the trigrams that became the *I Ching*. Suddenly people began connecting things. People were talking about enlightenment.

"The various wisdom traditions came into being around that time. We were starting to integrate the new forebrain into our former holistic way of seeing. We were completing the human brain, the human being. I think that's all enlightenment is, really. Just coming into focus. A few individuals were ahead of the curve and got there first, and if you look at their teachings, they were just trying to clue us in. Of course, we could only understand in terms of fear and superstition, and it all got turned into religion. But look at any religion anywhere, and you'll see that it began with *one* guy who arrived in himself."

"Ding!" says Tree, lifting the primordial *I Am* bunny and unwrapping it.

"Tree's eating the Godhead," I complain.

"Notice," says Tree, "how the dates are getting closer together. Time is speeding up, people."

"Definitely," says Xu. "The historical spiral is getting tighter. That would place the next step, the Five, the Pentagram, roughly twenty-three hundred years ago. There's a lot of historical information about that period of time. The Five seems to be all about complexity. Suddenly we're dealing with simultaneous waves and interference patterns and competing discourses. Different levels of consciousness are working themselves out.

"As a species, we were just beginning to integrate the Three, and now suddenly we're at Five. We think of that time now as the dawn of science. Socrates, Plato, Aristotle, Pythagoras, Euclid—this *explosion* of highly disciplined rationalism expressing into public life. Suddenly we have architecture and oratory and universities, and intentional governmental design. The whole world changed because our ideas about the world had changed, and you can see that it all came about very, very suddenly."

A line appears between Xu's eyes. "Now it gets really trippy."

He places the next chocolate bunny right beside the last one, even nearer the center of the table. The two are almost touching. "The Eight comes *right* on the heels of the Five. Remember, it took over thirteen billion years to get from the third bunny to the fourth. Now we have the Eight less than two thousand years behind the Five. According to this spread, we arrived at the Eight in June, 1905."

"Einstein's first paper on relativity," I say.

Xu nods. "Until that moment, everything was direct observation and deduction. Common sense. Einstein's work—and that of the others working at that same time—began at the exact point where rationality hit the wall. We discovered the limits of classical observation and deduction. Einstein's first paper demonstrated that the rational process is limited to its own conventions. We can escape those conventions but only in very small bursts and by the most extraordinarily energetic of means.

"At the same time, our instruments were getting more and more sensitive. Now we could catch glimpses of counter-intuitive things like dark matter and anti-matter and so on. Now we were using mathematical formulas to illuminate that landscape because it was so far beyond our powers of apprehension. Suddenly we're discussing alternative universes and strings and wormholes and multi-directional time." Xu shakes his head in wonder. "That's the Eight."

"Turn a figure eight on its side," says Tree, "and what do you have? Can you say we're not in Kansas anymore?"

Xu nods. "What came into question with the Eight was the very *eyes* we're seeing with. We were born under the Eight, so it's our zeitgeist, our paradigm. And yet—"

Xu leaps to his feet and bounds across the room. "And yet," he says, turning to face the table, "at the same time, we are *so* close to the center of the spiral now—right now in 2003—that we can actually feel it. Whatever is pulling us toward itself is casting its shadow back in time, and that shadow is touching our faces at this very moment." He blinks wonderingly. "To me, that's rather stimulating."

"By the way," I say, "what *is* at the center of the spiral?"

"To find out," says Tree with a smile, "follow the rabbit."

"Umm," says Xu, peering into his empty paper sack, "we seem to be fresh out of rabbits. Let's just say that the center of the spiral is acting as an attractor. I don't know how else to talk about it. Except that it's the Twenty-One. That's the last Fibonacci number that can be spoken of because the Twenty-One occasions a turn."

"A turn?" I say.

"It has to. But we're getting ahead of ourselves. First we have to pass through the Thirteen. Imagine another chocolate bunny so close to the last one that they nearly occupy the same spot. That's where we enter Thirteen."

"Hold on," I say. "The Fibonacci spiral is an *expanding* spiral, okay? The numbers get larger and spaced out ever wider. You've saying that history is a contracting spiral that's about to turn?"

"Actually, I think it's we who turn," says Xu. "An expanding spiral and a contracting spiral are really the same spiral viewed from different perspectives. It depends on the direction that you as an observer are traveling. I believe we change our direction entirely when we hit the Twenty-One."

"When does that happen?" asks Tree.

"We're getting there. First comes the Thirteen, which is the first double-digit number in the Sequence. I think that may be really significant because it combines the resonances of One and Three and their sum, Four. Who can really say what all that means? Four is a completely new integer to the Sequence. Add Four to the previous number and you get Twelve, which is like a tangent forking off in a whole—"

"You're hurting my head," I complain.

"Well, anyway," says Xu, "we'll find out about the Thirteen soon enough because it arrives in exactly nine days."

The kitchen is very silent for a moment.

Xu looks at his watch. "Eight days, seventeen hours, twelve minutes, and nineteen seconds. That's three minutes past twelve noon, Beijing time, on May eleventh. Interestingly, the sun will be in total eclipse at that very moment."

Another silence.

"Just think about that," whispers Tree. "At the very instant that this new consciousness arrives, the sun, the earth, and the moon will be lined up in a perfectly straight line."

"Syzygy," I mutter.

"What?" says Tree.

"Exactly," says Xu. "Syzygy is when three spheres line up such that their centers form a straight line. As it happens, at the moment of full eclipse that line will strike the surface of the earth somewhere very near Beijing. I'm trying to calculate exact ground zero, meaning the spot where the moon's shadow will be centered when the sun, the earth, and the moon are perfectly aligned. It looks like ground zero may turn out to be Beijing itself, which would certainly be interesting."

"And what would that mean?" asks Tree.

Xu smiles. "Good question. Personally I plan to be standing at that spot at that moment, once I find out where it's going to be. Of course, you're both welcome to join me, and Mrs. Mancer as well."

"I'll be in Memphis," I say. "Thanks for the thought."

"You've no idea where you'll be, Jules," replies Tree.

"Actually I have a pretty good idea."

Tree bristles. "Julian! This man is going through a lot of trouble to clue you in on something absolutely—"

"Tree, you said the same things about the Three—"

"Would you *please* forget—"

"Something did happen on March third," interrupts Xu. Tree and I turn to stare at the man with the wooden leg.

"That's what I came here to tell you," he says to Tree. Turning to me, Xu continues, "You know my random number generator? Sounds an alarm when a strong anomaly occurs? Well, I began noticing something in March. The alarm was going off all the time. I ran a printout of the data to see what was happening, and I found a lot of nine-clusters. Nines were coming out of the woodwork. After several days of this, I wrote more sophisticated software to comb the data, and there were anomalies *inside* anomalies, all of it related to nine. Nested clusters. Elaborate algorithms. Incredible stuff. Just before I left Sydney, I did a calculation and the occurrence of nine has been—get this—999.711 percent above random. I've a hunch that, given time, that number will settle in at 999.999." Xu lifts an eyebrow.

"Jesus, Joseph, and Amaterasu," says Tree. "*That* started on the Three-three-three?"

He nods. "I checked back, and March third was when the anomalies began."

"Of course!" says Tree. "Three-three-three. Nine. Each is an expression of the other."

"What is all this supposed to mean?" I ask no one in particular.

"I was hoping you might tell us," replies Xu. "It certainly has nothing to do with Fibonacci."

"What's the meaning of nine in numerology?" asks Tree.

Xu thinks for a moment. "In both Chinese and Hindu numerology, the prime significance concerns completion."

42

I never was much of a fan of Nine. For a while I tried convincing myself it was an upside-down six. How exactly do you trust a number that, multiplied by *anything*, reduces to nine? Seven times nine for instance is sixty-three, and six plus three equals nine. Any multi-digit number, meanwhile, when reversed and subtracted from itself always results in a number divisible by nine. Want more? There's lots more. I once devised a base-eight mathematics so as never to see the abominable thing again.

So now we're given to believe that nines are popping up in our composite reality like so many loaves and fishes, and all I can say is, when does the water turn to wine?

I'm kneeling in Lillian's kitchen, using a chlorine powder to scrub away the Julian *film*, as it were. Meanwhile, a distant piano tinkles, or does that summon the wrong image? I've heard these same faint Joplinesque piano noodlings on other evenings and wondered whose fingers warm the keys, and whether a martini glass waits on a nearby napkin or across the room sits an old woman, her eyes focused on some other time, some other place. Like the mournful trombone of afternoon, it's one more spoon to stir this soup of neighborhood sounds announcing the end of day, and loose, cigarette-tapping tales of remembered things.

From this spot in Lil's darkening kitchen, I can gaze into a hundred windows, each one uncurtained and naive with trust. Sometimes I switch off the kitchen light and just stand here, scanning these collected volumes, hoping still to find some clue as to how it's done, this *living* business that other people seem to know so much about.

Two men came today. It was the same two guys who re-placed the bathroom door. This time they wanted to re-lay the buckled tile flooring. Fine with me. Reverse *feng shui*, says Tree. If your life can reflect your home, why can't your home reflect your life? "Your grids are coming unfrozen," she told me. "I see it in your face. You're coming to life, baby."

It hurts like hell when your grids come unfrozen, especially when you've recently stopped drinking railroad gin. All at once I can't stand the thought of alcohol. The vaguest scent is enough to send me scampering to the squatter. It must have been that final evil mushroom that did it. Whatever *it* is.

Before the two workmen left, they put the mattress back on the box springs for me. I immediately went around picking up my clutter and ripping down what remained of the get-well art and just generally tidying up.

The place echoes now.

Everything here echoes with recollections of my tortured tenure at Shenzhen High School of Electronic Indifference. I just subbed my final three classes. Nimbutsu Nimbutsu Blind Lemon Jefferson. The students were in their usual Friday humor, i.e., utterly unaware that a teacher was in the room, so I decided against lengthy speeches. Let them figure it out for themselves when Lil shows up on Monday. In fact, it may be Wednesday before most of them realize it's Lil up there.

Anyway, I fully admit to feelings of both relief and, um, *poignancy* when the final bell sounded and I yelled, "Dismissed!" over the groaning of chairs. One learns to say dismissed at just the right moment, namely when the students rise to leave. It produces the illusion of being obeyed. Anyway, off they went and there I stood clapping chalk dust off my hands for the final time, thinking *gee* I wish I'd had sex with more of those girls.

The war's over, by the way. Not that Iraq surrendered. There *is* no Iraq to surrender. We ran out of villages to overrun and were down to shooting the stray individual, so we decided to declare it over ourselves. Good move, I say. The folks back in Duluth like long undies and short wars. Uh, operations. Myself, I'm into really spiffy kitchens, as my sister is coming back and not in the best of moods.

I'm glad there's a piano in this neighborhood and that it's not too near. Until it's named, a song is every song, a kitchen every kitchen, the faintly green-tinted night sky every possible sky. The pianist doesn't play often, and I like it that way, standing here in Lil's kitchen, hands wet, gazing out at the glows of kitchens across the way, monitoring the *kai xin gou* at the windowsill, its new leaflets patiently opening.

I'm not quite sure how I'll replace all this once it's gone.

I called her Lilly. When we were kids I called my sister Lilly.

"*Oh*? And how exactly did you arrange that?"

That's what I said to Arnie this afternoon when he called to say he'd just been fired by his school.

"My boss called me into his office," he explained, "and said all the foreign teachers in Nanshan District have just been released effective immediately. So how soon can I be packed? Of course, it only took a couple of phone calls to find out he's lying out his ass. I'm being fired 'cause I like to party in Hong Kong and he can't stop me. But that's the whole Chinese thing, right? Nobody cares that it's an obvious lie, just so long as it greases things along. Whatever. I got a nice severance check and I'm headed for Bali. See ya."

Arnie might run into Meng Xue Nong and Jiang Wen Kang there. They were mayor of Beijing and national health minister, respectively, until a few hours ago. I wonder if they were told that *all* the mayors and health ministers were being released effective immediately.

"This country seems to be really good at just two things," said Arnie before hanging up. "Under-reacting and over-reacting. First there *was* no SARS. Remember? Now they're shutting down restaurants and hotels. They're quarantining international flights. They're incinerating bodies without notifying next of kin. They're even refusing to turn over the ashes. Do you know how many people have died from SARS? Total?"

"Not exactly."

"Three hundred and seventy-two," said Arnie. "You know how many have died from AIDS in the same period? One and a half million."

It's tough out there.

Arnie closed the conversation by telling me to take care of myself. I asked him what he meant by that.

"Eat more," he said. "Think less."

The American mantra.

I hung up the phone feeling an odd mixture of things. It was a little strange not saying anything about my own pending departure, but I couldn't quite get it out. I haven't told anyone outside of Joe. I don't know what to say anymore. My *grids* are coming unfrozen?

The clock says it's eleven. I decide to turn on the news. Anything for a little comic relief. The first thing I see is the mayor of Hong Kong and his deputies, all elbows and assholes mopping the floors of their offices for the benefit of the cameras. You think they didn't get the message with the firings in Beijing? Next up is footage of beaming schoolkids holding up posters with helpful hygienic hints.

One poster shows a man spitting on the sidewalk while a family recoils in horror. You can get a twenty-buck fine for spitting on a Chinese sidewalk these days. Just think of the revenue. Now we're seeing various shots of the streets of Beijing, which looks totally dead. At a nearly deserted train station, passengers take turns passing through a temperature scanner. I switch off the TV. It's time I got out of this country before someone forces me to floss.

At least we're getting a few decent jokes out of this:

"SARS has a ninety percent survival rate. That's a higher survival rate than just living in China."

"People with SARS shouldn't be ostracized. Many SARS patients live happy, productive lives for three days before their lungs fall into their underpants."

"I've always said the Chinese can't handle a crisis. Have you seen their fire drills?"

"Finally they've hit upon a workable method of population control."

"So far, eight Canadians have died of SARS. With the exchange rate, I think that's five Americans."

And this verse, which borrows the melody of "When You Wish Upon a Star":

> When you kiss a girl with SARS
> You'll get pulmonary scars.
> If you dare go French with her
> Your note comes due.
> When she sneezes, don't inhale.
> Send her greetings through the mail.
> When you kiss a girl with SARS,
> They'll quarantine you.

I decide to take a late night stroll.

It's Friday, thus all one point three billion Chinese are outside lolling, hocking, all the usual, many of them shirtless or in PJs, every one of them blissfully unaware of the obvious, namely that the world around them is coming irreparably unglued due in large part to themselves. With all the coal this country burns, China could almost be America the Sequel but for the uncanny contentedness here. All along the broad Friday night sidewalk, children scamper and gurgle and power plastic trikes, and clutches of women ballroom-dance in tiny white sneakers as their husbands stand together and congratulate one another on their acumen. Not a single serotonin uptake inhibitor among them. Not *one*.

I've said that China is a hard place to be if you're Chinese, and by day it certainly is. Still one has to wonder at the unanimity these people must feel. To be both in and *of* a place of such monolithic self-same, to be swallowed whole by the enormity of this one thing that you are.

Chinese-y.

I turn into an unexplored neighborhood and enter the darkest *lu* I can find, hoping to get lost or at least mislaid for a while. I let narrow alley lead unto narrower lane, each open window a bit nearer my face, many of them emitting the hot-oil munge of course number six or seven, most emitting the cathode-ray glow of Big Brother's face-splitting smile, at each tight corner a grotesque grocery of one bare bulb—all of it sewn tight with interlocked stitches into the vast sweet-toxic darkness by the knife-sharpener's song.

Once, just once, I caught sight of the knife-sharpener himself. He walked beside an old bicycle with a grinding wheel mounted on the back.

I try to shake myself awake. I am so China-numbed that I can no longer see this place. If ever I truly did. Tree is always singing the praises of these people, telling me how long and how many amazing truths they've discovered. How gracefully they've learned to move through life. Could be she's right. How would I know?

I mourn China already. I mourn the borrowed fourth-floor walk-up and its heavy-footed cross-breeze. I mourn the pert well-intentioned rappings at the hollow door, and my sister's hopelessly estrogenic things strewn about. I mourn the window song, the teeming unhurried murmur of one more hour in one more Chinese day.

I mourn pie-faced Nancy Drew.

Well, almost.

One block from campus, I decide I'm not quite ready to return to my sister's sad, echoing apartment. I take the scenic route through Lichee Park. Hands in pockets, legs a little heavy now, I pass through the broad meadow that by day is a weft of kite strings. I pause for a moment in a dark circular plaza, its polished tiles gathering every trace of light from the surrounding city. My last night in China, and there's no moon to give me a shadow for company.

I'd completely forgotten, but today there it was on Lillian's desk. Bobby's translation of Li Bai's signature poem. Not printed out but meticulously rendered by brush and ink on the handmade rice paper. At left were the original Chinese characters, at right the English words. I think I can recall them:

Drinking Alone in the Moonlight

Amidst these flowers, a jug of wine.
I pour myself the cup of aloneness.
Raising it high, I invite the bright moon
Then turn to my shadow, which makes of us three.
Because the moon does not know how to drink wine
She has given me this shadow for company.

So let our mirth keep pace with spring!
I sing and the moon begins to reel.
I dance and the shadow lurches grotesquely.
While I'm still awake, let us rejoice together.
Too soon each will go his own way.

Beloved friends, promise me
That we will forever dance, beyond all passion
And meet again far beyond the Milky Way.

Returning to Lil's school through the dense lichee grove, I gradually re-enter the noise of the twelve-lane. Before I reach the thoroughfare, my eyes catch the flare of a cigarette lighter that illuminates a man's face, and I stop in my tracks. That's odd. In the momentary flare of the lighter, I saw a face with a hooked nose and a pair of tiny black-rimmed spectacles.

Retreating into a shadow, I spend a few minutes watching the orange tip of the cigarette as it swings up and down, and ask myself why Bellamy would be standing in the shrubbery opposite the entrance of Lil's school. No reasonable answer comes forward. Bellamy, said Ralpho, belongs to the Wen Jiabao faction that suspected Lil and I of working against their interests. But Wen is no longer a Beijing wannabe. He's the Premier of China. Wouldn't that mean less generalized paranoia? Evidently not. The butane lighter flares again, and it's definitely Bellamy's face that checks the face of a wristwatch.

From my position in the shadows, the entrance to the high school is clearly in view, and a sudden movement at the gate catches my eye. I watch two men emerge from Electronic Excellence and walk briskly away. I've never seen either of them before. The moment the two are gone, Bellamy's face appears once more, lit by the glow of a phone screen. He utters a single phrase into the phone before snapping it shut and turning away to disappear in the lichee shadows.

43

After paying for my last lame lunch at the Sidewalk Fish Brains Café—the family at the next table may have had something to do with it—I mope my way back toward Lillian's apartment and my two packed suitcases. And whatever listening devices or bags of marijuana those two hoodlums may have planted there last night. I've lacked the curiosity to check.

The family at the next table, if you must know, included a baby attired in the usual split pants you see in this country. I was just delving into my stir-fry when number-one son needed to number-one, as it were. Alertly, his father lifted him and held him out at arm's length while he irrigated the sidewalk between their table and mine.

My shoes have since dried completely. Thanks for asking.

Entering the school gate, I pass through the temperature scanner, malfunctioning as usual. Today it's flashing random numbers as two guards scratch their heads. There's nothing left to do at the apartment. Just lock the door behind me. I was supposed to be out three hours ago, but Lil's flight doesn't arrive till five. All that remains is to wrestle my two bags down the stairs and grab a taxi to a cheap hotel. Tomorrow morning, I find an ATM to clean out my checking account—Miriam wired me airfare this morning if she's as good as her word—and book an evening flight to Memphis.

Memphis. Can't even imagine the place.

"Oh, Ju-wen, it's you!"

"And it's you, Marilyn."

At her elbow is a man wearing a nervous smile and a pumpkin-orange necktie.

"Ju-wen, this is my friend, Mr. Li."

He laughs shyly as we shake hands.

"I tell Mr. Li," says Marilyn, "that you are very famous writer."

"And you, my dear, are a very famous liar." Edging away, I say, "Wonderful to see you both."

"Ju-wen, please, how is your mother?"

"Better," I say, still edging.

"Oh, is so good."

"Isn't it though?"

Turning, I hurry into the shade of the dormitory building. So, Mr. *Li*, is it? Nice taste in ties. Actually I owe Marilyn one, if not three. She turned out to be quite a decent sport about the whole seafood dinner thing. When I returned her phone the following day, she was kind enough to interrupt my apology with, "Is okay, is not enough," then closed her apartment door.

Nicely put when you think about it.

As I approach the too-antiseptic American Teacher's Apartment, fumbling in my pockets for the key, what do I hear but the ringing of the phone? Who could be calling now, I think irritably, going through all my pockets twice. Finally I discover the key in my hand. That's embarrassing. As the phone continues to ring, I force the lock two turns in the wrong direction and have to make three turns back the other way. Finally the door opens. Bursting into the apartment, I grab the phone and say, "*Hao*?"

Rhymes with *ciao*.

"Sit down," says Tree.

"What?"

"It's Lillian. They have her. The Chinese have Lillian."

The voicemail is eighteen seconds long:

> "Tree, are you there? Please pick up. I'm at the airport in Beijing. They've quarantined my flight. I'm *not* joking. A passenger must be running a fever.

> I'm trying to find somebody to explain—excuse
> me, I'm talking to my—no, you may *not* have my
> phone. Tree, listen. Do something. They're taking
> my phone, which they have no right—*hey*, you may
> *not* take my goddamn—"

I set Tree's cell phone on the white tablecloth between us. I've listened to the message four times. It isn't getting any better.

"What do you think?" asks Tree.

As I ponder my reply, a waitress brings two cellophane cups of jasmine tea and Kenny J's saxophone describes the thought process of a sheet of Sta-Fluff Fabric Softener with Stati-Gard. I'm not sure what to say to Tree. She has already made calls to the American Consulate and the supervisor of the teaching program and Lil's headmaster. I already know those three calls will result in exactly nothing. The SARS machine is a runaway train. No one can stop it, not even the Chinese. Both Tree and I tried calling Lil's cell phone. Subscriber not available.

"I don't know," I say at last, running my hands through my hair. "Maybe a passenger really is running a fever. That would be bad enough. That concentration camp outside Beijing worries the crap out of me. Ten thousand people jammed together in close quarters, stress levels off the charts. You wouldn't need more than one or two actual cases . . ."

My voice trails off.

"Or?" asks Tree. "What else could be happening up there?"

"How should I know? Are you still trying her phone?"

Tree leans forward. "Yes, every fifteen minutes. And I do not wish to be misdirected. What are you thinking, Julian?"

I take a deep breath and let it out. "It's just the climate up there, okay? The rules don't apply anymore. Assuming there were rules to begin with. Now? Since 9/11? Since SARS? Governments do any fucking thing they want."

"And?" demands Tree.

"And they may have locked down that flight to get Lillian."

Tree looks confused. "You think they would quarantine a whole flight to—to do what? What would they want with our Lillian?"

"It's complicated."

"You mean all that cloak and dagger stuff?" asks Tree.

"That's exactly what I mean."

Tree shoos away a fly. "No, that's crazy."

"Absolutely," I reply. "But that doesn't make it not true. We have to consider the possibility. That's all I'm saying."

I take a moment to stir my jasmine tea. "I had a beer one night with a Beijing reporter," I say at last. "High profile guy. Part of his job is covering the big government hospital. Somewhere around beer number whatever, he told me about seeing body bags dragged out of back doors and thrown into trucks. No records, no reports, no names, no nothing. Just bodies loaded into trucks."

Tree strains to understand. "You're saying those people died from SARS?"

I shake my head. "This was before SARS. You're missing my point. I'm telling you something about the people we're dealing with. Now with the whole SARS thing, they've got all the cover they need to do anything they want.. Even to Americans because . . ."

"Because . . . ?" says Tree.

"Because they're burning the evidence. The gloves are coming off, Tree. I think we may have really gotten ourselves caught up in something this time."

Tree's eyes are locked onto mine. "We didn't get caught up in anything, Jules. We were *airdropped* here. We came here with a purpose and—"

"Don't go grandiose on me, Tree," I growl. "Not now. Not fucking now."

Tree startles. "Grandiose? Did you just accuse me of *grandiose*? Who do you think you are talking to? What do you think might happen if I take off *my* gloves?"

I glance nervously at the woman across the table. I once saw Tree Carter wade into a Memphis street-corner disagreement between an intoxicated pimp and a young employee of his distantly related to Tree. He only slapped her once. That's all the time he had. A moment later he'd been launched from his spot on the sidewalk to a brick wall across the street.

Across the *street*.

"Let's not go there," I tell Tree as soothingly as possible.

"And who do you think *I'm* talking to?" she demands, fiery-eyed. "You have no idea of the power you hold in your hands, Julian Mancer. Well, the time is fast approaching when you will either discover that power, or we will *all* perish, do you hear me?"

"Uh, can we just focus on Lil?"

"The battle is *joined*," says Tree, her eyes still blazing.

"Okay. The battle is joined. Now how do we get Lil out of that place?"

"We go there," says Tree, pushing her teacup away.

I push mine away, too. "Fine. Agreed. Sounds like a plan. But, oh, wait. We haven't decided what to do *after* we go there. Any ideas on that?"

A thin smile appears on Tree's lips. "I am speaking to *Tlecort*."

I cry out in anguish, doubling over so uncontrollably that my nose hits the tabletop. A moment later, my chair is clattering across the floor and I lie wheezing partly under the table.

Two waitresses come running.

Glaring at Tree's knees, I say, "*What* did you just do to me?"

I allow the two waitresses to right my chair and put me back into it. "Maotai," I gasp and they scamper away.

Rubbing my sore right shoulder, I demand, "What did you just *do* to me?"

Tree, still smiling thinly, doesn't reply.

"Never mind," I say. "I'm going to pretend it didn't happen."

A moment passes.

"That's not going to work," I decide. "What did you just do to me?"

"What did I inscribe on your cast?" she asks.

"Don't be obscure. You just called me some kind of name—*don't* say it again—"

"And what happened?" says Tree.

"You saw what happened."

"What happened inside you, Julian? Where did you go?"

One of the waitresses reappears with a small glass of mao-tai. One whiff, and I recoil.

"Never mind," I say, shooing. "Go, go. Take this with you."

Leaning on my elbows, I close my eyes and rub them with my knuckles.

"Where did you go?" Tree asks calmly.

Reluctantly I go back into a vision of one fleeting instant. And the searing pain that accompanied it.

"I was wearing a toga," I reply blearily. "With epaulets."

"Who were you?"

"I don't know."

"Who *were* you?" repeats Tree.

I sag. "I think you may have just voiced my name—*don't* say it again."

"How did you feel?"

"Like maybe I'd just messed something up pretty bad."

"Good," says Tree.

I open my eyes. "Tree? What happened in Cetus?"

"Lots of things," says Tree. "What's important now is what's happening on Earth. How are you feeling now?"

"Horrible. Tell me what happened in Cetus."

Tree shrugs. "You were a warrior. You are a warrior. Not much has changed. Just the way you see yourself. Did something not turn out exactly right? We both know the answer to that. Ever since, you've been in a tailspin. And you have milked it for everything it's worth."

I give her a cool glance. I'm reconsidering the maotai.

"You *begged* for this chance," continues Tree. "You like to play like you're just tagging along—and I'm not just talking about China."

"I'm quite sure I didn't beg."

Tree sits back in her chair and folds her arms over her chest. "You were a math warrior. Your weapons were formulas so powerful they shattered their own fields and distorted dimensional space. Your equations opened vortexes that sucked down whole armies. You could change the trajectory of missiles. You could make a whole fleet of warships disappear into loops of extracted time. Wars stopped happening because of your work, Julian. Peace came to the whole planet. After that, you devoted your energies to architecture. You used your genius to design structures made out of pure thought. Then you turned inward and began designing structures for internal exploration. Temples, Julian. You built the most *incredible* temples." Tree's eyes glisten. "I know. I came into my own power in one of those very temples. Lillian did, too. We both owe you."

Tree refills both our cups from the teapot. "Well, there are always elements in the military that see all the wrong potentials of that kind of power. So they asked you to build a structure that would have been capable of generating too much power for *anyone* to control, and you knew that. And you built it anyway."

I nod. That part, at least, sounds like me.

"You knew those people were going ahead with you or without you, and you didn't trust them to do it right. You decided it was an idea whose time had come, and you were right. But it didn't have to be built by *you*, baby. That part was your own choice, and it has cost you a lot."

"I don't think this has a happy ending," I say.

"The truth is, you couldn't resist it," says Tree. "You were seduced by your own genius. The structure you came up with was even crazier than the original idea. It used the whole planet as an amplifier. Before anyone knew it was operational, you sent the construction crews home, and you activated it yourself."

Tree gazes at me. "Nobody in his right mind would have dreamed of firing that thing up without some kind of controls."

"I would've."

"When we don't have a clear and conscious purpose, Julian, what we are operating on is clear and *unconscious* purpose. That puts the shadow self in charge."

"I blew up Cetus?" I ask.

"Look through a telescope. It's still there. But you did give everyone a very interesting day. Earthquakes. Floods. Cities destroyed. Civilizations that are no more."

"Oooh."

"In the end," says Tree, "your temple destroyed itself. And you with it. You've been running from yourself ever since. Running from your power. It scares you. A lot of time went by, and you heard about a mission. You heard about a very dangerous three-soul mission to Earth, and you saw a chance to redeem yourself."

A little like Heracles, comes the thought. I quickly banish it.

"And yes, you did beg. You had to. Lillian and I wanted nothing to do with you. But we also knew what you're capable of. And we did owe you."

Tree waves for the check. "That's enough for now. Just know this, okay? You have worked *very* hard for this chance. Don't waste it."

I sigh. "Can we just keep it on the level of checking Lil out of the hospital?"

"Whatever you say," replies Tree, squinting at the check. "Go home and get some sleep. I have a feeling tomorrow is going to be a day."

My feeling is Tree's feeling doesn't even touch it.

We walk to the nearest bus stop, the night sky threatening rain. "You're sure the travel agency opens at seven-thirty?" I say.

"Seven days a week," replies Tree, searching her purse for change.

"We don't book anything at the agency," I remind her. "We just check flights and seats. We buy our tickets at the airport. Once we're in Beijing—uh, actually we haven't quite penciled that in, have we?"

Bus 207 squeals to a stop before us, and Tree squeezes my hand. "We'll know what to do when we get there. Go on home and get some sleep."

Tree on board, the doors close with a hydraulic sigh, and the bus hammers away into the night.

We'll know what to do when we get there. I actually let her get away with saying that. Then again, I decide, hurrying toward the corner, why bother with elaborate plans that have absolutely no possibility of working? It seems to be open season on Mancers and quite possibly Carters. Even if Tree and I are lucky enough to make it all the way to Beijing, our chances of getting past Arrivals are maybe one in seventy-two.

Just behind me, a car squeals to a stop. "Mr. Mancer?" I hear.

Turning, I look into a familiar pair of pale blue eyes. In the back of a taxi is everyone's hero, John the Fulbright Scholar.

"Get in," he says. "I have information about your sister."

John is as I remember him. Thick neck. Decisive chin. Not much of a sense of humor.

"The driver's dropping us in Dongmen," he tells me. "We'll talk once we're there."

"What can you tell—"

"We'll *talk* once we're there," he snaps.

It's a long drive to Dongmen Shopping District. Too many questions I can't ask. Too many answers he probably can't supply. John, looking snappy in pleated Bermuda shorts and a golf shirt, doesn't speak except to murmur a few words of Italian into his phone. Finally the taxi dumps us at Dongmen's busiest intersection in full Friday-night fury.

Guiding me into the sidewalk throng, John says, "Sorry to surprise you like this again."

"What do you know about my sister?" I ask.

In reply, he herds me into a three-story rat-maze of tiny shops offering fashions and accessories. We twist our way along a narrow corridor onto an escalator, exiting onto a different street entirely.

After a block of brisk walking, John slows his pace and turns to me. "Mr. Mancer, your sister has been taken to a quarantine hospital outside Beijing, along with the other passengers of Flight 261. We know that she's all right. Of course you're worried, but our advice is to remain here in Shenzhen, where we can keep you—"

"Excuse me, John. Is it John?"

"John's fine," he says.

"John, how do we get Lillian out of that place?"

The decisive chin juts toward me. "Listen, I know you're worried but—"

"I don't want to hear *worried*," I reply. "I want to hear how we get Lillian out of that place."

"For now, we watch and wait. We're monitoring the—"

"What do they want with her?" I ask.

John considers his answer for a long moment. "The Chinese are aware of your sister's special abilities, but we have no reason to believe that she's being interrogated. This may be an actual quarantine situation. Let's turn here," he says, checking over his shoulder and pulling me onto a side street.

"And you could be in China on a scholarship program," I reply, "but I doubt it. If something weren't going on, you wouldn't be talking to me right now. So, what's going on?"

"The reason I'm talking to you right now," John says evenly, "is to keep you from doing anything stupid. Suppose they *are* questioning your sister? Why talk to one Mancer if you can have them both?"

"If the Chinese really wanted me," I reply, "they'd have me already."

John shakes his head. "You don't know how closely we're watching you. Want to know the truth, Mr. Mancer? We'll all be very happy when you and your sister are back in Tennessee."

I turn to glare at him. "Is this the part where I apologize? *John*? Tell me something, how does it feel to be someone's flying monkey? Or is that too personal a question?"

John doesn't flinch. He also doesn't slow down. "Let's turn here."

"Why? Where are you taking me?"

"We need to keep moving," he replies. "Listen, we know that you and Mrs. Carter plan to fly out of here in the morning. If we know it, everybody knows it. Anything you do at this point will only make things more dangerous for Lillian, so—"

"Don't call my sister by her first name."

"Not a problem," replies John. "Now, if you don't mind I have a couple of questions."

"Not until you answer one for me."

John says, "If I can."

"What do you know about Timothy Dobbins?"

He shakes his head.

"How about Jerome Stiles?" I ask.

"Sorry."

I stop walking. "I guess you've never heard of Hydrangea Laboratories either, which would make you the most ignorant person I've spoken to in some time. I'm going back to the American Teacher's Apartment."

John raises his hands. "Mr. Mancer, giving you unnecessary information will *not* help me protect you. Can you grasp that?"

"I'm not going to cooperate until you answer my question," I reply. "Can you grasp that?"

"Let's keep walking," John mutters, glancing around.

"Not until you tell me what you know about Timothy Dobbins."

The cool blue eyes become ice cold. "Dobbins steals things. He and two others stole something they should have left alone."

"What two others?" I ask.

He shrugs. "Thieves. Small fries. What does it matter?"

"A white guy and a Latino?" I ask.

John looks away. I take that for a yes.

"Then Dobbins cut them out," I say, "so they're after him, same as everybody else?"

"Can we walk now?" answers John.

I don't budge. "What did he steal?"

"I'm not going to tell you that."

"It was the virus, wasn't it?" I ask.

John looks at me in surprise.

Shit. "Is he really my father?" I ask, trying to recover.

"We shouldn't be standing here," replies John. "Come on. I'll tell you what I know."

I don't budge. "*Is* he my father?"

"You already know the answer to that, Julian."

"How many others are there? Half-siblings? How many?"

He shakes his head. "I don't know the number. Your father couldn't get funding, so he made money any way he could. Patent theft mostly. Then he stole the wrong thing. That's all I'm going to tell you."

"Why was I . . ."

I can't quite bring myself to say it.

"Why was I . . . created?"

John says, "Look, we shouldn't be standing here."

"Why was I *created*?"

"Want to take a look at your skin?" he replies cuttingly. "Want to take a look at your sister's skin? What do you see? Any clues? Could you possibly be any whiter? Could you two possibly be any taller? Any smarter? Any more psychic? If you were creating a master race, Julian, what would it look like? Some people think it would look a lot like you."

I stare at him.

"He got excited when he got the first pair of twins," says John. "He started trying to turn out more, but you couldn't sequence genomes back then. It was a crap shoot."

"Tim Dobbins is a white supremacist?"

He shrugs. "I wouldn't call him that, exactly. He never went to rallies or anything. But he does like white. The whiter, the better. We have to go now."

"I don't believe this shit. How could—"

"We *have* to go now," insists John, grabbing my sleeve.

We turn two corners in quick succession, my mind reeling. *Master* and *race* are definitely two words that should never appear in the same sentence. And who in his right mind would want to envision an entire planet populated by myself and my sister?

"Mr. Mancer," says John, "I have an important question. What did Dobbins give you that night?"

"Nothing," I reply irritably.

"Nothing? He exposed himself in public like that just to give you nothing?"

"There was something in the bag," I answer, "but I refused it."

"What was inside the bag?" asks John.

"I didn't look."

"What did he *say* was inside the bag?"

"Bird's nest soup. I don't know what was inside the goddamn bag."

My companion stops in a shadow, creating a space between us. "That doesn't seem fair. I answered your questions, and you didn't answer mine."

I stop and look around. We have left the busy shopping district. John and I are alone in a narrow unlit lane. Suddenly two Chinese men emerge from the shadows and position themselves behind me.

John steps a little closer. "What was that you said about . . . a virus?"

"I've been meaning to ask you something," I reply. "Who exactly do you work for?"

"What kind of virus?" asks John.

"You stopped the Chinese from arresting me in Beijing," I say. "That seems to leave out China."

"You have fifteen seconds to convince me you're worth keeping alive."

"Unless," I continue, "you work for one of the Chinese factions. Or—could it be those happy North Koreans?"

"Ten," John says, looking away.

"Did I ever tell you that you represent the lowest form of vertebrate life?" I say.

John pulls an ice pick from beneath his shirt and examines the tip. "Five."

"And you look stupid in shorts. And your ears don't match."

"Three . . . two . . . ," he says, stepping forward.

"I have the protocol," I tell him.

John's eyes flicker. "What protocol?"

"The one that shut down the Chinese remote viewing program. Haven't you heard? We're going to shut down the North Koreans in less than a month."

"Neither you nor your sister will be alive a week from now," he replies.

"I don't know who you work for," I say, voice steady, "but I know they want this protocol."

John studies my face. Finally he says, "Okay, tell me about it."

"First let's talk about my sister."

He mutters a phrase of Mandarin, and an unseen lightning bolt penetrates my right kidney. I crumple to the pavement, gasping for air.

John's footsteps echo in the empty street as he circles me. "The protocol, Julian. What does it do?"

My hands search for something, anything.

"Julian?" says John.

My left hand closes around something familiar. It's the handle of a wooden chopstick. I search for its mate.

John stops pacing. He's standing at my head. "I don't think you have any protocols, Julian. I think you're a totally annoying waste of time. The Chinese are probably reaching the same conclusion about your sister."

I find the other chopstick. I take one in each hand.

"And that virus you're dangling?" he continues. "Old news. SARS is dying out. It's a non-issue."

A sudden noise echoes in the empty street.

John speaks a few words of Mandarin, and the two Chinese men turn and run in the direction of the sound.

"Julian, get up on your knees," he tells me, "quickly."

I don't move.

"Julian. Get up on your knees. I'll kick you if you don't."

With a groan, I hoist my butt into the air. John grabs me by the back of the collar and yanks me up. As I rise, I thrust the two chopsticks where his eyes should be. He lurches in surprise, and I turn and run. Stumbling along the darkened street, I realize that I'm headed toward the two Chinese men. Skidding to a stop on the damp pavement, I spot a narrow alley and hurry toward it, John's footsteps now behind, running.

Entering the alley, I encounter the silhouette of a man in a fedora. When I try to stop, my feet go out from under me. Lying helpless on the cobblestones, I watch the silhouette step closer and remove something from a pocket.

"Wait! No!" I cry.

He doesn't wait. Striding past me, the fedora-ed silhouette meets John the instant he turns the corner. I hear the whistling of steel and a cry of pain. Unwilling to discover what comes next, I begin limping in the opposite direction.

Rounding a corner, I burst into the street right in front of a racing taxi. The taxi squeals to a stop, horn blaring. I jerk open the passenger door and throw myself inside.

44

I awake at first light to pee a little more blood into the third-floor squatter. Stepping on the rusty handle, I try to get a flush but the blood-stained pee just swirls around a little. This is a zero-star hotel. Toilet down the hall. The drawers either don't open or don't close. On the other hand, there's no "Approved for Foreigners" sign in the lobby, which should make this place relatively safe, *relatively* being the hinge word. Returning to my room and its sullen cot, I lower myself as gently as I can manage. No broken ribs, as far as I can tell. I double the pillow behind my head and take a moment to review the plan concocted during the hellish night.

It's a thing of beauty, this plan.

Actually I think I'm functioning surprisingly well. Before exiting the taxi last night, I removed my shoes and stuffed them under the passenger seat. The bad guys always plant little transmitters in your shoes. Then I had the driver drop me at a shoe store where I walked right into a pair of faux Kenneth Coles. As far as I know, my former shoes are still motoring the greater Shenzhen metropolitan area. Here in my room, I went through my wallet, my belt, my everything, in search of additional bugs. There were none. I was almost disappointed.

Beyond the uncurtained window is enough light to declare dawn. Moaning, I roll to one side and push myself upright to begin the work of getting into my new shoes. Never break in a pair of shoes with a minced kidney.

I don't particularly like that John character. The next time he offers me a taxi ride, I'm saying no.

Quite slowly, I descend the unlit staircase to greet the day. As usual, it doesn't greet me back. I inform the desk clerk that I'll be staying another night. I hope I lie better than I salsa.

The empty street is aswirl with a fine drizzle. Ducking into the foyer of a nearby branch bank, I try all three ATMs. Not one is working. I really need to clean out the bank account, which includes not only my return plane fare from Miriam but also my last paycheck from Lil's school. A king's ransom, no, but we're not ransoming kings here.

On my third effort, one of the ATM malfunctions badly enough to spit out a random amount of cash. I grab it before the machine changes its mind.

Walking away, I see that the ATM gave me half-again what it should have. Smugly stuffing the cash into two pockets, I awaken a cabbie and hand him a written address.

We zip through the wet streets to the most affluent section of Shenzhen. I happen to know that Phoebe Sternbaum frequents an early aerobics class atop the Guanghua Building. I also know that the class dismisses at seven o'clock. By the time the driver drops me near the entrance of the building, the rain has completely stopped. I check my watch. Right on time.

Across the street from the Guanghua Building is a beef-and-noodles place. I dash in and take a table near the window. After ordering a tea, I monitor the street for any sign of a beautiful woman in a black leotard. Of course it'll be black, as will her shoulder bag. Phoebe's long shiny hair, meanwhile, will be loose at her neck. I find myself anticipating her exact scent after an hour of prancing at the gym. Funny how absence makes the olfactory nerve grow fonder.

Suddenly I spot her beneath a black umbrella. Phoebe's outfit is charcoal and her raven hair loose, much as I'd pictured it. Hurrying outside, I fall in behind her and time my approach so as to reach her just as she takes the car keys out of her purse.

"They say that regular exercise leads to increased libido," I announce.

Turning, the woman in the leotard does a double-take. "Julian."

I do a double-take of my own. Though Phoebe has arranged her hair to partially cover the swelling and discoloration, her left jaw is badly bruised.

"My God. What happened to you?"

Phoebe attempts a laugh. It doesn't come off. "Just fall down my bathtub," she says. Her face sobers. "Why you no meet me? Why you don't—"

"Could you drive while we talk? I'd like a ride, actually, if that's at all possible."

Wordless, Phoebe unlocks the car and we sit inside. Neither of us speaks as the Buick backs out of the parking space and enters traffic.

It's presently impossible not to recall the last time we sat side-by-side in this car, Phoebe revealing her fear that her husband would kidnap their daughter, if not something worse. I don't think my response was all that helpful.

Finally I turn and say, "Phoebe, I know I've been a bit of an ass. No excuses, okay? But I'm here to tell you something, and I hope you'll listen. If you still want to go to Beijing, I'll go with you."

The woman behind the wheel levels a cool gaze at me. Even without makeup, even with the swollen jaw, this is still one beautiful woman. Her eyes go back to the road. She says nothing.

"Did your husband do that to you?" I ask.

"Why you so much care?" she replies. "I tell you he want kill me, you don't care nothing."

"I told you to get yourself some help."

"I come to *you* get some help," she says.

"Phoebe. I'm a substitute teacher. You have powerful friends in Beijing, and you come to a substitute teacher?"

"That why I *come* to you," she replies angrily, jerking the wheel at an intersection. "You just nobody, not connected nobody, not tell nobody, not tell my husband and his . . ." Her voice trails off.

"Phoebe, I didn't know that he—that you were being—you should have said something, okay?"

More silence for a minute. I knew this wouldn't be easy.

"Why you want go Beijing?" Phoebe asks coolly.

"You said you have some friends there. Maybe those friends can help my sister."

"What kind of trouble your sister?"

I give her the short version. Lillian's flight was quarantined. I'm afraid she'll catch her death. "Your government won't help me," I say, "and my government can't. I need some help from outside the government."

Phoebe gives me a wry look. "You think I know those kind of people? Outside the government? Who tell you this?"

I return the look. "You did. You said they'd find your husband, no matter where he hid."

She stares straight ahead. "Maybe I tell you a lie."

"That still makes you the best shot I've got," I reply. "Phoebe. Look at you. You need to do something before it's too late."

We cover several blocks in silence.

"When you want go?" asks Phoebe.

"Can you be ready in an hour?"

"*What*? An—"

"I can't wait. My sister needs help now."

Phoebe blows out a blast of air. "One hour to change my whole life. What else you want?"

"Harold's credit cards."

Her mouth falls open.

"And any cash you find lying around."

"*Shit*," she hisses.

I can tell from her voice. She's in.

"And don't tell anybody," I say. "No calls, no notes, no emails. Nothing, you hear? Who's watching your daughter?"

Looking a bit pale, Phoebe says, "My mother."

"Good. Act like everything's normal. And it is, actually. More or less. All this will blow over in a few days."

"When I first meet you," says Phoebe weakly, "I think, this one is trouble."

I place my left hand on her right. "Phoebe, I—"

She pulls her hand away. "Is something I not tell you."

"What?"

"I still not tell you," she says.

Fair enough, considering everything I'm not telling her.

"Drop me at this bus stop," I say. "At eight-thirty, meet me at this address." I slip the note inside her purse. "Don't park. Just stop the car. I'll be watching for you."

Gritting my teeth, I unfold myself from the passenger seat. "And remember the cash," I say, closing the door.

Aboard Bus 126, I check my watch. Seven-twenty. Plenty of time to make my eight o'clock appointment with Tree at the travel agency. Not that I intend to keep it.

My sleepless night was just what I needed for elaborating a plan that takes into account the near certainty that Tree's and my intentions are now common knowledge. Thus, I will not meet her at the travel agency but intercept her before she gets on the bus. If memory serves, near Tree's bus stop are two or three small diners at the mouth of a narrow alley. At one of those diners I'll sit behind a newspaper and watch for Tree's approach. As soon as she shows, I grab her and we make haste to the other end of the alley where we jump into a taxi, and off we go to meet Phoebe's splendid Buick.

I think people make too much of this spy business. It's just common sense.

Truthfully I'm less than confident that Tree so much as made it back to her apartment last night. I certainly didn't. But what else am I supposed to do?

What it comes down to is—and I've had to get really clear with myself about this—I can't imagine taking on Beijing without Shatrina Carter.

Or with her, for that matter.

No, I haven't exactly *mentioned* Tree to Phoebe yet, but there's still plenty of time for introductions.

Through the window of Bus 126, I see we're drawing near the narrow alley in question. I make my unsteady way to the rear door and push the button. Moments later I'm on the sidewalk, still a short hike shy of where I need to be. Seven twenty-nine. Still plenty of time.

I flag a taxi, and right away the driver is pointing to his fare meter and wagging his head. I glance at the display whose LED readout is flashing uselessly. We settle on a fare, and off we go.

Of course, the sticky part of my plan isn't here in Shenzhen or even along the thousand-odd kilometers of China's various highways and highwaymen but the city variously called Zhongdu, Dadu, Daidu, Cambuluc, Beiping, Yanjing, Peking, and Beijing. Either Phoebe's connections there turn out to be in a really generous mood, or we've got a problem.

Nothing new there.

"Here! Here!" I tell the cabbie, who drops me at the discreet end of the narrow alley in question. He slaps at his useless meter as I collect my change and slowly unfold my body from the rear of the taxi. Both street and alley, still wet from the morning rain, have a bright just-polished sheen.

Come with me. Hurry.

What? I look around. Various people are striding past, some near, some far, some with their heads beneath rain hoods. Did one of those people just speak to me? The words were so brief and hushed, they almost could have been my own thought. Except that they came wrapped in a woman's voice. An Englishwoman's voice. A very *particular* Englishwoman's voice.

My eyes fix on the rapidly vanishing body of a woman wrapped in a tan hooded raincoat, hurrying away. I begin to follow her. It isn't easy. Whoever she is, this woman is really covering some ground, and I may have a fractured rib after all. After a difficult block, the woman throws a quick glance over her shoulder. It's too brief to reveal her identity, but I think I catch a glimpse of white skin. She rounds a corner, and I do as well, just in time to see the woman enter a wrought-iron gate. Turning toward me for an instant, Ana Manguella throws me a very deliberate stare before vanishing. I follow through the gate and up a flight of iron stairs to a small fire escape cluttered with the branches of a nodding eucalyptus.

Finally arriving at the spot where she stands, I open my mouth to speak, but Ana whispers, "Shhh." As I catch my breath, she peers down at the street corner we've just rounded. Impatient, I check my wristwatch. Now I give it a shake. It doesn't seem to be working.

"Might I ask," says Ana, removing her hood and shaking out her hair, "what you call yourself doing?"

"And might I ask," I reply, "how you knew I'd be getting out of that taxi at that street corner at that moment?"

"I told you I work in security."

"No," I say, "you told me you're in charge of security. I think I'm starting to figure out what that means."

"Julian, the whole world knows about your eight o'clock appointment with Shatrina Carter. There are practically TV crews standing by. And here you just *step* out of a taxi."

"Well," I begin defensively, "I chose a good, safe spot to step out of that taxi."

"Which is why it was so hard for me to find you? I won't save you again. You need to understand that."

"That's too bad," I tell Ana, "because I'm on my way to Beijing and I think I'm going to need quite a bit of saving."

"Why Beijing?" she asks brusquely.

"They've got my sister."

"They've got a lot of people, Julian. What exactly does your soul group intend to do in Beijing?"

"*What* soul group?" I demand. "The only soul group I know anything about is the Temptations, and they broke up a long time ago."

The blue and the green narrow suspiciously. "I think you told me a very different story before."

"About the Temptations?"

"About your work," says Ana.

"Forget that nonsense. All that world-saving business came to exactly nothing. All we care about now is getting out of this as alive as possible."

"Then why do things keep getting stranger and stranger?" asks Ana. "And why does my intuition keep pointing directly at you?"

"I, too, have something that keeps pointing directly at you. Still in all."

"What are you doing to the numbers?" asks Ana.

"What numbers?"

"What time is it?" she says.

"I don't know. My watch isn't working."

Ana raises one sleeve of her raincoat. There are at least a dozen watches strapped to her forearm. Suddenly I expect her to offer me a very fine deal on a Rolex Cellini. Looking a bit closer, I note there are thirteen watches on Ana's arm, all but one malfunctioning much the same way as mine. Troubling. I think back on my morning. The malfunctioning taxi meter. The balky ATM machines. My own cheap-ass wristwatch. I strain to remember when and where I last saw a correctly displayed number. It seems I got into a taxi at seven twenty-nine.

On reflection, I'm not crazy about that particular three-digit number. Add the three digits together, I note, and you get eighteen, which reduces to nine. Before the taxi, I'd boarded a bus at—what was it?—seven-twenty. Nine again. What's more, the bus was a 126.

"I'm waiting for your answer," says Ana.

"Do you have an abacus?" I ask.

She gives me a weary look.

"How about a Rubik's cube? A Ouija board? Have you ever listened to the Double White album really stoned?"

"Julian."

"Just a moment."

Again studying the watches on Ana's forearm, I note that each displays a time that reduces to nine. All except one, an analog. I look more closely at the two hands of the analog watch. The date box displays a three and a six.

That's just creepy.

"May I borrow this for a moment?" I ask, unbuckling the analog watch from Ana's arm. Xu says nines started cropping up on his random number generator on March third. I'd say whatever process began on that day is putting on speed.

"I'm still waiting," says Ana.

"I'm not doing anything to the numbers," I tell her, examining the analog watch closely.

"Wasn't it you," Ana says accusingly, "who said you enjoy playing stupid math games? Wasn't it you whose soul group disapproves strongly of this planet's structure of duality?"

"That's a misquote."

"And now you don't have a *single* clue as to why all the numbers are changing?"

"Exactly," I say, replacing the watch on her forearm. "I like the way you put it."

Actually it wasn't the analog I returned to Ana but my own useless one. The analog is now on my own wrist.

Ana exhales forcefully. "Julian, I have something to say to you, but first I owe you an apology."

"You're goddamn right you do."

"I was guilty of mixing work with pleasure," she says. "I think I made a bit of a mess, actually, and I'm sorry. And I really do wish your sister well. Now."

Ana spreads her feet slightly. "Julian Mancer, because of possible violations of Articles Four and Five—damn, another nine—of the Intergalactic Code, you are being sidebarred for questioning."

Ana's right forefinger touches the center of my belly. At the same moment, I see an enormous flash of ruby-tinged light and everything goes to black.

99

The flatulent drone of a semi-truck reducing speed. A dim overhead moon screened by a bank of altocumulus clouds.

Gradually I am aware that night has fallen. Suspended above me is a brightly lit sign reading, "Probability Motel—SAT TV." Beyond the sign, a scant scattering of stars.

Looking down, I realize I am floating just above the concrete balcony of said motel. I am an escaped birthday balloon bobbing along an open corridor punctuated by open doorways emitting a yellowish light.

The first door I pass reveals a room all but empty, at its

Nine ninety-nine. Nine nine *nine* nine-nine. Nine nine? Nine point nine-nine-nine. Nine! Nine nine nine. Nine ninety-nine. Nine nine nine nine, nine? Nine nine nine ninety-nine.

"Nine?"

"Nine nine."

Nine nine ninety-nine nine, nine nine nine. Nine nine nine nine. *Nine* nine nine. Nine? Nine nine nine nine. Nine nine nine nine nine, nine nine nine.

Nine nine nine nine. Nine nine nine/nine nine, nine nine nine.

"Nine?" nine nine. "Nine nine? Nine, nine nine.

Nine your pants ninety-nine nine. Nine nine nine. Nine nine or?

Or nine, nine nine.

Nine nine ninety-nine nine, nine nine nine. Nine nine nine nine. *Nine* nine nine. Nine? Nine nine nine nine. Nine nine nine nine nine, nine nine nine. Nine ninety-nine. Nine nine *nine* nine-nine. Nine nine? Nine point nine-nine-nine. Nine! Nine nine goddamn nine. Nine ninety-nine. Nine nine nine nine, nine? Nine nine nine ninety-nine. Nine nine ninety-nine nine, nine nine nine. Nine nine nine nine. *Nine* nine nine. Nine? Nine nine nine nine. Nine nine nine nine nine, nine nine nine. Nine nine ninety-nine nine, nine nine nine. Nine nine nine nine. *Nine* nine nine. Nine? Nine nine nine nine. Nine nine nine nine nine, nine nine nine.

"Nine?"

"Oh, *nine!*"

Nine nine ninety-nine nine, nine nine nine. Nine nine nine nine. *Nine* nine nine. Nine? Nine nine nine nine. Nine nine nine nine nine, nine nine nine.

Nine nine nine nine. Nine nine nine/nine nine, nine nine nine.

"Nine?" nine nine. "Nine nine? Nine, nine nine.

Nine ninety-nine. Nine nine *nine* nine-nine. Nine nine? Nine point nine-nine-nine. Nine! Nine nine goddamn nine. Nine ninety-nine. Nine nine nine nine, nine? Nine nine nine ninety-nine.

Nine nine ninety-nine nine, nine nine nine. Nine nine nine nine. *Nine* nine nine. Nine? Nine nine nine nine. Nine nine nine nine nine, nine nine nine.

Nine nine nine nine. Nine nine nine/nine nine, nine nine nine.

"Nine?" nine nine. "Nine nine? Nine, nine nine.

center a hospital bed whereupon a gaunt old woman lies curled like a toenail clipping. She looks a tad green. In the adjacent room, a Chinese boy in heavy glasses practices scales on a trombone.

The light emitting from the third room is a harsh red. As I float past its open door, I see a narrow cot and dresser beneath a bare light bulb. A teapot lies broken on the floor.

So, the Probability Hotel. I'm currently wondering at the probability of finding both Schrödinger and his cat floating face-down in the pool. Which is to say none of this strikes me as particularly probable.

I drift past an ornately decorated room with a fireplace mantel before which stands a small bespectacled man in a white three-piece suit, holding a martini. With a smug glance in my direction, he inquires, "Did you think you could get rid of me so *eeee*asily?"

This place will rent a room to anyone.

I notice that I'm not the only one bobbing along the balcony. Floating toward me and making momentary dazed eye contact is the American Teacher's Rat. This place *will* rent to anyone.

Now comes a corner. I turn it as through borne along by a brisk wind, passing an ice machine and a vending machine offering packets of laundry detergent and disposable small-caliber handguns. Neither machine sings in any language. Gazing ahead along the long corridor, I see only doors extending to infin-

Nine ninety-nine. Nine nine *nine* nine-nine. Nine nine? Nine point nine-nine-nine. Nine! Nine nine nine. Nine ninety-nine. Nine nine nine nine, nine? Nine nine nine ninety-nine.

Nine nine ninety-nine nine, nine nine nine. Nine nine nine nine. *Nine* nine nine. Nine? Nine nine nine nine. Nine nine nine nine nine, nine nine nine.

Nine nine nine nine. Nine nine nine / nine nine, nine nine nine.

"Ninety-nine?"

Nine nine. Nine nine? Nine, nine nine. Nine ninety-nine. Nine nine *nine* nine-nine. Nine nine? Nine point nine-nine-nine. Nine! Nine nine goddamn nine. Nine ninety-nine. Nine nine nine nine, nine? Nine nine nine ninety-nine.

"Definitely nine."

Nine nine ninety-nine nine, nine nine nine. Nine nine nine nine. *Nine* nine nine. Nine? Nine nine nine nine. Nine nine nine nine nine, nine nine nine.

Nine nine nine nine. Nine nine nine nine nine, nine nine nine.

"Nine?" nine nine. "Nine nine? Nine, nine nine.

Nine nine ninety-nine nine, nine nine nine. Nine nine nine nine. *Nine* nine nine. Nine? Nine nine nine nine. Nine nine nine nine nine, nine nine nine.

Nine ninety-nine. Nine nine *nine* nine-nine. Nine nine? Nine point nine-nine-nine. Nine! Nine nine god-damn nine. Nine ninety-nine. Nine nine nine nine, nine? Nine mother-fucker nine nine ninety-nine.

"Nine."

Nine nine ninety-nine nine, nine nine nine. Nine nine nine nine. *Nine* nine nine. Nine? Nine nine nine nine. Nine nine nine nine nine, nine nine nine.

Nine nine nine nine. Nine nine nine nine nine, nine nine nine.

"Nine nine nine."

"Nine nine? Nine, nine nine."

Nine ninety-nine. Nine nine nine nine-nine. Nine nine? Nine point nine-nine-nine. Nine! Nine nine Nine nine nine nine nine, nine nine nine. Nine ninety-nine. Nine nine nine nine, nine? Nine nine nine ninety-nine.

Nine nine ninety-nine nine, nine nine nine. Nine nine nine nine. *Nine* nine nine. Nine? Nine nine nine nine. Nine nine nine nine nine, nine nine nine.

Nine nine nine nine. Nine nine nine / nine nine, nine nine nine.

"Nine?" nine nine. Nine nine.

Nine ninety-nine. Nine nine *nine* nine-nine. Nine nine? Nine point nine-nine-nine. Nine! Nine nine nine. Nine ninety-nine. Nine nine nine nine, nine? Nine nine nine ninety-nine.

ity. Rooms without number.

The breeze pulls me a bit farther be-fore sucking me into a room crowd-ed with cheap un-matching furniture, family photos, and domestic clutter. A television plays loud-ly.

Asleep in a reclin-er is an elderly man in a plaid wool shirt. Nearby sits a young dark-haired woman busily shelling nuts. On the floor is a sack filled with un-shelled pecans.

Before her on a coffee table are two large bowls, one fill-ed with bits of bro-ken shells, the other with pecan meats.

"Hi, Julian," the woman says dis-tractedly, clearing a spot near her on the sofa. "I'm Marisol, and this is my fa-ther, Edward. You can sit here if that's okay. I hope you don't mind if I keep doing these pecans while we talk. My husband's on his way back from roundup, and it was his birthday last week, so I'm making a cake. How was your trip here? I hope not too bad."

I look down. My body is now parked beside Marisol on a brown vinyl sofa. Near my feet is a green plastic bassinette complete with baby, its dark eyes fixed on mine.

I gather from the reddish brown of the three faces and the clear, shaped notes of Marisol's voice that this is an American Indian family. Northern Plains tribe, I'd say.

"So, listen, Julian," says Marisol over the din of the TV, "we just needed to talk to you for a minute. There's some really disturbing stuff going on, and we're trying to figure out—"

"You're Ana's soul group?" I interrupt,

"Nine, or at the very least nine."

Nine nine ninety-nine nine, nine nine nine. Nine nine nine nine. *Nine* nine nine. Nine? Nine nine nine nine. Nine nine nine nine nine, nine nine nine.

"Nine nine."

"Oh, nine point nine."

Nine nine ninety-nine nine, nine nine nine. Nine nine nine nine. *Nine* nine nine. Nine? Nine nine nine nine. Nine nine nine nine nine, nine nine nine. Nine nine ninety-nine nine, nine nine nine. Nine nine nine nine. *Nine* nine nine. Nine? Nine nine nine nine. Nine nine nine nine nine, nine nine nine.

Nine nine nine nine. Nine nine nine / nine nine, nine nine nine. Nine nine. Nine nine? Nine, nine nine. Nine ninety-nine. Nine nine nine-nine. Nine nine? Nine point nine-nine-nine. Nine! Nine nine goddamn nine. Nine ninety-nine. Nine nine nine nine, nine? Nine nine nine ninety-nine.

"Nine."

"Nine nine?"

Nine nine ninety-nine nine, nine nine nine. Nine nine nine nine. *Nine* nine nine. Nine? Nine nine nine nine. Nine nine nine nine nine, nine nine nine. Nine nine nine nine. Nine nine nine / nine nine, nine nine nine.

"Nine," nine nine.

Nine nine. Nine, nine nine.

Nine ninety-nine. Nine nine *nine* nine-nine. Nine nine? Nine point nine-nine-nine. Nine! Nine nine nine. Nine ninety-nine. Nine nine nine nine, nine? Nine nine nine ninety-nine.

"Oh, *nine!*"

"Nine nine."

Nine nine ninety-nine nine, nine nine nine. Nine nine nine nine. *Nine* nine nine. Nine? Nine nine nine nine. Nine nine nine nine nine, nine nine nine.

Nine nine nine nine. Nine nine nine / nine nine, nine nine nine.

"Nine?" nine nine. Nine nine? Nine, nine nine.

Nine nine ninety-nine nine, nine nine nine. Nine nine nine nine. *Nine* nine nine. Nine? Nine nine nine nine. Nine nine nine nine nine, nine nine nine.

Nine ninety-nine. Nine nine nine nine-nine. Nine nine? Nine point nine-nine-nine. Nine! Nine nine god-damn nine. Nine ninety-nine. Nine nine nine nine, nine? Nine nine nine ninety-nine. Nine nine ninety-nine nine, nine nine nine. Nine nine nine nine. *Nine* nine nine. Nine? Nine nine nine nine. Nine nine nine nine nine, nine nine nine.

"Nine nine."

Nine nine ninety-nine nine, nine nine nine. Nine nine nine nine. *Nine*

gazing at the old man sleeping in the chair, his mouth open.

Marisol says, "She told you about our group? Good. Well, the thing is, we're trying to figure out what's happening with the planet right now—would you mind handing that juice to Stephanie? See the bottle on the floor there?"

I bend to lift a plastic bottle of apple juice. Wiping away a couple of hairs from the nipple, I offer it to the baby's open mouth. The two eyes watch me intently, but the mouth doesn't close.

Accordingly, I set the bottle on Stephanie's lap. Marisol meanwhile is shelling and talking distractedly. She mentions the usual list of unsettling earth changes.

". . . and the glaciers are melting, like, really fast now.

That's caught everybody by surprise. Those glaciers hold a lot of information, you know? They're like memory banks of what was happening when they froze, and now that's starting to be lost.

"And the old trees, too. Those trees hold a lot of information. We feel like this planet is very vulnerable right now, and we just picked up on something that could be pretty serious. It seems to be coming from—just a minute."

In response to a whistling teapot, Marisol hurries away. I glance vexedly at the loud TV. Steve Reeves is in a red toga. No epaulets.

"Can I make you some coffee, Julian?" Marisol calls from the kitchen. "It's just instant, but . . ."

"No, thanks."

nine nine. Nine? Nine nine nine nine. Nine nine nine nine nine, nine nine nine.

Nine nine nine nine. Nine nine nine / nine nine, nine nine nine.

"Nine nine."

Nine nine ninety-nine nine, nine nine nine. Nine nine nine nine. *Nine* nine nine. Nine? Nine nine nine nine. Nine nine nine nine nine, nine nine nine.

"Nine nine? Nine."

Nine ninety-nine. Nine nine *nine* nine-nine. Nine nine? Nine point nine-nine-nine. Nine! Nine nine goddamn nine. Nine ninety-nine. Nine nine nine nine, nine? Nine nine nine ninety-nine.

"Nine nine."

"Very well, nine."

Nine nine ninety-nine nine, nine nine nine. Nine nine nine nine. *Nine* nine nine. Nine? Nine nine nine nine. Nine nine nine nine nine, nine nine nine.

Nine nine nine nine. Nine nine nine / nine nine, nine nine nine. Nine? Nine, nine nine.

Nine ninety-nine. Nine nine *nine* nine-nine. Nine nine? Nine point nine-nine-nine. Nine! Nine nine goddamn nine. Nine ninety-nine. Nine nine nine nine, nine? Nine nine nine ninety-nine.

Nine nine ninety-nine nine, nine nine nine. Nine nine nine nine. *Nine*

nine nine. Nine? Nine nine nine nine. Nine nine nine nine nine, nine nine nine.

Nine nine nine nine. Nine nine nine / nine nine, nine nine nine.

"Nine?" nine nine. "Nine nine? Nine, nine nine.

Nine.

Nine your pants ninety-nine nine. Nine nine nine. "Nine nine or . . ?"

Nine, nine nine nine.

Nine nine ninety-nine nine, nine nine nine. Nine nine nine nine. *Nine* nine nine. Nine? Nine nine nine nine. Nine nine nine nine nine, nine nine nine. Nine ninety-nine. Nine nine *nine* nine-nine. Nine nine? Nine point nine-nine-nine. Nine! Nine nine goddamn nine. Nine ninety-nine. Nine nine nine nine, nine?

Nine nine nine ninety-nine. Nine nine ninety-nine nine, nine nine nine. Nine nine nine nine. *Nine* nine nine. Nine? Nine nine nine nine. Nine nine nine nine nine, nine nine nine. Nine nine ninety-nine nine, nine nine nine. Nine nine nine nine. *Nine* nine nine. Nine? Nine nine nine nine. Nine nine nine nine nine, nine nine nine.

"Nine? Really?"

Nine nine ninety-nine nine, nine nine nine. Nine nine nine nine. *Nine* nine nine. Nine? Nine nine nine nine. Nine nine nine nine nine, nine nine nine.

Stephanie is still staring at me. The old man is beginning to snore.

"So, anyway," says Marisol, returning with a smiley-face mug, "we just wondered if you knew anything about it."

I turn toward her. "Me? It?"

Marisol bends to offer the bottle of apple juice to Stephanie.

"Listen, I'd really like to help," I say, "but I'm experiencing some real family-of-origin issues right now. If anything comes up, I'll be sure to let you know."

"Come on, Steph," coos Marisol. "Hold onto it, sweetie." Returning to her pecans, Marisol says, "What about your friends?"

"I don't have any friends. I have a sister. My sister has friends. Look, seriously, if there's anything you can do to help my sister—"

"She's okay for now," says Marisol, "but we're all in trouble if we don't figure out what's going on with the numbers. I assume you know what I'm talking about."

"I know exactly what you're talking about," I reply, "and I don't know who's doing it or even what exactly it is they're doing."

"Well, it doesn't look very good. Somebody is, like, changing the code that this whole planet is written on. Imagine somebody deciding to alter the time-space grid beneath a densely populated planet. I mean, who would do something like that?"

"Uh . . ," I begin. I'm stopped by an image on the TV screen. Steve Reeves has just pulled a lion skin over his head. This is a movie about Heracles.

Nine nine nine nine. Nine nine nine / nine nine, nine nine nine.

"Nine?" nine nine. "Nine nine? Nine, nine nine.

Nine ninety-nine. Nine nine *nine* nine-nine. Nine nine? Nine point nine-nine-nine. Nine! Nine nine nine. Nine ninety-nine. Nine nine nine nine, nine? Nine nine nine ninety-nine.

"Nine nine nine."

"Oh, ninety-nine or nothing."

Nine nine ninety-nine nine, nine nine nine. Nine nine nine nine. *Nine* nine nine. Nine? Nine nine nine nine. Nine nine nine nine nine, nine nine nine.

Nine nine nine nine. Nine nine nine / nine nine, nine nine nine.

"Nine?" nine nine. "Nine nine? Nine, nine nine.

Nine.

Nine your pants ninety-nine nine. Nine nine nine. Nine nine or?

Or nine, nine nine.

Nine nine ninety-nine nine, nine nine nine. Nine nine nine nine. *Nine* nine nine. Nine? Nine nine nine nine. Nine nine nine nine nine, nine nine nine. Nine ninety-nine. Nine nine *nine* nine-nine. Nine nine? Nine point nine-nine-nine. Nine! Nine nine nine. Nine ninety-nine. Nine nine nine nine, nine?

Nine nine nine ninety-nine. Nine nine ninety-nine nine, nine nine nine. Nine nine nine nine. *Nine* nine nine.

Nine? Nine nine nine nine. Nine nine nine nine nine, nine nine nine. Nine nine ninety-nine nine, nine nine nine. Nine nine nine nine. *Nine* nine nine. Nine? Nine nine nine nine. Nine nine nine nine nine, nine nine nine.

"Nine?"

"Or else nine."

Nine nine ninety-nine nine, nine nine nine. Nine nine nine nine. *Nine* nine nine. Nine? Nine nine nine nine. Nine nine nine nine nine, nine nine nine.

Nine nine nine nine. Nine nine nine / nine nine, nine nine nine.

"Nine?" nine nine.

"Nine nine? Nine, nine nine."

Nine ninety-nine. Nine nine *nine* nine-nine. Nine nine? Nine point nine-nine-nine. Nine! Nine nine nine. Nine ninety-nine. Nine nine nine nine, nine? Nine nine nine ninety-nine.

"Oh, *nine*!"

Nine nine ninety-nine nine, nine nine nine. Nine nine nine nine. *Nine* nine nine. Nine? Nine nine nine nine. Nine nine nine nine nine, nine nine nine.

Nine nine nine nine. Nine nine nine / nine nine, nine nine nine.

"Nine?" nine nine. "Nine nine? Nine, nine nine.

Nine ninety-nine. Nine nine *nine* nine-nine. Nine nine? Nine point nine-nine-nine. Nine! Nine nine god-damn nine. Nine ninety-nine. Nine

"What can you tell us about Atlantis?" asks Marisol.

I turn to give her a frown. "Atlantis didn't exist. It's been proven."

"There's a room for everything, Julian," says Marisol.

"How did I know you were going to say that? Actually I have it on very good authority that I was causing trouble in a completely different galaxy at that time."

"Then how can you know what I'm saying?" asks Marisol.

I stare at her. "Why would I not know what you're saying? We're speaking Standard American English."

"I'm speaking Atlantean," she replies. "So are you."

I continue to stare. Short-term memory still holds the aural images of the words just spoken, and I take a moment to examine them. Surprised, I find that they were no variety of English at all, nor any other language I readily recall. In fact, I'm not certain that we've spoken to each other at all.

"That's . . . interesting," I say.

Or seem to say. My lips did not move. Marisol and I are speaking telepathically.

"Now you want to tell me what happened on Atlantis?" she says wordlessly.

Stephanie tosses her bottle onto the floor.

"I don't know what's happening in this *room*," I reply.

"It's just a room," says Marisol. "Everything you see here is virtual, Julian. This conversation is taking place on many levels, and it's being looked into on many levels, and you *do* need to answer the question."

"I've no idea," I reply, "what may or may not have occur-

nine nine nine, nine? Nine nine nine ninety-nine.

Nine nine ninety-nine nine, nine nine nine. Nine nine nine nine. *Nine* nine nine. Nine? Nine nine nine nine. Nine nine nine nine nine, nine nine nine.

Nine nine nine nine. Nine nine nine / nine nine, nine nine nine.

"Ninety-nine?"

Nine nine. Nine nine? Nine, nine nine. Nine ninety-nine. Nine nine *nine* nine-nine. Nine nine? Nine point nine-nine-nine. Nine! Nine nine damn nine. Nine ninety-nine. Nine nine nine nine, nine? Nine nine nine ninety-nine.

"Nine."

Nine nine ninety-nine nine, nine nine nine. Nine nine nine nine. *Nine* nine nine. Nine? Nine nine nine nine. Nine nine nine nine nine, nine nine nine.

Nine nine nine nine. Nine nine nine nine nine, nine nine nine.

"Nine?" nine nine. "Nine nine? Nine, nine nine.

Nine nine ninety-nine nine, nine nine nine. Nine nine nine nine. *Nine* nine nine. Nine? Nine nine nine nine. Nine nine nine nine nine, nine nine nine.

Nine ninety-nine. Nine nine *nine* nine-nine. Nine nine? Nine point nine-nine-nine. Nine! Nine nine nine. Nine ninety-nine. Nine nine nine nine,

nine? Nine motherfucker nine nine ninety-nine.

"Nine nine nine."

Nine nine ninety-nine nine, nine nine nine. Nine nine nine nine. *Nine* nine nine. Nine? Nine nine nine nine. Nine nine nine nine nine, nine nine nine.

Nine nine nine nine. Nine nine nine nine nine, nine nine nine.

"Nine nine? Nine, nine nine."

Nine ninety-nine. Nine nine nine nine-nine. Nine nine? Nine point nine-nine-nine. Nine! Nine nine goddamn nine. Nine ninety-nine. Nine nine nine nine, nine? Nine nine nine ninety-nine. Nine nine ninety-nine nine, nine nine nine. Nine nine nine nine. *Nine* nine nine. Nine? Nine nine nine nine. Nine nine nine nine nine, nine nine nine.

Nine nine nine nine. Nine nine nine / nine nine, nine nine nine.

"Nine?" nine nine. Nine nine?

Nine ninety-nine. Nine nine *nine* nine-nine. Nine nine? Nine point nine-nine-nine. Nine! Nine nine nine. Nine ninety-nine. Nine nine nine nine, nine? Nine nine nine ninety-nine.

"Nine ninety-nine?"

Nine nine ninety-nine nine, nine nine nine. Nine nine nine nine. *Nine* nine nine. Nine? Nine nine nine nine. Nine nine nine nine nine, nine nine nine.

"Nine nine."

red on Atlantis. I'm presently focused on what's occurring in a *highly* probable Beijing."

Marisol says, "Your friend won't be keeping her appointment with you. I guess you know that."

"Tree? Where is she?"

"Safe, for now. I know you're worried, Julian, but our policy is non-interference. We only step in when a problem is like really global."

"It's feeling pretty global to me right now."

Marisol sets down the nutcracker. "Let me make sure I understand you. You have absolutely no memory of anything on Atlantis, and you're doing absolutely nothing with the numbers?"

"That's exactly what I'm saying."

"You're not doing any music work?" she asks.

"Music work?"

"You don't seem to have a lot of self-awareness, Julian. You've done a lot of music work in a lot of places. That's one reason we're talking to you now. There's a huge tie-in between music and numbers."

"No, Marisol. I'm not doing any music work right now."

The young woman is very still for a moment, as though peering beneath my skin. "Okay," she says at last.

Turning to the old man in the recliner, Marisol calls, "Daddy. Daddy! Julian Mancer's here. Did you want to talk to him?"

The man awakes, snorts a couple of times, and struggles to push himself to his feet. I watch him walk, bent, past the sofa. He signals for me to follow.

I accompany Edward into a small kitchen whose walls smell of grease. I

"Oh, nine."

Nine nine ninety-nine nine, nine nine nine. Nine nine nine nine. *Nine* nine nine. Nine? Nine nine nine nine. Nine nine nine nine nine, nine nine nine. Nine nine ninety-nine nine, nine nine nine. Nine nine nine nine. *Nine* nine nine. Nine? Nine nine nine nine. Nine nine nine nine nine, nine nine nine.

Nine nine nine nine. Nine nine nine / nine nine, nine nine nine. Nine nine. Nine nine? Nine, nine nine. Nine ninety-nine. Nine nine nine-nine. Nine nine? Nine point nine-nine-nine. Nine! Nine nine nine. Nine ninety-nine. Nine nine nine nine, nine? Nine nine nine ninety-nine.

"Nine nine."

Nine nine ninety-nine nine, nine nine nine. Nine nine nine nine. *Nine* nine nine. Nine? Nine nine nine nine. Nine nine nine nine nine, nine nine nine. Nine nine nine nine. Nine nine nine / nine nine, nine nine nine.

"Nnumber nine? Number nine? Number nine?"

Nine nine. Nine, nine nine.

Nine ninety-nine. Nine nine *nine* nine-nine. Nine nine? Nine point nine-nine-nine. Nine! Nine nine nine nine. Nine ninety-nine. Nine nine nine nine, nine? Nine nine nine ninety-nine.

"Nine nine."

"Oh, for the love of nine."

Nine nine ninety-nine nine, nine nine nine. Nine nine nine nine. *Nine* nine nine. Nine? Nine nine nine nine. Nine nine nine nine nine, nine nine nine.

Nine nine nine nine. Nine nine nine / nine nine, nine nine nine.

"Nine?" nine nine. Nine nine? Nine, nine nine.

Nine nine ninety-nine nine, nine nine nine. Nine nine nine nine. *Nine* nine nine. Nine? Nine nine nine nine. Nine nine nine nine nine, nine nine nine.

Nine ninety-nine. Nine nine *nine* nine-nine. Nine nine? Nine point nine-nine-nine. Nine! Nine nine goddamn nine. Nine ninety-nine. Nine nine nine nine, nine? Nine nine nine ninety-nine. Splendid nine nine ninety-nine nine, nine nine nine. Nine nine nine nine. *Nine* nine nine. Nine? Nine nine nine nine. Nine nine nine nine nine, nine nine nine.

"Nine nine."

Nine nine ninety-nine nine, nine nine nine. Nine nine nine nine. *Nine* nine nine. Nine? Nine nine nine nine. Nine nine nine nine nine, nine nine nine.

Nine nine nine nine. Nine nine nine / nine nine, nine nine nine.

"Nine nine nine nine nine."

Nine nine ninety-nine nine, nine nine nine. Nine nine nine nine. *Nine*

watch the old man take something from the refrigerator. Opening a plastic bottle of red soda, he takes a long drink, replaces the cap and closes the door.

Turning to me, Ed-ward says, "They got me on blood medicine." His foggy eyes try to sharpen. "I can't never wake up. You from Memphis?"

I nod.

He smiles and noisily fingers the white stubble at his chin. "I knowed a cowboy from Memphis. Rode bulls. Name was Robert. John Robert. He got killed by a bad bull in Arkansas." The old man's smile fades.

"You say you gotta get to Beijing. What do you think you can get done up there?"

I study the dark eyes. Sleeping or no, this man seems to have caught every word of my conversation with Marisol.

"Probably noth-ing," I reply telepath-ically, "but I have to try."

Edward leans heavily against the refrigerator door. "Tell me something. Or don't tell me. Whatever you want. But I'd really rather you told me." Both blurry eyes peer into mine. "Just what in the hell are you, and what are you doing on this here planet?"

I look him square in the eyes. "I don't know. What are *you*, Edward?"

We gaze at each other for a long mo-ment. Finally the old man chuckles. "Well, we try to keep an eye on things best we can."

"Now I have a que-stion for you," I say. "Completion. What is it?"

"We were kinda hoping you could tell us."

I lean back against the wall. "I don't know, man. It's just

nine nine. Nine? Nine nine nine nine. Nine nine nine nine nine, nine nine nine.

"Nine nine? Nine."

Nine ninety-nine. Nine nine *nine* nine-nine. Nine nine? Nine point nine-nine-nine. Nine! Nine nine nine. Nine ninety-nine. Nine nine nine nine, nine? Nine nine nine ninety-nine.

"Nine nine."

"Okay, nine it is."

Nine nine ninety-nine nine, nine nine nine. Nine nine nine nine. *Nine* nine nine. Nine? Nine nine nine nine. Nine nine nine nine nine, nine nine nine.

Nine nine nine nine. Nine nine nine nine nine, nine nine nine. Nine? Nine, nine nine. Nine ninety-nine. Nine nine nine nine-nine. Nine nine? Nine point nine-nine-nine. Nine! Nine nine nine. Nine ninety-nine. Nine nine nine nine, nine? Nine nine nine nine-ty-nine.

"Oh, *nine!*"

Nine nine ninety-nine nine, nine nine nine. Nine nine nine nine. Nine nine nine. Nine? Nine nine nine nine. Nine nine nine nine nine, nine nine nine.

Nine nine nine nine. Nine nine nine nine nine, nine nine nine.

"Nine?" nine nine. "Nine nine? Nine, nine nine.

Nine ninety-nine. Nine nine nine nine-nine. Nine nine? Nine point nine-

nine-nine. Nine! Nine nine goddamn nine. Nine ninety-nine. Nine nine nine nine, nine? Nine nine nine nine-ty-nine.

Nine nine ninety-nine nine, nine nine nine. Nine nine nine nine. Nine nine nine. Nine? Nine nine nine nine. Nine nine nine nine nine, nine nine nine.

Nine nine nine nine. Nine nine nine / nine nine, nine nine nine.

"Ninety-nine?"

Nine nine. Nine nine? Nine, nine nine. Nine ninety-nine. Nine nine nine nine-nine. Nine nine? Nine point nine-nine-nine. Nine! Nine nine god-damn nine. Nine ninety-nine. Nine nine nine nine, nine? Nine nine nine ninety-nine.

Nine nine ninety-nine nine, nine nine nine. Nine nine nine nine. Nine nine nine. Nine? Nine nine nine nine. Nine nine nine nine nine, nine nine nine.

Nine nine nine nine. Nine nine nine nine nine, nine nine nine.

"Nine nine? Nine, nine nine.

Nine nine ninety-nine nine, nine nine nine. Nine nine nine nine. Nine nine nine. Nine? Nine nine nine nine. Nine nine nine nine nine, nine nine nine.

the fucking end-game everywhere I look. There's no avoiding it, and there's no delaying it, and it's waiting for me in Beijing. I've got to go there."

For a moment, the old man seems to listen to a voice beyond my hear-ing. Finally he says, "I guess everybody needs to find their own kind of com-pletion. That fellow John Robert found his in Arkansas. Looks like you'll find yours in Beijing."

Before I can con-jure a reply, I realize that Edward's fore-finger has found the center of my belly.

An instant later I am enclosed in a fire-ball of ruby-tinged light that fades to to-tal darkness before gradually brighten-ing once more—to become the spar-kling green and de-bilitating blue of Ana Manguella's eyes.

45

"There," says Ana, withdrawing her forefinger from my belly. Again I find myself on a eucalyptus-scented fire escape in Shenzhen.

"Sorry for the sidebar," says Ana. "There's an outside group interfering with some very delicate earth cycles, and we're having to check out every lead. As soon as you feel grounded, you may go."

I look around dizzily. "Where the hell did you just send me?"

"You didn't leave this spot, Julian, and no time elapsed. You were looked into, nothing more. I hope you'll forgive me if I'm rather abruptly on my way. All the best to your soul group, and I do hope you're able to help your sister."

"Wait," I say, taking hold of Ana's wrist.

She gives me a cool look. I let go in a hurry.

"Sorry. Do the Chinese have Tree?"

Ana sighs. "Yes, they've got her, and no, there's nothing I can do to help you. I'm sorry."

Before I can decide on my next question, the woman in the raincoat has turned and hurried away. Half a moment later, she is down the stairs and halfway across the patio below.

"Thanks for not breaking my back just now," I call to her. "I know it crossed your mind."

Turning, Ana Manguella gives me a half smile before covering her head with the hood of the raincoat. A moment later, she has disappeared down the glistening sidewalk.

So.

They have Lillian *and* Tree. I close my eyes and try to focus on something / anything intelligent to do. As usual, nothing comes to me. Re-opening my eyes, I start down the stairs. Before I've reached the second step my eyes catch sight of something on the sidewalk below. Or, loosely speaking, someone. Sans earring, Agent Barnes is walking briskly along the same stretch of sidewalk just graced by Ana Manguella, and in the same direction. Either our girl is being tailed by the Truth Guy or we have ourselves a coincidence.

I think for another moment just in case there's something heroic to be done and I'm man enough to do it. Could be, I decide, and most definitely not. Anyway it's not entirely clear which of the two more urgently requires protection from the other. I wait a few minutes, watching the sidewalk for any other of the usual suspects, asking myself meanwhile what happens should Phoebe fail to show at the appointed time and place. Not to worry, I conclude. She'll be there. The woman has a thing for me.

Finally I decide it's more-or-less safe to descend to the wet street below. I flag the first taxi that passes, this one equipped with a reasonably functioning fare meter. By the time I'm dropped at the rendezvous, though, it's spitting out bubblegum. The sun, meanwhile, has penetrated the clouds. The sidewalk is almost dry. After paying the cabbie, I survey the busy intersection, hoping to catch sight of Phoebe's Buick. Nothing doing.

Concealing myself in a doorway, I check the analog watch on my wrist. A woman like Phoebe, I remind myself, has carte blanche to be forty minutes late anytime anywhere, and she knows it quite well. Further minutes pass. I'm beginning to cast about for a plan C when all at once the Buick appears at the curbside. Elated, I forget my bruised kidney long enough to dash to the passenger side of the car, rip open the door, and *cast* myself inside—very nearly crushing Phoebe Sternbaum's daughter.

Beneath me, five-year-old Ling screams in C-sharp. Very sharp.

"Uh, Phoebe," I say, removing my great white ass from her daughter's face, "you didn't tell me that Ling was coming along."

Phoebe doesn't reply.

"Phoebe?" I shout over Ling. "You didn't *tell* me that—"

"Plenty time I introduce you now," says Phoebe, not turning. "Is my daughter, Ling. She so nice to meet you."

The Buick hangs a left.

"Uh, Phoebe? Your husband isn't going to take this very well. He'll call the police, okay? They'll put out an APB, which stands for Absolutely Positively Busted."

Ling continues to bawl, her eyes tightly shut. I don't think she likes me very much.

"Phoebe?" I try again. "I can't have the police involved in this. If you bring Ling, I can't come with you."

With a screech, Phoebe halts the car at a curb, imperiling half a dozen bicyclists. She switches off the engine, sets the hand brake, and gives me a fierce stare. "You go you don't go I don't care I just go without you. But *nobody* go without my daughter."

We stare at each other. Ling meanwhile reaches for high-D. She's very nearly on the money.

"Next you're going to tell me you forgot the cash," I say.

"Hah-row use credit cards," says Phoebe.

"Did you *get* the credit cards?"

"Har-roh have always with him."

I stare through the windshield, mulling over my alternatives. It doesn't take me very long.

"Okay," I say. "But you have to drive on back roads. Do you understand *back roads*?"

"I know this," says Phoebe, cranking the car and slamming the gearshift. "You think everybody stupid but you."

I spot a cell phone kiosk. "Wait. Park the car. I need to buy a phone. I need to buy three phones."

"Buy what?"

"Just stop the car. It's all part of the master plan. And could you *do* something about your daughter?"

Phoebe mutters a little Cantonese through her teeth.

This is going to be a really pleasant ride.

By the time we exit the car, Ling has transitioned from hysterical to totally composed. "Is she always like that?" I ask Phoebe, guiding our travel party toward the phone kiosk. "Sudden extreme mood changes? Psychotic episodes? Maybe I should know now."

"What you want buy?" asks Phoebe irritably.

"Three phones small enough to carry here," I say, patting one of the cargo pockets of my khakis. "Service all over China."

Phoebe helps me select a small flip-phone and establish service under a false name. I choose Lowell P. Nightsong. The phone company assigns me a number with five nines and a pair of fours. Decent poker hand. Phoebe doesn't go for it.

"*So* unlucky," she says. "Have two fours. Four is mean death, and nine mean the end. Nobody China want this number."

"What would a lucky number be?" I ask.

Phoebe shrugs. "Eight is mean get rich."

"What is mean stay alive?" I want to know.

It takes the kiosk owner several tries to acquire a number with neither fours nor nines. It costs triple. Now he's showing me how to place a call, which with my large hands is comically difficult. I always knew I was avoiding phones for a reason.

"Okay," I say to Phoebe, pocketing the phone, "I need two more."

"Just get them here," she says.

"Not here." I spot a sign on a nearby department store window and begin walking. Inside I acquire a second phone under another false name—I decide to go with Ted Williams— choosing the smallest model available and paying way extra for no fours or nines. Ditto a third phone purchased at a nearby supermarket. The third kiosk owner is unable to obtain a phone number without nines. I wind up with three of them and one four. That makes me only slightly dead.

"Let's stop here," I tell Phoebe, leading her and Ling toward an ATM machine. "I need you to withdraw some cash. As much as it'll give you."

The ATM is balky, as expected, but in the end spits out 33,939 yuan, exactly triple Phoebe's request. Good thing. Neither of Phoebe's other cards work at all. By the time we walk away, the ATM is flashing sporadic error messages. I grab all three cards from Phoebe's hand and drop them into the slot of a nearby mailbox.

"What you *do*?" she cries, her hands covering her face.

"You can't use those cards again," I say, walking toward the car.

"You *crazy*!" shouts Phoebe.

"And no more phone calls," I add over my shoulder. "Turn your phone off now so we can't be tracked. In fact, take the battery out. Understand *battery*?"

"Understand asshole tell me everything I do," mutters Phoebe, unlocking the Buick.

Ignoring her, I activate the least expensive of my three phones and, walking away from the car, dial Tree's number.

"Hello?" answers a man's voice. The accent is Chinese.

"Where is Shatrina Carter?" I demand.

"She cannot come to the phone now," comes the careful reply. "May I ask who is calling?"

"You may kiss my pit bull's ass," I answer. "Is that in your phrase book?"

After a hesitation, I hear, "My name is Wu Shu Rong. I am a detective with the Shenzhen Police Department. Professor Carter we think is possibly in some kind of danger. Therefore we have placed her in our protection. Please may I ask—"

I hang up then dial two phone numbers from my wallet. The first connects me to the US Embassy in Guangzhou, the second to the coordinator of Lil's and Tree's teaching program. I give the same information to each: Shatrina Carter is missing and probably wrongfully detained. I give them the name of Wu Shu Rong, in case it turns out to mean anything. Clicking off the call but leaving the power on, I toss the phone onto a pile of turnips in the back of a passing truck.

That done, I turn and hurry toward the waiting Buick. It's like I said. This secret agent stuff's overrated.

46

I turn to glance at Phoebe's daughter in the back seat, asleep with her mirror in hand. Ling has a thing for a small, round make-up mirror, pink, that she holds in her right hand and consults frequently, bringing it very close to her face, her small lips moving silently. Ling has Phoebe's high cheekbones and strong features, along with the fair complexion and hazel hair of her Western father.

This entire day this girl has uttered fewer than a dozen words, all of them Mandarin, though I'm told she's as proficient in both Cantonese and English, having picked them up from her father and grandmother, respectively. What Phoebe has told Ling about this little adventure of ours I can't begin to guess, but thus far the latter seems to be taking it at least as well as the former. She may yet turn out to be a reasonably well-balanced child when no one is sitting on her head.

I glance at the gas gauge, disturbingly low, but I say nothing. Gas stations are very few along China's rural roads, as Phoebe is fond of pointing out, as are restrooms of any and every stripe. Phoebe's pretty fond of pointing that out, too.

The sun is now an orange lantern behind Phoebe Sternbaum's haloed head, and the banana groves of Guangdong are far behind us. We're now three tiny grains in China's vast rice bowl. It would be really nice to have a map and a compass. More pressing just now are gasoline, a restroom, and a hot meal at a roadside inn with beds but without bedbugs.

Suddenly and for no apparent reason, Phoebe whips the steering wheel to the left and forsakes our rural highway for a rough one-point-five-lane road through hard-scrabble feed corn. A minute later she's stopping at an unmarked crossroads and looking in each direction. I'm looking, too, and I can tell you there's absolutely nothing to see except ugly.

Phoebe decides to take a left.

I'm holding a bit of my bodyweight on my hands now, as my bladder is quite swollen and Phoebe is *the* typical woman driver. Utterly oblivious to what she's putting her passenger through. Men understand that non-drivers have no steering wheel to steady themselves and so take pride in finessing the controls, reading each nuance of the road so as to never displace a hair on the precious passenger's head. A woman, given the least opportunity, will crash your head against the roof of the car *and* the side-glass within the same breath and never muster the curiosity to notice.

Not that I'm becoming irritable. With so much of this journey still before us, and two females sealed into this tiny capsule with me, irritability would be a poor life choice.

At each and every red light, Phoebe shifts into park, applies the parking brake, switches off the engine and stares fixedly at the light. I'm a little surprised she doesn't take the keys out of the ignition and put them in her purse. The moment the light turns green, she's scrambling madly to crank the engine, disengage the brake and shift into gear before we are into late autumn.

Not that it irritates me.

When Phoebe backs downhill out of a parking place, she uses the reverse gear. I'm careful to say nothing. No sly references to Newton. Not a word.

The Buick meanwhile takes us ever deeper into the feed corn. I give a glance to the right side mirror, wondering whether anyone could be stupid enough to follow us here, and of course no one is. All that icky business seems quite far behind us now. If we can just conjure a little gasoline, I'd say we're a slam dunk to make Beijing. What happens once we're in Beijing could still constitute a bit of a problem.

Phoebe, grim-faced, continues to burn our remaining gas. I distract myself by wondering which bad guy does what and to what general end. Bellamy, for example. Is he the kind of bad guy who just stands in the bushes while his friends go through your underwear drawer or does he, like John Fulbright, occasionally morph into something truly appalling? And I don't even want to speculate on Agent Velázquez's power-tool collection. On balance, I'd have to say this country has more Peter Lorres per square meter than pinkos, and personally I'm beginning to tire of it.

I steal another glance at the gas gauge, purposely avoiding seeing the odometer, which probably displays a nice row of nines just about now. The gas gauge seems to have bottomed out. My thoughts drift to Lillian, and I feel a stab of anguish. I've tried finding her a time or two. In the *glow*, I mean. It doesn't seem to be glowing these days. Or maybe I'm just not very psychic after all.

Phoebe decides to hang another left. Good move. One more and we'll be within sight of our own tailpipe.

We pass an untidy farmstead enclosed by a crumbling wall. Through the open gate is a view of meandering chickens and rotting scrap lumber. The Wang Chang Snopes family.

"That sign was say buy some petrol on this road," mutters Phoebe, "but I don't see. You tell me go the back roads, now you see back roads has nothing everywhere."

"Look," I say, pointing to a homemade sign attached to a utility pole. "What does that say?"

"It say don't come here."

I look at her. "Don't *come* here?"

Phoebe shrugs. "I think something about the SARS. Don't worry about this."

I nod, infinitely comforted. We're running out of gas just as night falls on the Mississippi of south-central China where the pitchfork-to-human ratio is exactly one-to-one, they're posting warnings in the feed corn, and I'm supposed to worry?

Before Phoebe can hang another left, we encounter a crude wooden barricade, beside which two men sprawl in folding loungers rigged with makeshift canopies. At our approach, their heads jerk up. When Phoebe stops the Buick, the two men jump to their feet and make shooing gestures. Phoebe motors her window down and gives them a blast of impatient contempt. That's the Chinese way of asking someone a question.

"Ask them where we can buy some gas," I suggest. I suggest it three times but she's busy arguing with the men, who seem to be getting more and more animated. One of them picks up a length of steel pipe, and Phoebe shifts into reverse.

"Did you find out about buying some gas?" I ask as Phoebe spins the Buick in a diorama of dust.

"Those men so *stupid*," she says bitterly. "I tell them, 'Just go buy some petrol bring it here we give you money lots of money.' Everybody in China understand money but those men just stupid understand nothing."

Now awake in the back seat, Ling says something in Mandarin. I recognize the word for bathroom. Her mother gives a terse reply. Again the Buick encounters the sagging farmstead we've just passed. Wang Chang Snopes and kin. The car slows to a stop just outside the open gate, and Phoebe switches off the engine.

"I talk to these people," she says miserably, removing her earrings and bracelet and placing them inside her purse. With a tissue she removes most of her lipstick and gives me a here-goes-nothing look.

I watch Phoebe disappear through the gate. Immediately comes the startled yipping of a young dog. Two other dogs join in. Maybe I should move to the driver's seat. Actually I see that Phoebe has taken the keys.

"Where is my mother?"

I'm surprised by the perfect English issuing from the back seat.

"Talking to some people," I tell Ling without turning. "We need gas. Petrol. Fuel. Essential oil of dinosaur."

We need a good many things, including a good defense against pitchforks. Or, it occurs, these could be progressive farmers. Maybe we'll be passed through a hay-baler and stacked on a wooden pallet.

"I need a bathroom," says Ling.

"Just a little longer," I reply over my shoulder.

Your mother insisted on taking the back roads.

Frankly I'm feeling a little guilty about dragging a five-year-old into all this, whatever this finally turns out to be. I've more or less rationalized involving her mother. Here after all is a physically and emotionally abused woman in fear of wrongful death at the hands of a philandering husband who doesn't floss. Chances are, given the context, I'm the best thing to happen to Phoebe Sternbaum in quite some time.

I wonder what's taking the girl so long. Daylight is fading quickly and it's hard to bale hay in the dark.

Ling speaks once more.

"Pardon?" I ask, half turning my head.

No reply. I turn fully to gaze into the back seat. Ling lies curled, eyes closed, fast asleep. Strange. I don't remember now what she said.

Phoebe bursts through the farmyard gate, followed by a populous Chinese family. No pitchforks, I note with satisfaction. In fact, everyone is smiling. Even better, there's a gasoline can in the hands of a boy wearing a John Denver tee.

John's smiling, too.

47

Last night I dreamed of being back in Memphis, strolling naked along Poplar Avenue—a common theme, actually—and trying to be quite nonchalant about it when my sister approached me in a pair of bib overalls. She had a red chiffon dress draped over her arm.

"Put this on," she said. "We have to talk."

"It's a dress," I told her.

"It's all I have," said Lillian.

I put on the dress. It felt kind of naughty with nothing beneath.

"*What* is taking you so long?" demanded my sister. "I'm rotting in a Chinese prison, in case you've forgotten, and yes it's definitely a prison. My anxiety attacks are having anxiety attacks, and here you are *streaking* along Poplar Avenue."

"I'm on my way to Beijing," I told her. "Just—"

"Just nothing. These people are scary, Doo, and I don't know what it is they're after. Where's Tree?"

"That's something else I'm working on."

"I *hate* this," said Lil, sweeping the bangs from her eyes, "our being scattered all over the place like this. I don't know what the fuck we're supposed to do now."

I couldn't quite take my eyes off my sister, whom you'll recall I hadn't seen in some time, awake or otherwise. Her eyes were more emerald than I'd recalled. Startling. I very nearly told her so.

"I'm really sorry about the whole dad thing," I said. "I wanted to tell you about it."

"Just come get me, okay?" snapped Lil. "And be careful. There's someone following you."

"I've shaken those people," I said.

She shook her head. "I don't mean physical people. Find Tree. She'll know what to do."

Lil began to laugh.

"What?" I said.

"The dress. You should keep it."

I awoke with cotton mouth and an acute case of gender ambiguation. I looked around. I was lying on a few folded blankets on the wooden floor of a cabin in whatever province we're in. Phoebe and Ling lay asleep on the double bed. I began to stretch, which wasn't the best of ideas. *Riveting* cramp in my right kidney. My arm was aching, too. And I missed that red dress. It's so hard to find a dress that hits my shoulders right.

After a quick breakfast of beef and noodles and enough MSG to dissolve the nervous system of a yak, we've managed to make admirable time. At least, so far as I can determine, not knowing whether to trust my—uh, Ana's—watch. The sweep hand is sweeping, at least. The sun is only a couple of hours past the zenith and we recently passed a road sign announcing Jiangxi Province, whose northern boundary I think is the historic Yangtze River. That would mark roughly halfway. That's the good news. Less encouraging is the growing evidence that Phoebe has defected to the people's interstate highway system.

"I thought we were going to stay on the back roads," I say. "By my count, this highway has eight lanes."

"All Chinese road back road," she replies stiffly.

"This is feeling kind of conspicuous."

"All Chinese road bi-bicious. You want go Beijing, we go Beijing."

We pass a road sign that puts us alarmingly near Nanchang, which is a city the size of Chicago. If I were lying in wait for this car, I would be parked along this exact stretch of highway.

"Phoebe, don't you think they'll expect us to go through Nanchang?"

"Who *they*?" she snaps. "We just go Beijing see some friends. Nobody care about this."

"I think your husband care very much about this."

Phoebe shoots me a glare. "You forget somebody here very understand English."

The car becomes silent except for the whap-whap-whap of the paving sections passing beneath us. I've been waiting for the right moment to suggest that we drive all night. Probably this isn't it.

We pass another road sign and Phoebe hits the turn signal. "Oh, we stop now this place very famous Chinese history."

"History?" I say. "We have time for history?"

"First communist government start here. I show my daughter this."

Beyond the off ramp, the road is a narrow, smooth meander of pleasant, round-shouldered hills. No traffic at all. My tension vanishes, and I consider the possibility that Phoebe may be exactly right. A little break could be just what we need before taking on Nanchang.

The Buick turns onto a small lane with an unmanned guardhouse, a notice pasted to the glass window.

"Government is close this place because SARS," reports Phoebe. "Don't nobody here."

Beyond the guardhouse is a tantalizing view of breeze-enlivened wooded slopes and grassy meadows. We could be in east Tennessee. We enter a pastoral dream of new grass and bouncing butterflies. Neither cars nor humans are anywhere in sight. The Buick glides to a stop in a hill-sheltered parking lot. Before us lies a twisting foot trail.

"Is where communist soldiers have the camp," says Phoebe, excitedly reading the sign. "We can go walk this place."

Phoebe opens the driver's door and bounds outside. I open the door but I can't move. It takes both Phoebe and Ling, both of them laughing, to pull me out.

Struggling to walk in the bright sunlight, I turn a complete circle, looking for something to be worried about. I don't find it. Closing my eyes, I inhale the intoxicating scent of newly minted grass. Ling runs ahead. Phoebe stands smiling at the head of the trail, waiting for me. A moment later we're walking hand-in-hand.

"You like this place so beautiful?" she asks.

I look at her. "I like."

A pair of yellow butterflies swirl before us, nearly touching our faces. Phoebe inhales and gazes straight up, showing her lovely throat.

"See how *high* the sky? Ninety-thousand *li*. Old book *Yi Wen Lei Ju* say that first everything everywhere is all together, very small, then *boom* everything get bigger sky is move away from the earth this take eighteen thousand years. Between the sky and earth is a man. He is Pangu. Pangu is go through nine changes every day, become so smart the sky become so high earth become so thick now. This is how everything start. Then come the first three emperors." She smiles. "Everybody China know this story."

Phoebe shouts ahead to Ling, who stops to wait for us.

"Why," I ask, "does every number in that tale reduce to either three or nine?"

"Because everything start with one, get ready with three, get finish with nine. You don't know this? Don't believe this? My husband say Chinese so silly, I say it make you *happy* believe something. Haw-row always believe nothing, just angry." A shudder goes through her. "I not want think about this now."

Our footpath enters a broadleaf forest. Here too is an overpowering scent of new spring foliage. We trace a cut between two hills, and the trail ends at a locked gate. Ling scampers up the wooded hill to our left and shouts for us to follow. We do follow and are rewarded by a vista of a lakeside bathed in sunlight. Beneath the shade of oaks, a carpet of grass leads right to the water's edge.

A moment later, Phoebe and I are sprawled in the soft grass watching a lone crane glide into the west. Ling tosses pebbles into the water. I feel Phoebe's body move slightly closer to mine. Our hips touch, and my body explodes in bliss.

"God in heaven," I say.

"What?" asks Phoebe, relaxed and smiling.

"What happens to us?" I whisper, astonished at myself. "How can we forget how beautiful this world is? It's like . . . it's like permanent temporary insanity. You go into town to buy a tin of tuna, and the next thing you know a decade has passed, your body has become a breakfast sausage, the Republicans control both houses of Congress, and you still don't have the tin of tuna." I turn to her. "Please tell me you know what I'm talking about. Even if you don't."

Phoebe's forefinger jabs my chest. "You say no *time* we stop here. Now you see. American people all the time so serious so hurry only get the bad health. *You* worst American."

She runs her fingers through my hair. "*Worst*," she whispers, bringing her smile so close to mine I'm certain they'll touch. At the last instant, she turns to see Ling run toward us crying, "Look!" In her tiny left hand is a fossilized stone.

I accept it from her hand. Seems an asterisk-shaped creature once drew breath very near where we lie. Now just an empty space. So it goes.

Ling runs back to the lakeshore and I ask Phoebe, "What will you do? Where will you go when all this is over?"

Her smile vanishes. "Don't know this."

Wrong question. I close my eyes, letting the moment dissolve, letting the lazy late-spring aromas induce a sleepy reverie. What does happen to us? And what do we do once we know it's happened?

I once developed a sci-fi story about a minimally evolved species of primate on a rock somewhere who didn't feel safe sleeping in the open, so they decided to sleep in little boxes. Eventually they became really good at box making. Soon their boxes were big enough for the whole family. Then a smoke-hole were added, and soon there were fewer and fewer reasons to ever leave your box. Soon you had clusters of boxes, then clusters of clusters. Life became about your box. Who had the biggest one or the one located nearest the really important boxes.

There were work boxes that everyone reported to, and entertainment boxes, and boxes where you went to buy things for your box. Finally little mobile boxes came along that took everyone from one box to another. There were boxes where you were born and boxes you were put in when you died, so you never really had to be without a box. Unless you belonged to the lowest rung of society. The boxless. Of course there were neuroses and illnesses that came with always being inside a box, but not to worry.

There were enormous boxes where all the broken monkeys were attended night and day—that each might someday return to his or her own box. Sometimes after a round of drinks, one monkey might inquire of others whether they had any interest in *the outdoors*. The reply was nearly always yes, as the outdoors was a popular notion among people with really nice boxes.

For some reason, that story was never published. I was told the premise was too unbelievable.

I steal a glance at Phoebe. Her eyes are closed. I wouldn't mind kissing those eyes. I like her nearness. Her faint scents. The soft breathing. The way it animates the two unseen breasts. I note that the swelling around her cheekbone has all but vanished. The bruising has begun to fade.

"What *you* do?" asks Phoebe suddenly, eyes still closed. "Where you go after everything over?"

"To a high-school baseball game," I reply sleepily. "I'll buy a bag of unshelled peanuts and choose a bleacher seat along the first base line, behind the women in the lawn chairs. I'll listen to what they say to each other about their sons and the coaches and their doctors. I'll watch the boys line up in the mud in their cleated shoes to drink from the water faucet. I'll hear that perfect popping sound that leather makes on leather." I blink. "You have no idea what I'm talking about, do you?"

Phoebe Sternbaum's hair is a tangle of temptation. She shrugs listlessly. "See the game, eat the peanuts, I know this."

I laugh at her and she looks at me in surprise. I think we're both surprised. As I watch, the perfect amber face spreads in child-like pleasure. "Ju! I never hear you laugh before."

She rolls toward me and the top of her head digs into my chest, Suddenly her head is resting against my shoulder. My long arm encloses her waist. By tender degrees, my thoughts dissolve into what they have been all along. Nothing.

My breath catches. Alarmed, I open my eyes and look around for Ling. She is a perfect picture of poise, seated on a log and gazing across the lake. A soothing sight. My eyes roll closed. Maybe I'm nodding off just a little. Suddenly Phoebe is standing over me.

"Ju? We go now buy the petrol eat some restaurant okay?"

Reluctantly, I stretch my body. My bruised kidney flinches. I decide to take my time rising to my feet.

"I have a funny dream," Phoebe tells me. "Funny dream about some big place, lots of people and some girl help us. Ling!"

"What girl help us?" I ask.

"I don't know this girl. Ling!"

Ling, scampering far ahead of us, stops to wait. "*Somebody* need help us," mutters Phoebe, her face suddenly dark.

"What about those people you know in Beijing?" I say.

"Not talk about this now," says Phoebe. "Ling!"

We join Ling at the foot trail to retrace our steps along the shadowed cleft. The sun is half fallen to the horizon. We've lost two hours, more or less, but maybe we've gained the heart to continue. All night hopefully. Two days and we're not yet halfway to Lillian.

I gaze at Ling, again scampering ahead. Now she stops and awaits us. When we rejoin her, she insinuates herself between Phoebe and myself and grabs our hands. Now she's pulling us toward a side trail. "This way," she insists.

I don't argue. Ling all but dragging us, we enter a denser neck of the forest.

As the treetops close over us, I feel a fresh pang of worry about Tree. I'd like to blame Tree for all this, but if Lil and I hadn't come to China, none of this would have happened. And Tree wouldn't be where she is now, wherever that is. I feel a pull toward Beijing that's almost palpable. The imagined scent of the place is enough to make me shiver.

Gradually the trees part before us. We're nearly back to the meadow and the parking lot, though by a different route. We've nearly burst into the meadow when—

I pull Phoebe and Ling to a stop. A dozen meters before us, parked within the shadowy canopy of the forest, its nose facing away, is a late-model silver Toyota with two silhouettes seated inside. I pull Phoebe and Ling back into the shadows.

"What?" says Phoebe.

"Shhhh."

Lowering my head, I peer through a gap in the bushes. The Toyota sports a Guangdong license plate. I don't like the look of it. I definitely don't like the look of the six-foot whip antenna attached to the rear bumper.

"Stay here," I whisper.

"But—"

"*Shhhh.*"

Carefully avoiding the mirrors of the Toyota, I pick my way ahead until the two men are in view. I don't recognize the driver, a young Chinese man in sunglasses. The man in the passenger seat, though, rings a very definite bell. Hooked nose. Round black-rimmed glasses. Never out of style.

I pick my way back to Phoebe and Ling. "Let's go back the other way," I whisper.

"Why we go—" begins Phoebe.

"Love session in progress."

Phoebe's mouth falls open. She tiptoes, trying to see more, but I drag her away. We retrace the side trail, my mind racing. *He uses lots of names*, Ralpho told me about Bellamy. *Belongs to Wen Jiabao. Everything you say around him goes into a report.* It never made sense to me that China's most important figure would take the slightest interest in my person. It makes even less now.

But somebody's sure going through an awful lot of trouble. I console myself that Bellamy and his driver don't seem to have outright murder in their immediate plans. Certainly they could have done anything they'd wanted with us before now. Maybe it's my scumbag father they're after. Still it's hard not to recall that lovely Chinese saying. Once the squirrels are dead, the dogs that tracked them will be cooked.

It takes a lifetime to cross the meadow to the waiting Buick.

"Give me the keys," I tell Phoebe.

"You want drive? Why you—"

"I'm in the mood," I say, yanking the keys from her hand. "Get in."

"What you so crazy? Take my keys like some kind—"

"Get in, Phoebe. Ling, get inside the car."

Throwing the driver's seat back as far as it'll go, I collapse inside. Pouting, Phoebe takes her time walking to the passenger's side. It's a real effort not to squeal a doughnut and burn rubber out of there. I manage to drive more or less normally until we're out of sight of the parked Toyota. Turning left onto the highway, I stomp the accelerator. The Buick swerves so badly that an old man on a trike decides to take the ditch. We top a hill, and the Buick is practically airborne.

"What you *doing*?" demands Phoebe.

"I'll explain in a minute."

I check the rearview mirror. No silver Toyota.

"Someone follow us?" asks Phoebe, turning to look through the rear window. "Who follow us?"

"There's a silver car behind us. It's important we lose them."

Scanning the highway ahead of us, I see a rough unpaved road ascending into a pine forest. I hit the brake pedal and yank the wheel. The Buick swerves onto the narrow road. A moment later we're wheeling into an impromptu garbage dump among the trees. Confident we can't be seen from the highway, I turn the Buick to face that direction and switch off the engine.

Phoebe is staring at me, astonished.

"Watch," I tell Phoebe, pointing to the highway. "You'll see a silver car with two men inside."

"You crazy," she replies, turning in the seat to gather Ling into her arms. "I crazy as hell go Beijing with you."

"Just watch, okay?" I say, knowing already that the car will not appear. Ten minutes later, it's official. No Toyota.

"Nobody follow us," says Phoebe. "You make me so scared I almost shit everywhere."

Ignoring her, I puzzle over the non-appearance of Bellamy. Why would he tail us all the way through southern China just to let us get away? It's as though he has no doubt he can find us again any—

Ah. The six-foot whip antenna. Decisively I yank the hood-release of the Buick and step outside.

"Where you go?" asks Phoebe.

"To look for something."

It doesn't take long. The transmitter, hardly larger than a dime, clings magnetically to a wheel strut.

Pocketing the bug, I begin walking toward the roadside below. "I'll be back," I tell Phoebe over my shoulder. Picking my way through the pines, I make my way to the roadside below. If I recall correctly, I spotted a gas station not too far from here.

Indeed there is a gas station less than a quarter mile away. I make my way through the shrubs at the forest's edge. Arriving, I see a bright-orange seafood-delivery truck parked at the lone gas pump. No one sees me skitter into the clearing to attach the electronic bug to the underside of the truck and scurry away.

The plan now, I tell myself, huffing back up the hillside, is to find an inconspicuous route either southeast or southwest. Away from Beijing. By the time Bellamy realizes he's tailing a quarter ton of prawns, we'll be impossible to find. Eventually we'll hook up with a northbound highway and drive non-stop to Beijing.

Nearing the garbage dump, I pause to catch my breath. One way or another, I tell myself, Bellamy and his whip antenna are beside the point. I've had spooks following me since the Three Sovereigns and Five Emperors. The real road hazard here is Harold Sternbaum. Here's a man who's just had his daughter stolen. And his wife, come to think of it. As I pick my way once more through the unkempt forest, I wonder what kind of reception he may be planning for me, should our paths cross in Beijing. Let's see if we can avoid finding out. Finally stepping into the garbage-strewn clearing and looking around, I find one thing inescapable. The Buick is gone.

48

I heard a story about a rooster who one day looked up to find that his hens had vanished. He checked in the barn. He checked under the house. He checked in the treetops. No hens. The rooster went to the pig and said, "You know what happened to my hens?" The pig replied, "They tired of your attentions. They went to live with the hawk." The rooster was surprised. "The hawk will eat them," he said. The pig replied, "Yes, but at least it is their own choice."

I'm not sure why that story comes up just now. Maybe it's because I've been standing in a garbage dump for most of an hour, and will continue to do so for the remains of the day and likely the whole of the night. By dawn, as the thinking goes, the fish truck will have lured Bellamy and company far enough away from here for me to safely descend to the roadside and negotiate my way to a bus depot.

Or not.

Actually I'm not standing in the aforementioned garbage dump so much as circling it warily. For one thing, I'm dimly hopeful of discovering something/anything approximating a ground cloth. So far, my efforts have yielded nothing beyond the following two observations. First, every direction in China is downwind. Second, nothing of value is ever, *ever* abandoned in this country. I don't think a single item here would qualify for an American garbage dump. It's more like things you'd scrape off your shoe. And I think I hear something approaching. A half-muffled gasoline engine seems to be headed this way—not from the highway, curiously. It's most likely an Abrams M1A1 tank with Bellamy's head sticking out.

Ah. Appearing beneath my feet, partly buried beneath a rusted-out steel drum, is what appears to be a large sheet of plastic. I decide to give it a mighty tug. The sheet of plastic doesn't budge. Finally I apply a truly heroic yank and the plastic sheet comes free. It's covered with something very like rendered hog concentrate. Disgusted, I toss it and wipe my hands on my pants.

I've touched China.

The half-muffled gasoline engine is getting closer. Definitely not an M1A1 Abrams, I decide. More like Italian Armored Division 1946. Maybe I can hitch a ride to Palermo. All at once the approaching sound becomes a shuddering roar and I look up to see a boxy truck-looking contraption labor into the clearing. It wheels around, shifts into reverse, backs up to the rubbish pile and goes silent. Stepping out is a man in a straw hat. After stretching his back, he notices my presence and gives me a gape. I gape back. Yes there *is* a platinum, green-eyed, six-foot-four mutant standing in the garbage dump. And what do you intend to do about it?

After what seems a full minute of gaping, the farmer opens the tailgate of the truck and rakes out a mound of yuck. No groundcover. Finally he tosses his rake into the truck bed and, with one more uneasy glance at me, slams the tailgate. The truck hammers away.

Unexpected Encounters with Avenging Ghost of Environmental Responsibility and Edict.

To my surprise, just as the truck exits the clearing, another vehicle enters. This one is GM quiet. As I watch, Phoebe Sternbaum's Buick circles around to offer me the unlocked passenger door.

I climb in. What would you do?

The car begins to move. No one speaks. In the back seat, Ling is whispering to her make-up mirror. Phoebe stares straight ahead. As we approach the highway, she jerks her head toward the back seat and says, "*She* is make me come back here."

"I don't want to talk about it," I reply.

"I think you tell my daughter some crazy story," accuses Phoebe. "Now she no listen her own mother."

"How much did you pay for this car?" I inquire. "I think, too much. Somebody just make this Mexico."

"Which way we turn?" Phoebe asks glumly at the edge of the highway.

I point to the left. It's a direction. "We're driving all night," I tell her.

No one speaks for a good hundred kilometers. That's what makes them good. I spend the time imagining what I might attempt to do once in Beijing, assuming we eventually get there. A change of clothes would be nice, but I mean other than that. I don't think I've ever rescued anyone before. I think it begins with finding the person you're going to rescue, preferably without placing an ad in the paper.

I throw Phoebe a suspicious gaze. I'm not so sure this woman is capable of connecting me to the higher rungs of anyone's organized crime ladder. Her rung may in fact have more to do with schoolyard cigarette extortion than influencing heads of state. But my only other option is to throw myself at the feet of Ralpho and hope he knows more about China's power elite than about their moon bases.

Phoebe stops the Buick at the lone pump of a rural gas station and opens her door.

"Buy some snacks," I tell her gruffly. "We're not stopping for dinner."

Phoebe slams the door.

As an attendant fills the tank, I survey the parking lot. No silver Toyotas in sight. I turn to glance at Ling, napping in the back, her tiny head resting against the car door. I try to picture this five-year-old convincing her mother to return to a garbage dump for a foreign devil who sits on little girls' heads. Suddenly Ling's eyelids roll up, displaying the whites. They seem to be looking straight through me. Shuddering, I turn away.

The attendant has finished filling the tank. Where's Phoebe? Irritably I survey the parking lot once more. My heart stops. Now pulling into the station is a delivery truck. Very large. Very orange. Very seafood.

Panting, I search in every direction for a silver Toyota. None in sight. A moment later, Phoebe returns, smiling, a plastic shopping bag in her hand. "We have a problem," I announce when she opens the door.

Phoebe gives me a wary frown. "You start this again? Next you tell me some silver—"

"I need to drive."

"You no drive my car again."

"Fine. Just hurry, okay?"

Phoebe's definition of hurry includes waking her daughter for a purple ice-cream snack in the form of someone's left ear. It's at least forever before we're back on the highway. I turn to check the road behind us, and *hello*. There's a silver Toyota attached to our rear bumper. The guy in the sunglasses is driving. In the passenger seat is Bellamy, his game face on.

"Uh, Phoebe, we need to find some help."

She eyes me nervously. "Ju? Why you—"

"Look in the rearview mirror."

"Who those men?" she asks.

"Not the Sisters of Divine Providence. We need a town. We need witnesses, as many as possible."

"Don't know nothing witness Jiangxi Province," she replies irritably.

The Toyota appears at our left, Bellamy's game face inches from Phoebe's nose. At this sight, Phoebe screams and panic-stops, whipping the wheel first one direction then the other. After a spin and a half, the Buick rocks to a stop in the exact middle of the highway, pointed in the opposite direction.

"Go! Go!" I yell, and Phoebe applies the gas.

By the time the Toyota accomplishes a one-eighty, we're nearly back to the filling station. I instruct her to hang a right onto a two-lane road that seems to promise the beginnings of a village.

"*Who* those men?" she demands.

"Just drive," I answer. "Whatever you do, don't stop."

Behind us, the Toyota is burning rubber. Bellamy, it would appear, has no intention of losing us again. We round a curve, and I spot a two-story building with a big red flag out front.

I love flags.

"Stop here," I order, as the Toyota re-attaches to our bumper.

"You tell me no stop," wails Phoebe.

"Stop, stop, *stop*!"

Phoebe brakes so hard the Toyota has to veer around us. When the Buick comes to a halt, there are two smoking tires on the sidewalk. I grab Ling from the back seat. "Inside, quick!"

The three of us hurry into the glass doorway of a governmental office where a uniformed man is seated behind a desk. He gazes at us curiously.

"Tell him, uh—" I pant. "Tell him we need directions. Make up something."

Phoebe tidies her hair and laughs apologetically. I return to the door to look outside. Bellamy is opening the driver's door of the Buick and releasing the hood latch. As Phoebe babbles with the uniformed man, I watch Bellamy remove a wire from the engine of the Buick, close the hood and walk away. That can't be good. Bellamy is also carrying Phoebe's purse. That can't be very good either.

"Tell him we're going for a stroll," I instruct Phoebe. Before she can get the words out, I'm dragging her and Ling toward a door at the rear of the building. We burst through the door into a narrow alley.

"This way," I say, lifting Ling. We run along rough cobblestones.

"Where we go?" asks Phoebe.

"Away," I say, turning left then right along a maze of alleyways, suddenly finding ourselves at the edge of a canal. On the other side is a bamboo thicket and a cornfield.

"This way," I say, heading toward an arched footbridge.

As we cross and enter the bamboo thicket, a footpath follows a small brook along the edge of the cornfield.

We pick our way along the well-trodden path, passing branching side paths. Unable to carry Ling any farther, I set her down and take a look around. An almost unnoticeable footpath twists its way up a wooded hillside. "This way."

Minutes later, we are panting to a hillcrest overlooking a patchwork of small corn and vegetable plots. In one of them, a lone farmer, facing away, hoes fertilizer into a row of sprouts.

Phoebe throws herself to the ground with a sob. "My husband send those men kill me, kill everybody! Aaawwwgh!"

I glance at Ling, remarkably collected as she seats herself on a boulder.

"We're good," I tell Phoebe. "We're very good. We just need to find a ride to Beijing."

Phoebe shakes her head. "We need go back. I talk to Hah-row, explain everything."

"Back?" I say. "*Back?*"

"I tell Hah-row just some big mistake, I take you see countryside and everybody get some wrong idea."

"Phoebe. Focus. We've got to get to Beijing. Once we talk to your friends—"

"I not tell you something about this," she says, wiping her nose on a sleeve.

"You not tell me something about what?"

"Not tell you something about the friends Beijing."

"I think I feel it coming now."

"Those men not my friends. I meet them because my husband know."

I'm staring. "Your husband know?"

Phoebe begins to whine. "I think maybe I go there tell them he so *bad* to me, just forget about me go have some girlfriend, maybe they talk to him."

"But you told Harold—"

"I just tell Hah-row some lie," wails Phoebe. "Just some Chinese woman, nobody care about me."

I give Phoebe a minute to collect herself, trying meanwhile to construct what to say to her first. At length, I decide on, "Phoebe, there's a difference between having connections with the Triad and your *husband* having connections with the Triad, especially when you're making off with his daughter."

Phoebe, blowing her nose, nods.

"I'm glad you're getting this. What does your husband do, anyway?"

She honks again then throws a glance at Ling. "Businessman."

"What kind of businessman?"

"Is kind of businessman the wife don't ask him this."

That says a lot, actually. I watch the farmer hoe his dung for a while. Even if I somehow elude the various secret services vying with one another to hominy my grits, I conclude, I probably still get a Sicilian necktie courtesy of the Chinese Mafia. It's so unfair.

Phoebe wags her head. "Ju, I so sorry tell you some lie. I take you to bus station now. You can—"

"*Bus* station?" I explode. "*Bus* station? They're chasing us with rocket launchers and zip guns and you want to drop me at the *bus* station?"

"No, no," she says, "my husband just want his daughter. We go back Shenzhen, nobody bother you, I promise this."

She promise this.

"We can't go back to your car. They did something to the engine. And they've got your purse."

Phoebe's mouth opens. "My *purse!*" she squeals, collapsing once more in sobs.

Across the fields, the dung farmer pauses to lean on his hoe.

It's a situation. Lil in a concentration camp. Tree locked up in Shenzhen. Bellamy on his phone calling in bloodhounds and scatterguns. And Phoebe without her purse. Yet, looking at Ling sitting poised on her boulder, I can't quite find my agitation. Which is irritating. Puzzled, I study the child's placid features for a moment and suddenly—

Suddenly I think I know something. I think I know why the child's voice was so clear in my head. In the car I thought I'd heard her voice, but the words didn't come from her mouth. They were inside my head. I step a little closer to Ling. Her gaze is softly focused, as though upon an inner landscape. I soften my gaze, too.

"Ju, what we do now?" asks Phoebe, dabbing at her eyes.

I don't reply. I'm beginning to catch sight of a fine mist surrounding the little girl on the boulder. Almost . . . a glow.

"Ju?" says Phoebe, rising to dust herself. "What we do now?"

"We stay together," I reply, trying to probe my way into the mist that now seems to be fading. I re-adjust my eyes, trying for just the right amount of unfocus. Another moment and I see nothing at all around Ling, who now says something in Mandarin. Her mother replies sharply. They continue for a moment, Phoebe increasingly vexed. I think they're discussing what my head might bring on the open market and whether they'd prefer large bills or small. Phoebe seems ready to settle for a TV dinner and a bicycle with a bell. Sighing, I turn away to watch the dung farmer. He stands gazing in our direction, leaning on his hoe.

"What you tell my daughter?" demands Phoebe.

"I didn't tell your daughter anything."

"You tell my daughter something. She say go with you. Crazy go anywhere with those men—" Phoebe shudders.

"She's right," I reply, studying the dung farmer now walking purposefully toward us, using his hoe as a walking stick.

"But don't *know* nobody Beijing," whines Phoebe.

"We'll figure something out when we get there," I say.

Or I think it was me.

Ling too watches the farmer's approach. She says matter-of-factly, "That man will help us."

49

The cicadas of dusk beginning their trill, Phoebe, Ling, and I follow a farmer named Yang along a pathway through tipping fields of sprouting corn and squash. At length we cross a plank footbridge over an irrigation ditch and enter a walled farmstead shaded by three immense ginkgoes. Inside, a few smallish pigs wander among chickens.

Washing his hands in a bucket, Yang calls out and a woman appears in a doorway. She is much like Yang, small and sturdy with a burnt-orange complexion and a thicket of graying hair. After a gape at me, she vanishes. Kitchen sounds commence.

Drying his hands on a worn towel, Yang smiles broadly, revealing two missing molars.

"He say," translates Phoebe, "we drink some beers before have the dinner."

I'll force myself.

Yang seats us at a wooden table in the courtyard. His wife appears with three brown longnecks. The bottles, capped with graying corks, are warm to the touch. Homebrew. Sharp on the tongue. I quickly drain mine, and a replacement appears. Ling abandons the table to range among the animals.

"He is tell me," Phoebe says of Farmer Yang, "he see you think you some kind of strange animal from the mountain. His eyes not so good, so look again, see you are Westerner. This make him feel very happy."

Yang smiles in seeming earnest.

"Can he help us get to Beijing?" I ask.

"Is not polite we talk about this now," replies Phoebe, her smile fixed. "Not so easy understand this man. In Jiangxi Province have the Kan dialect. So different."

I glance at Farmer Yang. Surely he must be curious. Phoebe has only told him that our car is broken and we need to get to Beijing. That we're in a spot of trouble, I think, speaks pretty well for itself. Thus far I'm surprised at the old man's readiness to invite total strangers into his home. Then again, his interest may turn out to be the TV dinner and the bicycle with the bell.

You may have heard the tale of the tigress who one day looked up to discover a very large creature standing nearby. The tigress had never seen such an animal. You and I would call it a donkey. The tigress circled ever closer, sniffing and watching, alert to any movement. The donkey only munched at the foliage. The tigress finally decided that the creature was a fool. She ate the donkey.

I *do* have an idea why that story comes to mind just now.

Night gathers. The cicada song thickens. Dinner smells erupt from the kitchen. Ling, comfortable among the chickens and piglets, squats with a stick to draw in the dirt. Beer number three arrives, and I study the relaxed face of Farmer Yang, eyes sparkling as he holds court amid his boughs and crumbling walls. I note that the wooden table where we drink is large enough to accommodate a large family.

The Chinese ideal is—or was, before Mao—four generations beneath one roof. Even now, the one-child policy is relaxed in the hinterlands where child labor is a necessity. I wonder why the Yangs' table is not surrounded by family. Halfway through beer number four, I ask. After Phoebe's timid translation, Yang replies at length.

"He say their son go work Harbin factory," reports Phoebe. "Their daughter go Shenzhen with husband, look for job, just live in some boat and hide in the trees. So many Jiangxi farmer go Shenzhen like this. Police find his daughter, make her have the—how you say? Not have the children?"

"She was sterilized?"

Phoebe nods. "They do this."

I gaze across the table at Yang, his face impassive.

The government uses the term *floating population* for the two hundred million out-of-pocket Chinese seeking something better. They aren't valued. In the US the homeless are a nuisance, in China a threat. Two hundred million people can bring a government down.

Farmer Yang says something to Phoebe.

"Yang say he always member of Communist Party, but now tell them, 'I am too old.' Really he is not want."

Mrs. Yang appears with course number one.

In very short order, I have demolished my serving of noodles and pork. A peppery chicken dish replaces it. I obliterate that, as well. Next is a fish-head soup, which I slurp down as noisily as possible. The Yangs seem quite pleased at my display. Finally we are served sliced and salted plums from the Yangs' own orchard. I leave nothing but the chopsticks. In fact, one of them seems to be missing a small section.

By the time I fall back in my chair, quite sated, the night is deep and an oil lantern is sputtering on the table. A chorus of crickets has overtaken the cicadas. Mrs. Yang, who has yet to take a seat at the table, let alone utter a word, now stands in the kitchen door, wiping her hands on a cloth and smiling. Her husband, drunk now, slams an empty bottle against the table and leans toward me.

"Yang say," Phoebe translates, blanching slightly, "he very hate the Party, very hate Mao Zedong. Mao only care about Mao, tell all the people some lies, kill everybody with some bad lies."

Yang, his eyes intense, seems to have waited quite some time to unload these sentiments. He speaks rapidly, and Phoebe struggles to keep up.

"Yang want tell you," says Phoebe, "when he is young, go to army, go Korea help fight Americans. He is believe the Party then, think Americans so bad, want kill some Americans.

He there for one year, so cold, just miss his family, not see any Americans. This make him very unhappy. He go somewhere alone, take his gun. After three or four days, he see some American soldier beside a river read a book. He kill this man. Nobody know he do this. Nobody is still know it. Only tell you."

Yang's face is flushed, but the two eyes remain soft and moist in the lantern light.

"Yang say he cannot sleep after do this," Phoebe goes on, "cannot eat the food, only feel so bad, so ask Guan Yin make this go away, but nothing work, so he say to Guan Yin, 'Give me chance help some American.' He think this cannot happen, wait fifty years, look up and see you on the hill, look like some strange animal. He cannot believe. Still cannot believe."

The farmer sits back in his chair with a sigh. His eyes close, and he massages them with the backs of his hands. Now he speaks to Phoebe.

"Yang say in the morning he take us to his brother. His brother have a truck, take us Anhui Province, see their uncle. The uncle help us go Beijing."

Phoebe's shoulders sag slightly in exhaustion.

Yang pops open a fresh bottle of homebrew and announces a toast.

"Yang say," reports Phoebe, "no more kill some stranger because somebody is tell you those people so bad."

Three bottles clink together in the glowing darkness. As I tip my head back, I take in the measureless and moonless sky. Or does it include me? *Beloved friends, promise me*, wrote Li Bai's brush on a night something like this one, *that we will forever dance, beyond all passion, and meet again far above the Milky Way.*

50

As we hammer across the broad Yangtze River into Anhui Province, Phoebe tells me about the recent sting operation that caught three hundred thousand Anhui civil servants
with their hands in the till. But what barrel is without its one
or two bad apples?

Phoebe has to lean toward me and shout this news over
the horrid *blat-blat-blat* of the truck engine. But there are
worse things than having Phoebe Sternbaum's face a few cen-
timeters from my own. I lean a little farther into that close-
ness, luxuriating in the sudden openness of this woman as
changeable as a puppy and with much better breath. Even better, we're lying close beside one another on a bed of straw,
Ling curled at our feet. Beneath our canvas tarp, we're unde-
tectable as we inch our way north, in tow behind what could
almost pass for a very old pick-up.

We reach the other side of the antiquated one-lane bridge,
and the road becomes an empty patchwork two-lane. Phoebe
and I celebrate by throwing aside the tarp that has concealed
us throughout the long morning, to revel in a springtime fantasy of pristine air, sky-reflecting rice paddies, and ranked
terraces of new wheat and budding yellow-green corn. Our
driver, the teenaged grandson of Yang's brother, whistles to
us through the glassless rear window of the truck and hands
back snacks prepared for us in the chilly pre-dawn. Leftovers
from last night's feast, they are wrapped in this morning's
griddlecakes.

"Is *so* good," sings Phoebe, "this food from countryside.
No find this kind of food anywhere. Is like I take you to coun-

tryside wedding, you learn so much real Chinese people of countryside always live the hard life but have *good* life. Why you always so worry, Ju? You see we get Beijing now, everything just good."

I try to smile. I'm not sure how to accomplish it. My mind is already in Beijing, where Lillian is going through God-knows-what.

Phoebe's face comes a little closer. "Ju, this so special moment. Look, look everywhere. You see?"

"I see."

I dreamed again of being back in Memphis. This time I was strolling naked on Beale Street. At least it was early morning. The only people around were street-sweepers, their heads down. I heard my sister's voice behind me and turned to see her trotting toward me in a jogging suit, her hands closed in little fists. The red chiffon dress was draped across her arm.

"You remembered," I said appreciatively.

I put on the dress. I'm starting to feel like one of the Chiffons.

"What seems to be the problem," asked Lil, "with getting me out of that concentration camp? Not that you've ever functioned very well on your own. Every day somebody new questions me, and every day it's someone creepier than before. Where's Tree?"

"I'm still working on—"

"Find her. And lose that deer-in-the-headlights expression, okay? It doesn't inspire confidence."

"Thanks so much for the confidence boost," I said, adjusting my shoulder strap. "That's going to come in handy when I take on Beijing single-handed. And I do *quite* well on my own. You were in Italy for six months, you'll remember, and I did perfectly fine."

"Three months," said Lil, "and you had to be institutionalized."

"It counts."

"You get your big ass up here and save me," said my sister. "Remember me? The one on the right?"

"I remember, Lil."

"And be careful. Something's stalking you."

"Exactly what is stalking me?"

"I don't know. I think it has to do with that whole catastrophe thing in Cetus. Find Tree. And get me *out* of that horrible place."

"I'm on it."

The last thing my sister said before jogging away toward First Street was that she and Adrian were taking a little break. "He wants some kind of commitment, and I'm like *I* don't know, man. He used to have a Bush sticker on his car. You can see where he tried to get it off."

Away jogged my sister, her white fists held high. I awoke with a renewed sense of responsibility and a yearning for something / anything slinky.

Now suddenly *blat-blat-blat* becomes *whackle-churf-bluff-thonk*, and the truck dies miserably at roadside. I watch Number One Grandson open the hood and stare at the engine as though he's never seen one before. I try handing him one of my two flip-phones, and he gives it the same stupefied look.

"We could have a problem," I mutter to Phoebe, returning the phone to my pocket.

Not that we were moving that much faster when we were moving. This truck has two forward gears, and they're both grannies. We're still a good three-hour hayride shy of Honorable Uncle, and here we are at roadside with the Barney Fife of emergency automotive repair.

As Barney and Phoebe discuss our options, which don't appear to be many, Ling squats at the edge of a roadside ditch, singing to herself and stirring the water with a twig. Joining her there, I notice that the water is alive with tadpoles. Ling's song seems to be for them. If I weren't so uncomfortably sober, I'd swear the tadpoles were drawing close to her, all but boiling in the water at her little feet. Strange. Even stranger, this doesn't surprise me.

Phoebe appears beside me. "We walk."

"We walk where?"

"Just walk," she says listlessly.

Moments later, Phoebe is leading the four of us toward whatever is next. I hope it turns out to be a Jacuzzi. Meanwhile, I'm enjoying the view, meaning Phoebe Sternbaum. I'm already growing nostalgic for our little hayride across the Yangtze, that pouty mouth so close to mine.

Actually I managed to do a little thinking during those morning hours. Maybe it was the clear country air, but during that time a matter previously vague/troubling became troubling/troubling. Having to do with a certain Beijing tourist attraction. The energy surrounding the Temple of Heaven, said Tree, was so overpoweringly twisted that she had nearly succumbed. Curiously, neither Lil nor I had had any trace of trouble with the place. In fact, now that I'm en route to Beijing, I feel practically *giddy* at the possibility of revisiting that park. I see, in particular, the three ornamented gates leading to the Circular Mound Altar, at its center the Heaven's Heart Stone.

There's something very peculiar about that place.

First of all, I never feel giddy. Secondly, if we even need a secondly, recent personal observations point out a growing problem with a certain *integer* not easily given to tables, chairs, nor the requirements of convenient music, an integer built into the Circular Mound Altar with a zeal bordering on psychosis, an integer that has no place in the Fibonacci sequence yet which *does* insinuate itself quite nicely between two Fibonacci numbers that may, if Xu knows anything, very succinctly describe this moment in time.

Before I can press on to thirdly, my thoughts are interrupted by the extended hiss of bald tires sledding to a stop. I look up to see a heavy flatbed truck rocking to a halt. Crammed into the cab are four men, each of them staring at me in astonished revulsion.

I glance down to make sure I'm not wearing the dress.

Dozens of other men, until now seated on the flatbed, rise to their feet and scramble to the nearer side to gawk, and the truck tips a little toward us. All the men are wearing the same outfit—white canvas coveralls with bold blue stripes. Convict labor.

Phoebe begins shouting questions to the driver, who doesn't seem to hear. Like all the others, he's still staring at me, mouth agape.

"How *is* everyone?" I shout, flashing two peace signs.

No one answers.

51

The truckload of felons decides they can't quite go on without us. Seating assignments are reordered, three of the convicts inside the cab clambering onto the roof, leaving spaces for Phoebe, Ling, and myself. Number One Grandson is tossed into the back like a suitcase. The rooftop felons now smile upside-down at us through the windows as the truck barrels north, all the others crowding forward to listen as Phoebe explains our situation, or some version thereof. If these men are stupefied by me, they are slain, slaughtered, and *skewered* by our Mrs. Sternbaum, whose vanity is rising admirably to the occasion. Ling, seated between the two of us, seems at home. Meanwhile, I try to arrange myself around a steel spring protruding through the seat.

Two things of minor note. First, concerning Chinese convict-labor attire, the stripes run vertically as opposed to horizontally as in the States. Thus a Chinese convict cannot impersonate his American equivalent without lying down. Second, the driver is wearing the very same outfit, meaning these men have no actual supervision.

"They take us almost Xuan Cheng," Phoebe informs me. "They not have permission ride somebody like us, so we get off outside Xuan Cheng."

"Tell me something," I reply. "Why isn't anybody watching these guys? Couldn't they all just run away?"

Phoebe is baffled by the question. "Run where? Have no papers, can't get the apartment, can't get the job, can't get nothing. Only somebody catch them, make them so sorry they do this."

I recognize the logic. Once government has made their ID mandatory for every action and transaction in life, you're utterly dependent on the pleasure of the state. The next step, as we all know, is to chip everyone. They push a button, your chip goes dead, and so do you.

This program is already underway in the States. Your passport has a chip in it.

I ask Phoebe what she told the driver about us.

"I just say we go visit somebody Hubei, have trouble with the truck. "

I lean closer. "You know, it's possible these men could help us. Think about it. They may have valuable contacts in Beijing."

"This whole truck," replies Phoebe, "is full of people get catch."

Valid point.

"Excuse me," says a voice from outside the passenger window.

I turn to see the smiling—sideways—face of a graying bespectacled man. His is one of four faces in that particular window.

"I'm sorry. I overheard your conversation," he says. "Please be careful what you say to the driver. He will tell the authorities anything he believes they may find useful."

I stare into the sideways face, struck by the intelligent eyes behind the cracked and scratched horn-rims.

"I am the only one here who speaks English," continues the convict, "so we can talk privately if you have some kind of problem. Some of these men have relatives nearby."

The driver barks some Mandarin at the bespectacled man, who answers briefly before telling us, "You should come to the point quickly."

Phoebe and I exchange a glance, and I turn back to the man. "We need to get to Beijing in a hurry without being noticed."

"Give me a minute," he says, disappearing.

The driver makes a sneering comment, and I ask for a translation.

"He say this man is always tell some kind of lie, just make the trouble," replies Phoebe.

I take a closer look at the driver. He looks like someone who'd have sex with your Chihuahua while you're in the bathroom brushing your teeth. When he turns to gawk at me, I give him a big grin and a wink. He is delighted. We laugh together like two old drinking buddies, and all the men around us cheer.

I survey the bright, eager faces filling every window of the cab. Aside from the driver, all these men seem quite innocent. Beijing doesn't divulge their numbers of incarcerated, but estimates run into the millions, probably a third of them political prisoners. All are forced to work. Mortality is high. The US complains about this regularly, to which the Chinese reply quite accurately that America leads the world in incarceration, specializing in the dark-skinned and poor.

The bespectacled face reappears. "In Xuan Cheng, look for Taxi 117. It is usually parked outside the museum. Tell the driver that his brother sent you."

"What museum?" I ask.

"You will see it on this highway."

Phoebe asks, "And what we can do for you?"

The man laughs in embarrassment. "I'm so sorry. I don't want to trouble you."

"Don't waste the time," she tells him.

The smile vanishes. "Perhaps it would be helpful if my family could hear some word from me. You could tell them that my health is good. You might also tell them"—he laughs to cover his embarrassment—"that I think of them very often."

"They don't let you talk to your family?" I ask.

"I am a special category of re-education," comes the reply. "In thirteen years, I have not been allowed to contact my family or a lawyer."

Thirteen years, I reflect, is a long time in modern Chinese politics. If he could get the attention of a lawyer, his case might well be reviewed.

The driver speaks sharply.

"I cannot give you my family's phone number," he tells us hurriedly, "or it will be overheard. Maybe if you have a pencil or—"

"Why were you arrested?" I interrupt, reaching into my pocket.

He blinks. "Someone gave my name. One of my students, I think. I was a professor at the time of the Tian—the big demonstration. You had to name someone, you see. You are beaten until you do. I named someone also."

I say to Phoebe, "Turn around and smile at the men."

She gives me a stare.

"Just do it," I tell her. "Turn around, knock on the glass, and wave."

Sighing, Phoebe turns in her seat.

"The other way," I correct her. "Toward the driver."

After chilling me with another stare, Phoebe turns toward the driver, brushing slightly against him. The truck almost leaves the road. Now she smiles and waves through the rear glass. All the men cheer wildly.

"It's very nice to meet you, Professor," I say, offering my hand.

With difficulty, he frees his right hand for a handshake. His face blanches when he feels the phone against his palm.

"You can use it one day only," I whisper, "then you must destroy it and get rid of all the pieces. Do you understand?"

After an uncertain moment, he closes his hand around the phone. The face vanishes from the window.

I stare straight ahead for a moment, inexplicably shaken. I'm no longer quite sure who I am. "Okay," I tell Phoebe. "That's enough."

"These men so *lonely*," says Phoebe as three dozen men try to climb through the window glass.

"Phoebe. That's enough."

The truck down-shifts at the base of a steep hill, and we snake our way up a heavily forested mountain. A rain shower appears from nowhere. The men outside shout happily in the momentary downpour, which leaves the air intoxicatingly rich.

"The driver tell me we need get out now, walk to Xuan Cheng," Phoebe reports when we reach the crest of the hill. Moments later, the truck is laboring away and all four of us are extending double peace signs. Every convict replies in kind, arms fully extended. When the truck shifts to second, a few of them almost tumble off the back of the truck.

"Damn," I say as the truck disappears, "that was almost cool."

"*So* hungry," Phoebe complains, walking away along the highway.

As we try to keep up with Phoebe, Number One Grandson speaks to her at length.

"He want find somebody come fix the truck now," Phoebe translates, "or somebody just steal it."

I reply, "Wish him the best of luck. We're looking for Taxi 117."

"Go Beijing in taxi so expensive?"

"Phoebe—" I begin.

"No talk about this now. My head hurt so bad."

No need to talk. Between the two of us we've enough colorful Chinese cash to ride in separate taxis, and we're spending it. Separate taxis could be exactly the ticket, now that I think about it.

As our group rounds the first curve, a large tile-roofed structure rolls into view. Perhaps this would be our mythical museum. No sign of Taxi 117. We come upon a sizeable parking lot, quite empty. At its entrance, Number One Grandson and Phoebe pause to talk things over. Ling says something into her mirror. I look about once more for Taxi 117. Somehow I've got to get at least one of us inside a northbound vehicle before night falls. Number One Grandson begins to walk away along the highway.

"He go find the town," says Phoebe, "find somebody fix the truck." Shading her eyes to survey the area, she says, "I think we get some food that place."

Phoebe begins striding across an overgrown meadow beyond which a couple of picnic tables are strewn near a dilapidated house. I take Ling's hand, and we follow a vague footpath among tiny blue wildflowers and throbbing insect song. The brief shower has awakened a plethora of scents, each bearing urgent messages that Ling, her head canted, seems to be browsing. Ahead of us, Phoebe approaches the dilapidated house and shouts for service. As we join her, an old woman comes jogging out of the house, tying on an apron. After a brief exchange, she hurries back inside.

"She make us some food and tea," says Phoebe listlessly, seating herself on a rough wooden bench. "I don't think taxi come here. This place just closed like everything else."

"What kind of museum is it?" I ask, gazing once more at the tile roof among the willows.

"Some famous history I think. We go Beijing tomorrow bus."

"We go Beijing now taxi," I reply.

"Ju, why you so *hurry*? Your sister is stay in good Beijing hospital. Chinese always take so good care Americans, everybody know this."

Our waitress returns, bearing tea. Ling complains that she wants a cola. When Phoebe disagrees, Ling collapses on the ground in a tantrum.

"My head almost blow up," cries Phoebe, gathering her exhausted daughter into her arms and rocking her.

By the time we're served a thin fish soup with green onions, Ling is asleep. Phoebe places her daughter down on a shaded spot of ground and returns to the table. "I feed her after nap. You see how tired everybody? Go Beijing tomorrow, don't tell me nothing."

I ignore her, eating on my feet, alert for any sign of a cruising taxi. Actually Phoebe could be right. That convict may have been locked up for twenty years. His brother could be working for Citibank by now. And with much of the country shut down by SARS, who knows?

The waitress reappears bearing foam plates of greasy fried rice and tough bits of pork. I manage to down half of it before tossing the plate onto the picnic table. "I'm taking a walk," I say, heading toward the overgrown meadow.

"Then we find hotel," Phoebe shouts after me.

I'm curiously curious about the museum beyond the meadow. The building is surrounded by willows that may enclose a garden at the rear. I walk in that direction and soon make out a lush garden among the willows, its centerpiece a finger of white granite pointing to the sky.

As I draw nearer the museum grounds, the finger of granite gradually takes the form of a man. At his feet is a thriving lily pond, its water circulated by a fountain. The wind seems to have caught the folds of the man's granite robe, which billows behind him like a sail as he gazes skyward.

Arriving at the water garden, I find that the two granite hands are clasped behind the figure. He is deep in thought. The white chest is arched forward and the chin lifted high, as though something in the heavens enchants the man. As I gaze at the upturned face, the noble tragic features, the thin mustache, I'm quite certain whose chiseled image awaits the next appearance of the moon.

"'Amidst these flowers,'" I whisper, "'a jug of wine. I pour myself the cup of aloneness . . .'"

How well I know this cup.

Engraved in the pink granite at the poet's feet is a stanza of verse, and I follow the strokes of each character with my eyes, imagining that I taste their meanings. For some reason, I don't startle when I hear the eruption of a rough Midwest voice behind me.

"You're late."

Without turning, I say, "What is *completion?*"

"It's what you're living for," answers Timothy Dobbins. "How's the kidney?"

"The left one's fine, thanks. What exactly is it I'm living for?"

"No ribs broken?" asks the leathery voice.

I turn to face the wrinkled man half hidden in the foliage. Tim Dobbins is seated on a camping stool. One long leg is crossed over the other. He's wearing the same safari hat as before; ditto the desert boots with checkered laces. A bulging daypack lies at Dobbins's feet. In his lap are three cell phones and a liter bottle of drinking water, half gone.

"How did you know I was coming here?" I ask.

"I know a few things."

"*I* didn't know I was coming here."

Dobbins smiles. "Good. You're finally starting to get it." He gathers up the three phones. "There's a car waiting less than a kilometer from here. We have to walk."

"I know about the Temple of Heaven," I say.

Dobbins stops gathering. He sits back in the chair, his eyes fixed on mine.

"I knew the moment I walked into that place," I tell him. "It's just taken a while to sink in. There's a built-in trip wire that senses the position of the sun. It was set to activate last March third. You're using the Circular Mound Altar to hack into the Fibonacci sequence."

"Am I?"

"You're using the nines to hack in between the Eight and the Thirteen."

I step closer to peer into the cold green eyes. "And I know about the others. The other little Dobbinses now headed this way. You trip-wired us, too, didn't you? Installed something in us that activates at that same moment? Only the Mancer twins came a bit early and got tangled up in your little depopulation program."

"Not my depopulation program," says Dobbins. "Forget all that now. SARS has run its course. The mutations have weakened it. Did you and Lillian show up earlier than I'd planned? Yes, and you imperiled a great deal beyond yourselves. The problem now," he says, checking his watch, "is that you're no longer early. You're very late."

"But *why?*" I say. "Why screw with Fibonacci? Why interrupt the pattern of evolution that has governed this planet for—"

"*Mis*governed," interrupts Dobbins. "The whole ecosystem here is about to go right over the edge, Julian, taking you and Lillian with it, along with every other bio-form worth having a conversation with, and you well know it. I can either let that happen, or I can do something about it. Look, once we're in the car, I'll explain everything. There's only one thing you need to understand right now."

Dobbins's face softens into something like a smile. "All of this is for *you*. Every single thing I've done has been for you and Lillian. And the others, of course. Here's my proposition. Take a ride with me, and I'll answer every question you ask. A plane is waiting in Shanghai. Once you've heard what I have to say, you can either get on that plane and begin your true work, or you can go your own way. But first, don't you owe it to yourself, to all of us, to listen?"

"Where is my sister?"

"I'm working on that. I'm working very hard on that."

"Where is she?"

"You know quite well where she is," says Dobbins. "She's in that medical menagerie north of Beijing, and every minute I waste sitting here could be better used getting her out."

Dobbins places both long feet on the earth and leans forward. "Julian, you've spent your whole life drifting without purpose, no real family, no match whatsoever between your gifts and the world around you. I know it's been hard. I've helped you as much as I dared. But all that is about to change.

I'm going to introduce you to your true family, your true purpose. A *brilliant* destiny awaits you, one absolutely perfectly matched to your gifts, a role that no one could possibly fulfill as well as you, Julian. This is the day you've been waiting for your whole life. All you have to do is ride and listen. Will you do that?"

Dobbins goes silent, sincerity pouring from his eyes. Either that or high thread-count cunning.

"And if I refuse?"

He shrugs. "You and your sister have been a rich surprise to me. Quite frankly, you bring qualities to the table that I never anticipated. But either you make it in, or you don't."

"In?" I say.

"Listen to me very carefully. In less than twenty-four hours, matters at hand will reach a crisis point beyond which there are absolutely no precedents. Things will either go very well or very, very wrong. Either way, you'll need to be beneath my protective wing. Unless you'd rather be one more dazed refugee picking through the rubble. Clear?"

"Why does the word *diabolical* keep occurring to me?"

Dobbins sighs. "We long ago passed the point of mild measures, Julian. I'm trying to change the trajectory of this planet in a way that enhances life, *advanced* forms of life, far more promising human life-forms than"—he sneers at the statue above us—"the current model."

With a groan, Dobbins rises. "Can you manage my bag with that sore kidney of yours?"

"First," I say, "help me get one thing straight."

"Make it quick."

I gaze into the serpentine eyes. "You designed me, right? In every detail? Wouldn't that mean you know me better than I know myself?"

Dobbins smiles resignedly. "It's true, Julian."

"Then how do you explain this?" I say, turning and walking away.

"Julian," says Dobbins. "Julian! You're wasting time that we don't have. There *is* a part of you that will fight to survive, against you if need be."

"Don't try following me," I say over my shoulder.

As I exit the garden, I hear ironic laughter behind me. "Why would I follow you?" shouts Dobbins. "I know exactly where you're going."

52

The driver's cruising speed is ninety, and that's not kilometers. Taxi 117 is a metallic-green Peugeot with electric seats and a not-bad sound system. The driver, Ma Tian Xi, looks quite regal at the controls, his dark hands on the leather-wrapped steering wheel. For the better part of the night, Ma has entertained us with stories of his life and that of his family, Phoebe serving as translator.

When he's not piloting Taxi 117, Ma is busy in his family's plum, fig, and apricot orchards on the small farmstead where six generations of Mas have cultivated the land. Since the economic reforms of 1989, there's been a steady income from the orchards, enough for Ma Tian Xi to afford the Peugeot and a taxi license. Not that he really required an additional income stream, but Ma had found himself with a little time on his hands. He now relishes every opportunity to ferry locals to nearby Lu'an and, farther down the road, metropolitan Heifei. He is even willing, we learn, to make the occasional all-night drive to Beijing.

Ma's younger brother, he has told us, is a scant year into a twenty-year sentence for murder. The brother, Ma Tan Shou, had been a carefree bachelor who operated a successful Korean barbeque restaurant in Xuan Cheng, providing hearty lunch portions for all who came, and many did. Tan Shou always closed shop at five sharp to wash up and spend his evening at a bordello outside of town. As often happens in such cases, Tan Shou developed a special affection for one of the ladies there, and it came to be understood that she was to be his companion whenever he called. Tan Shou was also a lover of cards, unfortunately, and one night he made the mistake of winning a lot of money from a particularly bad-tempered local bureaucrat. That man took his revenge by buying the aforementioned woman's services for an evening and beating her rather badly.

Everyone in town heard about this atrocity and wondered what Tan Shou's response would be. Wisely, Tan Shou controlled his rage. After a few weeks had passed without retaliation, the bureaucrat decided that he was untouchable. He presented himself at Tan Shou's restaurant to gloat, ordering Tan Shou around like a house servant. That, our driver told us, shaking his head, was a mistake. His brother, like all men, has a limit. Tan Shou poisoned that man. The bureaucrat died a horrible death in front of everyone, crawling out into the middle of the street to expire in grotesque convulsions. Everyone in the town had hated that awful man and completely loved the restaurateur, so he received the lightest sentence possible.

If Tan Shou can manage to survive nineteen more years of labor, the driver told us, he can return home at the age of sixty-three and spend his final years in peace. With this, Ma went silent. A bit stunned, Phoebe asked whether the brother's girlfriend was waiting for him, and Ma sucked his teeth.

That's a very sad part of the story, he said. The day after Tan Shou went to prison, she took down her clothesline and hanged herself. They found her with clothes pins all around her pretty face. Everyone in town contributed money for the funeral. It was the nicest funeral anyone could remember, said our driver, nodding.

Such terrible news, said Phoebe, to find out in prison. Oh, said the driver, no one has told him. We don't want him to lose hope. Every time Ma visits the prison, his brother asks about her, and every time Ma says she is well and waiting for him.

Ma sucked his teeth again and said, if his brother does survive his prison sentence, he, Ma, will certainly never eat at his restaurant again. Too risky. And that's a real pity, he concluded, turning to give us a sincere gaze, because no one does Korean barbeque better than his brother.

After that story, Phoebe lost interest in translating. She passed most of the night curled up in the back with Ling. Undeterred, Ma continued to regale me with stories—quite interesting ones, I imagine—knowing quite well that I didn't understand a word. For many men, driving and talking are one and the same. If we could get them to admit it, they talk when driving alone. Finally, the car was silent.

The final hours of night pass in a soft blur. I lose track of time and space. I actually doze off for a minute and awake with a start. I just had a dream in which a wide-eyed Lillian lay strapped to a gurney, a nurse looming over her with a huge syringe.

My heart pounding, I demand of Ma how soon we'll be in Beijing.

He points through the windshield and says, "Beijing."

"Beijing?"

I gaze through the windshield but see only traces of traffic along an anonymous four-lane. Grayish light is gathering at the edge of the sky, but there's nothing to illuminate but the occasional unlit gas station. Phoebe stirs in the back seat and struggles to sit up. Stiffly I turn to her and say, "We're there."

"Bathroom," she replies blearily.

"Did you hear me? We're in Beijing."

At length, Ma finds us a gas station that's open. He fills the tank and we all drink colas to open our eyes.

"Tell Ma he's dropping us at Peking University," I tell Phoebe when we're back in the taxi. "I'll find a hotel room for you and Ling near the East Gate. I have to go take care of a couple of things."

"Why we go university?" she asks.

"It's the only part of town I know."

When our taxi penetrates Fifth Ring Road, I begin to understand why reporters are describing this city as a ghost town. At dawn, the merest scattering of cars and delivery trucks dart along broad thoroughfares. Even inside Fourth Ring Road, streets are dead and buildings plastered with notices. It certainly appears that most, if not all, Beijing hotels are closed. Finally, near the East Gate of Beijing U., we find an open hotel, its lobby brimming with frustrated businessmen in need of a room. In their green surgical masks, the desk clerks are unyielding.

Phoebe tells me, "They say everybody go to hospital for examination, maybe four five hours, get certificate of health. Nobody want do this. I no want do this too."

I pull her toward the exit. If there's anything likely to kill you outright right now, it's spending half a day at an overrun Beijing hospital.

We enter the crowded lobby of a second hotel. Same frustrated hordes. Same story. No certificate, no room. I check the key display behind the desk. Some two dozen electronic keys are hanging there. "Let's go," I say.

I tell Phoebe to instruct Ma to find us a funkier hotel, preferably one unauthorized to serve foreigners. Ma replies that he can't remain in Beijing much longer, as his license isn't valid here. We encounter a multi-story hotel with rusting fire escapes and a faded plastic sign, and I say, "Here."

"Ma say he can't wait," reports Phoebe as the taxi stops.

"Fine," I say. "Ask him how much."

As Phoebe negotiates, I drag a sleepy Ling from the backseat. Next thing I know, Phoebe, Ling, and I are standing on the sidewalk and Taxi 117 is disappearing down the street.

"What happened?" I ask.

"He no want money," says Phoebe. "Just laugh."

"Just laugh? What did he say?"

"Chinese expression," she replies, trying to arrange her hair. "Is better talk like duck than just give some old shoe. We go inside."

Mechanically I follow Phoebe and Ling into a small lobby. This is a zero star hotel, but the lobby is filled with men, many of them shouting at the two grim-faced desk clerks. Even here, it's no health certificate, no room. Phoebe looks at me wearily. Most of the rooms are empty, I note, scanning the key display behind the desk. The keys are the old-fashioned metal kind, and all the available rooms are located on the upper floors.

"Follow me," I say.

In the general bedlam, no one notices that Phoebe, Ling, and I exit the lobby by means of the carpeted stairs.

"Ju? What we do?" says Phoebe.

"We're checking in."

We're all panting by the time we arrive on the fifth and topmost floor of the hotel. The air is stale. I lead the way to the room farthest from the stairs. Good, I think, examining the lock. Room 513 has been jimmied on more than one occasion.

I go through my wallet. There's nothing remotely resembling a credit card. I recall that Phoebe has none, either, my having deposited them in a post box. Now my hands come across something. It is a glossy image of Guan Yin, Goddess of Mercy and Illegal Hotel Room Entries. *Is for make the miracle*, I was told at Lijiang train station. *Or maybe just don't do nothing*. The card is very worn now, the inner metal core exposed at one edge.

I insert the card between the door and the frame and try to slide it past the lock. Nothing.

"*Shit*," mutters Phoebe, looking nervously up and down the empty corridor.

"You can relax," I tell her. "There's no one on this floor or the floor below us."

I try again, this time simultaneously rattling the loose knob. The lock pops open. The door falls opens with a dry groan. We three gaze into a dismal but tidy room. An ancient window air-conditioner. Two double beds. A roach electrocution device. No settee by the window. It'll do.

Ling runs past her mother to leap onto one of the beds. She doesn't even bounce once. Phoebe still stands worriedly in the hall. I pull her inside and close the door.

"Keep the door bolted," I say to her. "Keep the curtains closed. Don't go anywhere and, for God's sake, don't call anybody. Take this money. I'll be back after I take care of—"

"You not coming back," says Phoebe, turning away.

"I'll be back."

"You not coming back," she says again.

"Fine. Have it your way." I place a stack of banknotes on the bureau. "If I'm not here by nightfall, wait as long as you can, then—"

Phoebe grabs the money and flings it into my face. "You just want get *Beijing*," she shouts. "Now you Beijing, leave me, leave my daughter, don't even care what happen."

"Could you possibly say that a little louder?"

Phoebe hisses something in street Cantonese.

"Whatever," I say, bending to pick up the cash.

Now she's kicking at me. "Just like my husband!" accuses Phoebe, still kicking. "Just like *all* the men, lie me, lie my daughter, lie everybody."

Ling, sprawled on the bed, begins singing to the ceiling.

I decide to leave the money where it lies. Backing toward the door, I see Phoebe fall onto the other bed, sobbing. I glance at Ling. She's still singing. She's also holding a scrap of paper in her hand, holding it out toward me. I walk to her and take the worn, folded piece of paper from her hand. Opening it, I discover several handwritten Chinese characters. I've seen this note before.

"Ling?" I ask. "What does this say?"

She doesn't answer. Now I recall that Ling is a preschooler. "Phoebe? What does this say?"

She's too busy sobbing.

"Phoebe."

Still crying, Phoebe snatches the note from my hand and gives it a look before tossing it. "Just say please help this person so much."

I bend to recover the scrap of paper. It's all coming back to me now. Again I see the smiling young couple in the Beijing moonlight, the pretty face with the determined expression, a law student with a passion for women's issues. *This shelter begin help all the women children of the abuse.* I'm watching a delicate hand scrawl a note of introduction for me, a note that I've never quite brought myself to throw away.

"Where did you find this?" I ask Ling.

"In the hall," she says to the ceiling.

I pat my pocket to make sure my titanium-covered journal is still there.

"Okay, change of plans," I announce. "Phoebe, I want you and Ling to go to the university lunchroom today with this note and ask for this woman."

Phoebe, blowing her nose, doesn't respond.

"Are you listening? There's a girl who works at the lunchroom. I want you to give her this note and tell her about your problem."

Phoebe turns to face me. "Lunchroom girl? How some—"

"Just give her the note, okay? If you won't listen to me, listen to your daughter."

Phoebe glares at me. "Why my daughter know something you no tell me?"

"I didn't tell your daughter anything."

"Then how she know?"

I shrug. We both turn to gaze at the five-year-old on the bed singing softly to the ceiling.

Phoebe shakes her head. "Sometimes this girl worry me so much."

I hold the note out to Phoebe, and she stares at it.

"I take this," she says, "you not come back."

"That could actually be a good thing," I say. "A lot of people are looking for me. Sooner or later they'll find me."

I set the note on top of the TV. With a sigh, I step over the multi-colored bank notes and open the door. Before I can close it behind me, I hear Phoebe's sullen voice.

"Trouble," she says. "When I first see you, I know this."

I take one last look at Ling, her plastic make-up mirror in her hand. I'd thank her. I'd thank both of them if I only knew what for. Reluctantly, I close the door behind me.

53

This zero-star hotel has only one exit. Fortunately the lobby is too chaotic for anyone to notice me descend the stairs and slip out the double doors.

On the sidewalk I stretch out my stride, putting as much space as possible between myself and a certain woman and her daughter. That's the better part of the current plan.

In fact it may be the entire current plan. The only other thing that occurs just now is the one most likely to get me tied to a chair somewhere. That would be appearing at the razor wire-swathed gate of the Peoples' Beijing SARS Treatment and Quarantine Hospital with an earnest expression and a nice bouquet.

Actually there is one other idea that occurs, but I'm determined not to acknowledge it. The Temple of Heaven Park and its Circular Mound Altar are so close now they're speaking to me with each step. Not that I'm listening. I've half a mind to show up at that Irish bar on Third Ring Road, assuming it would be open at this, or any other, hour. Not that Ralph O'Malley would likely constitute much in the way of substantive aid, but I don't know anyone else in Beijing.

As for now, I'd feel considerably less conspicuous inside a taxi, whatever its destination, if only this broad, empty thoroughfare offered one. I think I'm reasonably near a subway station. Reaching an intersection, I peer in each direction, distracted somewhat by a persistent tinny screeching approximating the human voice. Finally turning to glare in the direction of the sound, I encounter a most unwelcome sight. A singing condom machine. Half-panicked, I scan the streets for additional troubling signs. I find them.

Strung along the sidewalk are three women beneath three parasols. Five, no, but we take what we can get nowadays. Beyond all possible doubt, mere seconds from now, those women's steps will fall into perfect sync and I will vanish into the maw of a room with neither a view nor room service.

I dash into the nearest shelter, the open door of a shop. It turns out to be an herbal pharmacy, a crowd of women pressing against a counter behind which white-clad pharmacists scoop medicinal herbs onto old-fashioned scales. I pretend to read a poster on the wall, a government-issued one that goes into some detail about how, in a moment of madness, one might wash one's hands. I study it for a full minute, hoping that the incoming *penetration* might find someone else to skewer, the last thing I'm needing right now being a fresh complication.

Finally, timidly, I peek outside the door. The street is relatively normal, all except for one thing. As my eyes tip up, I notice that the multi-story building across the broad avenue is topped by a series of red plastic Chinese characters, each erected on a rusting balustrade. The penultimate character is missing, and I stare at this display with some displeasure. *Déjà vu* was never very high on my list of favorite things. In most instances, the event wasn't all that much fun the first time around. Yet I've no question that I have looked upon exactly this sight before. I believe it had something to do with a very menacing red toadstool and a room composed of eyeballs and not a whole lot else.

There's nothing to do, I decide, but follow the rabbit. My eyes still on the too-familiar rooftop, I exit the pharmacy and trace the sidewalk in a direction that would provide the remembered angle of view. This requires turning a corner, then another, which places me on a quite narrow street with no view of the building at all. Still, the angle should be more or less correct now. I begin backing across the street, and a truck, horn blaring, nearly runs me down. As the truck barrels away, I note that it is an orange seafood-delivery truck. License tag 999-

333. I turn to examine the nearby street number. The nearest doorway is ninety-nine.

That's so nice.

Crossing the street, I tiptoe in vain. Were I a couple of floors higher, I think I'd be gazing at that storm-damaged rooftop from roughly the same perspective as I recall. Turning, I discover that I'm standing beneath a broad third-story balcony, perhaps that of an apartment, judging from the draped ferns. The anonymous building offers no other balconies, just the one. That's a bit odd. In Chinese cities, it tends to be either hundreds of apartments or none at all. Someone of means, it seems, has created a solitary domicile above a street of anonymous offices and warehouses. My curiosity piqued, I drop my gaze to street level. Directly beneath the balcony and its ferns is a steel door with neither buzzer nor intercom.

I look about the street for pebbles to toss. Nothing. Backing up a bit, I see that one of the sliding glass doors of the apartment is open. I consider shouting something, but what exactly does one shout? *Hello in the apartment? Throw down the chocolate? Ever occupied while stabling?* Cupping my hands, I call out the only words likely to stir a response, the words once shouted at me during a too-close encounter, not that I've a clue what they may signify.

"We are the Hydra!"

No reply. After a long moment, I shout again, more insistently, "*We* are the Hydra!"

Still nothing. I glance nervously up and down the street. All is cemetery still. I let a full minute pass before cupping my hands, taking a deep breath, and shouting, "We are the Hydra! Couldn't be prouder! If you can't hear us, we'll yell a little louder! WE ARE THE—"

The steel door below the balcony motors slowly open. Once fully open, it stops and I gaze inside a tiny foyer containing only a metal ashtray attached to a wall, above it a wordless no-smoking sign.

A bit nervously, I step inside and the steel door motors closed behind me. An elevator begins to descend noisily. While I await its arrival, I look about for some clue as to where I am. There's nothing to see. I check inside the ashtray. No sign that it's ever been used.

The door of the elevator opens. I step inside. There's no button to push. The door closes on its own, and the elevator ascends to what seems to be the third floor. I watch the door open upon a cluttered room that doesn't quite qualify as either apartment or office. Clearly someone spends a lot of time here. I'm gazing into a large, unkempt workspace with a broad balcony dotted by potted ferns—beyond which is exactly, precisely the view I recall.

I step inside the room. The elevator door closes behind me.

Separating the workspace from the balcony is a wall of glass and two tripod-mounted telescopes aimed at the heavens. I also take note of a row of ceramic pots, some of them bearing a low-growing cacti fully appearing to be *lophophora williamsi*, better known as peyote. Several other pots offer fully mature marijuana plants, and my eyes admire the heavy, drooping buds. Now I notice a cluster of small aquariums in a dark corner of the room, each bristling with variously hued mushrooms. I ask myself whether I might arrange to sublet.

Along every wall of this room are shelf after shelf of books and beneath them worktables bearing new and old computers and countless sticky notes, some of them faded. There's also a scanner, a laser printer, a microscope, an electron microscope, and a tray of dried mushrooms. Various messy notebooks lie open. An overfull trash can is surrounded by paper wads.

Aside from the bookshelves, nothing at all adorns the walls of this anomalous space with the exception of a single publicity poster proffering the words, "*A Room of Eyes*, by Bi Yu Nu." I step closer to study the poster and its illustration of an all-enclosing wall of eyeballs. Somehow I manage not to shudder.

"How did you find me?"

I turn to face a doorway where an elderly Chinese man sits in a wheelchair. Despite the deep lines of the pallid face, the man is robust. His most arresting feature is the matching pair of almond-shaped eyes, shockingly large and bright with a sickly yellow.

"That," I reply, gesturing toward the view beyond the balcony.

"That?" says the man.

"The view," I say. "I've seen it before."

Using his large hands to maneuver the wheelchair to the center of the room, the man stares at me, unblinking. There are green flecks in the enormous eyes. I was wrong about the color. Not a sickly yellow, they're a dull gold.

"Ah," says the man. "You were lying on a bed in a dark room. You were protecting your right arm. Before you ran away, you saw something and now that something has brought you here. Amazing." He rolls a little closer. "Positively amazing."

"You're Bi Yu Nu," I say.

The old man scowls. "My name is the least important thing you could possibly be asking me right now."

"You're right. Would you have a spot of English gin? Never mind. I don't drink."

"I know you're one of them," says Bi harshly. "Do *you* know you're one of them?"

I look around. There are no chairs in the room. I lean against one of the worktables and reply, "My name is Julian. Thanks for asking. And that's okay, I prefer to stand. One of whom?"

"The reason I know," he continues, "is because I am repelled by you. Aren't you by me? You can be completely honest."

"If we're being completely honest," I say, "you could use a housekeeper. And I've no interest in you at all."

"Did you learn nothing at all in the Room of Eyes?"

"I learned to never again eat the whole mushroom. I think I may have also stumbled onto an interstellar neural network, if that's what you're gesturing toward."

Bi nods slowly, measuring me. "That's how they found this place, you know. This planet? They found it through that network."

"Who's they?"

"Whose name were you shouting on the street a moment ago?"

"The Hydra?" I say. "That's a mythical creature from very long ago and therefore not on my current list of worries."

"The Hydrae, plural," replies Bi, "is a nomadic hominoid race from elsewhere in this galaxy. They are obsessive colonizers and interbreeders. The story of Hercules and the Hydra arose from early encounters between our race and theirs. They come in pods of nine. Thus, the nine heads of the Hydra. Now you're going to ask me *why* they are obsessive colonizers and interbreeders."

"Not really, but you go ahead."

Bi seems to warm to the subject. "The Hydrae are exquisitely murderous by nature, specializing in their own family members. It seems to be the pheromones that set them off. The more identical the genetics, the more agitated they become. You know the story of Cain and Abel? Hercules's murder of his family? Those aren't just stories."

Bi and I share a gaze. "So the Hydrae's only means of averting extinction," I venture, "is to put as much space among themselves as possible? That's why they're colonizers?"

Bi nods. "As soon as a healthy male reaches adulthood, he's sent away as part of a nine-pod composed of as dissimilar genetics as possible, making it less likely that they'll tear each other to pieces before their work is accomplished. That work is interbreeding, crossing themselves again and again with more docile hominoids wherever they find them."

"I gather their success here has been somewhat mixed."

"There's been some progress. Genocide is slowly giving way to domestic battery. The Hydrae seem to be reasonably encouraged. They return here every few thousand years to tweak the genetics." Bi rolls his chair a little closer. "Did you know your father?"

When I don't reply, Bi smiles icily. "Oh, I'm sorry. I see the question disturbs you."

"I'm already disturbed, thanks. You're telling me the human race is directly descended from the Hydrae?"

Bi shakes his head. "Our planet was originally seeded by a far older civilization. They come around every so often, too, but not often enough I'm afraid. Other civilizations have stepped in and made a hash of things, none more so than the Hydrae."

I give Bi a cool gaze. "No, I didn't know my father. What of it?"

"Do you have unusually high intelligence?" he fires back. "Let me guess. Your IQ is off the charts, you've never been sick a day in your life, and you're a bit telepathic. Or maybe a lot telepathic?"

When I don't reply, Bi smiles chillingly. "I don't suppose you're ever drawn to the occasional little *taste* of violence?"

"Only against myself," I reply. "As for the rest, how did you know?"

The unblinking gold eyes gauge me carefully. "Are you telling me that you are not given to unprovoked acts of violence?"

"Sorry. Actually I'm experiencing a sister problem, and I wondered if—"

"You have a sister?" interrupts Bi, "and you haven't killed her?"

"I gave her a hickey once, but she really deserved it. And this may be the strangest conversation I've ever had."

"You're mocking me?" whispers the man in the wheelchair. He begins to tremble, his face flushing. Bi seems to double in size. All at once, it appears inescapable that he will either launch himself at my jugular or fall dead at my feet. Finally Bi's breath catches and he falls back in his chair, wheezing. As he fights to regain his composure, I ask myself how close I just came to annihilation at the hands of a crippled senior citizen with a row of *really* nice pot plants. I also wonder how he knows so much about me.

"Your sister," pants Bi, wiping a tear from an iridescent eye. "Is she younger or older?"

"Yes," I reply. "We're twins. And I think I should probably be going."

"Twins?" gasps Bi, rolling closer still. "You said twins? And you're both alive?"

I back away from the wheelchair, which appears very close to creasing at least one of my feet. "Uh, you seem to know quite enough about me already, if you—"

"*We* are the Hydrae. You and I. Your sister, as well."

With a little leap, I flee to the other side of the room, and Bi turns his chair to face me. "I was one of three brothers. We never knew our father. Not a word was ever spoken about him. When my older brother was twelve, he lost his temper and killed our mother then himself. My younger brother and I weren't present, or I'm sure he'd have killed us as well. Shortly thereafter, my surviving brother and I fell very ill. Poisoned, I believe. Culled by the Hydrae as failed genotypes. My brother died. I survived to be passed from one relative to another. Finally I was placed with a wealthy family with the resources to deal with a very sick child. The Hydrae lost my trail."

Bi looks up at me. "My privileged circumstances have meant unlimited access to books and tutors. I've used those resources to help me understand what happened to my family and what could still happen to my new adoptive one. I'm not so different from my older brother, you know. I, too, am capable of murder." Here he almost giggles. "I think I might like it, actually. So I determined that it would never happen. Never. As soon as my writing income allowed, I left my adopted family and assumed a series of false identities, moving frequently, all the while continuing my research, looking into myth and history and archetype and ancient architecture, unearthing all I could about these . . . " Bi's gaze flickers. "About these monsters we are."

"You're telling me that you are a failed genetic experiment among extraterrestrials?" I say. "And that I am a more current one?"

"Everything here is extraterrestrial," growls Bi. "Even the planet itself. What is a planet but a coagulation of interstellar gases and minerals caught up in the orbit of a newborn star? After the initial coagulation, other foreign things—meteors, asteroids, bits of emerging life—are attracted. Much later, more advanced forms of life come along. But it all begins somewhere else, don't you see? Every bit of it."

"Is there a nine-pod of Hydrae on Earth now?" I ask.

Before answering, Bi slumps in his wheelchair, exhausted by his recent rage. "They've been here for some time. I think they're near the end of their lifespan, perhaps down to a lone survivor. I'm fairly certain they arrived here six to eight hundred years ago, here in China, and established deep political connections in Beijing. I think they're still here, what remains of them."

Bi stares at me for a moment. I fear that he's going to tell me something I don't wish to learn.

"I think they're desperate," he continues. "Once there's only one remaining pod member, that survivor must posit his DNA somewhere, must keep it going by any means possible. It's their most compelling racial imperative. It's a madness, really. That's why the ninth head of the Hydra is said to never die but remain lodged beneath a rock somewhere." Bi smiles icily. "Earth, in the present instance."

For a moment I ponder this thing *compelling racial imperative* and ask myself to what extent I myself am operating on compulsion and, if so, whose? I keep telling myself I've no idea what my next move will be. And yet it really couldn't be much clearer where I'm going. Finally I come out with the question that's been gnawing at the edges of my awareness. "What can you tell me about the Circular Mound Altar?"

Bi's eyes brighten. "At the Temple of Heaven Park? Why would you ask me about that?"

"I seem to be headed there. Not that I've decided to go. I'm not sure when I last decided anything, to tell you the truth. That place means nothing to me. Yet I can scarcely close my eyes without seeing it. And when I look back on the past three or four days, I don't know how I could be beating a path there any faster."

Neither of us speaks for a moment. Unwilling to gaze into the unblinking yellow eyes, I look through the window-glass at the cityscape that so improbably and unfailingly delivered me to this singular conversation. I've held fast to the belief that my mad dash to Beijing has been all about Lillian, about freeing her from that hospital from hell—and of course it is.

But freeing her for what exact purpose?

Finally Bi speaks again, his voice gravelly. "The truth about the Temple of Heaven is there for anyone to see. Just read the dedication. The temple is dedicated to 'The Supreme Ruler of the Universe' whose home is in the heavens. I've little doubt that the Hydrae themselves designed that altar as a way of re-invoking their dominion here. Think about it. The most exalted man in the world, the emperor himself, was required to go to that place three times yearly, humbly and on foot, and offer human sacrifices to the glorious ruler of the sky." Bi's mouth curls in disgust.

"It's more than that," I tell him. "That structure is composed entirely of materials selected for their piezoelectric signature."

Bi stares, transfixed, and I swallow hard. I've very little idea what I'm talking about.

"Very similar really to the paramagnetics and diamagnetics of the Great Pyramid of Giza. This focuses a very clear geometric signal into the bedrock below, in effect making of the entire planet an amplifier."

The gold eyes narrow. "You're telling me the Circular Mound Altar is focusing a signal into the Earth? What kind of signal?"

"A bad one. It's a Trojan Horse just about to whinny, and it seems to have something to do with me. Or I with it."

"Go, then," says Bi, "but you'll find it locked. The whole complex is closed indefinitely, supposedly because of SARS. But that doesn't quite explain the newly-installed razor wire or the thumbprint-reading device now placed at the main entrance."

Bi rolls his chair closer to me, close enough for me to see tiny flecks of red in the unblinking gold irises. "Maybe that means nothing. It certainly suggests the Hydrae have re-established their connections within the Beijing power elite. I've felt for some time that they're waiting for something. Some opportunity. Could it be that *you* are that opportunity?"

Bi wheels suddenly closer, using his chair to pin me against the wall. "Monster!" he snarls. "Fool! You think you can play with these creatures? You've no idea what you're up against. They're inside you, Julian!"

I struggle to free my legs from the wheelchair, but Bi grips my wrists with two powerful hands and yanks my face closer to his. I wince at his breath.

"It's not enough to look for them out there!" he snarls. "You have to start by finding them inside you. As I have my entire life!"

Pulling away, I stumble toward the elevator and push the button to open the door.

Bi wheels to point a trembling finger at my face. "You have a decision to make, Julian."

I dart inside the elevator. As the metal door begins to close, the man in the wheelchair sneers in my direction as though wishing me a truly unpleasant day. Just before the door closes, he whispers hoarsely, "Who is your family, Julian?"

54

Hurrying along the barren street, I tell myself that I'm walking toward the nearest subway station. It gives me a sense of purpose. I find that if I bounce on the balls of my feet, I can be just another guy on the street going about his truly unpleasant day. No intention at all of *lurching* to the Temple of Heaven Park with a glazed expression and a secret password that I don't know that I know.

That Bi Yu Nu interview was creepy. I did, though, like the touch about Lil and myself being galactically coveted on the basis of mutual amity. I'd say the world is getting stranger by the moment. Finally there's only the next step, the next breath, the next alarming oddity.

No sooner does this thought register than I see something no man should ever live to see: a red-bearded East Texan walking toward me with a sawed-off shotgun.

"Get down," says Ralpho, raising the barrel to the level of my chest.

I oblige, actually grabbing my head with both hands and collapsing onto the sidewalk with a sputtering wail. Immediately comes a horrendous *BOOM!* followed by the clatter of a spent shotgun shell falling quite near my head. Ralpho's scuffed boots stride past me.

Turning to look, I discover the crumpled and bloodied remains of a matronly Chinese woman gasping for breath. Beside her on the sidewalk is a pair of powder-blue cat's-eye glasses. Ralph O'Malley takes a decisive step back and fires another blast into the woman's body, which spasms violently then falls still.

"*What* in the name—?" I cry, crawling away from the bloody corpse.

Looking left and right, Ralpho slides two more shells into the magazine and says, "Who else is following you?"

"What?" I reply, dazed. "You want the whole list? Why did you kill Madam Wu?"

Ralpho's boot kicks something toward me. It's a stiletto.

"You were just about to receive a kidney donation," he says.

I grab both kidneys protectively. "Why would—" I begin. "Why should—"

Ralpho says, "I told you, Julian. There's a lot of people interested in you. Now that you're officially off the reservation, it's simpler all around to have you dead. Watch this."

Bending with a groan, Ralpho pulls at the woman's thick head of hair. It comes away in his hand, revealing a buzz cut over a scalp roughly as pale as my own. I'm looking at the head of a man, a Westerner and someone I have personally met. With a start, I recognize Barry Scribner, the Latter Day Charlestown attorney—or someone, it now occurs, who *pretended* to be.

Ralpho tosses the wig. "It's steady work keeping you alive, dude," he says, turning to stride away.

"Wait!" I cry. "No, never mind. Don't wait."

Stumbling to my feet, I hurry in the opposite direction. The next thing I know with any clarity, I've entered a subway station, passed through a dysfunctional infra-red temperature scanner, trotted down three flights of stairs, and huddled against the least conspicuous wall available. As I try to sort through my thoughts, a gathering rumble becomes a clattering burst of sound. A train slows to a stop. Mechanically I step onboard and claim a seat. The other passengers, most of them wearing surgical masks, eye me suspiciously. The current round of gossip seems to have Westerners once more at the head of the bad list.

Only gradually do I understand that this train is northbound, meaning I need to change trains only once to reach the northernmost end of the line. That would put me reasonably near Lillian's place of detainment. I guess that's my next move.

Now I'm walking dazedly through another near-empty station plastered with notices, most of them bearing the characters for "disinfected." I pass through one then another abandoned infra-red temperature scanner, their displays showing nothing but a throbbing string of nines. Every face I see stares accusingly, and I examine my hands and clothing to see whether I'm carrying any bits or pieces of Madam Wu. Or whoever that unfortunate cross-dresser was. I find no trace of her/him and for a moment I wonder whether I might have imagined the entire episode. And hopefully Bi Yu Nu's apartment before that. I have to dismiss the question. Were that the case, I'm imagining this train station, as well, which leaves me no place at all to stand.

The second northbound train dumps me, or fully appears to, at a small above-ground station where a lone attendant sits inside a glass booth. I hover near that booth, trying to formulate a means of asking directions—when I hear something arresting.

Arresting doesn't even say it. I turn a complete circle, trying to establish where a certain voice is issuing from. I'm reasonably certain that someone is speaking Mandarin with a West Tennessee accent and a strong dose of Lower Midtown attitude. I begin to walk, peering one way and another, increasingly aware of a voice that at some moments is an emphatic *purr*, sweet yet gritty like the honey at the mouth of the jar.

I approach a city bus stop, and the string of syrupy Mandarin words gives way to a spirited bar of "I Loves You, Porgy." I'm looking at the backside of Tree Carter, who is verbally engaged with a bus driver blocking the entrance to his bus. Still a bit dazed, I watch the driver secure the door then give Tree an imperious stare through the glass while wiping his hands on a cloth from his pocket. A moment later, the near-empty bus has whooshed away down the street.

Tree, alone at the bus stop, sighs loudly and says, "Leave unto Caesar what is Caesar's." She takes hold of the handle of her rolling suitcase. Turning, she finds herself looking straight at me.

"Did you say please?" I inquire.

Tree's mouth falls open.

"No hugs," I tell her.

"Oh my *God!*" exults Tree, abandoning the suitcase.

"I said no hgg*ghhhh—*"

Tree's embrace forces all the air out of me and damages a few additional ribs.

"My Julian, my *Julian!* I knew it, I knew it, I knew it! I knew we'd be put together somehow, and here you are."

Gasping, I say, "I don't suppose you can guarantee that I'm not imagining this?"

"Did you see that bus driver?" asks Tree. "Did you *see* that? Come on, let's find us a taxi."

"What exactly is the plan?" I ask, more or less knowing the answer.

Grabbing the handle of her suitcase, Tree sings, "We are committing our *foot* to the path, and the road shall appear beneath our feet."

"I was afraid that would be the plan."

As we scout for a taxi, I learn that Tree was picked up at her apartment by Shenzhen detectives shortly after our last meeting. "Didn't bother me," she says. "I knew that the forces of darkness would appear, and I knew that they would not prevail. Sure enough, two men came from the Consulate and told the po-lice they couldn't hold me one minute longer. Those kind-hearted men refused to leave without me, praise be to God. They even escorted me to the airport and put me on the plane, and I haven't had a single problem since."

Of course you haven't, comes the thought. They're using you to find me. "You're sure you aren't being followed?"

"Goodness and mercy shall follow me *all* the days of my life," trumpets Tree.

"Actually, I wasn't thinking about goodness and mercy."

As we circle the station in search of the inevitable line of taxis, I give Tree the short version of my story. I got a lift to Beijing from a friend whose organized-crime connections didn't quite connect.

"You were going to talk to the *Triad*?" asks Tree, trying not to laugh.

"I had planned," I reply irritably, "to *consult* with the Triad."

"You had planned to consult with the Triad," she repeats before surrendering to an extended sputter.

"I'm glad it makes you so happy," I say.

"Don't you get it? You *knew*, Jules. You knew all along that the answer is in the triadic. You just took it a little too literally, baby."

"Tree, not now."

She looks at me in surprise. "What do you mean, not now?"

"I mean, not now that whole wad of *goo*, okay? There is no triadic. All there is, is a very bad case of the nines, and I certainly hope you aren't going to gild *that* particular lily."

"You can still doubt it?" says Tree, amazed. "You can doubt that Spirit is at work here? After we just walked *straight* to each other in a city of thirteen million people?"

I look away.

"*Mighty* armies are arrayed around us, Julian Mancer!" thunders Tree in her radio voice.

"Got it," I say, noting a nearby policeman now turning to stare.

"*Mighty* forces of light and darkness are being brought to bear all around us!" shouts Tree. "It's coming to a head right here and right now, and you had better prepare your weapons. Are you *hearing* me, Julian Mancer? Are we communicating?"

"Wall to wall, dearest," I say, pulling Tree along.

"You need to understand something," she adds. "We are about to reunite with Lillian, and you need to be ready for that. You have no idea what the three of us can do when our intentions are aligned. All we have been waiting for all along, baby, is *you*. Waiting for Julian Mancer to finally come onboard, and I'm feeling that now. All this mess, all this trouble, is just what was required to finally get your attention. Are you seeing that?"

I don't reply. I'm not up to any more of Tree's saccharine and brimstone just now. We're just about to go confrontational with more or less every bad guy west of Spokane, and I seem to be the only one around here who gets that. One thing Tree does seem to have right, though. Mighty armies are arrayed around us.

Turning a corner, we find a long line of red taxis. We approach the first in line, but before we can touch the door handle the driver waves us off. The second and third drivers do the same. The fourth cabbie allows us inside until Tree declares our destination. We are ordered out of the cab. As we exit, I see him aerosol-spraying the interior.

A horde of starving taxi drivers now swarms around us, grabbing, shouting, jostling, their dirty gauze masks slipping down their faces. Tree shouts our intended destination, and all but one of them walks away. The remaining driver, who looks all of sixteen, goes a bit pale but he's still standing here. He and Tree negotiate at length in Mandarin.

"He'll take us nearby," Tree tells me at last. "We'll have to walk the last half a kilometer or so. We're paying triple the meter."

I nod agreeably, knowing that the meter won't work.

Tree takes the rear of the taxi and I the front. The taxi zips along suburban Beijing's broad, empty thoroughfares, the driver all the while slapping his useless meter. The driver exits the main road just before we reach a roadblock where, I note with pleasure, the bus that just refused Tree is mired in a long, unmoving line. The cabbie, grimly silent, turns onto a succession of ever-more-lonely two-lanes. My eyes take in shop after shuttered shop, many of them plastered with humorless black-on-white notices. Finally I submit to the urge to turn and check the road behind us. A taxi seems to be following at a distance.

"Is your past catching up?" asks Tree.

I ignore her and she laughs.

"Listen, Jules, I need to tell you something," says Tree. "Your past is tracking you. It's tracked you all the way here, and the last thing we need is to have your past in our present. Understand?"

"No, I don't. Who is tracking me?"

"It's someone who used to work for you. He was your right-hand man. You sent him away just when you needed him the most. I think he ain't over it."

"Are you talking about Truman?"

"Truman was a mask, Julian. I'm talking about the spirit behind the mask. I'm talking about where that energy is coming from, and it's coming from your past. Be careful. He may have plans to mess with your big finale."

"I have a big finale?" I say.

"You better have."

I feel Tree's hand on my shoulder. "I took a chance on you. Don't make me out wrong."

"This isn't helping," I say irritably.

"And one more little thing," says Tree, and her hand disappears. "All that stuff I said happened on Cetus? It didn't happen on Cetus."

I turn to look at her. "You mean the civilization I destroyed?"

Tree says, "I didn't think you were ready to hear it. Maybe you're still not ready, but all that stuff happened right here on Earth."

"Why did I know you were going to say that?"

"You're returning to the scene of the crime, Jules. Your day of redemption has come at last."

The driver brakes in the precise middle of nowhere, slams off the dysfunctional meter, and points straight ahead. I look straight ahead. There's nothing to see except an empty two-lane, a few abandoned buildings, a weedy lot, and a tailless cat. Tree questions the driver, but he just keeps jabbing his forefinger straight ahead.

Moments later, the taxi is turning and speeding away, and Tree and I stand gazing around ourselves at a ramshackle industrial area, evidently idle for quite some time. I take one look at the pitted pavement and pull out the shoulder-straps of Tree's suitcase.

"Help me with this," I say, squatting while Tree helps me into the straps. I turn to check the road behind us. There's a taxi parked some two hundred yards back. That's nice.

"Let's go," I say.

Beneath the haze-filtered sun, we walk within an eerie silence that makes every footfall seem slightly absurd. I offer my water bottle, and Tree shakes her head.

"You're dehydrated," I tell her.

"You tend to yours. I'll tend to mine."

I point to a wooden sign just ahead of us. It's covered with strident red Chinese characters. "Can you read that?" I ask.

"You know my eyes are bad," replies Tree.

Just as well, I decide. I just checked behind us again, and there are two taxis creeping along a hundred meters behind us.

"Where's the traffic?" I ask irritably. "A ten-thousand-bed hospital has to generate more traffic than this."

"Many paths to the mountaintop," says Tree, beginning to wheeze, rivulets of sweat starting down her face.

She could actually be right. The taxi driver may have chosen a seldom-used route, a back-door approach that the various welcoming committees may not anticipate.

A moment later, Tree is squinting at the sign. "It's the characters for SARS. The last character means 'warning.' I'd say we're getting close."

She turns to me. "Julian, I have to say something—"

"I'm not listening."

"What happens today will—"

"I'm not *listening*," I say testily. "I am what I am, and I do what I do." I extend the water bottle. "Put this in your mouth."

Tree smiles as she accepts the water bottle. "That's all I needed to hear, baby. You're standing in your power. Halleluiah and praise God."

As Tree takes a modest sip, three equally-spaced gunshots erupt behind us. I turn to see one of the two taxis squeal a one-eighty and make haste back toward Beijing.

"Fireworks," I say.

55

A red taxi passes Tree and me only to stop some ten meters away. Out steps a middle-aged Westerner in a golf shirt. There he stands, smiling broadly, hands on hips, awaiting us. Call me psychic. I know at a glance that this man is Harold Sternbaum.

"Keep walking," I whisper to Tree. "Don't say a word."

"You have picked one very hot day for a stroll!" the man calls to us, his white teeth gleaming. "You might at least be following a golf ball around, for heaven's sake."

As we draw closer, the man opens the rear door of the taxi. "Climb in. I'll take you where you're going, not that it's likely to do you much good. My name is Harold Sternbaum, and I'd—"

Tree and I walk wordlessly past.

"Uh-oh," says Sternbaum. "We aren't being pleasant."

Closing the door, Sternbaum falls into step beside me, and the taxi follows.

"Listen, Julian," says Sternbaum, "I know why you're here, and I know what you're up against. There's no way in hell you're getting your sister out of that hospital without a lot of help, okay? That's what I am. I'm a lot of help. But first, I need a little something from you."

Tree begins to hum a spiritual.

"Oh, we're musical!" says Harold. "How exciting! Would you care to know, Mrs. Carter, what your Julian did just before leaving Shenzhen? He stole my daughter. Not to mention my wife. I take it from his manner that he doesn't intend to give either of them back. How do you think that plays with me, Mrs. Carter? Any guesses? Hah?"

Harold takes out a handkerchief and pats his temples. "You will notice that I'm working very hard here. Considering the flow of events, I would call my approach extremely cordial thus far. But I've always believed in approaching complex problems like a rational adult. Julian needs a sister. I need a daughter. We can work at cross purposes, or we can help each other out. I say we help each other out. Would *someone* please say something? I'm a voice crying in the wilderness, for the love of God."

Tree continues to hum her spiritual. The warm, throaty melody unfolds before me like a vision. I find myself clinging to each note.

Sternbaum leans closer to my face. "Just like your father, hah? Smarter than everybody else. Got to do it your way. Did you know I've done business with your father? I helped him get into that tobacco deal in Guangzhou. He wanted to hybridize a more addictive tobacco strain. Can you believe that? A more addictive tobacco strain?" Sternbaum laughs gaily. "I couldn't work with the man. Everything's got to be his way."

Sternbaum digs his pointy shoulder into my arm. "Know those two fucking pickpockets who were after your father? Barnes and somebody or other? I hear they got a little too close to the action. The cops found them in their room this morning, hog-tied with syringes stuck in their necks. What do you think about that? *Hah*?"

I turn and look at him for the first time.

"Oh, my God!" cries Sternbaum. "He's looking at me! Any moment now he'll begin to speak!"

I turn my head away.

"Okay," says Sternbaum. "It's Plan B then. I'll have my friends shoot you both like the fucking dogs you are, right here on the road, and the Chinese can do what they want with the milk maid. What do you think about that? Hah? Takers?"

Sternbaum leans into me again, his rat-like face inclined. I smell his aftershave. "What kind of man would take something that belongs to someone else? What kind of man would take another man's wife and daughter? What should be done with a man like that, Julian?"

The remaining phone in my cargo pocket begins to ring. I find that altogether curious, as not even I know the number. I open the phone and punch up the call.

"Hao?" I say. Rhymes with *how.*

A calm, husky American voice replies, "Would you please tell Harold Sternbaum that, if he touches my son once more, he'll soon be parting his hair at the eyebrows?"

"You're a fucking ET," I say into the phone.

After a momentary silence, Dobbins says, "We're all extraterrestrials here, Julian. Now would you please—"

"At least you're dying," I add. "Wouldn't you say you're dying? And the whole pod thing with you?"

Dobbins sighs. "Everything here is dying, Julian. You are the last remaining hope for any of us. Come in. There's a shelter. Everything has been prepared."

I say, "Let me guess. The shelter is located beneath the Circular Mound Altar, it's designed for exactly nine occupants and, once everyone is strapped in, the structure transforms into a spaceship that—"

"Please," says Dobbins.

"What? Too much?"

Harold Sternbaum says, "Who the fuck are you talking to?"

"Actually, it's for you," I tell Sternbaum, "if you'll just wait a moment." I turn back to the phone. "Okay. Now, what exactly is the status of Lillian?"

"Forget Lillian. It's about you now," says Dobbins.

"Been really nice talking to you." I hand the phone to Harold Sternbaum. "Don't use all my minutes."

"*Who* is this?" Sternbaum barks into the phone. A moment later, he spins, looking in every direction. After a few angry sputters, he throws the phone as far as he can into the weeds.

"To hell with all of you," snarls Sternbaum, signaling to the cab driver. "I'm not dirtying my hands. Let the Chinese and North Koreans fight over who gets to hang you up by the fucking thumbs."

Before climbing into the taxi, Sternbaum shakes a fist at me. "If *one* hair of that child's head is harmed, I will personally buy you from whoever has you. Do you hear me, Julian? I will *buy* you."

He slams the door, and the taxi burns a one-eighty and disappears.

Tree's hum becomes a relieved sigh, followed by silence. Again, the silence is too complete. Something is missing. I don't know what. Now I hear a chortle.

Tree says, "People love you everywhere you go, don't they, baby?"

"All over the world."

Tree was right about different paths to the mountaintop. We're now approaching the ass end of the Peoples' Beijing SARS Treatment and Quarantine Hospital. No welcoming committees. For now at least.

"Let me do the talking," pants Tree, limping noticeably. "Don't say anything. Don't do anything. I got us in that taxi, and I'll get us in that hospital. Are you hearing me, Julian Mancer?"

The first thing you see are the light towers, sixteen of them, each at least a hundred feet high. Approaching closer, you notice the gleaming coils of razor-wire atop a forbiddingly tall chain-link fence. Beyond that, ranks and files of anonymous pre-fab barracks brood in the hazy sunlight. All around them, bulldozed earth lies bare where just weeks ago yawned a fallow field. When the Chinese decide to get something done, it's done in a hurry.

The third thing you notice is the saxophone music oozing from the horns mounted on each light tower. Struggling to not hear it, I study the compound before us. No trace of a rear entrance. There's no choice but to follow the unpaved perimeter road that skirts the chain-link. This we do, feeling the stares of the masked and heavily-armed guards patrolling the other side. The saxophone music is louder now. I feel it penetrating my DNA, tugging at the strands. I clamp my hands over my ears. It doesn't help.

"You're always hating on Kenny J," complains Tree, panting. "All in the world that boy is doing is trying to make a living with his horn."

Blood will fly. That's all that matters. It no longer matters whose. Something in me is beyond that now. That part doesn't want an easy solution. I fear there can be no solution because I've come too late. So let the various players play it out. Let them fuss over which government finally gets to out-creep all the others, which strain of cooties gets to sing the final stanza, which monkey-grotesque gets to write history for a little while.

I no longer even want to know whether it was the kind-hearted people of Shreveport, Louisiana, and Hot Coffee, Mississippi, who did or did not wittingly or unwittingly loose *what* upon the world's most populous society in their most vulnerably human moment. If there are even any humans here. Maybe Lillian was right all along. It's fucked. There's a part of me that wants it to be fucked.

Tree and I round the final corner, and the entrance of the compound swings into view. Before two gatehouses waits a long queue of trucks. Outside the gate sprawls a forlorn encampment of people napping on newspapers, slouching beneath parasols, awaiting, it would appear, news of family members brought here against their will.

Tree and I approach the gate, working our way through a knot of people confronting a row of soldiers. Behind the row of soldiers is another row of soldiers. All are helmeted and gauze-masked, and each brandishes a bayonet-tipped automatic rifle. Behind the two rows of soldiers is a second gate, bracketed by another pair of gatehouses. Between the two gates, inbound and outbound vehicles are being searched, drivers' temperatures checked, and clipboards consulted. Razor-wire swaths everything.

What comes to my attention now is a song. Tree is singing it.

"*Ohhh*-hhhhh, Pharaoh," she intones throatily, hands spread and fingers skyward. "Let my pee-EEE-eee-eople go."

Tree, still moving forward, takes a huge breath, seeming to double in size.

"OhhhhhHHHHHHHHH-HHHHHHhhhhhh, Pharaoh . . ."

Every head turns. The crowd begins to part before Tree, who half-walks half-floats toward the compound gate.

"Let my PEEEEEEE-eeeeeeeee-*EEEE*-eee-eople go."

The crowd scatters. Two men actually fall down trying to get out of Tree's way. She reaches the first row of soldiers, their rifles and bayonets leveled. Inhaling deeply, she reaches for a new octave.

She finds it.

Hands raised, eyes closed: "Oh PHAAAAAAAAAAAAAAA *AAAAAAAAAAAAAAAAAAAAAAAAAAAAAAAAAAA*. . . ."

Everything stops. Vehicle inspections. Breathing. An overhead light-bulb explodes. The saxophone music sputters, pops and goes dead.

"—AAAAA-ROHHHHHHHHH-*HHHHH*-hhhhhh—"

Suddenly wobbly, Tree steadies herself against a lamp post.

I step forward until I feel against my chest the point of the nearest bayonet. Beneath the military helmet before me is a pair of dark eyes wide with uncertainty. "What have you done with my sister?" I demand of the darting eyes. All the soldiers before me are young and unsure of themselves. It doesn't matter. We're beyond that.

Tree begins to speak in Mandarin, carefully articulating Lil's name.

"It's too late for talking, Tree," I interrupt, hearing once more the strange emptiness in the air. I know what it is now.

As though hearing the thought, Tree turns questioningly to me.

"She's gone, Tree," I say. "Check for yourself."

A frown line appears between Tree's eyebrows. Raising her hands, she uses the palms to scan the area in front of her. "Show me Lillian," she whispers, closing her eyes and panning her open palms left to right and back. Baffled, Tree shakes her head and scans the area again. Finally the two hands drop to her sides. Tree's eyes roll open.

An ominous roaring sound begins in the sky. Looking up, I discover a black cloud forming above Tree Carter's head. As I watch, a funnel shape descends from the cloud, pulling a halo of dust and debris into the air. Tree gworls in Mandarin, repeating Lil's name. An officer runs out of a guardhouse, looks skyward, and begins to shout.

All at once wind hits me like a speeding train. I find my-self sprawled on the ground several meters away, bits of sand stinging my face. Wiping my eyes, I see a truck turned on its side, wheels spinning. The chain-link fence and guardhouses are bucking violently. The soldiers all scatter, their helmets flying.

"Tree!"

I begin stumbling toward Tree Carter. Suddenly I know something. Or realize that I already knew. Reaching her, I cry, "Tree! She's not here! Lil's alive. She's just not here."

Slowly Tree turns her face toward mine. Her eyes are glow-ing orange-red.

"She's at the Temple of Heaven," I say. "I found her in the glow."

56

"I don't know why I did it," Tree laments hoarsely. "I just did it, Lord God in Heaven."

"You did it, all right," I say, fanning the good doctor with the city map of Beijing. We are in a taxi speeding toward the Temple of Heaven Park, having flagged the driver just as he arrived at what was recently a serviceable hospital gate. Everyone who witnessed Tree's little tantrum is still running, as far as I know.

Some Chinese can really move.

"You're totally dehydrated," I say, offering Tree the two fingers of water remaining in my bottle. She takes a tiny sip. As I fan her face, I look out at a cityscape that seems somehow very odd. The light, perhaps. I've noticed for some time that a hollow, yellow-green dusk seems to have settled over midday. For a moment, I wonder whether Her Tree-ness may have damaged the solar system. The cabbie shouts something. I ask for a translation.

"He says the Temple of Heaven Park is closed," reports Tree.

"I know it's closed."

There's no alternative now to following my desperate gut-feel that Lil is alive and waiting, that Tim Dobbins has somehow leveraged the Chinese into smuggling her out of that place in an extra-large body bag, to be delivered—where else but the Temple of Heaven Park? To whatever awaits us in that chamber beneath the Circular Mound Altar.

Suddenly I know something else, or suspect it. Just like everything else at the temple complex, the Hall of Abstinence may serve a dual function. Ostensibly a place for the emperor to spend three nights of fasting before the Worshiping Heaven Ceremony, that place could have been designed, as well, to accommodate nine fledgling Dobbinses as they prepare for their own little ceremony. I ask myself how many of the intended nine are actually waiting there. Is Lil now self-disclosing before a whole new set of siblings? Or did they rip each other to pieces at first scent? Again, there's nothing to do but go there.

"I'm done, baby," says Tree, drooping. "It's all on you now."

"Why is the light so strange, Tree?"

"It's the eclipse."

My breath catches. The eclipse. I've forgotten about it. Turning to peer through the side window of the cab, I try to catch sight of a shadow. There's a very thin one alongside a passing truck. The sun is all but directly above us, and here I am, exactly when and where Timothy Dobbins wants me.

Our driver brakes and delivers us to the edge of an empty parking lot. When the taxi departs, Tree and I are alone—or very nearly. There is a lone figure seated near the huge ornamental gate. He seems to be gazing at us. I watch the man rise awkwardly to his feet.

"Is that who I think it is?"

"Who?" says Tree. "Where?"

Taking Tree's hand, I lead her toward an approaching bespectacled Chinese man in a white cotton shirt. Tree squints in his direction. A moment later, she cries, "Oh, my God!"

A smiling Cangming Xu limps into Tree's hug. Impatiently I wait as they blather and hoot for their usual minute and a half. Finally I insinuate my face before Xu's. "What are you doing here?"

"Recovering my strength," says Xu with a grin. "See the razor-wire along the top of that wall?"

I do, just as Bi Yu Nu said I would.

"It's electrified," says Xu. "I found out the hard way."

"But why *here*?" I press.

"I'm chasing an eclipse," replies Xu.

Freeing himself from Tree's embrace, Xu pulls a GPS from his pocket and gives it a shake. "This thing is practically useless now, but it's gotten me this far. The Thirteen arrives in"—Xu checks the three analog watches strapped to his arm—"twenty-seven minutes. At that moment, the moon's shadow will be centered ninety meters on the other side of that wall, directly over the Circular Mound Altar. How's that for a coincidence?"

"It's not a coincidence."

"Listen to this man," Tree says to Xu. "He knows his temples."

He blinks. "But how could—are you saying that someone anticipated this eclipse six hundred years ago? And built the Altar on that spot?"

"Five hundred, ninety-six," I correct him.

"But—why?"

"Ever heard of throwing a monkey wrench in the works? What if that structure were designed to take the incoming evolutionary energy—and give it a nice little twist?"

Xu's mouth falls slowly open. "The *nines*," he whispers. "They're intervening between the Eight and the Thirteen. And they're coming from here."

I nod. "More by the second. Not to alarm anyone, but when the center of the moon's shadow hits the Heaven's Heart Stone, I think there may be a problem."

"Unless we get there first," says Tree.

Xu, ashen, shakes his head. "There's no possible way to get over that wall."

Wordless, I stride toward to the thumbprint-reading device Bi Yu Nu was kind enough to alert me to. I place my right thumb at its center. A moment later, the enormous gate begins to motor noisily open. As I wait, I note that the dim overhead sun is more than half in shadow. *Because the moon,* scratched a quill some centuries ago, *does not know how to drink wine, she has given me this shadow for company . . .*

Tentatively Xu, Tree, and I step inside the gate. "This way," I say, starting along the smoothly paved promenade. As the gate begins to motor closed behind us, my eyes fix on the first triple gate ahead. To reach the Circular Mound Altar, one passes through a series of heavily ornamented gates arranged in sets of three, the center portal reserved for the emperor's feet alone. Since 1949, those central gates have been locked tight and the smaller ones opened for the use of tourists. To-day those smaller gates are closed and the central portal wide open, though arguably not for the emperor's feet.

As we pad along the promenade, the sky seems to darken another half shade, and I glance up at low, scatting clouds now boiling up beneath the hollow grey-green of the sky. We are arriving at syzygy. Through the approaching triple gate and the one beyond it, I see the sharp glisten of white marble.

"I'm feeling seriously strange," pants Tree, trying to keep up.

"Same here," says Xu.

"I've never felt better in my life," I say.

It's true. I could almost be walking downhill.

"You guys want to take a look at this?" says Xu, gazing at his three analog wristwatches. The hands of each now show nine minutes past nine. I look down at my own analog. Its hands read the same.

"I think we'd better hurry," says Tree.

We pause before the penultimate triple gate. I stick my head inside. A glance to either side reveals no one, yet I feel the farthest thing from alone. I step inside. Tree and Xu fol-low suit. Immediately they begin to reel.

"*Oh* my God," says Xu.

"Oh my God," echoes Tree.

A third voice says, "Julian! I might have known."

As one, we turn to look behind us, but no one is there. I look up. Above the doorway we've just entered, clinging like a ninja to the ornately sculpted lintel, is a human. With a very green eye. And a very blue one. Both stare at me accusingly.

"My intuition has pointed to you all along," says Ana Manguella. "Now I see why."

Ana, her clothing the exact color and texture of the wall, drops to the pavement and pulls off a tight cap, loosing a tumult of dark tresses.

"It wasn't enough to bring down the Earth's most advanced civilization twelve thousand years ago," she says to me. "Now you've come to destroy what little remains."

I cover my belly with both hands and back away. "You stay away from me."

Ana takes a menacing step closer. "Do you deny that you are Tlecort, architect of the Great Temple of Atlantis?"

"This man," says Tree authoritatively, "has permission to be here."

We all turn toward Tree. She just spoke aloud yet I, for one, didn't hear her voice.

"I've received no such notification," replies Ana.

"You're receiving it now," says Tree.

A look of irritation crosses Ana's features. Meanwhile I shake my head. Either these people are speaking telepathically or I've gotten a really bad eggroll.

Tree says, "This man is here *because* he designed the Great Temple of Atlantis." She points toward the innermost triple gate. "Inside that gate is an architectural weapon aimed directly at the heart of this planet. Who would *you* send in there to disarm it?"

All eyes go to me. I back up a little, bringing me slightly closer to the Altar.

Ana says to Tree, "My soul group knows nothing about any of this. Whoever you are, you've entered this planetary space under false—"

"We had to, sweetie," replies Tree softly, using her voice. "And now you have to manifest some faith because we are slap running out of time. Either this man gets to that altar before the—"

"Why so impatient, Julian?" interrupts Ana.

"Who, me?" I've just taken another step closer to the Altar.

"And why is it," says Ana, "that only you seem to be comfortable here?"

"It's complicated," I say.

"It's way complicated," say Tree. "Julian's body, his genetics, were designed with this place in mind, okay? To jibe with this energy. That's why only he can do this. He's the only one of us who can go up there."

Tree turns to me. "Sorry, Jules. I knew all along, but I couldn't say anything." She teeters for a moment, steadying herself against the gate. "Listen, honey," she says wearily to Ana, "there's nothing we can do now but send that boy up there and trust that the higher angels of his nature *will* prevail. Jesus, Joseph, and Aphrodite."

Ana shakes her head. "I've seen that altar up close, and no one here is prepared to deal with it—least of all you, Julian. Each of the three tiers takes you deeper into—"

Ana's voice falters. After a moment, she wipes her face with both hands and continues, "It's a mythical space. Up there, even the smallest thing opens out into an epic story. Any flaw in your intention can become exaggerated beyond all proportion. I threw something up there. Just a pocketknife. What landed there was not a pocketknife but a gold-hilted double-edged sword. From a pocketknife, Julian. God only knows what will happen if we send you up there."

Xu says, "Uh, there's not much time."

We turn toward Xu, who just spoke telepathically and seems a bit surprised at it. He's staring at his forefinger, which appears as a *bouquet* of forefingers. Nine of them, to be exact.

We each examine our own multi-forefinger arrays. I resist the urge to check inside my pants.

Folding her blur of fingers into a fist, Ana says, "Is it true, Julian? Can you really stop that thing?"

"Umm . . . ," I begin.

"Don't give me *umm*," she snaps. "Your intention has to be very pure up there, or we are done, understand?"

Tree places a hand on Ana's shoulder and says, "He's all we got, baby."

Ana's eyes close for a moment. When they re-open, she says, "Okay. Julian, you're on point. Nothing sudden, nothing stupid. You two," she says to Tree and Xu, "stay here."

"Nobody's staying anywhere," says Tree, grabbing a hold of Xu for support.

"We're right behind you," says Xu, gazing uncertainly at the final triple gate before us.

Not until we pass inside the innermost wall do we fully see what it encloses. The three-tiered obelisk of the Circular Mound Altar, open to the brooding sky, is now *nine* charming obelisks, each glowing a different red-orange hue, each seemingly afloat upon the fetid air, each overlapping the others, no one of them evidently substantial enough to step on. Between the gate we have just entered and the floating nine-fold array before us wafts the foul smoke of a nearby sacrificial oven. I can't help but wonder who's for lunch.

"What do you think, Julian?" asks Ana, her eyes foggy.

I don't reply. I'm busy scowling at the sculpted gargoyles guarding the first tier. And yet I feel a nearly irresistible urge to *taste* those cool marble steps with the bare soles of my feet.

I hear a gasp. Tree has fallen against one side of the gateway. She sinks slowly to the paving stones. Trying to assist, Xu grabs at her and goes down, as well. Ana's knees, meanwhile, are visibly shaking. "What do you know about that structure?" she asks me.

"There's an underground chamber. Inside are some people. Loosely speaking."

"What else?"

"That's all I know. What do you know?"

Ana shakes her head. "Could be we're seeing a probability array. Once you put your foot down on one of those altars, maybe they all collapse into one. But be careful. My soul group is telling me that, up there, things are not what they are but what they are becoming. You have to read the metaphor, find a doorway into the story."

"A doorway into the story," I say, edging a bit closer to the Altar.

"You're sure to encounter a portal guardian," she says, and I stop edging.

"What kind of portal guardian?"

"I don't know," replies Ana. "If we're dealing with an underground chamber, it may be the Guardian of the Underworld."

She gazes at me. "More commonly known as the Hydra."

I really stop edging.

"If so," Ana continues, "you can only survive the encounter as Heracles. That's your doorway. You'll need a club and a lion-skin." Turning to Tree and Xu, Ana calls weakly, "We need a wooden club."

Tree and Xu, sprawled side-by-side on the paving stones, give her a dazed look.

"Listen, Julian," continues Ana. "I don't—" Her voice breaks into a ragged cough. A moment later, she is on her hands and knees, blood bubbling from her nose.

"Ana?" I say, kneeling beside her.

Wiping her face on a white sleeve, she says, "Listen to me. I don't know what nine means anywhere else, but on this planet it means completion leading to rebirth. It's the end of one cycle and the beginning of another. That's the way it's done here. The epochs build one atop the other, no interruption, no going back. Civilization after civilization, apocalypse after apocalypse, cycle after cycle, lesson after bitter, failed lesson—*and* success after incremental success. Each step takes us farther along an evolutionary arc that must—"

Ana surrenders to another horrid fit of coughing. Xu appears, crawling. He hands her something that would appear to be a wooden leg. "Maybe this can work?" he says.

Ana grabs the prosthesis and tells me hoarsely, "Take this. It's your club."

"Thanks so much," I say as Xu crawls away on all threes.

Ana struggles to her knees. "Julian, Earth *must* survive. The experiments here must go on. We are the free will planet. We take freedom of choice farther than it's ever gone anywhere, and we've not even begun. The work here must find completion."

Ana rips a sleeve from her bloodied white shirt. "Here. Heracles tied a cloth over his face for protection from the Hydra's breath." Now she hands me a small butane lighter. "Heracles had a helper, a cousin named Iolaus who used fire to cauterize the—"

Ana, listing to one side, now begins to fall. I grab her just before her head strikes the pavement. "Ana!"

I drag the limp body back to the triple gate.

She croaks, "You'll have to do without an Iolaus. Give me everything from your pockets. Whatever you carry up there will take on a life of its own."

Handing her my wallet and personal pair of chopsticks, I ask, "What's going to happen to me up there?"

"I don't know," she says. "The watch, too. And the moldavite. What else do you have?"

With a sigh, I hand over my titanium-bound journal.

She extends her hand again.

With another sigh, I hand over the last two good German-made pencils in all of China. "Listen, Ana. I'm sorry about the whole boy-girl thing. I wish it had turned out—"

I'm interrupted by a rude slap across the face. "Cowboy up," says Ana, her eyes blurry. A moment later, the eyes roll close and the bloody head falls back against the earth.

Eyes widening, hand on my stinging check, I rise and turn to face the Circular Mound Altar. Gazing straight up, I see that the low, scatting clouds have gathered in a broad, eddying circle, their center point directly above the swirling multi-altar display. I lift Xu's prosthesis and begin to walk.

Life is so whatever.

"And don't you take *no* mess," calls Tree's gritty voice, "from no ugly monster. You hear me?"

I pass the sacrificial oven, my nostrils burning with the acrid smoke. I'm close enough to see the charred remains on the grate. On the paving stones beneath the oven is a half-melted pair of spectacles, their frames black and perfectly round.

I never did like Bellamy all that much.

57

Ana was right. The closer I draw to the nine-fold Circular Mound Altar, the more the multi-dimensional display collapses into a single structure. Finally it is a solitary step that invites my tentative toes. Unable to quite set my foot on the step, I back away and take a deep breath. Maybe I should have given this whole matter a bit more thought.

Reaching into a pocket, I extract Ana's butane lighter, rear back and throw it onto the upper terrace. I can't see it land, but what I hear is a series of loud metallic clangs. Jesus, what arrived up there, a fire truck? Ana was telling the truth about this place. Things up there are what they're becoming.

I'm becoming somewhat reluctant. In fact I'd toss this chunk of eucalyptus and *book* if not for that gut-level pull that seems stronger by the moment. Despite everything, I find myself leaning forward. As though by its own volition, my foot lifts itself to step.

The moment my toes touch down on the white marble, a bright light erupts from the center of the uppermost tier, silently shooting straight into the sky, piercing the expansive circle of low clouds to seemingly touch the shadowed moon herself at the sky's zenith.

Squinting, I ascend the second step and the third, increasingly awash with an inexplicable sense of arrival. Belonging, even. I don't even know what that word means, but I know this place well, and it knows me. By the time I arrive at the first marble terrace, I recall my father's words. How could there be any solution to the quandary of my life beyond its original blueprint? How can there be an impulse truer than the one now tugging at my bowels? That same impulse has drawn me to the far side of the world and then across half of China and finally, inexorably, to this very spot.

Or is there *another* pull, one even older, a blueprint drafted by another hand entirely? Do two voices now sing inside my head, a fifth apart? What happens, I ask myself, when those voices retreat unto separate scales to whisper into opposing ears? What happens then, when dust is merely dust and regret just another case of regret? I only know that I've spent my whole life longing for something, *wasting* in the agony of its absence. I've never felt closer to that something than right now.

And closer to losing it forever.

Decisively I mount the nine steps to the second terrace. The instant my foot contacts its white marble, I am filled with an elation that I've never so much as glimpsed before. An uncanny sense of completion strikes me more deeply and personally than anything I've ever known. The completion that all events have been racing toward? Now I know it is my own.

Teetering a bit, I close my eyes to consider the finer-grained details of my experience, which seems to expand further each instant, subsuming everything that I thought that I thought that I knew. There is no drop-off in the elation, only an ever-rising tide that threatens to obliterate obliteration itself.

Who is your family, Julian?

Opening my eyes, I try to find my bearings. Pulling myself taller, I begin to ascend the final nine steps, stopping just short of the ultimate terrace, where three hundred sixty balustrades support a circular lintel that frames an obelisk composed of concentric rings of cut stones, each ring nine-divisible until exactly nine stones embrace the Heaven's Heart Stone—now glowing brightly from within. It is from here that the beacon of light arises. I look up to follow the beam until it touches the shadowed moon's tender underbelly. Only a tiny sliver of white remains of that moon. We're now arriving at full eclipse. *Intention, Julian,* says a voice inside my head. But whose? And if mine, which mine?

No matter, I reply to the thought. There can be no direction now but forward. Tentatively yet decisively, I place one foot on the upper terrace. In response, the central stone spins ever faster until it dissolves into light, and the nine stones embracing it fall away, revealing a brightly lit entryway leading into the depths of the Circular Mound Altar. The voice comes from everywhere at once.

"My son. You're here."

Timothy Dobbins's soothing voice is indistinguishable from the crystalline euphoria that continues to build within me. Fighting feebly against the ferocious tide, I turn in every direction but there is no Timothy Dobbins. From the upper terrace of the Circular Mound Altar, it is said, even the quietest whisper comes back from all directions. Dobbins must be below, speaking into a microphone.

"Just another few steps," coos the husky voice. "You're almost home."

A tear wells in one eye. How long have I traveled? How long and how friendless? The twisted road behind me seems now to fall away like a withering umbilical, never again to be needed. Can it be possible that I've finally arrived somewhere? Through the teary eye, I gaze at the open portal before me, and my bodyweight shifts forward, readying itself to step.

And now I freeze. A raw shudder overtakes me. Again I close my eyes and try to focus, try to find some strand of myself within the impenetrable blizzard of incoming sensation and—and suddenly I realize that it *is* incoming. Unlike the pleasure discovered at my center in Ana Manguella's bed, that gently glowing coal in my body's core, a self-intelligent flow of *being*—what I feel now presses in from some other place, seemingly from the marble beneath my feet.

Straining, I try to discern the intelligence behind that blizzard, the living heart at its center that opens unto ever-broad-er, all-inclusive knowing. I don't find it. At the center of this sensation is only a desperate need to control. To latch onto neural receptor sites designed for a higher purpose. At the center of this euphoria is but an ever-tightening fist. It is fear. The instant my body knows this, I feel something within me pull away and steel itself. Opening my eyes, I wipe away the trail of the tear and withdraw my foot from the upper terrace.

"Julian?" says Dobbins's voice.

"Send my brothers and sisters out," I hear myself say. "I'm shutting this thing down."

"You know you can't do that," the voice replies almost kindly. "All you can do is shut yourself out."

"I'm armed," I reply, lifting Xu's prosthesis. "Or legged, as the case may be."

A moment later, the white marble stones at the Altar's center begin to converge, covering the stairway. "I tried, Julian," whispers Dobbins's voice.

As I watch, the re-materialized Heaven's Heart Stone grinds to a halt. For a long moment, all is silent. Drawing a deep breath, I tighten my grip around Xu's wooden ankle and step onto the upper terrace, the rush of pleasure now gone. Instead is a strong foreboding. Something has shifted, probably not for the better.

Cautiously I advance toward the glowing Heaven's Heart Stone, stepping around a double-edged sword and a white-hot firebrand. Beneath my feet, eighty-one perfectly cut stones give way to seventy-two, then sixty-three, then fifty-four. I pause before the ring of forty-five stones. Something has definitely shifted. Now I notice something. The light above the terrace is changing, breaking apart as though through an unseen prism. At the same time, something begins to swell. The ever-building pressure almost pushes me back.

As I watch dumbfounded, the vertical beam of light breaks into nine razor-sharp spears that now spawn competing geometric planes. Appearing in the air above the Heaven's Heart Stone is a towering, burnished gold tetrahedron, its four points as sharp as daggers. A moment later, I'm looking at a sparkling emerald cube. Which as quickly pops into an octahedron in a fiery blue—and now a rotating purple icosahedron. The multi-dimensional space above the Altar is crystallizing and re-crystallizing into ever greater complexity until the icosahedron becomes a full-on dodecahedron bristling with identical pentagonal facets of a blazing red-orange.

I step back, shielding my face, as the red-orange light waxes ever brighter. Squinting, I watch the sharp edges of the dodecahedron morph once more, the crisp facets gradually becoming undecipherable limbs and horrid appendages. Before me, looming above me, *menacing* me with the stares of multiple cold eyes—is the mother of all Hydrae.

Poised before me, its four clawed feet gripping the white marble, is a huge, scaly grey-green creature with a writhing serpentine tail. Erupting from its shoulders is a cluster of long, oily necks bearing feathered heads, each with a pointed snout and a massive jaw. The stench is overpowering.

As I gawk, the nearest of the nine heads gathers itself as though to strike. I jump back an instant before my body would have been snapped in half. Before I can catch my balance, another of the heads lunges, and I dodge nimbly to one side. As quickly, the creature spins, its long tail sweeping at my legs, and I go airborne.

Airborne.

I find myself spinning through the air like a gymnast, sailing above the charging Hydra and swinging my club to deliver a blow to the rearmost head as I pass. Landing behind the creature, I wheel, my weapon at the ready. Only now do I realize that Xu's prosthesis is now a massive club, its gnarled handle perfectly shaped to my hand. I catch a momentary glimpse of my body, which is beautifully muscled and draped in a flaming red toga. Before I can register surprise, the Hydra spins again and three heads rear simultaneously, every nostril flaring. The creature's body swells as it inhales to give me a triple dose of excellent poison breath.

Just as the three heads spew their noxious blasts, I again go airborne, my club whistling to punish the first of the heads. With my other hand, I pull Ana's sleeve tighter around my face—but a fourth Hydran head now stretches its long, scaly neck to snap me out of the air. Just before its jaws close around me, I feel something like an explosion, and I am sent spinning to the white marble, where I crash hard, my ears ringing.

"Behind you!" cries Xu's voice.

I roll to one side, narrowly escaping the lunge of a second Hydra, appearing from nowhere. As it recoils for a second strike, I realize that the air is filled with Hydrae, each menacing me from a separate dimension. Two Hydran heads lunge simultaneously, and I turn sideways, launching myself between their respective dimensions, and their jaws snap at nothing. I find myself landing on my feet in yet another dimension, gazing around as though through a massive crystal, each facet domiciling another multi-headed creature with aggressive-compulsive disorder. Meanwhile, seven other Hydrae, each as fierce as the other, wheel and search frantically for me.

Actually, seven plus one.

Sensing the attack before it comes, I jump to one side just as a massive serpentine tail slams down on the spot where I was standing. I turn to encounter Hydra number nine, which doesn't give me time to recover but spins, its nasty tail whipping around to strike again. Inexplicably, I know exactly what to do.

I begin to sing.

The war song erupts from my solar plexus like a missile, its trajectory every possible direction, its aim utterly true. The song *hurling* itself from my deepest center is both the ultimate weapon and every weapon's negation, for it distorts time and space, rendering every trajectory a failed hypothesis. Hydra number nine now exhales a fresh blast of poison, but it arrives at every conceivable nowhere. At the same instant, three other Hydrae attack from their respective dimensions, but their vectors become entangled. I am removed from all access, dancing in every possible position at once, and none of them, for mine is the song that writes the code of the moment.

I dance and the shadow lurches grotesquely.
I sing and the moon begins to reel.

Suddenly Tree's voice is layered over mine. I catch a glimpse of her standing leaning against the innermost gate, arms raised to the heavens.

"Rock ooo-aaaahhhh-AAAAH-ffff Ages-SSSS-sss . . ."

I dart in and out of Tree's unfurling melody, harmonizing in an unknown scale. Eighty-one Hydran heads rear in rage, confusion, and astonishment. As I zip past them, my lips plant a kiss on the top of each hairless head at the same instant, and they wheel furiously, searching for what is not there.

Maybe that was a little much. Hubris, actually. But the math is *so* easy, reality so readily rewritten, sucked into eddies and swirls and impossible-to-follow vortexes. One dimension or nine, it's the same playhouse. I dart once more amid the multiple Hydrae, dropping my song into an easy Aeolian scale, allowing the creatures to catch sight of me. The monstrous heads lunge simultaneously, jaws opening, and as suddenly my war song shifts, the melody unexpectedly banking off Tree's, and when the Hydran heads try to follow, they become entangled, forming knots as they struggle against each other.

That, too, was probably a little unnecessary. But nice.

"Clefff-FFF-*FFFF*-ffttt for meee-EEEE-eeeee . . ."

I let my song fall back into sync with Tree's unfurling hymn, and the various entangled Hydran heads struggle, pulling tighter the knots that progressively strangle them. In desperation, those heads now attack each other, their foul blood flying in every direction.

Suddenly I'm aware of something behind me. Instantly I shift scales and octaves, but that same something shifts with me, seemingly locked onto my every thought. I reverse directions and head back into the music just unleashed, making counter-harmonies in reverse time, creating sub-currents within which I now plummet, leaving no trace.

It's all coming back to me now.

But somehow this maneuver, too, has been anticipated. That same something on my tail is now before me, its maw opening.

I recognize that maw, that face.

Incredulous, I react almost too late, sending forth a burst of pure silence and darting into the Debussian void just before being gulped down by—

Julian Mancer.

"Let me hiiiii-iii-*IIII*-ide myself in theeee . . ."

There is a part of you, I was recently told, *that will fight to survive, against you if necessary.*

Again the awful ogre is on my tail, reading my thoughts almost before I can think them, uncannily telepathic, diabolically intelligent, intrinsically evil—and every bit his father's son. I must face the fact that some element within my own mind, perhaps even its greater measure, now wars against me. And rather well.

Before I can respond to this unhappy realization, I see that I am not merely hounded but have been turned, like a fleeing fox by whippets, back into the midst of the multi-dimensional array of Hydrae. Every vile reptilian head not presently occupied with tearing at the others now catches sight of me, and I turn sideways, my song quavering as I veer among them. Again Julian Mancer has anticipated my maneuver. I feel his hot, stale breath close behind me. In this space, said Ana Manguella, every flaw in one's intention is magnified. Could there be some tiny defect in my intention?

Nah.

Again I reverse directions in time, but Julian Mancer has anticipated me. I have to spin out of control to avoid annihilation, the colorless and pitiless mask of my own face snatching the club out of my hand and splintering it.

Desperate, I dive into an alternate tempo, darting among the beats, noting as I go that the long, bloody stumps that once were Hydran heads—are now re-sprouting, *two* heads for each one lost. It's a situation.

"Let the waaaah-AAAAH-aaa-ter and the bloo-ood . . ."

Remembering that I am darting through metaphorical space, I pull in my arms like a figure skater and, spinning ever faster, I plummet into Tree's lyrical landscape, finding myself in the depths of an immense ocean. It's cold here, and dark. No hint of sunlight. I gaze in every direction, recognizing neither up nor down. At least I'm able to breathe. Gradually, my eyes adjust, and I sense a vague glow emanating from one direction. Decisively I turn and head toward that glow, my body whipping effortlessly through the dark currents like that of a dolphin.

Good thing Tree isn't singing "Okie from Muskogee."

As the light before me grows gradually brighter, I begin to make out the beginnings of icy blues and shimmering aqua greens. The colors seem familiar, almost welcoming, and I increase my speed. I seem to have exited the pitched battle on the Circular Mound Altar along a tangent of no-time. If I'm right, time on the Altar will not move forward until my return.

Here within the embrace of Tree's image of healing waters, I may have found a much-needed refuge, an opportunity to renew my strength. The waters feel ever warmer as I approach the shimmering blue-green light. I increase my speed once more, sensing something quite compelling now in the iridescent colors. I sense a vague, nagging worry, as well. Something just beyond recall.

As I gradually enter the soothing, sparkling warmth, the green and blue become almost blinding, and I strain to make out their source. Feeling increasingly groggy in the sun-warmed waters, I almost fail to notice that the blue-green iridescence is closing behind me, sealing me into a dazzling embrace.

What was that lyric Tree was singing? There was nothing about color but only water. And blood. Here is water aplenty, but no blood to speak of, except for—

My own.

Suddenly, my eyes detect a wave of movement in the blue-green sheen closing ever tighter around me—and I take hold of that certain nagging something beyond my recall. A rhyme, actually. Four beats, stress on the second. *Beware the sheen of the blue and the green.*

At the last possible moment, I burst into explosive song, churning the surrounding waters and throwing off the simultaneous attack of thousands of needle-toothed carnivorous fish, their oily blue-green scales reflecting the overhead sun. I bolt from their midst but not before catching a fleeting flash of the numberless frenzied faces. Colorless. Pitiless. Uncannily telepathic. Julian.

Putting on speed, I zip dolphin-like toward the cold, dark waters below, hoping that the teeming predators at my heels are not bottom-feeders. Then again, I know who I'm dealing with here. The manifold Julian Mancer gives spirited chase, and I realize that he is following a blood scent. Along my right side is the burn of salt in an open wound, and my hands go there, probing. Not too deep yet a problem. I realize that the next line Tree's lips are poised to deliver is: *From thy wounded side which flowed.* I wonder if it's too late to request "Okie from Muskogee."

"Did you think you could get rid of me so easily, my General?"

The voice is almost familiar. Turning, I discover at my side the mocking smile of a young man, quite naked, his blond hair streaming behind him as he swims along my port side. Quite close behind us, the waters churn with the pursuit of countless needle-like teeth.

"I couldn't stand by and see you destroy yourself again, my General," I am told telepathically. "Are you seriously wounded?"

"Have we met?" I reply.

"We have."

"Is it you who's been trailing me? With an old score to even?"

The young man gives his blonde head a shake. "With an old debt to repay, my General. I owe you everything."

"It was you who played the part of Truman?"

"No time to talk, my General." The young man nods toward the school of man-eaters nipping at our heels. "I don't think you can out-swim these guys."

"Bicycling seems out of the question," I reply.

"Chapter Thirteen."

"Come again?"

"As you've known all along," says the young man, "the solution lies in Chapter Thirteen. See you at the Circular Mound Altar."

Before I can say *what* Chapter Thirteen, the naked youth has vanished in a burst of tiny bubbles, and I am alone in the cold, dark waters, save for the multi-maniacally pursuing Julian Mancer. It seems I'm now supposed to recall something I've known all along from an incinerated and never-to-be completed, *utterly* deleted novel from hell and its immediate outlying environs—while bleeding and fleeing myself in carnivorous fish form.

Nothing occurs to me, but as the nips are coming quite close to my heels, I decide to emit another explosion of song, its vibration calculated to splinter the tiny bones and appalling teeth of this ill-timed cult following. I let fly, and the burst of song roils the cold water into a cloud of foam, jetting me forward. For a moment, I see nothing at all behind me—but once more, my dark side has anticipated me.

The frenzied fish re-emerge from the foam unfazed, their ranks and files re-formed into a confectionary swirl, and I realize that Julian Mancer possesses my own understanding of wave dynamics and is using that knowledge to *dip* between the dip slopes of my attack.

Ah. Dip slopes.

The beginning of Chapter Thirteen, I now recall, goes into quite some detail about untangling the syncline and anticline of concurrent tectonic vectors by means of reverse osmosis, past life regression, and spare rubber bands. What are the chances, I conjecture, that a solution to the current quandary might lie in those very details, and what that might mean in terms of fish food? No matter. The water is chopping with Julian Mancer's German-made-pencil-like teeth, and my strength is fading. Time to find out whether that fair-haired boy might actually be onto something besides the divan.

I begin to move through the water in such a way as to create syncline/anticline currents, to which my school of followers respond as one, simultaneously proving and disproving Sandborns' Unified Wave Theory as each fish is intent on remaining in sync with the others and simultaneously in sync with me. Little do they know, this introduces a breach between undertow and overtow in a way that opens a probability window through which I might actually manage to wriggle, escaping these dark waters of geologic unknowing.

Which is to say, I've no idea how Chapter Thirteen might apply here, but I've had quite enough of this aquatic rudeness and so dip *quite* suddenly between the two presiding probabilities, which are that I am either (a) eater, or (b) eatee. It now tumbles to the center of my awareness that I am, in fact, whichever I elect to be. That is, while the situation is inescapable, I am at choice as to what perspective to experience it from.

Let's not be the eatee.

No sooner postulated than all is reversed and I am no longer pursued but pursuer. I *am* the terror that now opens its fiendish maw to rip at the white flesh of Julian Mancer with his own needle-like teeth, *his* horrid blood now uncoiling in the dark waters like a toxic cloud—and it is I who spins away from his pitiful death throes to zip alone through the anonymous waters, one with their blackness, with *my* blackness.

Ever farther behind me falls Julian Mancer's shrill, bubbling wail, rising in pitch until it is indistinguishable from the churning of the deadly waters.

I crash clumsily onto the white marble of the uppermost terrace of the Circular Mound Altar. The neighborhood hasn't improved much in my absence. Foul-tempered Hydran heads still rear from simultaneous directions and dimensions.

Tree, still leaning against the innermost gate, croons, ". . . From thy WOUNN-*NNN*-NND-ed side which flowed . . ."

A familiar voice cries, "My General!"

Just before it takes off my head, I pluck from the air a spinning double-edged sword, until recently Ana's pocket-knife. Standing in the midst of the maelstrom is our fair-haired boy, no longer naked but wrapped in a red toga and silver chain-mail. I realize it is Heracles' nephew Iolaus I behold, in his right hand a white-hot firebrand.

But wait. Two serpentine heads are now coiled to strike at Iolaus from behind. I spring into action, spinning through the air to hack off both heads in a single stroke, the cold blood splashing my face. As quickly, Iolaus cauterizes the stumps, and I turn to face a new attack from three overlapping dimensions. The three Hydrae strike at the same instant, and I spin again, my sword describing a deadly arc. Again, the white marble is stained a dirty red, and the firebrand sends up a hissing cloud of steam.

"Be of sin-nnnn," sings Tree, "the double CUURR-RRre."

We're doing our best, sweetie.

Above the Altar, the air becomes thick with a stinking grey-brown cloud of vapor as Iolaus and I spin and deal death until the terrace is all but covered by severed Hydran heads that lie twitching and spurting blood.

"Save from WRATHhh-hhhh," sings Tree, "and make me puu-uurrre."

Finally the air clears to reveal exactly nine remaining Hydrae, each with one remaining head. Those nine heads, though presently stunned, would be the immortal ones, I'd say, which cannot be killed but only trapped beneath a rock. If only we had a . . .

Iolaus and I share a questioning look. Now we turn to gaze at Tree, who is inhaling deeply, preparing to deliver her money line.

"Rock of Aaaa-AAAAAAAAAAA-ages . . ." she cries, and I drop my sword to join in, a third above. Iolaus drops his firebrand and hits the fifth.

We're not half bad, this trio.

At this moment, all nine Hydran heads gaze skyward, their maws slack. They can't like what they see. Directly above the Circular Mound Altar, arcing through the sickly green firmament at an alarming velocity, is a spinning and smoking rock. Of ages, one assumes. With a shrill hiss of alarm, the nine Hydrae scramble together, collapsing into one creature which tries desperately to claw its way beneath the Heaven's Heart Stone.

"Cleft for me-EEE-eeee-*EEEEEEEE*-eeeeee . . ."

As we push our quavering notes quite near the breaking point, the enormous descending rock *clefts* into two precise pieces, the smaller one flaming out quickly but not before deflecting the larger piece ever so slightly. That larger chunk now hurtles directly toward the center of the Circular Mound Altar. I decide I've seen enough. No longer singing, I'm flying through the air, making haste for the nearest exit.

I don't quite get there.

A horrific blast shatters my senses. The whole upper terrace of the Altar leaps skyward in a billowing cloud of crushed white marble. I seem to spin through the air for a foolish eternity before coming to rest on my back amid a downpour of debris and finally a suffocating powder-like dust. The only sound now is a fading series of echoes of the calamitous crash, leading gradually to an eerie silence broken only by a curious sizzling, popping sound. Now I hear coughing. Gradually I realize it is my own.

Slowly and painfully, I rise to my knees in what seems a moonscape. No longer someone's sing-song superhero, I am a dust-covered man in torn khakis. The air feels oddly empty. There's no trace of the shrill energy that quite recently gripped this place. Wiping the dust from my face, I rise and look around myself. It appears I am alone. No fair-haired child, no severed heads, no bloody remains. Gone is the entire detritus of what seemed a very real battle, now no more than a dream. Dazed, I find myself ascending what remains of the rubble-littered steps of the upper terrace of the Circular Mound Altar. On the top step, I stop and stare.

Embedded at the center of the obelisk is an enormous, irregular grey-green meteorite the approximate size of a road grader. It's from this prodigious rock that the hissing and sizzling sounds emanate.

Now my eyes catch sight of something. At the base of the meteorite are two feet wearing tan desert boots with checkered laces. The remains of the late Timothy Dobbins, it would appear, lie crushed beneath the steaming meteorite.

So it goes.

Again, the sound of coughing. This time it isn't from me. Following that sound, I pick my way around the overheated boulder to discover a dusty head and shoulders struggling to emerge from the debris. Those shoulders, unless I'm very wrong, are draped with very long, very platinum hair.

"Lilly?"

Dropping to my knees, I toss aside a clutter of white marble. Finally I take hold of two white hands and pull my sister from the rubble.

"Lilly! Are you okay?"

Lillian, clad in a hospital gown, finally croaks, "*God*, I need a cig. What the hell just happened to me?"

"Where are the others?" I ask.

Wiping dust from her eyes, Lil replies, "What others? All I know is somebody hits me with a needle and I wake up in Chernobyl."

"Is that my *baby*?" cries a familiar voice.

We turn to see the approach of Tree.

"Oh my precious Jesus!" she cries.

"Tree!"

"Aaaaaaaughh!"

"Aaaaaa-AAAUUGHH-hhh!"

Laughing and crying, a white-faced Tree and a whiter-faced Lil embrace. I peer, meanwhile, at the anonymous mound of debris. No new siblings after all, it seems. I was kind of counting on a sister upgrade.

"You see what happens," Tree says to me, still clutching my sister, "when you call upon the Rock? You *see* what happens, Julian?"

What I'm seeing is an enormous green crystal embedded in one side of my favorite meteorite. That crystal is moldavite. As I watch, the cooling green crystal pops loudly and a large piece breaks off, clattering onto the marble.

"*Thank* you, Jesus," says Tree, examining her fingers, which once more number exactly ten.

I check inside my pants. No real changes.

Thank you, Jesus.

Suddenly comes the unwelcome sound of a racking shotgun, followed by an East Texas drawl. "Move away from the mutants, ma'am."

58

"Ralpho?"

"Nothing personal, Julian," replies the man on the other end of the shotgun. "I knew you'd eventually lead me to the nest. The hard part was keeping you alive. I've never known anybody with a stronger death wish."

"Uh, there *is* no nest, Ralpho," I tell him. "In fact, I think you'll find things here largely under control."

Ralph O'Malley answers, "Dr. Carter, would you kindly move away from the mutants?"

"Ralpho?" I say again.

"This ends exactly here," he says resolutely.

A furrow appears in Tree's dust-covered brow. "I have had too crazy a day for this. Why don't you put that *ugly* gun somewhere out of my sight?"

Lillian moves a little closer to Tree. "She means it, man."

I notice a movement behind Ralpho. It's Xu, sans wooden leg, crawling toward Ralpho. He's hopelessly far away.

"Actually we're all mutants, Ralpho," I say. "And no one here is a vegetarian, so . . ."

"Is that Dobbins under that rock?" asks Ralpho, pointing with the shotgun.

I nod. "So it goes. But we have important things to discuss. Like . . ." I look at Lillian.

"Anthropomorphism," says Lil.

"Yes, anthropomorphism. Agree or disagree. It's humanizing and dehumanizing at the same time."

Xu, now upright, tries hopping toward Ralpho. He'll never make it in time.

Ralpho levels the shotgun. "Either move away, Mrs. Carter, or I'll have no choice."

Pulling Lil and myself closer to her, Tree says resolutely, "We are always at choice."

I raise my hands, palms open. "I know. Let's all *think* about this for a minute."

Ralph O'Malley spreads his feet and drops his center of gravity. "Three . . . two . . ."

Desperately Xu extends his arms and his one leg, becoming a rolling hoop.

"One . . ."

At the end of his final cartwheel, Xu delivers a solid kick to the side of Ralpho's head, and the shotgun goes off. At the same instant, a white shape flies through the air, intercepting the tight pattern of buckshot.

It's Ana Manguella, Director of Security.

"Ana!"

Shotgun blast still echoing in the air, I run to the bloody form lying in the rubble between myself and the unconscious Ralph O'Malley. Turning Ana's crumpled form over, I search frantically for a wound, finding only a ragged and singed hole at her breast pocket. Amazed, I pull from the pocket a badly deformed yet basically intact titanium-shielded journal.

"Crap," I say, looking at the remains of my journal.

"Shit," moans Ana, curling around her bruised chest.

"Geezly," says Lil, kneeling to examine Ana. "It looks like all that blood's from her nose. I think she's okay. You hear me, hon? You're going to be okay."

Checking Ana's other pockets irritably, I say, "Where are my pencils?"

Again, the racking of the shotgun. I look up. One by one, Xu is ejecting the unspent shells, which rain down on a motionless Ralph O'Malley.

"Mr. Xu," says Tree, "would you please place that *thing* as far away from us as you can? We'll have no more of those in the world now being born."

Xu flings the shotgun. Placing his hands on his hips, he smiles broadly. "The Thirteen. It's here. Look around."

I look straight up into an unclouded sky. It's actually blue. Along one side of the reappearing sun is a newborn brightness. I almost imagine that I hear a bird.

As Xu begins searching for his wooden leg, a smiling Tree dusts the powdered marble from her face and says, "It's time to rededicate the temple, kids." She extends both her hands.

Lillian steps forward and accepts one of Tree's hands before turning to me. "Doo?"

"Jules?" says Tree, waiting.

I look at both the extended hands. Oh what the hell. I accept both hands, and they pull me into a tight embrace.

"My boy and my girl," coos Tree.

I have to strain to keep my forehead from touching theirs. A moment later I'm straining a little less. Finally I'm not straining at all. The three warm foreheads meet. I feel it now. Despite myself. Despite everything. I know it for the first time. Completion.

On this ancient altar, amid the ruins of every possible blunder, every foul betrayal, our feet seemingly melting into the cool white marble, eyes closed yet filled with an unmistakable inner brightness—we are here at last.

Everything we thought we knew, everything we thought we doubted, falls gently away, leaving us empty and transfigured, our arms entwined, our warm breaths mixing. All at once, we three are a vast column of light connecting sun and earth through the soft, intervening half-brilliance of that which we are.

"We send a voice," says Tree Carter, her breath hot and sweet, "unto all who have come to this world to struggle and to live, to laugh and to cry, and we say, 'Have *heart*, loved ones.' We send a voice to our own past, to our very ancestors, and to those whom we ourselves have been, and say, 'Persevere, loved ones. Every tear that falls upon your precious feet will someday nurture the hearts of those whom you shall become.' Holy Lord God Nimbutsu Nimbutsu."

"Holy Lord God Nimbutsu Nimbutsu," echo Lil and I.

"We send forth a voice and a *song* to our future selves, those mighty ones whom we shall one day constitute and construe, conjugate and corroborate, and we say, '*Believe* in us. Wait for us. Help us.'"

I open my eyes. There's no frown-line between Tree's eyebrows. Her dusty face is as smooth and unlined as a baby's. As I watch, the golden light of the newborn sun falls across her features.

"We say unto all," continues Tree, "and unto our own selves: this is a new world. Not someday. Not somehow. Not someone else. Right here, right now, right or wrong, all the way. *We* are the new temple. This is a new world and we shall never, ever go back to where we have been. Thanks be unto all who shine, and all who shine, and *all* who shine. Be it hereby and forevermore so."

"Be it hereby," say the Mancer twins, "and forevermore so."

Jesus Jehosefat Archbishop Tutu.

Epilogue

I've discovered a new room. Sometimes at night I throw open the curtains and windows of my new room to gather in the neighborhood scents and sounds that I never cared to know before. There's a lot about Memphis that I never cared to know before, beginning with this small apartment on a poplar-lined street, my home during the closing years of an old epoch and the beginning of a new one.

Thus far I'd have to say that not much has changed. There are still winos in the parks and panhandlers on the street. There are people with good hair on television and ball games on Saturday. Maybe it's only I who has changed.

I've taken to carrying cigarettes for them, the panhandlers, the unshaven men of the streets and toppling downtown parks. I hold the flame steady as they cup their shaky hands. Sometimes their fingers touch mine and I am reminded of something or someone just beyond recall.

By afternoon I wander Memphis by foot, looking for a way to enter. I'm too alert for the bar and grills, too tragic for the bookstore cafes, too abstract for the polished supermarket aisles and shopping mall benches. You have to find a doorway into the story, I was told late in the last epoch.

My mother is awake, say the nurses, though she doesn't speak. There seems to be a point where we have said enough. I think I have a personal understanding of that.

Tree still teaches small children and satellite-feeds her weekly radio show. My sister has resigned her position at Stuebans, Stuebans, and Rehnquist. Her immediate plans are to quit smoking and begin a counseling service for recovering conservatives IHW.

I too have resigned my post, that of providing fraudulent articles to Miriam Goldfarb's glossy tax-write-off of a magazine or fully intending to. I never was that kind of writer. If I never pen another word, my journal has already served to save the life of the most exquisite woman alive, wherever she may be and whomever she's sidebarring now.

Harold Sternbaum is dead. So it goes. He was the central launderer of money for the Triad, they say, before it was decided that he used a little too much starch. After handling the details of his considerable estate, Phoebe vanished along with her mother and a hazel-haired child with a thing for plastic make-up mirrors.

The Temple of Heaven Park is closed indefinitely, "for maintenance" say the Chinese. My own sources whisper that the remains of seven tall, blond Westerners were discovered in the Temple of Heaven's Hall of Abstinence shortly after the beginning of the new epoch. Poor devils, it appears they fell upon each other in a frenzy shortly before my sister's arrival. Amid the bodies was found a chocolate bar, one bite missing.

Seven mutants. One chocolate bar. Unfortunate ratio.

I like my new room. I enjoy haunting the ballparks on Saturdays, warming the first-baseline bleachers, shelling peanuts and listening to the perfect pop of leather on leather. I feel as though I'm waiting for something without knowing exactly what it is. There's just a certain curiosity about the next moment, as though something splendid might happen.

About the Author

Author William Broughton Burt grew up in Greenville, Mississippi, home to authors such as Ellen Gilchrist, Shelby Foote, Hodding Carter, William Alexander Percy, and Berne Keating. Burt began writing at age sixteen, honing his craft while pursuing a career in radio announcing.

Burt attended Mississippi State University, promptly winning a literary scholarship and various awards that brought his work to the attention of established writers such as John Grisham and Padgett Powell. Upon receiving his masters from the University of Memphis, Burt was enlisted to teach English for a year in Shenzhen, China. During that year, the SARS epidemic broke out, and Burt's experiences became the basis of his first novel, *The Year of the Hydra.*

Among William Broughton Burt's interests are various martial arts, including Tang Soo Do, in which he holds a second-degree black belt, and Tai Chi, which he taught for decades. Burt's non-fiction book, *Moving at the Speed of Truth: Tai Chi Decoded*, is his personal synthesis of the underlying principles of the ancient art.

Now living in Latin America, Burt is a university professor, essayist and musician.

Connect with William

Fans can write to William at the following addresses:

William Broughton Burt
c/o Grey Gecko Press
565 S. Mason Road, Suite 154
Katy, TX 77450

wbburt@greygeckopress.com

Grey Gecko Press

Thank you for reading this book from Grey Gecko Press, an independent publishing company bringing you great books by your favorite new indie authors.

Be one of the first to hear about new releases from Grey Gecko: visit our website and sign up for our New Release mailing or All-Access email lists. Don't worry: we hate spam, too. You'll only be notified when there's a new release, we'll never share your email with anyone for any reason, and you can unsubscribe at any time.

At our website you can purchase all our titles, including special and autographed editions, preorder upcoming books at a discount, and find out about two great ways to get free books, the Slushpile Reader Program and the Advance Reader Program.

And don't forget: all our print editions come with the ebook absolutely free!

www.GreyGeckoPress.com

Support Indie Authors & Small Press

If you liked this book, please take a few moments to leave a review on your favorite website, even if it's only a line or two. Reviews make all the difference to indie authors and are one of the best ways you can help support our work.

Reviews on Amazon, GoodReads, GreyGeckoPress.com, Barnes and Noble, or even on your own blog or website all help to spread the word to more readers about our books, and nothing's better than word-of-mouth!

http://smarturl.it/review-hydra